A TIMELESS YEARNING

One arm firmly molding her slender body to his, Zach reached up to stroke the satin softness of Elyse's cheek. He felt his heart turn over as her lower lip quivered with sudden uncertainty. "What are you afraid of?" he asked quietly.

"I'm not afraid." Elyse bit back the truth and tried to control her trembling.

Zach's head lowered and his eyes closed as his mouth brushed hers. "Lis." He whispered the endearment with overwhelming tenderness as he surrendered to something indefinable, feeling himself drawn into some other place and time. The desire that burned inside him was like a litany of something from his own past aching to be remembered. . . .

"MEMORY AND DESIRE is such a wonderful, curl in your chair book I found myself reading it twice to be sure I didn't miss anything. I wish I had written it. *Bravo, Ms. Simpson!*"

— Fern Michaels,
author of TEXAS HEAT

MEMORY AND DESIRE

CARLA SIMPSON

ZEBRA BOOKS
KENSINGTON PUBLISHING CORP.

ZEBRA BOOKS

are published by

Kensington Publishing Corp.
475 Park Avenue South
New York, NY 10016

First printing: September, 1988

Printed in the United States of America

Through the travail of ages
across the millenniums far,
we desired and loved and parted
countless times among the stars.

From the swirling mists of time
you return and now I see,
we loved in many places, by many names
but always you and me.

Carla Simpson
May, 1987

Prologue

February 7, 1856
Coast of Cornwall, England

"Regina, you must come away. It's of no use." The elegantly
dressed gentleman wore his sorrow and concern in the deep lines
etched on his face. He couldn't bear to see his dear friend tormenting herself, hoping against hope, as she continued staring out
across the ominous sea with stricken eyes. Stoically, she shook her
head, pulling the heavy folds of her voluminous cloak more securely around her sagging shoulders.

"I can't give up," she whispered brokenly. "As long as there's even
the barest chance one of them may have survived." Lady Regina
Winslow turned to her companion in desperation. "Please, Cedric,"
she implored, "can't you understand? They're all I have left in the
world." Grief hung heavy in her voice, as she turned her gaze back
to the churning sea.

Sir Cedric Chatsworth nodded grimly. He knew she'd never
cease her vigils on that bluff high above the crashing sea until
something was found—something or someone.

An icy wind assaulted the bluff, its cold blasts stealing through
their heavy clothing. Behind them waited a stately black coach
bearing the Winslow family coronet, and four perfectly matched
bays. Heads down, tails and manes blowing in the frigid wind,
their dark coats seeming almost black, the horses stood eerily still.
The coachman, dressed in the finest burgundy livery, huddled
against the cold as the storm-filled sky threatened to burst upon
them. He sat rigid, collar turned up almost to the brim of his black
silk hat, his eyes nothing more than two narrow slits. And he
watched and waited as they'd all done for two days.

"At least come and wait in the coach, out of the wind. What
good will it do if you catch your death out here?" Sir Chatsworth
implored. His question was met with silence, for Regina continued

to gaze over the edge of the bluff which dropped away to the seawall below. One hand reaching to steady his hat, Chatsworth turned and walked toward the coach. The coachman stirred and jumped down stiffly as he approached.

Sir Chatsworth took from the vehicle the thick fur lap robe. Then he returned to Regina's side, and laid it gently about her shoulders. Her trance was momentarily broken as his hand lingered lovingly on her back.

"Thank you, Cedric," Regina whispered so softly her words were almost lost on the howling wind, which seemed to hesitate then swirl about them with renewed urgency. Her large blue eyes were weary, and lines were etched in the softness of her face. For a moment she gazed at him searchingly, as if silently begging him for something; then she turned wistfully back to the angry sea that pounded the rocks below with relentless fury.

The villagers of Land's End said it was the worst storm in memory. For two days the sea had seemed to curse and scream, hurling its rage against the coastline, destroying anything that dared venture forth. Days earlier, the waves had roiled and built like avenging demons, and the sky had turned so gray and ominous it seemed that day was night. A howling wind pelted the village with stinging, icy shards of rain, and at noon it was as bleak as night, clouds churning overhead, the ocean heaving and spewing until it and the clouds met and seemed inseparable.

Then, two days ago, a feeble light was seen in the darkness. A ship, struggling against sea and wind and rain, plunged through the teeming waters, sails rigged taut, trying desperately to turn away from the breakwater. Over the roar of the ocean and the howling of the wind, the villagers cringed and offered fervent prayers as they heard the ominous sounds of the wooden hull splintering and cracking on the rock-strewn barrier.

Hearty fishermen braved the night, and crawled, lanterns in hand, to the bluff high above the breakwater. The light they'd seen earlier, bobbing in the storm, hung momentarily suspended like a lone star in the heavens. Then, as the villagers watched helplessly, knowing none dare venture into the stormy sea at night, cries were heard, or was it only the wind? A few of the strongest men crept down the rocky ledge to the breakwater below. The distant light lingered, flickered, and then vanished, so that none were certain they'd seen it at all.

At dawn, the villagers returned to the bluff above the sea. Out on the breakwater, the crumpled hulk of a brigantine clung lifelessly to the rocks. Splintered pieces of her hull and cargo floated

8

in clouded tidepools. The storm seemed to lessen with the dawn and several men attempted to reach the battered ship. As they drew near a wave crested and forced them back, but they could hear the ship groaning as she shifted and sank more deeply, until only a portion of her deck and two broken masts remained above water. Her sails hung like a maid's sodden skirts; her stern was completely submerged. There was no sign of life. It took all their strength and skill to return to the small inlet without capsizing. As they pulled their small craft from the water, one man whispered the name of the ill-fated ship, and the men turned as one to watch solemnly as the brigantine *Venturer* slowly gave up her struggle with the sea.

Lady Regina shuddered, grabbed at the fur robe with gloved hands. The wind, penetrating her heavy clothing felt like the chill of death stealing over her. She'd waited in Plymouth for news of the *Venturer*, then had made the hazardous journey to Land's End at breakneck speed when word had come of the wreck. Her eyes, the deep-dark blue of heather upon the moors, were glazed with unshed tears. Even when she and Cedric had arrived at the inn and she'd heard the ship's name whispered in hushed tones, she'd refused to believe. James, my dear son, she thought, a sob escaping her. Why had he insisted on returning with his family from the Colonies at this time of year? What was so urgent that it couldn't have waited until later, when the voyage would've been safer?

Her gaze wandered over the deserted bluff which men from the village had descended hours earlier to reach the seawall below. For two days, they'd searched the shoals and tide pools, braving a relentless sea and an equally unyielding wind, searching for survivors. And each time they'd trudged wearily back up the ledge, their heavy woolen coats clinging to their weary bodies like shrouds, the answer had been the same: no survivors.

The sky had turned to slate. If only Richard were with me, she thought, then caught herself. No, it would be no different if her husband were alive and here with her and Cedric. Richard had always been the stoic, proud and faintly overbearing. She smiled faintly at the memory of the friendship between her husband and Sir Cedric Chatsworth, one that had endured since they'd been at Eton together. They were a study of contrasts, always falling into some argument or another over some matter of government or foreign policy. Ceddy, as her husband called his dearest friend, was simply far too practical. Dear Ceddy, she thought, you've been such a friend to me, so dear all these years I've been alone, especially after James left for the Colonies. Her husband always

9

insisted the United States be called the Colonies. She realized old resentments died hard, even though the matter of the Colonies had been settled decades ago.

Dear James . . . Regina's gaze fastened on all that remained of the *Venturer*. Broken masts, all that was left of the brig, poked up through swelling waves. James . . . so dear to her and Richard after their firstborn son had succumbed to the fever. James had held such promise, and he'd so eagerly sailed off to visit the United States, taking it upon himself to personally oversee property Sir Richard Winslow had quietly and unobtrusively acquired over the years. James had met Anne in New York, and they'd fallen deeply in love. Regina's one voyage to the Colonies had been made to attend their wedding. Family obligations had demanded her quick return, so she'd not been there for the arrival of her first grandchild. But James and Anne had assured her they would make the voyage to England as soon as the baby was old enough. However, Anne quickly conceived again, and that birthing had not gone well. She'd lost the second child at birth, and had been confined to bed for weeks afterward. So the planned voyage to England had been delayed for almost two years. Tears welled in Regina's eyes, and her heart was heavy. She'd wanted so to see them again, had mentioned it in every letter. Now, for all she knew, her son was lost, along with his wife and child. Lady Regina caught herself, her resolve hardening. No! She refused to accept it! Dear Father in heaven, she'd never even seen her granddaughter, Elyse.

Cedric's hand tightened around her arm, steadying her as the first dark figure crested the bluff, followed by several others. Regina looked from one man to the next, her eyes searching their wind-chapped faces, as they trudged past her, shaking their heads wearily, mumbling some vaguely sympathetic words as they rubbed aching hands together. All refused to meet her eyes directly. The answer was the same as it had been for the last two days. At first she'd stoically refused to believe the wreck was the ship James and Anne were returning on. But when she'd reached the village of Land's End on the coast of Cornwall, her stoicism had ended. As the brig broke up on the rocks beyond the breakwater, bits and pieces of her were washed ashore, among them the captain's manifest and a list of passengers. James's name was still decipherable, indicating he'd come aboard the *Venturer* in New York with his wife and child. Upon seeing it, something inside Lady Regina Winslow seemed to die.

As long hours had become one day, and then two, her hope that James and Anne might have survived rapidly faded. Their deaths, along with those of the crew and the other passengers, seemed cruel, but the loss of a child, her granddaughter, was incomprehensible to Regina.

"Reggie, please." Using the nickname he'd given her when they were young, Cedric tried to lure her away. "It's no use, my dear," he gently begged. She clung to his arm for support as if all strength had suddenly seeped out of her. Slowly, she nodded.

"It's so difficult . . . I hoped that maybe somehow . . ." she whispered brokenly.

"I know," he soothed, tucking her arm through his and tenderly drawing her away from the bluff. He patted her gloved hand lovingly. "Perhaps tomorrow . . . there's nothing more to be done tonight."

A shout stopped them, and Cedric turned, squinting into the growing darkness. One of the men who'd just passed them ran back to the edge of the bluff.

"It's Quimby!" he shouted above the wind. "Come on, lads!" He cupped his hands, calling to the others. "Give us a hand! He's got something."

"Wait!" Regina pulled back, her fingers biting into Chatsworth's arm as she looked desperately to the cliff wall, where the men had gathered to assist their companion up the steep rock face.

The man was nothing more than a large, dark shape as he collapsed over the edge of the bluff, strong hands pulling him to safer ground, his friends surrounding him. He fought to breathe, his skin chapped raw from the wind and biting sea spray, and struggled to his knees, clutching the heavy jacket that burgeoned across his chest.

"Eh, Quimby, what yer got there?" One man threw a blanket around his friend's shoulders while another tried to help him stand.

The man addressed groaned from between chattering teeth, his eyes glassy with cold and fatigue. Then he got to his feet, opening his jacket for the others to see.

"God almighty! Will ya look at that! Where in bloody blue blazes did that come from?" one of the men exclaimed.

Regina tore from Cedric's grasp. The luxurious lap robe fell to the sodden ground and her voluminous cloak billowed from her shoulders as she braved the wind at the edge of the bluff.

Cedric called out, running after her.

Unable to stand, the man known as Quimby collapsed, his legs near frozen from wading in the frigid water below, but he raised bloodshot eyes to Regina, and opened the folds of his coat.

11

She cried out, her hand flying to her mouth. A small child was bundled inside the sodden folds of Quimby's jacket.

"Father in heaven!" Regina fell to her knees beside Quimby, clutching at his arm.

"I found her among the rocks, ma'am," he explained brokenly, his breathing labored. "We already looked there. She must have washed up after." He carefully opened his coat, surrendering the child.

Regina reached for the cold, seemingly lifeless bundle, folding the little girl inside her heavy cloak. She sobbed as her fingers wrapped around smaller, blue ones, almost transparent and rigid with cold.

"Reggie, what is it? Good God!" Cedric came up behind them. His cheeks sucked in as he struggled to draw an even breath. He leaned over, eyes widening at seeing the small, blue-tinged face nestled against Regina's ample breast.

Tears in her eyes, Regina looked up at him, snuggling the child against her own warmth. "Cedric, this is my granddaughter."

"What? Good lord, Reggie! Are you certain?"

Quimby rose shakily to his feet. "It doesn't rightly matter who the child is, guv'ner. We'd best get the wee one out of this weather and find out if there's anything left of her to save."

Cedric reached down to take the child from Regina. He knew she must be exhausted. But she met his gesture with defiant eyes, clinging to the sodden bundle.

"I'll carry my granddaughter," she cried out vehemently. However, the hard edge left her voice as it quavered. "Please, Cedric, she's so small and cold."

Chatsworth nodded, his arm going round her for support. As he held her close, trying to shield them both from the biting wind, he prayed the child, whoever she was, might still be alive.

Settling them inside the coach, Cedric quickly gave an order to the driver. When the door was closed, cutting off the stinging wind, he tapped firmly on the roof of the coach with his gold-tipped cane. The equipage lurched forward and turned, the driver setting a furious pace as he sent the horses flying down the road toward to village.

Sir Cedric's hand rested on Regina's shoulder as she knelt beside the huge down-filled bed. The child lay motionless in the center, barely visible in the feathery mass with blankets covering her. The local physician, a man of dubious talent, bent over her, his face a

12

mask devoid of emotion. Regina raised desperate eyes to him as he rose.

"It's too soon to tell," he informed them gravely. His mouth was pulled down severely at the corners, as it had been for two days, since he'd been summoned to the inn. He resented being ordered to remain there when he had other patients to attend to, patients who truly needed his care. But Lady Regina Winslow had been adamant that he stay. Now he looked at her with an expression very near grim satisfaction, as if to say I told you it would be of no use. As he repacked his crude instruments, he shook his head pompously.

"Where are you going?" she demanded, her fingers protectively pulling the heavy coverlet back over the child.

The physician turned, dismissed her with a shrug. "There's nothing more I can do. As far as I can see, there are no broken bones. She's alive, but that's about all. There's that nasty bump on her head and all those bruises. She must have been battered about in the water for a long time. It's beyond me she survived at all. Children that small are usually not good swimmers."

"You can't leave," Regina informed him determinedly, her eyes briefly leaving the child. "What must be done when she awakens?" Fear and apprehension were in her voice.

"I can't be certain that she will." The physician was cold, aloof, enjoying his transitory power over someone of wealth and position. "I've seen it before. Very often they never awaken with a head-wound like that." He sniffed indignantly. "You must prepare yourself to accept the worst."

"No!" Regina rounded the bed with purposeful strides, fists clenched. "She's not going to die, and you're not leaving."

"I have other patients in far greater need than this child. I've a woman waiting to give birth, and several men needing my attention." He tried to shame her by implying that she was responsible for the injuries of the men who'd tried to reach the *Venturer*.

But Regina wasn't fooled. She knew this man and the kind of people who lived in Land's End. They preyed on salvage taken from foundering ships. And many vessels sank off this wild and forbidding coastline. It was the promise of finding gold coin that had prodded villagers to search diligently for survivors. And they'd have their gold. She'd gladly pay it. The child's life was worth it.

The doctor brushed past her, giving instructions on what to do if the child should awaken, which, he said, he highly doubted. Regina's eyes hardened. Devil take him, she'd do without the man. She didn't trust a man who turned away from a stricken child to

13

tend the scratches and scrapes of strong and hearty men.

The physician stopped beside Cedric, loathing in his eyes. He was contemptuous of any man of better station. "This happens all the time," he declared unconcernedly. "The child is probably not even her granddaughter. She could be from any one of a half-dozen villages along the coast. They constantly wander down to the rocks, disobedient little beggars. We have at least one wash ashore every storm. The next year, their parents replace them with another." His voice was cold, unfeeling.

"Get the bloody hell out of here before I throw you out! You're not fit to breathe the same air as that child!" Cedric's eyes glittered with contempt, and he moved toward the physician, the man's words nonetheless churning doubts he hadn't wanted to admit. The child might not be Regina's granddaughter. The physician shrugged and quickly left the room, practically colliding with a young maid on the stairs.

The girl squawked, as she re-balanced a tray holding hot broth. "Watch it, guv'ner. Why's he in such a bleedin' hurry?" She entered the sparsely furnished room, deposited the tray on a small table, and came around the side of the bed to peer at the small face poking through the blankets.

"Not much left o' 'er is there?" The maid glanced uncertainly from Regina to Cedric, then quickly apologized at seeing Regina's stricken expression. "I didn't mean nothin' by it. It's just that she's so small, and she's gone through so much." She fingered the coverlet, smoothing the fabric. "She needs one of me maw's special potions. It always fixes us up right fine when we come down with a bit of the ague. It has a wee dram of rum in the mix, for medicinal purposes of course," she added.

Regina fixed the girl with a penetrating stare. "Rum?"

The girl beamed. "Right ya are, mum. A good dose of rum, sugar, saffron—"

"And a touch of camphor," Regina finished for her. She smiled at the girl's open admiration.

"Now how would a lady like you be knowin' about that?"

"My mother was from the moors." Regina smiled. "She always swore by the cure. If it didn't kill you, it would cure you. It's a far better cure than any that physician could offer." Regina's contempt for the man was evident. "Can you find the ingredients?"

"Sure enough!" The girl bobbed her head. "Me maw keeps a good supply at home. I'll have to see if I can get away. Ol' 'Arry don't like me sneakin' off during workin' hours."

"You tell the innkeeper I've sent you on an errand. He'll be

14

compensated for his inconvenience," Regina assured her. Then she turned to Cedric. "I'll need your help."

"Anything, my dear. Just ask." He pushed aside the physician's comments for the moment. Right then, it didn't matter who the child was. The doubts would return later, when the child recovered . . . if she recovered.

"We'll need lots of wood for the fire." She motioned to the small fireplace, where a meager blaze struggled to warm the room. "It must be made as warm in here as possible." Regina turned back to the girl. "What's your name?"

"Katy, ma'am." The girl dipped into a quick curtsy.

"I want a big kettle of water boiling over the fire, the biggest you can find. I want this room filled with steam." She shooed the girl to the door. "Move! We've got work to do!"

As Cedric followed Katy from the room, the girl turned and whispered over her shoulder, "Much as I 'ate that old bastard" — she referred to the physician — "he might be right; the child might not be 'er granddaughter." She'd obviously overheard the man's parting words. "The little ones all go down there. Me own brother Malcolm almost drowned down in that cove. I just hate the idea of Lady Winslow gettin' 'er hopes up."

Cedric patted the girl on the arm. "Nevertheless, we'll do as Lady Winslow asks. I've known her a great many years, and there's only one thing in this world or the next I fear more. She can be a formidable force when she wants something."

The girl stopped at the top of the stairs, staring at him in confusion. "A formi— What'd ya call 'er?"

Cedric sent the girl on down ahead of him, winking as she tried to repeat the word. "She can be a mighty determined woman."

"I gotcha, guv'ner." Katy smiled knowingly. She turned and shouted at the innkeeper. " 'Ey, 'Arry." Her voice carried over the din and noise in the tavern. "I gotta go to me mum's. I'll be right back." Without waiting for an argument, she ducked down the passage that led to the back door of the inn.

"Hey, just hold on there, yer work ain't finished yet." Harry started after Katy, but Sir Cedric stepped between the rotund man and the hallway that led to the back. "I'll be needing several things, my good man, and I'll pay well for them." For emphasis, he produced several gold coins from his breast pocket.

Harry stopped in his tracks. Gold was more important than a wayward girl. His eyes gleamed. "Whatever ya need, guv'ner, I got it."

The small room glowed golden, images of flames dancing on the far wall, as steam curled above the simmering kettle, making the heat damp and thick. When Cedric carefully closed the door behind him, Regina did not notice. She sat on the edge of the bed, spooning drops of a foul-smelling liquid into the child's small, birdlike mouth. Most of the concoction dribbled down the tot's tiny chin. He shuddered, thinking the cure must be almost as severe as the illness. Setting the bowl aside, Regina looked up, her weary eyes meeting his.

"Is there any change?" he inquired softly.

She shook her head. "She's alive and she's warm. I suppose that's all we can hope for right now."

"Reggie, please come down and try to eat something. You've been up here for hours," he begged softly, his heart breaking for this woman he'd admired for so many years. "You can't continue like this. I'll send Katy to watch the child. You must have something to eat, and then rest."

Regina smiled, but her eyes were filled with worry. "I can't leave. I want to be here when she awakens." Not if. She refused to acknowledge that her granddaughter might not awaken. Tenderly, she smoothed the coverlet. "What time is it?"

"Almost daybreak." Cedric came to stand beside her and look down at the pathetic child. Regina's son had written that the child favored the Winslow side of the family. And Reggie'd boasted about her granddaughter, showing the small hand-painted miniature portrait James had sent to anyone remotely interested. Truthfully, Cedric saw no resemblance to Reggie or James in the pathetic creature bundled in the oversize bed, a child so small she seemed to disappear in the voluminous folds of the covers. He supposed it was possible she favored her mother more. He'd never met Anne Winslow. She and James had married on the continent. Ill health had prevented Cedric from attending the ceremony. The physician's words came back to him. What if the child was from one of the surrounding hamlets? Could Reggie bear to face the truth?

"What about the men from the village?" Regina whispered brokenly, her fingers tenderly stroking the matted hair back from the child's small face.

"They've promised to take up the search again at first light. Perhaps they'll reach the ship today." He broke off, not saying what he was thinking. The *Venturer* was practically completely submerged. Even if the searchers did reach the ship, it was certain

16

there was no one left alive. His gaze fastened on the child. In two days of frantic searching, only this small girl had been found. Each winter along the Cornish coast it was the same. When a ship went down, her cargo was salvaged, but there were seldom survivors. This was a wild and forbidding stretch of land. The crew of the brigantine had made a fatal error, and had paid for it with their lives and the lives of their passengers.

Cedric looked down at the child. When they'd brought her to the inn, her skin had been a terrifying shade of grayish-blue, her breathing so shallow it was hardly there. Now, her color had brightened to crimson, and her breathing was hard and labored due to the fever that raged through her small body. He'd seen such fevers, and knew even the stoutest of those afflicted often didn't recover. He gently laid a hand on Regina's shoulder, trying to comfort her. Through the long night he'd been trying to think how he could express to her the doubts the physician had left in his mind.

"Regina, you need rest. And we must talk," he coaxed.

She spoke as if she hadn't heard a word he'd said. "I want Dr. Crestwell in London notified. He's the finest physician in England. And I want specialists to look at her, the best. Only the best for Elyse."

"Reggie," he said uncertainly. It was as if her mind was in that same faraway place that seemed to claim the child. She hadn't heard a word he'd said, or if she had, she'd chosen to ignore him.

"I want Mr. Quist to return to London." She asked him to inform her coachman. "And I want the townhouse opened. Everything must be ready when we arrive." She faltered. "I hate to leave. There might be word of James or Anne." Her voice trailed off, for she knew in her heart there was no hope.

Chatsworth seized this opportunity. "The physician said there are accidents every winter. Regina, listen to me," he implored. "The child may not be your granddaughter. Katy told me children wander down on the rocks all the time."

"No!" Regina turned on him, the storm in her dark blue eyes more threatening than the one beating against the shuttered windows. "I know my own granddaughter! This is Elyse!" She turned back to the child, her shoulders trembling with anguish. Then she crumpled onto the bed, burying her face in the folds of the coverlet and letting tears gush forth in a flood. "Dear God," she wept, "she is my granddaughter!"

"Dear Reggie." Cedric reached out to her, but his hand fell limply to his side. He knew her only comfort was to be found in the child, whoever she was. Cedric slowly closed the door. After giving Regina's instructions to her coachman, he slumped wearily into a chair downstairs and kept a vigil beside the fire. When first gray light of a new day seeped through the paned windows, the search party had already left to return to the rocky coastline. He knew they no longer hoped to find survivors. Their interest lay in the cargo that would wash ashore.

For three days and three nights, Regina refused to leave the child's room. Cedric spent long hours with her, placing fresh wood on the fire, conveying messages to Katy through the door, or waiting downstairs for word at the end of each day when the salvagers returned. Their mumbled replies were always the same: no survivors.

The hours slipped into yet another day, the child's condition remaining unchanged, fever raging through her frail body. But Regina refused to leave her side. Her elegant gown was wrinkled now, spotted with stains made by the foul-smelling medicine Katy prepared in the kitchen. The young maid refused to leave the inn even when her work was completed, saying she wanted to be near the child. And Quimby, who'd found the little girl on the rocks, refused to return to the rocky cliff, giving the excuse that it wasn't fit weather out for man or beast. Though a drinking man, he hadn't touched a drop since he'd pulled the child from the sea.

Cedric jerked upright from his dozing, his bloodshot eyes focusing slowly on the stairway.

"Regina?" His senses cleared. "My God, what is it?"

She smiled wanly, as she slumped into the chair across from him.

"She isn't . . . ?" He couldn't say the words. So many days they'd waited, even he had begun to hope.

"The fever broke almost an hour ago. Katy's with her." Tears welled in Regina's eyes, and she buried her face in her hands. "She's going to live."

Cedric was out of his chair and beside her in an instant. He wrapped an arm about her shoulders. "Has she regained consciousness?" he whispered hopefully.

Regina shook her head. "No, but she will." She turned determined eyes up to him, clinging to his comforting hand. "Ceddy, she has to live. After all this time, I know there's no hope for James or Anne, but I couldn't bear to lose that little girl, too."

"Hush, hush." Cedric soothed her, stroking her hair. "We'll just have to wait."

Sniffling, she motioned for a handkerchief. Cedric smiled. Never in all the years he'd known her had Regina Winslow had a handkerchief when she'd needed it. He handed her his.

"Did Mr. Quist leave for London?" She wiped her eyes.

"Yes, and he has returned," Cedric confirmed. He frowned slightly at the disturbing news the man had brought back but he decided not to burden Regina with it at the moment. He knew from the look in her eyes, she couldn't take any more right then. He forced back the frown and smiled gently.

"Everything will be ready when we get there."

Regina nodded, her head snapping up as Katy suddenly appeared at the top of the stairs.

"Come quick, ma'm." The girl gestured excitedly. "It's the little one!" Katy whirled back around and disappeared inside the small room. Regina flew across the tavern and up the stairs, Cedric immediately behind her.

"What is it?" Regina burst into the room, fear lining her face, her eyes wide and stricken.

"Look for yerself, mum." Katy pointed to the bed, where the child stirred among the heavy covers.

Crying out, Regina knelt beside the bed. Small and frail, the child weakly turned her head toward them. Her mouth opened and closed, the lips dry and cracked. One small hand reached from the covers. Regina felt her forehead. The child's skin was cool, her breathing regular and even.

"Dear God!" she whispered, her eyes filling with tears. "Oh, Ceddy, she's coming around." She bent over the little girl, talking in the soft, crooning voice she'd used when her son was a small child. There was the faintest trace of color on the child's cheeks, natural, healthy color, not the fiery crimson of fever.

"Sweet, sweet baby." Reggie stroked the child's face, holding its small hands in her own. "Grandmother is here, darling. I'm here, and you're safe. I love you so, and there's so much I want to share with you. Grandmother is here, Elyse."

From some deep, dark void of timelessness and space, strength seemed to ebb back into the small hands. Small fingers tightened around Regina's, eyelashes quivered, lips moved faintly. Then large round eyes opened slowly, searchingly. The little girl blinked once, twice, then stared at the faces looking down at her. As her confusion cleared, the pristine whites of her eyes surrounded blue so deep it was like the heather on the moors. The irises were large and black, fathomless as the ocean that had yielded her so reluctantly.

"Elyse?" Regina spoke softly not wanting to frighten her granddaughter. The child had suffered a severe blow to the head; the bandage was thick and heavy. Reggie couldn't be certain Elyse's memory would be clear. She wasn't certain she wanted her to remember.

As color flooded the little girl's cheeks, her eyes darted about the room with childish curiosity. She regarded the people hovering over her with a mixture of curiosity and amusement. There was no confusion or uncertainty in the depths of her crystal blue gaze. Her voice was small and breathless.

"Where is he?"

Regina's eyes glowed as she heard these first spoken words which she didn't bother to try to understand. With rapturous delight she squeezed her granddaughter's small hands, showering kisses on her small face. For her, there had never been any doubt that this was her granddaughter.

Cedric stared in disbelief at the child. His doubts had vanished the moment she'd opened her eyes, for they were as dark and vibrant as Regina's. There was no mistaking the resemblance.

The little girl continued to stare up at them as if wondering what all the fuss was about, and her gaze traveled from her grandmother to Katy, then to Cedric.

"Where is he?" she insisted, struggling up from the coverlet.

Regina smiled uncertainly at the inquisitive child who'd fixed her with such a determined stare, but her smile faded and she shot a stricken glance at Chatsworth. He? It suddenly occurred to her that Elyse meant James. Regina's eyes welled with tears. Gently, she smoothed the toddler's thick, dark hair. Her fingers trembled. Anne's hair had been that same color; her father's eyes, her mother's coloring. Elyse would be a striking beauty one day. Regina gathered her granddaughter close, her heart aching.

"They're not here right now, my darling," Reggie explained gently. There would be time to explain later, when Elyse was stronger. Right now she couldn't be certain of how much the child comprehended of what had happened.

Elyse fought back the covers, her eyes wide, clear, determined. She glanced about the room. "Where is he? He promised he would come back for me." Her voice was haunting, its aching melancholy tearing into their hearts. She crawled from her grandmother's grasp, heading for the edge of the bed. Tears filled Elyse's eyes as she gazed about her.

"He's been gone so long." Her childish voice quavered. "And he did promise; he said he loved me and that he would come back for me."

Katy reached for the child and pulled her onto her lap, cradling her like a baby. "There, there little one. It's all right now. Don't ya be frettin'," she soothed. " 'E promised 'e'd come back, and 'e will. I know 'e will." Katy rocked the child gently back and forth.

Regina stared in mute silence at Cedric. He patted her shoulder, then firmly took her by the arm, helping her to her feet. "You're exhausted. The child will be fine now. Come downstairs. You haven't eaten or slept in days." Cedric turned to Katy. "You'll see that the child sleeps?"

"I'll stay right 'ere with 'er, guv'ner. I gots me seven brothers and sisters. Me maw always said there was nothing like rockin' a wee one when they was troubled. I'll be down to get yer something to eat as soon as she dozes off."

Cedric nodded and then guided Regina from the room. Once she was out the door, she turned and crumpled against his shoulder. "Oh, Ceddy, will she be all right? She seemed so much better when she awakened. But what did she mean?"

Cedric held her close, stroking her disheveled hair. "She's been through a great deal. Give her time. We'll get her back to London and have Tom give her a thorough examination. I'm certain, in time, she'll be just fine. She did suffer quite a severe knock on the head."

"Yes, of course." Regina nodded. Her eyes were red from crying and lack of sleep. "That must be it. I expected too much. I'm afraid I'm greedy. After the last days . . ." Her voice broke, and she looked up at him, seeking the truth in his eyes. "You do believe she's Elyse?"

Cedric sighed heavily. He knew what she wanted to hear, and it wasn't necessarily the truth. Yet he had seen a resemblance when the child had awakened. "She has your eyes, my dear. I never met Anne . . ." He was fumbling badly.

"No, you didn't. She was so lovely, with hair that same color." Her voice quavered. "James loved her so. And he was so proud of Elyse. They couldn't wait for me to see her." She turned and gazed wistfully at the closed door, as if she couldn't bear to leave for even a moment, but Cedric firmly guided her down the stairs.

They sat at the small trestle table in a corner of the inn. Katy had brought them tea, and cakes she'd proudly boasted " 'er maw" had baked; then she'd gone back upstairs to watch over Elyse. Every so often Regina's gaze darted watchfully to the door at the top of the stairs. It was now two days since the child had awakened.

After eating a hearty meal, she'd slipped into deep, restful slumber, sleeping for almost sixteen hours. During that time, Regina remained by her granddaughter's bed, fearful that she might yet slip away from them. But with each passing hour, the child seemed to grow stronger.

Sadly, there was no trace of another survivor. So a somber Lady Regina Winslow accepted the truth, and turned her strength and determination to ensuring Elyse's recovery. She announced that they would return to London immediately, as if she couldn't bear to remain in Land's End a moment longer. Earlier that morning she'd gone alone to the bluff. Cedric hadn't asked why, he'd understood. Now he watched her from across the table. She'd donned a clean gown of deep aquamarine that set the color in her eyes to dancing. Her dark blond hair, faintly streaked with gray, was elegantly styled atop her head. The deepened lines at the corners of her eyes were the only outward signs of her grieving. Cedric was again reminded that Lady Regina Winslow was a very beautiful woman. He'd been aware of that for almost forty years, and strongly suspected it was the reason he'd never chosen to marry. There wasn't another woman alive to compare to her. And for twenty-two of those forty years she'd been married to his closest friend.

Cedric rummaged in the pocket of his elegant charcoal jacket, then replaced the cigars.

Regina looked up from her tea, a ghost of a smile playing around the corners of her mouth. "For heaven's sake, Cedric, go ahead and smoke your cigar. You know very well it doesn't bother me. I rather like it. Richard used to smoke them all the time." She spoke fondly of her husband.

"All right, if you're certain." Most women were given to a case of the vapors or to swooning spells at the first whiff of smoke. He took out a small cigar and twirled it thoughtfully between thumb and forefinger. He'd hesitated to tell her during the days of Elyse's recovery, but now that they were returning to London, he knew he could delay no longer.

"We've had news from London," he began thoughtfully, wondering if she was strong enough to hear it now. He preferred she hear it from him rather than one of her household staff upon their return.

"What is it?" Regina reached out and patted his hand. Ceddy had always been such a dear friend, always trying to shield her from life's little unpleasantries since Richard was gone. Her faint smile faded before his silence and somber expression. He seemed

22

to be searching for the right words. She'd never known him to be at a loss to express himself.

"What is it?" she whispered, fear congealing around her heart. "Ceddy?" she urged.

"It's Felicia." He spoke slowly, wishing he could spare her this.

"What's happened?" Regina's voice had a hard, desperate edge to it as she thought of her dear friend.

"Mr. Quist brought back word . . ." He hesitated. "I know you were very close."

"She's dead, isn't she?" Regina voiced what he seemed to be having such a difficult time saying.

Cedric nodded.

"Somehow I knew." Her voice was a hollow whisper. "She was sick for such a long time . . . and so very unhappy." She breathed a ragged sigh, no more tears left in her. "She was like my own daughter after her parents died. Her marriage to Barrington was arranged, and in spite of appearances not the happiest. She was in love with someone else, but she never spoke of it, not even to me. My poor, dear Felicia. She was a real friend. I hope she's at peace now." Regina sighed. So much sadness. So much loss. "When did it happen?"

"The evening of the fifth," Chatsworth remarked slowly, "the night the ship went down. According to Mr. Quist, within the very same hour." Regina only nodded sadly. If the coincidence registered at all, she showed no response.

Katy interrupted them, jauntily coming down the steps. "I swear that wee child has two 'ollow legs, she does. Why she eats more than me brother, Simon, and 'e's five goin' on six."

Regina smiled up at the girl, heartened by the good news. "Katy, you've been a godsend. I can't think what I would have done the last two days without you. I've been considering something." She hesitated. "How would you like to come back to London with us? You could help me care for Elyse."

"London? Me? Gawd almighty, what would I do there? Me maw says the place is dreadful wicked and there ain't a job to be had." She jerked her thumb over her shoulder toward Harry the innkeeper. "Ol' 'Arry might not pay much, but at least it's steady work. Men is always wantin' their ale." She winked.

Cedric was a bit taken aback by the girl's profanity and her candor. Regina didn't seem to mind either.

"Elyse has become very attached to you the last few days, and I'll need someone to help me with her. I'm a bit old to be starting over again with a child," she admitted.

23

"Right ye are, mum." Katy nodded, completely unabashed. "But there is me mum and me sisters and brothers to consider." She hesitated.

"You'll be well compensated. You'll live in London with us at the town house, and at the country house in York." Regina reached out, taking the girl's hand. "You're gentle and caring, and the only other person I've met who knows about saffron and camphor. Please, say you'll come. You'll make more money in a month than in an entire year here at the tavern. And I would like someone such as yourself around my granddaughter. She's going to need a great deal of love and caring to recover from her loss."

Katy's eyes widened as she considered Lady Regina's offer. Then she nodded and set her mouth in a firm line, her decision made. "I guess I'd be a fool to turn down an offer like that. 'Sides, who could refuse a position carin' for a pretty little thing like 'er." She shook Regina's hand very businesslike. "Ya got yerself a deal, ma'am." Then she blushed and dipped into a deep curtsy. "Sorry, yer ladyship. I gotta be honest with ya; I don't rightly know 'ow I'm gonna fit in. Me maw says me manners are right fine for a tavern, but not rightly what ye'd be needin' in a house in London."

Regina smiled. "You let me worry about that. It'll be refreshing to have someone with your honesty around. And I want to learn more of your mother's recipes, especially that broth you fixed the other evening. I think we both have a great deal to learn. I just hope I haven't forgotten how to raise a child."

Katy waved her off. "Ah, there ain't nothin' to it, ma'am. Ya just love 'em and squeeze 'em, and give 'em a swat or two on the bum just to let 'em know when they get a bit rowdy. That's what me mum always says. I best get home and tell her the good news. When are we leavin'?"

"First thing in the morning," Regina informed the girl.

Katy's eyes widened. "Boy, ol' 'Arry is sure gonna 'ave a conniption fit when 'e 'ears this." She waved, curtsied, and waved again, not quite certain what to do with herself. Then she giggled and sped out the back of the inn.

Regina looked up as Mr. Quist came through the front door of the tavern, a large man in tow.

"Excuse me, ma'am." Mr. Quist took off his hat and nodded his head.

"Good morning, Mr. Quist. Will we be ready to leave in the morning?" Regina asked her driver.

"Aye, yer ladyship." He twisted the silk hat in his hands. "This here is Mr. Quimby. He's the one that found yer granddaughter."

Regina stood, immediately seizing the large man's hand. She hardly recognized him. His face was all but hidden behind a stubbly growth of whiskers, heavy jowls, and a moth-eaten muffler.

"Mr. Quimby, I'm forever in your debt. I hoped we might have a chance to speak before I left."

The man bobbed uncertainly and shuffled his feet, obviously uncomfortable. "She's a fine little girl, ma'am. I wish the best for her, and you."

"Thank you, Mr. Quimby. I'd like to do something for you in appreciation. Do you have a family here in Land's End?"

"Me?" Quimby's eyes widened in surprise. "Hell no, ma'am. Beggin' yer pardon." He winced at his use of profanity. "It's not every day we have a fine lady like yerself so far from London."

Regina smiled. "It's quite all right. My late husband, the Earl of Larchmont, used to swear quite a lot." She gestured to his jacket. "That's a fine coat you have, Mr. Quimby." She eyed the shabby and torn fabric. "Perhaps you'd like another. When I return to London, I'll instruct my solicitor to open an account for you. The weather is severe here. Perhaps a new scarf too." She suggested carefully, not wanting to offend the man.

"Lord, I don't need such fancy trappings, ma'am. Not such as me." Quimby shuffled his large bulk. "It's enough just knowing the little lady is doin' well."

Mr. Quist intervened. "Quimby here is real handy. We had a loose coupling on the coach when I got back from London, and he fixed 'er right up. Folks say he can do almost anything with his hands. I was thinkin' maybe . . ."

Cedric coughed loudly to gain Regina's attention. He figured he might be able to find a place for the man with one of his acquaintances.

"Ceddy, perhaps you should have some of Katy's broth. You appear to be coming down with a cold," she said, politely dismissing him. Then she smiled. "I do quite a bit of traveling back and forth from London to the country. I seem to remember having the coach repaired just last October. Isn't that correct, Mr. Quist?"

"Quite right, ma'am". His eyes lit up.

"Then I think perhaps we should have someone who could take care of it on a regular basis. And of course there will be other responsibilities." Regina smiled. She liked this big gruff man who found words so difficult. When all the others had given up searching for survivors from the *Venturer*, he'd stayed behind and continued. His unselfish gesture had meant the difference between life and death for Elyse. "I hope you'll consider joining my household

25

staff in London, Mr. Quimby."

The man was completely speechless. What little of his face was visible through beard and muffler quickly turned a bright shade of crimson. "I'd like that real fine, ma'am . . . er, ah, yer ladyship."

"We'll cover that later," Regina reassured him. Then Mr. Quist grabbed the big man by the arm, and quickly led him out of the tavern.

"Regina, have you completely taken leave of your senses? You have more than enough staff in London, and at the country house." Cedric gaped at her. "I was about to offer to place Quimby with one of my associates."

"He wouldn't have accepted it," she informed him flatly. "Mr. Quimby may be lacking in a good many things, but he's obviously a man of strong principles. He'd be completely out of place working for one of your friends."

"And he won't be with your staff in London?" Cedric questioned.

"Not at all. For you see, if any of my people say a word against Mr. Quimby, they'll find themselves immediately discharged," Regina announced firmly. Then her voice softened. "I value a man with a courageous heart more than all the finely spoken words in the world. He risked his life to save my granddaughter. That's all I need to know of him."

"Regina, you're a remarkable woman." Cedric enfolded her hand in his.

"No," she answered simply. "It's just that I understand what it is like to live in a place like this. What future would a girl like Katy have here? And Mr. Quimby? God knows how the man lives. These people gave me back my granddaughter. Now I want to give them something—a chance at life."

Cedric took her hand in his. There was a spark of the Regina he remembered in her eyes. "You're right, of course."

"Thank you," she murmured. Slowly drawing her hand from his, she laid her palm lovingly against his cheek. "Thank you for being my friend." She turned and climbed the stairs, wanting to be with her granddaughter. She needed family about her to ease the ache of the grieving that had only just begun.

Mr. Quist tipped his hat, the sharp wind rustling his thin hair. "We're all ready, your ladyship."

Regina nodded and drew her cloak closed to block the wind. Their few bags were already loaded in the boot of the elegant coach. The innkeeper had been paid handsomely for his hospitality, farewells had been sadly mumbled, and Mr. Quimby sat atop the coach. He quickly scrambled down as Regina stepped from the inn. Cutting off Mr. Quist, he bowed low, sweeping his woolen cap from a balding head in a grand gesture of respect as he moved to open the door.

Cedric assisted Regina into the coach, settling himself across from her in the warm protective interior. Katy beamed at her from the corner in which she was carefully cradling Elyse. After the door was firmly latched, the coach dipped slightly under Quimby's cumbersome weight as he climbed atop. Mr. Quist followed and, seizing the reins, called out to the team of matched bays.

"Come on, Chester. Here Max! Ho there, Robbie and Dustin!" He gave a shrill whistle, snapped leather just over their heads, and the team came to life, swinging around and quickly matching pace. They were eager to be off, and the coach swayed into line behind them.

Regina pulled the heavy velvet curtain back from the window. Rain had begun to fall. How she hated this place, longed to be away from it. Her pain eased as her gaze wandered to her grand-daughter. There was no doubt in her mind as she looked at the sleeping child. The eyes, the shape of her face, the curve of her mouth were her father's; but her fair skin, finely shaped brows, dark hair, and small, straight nose were definitely Anne's. She was such a treasure, a mixture of the parents who'd loved her so.

Glancing out the window at the bleak coastline, Regina tapped on the roof. The coach rolled to a stop. Cedric watched silently as she gazed out the window at the churning ocean that still raged against the forbidding coastline.

A tear slipped down Regina's cheek. Somewhere out in that vast darkness, two souls she loved had gone to their Maker. Somehow, by some miracle or act of God, the tiny child nestled in Katy's arms had escaped. What had she endured? What fears and pain were locked deep inside her? She seemed to remember nothing of the storm or the loss of her parents. Whatever memories she had were tucked away, perhaps never to emerge; James's or Anne's name provoked no response. She was unafraid, not a hysterical child, but it was as if the life she'd known before the accident was a slate wiped clean. Tiny Elyse had no memory of her mother or father.

The child stirred, yawning softly and rubbing her eyes before she sat up. She smiled first at Cedric—he'd become an immediate favorite—then at Katy who tucked a woolen coat about her shoulders.

"Why have we stopped?" Elyse's small mouth curved almost into the shape of a bow. "Is he here?"

It was the same question she'd asked when she'd first regained consciousness. Regina gave Cedric a startled look. She reached out to Elyse, stroking her sable curls.

"You've been dreaming again, sweetheart."

Elyse glanced expectantly to the door, intelligence burning in her wide blue eyes. "He promised he would come back for me. Is he here yet? He promised."

Regina gathered her granddaughter against her side, tears filling her eyes. "It's all right sweetheart. He'll come back for you," she said soothingly.

Elyse turned her cherubic face up to her grandmother. "But when, Grandmama?"

Regina's heart turned over. It was the first time Elyse had called her that.

"Not now, but one day he will come to you," she promised, thinking of James and believing with all her heart that somehow loving bonds did survive the finality of death. She smiled lovingly down at Elyse. "He loved you very much, and he'll find you one day." She kissed the top of her granddaughter's head, more than ever convinced of the power of love. It was indefinable and enduring. Hadn't she found it again in this small, beautiful child?

Cedric tapped a signal to Mr. Quist, and the coach lurched into motion.

Chapter One

Christmas Eve, 1870
London, England

"And just what do you think you're doin', young lady!" Katy's mouth thinned into a disapproving line. The gray silk of her skirts crackled as she ascended the wide curving staircase.

Head poking through two spindles of the curving balustrade, Elyse looked at her, then jerked back into the shadows. Caught! She could try to reach her room, but what was the use. Katy had already found her out.

The maid reached the landing, her cheeks puffing from the exertion of racing up the stairs. It was a full minute before she was able to speak between gasps for air.

"And don't think I'll be acceptin' any of your excuses, sittin' up here like a common servant, actin' like you have no manners or breedin'," she scolded.

Standing her ground or rather sitting on it, Elyse fastened Katy with a beguiling smile that could charm pennies from a pauper. "I wouldn't think of offering any excuse. And it serves you right, being out of breath," she retorted playfully. "You shouldn't run up stairs." She was repeating a rule she'd heard cited countless times.

Katy's soft brown eyes narrowed as she wagged a finger at her young mistress. "Yer supposed to be restin' before the party."

"Oh, Katy, I can't possibly sleep." Elyse sprang to her feet, slipping her arm through the maid's as they turned toward the top of the stairs. "You know how I love Christmas, and Grandmother's made me stay up here all afternoon." She pretended to pout.

Walking with her to the bedchamber, Katy fixed on her a reprimanding look. "It's because you always poke all the packages, and shake them. Then you guess what's inside and spoil the surprise." She opened the door to Elyse's chamber, pushing her inside.

"And I'm usually correct." Elyse clasped her hands together as she whirled across the room, her dressing gown softly brushing the floor. The brilliant, peacock blue fabric set her eyes to dancing. "What do you think Grandmother gave me this year?"

Taking Elyse firmly by the shoulders, Katy pushed her gently down onto the seat before the dressing table, and picking up a brush, she waved it menacingly at her mistress. "It would serve you right if she gave you nothing. Sittin' at the top of the stairs like a common street urchin, in nothin' but your dressin' gown. Your behavior is appallin'. What would Master Jerrold say to see you acting like such a hooligan?"

"Indeed." Elyse fixed an innocent smile on her beautifully curved mouth, but the light in her eyes danced. She was anything but contrite. "What would he say?" She burst into laughter.

Katy forced her mouth into a thin line of disapproval. It wouldn't do for her to break out laughing. "Yer too bold fer yer own good. Yer grandmother has spoiled you rotten. Maybe marriage will settle you down." She shook her head, as if she sincerely doubted that possibility.

The pout returned, only to tilt into a breathtaking smile. "I don't see why," Elyse announced brazenly; then she grew more thoughtful.

"Why is it the moment a woman marries she becomes insipid and boring?" It was obviously something she'd given a great deal of thought.

Katy's surprised expression was caught in the mirror. "Now, whatever gave you such an idea? Yer grandmother is not insipid or boring." She directed the admonishment to the reflection of an exquisite beauty in the mirror.

"Grandmother is not married," Elyse hastened to point out. "She's, how do you say . . . keeping company with Uncle Ceddy."

"Don't be so bold. She and Sir Cedric are old friends. He was a good friend of yer grandfather's as well."

Elyse refused to be distracted from her train of thought. "Why is it that when a young lady is seen about with a young man she must have a chaperon? Who's to be grandmother's chaperon?" Mischief danced in her brilliant eyes, daring Katy to come up with an answer for that one.

The maid fumed. "Yer the ornery one today, aren't ya? It so happens that a lady of yer grandmother's position and age does not need a chaperon."

"But why?" Elyse persisted, warming to her subject. "After all, she's capable of a physical relationship. Surely such things don't end when you get older."

"Good Lord!" The hairbrush clattered from Katy's hand. "Whatever put such ideas into your head? It's not for you to be wonderin' what older folks are up to! Now, come along." She crossed the room toward the wardrobe. "It's time you dressed for the party. Sir Cedric arrived over an hour ago."

"I know. I waved to him from the stairway." Elyse laughed as she rose from the chair. Hands folded behind her back, rocking on firmly planted feet, she grinned, amusement dancing in her eyes. "I think age has little to do with it. Grandmother and Uncle Ceddy have been on very intimate terms for quite a while. There was the time I almost walked in on them—"

"Shame on you!" Katy whirled around. "Sayin' such things and eavesdroppin' on yer grandmother. You're an ill mannered chit." She wagged her finger until Elyse was certain it might fall off. "If her ladyship heard you sayin' such things—"

"God's nightgown, Katy!" Elyse burst out laughing. "Grandmother is the one who told me all about it afterward."

"Dear Lord, what is the world comin' too?" Katy collapsed on the dark blue satin coverlet draped across the bed.

Elyse crossed the room and knelt before the stricken maid. "Grandmother thought I should have one of those conversations that all brides have with their mothers when they become betrothed. One thing led to another, and well I just . . ."

"Asked?" Katy was too horrified to believe it was true.

"Well, you and Grandmother always said the best way to find out something was to—"

Katy groaned, her eyes rolling heavenward. "You did ask her! Lord have mercy, what will she think of me and what I've been teachin' ya?"

Biting her lip, Elyse practically choked from holding back laughter. "She thinks you're a good influence on me. She said just the other day that you keep me from becoming too serious about myself."

Katy fretted. "She'll ship me back to Land's End, I just know it."

"No, she won't," Elyse assured her as she rose and went to the small writing desk that stood before the window. She opened the center drawer and took out an envelope.

"I suppose I should save this until Christmas morning," she said, "and you were perfectly rotten to me on the staircase." Her mouth curved into an enticing smile. "But I never could stand the anticipation of waiting." Crossing back to the bed, she thrust the gold-embossed envelope into Katy's hands.

"What is this?" Katy eyed it suspiciously. "Me severance pay?"

"Of course!" Elyse teased. Dropping down onto the thick carpet at the maid's feet, she tucked her dressing gown around her long legs. Despite the grim expression on her face, lights danced in her eyes. "I persuaded Grandmother to keep you on until after the holiday. I thought it would be cruel to toss you out before Christmas." She watched Katy from the corners of her eyes.

"You're an impudent girl. It's a wonder young Lord Barrington offered his proposal." Katy teased her back, completely unruffled.

Elyse rolled her eyes and waved her hand through the air in a gesture of abandon. "How could he refuse? You know how determined Grandmother can be when she wants something."

Katy frowned. "I've changed me mind. Yer not impudent, yer just plain rude. I think that knock on the head when you was a baby addled yer common sense. Master Barrington won't be pleased with a sharp-tongued bride."

Elyse's eyes widened in mock horror. "Undoubtedly. He'll probably lock me away in the country and take a mistress here in London."

The maid discreetly refused to respond to this reference to what had been common knowledge about Jerrold Barrington before his engagement to Elyse. She couldn't meet her young mistress's gaze, having heard from some of the other servants that the situation hadn't changed.

"I believe mistresses are supposed to be quite fashionable. And don't frown at me so," Elyse admonished. "I know of the rumors about Jerrold's activities. There's no need for you to look like a prune-faced old crow." She fixed Katy with the wide-eyed gaze that more than once had caused the maid to wonder if there wasn't someone much older lurking behind it. "Well, are you going to open it, or must I do it for you?"

Frowning, Katy slipped a finger beneath the wax seal. It was obvious that Elyse was aware of the rumors, so she tried to lighten the mood that had suddenly descended on the room.

"If I'm to be cast off, I might as well start preparin' meself fer it."
She reached out and lovingly pressed a hand against Elyse's cheek.
A filmy piece of paper fluttered out of the envelope clutched in her
other hand. Katy picked it up and began to read. Then she thrust
it into Elyse's hands. "Well, I don't see me final pay. You read it;
you know I'm not so good on me letters."

Taking the paper, Elyse rose to her full height. "It's a deed," she
announced with great ceremony.

"Deed? To what, in God's name?"

"Katy, darling," Elyse chided teasingly, "you really must try to do
something about your language." She then became very serious,
her dark sable brows drawing together slightly.

"It's the deed to a house in Cheltingham, not far from here."
Upon seeing Katy's confused expression, she continued. "You see,
I have been eavesdropping just a little." She sat down beside the
maid. "I know that practically everything you earn goes to yer
family."

Katy nodded. "It's been hard on me mum ever since Pa died. He
was a good man, always did his best to provide for all of us. But
there was always a new mouth to feed. There were four new babes
after I left. Then, after he died . . . well, mum just couldn't do it
alone. The older kids try to help out, but there's just so much they
can do."

Elyse squeezed Katy's hands lovingly. "That's why I'm giving
you this deed. I know how you miss your mother." She stopped,
drawing in a deep breath. "I know how I would feel if my mother
were still alive and very far away." Her eyes glistened with sudden
emotion. She wiped at them, silently scolding herself. She certainly hadn't intended for this to be a somber occasion

Katy patted her charge's hand. She still didn't fully understand
the meaning of Elyse's gift. "You've been as dear to me as my own
since the day Quimby found you in that tide pool. I understand
what yer feelin'."

"I know you do, and that's why I want you to have the house."
Elyse wiped at the corner of one eye. Then, laughing at her own
foolishness, she rushed on to describe the house. "It's quite large
with several rooms, and an ample kitchen with a good stove. I
remember you telling me how your mother likes to cook. And
Grandmother still raves about her special soup."

"Aye, me mum's always been a good cook." Katy nodded. Then
her eyes widened, as the full meaning of the gift finally took hold.
"Good heavens!" She clapped her hands to her cheeks. "You're

serious about all of this!"

"Perfectly serious," Elyse reassured her. "And there's more than enough room for all the children and any guests." She became very thoughtful. "Of course, you may decide to live with her as well." There was a touch of wistfulness in her voice, but she hid it behind a bright smile. She wanted very much for Katy to be completely happy with the gift. "I know Grandmother would insist that you have the use of the carriage whenever you need it to get back and forth." She folded Katy's hands around the deed, hating the idea of losing a dear friend but understanding Katy's desire to be closer to her family. She'd considered asking her to go to Barrington House with her after she married, but that decision must be Katy's.

"But why . . . ?" Katy stammered. "This is so much. Whatever possessed you?"

"Because you've been a dear and wonderful friend. And I want you to have your family near you. I know what it means to feel alone."

Katy's eyes filled with tears. "Does yer grandmother know about this?" She smoothed the deed with trembling fingers.

Elyse sat down beside her on the bed, wrapping an arm lovingly around her shoulders. "Of course," she admitted smugly. "She helped me find it, and Uncle Ceddy made the necessary arrangements. She's been so excited about the whole thing, I didn't think she'd be able to keep it a secret until Christmas. "I did it because I love you, and you mustn't refuse." She squeezed Katy affectionately, then fixed tearful eyes on her.

Katy nodded, momentarily unable to reply. "Thank you, darlin'." She laid a hand against Elyse's cheek. "Thank you from the bottom of me heart. You're the dearest child. It'll mean so much to me mum. But I won't be leavin' here," she announced, sniffing loudly. "This is my home now, as long as you and your grandmother want me. Besides"—she hesitated—"as much as I love me mum, I don't think we could live in the same house together. She still thinks I'm fifteen years old." She dabbed at her eyes with a handkerchief.

"I was hoping you'd say something like that." Elyse rose from the end of the bed. "Then it's settled. After the holiday, I'll help you make the arrangements necessary to move your family. It'll be fun." She whirled across the room, as excited as Katy about the gift. A loud shriek stopped her dead in her tracks.

"What is that?"

Elyse whirled back around, her dressing gown swirling open

34

below her knees, and her gaze followed Katy's to the muddy toes of the riding boots protruding from beneath its hem. She quickly pulled the gown closed.

"Perhaps the latest fashion from Paris?" she suggested weakly, wincing at the ridiculous notion. Just how was she going to get herself out of this one? She'd been so excited about the preparations for the party and about Katy's gift that she'd completely forgotten about the boots until they'd poked incriminatingly from beneath the dressing gown.

"You've been out ridin' again!" Katy exclaimed, her gift now completely forgotten. "And by the looks of them boots, it's been real recent!" She threw her hands up in a gesture of frustration. "What will yer grandmother say?" She inhaled deeply, preparing to deliver a lengthy tirade on proper conduct for young ladies of society.

But Elyse whirled away, cutting her off. Once Katy got started, there'd be no end to it. "Katy darling, do you think the blue gown is right for this evening? Or perhaps the red one?" she questioned innocently, deftly changing the direction of their conversation.

Katy's eyes narrowed. "The red is scandalous." Her mouth snapped shut; she had been outmaneuvered. "No young lady should expose so much of herself in public. You'll fall right out of it. And quit tryin' to change the conversation around!" she scolded, her finger coming back into action. "You don't fool me a bit. I know what yer up too."

"Oh?" Elyse raised her delicate chin a defiant notch as Katy took a deep breath. "I suppose you're right, of course." Devilment sparkled in her eyes. She reached for the blue gown, and heard an audible sigh of relief. Her mouth twitched with suppressed merriment as she stuffed the blue back into the wardrobe and seized another gown.

"I'll wear the red," she announced. Behind her, the sigh became a startled gasp.

"Oh no you won't! You'll wear the blue!" Katy announced flatly, handily retrieving the blue gown. Whirling around from the wardrobe, she stood with feet planted as if ready to do battle, the expression on her face one of utter determination. Nothing less would be needed to see that her mistress wore the blue gown.

"Now, Katy darling . . ." Elyse cajoled.

"Don't you *Katy darling*, me. I know what yer up to, and I won't have it! I won't have it!" Katy's eyes narrowed determinedly.

* * *

35

Elyse swept down the wide staircase, brilliant red silk clinging to her slender figure. She stopped, taking a shallow breath and then quickly releasing it. Katy was right, of course. With every breath she took, she feared Katy's dire predictions would come true and she would spill out of the low-cut neckline. It was scandalous, and she loved it.

She greeted a distant cousin, and her smile deepened as she caught sight of her grandmother and Sir Cedric. Disengaging herself from her enraptured cousin, she crossed the room.

"You've outdone yourself, Grandmother." Elyse clasped her hands together in delight as her gaze swept the decorated room. "Everything is so beautiful." Her eyes glowed with excitement. Red and gold candles shimmered in every corner, and the mantel above the fireplace was draped with garlands of waxy green holly dotted with clusters of crimson berries. A fire crackled merrily at the hearth, its golden flames reflecting off polished wood. And the yule log waited, decorated with ribbons. It had become a tradition for Cedric to place the gigantic log on the fire just before midnight so that it might burn through the night, leaving warm embers for Christmas morning when he joined them for a large breakfast celebration.

A gleaming brass kettle simmered over the fire, a mixture of pungent spices steaming in the bubbling liquid it held. The concoction filled the room with fragrant scents, and spicy pine boughs hung at every window sash, bordered every table. But by far the most spectacular sight was the huge evergreen tree in the center of the drawing room that opened off the parlor.

With almost childish delight, Elyse approached for closer inspection. Her eyes glistened as she gazed up at the huge tree. Years before, Uncle Ceddy had explained the Christmas custom of the German people. Each Christmas at yuletide, they cut pine trees in the forest and brought them into their homes to be decorated. Candles were carefully placed on the tips of branches decorated with bows, strings of colorful beads, and hand-painted toys. Enraptured by the story, Elyse had pleaded with her grandmother that they have just such a tree for their next Christmas.

Now she inspected every decoration. She'd made most of them herself as a child. Hand-stitched dolls and toy soldiers clung to the branches along with the hand-carved wooden animals Quimby had made for her one year. They competed for space with fresh apples and oranges, while white candles in small gold holders winked from the ends of the branches. Atop the tree was a shining gold star. And below, peeking from beneath the lowest boughs, were colorfully wrapped packages.

"They're not all for you, my sweet." Lady Regina smiled lovingly. In return Elyse frowned teasingly as her grandmother took her hand. "How would it look if I spoiled you, by giving you everything under the tree?"

As he silently watched their exchange, Sir Cedric coughed behind his hand. "I'm afraid you don't have to be concerned with that, my dear," he said to Lady Regina. "You've already done it." Humor danced in his eyes as he pressed a kiss against Elyse's cheek.

"You look ravishing. I propose a toast." He took three goblets of champagne from a nearby tray, and raised his glass ceremoniously. "To the two most beautiful women in all London. One I consider as dear as my own daughter"—his eyes twinkled beneath the sweep of frosty white brows—"the other"—he hesitated, a devilish gleam sparkling in his eyes—"I should like to call my wife," he announced softly, his gaze fastened on Regina.

"Wife! Good God, Ceddy, have you taken leave of your senses?" Regina pressed her hand against her heart as the champagne threatened to go down the wrong way. Several of her guests glanced in their direction.

"Not at all." Sir Cedric smiled back at her, knowing the advantage was all his. "I've asked you several times, and I've decided it's now or never," he announced emphatically.

"Is that so?" Lady Regina recovered quickly. She fixed her eyes on him, a contemplative expression on her face. "You know very well I don't like ultimatums," she responded with equal emphasis.

Elyse headed off the impending confrontation. Both Ceddy and her grandmother could be unreasonably stubborn. "I think it's a grand idea," she announced, thinking she'd like nothing better than to see the two dearest people in her life together. "It's about time you made an honest woman of her." She smiled as she sipped from her glass.

"Well!" Regina blustered. "I can see whose side you're on, my dear! I think this is hardly the time or place to be discussing such matters. And I'll tell you both right now, I won't be manipulated into a decision."

Cedric ignored her last remark. "It's precisely the time and place." He reached for a nearby bottle of champagne, and refilled their glasses.

But Regina begged off. "Please, Ceddy, no more. You know how it affects me. I can't have you talking me into something when I'm under the influence of champagne."

Filling her glass with bubbling liquid, he would have none of that. "I want it to affect you, my dear. And I think there's no better time to discuss this. After all, Elyse is to be married in June. Then what will you do with yourself?"

"I hadn't thought about it. There's been so much to do lately. I suppose I thought we would continue as before."

"I'm afraid that just won't do, Reggie," he informed her matter-of-factly.

"You see, it's not a matter of my making you an honest woman, but of your making me an honest man. My dear, you've absolutely ruined my reputation, keeping company with me as you have the last several years." He shook his head with mock tragedy. As Regina's mouth dropped open at his outrageous announcement, he pressed his argument.

"Therefore, I insist that you accept this now." He slipped his hand into the pocket of his waistcoat, producing a small box.

Elyse watched in delight as he opened it, revealing the ring inside. A large gleaming emerald was set amidst smaller diamonds. It was the most beautiful ring she'd ever seen.

"If you don't accept it, I will. Actually, I can't think of anything I would like more than for you two to be married," she declared, and took another sip of champagne, a thoughtful expression on her lovely face. As if she'd been struck with sudden inspiration, her eyes widened. "We could make it a double wedding! Wouldn't that set London on its ear." She whirled around. "I must find Katy and tell her." She was off in a swirl of red silk.

"No, Elyse wait!" Lady Regina called helplessly after her granddaughter. Then she turned on Cedric, her eyes, so like Elyse's, narrowing. "You did that deliberately. Now everyone will know about it," she accused.

"That's what I'm counting on, my dear. It's a sorry situation when a man is forced to coerce a woman into marrying him." He smiled in spite of himself, quite satisfied. "Now you dare not refuse."

Lady Regina fought back a smile, her eyes sparkling. "I should be angry with you." She tried to remain very stern.

But Cedric wasn't fooled. "You should, but you won't. Because, my dear"—he took her arm, pulling it through his as he lifted his glass in a toast to her—"you know as well as I that it's time to get on with our lives."

Regina smiled softly. "You're right, of course. And I do love you, Ceddy." Her gaze wandered across the parlor to where Elyse was laughing gaily. Her granddaughter was beautiful, and Regina so wanted her to be happy. Her expression became pensive. "I had hoped Jerrold would be here by now. Lord Barrington gave his word he would come. I hope this isn't a sign of more difficulty." She frowned, wondering what diversion kept Elyse's fiancé from her side at this time. "There are times when I wonder if I'm doing the right thing in allowing her to marry him," she mused aloud.

"Allowing her?" Sir Cedric practically burst out laughing. "My dear, I've never seen a campaign to match yours in arranging this marriage. I thought it was what you wanted."

"I want Elyse's happiness." Regina watched her granddaughter thoughtfully.

"She seems happy enough." Ceddy's gaze followed hers.

"Yes." There was a note of hesitancy in Lady Regina's voice. "She seems to be happy. I just wish I could be certain. I wish she were more concerned about Jerrold's absences. But it's as if . . ."

Cedric raised her chin with his fingers. "She wouldn't have accepted his offer if she wasn't certain. Elyse is a strong-minded girl. I can't imagine anyone forcing her to do anything. She reminds me a lot of you in that respect."

Regina smiled faintly at his last remark, but she was still troubled. "I lay awake nights wondering if she's doing it for me. Jerrold's mother was a dear friend of mine, but God knows that's not reason to insist on a marriage. I just want her to be happy and secure when I'm gone."

"I know that, my dear," Cedric responded.

"She lost both her parents and has no other close family, so there's no one to look after her."

Cedric fixed her with an amused expression. "Somehow I can't imagine Elyse needing someone to look after her."

Regina acted as if she hadn't heard a word he'd said. "There are times when I look at her, hear something in her voice when she speaks of Jerrold or the wedding . . . she seems so casual about it all, so . . . accepting, as if she's resigned herself to it. That's not how a bride should feel."

"I would hardly call her resigned. Look at the girl, she is positively radiant."

Regina nodded, unconvinced. "Yes, she does seem happy, and she hasn't been bothered by the dreams lately. But still . . . there's something about her. Do you know she's taken to riding early in the morning? She leaves before anyone else is awake. I'm worried about her. She's always been such a responsible child. I'm at a loss to understand this restlessness in her lately. And every once in a while I find her looking out the window, as if she were watching for something . . . or someone."

"Have you tried talking to her about it? She really shouldn't be out alone."

"Yes, she doesn't try to lie about it, but she refuses to give it up, insisting that if she can ride in the country, she can ride when we're here in London. I've had Quimby follow her at a discreet distance. I'm uncertain whether she knows he's doing it."

"Then what have you to worry about? She's safe enough with Quimby about. God knows the man would give his life for her." Cedric tried to assuage Regina's fears.

"You're right of course," she admitted. "Still . . ."

"Are you worried about how it looks for the future Lady Barrington to be out alone, scamping about London?" he teased, knowing full well Regina had never given a fig about what other people thought. It was one of the things he loved about her. Since Elyse had come to live with her, she had made a distinct effort to observe certain rules of propriety, however, for she was determined that her American-born granddaughter would take her rightful place in society.

She gave him a capricious smile. "I do not care what people think about me, but I want the very best for Elyse. Look at her, Ceddy." Lady Regina's eyes glowed proudly. "She is lovely, isn't she?"

"Almost as lovely as her grandmother." He raised her hand to place a kiss across the backs of her fingers.

She squeezed his hand affectionately, but her worried expression lingered. "Perhaps after the holidays, she'll take more interest in the wedding."

"Speaking of weddings . . ." Taking the gift box from her hand, he removed the ring and carefully placed it on her finger. "I should like you to consider ours. Don't worry about Elyse. She'll be happy. And Jerrold will make her a good husband. There's too much at stake for him to fail. After all, Lord Barrington wants this marriage almost as badly as you do. And besides"—he paused, winking at her—"he'll have to answer to me if he doesn't."

Lady Regina smiled as she looked down at the ring. She prayed Ceddy was right. She knew Jerrold adored Elyse, and it did seem that lately he was curtailing some of his more indiscreet activities. In his circle, membership at White's, one of London's more elite men's clubs, was expected, as was occasional gaming or betting on horses at the private jockey club. That didn't bother her. What did bother her were the persistent rumors of his various liaisons since the betrothal was announced. Lord Barrington had assured her these were nothing to be concerned about, saying Jerrold's activities were merely a young man's dalliance before settling down into marriage.

"Have you given Elyse her gift yet?" Ceddy still held her hand.

Regina broke from her thoughts as soft music floated in from the adjacent room. "Not yet. I do hope she'll like it."

Cedric patted her hand. "Come along then, and let's give her at least one gift to open."

From beneath the tree, Regina selected a small package wrapped in gleaming gold satin paper and tied with a red bow. She looked up abruptly, a stunned expression on her face.

"Listen! Do you hear that?"

Cedric cocked his head in the direction of the music room. "Yes, and it's a very lovely piece. Although I can't quite place the melody."

"It's called 'Remembrance.' " Regina stood listening, her eyes suddenly quite somber as she recalled the title of the tune she hadn't heard in many years. "But it can't be. It's impossible," she whispered incredulously. She walked slowly toward the open music room, Elyse's gift clutched tightly in her hand.

Cedric followed her, a confused expression on his face. He'd never seen her act this way before. "Reggie? What is it?" He stood behind her in the doorway, listening with several other guests.

"My God! That was her favorite song," Lady Regina whispered, mesmerized by the soft music.

Elyse was seated at the piano in the center of the room, her slender hands moving with unerring grace across the keys. The notes filled the air, wrapping everyone in haunting sweetness.

Cedric was faintly surprised. "I didn't know Elyse had become so accomplished," he said to Regina.

"Nor did I," she admitted. "She always hated her music lessons. Katy had to stand over her just to make certain she didn't sneak off." Her voice caught. "How could she possibly know that melody? It's been almost twenty years." She stood watching, enraptured by the radiant girl who was lovingly playing the beautiful haunting strains.

41

"Obviously, she knows the piece quite well," Cedric conceded. As he turned to Regina, his eyes filled with concern. "Reggie, for God's sake, what is it?"

"That was Felicia's song." Her eyes were fastened on Elyse.

"I see no reason for alarm, my dear." He tried to comfort her. "It's obviously a well-known composition."

"No! You don't understand!" she insisted. "That was Felicia's song." Like the others in the room, she listened, completely captivated by the soft notes that were almost mournful. "Dear Felicia," she reminisced, "it's been so many years since I last heard her play it."

Cedric shifted uneasily, at a loss to understand why a beautiful but simple melody should disturb her so. "Perhaps Elyse came across the music somewhere."

"That's not possible." Regina turned on him insistently. "No music was ever written for it. Felicia composed it herself. Don't you see? It's not possible that Elyse could have learned it in her lessons."

"Dear Felicia." Her eyes grew misty. "I remember the first time I ever heard her play it. There was such a sadness about her, such a loneliness in the notes. I heard it once more, when I went to visit her after she became ill that last time. I remember she was supposed to be resting, but I heard music coming from the upstairs solarium. She was playing 'Remembrance.' When she finished, she said she would never play it again, because it was too late. I never knew what she meant by that. Only a few weeks after that, she was finally gone."

Regina turned to Cedric. "Do you remember? It was when James and Anne were lost in the shipwreck, and we thought Elyse was lost as well. Of course, we didn't find out until days later about Felicia, after Elyse had been found and was recovering quite nicely." Her gaze fastened on the beautiful young girl at the piano. "So much sadness that day. I thought afterward that Elyse's recovery was like a gift amid so much sadness and loss."

Cedric smiled gently. "It's Christmas, my darling. This is supposed to be a happy time."

She smiled up at him. "I know, and I am very happy. You and Elyse have seen to that. Thank you." Regina's gaze returned to her granddaughter. Yes, she was happy. She prayed Elyse would be as happy.

The melody ended, the last soft notes of the refrain haunting those in the room. After a moment of silence, Regina's guests clapped, obviously greatly taken with the stirring performance.

Elyse looked up, her surprised gaze locking with Regina's across the room. Her eyes glistened almost feverishly, and she smiled as if embarrassed, then nodding to their guests, she joined Ceddy and her grandmother.

Cedric complimented her lovingly. "That was absolutely stunning, my dear. I didn't know you were so accomplished."

Elyse laughed a little shakily. "Actually, I'm not. I always hated my lessons, and would do anything to get out of them. I don't know why I remembered that particular piece." She squeezed Regina's hand affectionately. "It must be the Christmas spirit. It's my gift to you." Elyse smiled softly at her grandmother.

Regina's breath caught in her throat, and her hand fluttered over her heart. "Those were her very words the last time she played that melody." She suddenly felt very light-headed, and her blue-veined hand reached for Cedric.

"Reggie, what is it?" His arm went around her for support when it seemed she might faint.

Elyse's eyes widened in alarm. "Grandmother! What is it?"

Regina's hand tightened over hers. "Where did you learn that melody?" she asked feebly.

Elyse looked from Ceddy to her grandmother, frightened by the sudden pallor on Regina's face. "I suppose Herr Lundgren taught it to me during one of my lessons. I really can't remember." She rushed on, her concern reflected in her soft blue eyes. "I didn't mean to upset you. I thought you would like it."

Regina hastened to reassure her, love shining in her eyes. "You haven't upset me. Quite the contrary, you've made me very happy. That particular melody has always been a favorite of mine. A very special friend once played it for me. Thank you, darling, for sharing it with us tonight. I can't think of a better gift."

Elyse smiled uncertainly at Cedric.

"I think it might have been the champagne," he suggested.

Mock horror showed in Elyse's eyes. "Grandmother!" She looked appropriately shocked. "Do you mean to tell me you're foxed?"

"Foxed!" Lady Regina immediately became more steady on her feet. "I should say not!" she responded indignantly. "Ceddy, how could you suggest such a thing? Quite the contrary. In fact, I feel the need for another glass of champagne, and"—she placed the satin-wrapped gift in her granddaughter's hand—"I have a gift for you."

Seeing that her grandmother seemed to be sufficiently recovered from whatever it was that had upset her so, Elyse indulged her curiosity. "What is it?"

"I'm surprised you haven't already guessed," Regina chided. "Open it." She drew Elyse down onto a nearby settee.

"Will you be all right, my dear? I see someone I would like to speak with." Cedric leaned over her, concern drawing his brows together. ●

"I've quite recovered," Regina assured him. Then she turned to Elyse. "Well? What are you waiting for? Aren't you going to open it? You've never waited this long before." Her merriment had returned, and was sparkling in those blue eyes so like her granddaughter's.

Carefully, Elyse untied the ribbon and undid the wrapping, revealing a small wooden box. As she lifted the lid, her delicate brows drew together in bewilderment. She couldn't imagine that her grandmother would give her another piece of jewelry. She'd already given her several and had said her granddaughter would have no more except as her inheritance.

Elyse turned back the velvet inside, her bewilderment quickly turning to astonishment. A pendant suspended from a strand of perfectly matched, luminous pearls lay on midnight blue satin. She'd seen the pendant several times, and knew her grandmother prized it highly. It carried some great sentimental value, although Elyse was uncertain of its origin.

"It's the most beautiful thing I've ever seen," she got out, though completely overwhelmed. The design was quite old-fashioned, but nonetheless spectacular. A wreath of twelve perfectly matched diamonds encircled the largest, most perfect pearl she'd ever seen. Another, smaller pearl dangled from the setting. The pendant was attached to the necklace by an elaborate fleur-de-lis fashioned from smaller diamonds. The piece was breathtakingly beautiful. Elyse raised questioning eyes to Lady Regina.

"Why are you giving this to me? I know how much it means to you."

"You're right," her grandmother admitted. "It does mean a great deal to me. It was a gift from a very dear friend of mine. Jerrold's mother."

Surprise filled Elyse's eyes. "Felicia Barrington?" She knew her grandmother had been acquainted with Jerrold's mother, but she hadn't known the pendant had belonged to Felicia.

"She was very much like a daughter to me. And she was a good friend. I admired the" — she hesitated, then went on — "the pendant once when I was visiting her. Then, after she became so ill, she had it delivered to me, insisting that I accept it. Though she never spoke of it, I'm certain she knew how ill she was. Within a matter of weeks, she was gone." Regina seemed to mentally shake herself free of that sad memory.

"Of course, the pendant wasn't attached to the necklace then. I added that later. I thought it such a waste to have something so lovely and not wear it."

"Did she wear it like this?" Elyse held the necklace against her throat.

Her grandmother shook her head. "I'm not certain." Again there was that hesitation. "I know it meant a great deal to her, and I've always valued it. Now it is yours."

Elyse grew thoughtful. "Jerrold has never mentioned it, yet he's seen you wear it several times."

"Men usually aren't concerned with that sort of thing." Lady Regina waved her bejeweled hand airily.

"Still, you would think he would notice something that belonged to his mother. I hope he won't object," Elyse mused thoughtfully.

"Nonsense. When you are Lady Barrington, all of the family jewels will go to you anyway. So it's only fitting that you should have this. And it would please me very much." She smiled at her granddaughter, knowing with those words she'd won their argument.

She watched Elyse, seeing something in her fragile beauty that reminded her of her dear friend, and she experienced the same feeling that had come over her when she'd watched her at the piano while listening to those haunting strains of music. She was convinced that if she closed her eyes and then opened them, she would find Felicia sitting beside her. But, of course, that was impossible. Elyse bore no physical resemblance to her friend. Still, there had been times in the past when she'd had the strangest feeling. . . .

Get a hold of yourself, Regina silently scolded herself. It means nothing. You're just becoming a sentimental old fool. Perhaps you should accept Ceddy's offer. At this rate, you'll need someone to take care of you very soon.

Again, she tried to shake off the feeling. And yet, as she watched Elyse's reaction to the pendant, she felt as if she were seeing someone else behind those startlingly blue eyes. It wasn't a frightening sensation. It was something else. There were moments when she saw something in Elyse—a look, a glance that was so completely different—and it seemed almost as if someone else was very carefully hidden away in her. It had been a long time since she'd

45

last had that feeling . . . until today. It usually came to her when Elyse had the dream she'd had as a child. But that was no longer anything to worry about. It had been a long time since she'd had that dream.

Elyse smiled softly at her grandmother. "I can't accept this, knowing how much it means to you."

Brought back abruptly from her silent musing, Regina chided her lovingly. "Of course you can accept it. Eventually, you shall have everything that is mine anyway, and it would give me great pleasure to see you wear it. Pretty things are meant to be enjoyed. To be very honest with you, it never looked right on me. Not everyone can wear pearls, you know."

She raised her hand, examining the elegant ring Cedric had given her. "Emeralds are much more to my liking." She looked up. "But you, my dear . . ." She seized the pearl pendant and reached up to fasten it about Elyse's neck. "You were meant to wear pearls. On some people, they seem to lose their luster, but on you . . ." She sat back to allow for a better inspection, cocking her head and smiling to herself. "Ah yes, you can wear pearls. See how they glow next to your skin." She drew Elyse to her feet before the mirror that hung over the fireplace mantel. "They seem to take on a life of their own."

The lustrous pearls did seem to glow when worn by Elyse. Almost luminous, they were a soft rose color, like satin against her skin.

"And," her grandmother continued, "it means a great deal to me that you have something of Felicia's. It's almost as if I were giving something back to her in giving this to you."

Elyse caressed the large single pearl, almost feeling its warmth. She couldn't refuse Regina something that meant so much to her. "Thank you," she whispered, tears glistening in her eyes. "I shall treasure it always." She squeezed her grandmother's hand, wishing she could always hold onto this moment of love.

"If I may be so bold," Cedric said as he rejoined them. He deposited a large package in Elyse's hands. "I also have a gift for you. And then I think we should rejoin our guests. Others have arrived, and your housekeeper, Mrs. Halverson, is insisting we sit down to Christmas dinner."

Regina casually inquired, "Has Jerrold arrived?" But the somber glow in her eyes belied her light tone.

"I'm certain he'll be along at any time," Cedric assured her, and they both noted Elyse's reaction.

She smiled at both of them, seemingly unaffected by her fiancé tardiness. "It is a pity he couldn't be here to see your gift to me, Grandmother. And if he doesn't arrive soon, he'll miss Mrs. Halverson's exceptional Christmas goose."

Her response was polite and proper, and completely lacking in concern. Regina frowned as her gaze met Cedric's.

"Come along then," he coaxed, taking her arm and then Elyse's. "By all means let's join your guests for Christmas dinner. I've heard the ugliest rumor that the queen has become aware of Mrs. Halverson's culinary reputation, and may try to steal her away from you. We don't want to keep her waiting, or we may just find her gone—spatula, apron and all."

Elyse ran. The mist swirled, sending trailing streamers after her. Like insistent fingers, they clung to her gown. Her clothes were cold and wet against her body. Her lungs ached.

A distant light shrouded in vapor lured her onward. The mist eddied and parted, the light becoming much brighter until it was almost blinding in intensity.

Elyse stopped, a smile softening her mouth as she willed the frantic racing of her heart to slow. Like an apparition, he emerged from the mist.

"I knew you'd come back," she breathed, her heart in her eyes. The light was the brilliance of the sun, emerging to bathe them in its glorious rays. It was suspended in an achingly blue sky, broken only by the upward thrust of two tall masts. There was a faint rolling motion beneath her feet as if she were on the deck of a ship. Her gaze fastened once more on the man. Slowly, she walked toward him, reaching for his outstretched fingers.

"I've waited so long for you." The words were an ache in her throat. "I was afraid you would never come."

His voice was like an echo from long ago as he drew her into his arms. His hand stroked her hair; his lips were against her ear, whispering of promises fulfilled and those yet to be kept.

Her eyes closed, the warmth of his body seeping into all the places deep inside her that had lain cold and empty for so long. At last, she felt as if she were truly complete, whole again. She leaned into him, her arms encircling his waist; becoming a part of this man who was an apparition from her dreams. It was as if their two souls ceased to exist and merged as one, bound across time, across the empty expanse of sky and sun and sea.

47

He gently cradled her head, the timeless yearning that was theirs returning with his achingly sweet touch. She waited breathlessly. His mouth touched hers tentatively like the barest whisper of love, as if he were reacquainting himself with the touch and taste of her.

As her arms stole about his neck, the wind and sun filled her senses, colliding with a longing that was equally timeless. Her mouth opened under his, breathing in the essence of him, remembering as his lips took possession. Emotions that had lain sleeping burst to life. Desire, from some millennium in time, jolted through her. This man, this moment—a thousand other moments remembered and once lost were theirs again.

Overhead the bright heat of the sun wavered as dark clouds appeared on the horizon. Rolling mist engulfed the deck of the ship. Her stricken gaze searched his beloved face, his eyes now haunted with longing and regret.

"No! Not this time!" she cried out as he pulled out of her arms, his lips forming silent words, tears falling from his eyes.

"Please stay! I can't bear it if you go!" Elyse reached for him desperately, the mist slipping through her fingers until nothing remained.

"Please! Don't go!" She ran into the mist, eyes wide, searching. There was nothing, only the aching loneliness once more.

Elyse collapsed onto the deck of the ship, but it, too, had once more been transformed and had disappeared into the mist. Hot tears flooded her eyes.

"You promised you would come back for me," she cried from the depths of her soul. "You promised."

Eyes wide, Elyse jerked upright in the bed. She yanked off the clinging blankets, struggling to draw a breath. She felt as if she'd run a very great distance; her lungs were aching. And, dear God, she was cold, unbearably cold. Her gown was plastered to her skin. In spite of the heavy blankets, Elyse shivered. The mist was gone now and with it, the phantom from her dream.

A broken sob escaped her as she collapsed back against the pillows. Across London, cathedral chimes rang out in the clear, Christmas night.

She'd almost begun to think the dream was finally gone. Now, she realized it wasn't gone at all. It was here and achingly real. Closing her eyes, she could almost feel the desire again, the strong arms closing around her, comforting, protecting.

"Who are you? What do you want?" she cried softly into the darkness. "How can you be so real to me and not be there?" She tried to hold onto the dream, but it was now only a lingering memory. Her fingers clutched at the pendant, the large pearl luminous against her skin.

"Please come back to me."

Chapter Two

Resolute Station
New South Wales, Australia

Eyes filled with pain and loss searched the land as evening stole across the fertile valley, last light glistening off the silvered ribbon of the river. Faint tendrils of mist shrouded the trees, making them seem like mournful women, draped in widow's weeds. The wisps clung to the earth, stealing through gulleys and hollows, guarding secrets, whispering to him with a soft rustling of leaves, the message unintelligible.

Beneath his feet, the ground cooled as night slipped over all. The scorching sun was gone now, hiding deceptively. Only in those last few moments of daylight, when the night air crept on cat feet and faint breezes stirred, did the land seem less harsh, almost peaceful. In moments like these, he could almost hear the voices. The aboriginals said they were the voices of their ancestors, speaking to them through the darkness of Dreamtime. For the natives, Dreamtime was the basis of all thought and practice. It was their cultural, historical, and ancestral heritage. In their minds, it was an age that existed long ago and yet remained ever present as a continuing, timeless experience linking past, present, and future. To them it was the dawn of all creation, when land, rivers, rain, wind, and all living things first began. Born and raised in this land, he accepted their beliefs, and now hoped they were true. He needed to believe that something from this life continued beyond the grave.

Shadows defined his sharply chiseled features as strong brows drew together over silver eyes that appeared almost catlike above the planes of pronounced cheekbones. His straight nose hinted of aristocratic ancestry, his mouth was thinned, uncharacteristically, into a tight line. A muscle flexed in his stubborn jawline.

50

"I should have been here for her." Zachary Tennant flattened his hand on the freshly turned earth, regret sharp in his voice. He smoothed the mound, as if he might still reach out to the woman buried there. Then his fingers closed, gathering the dry loam, trying to hold back death a little longer. Haunted eyes squeezed back tears. He wouldn't cry. Damn! She wouldn't want him to.

"Don't be so hard on yourself, lad." The voice came from the shadows beneath the gum tree. "She understood that you couldn't be here. The fight against the Crown means survival for Resolute, for all of us. You were needed elsewhere. She accepted that, just as she accepted this land."

"So far from her beloved Ireland," Zach lamented. "And she loved this land so much," he whispered brokenly.

"Aye, that she did, as your father loved it." The owner of the disembodied voice separated himself from the shadows, and Tobias Gentry, physician, stepped forward to bid silent farewell to a woman he'd respected and admired, and loved in his own way.

"Why, Tobias?" Zach fought the emotions that churned inside him. "How could she love a land that took so much from her?" He stared out at the vast valley that stretched away from the river, looked to the large white house framed in the growing twilight, as if he might find the answers there. In a sense he would. Resolute. True to its name, this land had been claimed from the wilderness by sheer determination and stubbornness.

Tobias straightened against the nagging infirmity in his back, and his pale blue eyes followed gray, searching for answers across the mist-shrouded land, finding different ones from the young man who mourned so deeply.

He grunted. "It didn't matter that the land wasn't her native Ireland. She loved your father, Zach, and everything that was him, including this land. She put her roots down deep, boy, and raised you here." Tobias laid a hand on the young man's shoulder, trying to think of something to say, offering comfort.

"Mourn her loss, boy, but don't mourn her love of Resolute. She pledged herself to this land just as she pledged herself to your father. It isn't likely she had any regrets." He fell silent, remembering the fair-haired young lass who'd come to Sydney so long ago.

They'd all begun in Sydney—he, Megan, and Zach's father, Nicholas. Dear Lord, had it really been so many years? He rubbed his hand thoughtfully across a chin grizzled with silvery whiskers. Time had a way of slipping away from you. He watched the boy, then smiled gently. Zachary Tennant was no longer a boy. He had to remind himself more often than not that he was twenty-seven now, a man full grown, very near the same age his father was when he'd arrived from England in the early years.

Zach swallowed, emotion hard in his throat. As earth fell from his fingers, his gaze returned to the valley. Herds of sheep swelled across the landscape, their bodies lean from clipping and recent lambing. He loved this land; loved its harshness, the unrelenting beauty and starkness of it. He knew Tobias was right. He could almost hear Megan's reproval of his anger. She'd loved Resolute almost as much as she'd loved his father.

Zach stood, eyes closed as he breathed in the pungent camphor of trees damp with early evening dew. This land was home, his parents were buried here in the wild place they loved. He understood the sadness of that and accepted it. But the restlessness he'd felt since Megan's death was less easily understood. Some vague thought, half-formed, nagged at him. He should have come back when he'd first learned she was gone. But Tobias was right, it would have served no purpose. Not then.

She'd always been Megan to him, never Mother or Ma. Just Megan. Perhaps it was because she had to be both mother and father to him, friend and family. She and Tobias and Resolute had formed the core of his life. And then, when she'd needed him, the one time he should have been there, England had denied them that, just as it had denied them so many freedoms.

Tobias waited silently. There was a time to mourn and a time to heal, a time to all seasons according to the Bible. He knew he must give Zach his time. And then he must fulfill an old promise. He shifted, feeling all of his sixty years as he watched the man beside the three graves, one new, the other two different in size and one of those marking the death of a small child, Megan's firstborn. Tobias sighed heavily.

Good God! Had Nicholas really been gone so long? Yes, yes of course, he thought. He'd been gone since just before Zach was born. The lad had never known his father, except through Megan's memories and stories. But then, Megan hadn't known everything.

He looked up as Zach walked toward him, brimmed hat in hand, the early evening breeze gently lifting golden hair so like his mother's.

"Come on, Tobias. Megan wouldn't want us wasting time. Minnie should have supper waiting, and I want to meet with Jingo first thing in the morning. There are stray lambs to be brought in." He wrapped an arm around the older man's shoulders. The bond

52

between them was deep. Tobias had been like the father he never had, making his home here at Resolute. They'd made an odd family; a widowed woman with a son to raise, an assortment of itinerant workers, and Tobias.

"Aye, lad." The older man nodded brusquely. "Yer mother never did hold with grievin' for very long. She used to say the land couldn't wait for such things. It just goes on and on, bein' what it is. Its needs don't change. She got that from yer father." Together, they walked from the small hill above the house, the wild grass damp and pungent beneath their boots.

Inside the dwelling, the smells of the evening meal bolstered them, reminding both men that, like the land, appetites didn't understand the need to mourn. A robust woman emerged from the kitchen, steely hair pulled sharply back from her face into a neat bun. A ladle was clenched in the hand she propped against an ample hip. Clad in men's work pants and clean white shirt, Minnie scrutinized both men.

"Dinner's gettin' cold," she announced. But her soft brown gaze lingered on Zach. "You all right?"

Minerva Halstead had been at Resolute since Zach was a small boy. Almost as wide as she was tall, she was chief cook and housekeeper. The two women in the house had been an odd pair, Minnie's robust girth overshadowing his mother's slender height. She'd arrived at Resolute over twenty years ago, a child tucked under each arm and no husband. She'd informed everyone she was a widow, although no one had ever bothered to verify that fact. She just arrived, went to work, and never went back to wherever it was she came from. It had been Megan's policy never to ask about a person's past. She'd always said nothing mattered but today and what tomorrow could bring.

Zach nodded, his smile not quite reaching his eyes, eyes different from Megan's soft blue ones. "Yeah, I'm all right. She wouldn't want me wastin' time."

"Right ya are. I never knew a woman like yer ma for work. Yer the same way." Minnie nodded. Suddenly thoughtful, she stared down at her boots. "I suppose you won't be stayin' long this time."

"We've got wool for the ships in Sydney harbor. The Queen's navy will be startin' their regular patrols, so I want to get two more ships out, and a very special cargo." Zach nodded. "I think Resolute's in safe hands for a little while."

"Megan wouldn't want you riskin' yer neck like the last time," she reprimanded with motherly affection. "Besides, my Tess is comin'

53

up from Adelaide." Her eyes sparkled with old mischief.

"She's turned into a right proper young lady in spite of herself."

Zachary laughed. "Still the matchmaker, Minnie?"

"My Tess would make you a fine wife. She's got a temperament to match yours, and it's about time you thought about settlin' down. It just ain't right for a handsome man like you to be shyin' away from the ladies," she scolded.

Zach watched her with amused eyes. It was a frequent topic of discussion, and she was right. He and Tess were of the same temperament; that was precisely why he was convinced life with someone as volatile as Tess would be pure hell. As long as he could remember, Minnie had been scheming to get them together. He tried imagining the high-spirited Tess complete with proper manners. The last time he'd seen her, she'd had her skirts hiked practically over her head, and was astride a nervous brush pony that threatened to unseat her at any moment. He'd ordered her off the beast for the animal's sake.

Tess had a wildness about her he found difficult to believe anyone could tame. He remembered how she'd followed him into the barn that sultry hot afternoon. There in the cool shade she'd stripped down to bare skin without so much as a flush appearing on her adolescent body. Raising her dampened, long blond hair off her sweat-beaded back, she'd calmly proclaimed she was hot all over. It was almost more than any man could be expected to endure. Yet Zach had endured it and politely refused, heaving her into a stall and covering her light body with scratchy hay. He could still hear the obscenities that had followed him all the way to the main house. Two days later, Minerva had bundled Tess off to a distant cousin in Adelaide and what she'd hoped was a proper education. With a faint twist of a smile, Zach wondered just who had been the instructor and who the pupil. It might be interesting to see what changes Tess had gone through, but more urgent matters demanded his return to Sydney.

The local parliament was allowing itself to be dictated to by the home government in London, on matters including the raising of impossible tariffs on all imported goods. As for exports, such as valuable cargoes of high quality wool, Mother England was rapidly taking the final steps toward monopolizing all shipping, the Barrington Shipping Company out of London being their approved carrier. All independent shipping lines were forbidden to carry any cargo for export to Europe. Slowly, but surely, the Crown was imposing an economic stranglehold on the colonies in Australia, and vast profits were making their way into the pockets of the powdered and pompous overlords in London.

Zach and some of his friends felt it was time to loosen that stranglehold. Some would call what they did in secret off the coast of Australia acts of piracy against the Crown. But loyal colonists considered it a bid for independence every time a ship of the Barrington line was attacked and sent to the bottom of the ocean along with its cargo. It would mean Zach's life and those of every one of his crew if they were ever caught or their identities were discovered. They'd known that from the very beginning, and they carried that haunting truth with them each time they sailed against an English ship. But their attacks had worked. In the past two years, they'd sent an impressive amount of shipping to the bottom of the sea. In short, they'd gotten the attention of the Crown. The penalties were high. Every man who sailed with Zach had a price on his head. But Zach was undaunted. He'd strike and strike again, until the mighty English lion was ready to listen to the colonists' demands for competitive shipping practices. Until that day came . . .

"Sorry, luv." Zach smiled at Minnie, a heartbreaking smile.

"So what are you waitin' for? My Tess is as close as you'll find to perfection," she hinted, her meaning obvious.

"Maybe I'm not looking for perfection," Zach argued playfully, and leaned around the large woman for a better glimpse of dinner.

She slapped at his shoulder. "You'll not set foot in my kitchen smellin' like range critters." Her eyes sharpened. "Just what are you lookin' for in a woman? Those fancy sportin' women in Sydney aren't for you. Why yer dear mother would turn over in her grave if you tried to bring a woman like that onto Resolute."

Zach almost burst out laughing. "Minnie, sportin' women are for sportin', not marryin'." He grew thoughtful, however, as his stomach grumbled at the delay of supper, and, placing strong hands on her ample shoulders, he gazed solemnly into her eyes.

"I'm waiting for the one woman meant to share my life." He pressed a finger against her mouth as she started to question just who that might be. "I don't know who she is. I haven't met her yet"—a faint smile teased his lips—"but I'll know her when I meet her."

"I suppose she's a woman from yer dreams," Minnie huffed indignantly.

"We all have our dreams, mine just happen to be a bit more elusive than most."

"Well, it can't be for not lookin' that you haven't found her yet," Minnie admonished. "Every woman in Sydney under the age of sixty and old enough to say yes is after you."

"Minerva"—he shook a finger at her—"one of these days, I'll return to Resolute with my bride flung over my shoulder and surprise everyone." He glanced over her shoulder, sniffing the aromas filtering from the kitchen.

"You'll most likely surprise yourself," she huffed, "and quit eyin' them biscuits. They're for dinner." She motioned to Tobias. "Go on and get cleaned up."

Zach nodded, then gave her an affectionate peck on the cheek. "Minnie, m' dear, I do believe you've lost weight. If you're not careful, you'll waste away to nothing," he teased.

"Go on with ya." She swiped at him with the ladle. "Don't you go bein' cheeky with me," she grumbled as she turned and waddled into the kitchen.

"Damned bossy woman!" Tobias muttered as he followed Zach to the closed-in porch off the kitchen, where a pump gleamed over a metal sink. "You'd think she owns the place."

"At times, I do," Zach admitted. "I don't know what we'd do without her."

Tobias rolled his sleeves. "Just don't go tellin' her that. She's impossible to live with as it is." He thoughtfully scrubbed his hands and arms; a habit he'd acquired when he'd been a physician, though many doctors had ridiculed the practice.

"There's something I need to talk with you about, But it'll keep till after supper." He cast a thoughtful glance at Zach as he reached for a nearby towel. "There's several things need to be discussed now that Megan . . ." His voice trailed off. "I'll meet you in the dining room. I need something from upstairs." He turned down the hallway and made his way to the stairs that led to the second-floor rooms.

Zach cut through a tender lamb chop, hardly tasting it as he popped it into his mouth. But he smiled his compliments to Minnie anyway. Then he drained the coffee from his cup and thoughtfully contemplated Tobias who was entering the room.

His old friend hesitated as if considering something of importance. Then, apparently having made a decision, he crossed the dining room, dropped into one of the straight-backed chairs, and set a small traveling case on the table.

Zach motioned to the satchel that looked much like a medical bag. "You thinking of startin' up your medical practice again?" he teased gently. Over the years Tobias had provided medical care for the workmen at Resolute and other families across the valley. The library was filled with medical texts, most of them brought with him from England years ago. Occasionally he ordered a new book from Sydney, but it took months to reach New South Wales from Europe. In all those years, he'd never chosen to set up practice in the bustling port town. It was another of those unexplained secrets from the past. Just as Zach had learned never to question Minnie's past, he'd never questioned Tobias about his. Someone's past was no one else's business.

Tobias gave him a thoughtful look, then shoved the bag across the table.

Zach waved him off, thinking he meant to teach him some new medical technique. "I don't have time. Those lambs need to be brought in to the feeding pens or we'll lose them. And there's wool to be loaded on the flatboats down at the river. The warehouse in Sydney is empty, and I want to get those ships out before Barrington Shipping and the Crown see fit to close us down." There was contempt in his voice.

Tobias patted the trunk solemnly, then took a cup of strong coffee from Minnie. "This won't wait, Zach. I promised to give you this once Megan was gone." His saddened eyes shifted down to the table.

Zach pushed his plate back. Toying with his coffee cup, he glanced across at the small satchel. "Promised who?"

Tobias's careworn eyes met his. "I promised your father, before you were born. I've kept this all these years. Megan never knew about the trunk."

Zach's gaze fastened on the scarred leather case. The aching emptiness he'd felt earlier, returned. They were both gone now— Megan and the father he'd never known. Nicholas Tennant had died before he was born, but Zach knew him as if they'd shared a life together. Tobias and Megan had seen to that, by telling him stories of the early days at Resolute, when his father had brought his new bride to the sheep station from Sydney.

The old man nodded. "Nicholas kept a journal, beginning on the day he left London. I imagine it's inside. There's a great deal you never knew about your father, a great deal none of us ever knew, not even Megan. That's the way it was in the early days. No one asked questions and no one volunteered information."

It was impossible for Zach to tear his eyes away from the satchel with initials etched in the cracked leather. It was old and scarred, its corners worn away. It had endured much handling.

"Minerva! Where is that woman when you need her?" Tobias bellowed.

"Right here, you old fool. Calm down, you'll get apoplexy." Without being told, she retrieved a bottle of whiskey from the kitchen cabinet. It was kept there for medicinal purposes on orders from Dr. Tobias Gentry. She poured a healthy draught.

Tobias looked up at Zach. "Megan and I told you about the years after he came to Resolute. But I first met Nicholas Tennant in Sydney. He never spoke about the past, felt it was best forgotten. Then those last months before he was killed, he seemed to change his mind, especially after he knew Megan was carryin' you. He hoped for a son, and I know he'd be real proud of you. He told me about the journal. He said if anything ever happened, I was to make sure you got it after yer mother was gone. He felt you'd have a need someday to know about all the years before he came here." Tobias took a liberal swallow of the *medicinal* coffee. Reaching out, he thumped the trunk.

"It's all in there; everything about when he was a young man. You read it."

"Megan told me everything." Zach's gaze impaled the case as if he might see the contents without opening it. A shiver throbbed along his nerve endings, almost as if he were reluctant to know what might be inside.

The old man rose from his chair, setting the drained cup down hard on the table. "She told you what she knew, what she'd been told by your father, what life was like after she came to Resolute. But it wasn't everything." Tobias slowly came back to the table. Leaning across it, he braced his weight on his knuckles.

"There's a great deal you don't know about Nicholas Tennant, because he never told anyone else. I only knew bits and pieces, as much as he wanted me to know, and I never questioned him. We all had our secrets in those days." He ran a hand over the trunk, regret lining his face; regret for the old wounds he feared the truth might bring.

"When you've finished, I'll be down at the barn. That mare's gonna foal anytime. Horses or babies, it doesn't make much difference." Grabbing his hat, Tobias shoved it down hard on his head. But he stopped at the door to the dining room and held out his hand. Frowning her disapproval, Minnie nonetheless held her tongue and handed him the whiskey bottle.

Zach stared at the satchel. After draining his coffee, he reached for the it and twisted the latch. It opened freely.

The dusty journal lay on top, its leather binding cracked and worn, the pages slightly faded. Zach read the opening entry:

London, England
June 7, 1839

   I begin this journey into hell. One day I will return and have my day of justice for the crime of which I am accused.
   I will reclaim my birthright from those who have accused me. And, God willing, Felicia will be waiting for me. I shall now be called Nicholas Tennant.

Zach stared hard at the neatly scrawled words of a man taking on a new identity. Turning the pages, he slowly began reading about the man he'd never known, his father, Nicholas Tennant. The words pulled at him, drawing him back to another time and place. Her name appeared again—Felicia. The night breeze stirred the drapes at the windows. Already, mist slipped heavily across the land, bathing it in unnatural light. Felicia. Her name was like a whisper across his soul.

He looked up. The soft glow of the lamp was creating golden pools in the room. His eyes ached from reading. The opening passages began with the voyage from England, and a detailed description of the squalid conditions aboard ship. Again that name appeared, almost like a litany spoken to ward off the suffering and longing of the young man who'd made the entries so long ago. As he read, Zach's fascination grew. Who was Felicia? And what was the crime his father had been accused of? Before, he'd believed his father was a settler who'd arrived like so many in the early years of the colonies. But the entries he read were hardly the words of a man at peace with his life or the land where he'd been thrust. Youthful anger and the desire for revenge leaped at him from the pages.

Zach sat back in his chair, the chair his father had once used. The name haunted him. Felicia. Who was she? Zach slammed the journal shut, not yet fully read. He reached for a thick bundle of neatly folded papers at the bottom of the satchel. They were official government documents.

One was an unconditional grant of land. Zach set it aside, knowing it was the deed to the land at Resolute. Scanning the other documents, he found one that was torn into several pieces.

His eyes narrowed as he tried to decipher the elaborately scrawled words on one piece. Then, as he held several pieces together, hard lines formed between his brows. The words *Form of Conditional Pardon* leaped off the paper at him.

The kitchen door slammed behind him as he stormed across the yard, mist swirling in his wake. Not finding Tobias in the barn, he rounded the paddock, throwing the door to the small office back hard on its hinges. Eyes blazing, he heaved the journal down on the desk. It hit the hard surface with a damning thud.

"My father was a convict!"

Tobias winced, the whiskey having failed to completely dull his senses. The accusation echoed in the small office, bringing back a flood of memories filled with secrets. He pushed himself back in the hard chair, squinting to focus his weary eyes. He sighed heavily.

"Megan's mare threw a fine colt," he replied dully. "That line will produce some good horses."

Zach descended on the desk and the man behind it. Hands twisting the front of Tobias's shirt, he hauled him upright. "It's true, isn't it!"

"Aye, it's true," the old man acknowledged, pulling himself free. "As were a lot of us sent to serve out our sentences."

The full impact of his response slowly registered with Zach. He let Tobias fall back into the chair. "You were a convict?"

Tobias nodded as he slumped wearily, shoulders sagging. "Aye," he admitted gruffly, his gaze dropping to Zach's clenched fists. "Those were hard times, harsh penalties."

"Why? In god's name, what was your crime?"

Tobias rubbed his bloodshot eyes. "My crime?" he repeated thoughtfully. And then he laughed cynically. "My crime was my profession." He waved Zach's next question aside.

"I was trained to be a physician at the Royal Academy of Medicine, a most prestigious school." With an almost conspiratorial air, he leaned forward in his chair.

"You see, one must have connections even to be admitted to the school." Laughing to himself at some private joke, he leaned his head into his hands. "My father wanted me to be a country gentleman, marry well. I had delusions of a profession, to the great horror of my aristocratic family." There was a note of derision to the last words. "But they finally relented. After all, I was not the firstborn son, merely the second. I was allowed to enroll at the Academy, where I quickly earned my degree. A most promising career loomed ahead of me."

"That is"—he paused—"until the day I accepted a very prominent and influential gentleman and his family as my patients." Tobias shifted, uncomfortable with the memory as he continued.

"The son was taken ill with a severe fever. The family delayed in contacting me, refusing to accept the seriousness of the boy's illness. When I was finally summoned, he was already very weak. He died two days later. Suffice it to say, the family was deeply grieved at the loss of their only son and heir. As a result, I was brought up on charges before the local magistrate. Because of the man's position in the House of Lords, I was tried and convicted of contributing to the boy's death. A brilliant career was shattered, a family ruined." With an absent wave of a hand, he continued, only the faintest trembling of his fingers giving any indication of the emotions that still held him prisoner.

"Because of my family's position, my sentence was reduced from hanging to a seven-year term at the penal colony at New South Wales, and permanent exile from England. I arrived in Sydney in the spring of 1817 to begin my sentence. I met your father there. We were men of a similar past. He told me only that he'd been wrongly accused of a crime. I never questioned him about it, and he never chose to speak of it again." Tobias opened a drawer to rummage for another bottle of whiskey.

"You're drunk," Zach accused, wondering how much he should believe.

"And I plan on getting a lot drunker before the night is over," Tobias announced, finding the bottle and turning it over appreciatively in his unsteady hands. "As a physician of dubious reputation, I'm certain of one thing"—he squinted a rheumy eye—"this is the only thing that dulls the pain."

Zach descended on him, the bottle shattering against the far wall. "No you don't!" He jerked Tobias back out of the chair, dragging him across the office and out into the open yard. Hauling him to a stop in front of a large wooden trough, he shook the old man until his head wobbled back and forth on his shoulders.

"I want some answers and I want you sober enough to give them!" he spat out the words with choking fury. Ignoring Tobias's feeble protests, he plunged him headfirst into the cool water, holding him under until bubbles frantically broke the surface.

Tobias's arms flailed wildly as he tried to free himself. Finally Zach jerked him up, coughing and spewing, allowing him only enough time to inhale a small amount of air before plunging him

61

back in again. He dunked the old man three more times, until his arms hung limply at his sides. Relenting then, Zach jerked him out for the last time and dropped him into the dust at his feet.

Gasping for air, Tobias clutched at his throat. "You tried to drown me!" he rasped between gulps for air. His reddened nose held the only distinguishable color in his face. The rest of his skin was a sickly, pasty green. Finally drawing a deep breath, he fell silent. Then his eyes widened. Scrambling to his knees, he crawled as fast as he could across the yard and rounded the corner of the horse barn.

Zach listened in disgust as Tobias was sick again and again behind the shelter of the barn. When he heard nothing but silence for a couple of minutes, he started around the barn, suddenly afraid he might have been too hard on the old man. Rounding the corner, he was stopped by a well-laid punch that caught him in the midsection.

The air rushed out of Zach's lungs in a whoosh. Surprise quickly turning to anger, he staggered backward into the dirt.

"What the bloody hell . . . !" His gray eyes turned the color of darkest slate.

Tobias stood over him, legs spread, chest puffed up like a banty rooster's. His clothes were soaked, his hair rumpled; but he'd obviously fully recovered from the unexpected bath Zach had given him.

"Just remember, boyo," he roared, his head beginning to clear, "I can still take you any day of the week!"

"Is that right?" Zach propelled himself up out of the dirt.

"Right!" The older man stood his ground as they came nose to nose, or rather nose to chest; he refused to be intimidated by Zach's height. "I seem to recall takin' yer father down a peg or two in me youth. I'm not too old that I can't put you in yer place as well," he shouted.

"In your youth," Zach reminded him, hands planted on his hips.

"In me youth, or now. It doesn't matter. I got a few tricks I can show you," Tobias blustered, knowing even as he did, he was getting himself in deeper and deeper. But, after all, a man could be pushed just so far.

Zach reconsidered, knowing he could beat Tobias in a fair fight. But what would it prove? That he was stronger and younger? He shook his head. "Not today, old man. I want you in one piece to answer some questions." He turned away, unaware that Tobias's shoulders sagged in relief.

Tobias followed Zach back to the barn, keeping a cautious distance between them. They collapsed into chairs on opposite sides of the desk. More stubborn than cautious, Tobias reached inside the bottom drawer, retrieving a third bottle. He held it up. "Drink?"

"Don't mind if I do." Zach winced faintly as he felt the bruised ribs that had taken Tobias's punch. He shook his head. "You throw one helluva punch for an old man." He frowned as he accepted the bottle, taking a healthy swig. He and Tobias had shared more than one bottle over the years. This was the first time they'd ever shared one as a peace offering to one another.

"You've got a wee bit more muscle than the last time I took ya on," Tobias conceded. "I'll have to remember that next time." Taking the bottle back, he raised it in salute.

"You drink too much," Zach criticized.

"Aye," Tobias agreed, "that might be true. I can't seem to throw as good a punch as I used to. A few years back, if you'd tried that stunt at the trough you'd have been picking yerself outta the dirt."

"I did pick myself out of the dirt," Zach reminded him with a wry smile, picking at the stained cloth of his shirt. His expression sobered.

"Who was Felicia? What did she have to do with my father?"

Tobias's eyes widened at the name. "Your father always spoke of returning to England, until the day a letter arrived from her. Her name was Barrington. I never knew the contents of that letter, but after that your father changed. He never spoke of her or England again. It was as if that letter cut off any ties he had there. But she meant somethin' important to him. I'm certain Megan never knew about her."

"The letter wasn't in the trunk."

"He destroyed it. I watched him as he tore it into pieces and burned it. I think most of your father's dreams must have been destroyed along with that letter. Not long after that, he accepted a post on a journey inland over the mountains from Sydney. He talked me into going with him. We traveled for months. Then we found this place, and your father named it Resolute. The provisional government saw to it he had an unconditional, full deed of title to as much land as he wanted out here. I suppose they thought if he was buried in the interior, they were well rid of both of us. And your father was content to remain here, except for occasional trips to Sydney. I think it was all because of her. Lady Felicia Barrington."

Zach leaned across the desk, retrieving the whiskey bottle. He took a long drink, then reached into his shirt pocket.

"What do you know about this?" He opened his fingers, revealing a diamond and pearl pendant. The fine metal and sparkling stones seemed to burn into his skin.

Tobias shook his head. "It never belonged to your mother. If your father had given her something like that, I'd have seen it."

Raking his long fingers through his hair, Zach stood. He stretched his long body, against the pain of bruises that could be seen and those carried deep in his soul, those that couldn't be seen. The pendant was clutched in his hand.

"Was my father serving his sentence when you met him?"

"Aye, seven years. The same as me. We were both given conditional pardon by the territorial government; we were free men, so long as we never attempted to return to England."

The brilliant diamonds and luminous pearls glowed with hidden light. Zach's cold fingers closed over the pendant, the glow stealing into his aching flesh. Felicia Barrington. Some half-formed thought lingered just at the fringe of memory, like something he'd once known and had now forgotten. It was the same feeling he'd had when he'd first seen her name in the journal, like a memory that refused to be remembered but teased at him nevertheless. It was like the night voices he often heard out in the wilds of Resolute, carried on the wind. The voices of Dreamtime.

He shook his head, unable to understand the nagging restlessness that pulled at him. Now that he'd come home, he realized the answers weren't here. He slammed the door of the small office behind him, the loud snap distant and remote, like the closing of another door, in another time and place.

Something indefinable turned his gaze in the direction of the mountains and beyond, to the sea. He'd promised . . . something. What, and to whom? His fingers slowly uncurled and he stared at the pendant, wondering about the woman it had once belonged to. Retracing his steps to the main house, he climbed the stairs and slumped across his solitary bed. Visions of a beautiful young woman filled his imagination and claimed his Dreamtime, echoing the promise.

"Yer daft, clean out of yer mind!" Tobias burst into the wood-paneled office in the main house. The collar of his shirt was askew, his thinning hair was mussed, and his skin had a blotchy pallor

64

due to the whiskey he'd consumed the night before. Bloodshot eyes fixed on the object of their attention across the monkey-wood desk.

"You can't go to England! Yer a wanted man!" He clutched at the desk edge, weaving slightly off center of firm footing as the room suddenly seemed to move uncertainly about him.

"Sit down before you fall down," Zach commanded gently. Reaching across the desk, he pressed a signed voucher into the hands of his foreman, Jingo Nymagee. "That should cover any expenses for Resolute while I'm gone. If anything else comes up, you're to see my solicitor in Sydney."

Jingo nodded, grunting out a response only Zach would have understood.

"When ya comin' back?" he mouthed, dropping letters that were more difficult to pronounce, his speech an odd mixture of pigeon English and a native slur. He was full-blood aboriginal and the best foreman Resolute ever had. His ancestors had roamed this valley for generations.

Zach Tennant had saved him from hanging at the hands of the Queen's regulars when both men were young and he'd hidden Jingo at a remote herder's cabin high in the hills. Loyalty ran deep among the natives. As Jingo saw it, Zach had saved his life, so he was bound to return the favor. Not wanting Jingo to risk life and limb, Zach had convinced him to stay on at the station. And so, Jingo was another who came to Resolute and never left. With Megan's approval, Zach made him foreman at the sheepherding station, and there was no one more knowledgeable about this valley or the mountains beyond. Over the years, Jingo proved his loyalty ran blood deep. He taught Zach the ancient tribal customs of his people, and Zach taught him how to twist the tail of the Queen's enforcers.

"It's a long voyage. We'll have good wind this time of year, but we'll be to sea at least four months. It may be as long as a year before we can get back; that is, if they don't catch me." Zach's twisted half-smile could have meant he was perfectly serious, or sharing one of his many jokes with his friend. Tobias came up out of his chair.

"Dammit to hell, man!" he exclaimed. "You can't go to England. They'll hang you fer certain!"

Zach chose to ignore him for the moment, giving Jingo final instructions. "Minnie will be here to supervise the house. Justin and Rufus will help you with the ranch."

"What about dat next season wool? Ya want for me to ship it

downriver to Sydney?"

Zach shook his head. "The political climate is too dangerous. When the shearing's done, have the wool processed for storage and transported to MacDonald's warehouses in Adelaide. The British will never look for Resolute wool that far from Sydney. It's a longer trip, but I want things to quiet down while I'm gone. That will make the watchdog fat and lazy. And make certain you keep the men working on that new area. Post guards if you have to. Just don't leave any witnesses if things get rough with the authorities."

"Right ya are, boss." Jingo tipped his sweat-stained hat, a sheepish expression fastening on his face. "Wish I be goin' with ya to that bloody England," he grumbled.

"I need you here, friend. I can't trust anyone else with Resolute now that Megan's gone."

"Yeah boy, she sure one fine lady boss. I'll take care everything here." He nodded, tucking the voucher inside his shirt pocket. Then he turned and left. Outward displays of emotions weren't characteristic of the aboriginals, and regard for women was given grudgingly by them.

"Now, Tobias, you were saying?" Zach settled into the chair behind the desk, carefully rechecking the list of intructions he'd made for the running of Resolute in his absence.

Tobias descended on the desk, weaving slightly as he leaned on the edge. "Just what the bloody hell do you think yer doin'? You can't go to England! Have you lost all reason, man?" he groaned at his own words, pressing the heels of his hands into aching eyes.

Zach swiveled in the chair behind the desk, turning away from Tobias's tirade to stare out the wall of windows. He only half listened as Tobias continued to argue. His gray eyes, weary from lack of sleep the night before, scanned the valley.

Felicia. In the light of day, the name still haunted him. What had she meant to his father? As he read the journal through the long hours of the night, he felt himself drawn by some intangible force behind the neatly scribed words on the faded paper. Questions with no answers. Instead of providing him with insight to the man his father had been, the journal had only opened more doors. Slowly, he turned the chair back. Tobias had finally worn down, the effects of the whiskey draining him of all energy. He launched one last verbal assault.

"Yer a wanted man!" Tobias pleaded with outstretched hands. Then he slumped into a chair opposite the desk and hung his head, shaking it slowly from side to side. "They'll hang ya, if you so much as set foot on British soil. It's too dangerous." He raised his head, bloodshot eyes imploring Zach.

"It's the Raven they want, not me," Zach responded with a faint smile.

"Then yer determined to go?" Tobias ran shaking fingers through his sparse gray hair.

Zach nodded. "I've sent word ahead to Sydney. The *Tamarisk* will be ready to sail when we arrive. We'll escort the other two ships to Lisbon and then continue to London."

"We?" Tobias stared, trying to focus his eyes, speechless for the first time in several moments.

"Of course." Zach rose from his chair, a devilish gleam sparkling in his gray eyes. "I've never been to London. I'll need someone to show me about if I'm to learn about my father's life there. You'll enjoy the visit, Tobias. You must have friends in England."

"I was exiled, banished from England forever! I'll be sent to Newgate if I return!" Tobias was flustered.

"Only, if you get caught." The smile deepened, glowing in Zach's eyes. Then he sobered. "I have to go, Tobias, with or without you."

"It's because of that bloody journal, isn't it!?"

"Yes, partly," Zach admitted. "But it's more than the journal." He reached inside the small trunk on the corner of the desk, his fingers closing over the pearl and diamond pendant. It wasn't the most expensive piece of jewelry he'd ever seen, although obviously quite valuable, but it was by far the most fascinating. Intricately designed and of great beauty, the pendant intrigued him, its diamonds winking at him secretively, its pearls possessing a luminous, haunting light.

"My father had another life, one we never knew about. I have to find out about it, Tobias. I want some answers to my questions," he admitted somberly, his voice filled with an emotion unusual to him, as his hand rested on the journal. He cleared his throat. "I never knew him. It seems no one know him completely, not even you. I have to go." The light in his eyes glowed dangerous and secretive.

"Besides," Zach's mood suddenly lightened, "I think it would be great sport to tweak the nose of the English lion in its own lair. Don't you?" He dropped the pendant into a soft leather pouch.

"And"—he caressed the journal thoughtfully—"I have to find a certain lady."

* * *

67

The lady he had in mind, when they reached Sydney eight days later by riverboat, wasn't Alice Mulroney at the discreet house on Cavington Street, but Zach went anyway. It would take another day to make the *Tamarisk* and the other two clippers ready to sail. He hoped in that time, with Alice's usual passionate attentiveness, he might purge his soul of the restlessness that had possessed him since he'd first read Nicholas Tennant's journal. Somehow, in the reading, he'd found it hard to think of the man as his father. A shadowy image had emerged from the pages, portraying a man neither his mother nor Tobias Gentry had ever spoken of. Perhaps more revealing were the events of this man's life that remained untold.

Zach stirred beside Alice. She was a winsome creature with pale skin, long golden hair, and silken limbs that twined wantonly around his waist. She fastened him with a long gaze.

"Didn't I please you, luv?" She bit at her lower lip. Her pleasure had come easily, as it always did with Zachary Tennant. But it didn't take an expert to realize their lovemaking hadn't been the same for him.

Zach threw back the covers and slipped from the bed. Dousing water over his face and hair, he turned, giving the lovely Alice an ironic smile. "It's not you. It's me," he admitted, running a hand across the stubble of beard on his chin. He turned back to the mirror over the elaborate dressing table. He was a fool and he knew it. Any number of rich, influential men in Sydney would like to fill her life as well as her bed, yet over the last six years, she'd contented herself with the infrequent visits he made to town. He didn't fool himself, he knew she saw others when he was away. It didn't matter. In fact, he encouraged her to do so, requiring only that she make herself available to him when he was in the city. He caught the reflection of Alice's saddened expression in the mirror. She slipped from the bed, draped in pink satin. Her covering slipped as she came up behind him to wrap her arms around his waist and press her breasts into his back.

"Why do I always feel as if there's someone else in that bed besides you and me?" she whispered against his skin, for the first time voicing the doubts that had haunted her for the last six years. It hadn't been easy loving a man like Zach Tennant, having to content herself with the three or four days each month that he spent with her. And then, there were times when he was gone for several months at a time.

Zach turned, wrapping his arms loosely around her slender

body, regretting that he hadn't been more attentive to her. He liked Alice, she was a beautiful, exciting woman. Any man would give his right arm just to be with her. He enfolded her in his arms, afraid she might see the lie in his eyes. He wasn't in love with Alice Mulroney, or any woman, and that was the problem. He smoothed her hair, pressed a kiss against her forehead.

"And just who might be in that bed with us? There wasn't room for anyone else last night," he teased playfully, trying to bring a smile back to her lovely face.

She pulled back within the circle of his arms, her gaze somber as she studied his face, looking for the truth behind the casual conversation. "I don't know. I wish to God that I did." She tightened her arms around him, laying her cheek against his well-muscled chest.

"It's not just last night. It's happened before. You're here, making love to me, and then somehow"—she paused, closing her eyes tightly, almost afraid to go on—"it's as if you've left me. You're still here, at least in the flesh, but I can feel you slipping away from me. There are times when I look in your eyes"—she pulled back from him again, her gaze searching his—"like last night and now, and you're not really here with me." She placed a slender hand on each side of his handsome face and shook her head. "You've gone away from me again, Zach. Even now, you want to be away from here. What are you searching for?" Or whom? Her heart cried out.

He wrapped an arm around her shoulders, and they stood silently for the longest time, both gazing out the window beside the dressing table. It was almost dawn, the first gray light illuminating the horizon. Alice's small house was on a hill, looking out across the harbor, and Zach's gaze fastened on the expanse of restless ocean that waited.

His arm dropped. "I have to go."

Alice Mulroney bit off her response. She couldn't send him away with harsh words and risk losing him forever. "Where is it this time?"

Stepping into his pants, Zach looked up. He could trust Alice. She had no more love for the British than he did. Still he held back on telling her everything. "We've cargo to deliver to Lisbon."

"When will you be back?" She silently cursed herself. Zach didn't like to be questioned, and she knew the reason. If she didn't know anything about his activities, she couldn't answer any of the magistrate's questions.

Pulling on boots, Zach tucked his shirt inside his belt. It was always the same. He'd never spent a full night with Alice. Something always compelled him to leave before they could share that lingering intimacy. He'd come to her only a couple of hours ago, and was now anxious to leave again.

Fully dressed, he hesitated, knowing he should say something to her. But the words refused to come. He feared if they did, they'd only be lies. "I'll be back." He kissed her brusquely and then slipped from the room, his boots treading softly on the luxurious hall carpet. Downstairs, the door closed with an impatient thud.

Alice Mulroney leaned against the turned wood post of her bed, already feeling the emptiness of his leaving. "Somehow, I doubt that this time, Zach Tennant," she whispered with regret.

The blue-green water sliced beneath *Tamarisk*'s hull as wind filled her burgeoning sails. Zach stared across the harbor, the masts of the other two clippers barely outlined in the early dawn. Within a short while they would be on the open sea and beyond the reach of the Queen's enforcers. Their course was set; orders had been given to the crew by the second mate. Zach smiled at the news that Tobias had come aboard sometime during the night, even though he'd sworn he'd never set foot on deck. One of the crew had informed Zach that he was below decks sleeping off the effects of a long night spent in one of Sydney's finer gambling halls.

Zach took the wheel, his fatigue slipping away. Beyond the horizon lay endless miles of open sea, and the force of the ocean beat like the heart of a restless creature as it carried them toward the rising sun, and England.

Chapter Three

"Yer courtin' the hangman's noose if yer caught!" Tobias stomped the length of the captain's cabin, hands balled into fists of impotent rage.

"I promised yer mother I'd look out for you. How can I do that when you insist on sailing right into London harbor? For God's sake lad, there's still time for us to be away! We can unload the cargo. There's no need for you to even go ashore," he implored. "We'll take on fresh supplies and be on our way. Think! What yer plannin' is madness!" His face was crimson, large veins prominent in his neck.

"Here come the lobsterbacks!" A disembodied voice echoed teasingly from the adjacent cabin. Tobias chose to ignore the jeering remark.

With a faint smile pulling at his mouth, Zach closed the journal. He'd come this far, he wasn't about to leave London without answers.

"I can't just leave, Tobias. We're here and I intend to find out about my father. At any rate"—he downed the last swallow of strong coffee, fastening his old friend with a wry grin—"I've always wanted to see England."

He became thoughtful, a wicked gleam lighting his gray eyes. "It'll be great sport dealin' directly with the Crown, without paying the usual import tariffs they impose on the colonies. And just maybe, it'll give me the opportunity to learn what the godalmighty English have planned for us in Australia." His eyes lowered, scanning the ship's manifest. It would take several days to unload cargo. Already, his first mate was ashore, locating warehouse space where they might store the wool from the *Tamarisk*'s hold.

Tobias shook his head solemnly. "This is no game, Zach. We could both end up in prison."

Again that disembodied voice mimicked their conversation. "Lash the bastard to the yardarm!"

"Will you shut him up!" Tobias thundered, his patience badly shaken due to too much whiskey and too little sleep the night before.

"You know as well as I that Sebastian says exactly what he pleases. And with his temper, I'm not about to tell him otherwise and lose some skin for it." Zach ignored Tobias's and Sebastian's gloomy predictions.

"Now, if you're quite through, I want you to go ashore."

"Not bloody likely!" the old physician blustered, Sebastian and his dire warnings momentarily forgotten. "I'm an exile! Do you know what they do to exiles who try to sneak back into the country?"

"They can do nothing if they can prove nothing. Haven't we learned that about the English?" Zach's smile deepened as he warmed to his plan.

"What do you mean by that?" Tobias failed to follow his line of thought.

Zach rose from his chair and, going to stand before the open porthole, gazed out across the harbor. "It's been over thirty years since you left England. You're not the same man you were then. You've changed." A teasing smile lifted the corners of his mouth as he turned to his friend. "You've put on a few stone the last few years." His amused gaze traveled over Tobias's portly frame.

"Insolent upstart!" Tobias glared at him, but there was a definite twinkle in his eyes. "So, you don't think anyone will recognize me, eh?" He passed a hand over the stubble on his chin.

"It's not likely any of us will be recognized. We're different men with different identities. Exactly as it was when you and my father first went to Sydney."

"You could be right there."

Zach nodded. "You'll notice when you go topside that I took the liberty of changing the colors. *Tamarisk* now flies the flag of Spain. I thought it a safeguard against too many questions."

"And you think we can fool the bloody boyos in red?"

Zach winked conspiratorially. "I've been lucky so far." He grinned and, crossing the cabin, slapped a hand on Tobias's back.

"The British fleet is far too busy searching every harbor town in New South Wales for the Raven. They'll not be concerned with the likes of us."

"Yer too bold, lad." Tobias shook his head. "Sometimes I think you like playing games with the devil."

Zach threw back his head and roared with laughter. "Why, Tobias, don't you know?" His silver gray eyes narrowed dangerously. "I am the devil." Then he sobered and went back to his small desk. "Now, we must make a plan for you to go ashore. You have some memory of London, whereas I have no knowledge of it whatsoever."

"I don't like it," Tobias complained, shaking his head.

"But you will go," Zach informed him gently.

"Aye, I'll go. But only because I know if I don't, you'll do it yourself and probably end up in some kind of trouble. London is no town for a stranger." The old man sighed resignedly. "What is it you want me to do?"

Zach sat down at the desk, opening the journal. "I need information." He pushed back thoughtfully in the chair, his fingers lightly drumming the worn pages of the leather-bound volume. "I need to know everything about the Barrington family, particularly Felicia Barrington." His voice hardened. "And find out what you can about Barrington Shipping. It's time to corner the lion."

Tobias shook his shaggy-maned head. "Yer always readin' that damned journal. I wish I'd never given it to you. Felicia Barrington has become an obsession with you. For God's sake, Zach, it all happened over thirty years ago!" He waved his arms in frustration. "You don't even know if she's still alive! And what are you goin' to do when you find her? She's a Barrington, remember? They'll not exactly roll out the red carpet for us!"

Zach sighed, his silvery eyes traveling back to the open porthole with an expression of inexplicable longing.

"I don't know," he whispered, lost in his own thoughts.

She was out there, somewhere. He could feel it, but even he was at a loss to understand his preoccupation with a woman his father had once known. "Aye, Tobias," he agreed, "she has become an obsession." He picked up the sparkling pendant, twirling it in the sunlight that poured in through the porthole. The rays invaded the stones, reflecting deep hidden facets, hinting at other secrets concealed within. "A magnificent, elusive obsession. And I won't rest until I find her."

* * *

"Suck it in, luv," Katy managed from between clenched teeth as she pulled hard on the corset strings.

"Katy!" Elyse squealed. "You're cutting me in half." She gasped, trying to breathe.

"Yer dressmaker said we have to get it down to seventeen inches for that dress to fit." Katy pulled harder.

Elyse clung to the post of the large bed, eyes closed painfully. Behind her, Katy wound the strings of the corset more tightly around hands reddened from pulling.

"Just a little bit more." She coaxed.

Elyse groaned. "A little bit more and I won't be able to walk."

"It's necessary." Katy gritted out, pulling the strings a fraction of an inch tighter.

Elyse's cheeks drained of all color. "Enough!" She swore inaudibly under her breath. Then, jerking away, she swung around, drawing a deep breath as the strings loosened and the garment gaped open down her back.

"No more!" she warned with outstretched hand. "I refuse to be trussed up like a Christmas goose." Determination glittered in her brilliant blue eyes as she backed away from the maid. "Eighteen inches will just have to do." She tossed her auburn hair defiantly over one bare shoulder.

Katy sucked in her cheeks. "Madame Duquesne won't like it."

"I don't care if France declares war on England!" Elyse announced. "No one will ever know it's eighteen inches and not seventeen."

"Eighteen won't fit," Katy announced. "Madame said it would have to be no more than seventeen or you'd never get the back of the gown closed."

Holding the front of the corset against her firm breasts, Elyse strode across the bedchamber. "Then I won't wear it." Head held high, she threw open the wardrobe. "It's as simple as that," she declared, surveying an array of gowns.

Katy threw up her hands. "Yer grandmother paid a fortune for that dress. The seamstress has been working on it for weeks." A satisfied smile tilted her mouth as she added a final comment, knowing the effect it would have. "Master Jerrold approved the fabric himself. He's expectin' you to wear this gown to the engagement party. I heard him say the lady who's to be the future Lady Barrington has to be properly dressed."

That did it! Elyse whirled back around, her anger concealed

behind a deceiving smile. "I don't care if Queen Victoria herself selected the fabric!" Her attempt at deception had ended. "Good Lord, can't I be allowed to choose anything for myself!"

She jerked first one gown, then another roughly aside, the lace-trimmed corset falling to the floor.

"Good lord, yer an indecent child!" Katy swooped across the room, seizing the corset and wrapping it about Elyse's bare body. "What if someone were to come in just now?"

"And who might that be?" Elyse demanded. "My fiancé, perhaps? I think not. No, indeed!" She answered her own question with more than a trace of sarcasm. "He's far too occupied selecting the proper fabric for my gowns," she mimicked. "Or responding to all the gifts we've received, or"—she inhaled deeply again, now that she was free of the restraints of the corset—"visiting his mistress at Brookfield Court!" Her color, now fully restored, spread vividly across her cheeks.

"I'll not have you talkin' about such things," Katy warned. Her mistress really had her temper up this time.

"Oh yes, I forgot, if we don't speak of *those* things, then perhaps they'll go away. Katy darling"—Elyse squared her slender shoulders—"mistresses don't go away, they merely remain discreet. Or perhaps not so discreet."

"You shouldn't say such things about the man yer to marry. Why, if anyone were to hear you, they'd think you didn't love him," Katy scolded gently, a concerned expression knitting her brows together.

Elyse only glared at her, remembering the evening at the opera several weeks earlier, when Jerrold's former mistress had approached them at intermission. Katherine West had been intoxicated, and Elyse had felt sorry for her escort. He'd truly seemed like a nice gentleman. But the realization that she hadn't felt the slightest twinge of jealousy was disconcerting. In fact, she'd been openly amused at the time. After all, how often could a woman actually claim to be socially acquainted with her fiancé's mistress?

She remembered the livid expression on Jerrold's face at her reaction. He'd been cool and distant the remainder of the evening, and she knew the reason. He liked dictating her responses to such situations, just as he liked dictating the gowns she was to wear.

Katy gave her a thoughtful look. "That's it, isn't it?" she asked somberly.

"What is?" Elyse remarked absently. Her hand closed over a new gown she hadn't yet worn. She pulled it from the wardrobe and

75

turned to Katy.

"I'll wear this one," she stated emphatically. "It's *my* favorite."

"Yer ignorin' me," Katy said accusingly, taking the gown from her.

"That's impossible, Katy luv." Elyse smiled, her eyes turning a darker blue with the lie.

"You don't love him, do ya?" Katy pinned her charge with an insistent gaze.

It was pointless to lie. Katy would see the truth despite any excuses she tried to give.

Elyse sighed heavily, wishing there were an easy answer. There just wasn't. "I don't know what I feel, Katy. I wish I did."

Eyes stark, Katy shook her head. "It's wrong marryin' a man ya don't love, even if he is the richest man in all England. All the money in the world can't buy happiness."

"It really doesn't matter, does it?" Elyse responded with brutal honesty. "After all, a proper lady would never break her betrothal simply because she wasn't certain of her feelings." Releasing an uncertain sigh, she tried to comfort the maid. "It'll be all right, Katy. Now, be a good girl and bring the gown, and be sure to lace me up to eighteen inches."

The gaiety in her smile was forced. "We have a party to attend. And please, work some of your magic." There was an odd catch in her voice, as she turned her back for the corset to be laced. "After all, everyone always expects the bride to look radiantly happy."

"You may be able to fool everyone else, including yer grandmother, but yer not foolin' me. I've known you since you were a small babe. Have you forgotten? I know everything about ya. And," Katy accused, easily tightening the corset to eighteen inches, "I know you've been havin' that dream again."

This time Elyse didn't even try to disguise the truth. "Why is it always the same? Why can't I remember anything else?" She closed her eyes, leaning her head against the post of the bed. "Who is he, Katy? Who is the phantom of my dreams?"

"Yer grandmother always thought it must be your father, because losin' your parents was such a dreadful shock." Katy held out pantalets for her to step into.

"No." Elyse shook her head. "There are portraits of him and of my mother all over the house. He's not the man in my dreams. It's someone else. Someone I know . . . if only I could remember." She closed her eyes, experiencing again the overwhelming peace she always felt with the dream, and the passion. . . .

76

"I feel so safe, as if I've finally come to the end of a very long journey." Her voice was hollow with longing. "And when he kisses me . . ."

Katy's head came up, a startled expression on her face. It was the first time Elyse had ever mentioned anything so intimate being in her dreams. Her voice was hesitant as she tied the strings at Elyse's waist. "It's natural to dream of the man yer to marry."

Wrapping her arms about herself, Elyse crossed the room to stand before the windows. She stared silently into the early evening darkness as if searching for something beyond the glass. The light in her eyes softened with some hidden memory. "I can almost see him through the mist. It's not Jerrold."

"But I'll know him when I see him." Her throat tightened with inexplicable longing. Sadness always accompanied the dreams, like a foreboding of some loss she couldn't understand. She found herself watching and waiting. For what? A man who existed only in her dreams?

She laughed softly as she turned to Katy, breaking the spell that had descended over the room. "You had a saying when I was little: 'If wishes were horses, then beggars would ride.' Well, it seems, Katy my love, that I'm without my 'horse.' I've lost him and can't seem to find him."

She smiled sadly. "It'll be all right, Katy, I promise. I won't spoil this for Grandmother."

The maid frowned, unable to dismiss the nagging doubts that had plagued her since Elyse's betrothal was formally announced. Still, she knew it was not her place to interfere. She was just a simple country girl with dreams of her own. What did she know of arranged marriages? All she was certain of was that a young girl, no matter her station in life, should have the right to make a decision of the heart when it came to marryin' with someone. Perhaps that was one of those things a girl gave up when she became a proper society lady. Still, Katy couldn't help feeling it was wrong somehow.

"Come along, darlin'," she whispered soothingly, "let's get you dressed. Jerrold and his father will be here soon. Which jewelry will you be wantin' to wear? How about the diamond and sapphire necklace Master Jerrold gave you for your birthday?" she suggested brightly.

Sighing, Elyse sat before the large mirror at the dressing table. She shook her head. There was only one piece she would wear that evening. She felt almost as if it were a good luck talisman.

"I'll wear the pendant Grandmother gave me." After all, she thought with a tight feeling that should have been happiness, tonight is to be a very special night.

Zach forged the elaborate signature to the contract. At least now he would have a place to store his wool. Only he and Sandy knew the true value of those tightly bound bales, for inside each was a heavy leather pouch containing something far more valuable— gold. It was a deception of course, hiding the gold but keeping it in plain sight.

He looked up as Tobias carefully made his way up the gangplank to step down on the more secure deck. Wiping beads of perspiration from his brow, the older man sat on a nearby barrel.

Zach nodded to his second mate. "Make certain guards are posted, but not conspicuously." He turned to Tobias. "What were you able to find out?"

"Give me a minute to catch me breath," Tobias puffed. Removing the top of an adjacent barrel, he seized a ladle and dipped into the cool water. He took a long, liberal drink, closing his eyes as his thirst was quenched.

Zach slammed a hand against the center mast. "Good God, man! What did you find out about the Barringtons?"

Tobias shifted his stout frame. Taking another sip, he narrowed his gaze thoughtfully.

"I found out that if you mention the Barrington name anywhere about London, you're bound to find out something."

"Such as?" Zach shifted impatiently.

Tobias's gaze dropped to his hands. "London hasn't changed much in thirty years. Most of the businesses are still here, though the faces have changed a bit." He smiled ruefully. "They're all younger." He chuckled to himself.

"Over thirty years," he murmured. "An entire lifetime. God, I didn't realize how much I missed England." There was an odd catch in his voice as he blinked back emotion.

"My sister's in Glenwood now," he added, running his hand thoughtfully across his chin.

"Sister?" Zach looked up, surprised. "You never mentioned your family. I assumed . . ."

"They were all dead?" Tobias finished for him. He frowned. "I'm sure they wished they were after the scandal of my trial. My mother died before all that nasty business, thank God. I received a brief notice about my father's death. I didn't find out about it until almost a year later. That's been almost twenty years ago." He shifted, experiencing an odd feeling at sharing all those old and painful memories. "But my sister seems to have made a good life for herself in spite of it all. She never wrote to me directly, always handled everything through the family solicitors. She's married now. To a fine gentleman as I understand. I can't believe it." He shook his graying head. "They have four children, all grown."

"Tobias, please." Zach patiently prodded him to continue.

"I'm gettin' to it, I'm gettin' to it." The old man frowned.

"What about the Barringtons? Were you able to find out anything about them?"

Tobias's eyes narrowed speculatively. "They're a powerful family, boy, old money, impeccable lineage. The name carried a great deal of power when I was a young man. They're not limited to shipping. They own a piece of the rail system, mining operations in south Wales, and a good portion of coastal fishing."

"I didn't ask for a banker's report," Zach replied caustically. "What about the family?"

"To understand the family, you've got to understand their place in society. They're powerful. Old Lord Barrington died several years ago. A son inherited the family fortune, and the grandson will inherit the title and the fortune he's built up."

"A great deal of it made from the sweat and blood of our people at Resolute and the other stations in New South Wales," Zach concluded, contempt in his voice.

Tobias continued to reveal the information he'd gathered throughout the morning. "They have a large town house here in London. The Barrington building is on Regent Street. Most of the family business is handled there. And there are several country estates; the largest is in Lincolnshire. And"—he paused—"they own practically every warehouse on this waterfront. You're probably renting space from them for that wool." He watched Zach carefully for a reaction to that last statement.

A wicked smile lifted the corners of Zach's mouth. "As you would say, my friend; 'not bloody likely'! I had Sandy make certain he found an independent warehouse." He was referring to his first mate. "I'm not about to pour any more money into Barrington's fat purse. Where is this London town house?"

"In the most elite part of the city, Highgrove. It's not likely you'll get an invitation to visit. Their usual houseguests include titled nobility, even a member or two of the royal family."

"There's always a way, Tobias. Have you forgotten how charming I can be when I want something?" Zach's eyes darkened to cold slate. "After all, we have something in common — Felicia Barrington."

Tobias blotted his upper lip with his handkerchief, wiping away beads of perspiration that formed nervously in the cool air. There was no point in holding anything back. If he didn't reveal everything, Zach would find out for himself. It was always that way. The man had an uncanny ability to ferret out things, as if he could see beyond a person's careful words.

"There's a fancy ball bein' given this evenin' in honor of young master Barrington," he added, replacing his dampened handkerchief in his vest pocket. He glanced at Zach speculatively from beneath the sweep of frosty eyebrows.

"A ball?"

The chill in those silver eyes could cut into a man's soul. It had been the same with his father. Tobias remembered that same look, long ago, in Nicholas Tennant's eyes. The memory sent an uneasy chill down his spine. The conversation held on that day had become too personal. He'd pressed too hard, freely giving information about his own past, then asking the same of his friend, to receive only that cold, killing stare in response. He'd never asked again.

"Lord Barrington's son is to be married. The engagement is being celebrated at a fancy dress ball," Tobias announced dismally, knowing full well what the next question would be.

"And where is the ball being held?" Zach didn't disappoint him.

"The bride's grandmother is hosting the event. Lady Regina Winslow is well placed in society. I believe the girl was originally from the continent, American born." Tobias straightened the fabric of his vest. "It's to be the social event of the season."

"No doubt," Zach replied, his eyes downcast. "It would be a perfect opportunity to meet Felicia Barrington. I want an invitation," he announced, his gaze meeting Tobias's squarely, a glint of challenge in it.

His old friend very nearly fell off the barrel. "It's impossible!" He was thunderstruck. "You must be daft, boy! Haven't you heard a word I've said? These are powerful people, titled and of the nobility! Invitations just aren't handed out to common people, much less . . ."

"Convicts? Or the son of a convict?" Tobias supplied with brutal honesty. "Ah yes. I'd forgotten the bloody class structure of Godalmighty England." He squared his wide shoulders, fixing Tobias with a secretive gaze. The light in those gray eyes hinted at a trace of deadly humor. "Then I suppose we shall just have to be certain an invitation is extended. Certainly an exception might be made for a member of the nobility visiting London."

"What the devil are you talking about?" Tobias came up off the barrel. "We don't know anyone like that. Yer talking madness! It's impossible!"

"Impossible?" Zach arched a golden brow. "That's what the Crown and Barrington Shipping said when the Raven lured all those ships out onto the Barrier Reef and scuttled them. They said it was impossible that it could be the work of just one man. But we know better, don't we, Tobias?"

"Yer mad! Yer bloody mad! You'll be caught and hanged."

"For attending the social event of the season? I think not." He winked at Tobias. "I merely want to give the happy couple my fondest wishes, and to find out what I can about Felicia Barrington." Zach had been leaning against the center mast. He stood upright.

"Take Sandy with you. I'll need a place to live while we're in London, perhaps in Highgrove," he added conspiratorially. "I believe you mentioned it's a fashionable place to live."

"You think you can just bloody walk in and buy a place? Those are old family homes of the aristocracy. They don't sell them unless there's a very great need."

"Tobias, I have a very great need." He pinned his friend with a calm gaze. "But I have no desire to own property in England. With the wealth of these people, surely one house can be found vacant, its owners vacationing elsewhere. Find such a place. And servants," he added as an afterthought. "Everything must be perfect."

"Is that all?" Tobias roared. "Surely there must be something else, you'll be wanting?"

Zach nodded. "I'll need a carriage and horses. Sandy will be my driver." His enthusiasm gained momentum as he laid out his elaborate scheme.

"I'll have need of a tailor. Send him to the ship. The rest can be taken care of tomorrow."

"Tomorrow! How generous of you!"

Zach raised amused eyes to his friend. "Inform the tailor that we'll need evening wear for two gentlemen. And please, do pick out a suitable fabric for yourself, your grace."

"My what!" The veins in Tobias's neck suddenly became visible

81

under florid skin.

Zach stood back, rubbing his fingers thoughtfully across his sharply angled chin, scrutinizing the older man.

"Yes, a marquis will do quite nicely; Spanish of course, since *Tamarisk* is flying a Spanish flag. That should be aristocratic enough to get everyone's attention. You'll go as my uncle, although some may question the family resemblance." He smothered back a laugh as he scrutinized his friend.

"You must affect a slight accent. Anything will do, so long as it's not English."

Tobias was incredulous. "A marquis! Now I know you're mad! It won't work, it just won't work! Even if your scheme had some merit, there's not enough time to accomplish everything. The ball is tonight! Only a few hours away!"

"Precisely so, my friend. But you've forgotten how vain and arrogant your English *friends* can be." He smiled coldly. "I intend to make certain the Barringtons are aware of the arrival of the Marquis Ramon de la Vida and his nephew"—his smile deepened—"the Count de Cuervo." He savored the title he'd bestowed upon himself.

"Yes"—he spoke, with great satisfaction, as if no one else were about—"money and a title will get me exactly what I want."

His thoughts returning to the present, he sobered. "And in plenty of time to attend the ball being given in honor of the engagement of young Lord Barrington."

"Elyse, my dear, you disappoint me," Jerrold Barrington whispered discreetly, as he smiled congenially at a grand duchess. "I had hoped to see you wearing the gold satin. Was there something wrong with the gown? Perhaps Madame was negligent in her duties to you," he suggested, an annoyed tone tinging his silky voice.

Elyse laid a gloved hand on his arm in what must have seemed to others an intimate gesture. "I'm sorry you're disappointed." She smiled up at him. "Madame is not to blame. Her work was perfect, as always. I chose not to wear the gown. It seemed—" she paused to seek the right word—"it seemed extravagant."

"Extravagant? My dear, of course it's extravagant, as I expect. You must remember that once we're married you will be a titled lady with all the social recognition that accompanies such a title. It is expected of you."

"Jerrold"—her words were equally silken, hiding the edge of irritation that always seemed to accompany their discussions lately—"I am already a lady," she reminded him. "And"—she paused for effect—"I will wear what I please."

A muscle worked irritably at his clenched jaw. "Of course, my dear. It's just that the Barrington name carries a great deal of importance. People in society look to us to maintain certain standards."

"Do you find my standards lacking?" Elyse coolly confronted Jerrold as his fingers closed bruisingly over her arm.

"Elyse, darling"—he inserted the endearment almost as an afterthought—"you're beginning to draw attention."

She fastened on him a look of wide-eyed innocence. "I thought you liked attention."

His grip tightened, bruising the pale skin beneath her gloves.

Equally determined, she impaled him with a defiant glare. "You're hurting me," she breathed between elegantly curved lips.

His fingers immediately relaxed, the expression on his face becoming suitably contrite. "I'm sorry, my dear. It's just that you have the most irritating habit of challenging me at the most awkward moments." His hand slipped to her waist, pressing her in to him possessively. "But I suppose that is why I desire you so completely."

Elyse stared at him, words frozen in her throat. Lately, he'd become much more demanding of her affections when they were together. This was not the first time Jerrold had made certain she was aware of his feelings. Her gaze lowered as she brought her churning emotions under control. She should have been flattered by his intimate attentions. Instead she found them as bothersome as his earlier criticism of her selection of a gown. She mentally berated herself. What was wrong with her for God's sake? After all, in less than two months they were to be married.

Elyse pushed that thought from her with almost silent desperation, as she had done numerous times over the past year. Almost as if she could will it away by ignoring it. But in her heart she knew it wasn't that simple. With each passing day she was fast approaching that irrevocable moment when they would be husband and wife, forever.

Disengaging herself from the circle of his arm, Elyse smiled and caught him in a trap of his own making. "We must be careful; someone may be watching." She reached up a gloved hand, touching his cheek, trying to feel some essence of the desire that glis-

83

tened in his eyes, and masking the twinge of disappointment in her own as her fingers curled into a small fist. Here was none of the desire that she felt so completely in her dreams.

"Elyse, darling." Her grandmother broke in on the silent battle of wills. "You and Jerrold must come along and greet your guests. Lucy Maitland has been looking for you. She mentioned a Spanish nobleman among the late arrivals. For the life of me, I can't remember such a name on the list of invitations." Regina had witnessed their uneasy exchange from across the ballroom. Again she was plagued by misgivings. She smiled, trying to give Elyse some of her confidence.

"It seems he's an acquaintance of your family, my dear." She turned to Jerrold.

He smiled disarmingly. "Then by all means, Lady Winslow"—he took her arm with the grace and dignity of a perfect gentleman—"we should attend to your guests. After all, this is the most important night of my life." He extended his other arm to Elyse.

Lucy Maitland smiled radiantly in greeting as they joined her. "You look absolutely beautiful tonight," she whispered discreetly to Elyse from behind the arc of her satin brocade fan. "But you really should try to smile. People will think you're not enjoying your own engagement party."

Elyse flashed her a pleading glance as Jerrold turned to converse with an acquaintance. "Oh, Lucy, what am I going to do?" she whispered miserably.

Lucy caught her by the arm and drew her away from prying glances. "Good heavens! You look absolutely miserable."

Elyse smiled unconvincingly. "It's nothing." She bit at her lower lip. "It's probably just the excitement of the party."

"I've seen more excitement from you over studying French essays at school," her friend commented.

Elyse sighed brokenly. She could tell Lucy just about anything. They'd attended academy together, and suffered over French as well as mathematics, going through it all with undying loyalty to each other. But how could she possibly tell Lucy about the doubts that nagged at her?

Elyse shook her head, "I don't know what's wrong with me." She made a gesture toward the brilliantly decorated room. "I should feel . . . differently about all this."

"What's wrong?"

"I don't know," Elyse murmured miserably, then she looked up. "Yes I do. I want to feel the way you do about Andrew. That's how it should be between a man and woman, isn't it?"

Her friend drew back in surprise. "Is that right?" A playful smile twitched at the corners of Lucy's mouth. "Well, let me tell you. He's off limits," she declared jauntily, "and I'll scratch out the eyes of any female who thinks otherwise."

Elyse groaned. "You know what I mean."

Lucy sobered. "Yes, I know precisely what you mean." She wrapped an arm around Elyse's shoulders, squeezing her lovingly. "You're probably just a little nervous about all this. After all, the Barrington name has been known to strike fear into the hearts of mortal men. That's quite a title you're marrying."

"A title," Elyse responded somberly. "Perhaps that's it." She shook her head, trying to find a way to explain her feelings. "When did you know you loved Andrew?" She looked up hopefully.

"I must have been about seven." Lucy tapped the tip of her closed fan thoughtfully against her chin. "Yes, I'm certain of it." Her eyes widened. "Do you promise not to laugh, if I tell you about it?"

"You were seven?" Elyse stared at Lucy, astonished, trying to smother a giggle. It seemed incredible that her friend, who'd been known to be rather wild, unmanageable, and unpredictable as a child, could have loved anyone for more than a week at the most, much less since she was seven years old.

"I warned you not to laugh."

Elyse fastened an appropriately solemn expression on her face. "I promise."

Lucy looked at her skeptically, then decided she could be trusted to keep her word. "Andrew and his parents were visiting us at Shelbourne. I was riding my pony and fell off, right into the middle of a mud puddle at his feet. I'll never forget the expression on his face. He laughed so hard."

Elyse couldn't restrain her laughter as she imagined Lucy sprawled in a mud puddle. It came out in a most unladylike fashion, and was quickly muffled behind her gloved hand. "You must have been furious," she managed to say, forcing back laughter until her eyes watered. "You've always had a dreadful temper."

Lucy glared at her. "I was, of course. But he just kept right on laughing. Well, he just has the most infectious laughter. How could I possibly resist? No one ever dared laugh at me before. I decided right then and there, he was the man I was going to marry. Anyone who would dare laugh at Lucy Devereaux was as crazy as I was, or had a strong sense of himself. But don't look so downhearted." She tried to bolster her friend's spirits. "Not everyone falls into love and a mud puddle all in the same day. Usually it's accomplished in much more conventional ways. It's not the same for everyone," she said encouragingly. "Everyone feels it differently. Now, if you were to ask Andrew, he'd come up with an entirely different explanation. Our first meeting wasn't like that at all for him. He thought I was an impossible, demanding child." She winked wickedly. "Now, he knows how demanding I can really be."

"But you fell in love right away, in a mud puddle of all things!" Elyse bemoaned. "Why couldn't Jerrold love me that way? Do you know what he'd say if I fell into a mud puddle?" She tilted her lovely head as she assumed a stern, disapproving expression. "My dear Elyse," she mimicked, her mouth pursing into a thin frown, "whatever will people think? After all, you have a position to maintain. You'll be the laughingstock of London. How will I ever live this down?" For added effect, she rolled her brilliant blue eyes in an exact imitation of Jerrold's most reproving glare.

Lucy choked back her own laughter. She'd known Jerrold Barrington a long time. They all moved in the same social circles, but despite that, Jerrold always considered himself a notch above everyone else.

"Oh, Lucy." Elyse sighed, wiping tears from the corners of her eyes. "Here I am making a joke about it." She smiled sadly. "It's no joke at all. I should feel something more, something like . . ." She paused, searching for the right word. It was there, from her dreams, but she wondered if Lucy would consider her completely mad.

"Like a bolt of lightning?" Lucy suggested, knowingly arching her brow. "I feel it every time Andrew and I are together. I'd die if I didn't," she whispered solemnly, and solemnity was rare for Lucy Maitland. Her gaze wandered across the ballroom to where her husband was involved in lively discussion with an acquaintance. "It's as if we were meant to be together." She laughed at the foolishness of the thought, and made a joke of it.

"You know, destined, written in the stars?" she said gaily, making an elaborate gesture through the air with her hand. Then, struck by a sudden thought, she seized two champagne glasses from a nearby tray, handing one to Elyse.

"Let's share a toast," she proposed as she raised her glass. "To your happiness, and lightning bolts." Crystal rang with false gaiety against crystal.

Elyse drained the glass, her eyes widening as Lucy coaxed her to enjoy just one more toast.

"I can't!" she declared. "Champagne affects me strangely."

"Strangely?" Lucy swallowed back her astonishment. "What happens? Do you change into some sort of wicked creature, casting spells on everyone?"

Elyse giggled. "If only it were true. Maybe I could cast a spell on Jerrold."

"And turn him into a frog," Lucy suggested, quickly handing Elyse another glass of champagne before she could protest.

"But then, I suppose you would have to start with a prince first. And my dear"—she leaned discreetly forward as if she were sharing an important secret—"Jerrold is no prince."

"No, he's not," Elyse replied sadly, her laughter fading. She knew Jerrold would disapprove of such behavior. But why shouldn't she share another glass of champagne with her dearest friend one last time?

Tobias tugged warningly at Zach's sleeve. "We'll never pull it off! It isn't enough that we've lied and bribed our way this far," he muttered under his breath, casting a worried glance at the English gentlemen and their ladies, "you insist on wearin' that damned eyepatch. Be subtle you said; blend in with the crowd! We stick out like whores at a church social in these flashy clothes with all this fancy braid and these colorful medals. There isn't enough gold in all of New South Wales to buy our way out of this if we're caught!"

"Easy, old friend." A smile pulled at Zach's mouth as he separated from Tobias. "And stay away from the tables. I want you perfectly sober."

"Sober?" Tobias whispered in his wake. He made a feeble move to follow, then thought better of it. If one was caught, the other might still get away. He turned with an appreciative eye toward the elegant, embossed silver serving bowls set upon linen-covered tables along the wall. He frowned. The last thing he wanted was some weak punch. God! He needed a drink.

Zach's silver gaze swept the ballroom, taking in the understated wealth of the immaculately dressed men and their elegant but overstated ladies. He'd inquired discreetly about Lady Barrington, but had received only vague equally questioning responses.

An uneasy feeling slipped down his spine. Perhaps Tobias was right. Felicia might not be alive after all these years. Tobias hadn't been able to learn anything about her since their arrival.

Contrary to his suggestion to his old friend, Zach took a glass from a tray offered by a passing servant. When he made a remark about something more substantial than champagne, the servant disappeared with a nod to reappear a few minutes later with a bottle discreetly wrapped in fine linen. The amber-colored liquid splashed reassuringly into a heavy crystal tumbler. As fine French cognac slipped warmly into Zach's stomach, he looked up, and, across the rim of the glass, saw her.

Unbidden, a thought occurred to him. *I would have known her anywhere.* It was there in the slender arch of her neck, the delicate contours of her face partially turned away for she was in conversation. It was like a memory, illusive, teasing, bittersweet. Something he couldn't name or fully recall. *And her hair . . .* an undefinable pull drew him to her, as if a spell was cast on him.

Drawing a deep breath, Zach turned away, trying to bring his thoughts under control. Something white-hot slipped across his senses. It was impossible! He knew none of these people. He didn't know *her*.

Yet, even as he denied it, he felt himself turn and search for her with almost passionate desperation. It was insane! He'd known countless women, some as forbidden to him as England. Yet he crossed the ballroom like a sleepwalker, compelled by something he could neither understand nor escape to seek her out.

Speculative whispers followed him across the room as he walked with quiet grace, threading his way through the guests, the black worsted wool of his dress suit brushing against satin and lace. Several elegantly coiffed heads turned in his direction, and glances, no longer discreet but openly appraising, took him in. His gaze was only for *her*. Like soft music reaching through darkness, her voice was low, silky. Her faint laughter reached subtly inside him, touching hidden thoughts and half-forgotten responses. As he reached out, his fingers brushed her arm, and something very like an echo of memory moved ghostlike across his soul.

The touch was so faint, she might not have felt it at all. It was like the feather-soft beating of wings, or the rush of an uncertain heart.

"Lady Barrington?" Zach said.

Elyse turned. "Oh my God!" she whispered, her fingers flying to the diamond and pearl pendant at her throat.

She was only vaguely aware of the curious stares turned in her direction. The soft murmur of conversation around her suddenly grew silent. The brilliant light from gas lamps and candles wavered, then surrendered to darkness. For a moment or perhaps a millennium in time, it seemed she was plunged into a world devoid of sight or sound, of everything but this man and the promise of her dream.

Tears filling her eyes, Elyse whispered from the depths of her soul, "I knew you'd come back to me."

Chapter Four

Elyse was only vaguely aware that Lucy was making the necessary introductions. The room swam about her like a sea suddenly gone stormy. A strange numbness reached up from deep inside, engulfing her; a loud roar flooded her senses. For the briefest moment in time she felt as if she were standing outside herself, watching everything and everyone from afar. And the one person who held her fascinated was the mysterious stranger who'd appeared like the phantom from her dreams, like a bolt of lightning.

"May I present the Count de Cuervo," Lucy began uncertainly, glancing around the circle of surprised people. But their reactions could not match her own surprise at Elyse's response to this handsome stranger. She tried desperately to salvage what she might of a terribly awkward situation.

Zach inclined his head politely at the introduction, his eyes fastened on the young woman who'd reacted so strangely to him a moment before, and on the magnificent pendant she wore around her neck. Recognition was like a shaft of blinding light, stark to the senses. It was identical to the pendant he'd carried from Resolute!

"Elyse?" Lucy whispered with growing urgency behind her polite smile. "Are you all right?" She paled visibly.

"My God, I think she's going to faint," someone said.

Elyse turned to her friend, trying to reassure her. She reached out unsteadily and her gloved hand was immediately seized by strong fingers that closed over it in gentle support.

Zach stood beside the beautiful young woman. The strength in her fingers belied the paleness of her skin. That sense of inexplicable familiarity he'd first felt washed over him again, as if he knew her, knew her touch. The feeling was disconcerting and he carefully masked it as a dark-haired man also came to Elyse's assistance, the expression on his thin face reflecting several emotions.

90

Concern was not one of them. Displeasure was obvious in the annoyed downward turn of his mouth.

"For God's sake, Elyse," Jerrold Barrington hissed, "you're making a spectacle of yourself." The whisper was insistent, like the loathsome warning of a viper. "I certainly hope you're not thinking of fainting."

Elyse's head came up, her thoughts clearing with the harshness of his words. Thinking of fainting? How in God's name did someone think of fainting? She inhaled deeply, trying to overcome the coldness she remembered so well from her dreams. She was still shaking, but Jerrold's scathing remark had had the effect of a dousing with icy water.

"You know very well I never faint!" Elyse responded, with more strength than she felt. She tried to concentrate, her gaze fastening on the lean, strong fingers supporting her left arm. It was the gentlest touch, but she felt comforting warmth in those fingers. She looked up, following the cut of the immaculate evening coat, until it was broken by the stark white of an elegant shirt decorated with perfect tucks across the width of chest, and the more dazzling white in the smile that curved a maddeningly inquisitive mouth. He was real! As was that intense gray gaze fastened on her with a mixture of amusement and concern. The scrutiny was emphasized by the slash of the black patch across one eye. On anyone else it would have seemed ridiculous, but Elyse was certain no one ever ridiculed this man. The patch gave him a rakish air, like that of a brigand or perhaps a pirate. She could almost believe she might have imagined him, but the strength in those fingers was more than just imagination.

"Well, you certainly gave me a scare. You could've fooled me about not fainting." Lucy fluttered her brocade fan with a nervous gesture, as she silently wondered just what had gotten into her friend. Elyse had been right when she'd said she never fainted. She had the constitution of a horse.

Jerrold lifted a condescending brow. "Perhaps you would like to rest for a little while. With all the excitement of the evening . . ." he suggested with a maddening air of authority.

"Not at all, Jerrold." Elyse gave him a quick smile as her curious gaze returned to the stranger beside her. "We haven't been properly introduced."

"Is there an improper way?" Zach's concern for this beautiful young woman shifted to faint amusement. Whatever had caused her first reaction to their meeting certainly wasn't affecting her

91

now. She seemed to have fully recovered. He wished he could say the same for himself. He couldn't shrug off the feeling that somehow this wasn't the first time they'd met.

Jerrold frowned at the offhand comment, considering it as out of place as this stranger. "May I introduce myself, since I have not had the honor?" He looked on the stranger with condescending aloofness, the tone in his voice faintly mocking, as if to say he was already acquainted with anyone of importance. "Jérrold Barrington," he announced with such authority that Elyse glanced up at hearing him use this tone with one of their guests.

The man with those unreadable, gray eyes and the damning calm accepted the introduction with a faint inclination of his golden head, as if he were listening to the idle buzzing of a bothersome insect. Elyse's eyes widened as her thoughts came back under control. She couldn't for the life of her explain her initial reaction to him, but whoever he was, he was not the least intimidated by Jerrold.

He smiled, almost as if he found something very amusing in Jerrold's manner. "I'm a visitor to your country, señor." He said this as if it were an afterthought. Elyse's eyes shaded to soft blue with her appreciation of his attitude.

The curve of Zach's smile deepened. Bending forward from the waist, he gently raised her gloved hand. Grazing a kiss across the backs of her fingers, he turned his head slightly, to steal a glimpse of the man who'd suddenly appeared beside her. Barrington was tall and dark, with the sort of looks that were almost too polished, too perfect, as if he spent a great deal of time making certain they were just that. Zach's smile quirked. Unless he missed his guess, the heir to the Barrington family fortune was more than a little displeased with the young lady's outburst a moment earlier.

As he brushed his lips across her glove's smoothness, his mouth turned into a secretive smile. So, it seemed Mr. Jerrold Barrington was a man given to propriety and appearances. As Zach knew well, it was easy to act the part of the perfect gentleman. But the young lady who'd captivated him with her unpretentious greeting was less easily understood. She was elegantly beautiful in the blue gown. The fabric caught and held the depth of color in her eyes, making them seem large and almost mournful. A dark light filled his gaze as it fastened on the diamond and pearl pendant at her neck. It was identical to the one he'd found in his father's trunk. He was certain of it. Only it looked different on her than he might have expected. Yes, except for the pendant she looked . . . *just the way she'd looked the last time he'd seen her.*

He held onto her hand, knowing how it must look to the others who stood about, yet somehow afraid if he released her, she would simply disappear and he would never see her again, like some ethereal creature he'd only imagined. She was so very beautiful, familiar to him and yet not, as if they might have met before and were now meeting again. And yet, if he had met her before, Zach knew he would remember it. Jingo Nymagee would explain it as part of the Dreamtime; now, or then, or tomorrow. All time, and each a part of yesterday, today, and tomorrow. Zach didn't know how much he believed of the legend of the Dreamtime. He was only aware of this woman, this moment somehow captured by them alone, and all the moments he might yet steal of tomorrow.

He watched the play of emotions across her face, surprise followed by embarrassment. A revealing pink spread across wide cheekbones. Those magnificent eyes rimmed in feather-soft, jet black lashes tilted faintly at the corners. Again he was fascinated by the curve of her jaw above the elegant curve of her neck. Something pulled at his memory, something that seemed somehow different. Her hair was pulled up and piled in soft layers on top of her head, like a crown of rich, dark sable. *You promised to wear it down for me.* The thought intruded, just as the elusive memory had intruded earlier, filling him with an inexplicable sense of sadness.

Zach's smile immediately faded as he abruptly released her hand. Who was this woman who seemed to claim his thoughts? Jingo would say he was lost in the Dreamtime, reliving another day and time. Like the aborigines, his people, Jingo was deeply influenced by legend and myth.

He forced himself to meet her eyes, desperately needing them to be a less haunting shade of blue, desperately hoping they would be just as he remembered them.

"Miss Winslow is soon to be Lady Barrington." With equally imposing formality, Jerrold Barrington established boundaries.

Soon to be fixed in Zach's mind as he raised his head above her hand. "Then congratulations are in order." That was the reason his inquiries had met with such surprise. He glanced down, unable to understand his disappointment at learning she was this man's fiancée. He was aware of a faint trembling as he refused to release Elyse, and didn't know whether the uncertainty was hers or his own. He wouldn't have thought this magnificent creature to be the shrinking, withering sort. She tried to withdraw her hand, refusing to meet his gaze, and amusement deepened the soft creases at the corners of his mouth.

"I don't believe I've had the pleasure, sir," Jerrold Barrington prodded, fixing him with a glare of obvious disapproval.

Nor I, thought Zach, equally contemptuous. But then, he was quite accustomed to the condescending attitude of the British nobility. It helped remind him of his true feelings for all Englishmen, especially the Barringtons. His gaze returned to the *soon to be* Lady Barrington. She averted her eyes, but not before he caught the faint flash of response she couldn't disguise completely. So, it wasn't shyness he'd sensed in her after all. She was equally ill at ease with Jerrold Barrington's rudeness. And something more glistened in her eyes. Something very much akin to recognition.

His smile masked his contempt for the Barrington name. "We've never met, but we've had business dealings."

"You're not English, sir." Jerrold's patronizing air indicated mere tolerance.

Elyse stiffened, feeling the deliberate censorship of Jerrold's biting comment. It was maddening how much pleasure he got from belittling people, yet fascinating that this stranger seemed completely unaffected by him.

Zach smiled inwardly at the flash of disapproval he saw in those blue eyes. So, the soon-to-be Lady Barrington wasn't so easily manipulated by her fiancé. His words were for Jerrold Barrington, but his eyes never left hers.

"I have diverse interests, Lord Barrington," he said coolly, then, as if deliberately considering, he paused, selecting his words carefully. "And I've had some dealings with your firm. You seem to have crossed paths with an infamous fellow who goes by the name of the Raven. I understand you've lost substantial cargoes, not to mention several ships of the line, to this devil."

"Then you've had some dealings in the colonies of New South Wales. I do hope you weren't victimized by that pirate." The disdainful arch of Jerrold's brows lowered a notch. He wouldn't offend a possible client.

"Many have suffered at the hands of the Raven." Zach carefully maneuvered the conversation. "He seems to be such a very elusive pirate that I'm given to wonder if he truly exists. Perhaps the difficulty you British have had in New South Wales is aggravated by your inexperience in dealing with the people there."

"Dealing with the people!" Jerrold laughed incredulously. "I would hardly give the inhabitants of New South Wales the courtesy of that description. They're nothing but convicts and miscreants, not fit for human society elsewhere." His tone was gratingly superior. "The dregs of humanity, if you will. Of course, we anticipate certain difficulties in dealing with such riffraff. But we can and will control the situation. After all, there is a great deal of wealth to be obtained from that ungodly continent. It's beyond me, how those unsufferable Australians can even consider themselves of equal status to Englishmen; making the demands they do for their own home government, and with the entire country inhabited with those inferior savages."

"Yes, I've heard of their intense dislike for all Englishmen," Zach mused thoughtfully.

"It is a temporary condition, I assure you. Nothing more than a bit of misplaced arrogance. In time they will come to appreciate what England has bestowed upon them," Jerrold arrogantly assured them all. "As you'll recall we've been forced to deal with your people in the past. You did say you were Spanish?"

Elyse drew in a sharp breath at Jerrold's caustic remark, but the Count de Cuervo seemed completely unaffected. Her eyes widened at his deep, appreciative laughter.

"You are to be complimented on your sense of grace and humility, Lord Barrington. You are, above all, an example of the true Englishman."

Only Elyse seemed aware of the biting edge to the Count's remark. Like his words, his gray gaze sparked with something vaguely threatening.

Jerrold smiled oddly, thinking that perhaps he might have missed something in the exchange but unable to find anything in the Count's response at which to take offense.

Zach's hands itched to feel Barrington's throat beneath his fingers, but his smile was silken. "It is most fortunate for me that we have met. I should like to discuss a certain cargo with you. At your convenience, of course. It is a most rare and precious cargo, one I'm certain you will find of great interest. Certainly someone who has your expertise with the colonials of New South Wales might be able to advise me on a purchaser for it."

Wide-eyed, Elyse stared at the Spanish nobleman. He seemed to be praising Jerrold, but she knew for a fact how disastrous the last two years had been for Jerrold and his father. They'd had disastrous results with exporting and importing cargoes to Australia, losing one ship after another to a man they knew only as the Raven.

Their latest loss had been several ships heavily laden with cargo and armaments, at some remote place called the Barrier Reef. Most of the crew had escaped, but the financial loss of cargo and ships had been devastating to Barrington Shipping. She knew of the details only through the servants who exchanged gossip at the open-air market when everyone was in residence in London.

Elyse had used the heavy financial loss as an argument to persuade Jerrold that they wait until the following year to announce their engagement. But he'd adamantly refused, informing her that it was nothing for her to concern her pretty little head over. That he'd considered her suggestion and concern as little more than bothersome had irritated her. She wanted to know about such problems, and to be of help. But Jerrold absolutely refused to discuss anything remotely concerning business with her.

She hadn't been able to ignore the nagging feeling that there was more to his stance. She knew marriages were often made for financial advantage. Until that moment last winter when she'd confronted him about the trouble in New South Wales, it had never occurred to her that Jerrold might consider their marriage a financial arrangement. The Count de Cuervo seemed well informed about the Barringtons' difficulties, however. She could see the superiority waver in Jerrold's eyes, and couldn't smother a feeling of satisfaction as he tried to extricate himself from a conversation he could no longer control. Jerrold loved manipulating people to his own advantage. She remembered that she'd once thought of him as commanding and confident. Now he often seemed little more than arrogant.

"We have many ships, your grace." Jerrold struck a polite pose. "Traveling to virtually every port in the world. Undoubtedly, we've carried your cargoes. I should like to discuss this with you." He turned to Elyse, a trace of the old arrogance returning.

"Please come along, my dear; we have other guests. After all," — he paused for effect — "we will announce our engagement. This is a very special evening." He felt he'd very effectively cut the outrageous stranger from their conversation, and he frowned slightly when Elyse hesitated. He found indiscretion intolerable, especially in the woman who was to be his wife. He'd have to speak to her about this sort of thing.

Elyse pulled back on his arm, guided by some unseen force that compelled her to refuse to comply. "The count is our guest," she announced coolly as warm color slowly spread across her cheeks. She hated confrontations, especially when Jerrold enjoyed them so much, but he was being deliberately rude and overbearing. Instead of having the desired effect and bringing her under his control, his attitude grated on her. She found his behavior appalling.

Beside them, Lucy laughed with forced gaiety, obviously deciding diplomacy might be a better weapon. "The orchestra has begun another waltz," she said as she inserted herself between Jerrold and Elyse. "You know very well the announcement won't be made before midnight. Lady Winslow has planned everything perfectly." Lucy fastened Jerrold with a benign expression. "After all, it must be done properly."

Her words fairly dripped honey, only Elyse was aware of her subtle manipulation as she turned to the Count de Cuervo. "It is appropriate for the hostess to dance with her guests. And this is such a lovely waltz." Releasing a wistful sigh, Lucy smiled convincingly. Her intentions couldn't have been more obvious.

A conspiratorial smile played across Zach's mouth. "And we haven't had our dance yet," he said. He turned to Elyse, fastening on her a disarming and thoroughly captivating smile. "Soon-to-be Lady Barrington?" he teased, mocking laughter in his voice.

Elyse threw Lucy a murderous glare. She was being manipulated again, and for reasons she could well guess. "I should find my grandmother and help her greet our other guests," she said by way of apology. She looked to Lucy for aid, and immediately knew the cause lost.

"Elyse, you know good and well everyone who is anyone has already arrived. If someone comes late, your man Bascomb will let him in." She referred to Lady Winslow's intrepid butler.

Zach turned the full force of his persuasion on Jerrold Barrington. He still had many questions he wanted answered, and Miss Winslow might prove an excellent source. It would be advantageous to use Jerrold Barrington's fiancée to learn what he wanted to know. "Certainly you don't disapprove. I assure you, my family has a most impeccable background. And later, perhaps, we could discuss that cargo I was speaking of. It arrived just this morning aboard one of my ships. I managed to acquire a holdful of superior quality wool. I think we might strike a price even you would find profitable." He smiled inwardly as he saw capitulation in Jerrold Barrington's greedy gaze. The mention of wool was almost more than the man could stand. It was unheard of to find wool, unless of course it was obtained from someplace else, perhaps as contraband from the colonies in New South Wales. Zach knew he'd fed the man's curiosity, and he was certain Barrington was almost drooling at the expectation of picking up such a cargo. Jerrold seemed the sort who'd barter his mother if he thought there was an advantageous deal to be made.

Jerrold hesitated only a moment, then gave Elyse his assent. "By all means, my darling, you mustn't be rude to our guest. After all, it will only be for this one waltz, and then I'm certain the Count de Cuervo will return you safely to my side."

Zach could see the anger that immediately sparked in those blue eyes, anger at her fiancé's callous behavior. The man was worse than a fool; he was an absolute ass. He didn't even realize he was slowly losing what should have been his most prized possession. Miss Elyse Winslow was furious beneath her cool exterior. Zach smiled, thinking that if he had ever had occasion to meet her before, he would never have forgotten it.

Seeing that she was being efficiently handed over into the hands of the Count de Cuervo and had absolutely nothing to say about the matter, Elyse turned to Lucy who'd offered no reprieve whatsoever. In fact, her friend was responsible for all this.

"Please tell my grandmother I will join her and Lord Barrington immediately following this last waltz," she said, making everyone aware of her intention to see her social obligation to this stranger concluded as soon as possible.

Lucy choked back a sudden giggle and solemnly promised to deliver the message. "You sly little fox," she whispered in Elyse's ear, as she smiled wickedly. "Why didn't you tell me you had met the count before?"

"We haven't . . . I mean . . ." Elyse faltered. "Lucy, please!" she implored. Glancing up she found the Count de Cuervo watching her with that careful gaze. She gave both men an equally rebellious glare. She didn't like being dictated to or treated as a reward when Jerrold found it to his advantage. And she didn't trust the Count de Cuervo. But she knew if she were entirely honest with herself, it wasn't that she didn't trust him. Actually, she didn't trust the uncertain feelings he roused in her. They were all too familiar and disconcerting. She'd come to know them far too well from her dreams.

Despite her intentions, Elyse's breath caught in her throat as she saw something elusive behind his smile. There was no mockery in that gaze, only a curiosity to match her own.

I can't see his eyes, she remembered telling Katy, *but I'll know him when I see him.* Something very near fear shimmered down her spine. She didn't know him! It was impossible! She couldn't simply will someone to appear, to just step from her dreams. The man in her dreams didn't exist! Long ago, she'd made herself believe he didn't. And yet, at this very moment as she stood, caught by the gentle restraint of his hand, staring at a man she couldn't remember, she felt an invisible bond stronger than his hand. Dear God, what was the matter with her?

She pulled abruptly from his grasp, uncertain whether she gained her freedom, or whether he simply released her. She should have been relieved. Instead, she felt that same sense of loss and emptiness from her dreams. Everything in the large ballroom seemed suddenly distorted, as if she were standing still and the entire room, its lights and colors, whirled about her, out of control. No, not everything was out of control. *He* was there, calm in the eye of a sudden storm. She pressed her fingers against her temple. The room had become unbearably warm.

"Please . . . I . . ." She closed her eyes, hoping she could open them in a few seconds and find everything as it was before. Before he'd appeared with thick golden hair and eyes as impenetrable as mist.

"Elyse? Are you unwell?" Lucy's voice seemed to come from very far away.

"Of course not." Her voice quavered as she fought to bring her emotions under control. "Please, I'd just like some fresh air."

"Elyse, darling, if you're not up to this next dance, I'm certain the count would understand . . ."

Stepping between Elyse and Jerrold Barrington, Zach effectively cut off his solicitous speech. It fed his sense of recklessness to steal her away from her fiancé.

"I'm certain she'll be just fine. All she needs is a walk outside." Not waiting for anyone's approval, Zach artfully guided her from the ballroom and from Jerrold Barrington's objections.

Lucy Maitland's eyes widened, a curious smile turning her mouth as she and Jerrold were left standing at the edge of the dance floor. Watching the retreating couple, she flicked her brocade fan back and forth speculatively. Less than an hour ago, the most fascinating and mysterious man had arrived, sending every available female between the ages of fifteen and seventy-five into speculative fits of perusal. And he'd just chosen to make off with the intended bride, taking her right out from under Jerrold's nose.

Her smile deepened. "It seems you've lost her." She took great delight in the frown that comment provoked. For months, Jerrold had pranced about London, indiscriminately flaunting his mistress, an overly libidinous actress rumored to have an outrageous set of lungs. And for months, Lucy Maitland had railed against the injustice of it all to her husband. Well, it seemed Elyse had made a conquest of her own. And such a conquest! Lucy didn't usually participate in idle gossip, but in this case she just might slip in a discreetly placed word or two about Elyse and the count.

Snapping her fan closed, Lucy assumed an innocent expression. "Good heavens! Don't act like such a dolt. Dance with me, Jerrold. If you stand there staring after them, people will talk."

"Not now, Lucy." Jerrold seemed to think better of so easily turning Elyse over to a stranger. He tried to sidestep her friend so he might pursue the mysterious man who called himself the Count de Cuervo.

"Yes," Lucy insisted. "Right now." Her mouth curved into the enticing smile that never failed to get her what she wanted. She would have such fun telling her husband about all this later.

Jerrold began to object. "Perhaps Elyse—"

"Will be just fine," Lucy cut him off. "Jerrold"—she feigned incredulity—"you can't be jealous, or perhaps worried? He is a devilish, handsome man!" She smiled radiantly as she slyly maneuvered him further away from the French doors that opened onto the veranda. "Is the fit of the shoe a little tight?"

"What do you mean by that?" He turned to her indignantly, over her shoulder watching Elyse and the count disappear into cool evening shadows.

Lucy slipped her arm through his, coercing him out onto the dance floor. "I think you know exactly what I mean, darling." She patted his arm. "Don't look so devastated. I'm certain she'll be back in a little while. After all"—she smiled wickedly, fully enjoying her little part in Elyse's disappearance with another man—"what harm could there possibly be? It's all very innocent. You should know that, Jerrold." She pinned him with a knowing gaze, then smiled coyly at him. "You mustn't worry. Elyse will be the soul of discretion." There, she thought triumphantly! That ought to sufficiently irritate him.

Next she appealed to his sense of male pride. "You've danced with practically everyone here, including Constance Laughton. If you're not careful, you'll start rumors." Her mouth curved in whimsical delight at the game she was playing. Jerrold was actually beginning to look a bit uncomfortable, which was exactly what she wanted. Then he wouldn't have time to be concerned about Elyse, the mysteriously handsome Spanish count, and an incredibly romantic moonlit night.

"Everyone knows what a dreadful reputation that woman has," she continued, flashing her eyelashes convincingly. "Lady Winslow only invited her out of courtesy to Lord Laughton. He is such a dear man. Besides, Andrew isn't anywhere to be found. Do be a dear and say you will dance with me." Lucy knew she was being an outrageous flirt, and she loved it, especially when she was manipulating a pompous ass like Jerrold Barrington. Honestly, she just couldn't understand Elyse's commitment to this engagement.

Her eyes glistened thoughtfully. There were still a few weeks until the wedding. Anything might happen in that amount of time. After all, she herself had fallen in love in an instant, in the middle of a mud puddle. And bolts of lightning had been known to strike very quickly. She watched with restrained delight as Jerrold found it impossible to extricate himself from her demands.

A muscle tightened faintly in Jerrold's jaw, but he said nothing. After all, Andrew Maitland had substantial contracts with Barrington shipping. It wouldn't do to offend his wife, even if she had the aggravating habit of setting Elyse against him. Jerrold turned on the charm, smiling thinly as he coolly perused the woman in his arms. Lucy Maitland was a beautiful woman, with snapping dark eyes and pale, honey blond hair. He'd wondered more than once what it would be like to tumble her in his bed. But he'd dismissed the idea just as quickly. It would be far too dangerous. After all, she was Elyse's best friend, and seemed to be unswervingly loyal. Still . . .

Lucy's eyes narrowed slightly as she felt the subtle tightening of Jerrold's arm about her waist. Her hand rested on his shoulder, the closed brocade fan cocked just below his ear. She tilted the angle, slipping it firmly into his throat. At his startled look at the sudden pressure that momentarily cut off his air, she smiled beguilingly.

"You must be careful, Jerrold. You never know who might be watching." Then she laughed, fully enjoying his discomfort, and glanced discreetly toward the veranda. Oh, what she wouldn't give to be a mouse sitting in a darkened corner out there right now. Unless she missed her guess, there was more to Elyse's little spell than mere overexcitement.

Lucy had caught the briefest flash of something in her friend's eyes when Elyse had turned to meet the count. It had almost seemed as if she'd recognized him. And what was it she'd said? Oh yes, *I knew you'd come back to me.* Certainly not the typical greeting for a new acquaintance, but rather something someone might say to a . . . lover? She tucked it all away, promising herself to question

101

Elyse about it later. And here she'd been encouraging her to indulge in a little innocent flirtation! Flirtation indeed! Innocent? She wondered.

Elyse was a few steps ahead of Zach as he guided her through the doors and out onto the veranda. She stopped abruptly, causing him to practically walk into her. He towered over her, amusement dancing at the corners of his mouth as her hand came up to block a more intimate contact. "I'm really feeling much better now. It's not necessary for you to remain with me," she informed him in a rather shaky voice.

Though her hand was placed discreetly between them, he refused to acknowledge her polite gesture that he stand back. He knew it would make her angry, but he couldn't resist the temptation to see emotion spark in her cool blue eyes, first like ice, then like fire.

"I wouldn't dream of abandoning you." His voice was low, mesmerizing. "How would it look if I retreated too quickly?"

"Look?" She cleared her throat, drawing herself up to her full five feet and six inches, not including the small heel of her dancing slippers. Even at that his advantage was overpowering and more than a little disconcerting. "I really hadn't given it much thought," she replied honestly. And indeed she hadn't. In truth, the only thing she'd thought about since she'd first turned to find him looking down at her was this man.

"You really should, you know. It might be the beginning of something very scandalous. And Lord Barrington seems very conscious of such things," Zach teased, reaching to secure her gloved hand in his. He didn't want her retreating so easily.

In spite of her intentions, Elyse laughed. She'd met many foreigners on the Grand Tour, but this one certainly qualified as the most arrogant. No, "arrogant" was the wrong word. Jerrold could be maddeningly arrogant. This man was confident, to the point of nonchalance. She composed herself, forcing her eyes away from the sheen of the black eyepatch, but she was unable to rid herself of a growing curiosity about what lay underneath. Was he badly scarred, with only a gaping hole beneath the sweep of that golden slash of brow? Or had the wound been neatly closed, leaving only a white slit of a scar where once a compelling gray eye matched the one that regarded her now with such maddening calm. Had he lost the eye in an accident or a confrontation? There was something

102

about the eyepatch that bothered her.

It wasn't the idea of scarred or torn flesh, or even the possibility of a disfiguring hole. What she felt was a fleeting sadness that he might have suffered great pain. And the agony of that sadness was almost overwhelming.

"A penny for your thoughts." Zach smiled down at her, unable to resist the temptation of knowing what she was thinking at just that moment.

"I'm afraid a mere penny wouldn't do." She masked the sadness with a faint smile. "It may very well cost you an entire fortune."

"It would be a fortune worth the losing." There was something elusive about her smile, something almost lost and mournful in her eyes. And then it was gone. Maybe he'd only imagined it.

Elyse took a tentative step backward as she changed the topic of their conversation. "I have no intention of dancing with you," she informed him airily. "I don't dance with pirates."

Zach burst out laughing, to cover a sudden fit of coughing brought on by the incredible accuracy of her statement. Then he sobered. "Oh, I think you will, lovely lady. After all" — he suddenly became very solemn, but it was a teasing soberness — "a hostess is expected to dance with her guests. It would be very bad form for you to refuse."

"Do you always get exactly what you want?" Her delicate chin tilted slightly, and her lips parted questioningly beneath that straight, faintly snubbed nose he found delightful for its brevity.

"Usually." Zach smiled down at her. "You see" — he took that one step toward her, closing the distance between them once more — "I detest losing, but winning . . ." He paused.

"Yes?"

His gray gaze darkened to intense slate, as he thought of many prizes to be sought and won. "Winning is everything." He knew the exact effect his words would have on her. And he was right; a defiant light sparkled in those beguiling eyes. Barrington was twice a fool for his lack of caring for her. Zach smiled. Elyse was definitely feeling much better. Her color had returned. She pinned him with that compelling gaze. At this moment, her eyes were the exact color of exotic and rare lapis stones, shot through with faint golden light that hinted at her mood. His gaze lowered to the intriguing pearl and diamond pendant around her neck. The luminous jewels seemed to come alive against her skin, as if they'd been especially fashioned for her.

"Everything?" she whispered softly. Jerrold had always felt the same way. And she detested his overbearing, competitive nature. But there was nothing overbearing about the Count de Cuervo. Though he was keenly competitive, she understood that, he was vastly different from Jerrold. There was no cruelty in this man. Instinctively she knew it. She'd felt it in the unrestrained tenderness of his touch earlier. Now the thought of that touch, and the feelings it had aroused, made her wary. She took another hesitant step backward, only to be brought up short as the stone wall surrounding the veranda pressed against her back. Although he didn't take a step toward her, she felt inexplicably trapped and couldn't understand the reason for it. The veranda was well lit, and guests were mingling near the opened doors, well within calling distance. Yet she felt the exhilaration of danger with this man. Suddenly, she decided it would be safer to put even more distance between them.

"It really isn't necessary for you to remain here with me," Elyse informed him coolly, intimating that he should leave and at the same time hoping he wouldn't. "I'm really much better, and I can take care of myself."

"Yes," he admitted, his fingers slipping beneath her chin and tilting her head up so that he could look directly into her eyes, "and you never faint." His tone was teasing.

"No. Never," Elyse responded shakily. Her thoughts were suddenly confused again, and she had the vaguest feeling it had nothing to do with her earlier faintness. She lowered her gaze to the curve of his smile, and to the single dimple that appeared briefly. Color crept into her cheeks as she found it impossible to break away from the heart-stopping tenderness of his smile. His mouth curved upward, then turned down abruptly at one corner as if he found something oddly amusing. She moistened her lips, unable to hold back her curiosity when she knew more questions would only foolishly delay him.

"Why did you call me Lady Barrington?"

Gray turned to darkest slate in the muted glow that filtered from the expanse of the ballroom windows at the side of the house. The low light pooled softly on the veranda and wide, manicured lawns. "Why did you think you knew me?" he answered her with a question of his own.

"It was a simple mistake." She dismissed him with equal efficiency, but knew the question went unanswered for both of them. For the life of her, she couldn't understand why she'd said what she had. She tried to cover her uncertainty.

"I thought you were someone else."

Again the smile reappeared, creating a careful, disarming fa-çade. Zach thought he'd found the mysterious woman out of his father's past. The discreet inquiries he'd made upon his arrival that evening had all brought confused reactions. One imperious-look-ing woman, an odd expression on her face, had pointed this young lady out to him. Now he understood the confusion. The woman standing before him was far too young to be Felicia Barrington. He should have felt regret at having come this far and risked so much with this foolish scheme, as Tobias was constantly reminding him. Oddly enough, he didn't regret anything, not even the danger he'd placed them both in.

"You thought I was Lady Barrington?"

"As you said"—he threw her words back at her—"it was a simple mistake." He'd responded far too casually, and with equal casual-ness he reached up, slipped his fingers beneath the pendant that lay in the hollow of her throat.

As if she'd been burned by fire, Elyse jerked away from his touch. The clasp bit painfully into the tender skin at the back of her neck, then parted. As she pulled away from the disconcerting heat in those fingers, a flash of brilliant light shimmered in the evening darkness. Just as quickly it fell to the flagstones of the veranda, like a shooting star, brilliant and then gone.

Zach bent over, his fingers closing over the cool elegance of diamonds and pearls intricately set in an old-fashioned design. The muted light from the ballroom illuminated the stones; the pearls glowed softly. He frowned, lightly caressing the stones. They radiated warmth, as if they carried life in their shining depths.

"I believe you dropped this." He stood, his words halting her.

Turning slowly, Elyse squared her slender shoulders, and her gaze fell to his extended hand, from which her pearl and diamond pendant dangled with cool brilliance. Anger quickly turned to alarm. She reached out, her fingers lightly brushing his, like the breath of a kiss. She drew back abruptly as if she'd touched fire. Beneath her gloves, her skin glowed warmly, and she curled her fingers against the betraying heat.

"It's very unusual." His voice softened, as he caressed the pen-dant almost lovingly. "It looks as if it's very old."

"It was a gift." Elyse reached for it only to have it drawn further from her grasp.

Zach turned the pendant around and around in the light, in-specting all its luminous facets. "And like the owner, I would guess very . . . unique." Slowly, his gaze rose to catch hers, which, like the pendant, was filled with mysterious lights. "The clasp is broken. I must have it fixed for you. I feel responsible for breaking it."

"That's really not necessary," she reassured him. "If you'll just give it to me, I'll have it fixed myself."

"Was it a gift from your fiancé?" he persisted with maddening calm, keeping the pendant just beyond her reach.

"Jerrold?" She laughed softly in spite of wanting to be angry with him. "No, I'm afraid not. He prefers more ostentatious jewelry. He's given me several pieces."

"I'm sure he has," Zach remarked tightly. "Why aren't you wearing them?" The darkness of his gaze blended with the night shadows.

"I prefer the pendant. It's much more suited to my tastes." Elyse smiled softly. "And, it holds a special meaning for me." Her voice had softened.

His stunned expression was concealed from her, but Zach's eyes glowed. "Who gave it to you?" he whispered, his own voice hollow and aching.

"It was a gift from my grandmother." She could almost sense his disappointment. What had he expected her to say?

"It was given to her by a friend many years ago. Felicia Barrington."

Zach's gaze hardened at the sound of the name that had brought him thousands of miles to a country he loathed, and for a purpose he'd begun to dread. "Lady Barrington." He ran the name slowly over his tongue, the bitter edge to his voice evident, he repeated it. "Lady Felicia Barrington."

"Yes," Elyse answered uncertainly. The night had suddenly grown very cold. She shivered faintly. After all, what did she know of this man? Watching that single eye, she moistened her lips with her tongue, her fingers itching to snatch the pendant from his grasp. She wasn't about to leave without it.

"Who is Felicia Barrington?"

Elyse blinked uncertainly. It was an odd question to come from someone who'd informed them all only moments before that he'd had substantial dealings with Barrington Shipping.

"She was Jerrold's mother. But then you should know that. If you are who you say you are." She breathed in slowly, trying to calm the racing of her pulse. It had begun in her fingertips, coursed up her arms, and was now hammering in her heart.

"Was?" The single word fell like a blow. His gaze was fastened on the pendant. "What happened to her?" he ground out almost fiercely.

Once more that sense of danger returned, slipping like a warning down her spine. "She died many years ago. She was sick for a long time. I remember my grandmother telling me she died the night of the . . ." She hesitated. "The night my parents died." Elyse asked herself, why she had felt compelled to tell him that? Or to explain anything to him for that matter? She took a step closer to prove she wasn't intimidated by him, at the same time fully aware that she was.

"Now"—she tilted her lovely chin—"I would like some answers as well."

Zach's smile returned briefly at her show of bravado. "I suppose that's fair enough," he acknowledged gruffly, carefully burying his disappointment. Felicia Barrington was dead. Tobias had tried to prepare him for that possibility. After all, everything that had happened to his father before he'd arrived in New South Wales had taken place almost thirty-five years ago. It was a long time. Just as the years had changed his father and Tobias; they'd changed others.

"Who are you, really? And I don't mean that ridiculous title you gave everyone in there." Elyse pinned him with an insistent gaze that was far more confident than she was.

Zach stared at her incredulously. "You don't believe I'm the Count de Cuervo!" He assumed an appropriately injured expression.

"Not for a moment! You, sir, are a fraud!" Elyse informed him confidently, taking another step closer. Whoever this man was, she was going to enjoy exposing him, just as he'd taken great delight in drawing a response from her in front of Jerrold and Lucy. Lucy!

Dear God, how was she ever going to explain this to her? Her friend was undoubtedly deliberately detaining Jerrold in order to give them more time alone. Their meeting had seemed to feed Lucy's sense of romantic adventure. She just couldn't understand why everyone else wasn't as outrageously in love as she was. The trouble was, Elyse knew, she envied Lucy. She'd have given almost anything to be able to feel such emotions for Jerrold. She forced back other more startling emotions as she found herself staring into the cocksure gaze of this stranger who had the uncanny ability to completely unnerve her.

"You're quite certain of that?" Arms folded across his chest, he fixed her with a careful gaze.

"Yes." Of course she was certain! Yet her voice sounded less than absolutely confident.

"All right. Let's suppose you're right. Who am I?" Zach countered, wondering just how much she thought she knew, or had guessed.

He certainly had a way of turning the conversation around to his advantage, Elyse decided. She silently wondered what else he could easily manipulate. "That's supposed to be my question."

"I'm quite sorry. Please go ahead."

A smile teased with maddening tenderness at his lips. Elyse was completely undone by it. She moistened her lips again, her gaze wandering to the corners of his mouth where the smile lingered, teasing a faint dimple deeper still. Her dark blue eyes were then drawn to the black eyepatch. She decided he undoubtedly enjoyed that advantage.

"I don't believe you're Spanish at all," she challenged. "And the title is undoubtedly just as fake." Her confidence grew when he didn't bother to offer an argument. She was fairly certain his accent wasn't Spanish, although she couldn't quite place it. At this very moment, it was more a matter of what he was not than what he was. Elyse inhaled deeply, knowing she was venturing into unsafe territory. What he was . . . a maddeningly handsome man with the aggravating air of someone who did not give a damn about anything or anyone. And there was that faint flickering warning of danger about him, despite the spotless white shirt and the formal black waistcoat and pants that were an elegant contrast.

Slowly, he shook his head, his gaze lowering from her. For heaven's sake! She hadn't meant to embarrass him. Then she realized he wasn't embarrassed at all. When he raised his head, fastening her with that penetrating gray gaze, he was laughing at her!

"I don't see what's so funny," she announced in her most haughty tone. Usually it was sufficient to bring a man up short. But he only continued laughing, finding something very amusing about their conversation.

"What are you laughing at?" Elyse moved even closer, her fingers curling into tight fists. Oh what she wouldn't give to wipe the smile off his arrogantly handsome face.

"I'm sorry," he apologized, reaching to wipe what appeared to be a tear from the corner of his eye. Then he cleared his throat, trying to smother another fit of laughter. "It's just that you've found me out."

"I've what?" Elyse drew back in surprise.

"You've found me out. You're quite right, Miss Winslow," he said formally, bowing low from the waist. "I'm not a Spanish count. What would be your guess?" Zach delighted in the way her mouth twisted thoughtfully. Most women would have given him some wide-eyed, simple look and then played the confused, naïve young virgin. They somehow assumed that was what a man wanted. Perhaps some men did. As for himself, he found Miss Elyse Winslow, soon-to-be Lady Barrington, absolutely charming. She didn't give a damn about appearances, either physical or social, or she wouldn't have come out on this veranda with him in the first place. And, as it was, she had no idea just how close she'd come to the truth.

Leaning toward him, arms folded across the curve of her bodice, she mimicked his casual air. "With that patch, I'd say you're a pirate." The light in her eyes sparkled with hidden fire and secret promises.

Zach watched her carefully, only a trace of a smile lingering at the corners of his mouth. "A pirate—eyepatch and all."

"Of course. Which would explain why you found the pendant so fascinating. And"—she hesitated meaningfully—"why you still haven't given it back to me. You, sir,"—she leaned closer, her eyes widening with her sense of victory—"are undoubtedly a black-guard and a scoundrel, probably with a price on your head." Taking one quick step forward, Elyse's hand shot out, her target the pearl and diamond pendant still dangling from his long fingers.

With lightning swiftness, Zach closed his fingers securely around her wrist, and his other arm stole around her slender waist, pulling her full-length against his body. The game was over. Elyse gasped.

"And you, dear lady, are a thief." His breath was warm, mingling with the night air, and faint surprise shaded his words because of that first full contact with her slender body.

She was a thief all right. But he doubted she understood his meaning. She could steal a man's heart with those eyes that prom-ised something elusive. And unless he missed his guess, that something was desire.

One arm firmly molding her slender body to his, Zach reached up, stroking the backs of his fingers against the satin softness of her cheek as if she were a frightened animal and he could tame the fear from her.

"Please don't do that." She batted at his hand, only to find herself drawn more intimately against his muscular body. Something vague and closed away deep inside him opened to her, like a door once tightly shut now giving way. Zach felt his heart turn over as her lower lip trembled with sudden uncertainty. She'd tried to beat him at his own game and now found the stakes too high.

"What are you afraid of?" he whispered, feeling the trembling that arched her body away from him. "You did promise me a waltz," he reminded her.

Elyse bit back the truth. "I'm not afraid." Dear God, what was happening? Who was this man and why was he having such a devastating effect on her? More importantly, who was she allowing it. "But I've changed my mind. I don't care to dance with you."

"Do you regret your choice?" Zach's head lowered and turned. His eyes closed as he gently brushed the exquisite softness of her cheek with his roughened one. His lips brushed against her skin, his tongue tasting her sweetness. Somehow, he'd known she would be just that sweet and alluring, one taste never enough.

"It wasn't my choice. Stop that!" Elyse whispered brokenly, her eyes closing against the exquisite torture of his warm mouth. He'd called her a thief. Now she was a liar as well. She didn't want him to stop. She wanted him to go on caressing her like that . . . always and forever.

"Stop what?" Zach teased, grazing his lips against the line of her jaw, feeling the small muscles clenching and unclenching. Unable to resist tasting her lips, he turned his head, until his mouth lightly touched the corner of hers.

Elyse's hands flattened against the stark white of his shirt, her hips riding against his, satin-shrouded thighs brushing his. And his mouth. He was having a torturous effect on her senses as his lips tenderly traced her cheek until they lingered just at the corner of her mouth. She'd long ago ceased breathing. Her hands curled in the folds of his shirt, intent on pushing him away, yet desperate to pull him closer. As the wait became unbearable, Elyse lifted tortured eyes to his. His gray gaze swam in a mist of confusion and desire, his strong arms surrounded her, preventing retreat, yet refusing to pull her closer. He was so near, her vision was blurred and the only thing remaining distinct was the desire unfolding within her, weighing her down as if she had no will of her own. As her eyes met his gaze, she saw something very near sadness shimmering in that gray depth.

"Lis." Zach whispered the endearment with aching tenderness as he surrendered to something indefinable, feeling himself drawn into some other place and time. It had begun when she'd first turned to him with those heartfelt words that seemed engraved on his soul. Now the desire that burned inside him was like a litany of something from his own past aching to be remembered. Cradling her head in his hands, he let his thumbs caress the prominence of her high cheekbones, her silken skin; moving in hypnotic circles, almost as if he were reacquainting himself with the touch of her. His fingers trembled into the silken mass of her hair, stealing the pins, freeing the auburn strands until they tumbled below her shoulders like a luxuriant mane.

"Lis," he whispered again, lowering his mouth against hers, the whisper becoming a caress, a once-forgotten promise. *You promised to always wear it long for me,* echoed softly across his thoughts.

As if he struggled up from some dark void, Zach forced his hands from her hair. With almost aching tenderness, he released her.

Elyse tried to draw him back to her, a broken sigh escaping her lips. She felt as if something had been stolen from her. It was an intangible loss, even the more overwhelming in that it couldn't be seen or touched. But she felt it deep within.

"No," Zach whispered raggedly, struggling against equally shattered composure. "I won't hurt you again," he said softly, unable to comprehend where the thought had come from. Carefully he set her from him. The cooling night air moved between their bodies restoring some semblance of sanity. The pendant was still clutched tightly in his hand. The expression on his face was stark and filled with inexplicable pain.

Her own pain was acute. Elyse's gloved hand flashed through the air, landing dully against his cheek. "You're a cad and a lowlife." The pendant was all but forgotten in light of her wildly churning emotions. "You sneak in here with grand lies about who you are, asking questions about Lady Barrington. I want you to leave now."

Zach stiffened as if he'd taken a great blow. "I'm sorry if I offended you," he breathed out, extending his hand one last time to caress her cheek. "Good night, lovely lady."

And then he was gone, leaving her with a more aching sense of loss than any of her dreams.

Chapter Five

"How long did you say you would be in London, your grace?" J. Hollings, Esquire, looked down the narrow twist of an incredibly long and disdainful nose.

"I didn't," the Count de Cuervo replied curtly, causing poor Hollings to jump as he fixed him with a quelling stare.

Tobias shifted uncomfortably. His head hurt, his eyes ached, and his mouth felt as if it were stuffed with wool. The collar of the damnable shirt cut into his neck, his shoes pinched miserably, and he had the feeling Zach was taking great pleasure in drawing out this meeting unnecessarily.

"Mr. Hollings assured me there would be no problem in using the house while we're in London," he said. "I might add, I hope our stay will be brief." He irritably forced the words from between clenched lips. If he didn't sit down soon, he'd fall down. On second thought, maybe that would teach the young upstart a lesson, set all of London abuzz about the Count de Cuervo's uncle, the illustrious Marquis de la Vida. Tobias almost choked, thinking of the identity he'd been forced to assume. A Spanish marquis! Of all the idiotic, addle-pated ideas! The longer Zach kept up this charade, the greater the chance they were going to get caught at it. But the longer it continued, the more deeply submerged his young friend had become in the deception. It was as if Lady Felicia Barrington had some invisible hold on him.

Zach left the library, continuing his inspection of the first-floor rooms. The elegant manor house bespoke position, respectability, and wealth. He only had a need of the first two. His decision made, Zach turned abruptly to return to the library, almost tripping over the ubiquitous Mr. Hollings.

"It will do quite nicely. We'll only have need of the rooms on the ground floor. Our stay in London, will be . . . brief." He fixed on the solicitor an expression of cool disdain that was heightened by the black eyepatch obscuring part of his face.

Mr. Hollings coughed nervously and straightened his black satin cravat. There was something about this elegantly dressed gentleman with the odd accent that intrigued him. Though his title was that of a Spanish nobleman, his features contradicted such origins. The solicitor shifted uneasily. He learned early in his career the rewards of discretion. He never questioned the motives of the firm's clients, but this was a most uncommon situation.

"It is unusual that Lord Vale left no instructions that you would be visiting, your grace," he ventured in a squeaky voice that failed on the last word. Clearing his throat, he smiled weakly. "We've handled many transactions for Lord and Lady Vale in the past. It seems irregular . . ." Hands twisting nervously, he let his pale eyes drop from the questioning glance of the Count de Cuervo.

"My cousin wasn't aware of my precise plans. However, if you wish, we could send word to him that you prefer I remain aboard my ship until the matter is settled." Zach fastened the man with a chilling glare.

Hollings blanched. "Oh my, no! We couldn't have that! It wouldn't be proper . . . that is, what if his grace were to learn of the matter?" He looked as if he were about to faint. Removing a handkerchief from his breast pocket, he blotted at his upper lip. "No indeed. I wouldn't want Lord Vale to think we were remiss in our responsibilities to a member of his family."

When the mysterious Count de Cuervo offered no further information, he nodded jerkily. "If everything meets with your approval, I will make the necessary arrangements for the household staff to return immediately."

Zach smiled. "I will rely on your expertise, Mr. Hollings. And upon my 'cousin's' return, I will convey your competence in making my stay . . . pleasurable." It was amazing how people fawned over the titled, amazing how much could be gained with just the nod of a head or the raising of an eyebrow—amazing and loathsome. Still, he could endure it to get what he wanted.

"I would like to move in immediately. I'll have my things sent from my ship." His gaze wandered over the richly paneled library. It was elegant. Dark wood, dark velvet fabrics, and equally dark carpet. Like a mausoleum. The walls closed in worse than those of the cabin aboard the *Tamarisk,* making him silently long for the vastness of Resolute. He smothered the longing. Soon enough he would have the answers he'd come for and would conclude a very

113

special "business transaction" with Barrington. Whether she realized it or not, Lady Elyse Winslow would help him accomplish those ends. She would make the perfect pawn to get at Barrington. His mood carried an edge of anger. He turned on the cringing solicitor who was hesitating as if there were something else to be said but he was afraid to risk it. Zach cocked a golden brow to hint faintly at his irritation at finding the man hovering very near his elbow.

"Is there something more?" Zach enforced control over his anger. After all, this man had nothing to do with it. He recognized his irritation as an offshoot of the same emotion that had abruptly sent him from the engagement party two nights before and had prevented sleep each night since. He told himself it was merely anticipation at being so near the truth about his father and yet not knowing it. But just this morning, he'd turned his anger on Tobias and had felt badly for it afterward. His friend was suffering his own demons, drinking himself practically unconscious each night and then enduring the aftereffects each morning. He hated Tobias's weakness but he understood the reason for it.

He supposed his old friend was entitled to bitterness over the past. Bitterness like truth was often a harsh taskmaster. And like the truth, his own bitterness had begun to emerge when Tobias had given him that worn and battered trunk after Megan's death. Those two emotions were like shards of broken glass driven deeply into an open wound that festered and never healed. The wound his father had carried for years. It was something only Tobias fully understood, and empathy was mirrored in his bloodshot eyes. Zach was only just beginning to understand such feelings.

"Was there something else you wished to discuss?" he repeated.

"Not at all, your grace." Mr. Hollings dipped and bobbed like a puppet controlled by invisible strings. "I'm certain I'll be able to have the servants here before midday."

"Excellent." Zach preceded him to the front door.

Just beyond the portal, the solicitor hesitated again. "I suppose there is just one more thing—" The door slammed in abrupt dismissal, cutting off any further attempt to gain information.

"Good God!" Hand clasped to his sweat-beaded brow, Tobias buckled into a nearby chair draped with a dustcover. "I'm certainly glad that's over." His eyes closed wearily, his head rolled back against the Queen Anne chair. "And you standing there as if you couldn't quite make up your mind about whether you wanted the house or not! If that little pipsqueak starts snooping around, the constable will be our first caller."

Zach rested a shoulder casually against the doorframe, hands thrust deep into the pockets of his gray worsted pants. His mood was deceivingly calm. "One must always act the part, my friend. There's nothing quite like snobbery to win people over. Mr. Hollings won't ask questions. He's afraid of returning to his superiors without adequate information about our sterling characters, but he's more afraid of offending an important client. And therein lies the dilemma. Mr. Hollings is soundly caught between a rock and a hard spot. Instead of taking a stand, he'll just squirm around a little bit and hope we are the upstanding citizens we say we are."

"God help us if he finds the fortitude to investigate that information you gave him. A bank account in Switzerland of all places!" Tobias muttered, rubbing his eyes.

"Which shows just how much you know, my dear friend. It is a fact that the most reputable international businessmen, and even the royalty, utilize such accounts. The Swiss are known for their expertise and discretion in financial matters. At any rate, the account exists."

"It does?" That seemed to sober Tobias somewhat. He sat upright with a jerk, paying a severe price for moving so quickly.

"It does," Zach informed him. "I took the liberty of establishing it several years ago. I thought it necessary to secure certain funds that no one would be able to trace."

"That explains a great many things," Tobias mumbled. "At least I think it does. I always wondered about all those little account books you kept in the safe at Resolute."

Zach smiled secretly. "There's a great deal you don't know, my friend."

"Eh, what's that you say?" Tobias raised blurry eyes to stare at him a little unsteadily.

"I was talking about the marvelous coincidence of things that come in twos: gloves, shoes, and pendants." He subtly changed the conversation.

"Pendants? What madness are you talking now? I see only one . . . I think." Tobias closed his eyes. He could have sworn Zach held only one pendant in his hand. He groaned. "My hair hurts."

"It should hurt, considering the whiskey you consumed last night. But yes, my friend, only one pendant. But one of two." He twirled the pendant round and round, fascinated by its hidden facets.

"Yer daft, there's only one. Unless me eyes are playing tricks on me." Tobias squinted at the sparkling object Zach held aloft. He'd experienced it before; the subtle playing of tricks by the mind after excessive drinking. And ever since they'd left Sydney over four months earlier, he'd indulged in spirits to excess. He rose on unsteady feet only to slump back wearily into the chair.

"I think maybe you'd better go on without me to that appointment. I'll just stay here and wait for those servants that Mr. Hollings said he'd send over. God!" He rested his forehead in cupped hands. "I wish Minnie were here with one of her special tonics. Better yet, I wish we were back at Resolute." He sighed heavily, his head nodding forward onto his chest. "Soon enough, Tobias."

Lost in deep thought, Zach found himself answering his friend's question. "Yes, only one," he whispered as some vague, half-memory returned. It moved unbidden through his thoughts. *She was the one.*

He shrugged off the disconcerting feeling he'd had when he'd first seen her two nights ago, as if he were somehow seeing her again. Strange, how easily her name came to his lips. Lis. The endearment, something felt rather than thought, echoed softly through him.

The deep rumble of snoring filled the library. Tobias's head nodded forward onto his chest, his arms draped loosely over his ample paunch. Zach crossed the room to his friend. Lifting the older man's feet onto a stool, he tried to make him more comfortable. "One of these days, you must end your wicked ways, my friend. And one of these days, very soon, I will have the answers I want and we can leave England. Rest easy," he whispered gently. "I'll be back."

Zach hesitated on the first step of the imposing building. Austere brick towered overhead a full six stories. Gold leaf lettering on a bronzed plaque denoted Barrington Shipping. It spoke of old money, old family, and power. If he'd been anyone else, he might have been impressed. But a lifetime of different circumstance prevented that illusion. Still, there was a vague feeling of familiarity about the building, as if he might have been there before. He shrugged it off.

Trapping the lion in its lair. The thought he'd first shared with Tobias months ago came back to him. This was the lair, and the lion waited.

Jerrold Barrington rose in greeting as Zach entered the formal office. A faint smile played across his lips. It must be an affliction of the nobility, to surround themselves with rich furnishings. This office, like the library in which he'd left Tobias, was richly appointed to the point of surfeit.

"How pleasant to see you again," Jerrold Barrington declared. "Please, make yourself comfortable."

"The pleasure is mine," Zach responded, his real meaning hidden.

Jerrold came around the desk. Lifting the lid on a hand-carved wooden box, he offered his guest the finest of rolled cigars. "I hope you had no difficulty finding our establishment."

Zach shook his head. "Not at all." He declined the offer of the cigar, preferring one of the thinly tapered cigarettes he carried inside his breast pocket. The gesture was innocuous, but it had the desired effect. Barrington's brows rose at the refusal. He was obviously a man who wasn't accustomed to being refused.

"Your company is well known, Señor Barrington"—Zach's choice of words was faintly derisive—"in many ports of the world. I decided long ago that my business would be best served by dealing with you when I reached England. That is, if we can reach a mutually satisfying agreement." His statements carried far more import than the other man could possibly know.

Jerrold resumed his position behind the desk, establishing distance as he retreated to the thronelike overstuffed chair. "I find it somewhat surprising that a man of your obvious station should be concerned with matters of business."

Zach's smile deepened. "As with yourself . . . I find there are certain matters that only I am capable of facilitating." He rose, at ease in the lion's den. Standing before the sweep of windows that opened onto a view of the business district, he maneuvered the conversation.

"Certain transactions are best handled by me. I think you understand my meaning. The fewer who know of them, the better." He turned, leveling a speculative gray gaze on the watchful man behind the desk.

Barrington was careful, in his choice of words and his reactions. "You spoke of just such a cargo the other evening when my fiancée and I first met you." His hands, spread on the desktop, betrayed only the faintest tremor of anticipation. After that evening, he'd sent one of his men to learn what could be found out about the Count de Cuervo. The man had returned with little information.

It seemed the Count de Cuervo was a man of mystery. He had merely learned that the count was distantly related to Lord Vale.

"Ah yes, your fiancée," Zach recalled, carefully masking what he felt deep inside. "She is a lovely young lady. You are most fortunate." He forced himself to get beyond the loathing he felt for Barrington.

"Yes," Barrington admitted slowly. "The other evening, it almost seemed as if you might know each other."

"It was a simple mistake. I knew of Lady Felicia Barrington through a friend of mine."

"Most unusual. My mother has been dead for many years," Jerrold replied.

"Yes, so Lady Winslow informed me. I am deeply sorry. She must have been a very fine lady. My friend spoke highly of her."

"Who is your friend? Perhaps I know this person."

Zach turned to him. "It was someone I knew in the colonies."

"New South Wales? Such a wretched place. I sincerely doubt that, although I do have friends there because of my business dealings, and there are many English people there. It's possible one of them might have been acquainted with my mother."

Friends! Zach's gaze narrowed. A man like Jerrold Barrington wouldn't dirty his feet walking across the street to exchange pleasantries with a colonial, much less one who was a convict. He concentrated on the framed etchings of various Barrington ships that filled one wall as he slowly brought his anger under control.

Gypsy Moth came to mind. The name seemed to leap into his thoughts. Why in the devil had he thought of it? He knew of no ship by that name. He continued his slow perusal. A ship's sextant was encased in glass on a mahogany table. He was drawn to the sextant as another thought, more vague, remained just beyond his grasp.

His father taught him to use the sextant when he was a boy.

Zach blinked as he stared at the sextant. That wasn't right at all! His father had died before he was born. An old sailor by the name of McAndrew in Sydney had taught him how to sail and use the sextant to chart a course. What the devil was wrong with him! As easily as the thought came, it was gone and Zach turned to Barrington, hoping to learn something tangible from their conversation.

"I became acquainted with this man in New South Wales. His name was Nicholas Tennant." He watched carefully for any sign that Barrington recognized the name, and masked his disappointment when there was none.

"You said was?"

"He's dead now." Zach continued his slow tour of the office, feeling a restless need to keep moving. He pretended to study the etchings of ships. Most were of clippers or the slower frigates, although a more recent sailing vessel also boasted a steam engine as evidenced by the single smokestack protruding from her main deck.

His gaze narrowed at sight of a smaller sailing vessel. The artist had caught it at just the right moment, revealing the two masted ship heeling over hard amidst white-capped waves. The name *Gypsy Moth* was neatly scribed underneath, and the year 1814.

Jerrold Barrington rose from his chair and crossed the office. Standing very near Zach, he noticed the focus of his interest. "I first learned to sail aboard her. Wretched, beastly little craft to handle in rough seas."

"Where is she now?" Zach's voice was hollow as he fought off something vague and a little unnerving. How could he possibly have known the name of the vessel?

"At our summer beach place near Dover. Father goes there quite often. I haven't in years. But as you can see," he went on boastfully, "our interest lies in bigger ships, and their cargoes."

"The other evening it seemed you might be acquainted with Miss Winslow," Jerrold probed subtly.

"A most delightful young lady. But no, I'd never met Lady Winslow before that evening," Zach assured him.

"That's strange. She seemed to think she knew you," Jerrold mused, unable to suppress a nagging irritation that perhaps this man wasn't telling him the truth.

"A simple mistake." Zach smiled faintly. "I'm often mistaken for someone else."

Barrington frowned. Mistake indeed. Only a fool would mistake this man for anyone, not with that damned eyepatch. He wanted to know a great deal more about him, and the business transaction he'd spoken of.

Jerrold Barrington smiled congenially, reminding Zach of a lazy boa constrictor before it moves in for the kill. "You mentioned a business matter the other evening," he said. He tugged with great authority on the satin rope mounted at the wall beside the desk, and then looked up as an older man entered.

"Hobson, we'll take brandy in the library." He turned to Zach.

119

"If you'll join me. The library is much more comfortable and is a discreet place for discussing business." Indicating a door in the mahogany-paneled wall to the right, he led the way into the library.

"Since you seem so well acquainted with Barrington Shipping, you're undoubtedly aware that we are experienced in handling a variety of cargoes for both import and export to virtually any port in the world."

It sounded like a well-rehearsed speech he gave often. When the brandy was brought, he dismissed his employee and poured the amber liquid into squat glass tumblers.

Zach smiled as he accepted the proffered drink. He had Jerrold where he wanted him. Barrington was curious and greedy. He would not turn down the offer Zach was about to propose. And it was all so perfect. A precious cargo was carefully disguised and quite safe. What Barrington didn't yet know was that it was actually his cargo, first sold to him in New South Wales for a mere fraction of its true value.

Barrington controlled all shipping, and thereby controlled prices on all commodities. It was a lucrative arrangement that had the effect of maintaining an economic stranglehold on the colonies.

But this particular cargo had a unique history. It had first been sold to Barrington Trading Company, then loaded in the hold of a Barrington ship bound for England. Mysteriously, the ship never made her destination. Her crew, as well as her cargo, were lost off the treacherous coast of Australia as were so many ships over the past two years. Now that cargo had just as mysteriously reappeared in the hold of the *Tamarisk*, to be resold to Jerrold Barrington at an exorbitant profit. It was a scheme the Raven would envy.

Zach smiled secretively. "As I explained, I am a stranger to England. But I thought you might be able to acquaint me with someone who might be interested in a certain cargo."

Jerrold's demeanor was almost condescending. "I will try. Of course, there is the possibility my company might be interested as well. That would depend on the cargo, and whether or not there is a ready market for it."

"Of course. There's always a market for this particular cargo. I acquired it from a man in the colonies; however, I'm not at liberty to divulge his identity." It was a game of cat and mouse, and Zach loved it.

Jerrold nodded, as he lifted an etched-crystal tumbler of brandy to his mouth. Contraband. But then it wasn't the first time his firm had dealt in such commodities and it wouldn't be the last. There was a great deal of profit to be made in it. "What is the cargo?"

Zach lifted his own glass in a faintly mocking salute. "Four and a half kilos of raw, unrefined gold, taken from one of the richest ore deposits in the world." He suppressed a faint smile as he revealed the exact amount of gold lost aboard that Barrington ship off the coast of Australia only. months earlier.

Jerrold Barrington broke into spasms of coughing. When he had sufficiently recovered, his dark eyes narrowed as they studied his guest. "I think perhaps we might be able to strike a deal, *señor.* Where did you say you came by such a large amount of gold?"

"I didn't."

There wasn't a trace of warmth in Barrington's smile. He reminded Zach of a sly wolf.

"It hardly matters. As you said, there is always a market for such a cargo. What price did you have in mind?"

Barrington never flinched when Zach named a price that was just below the market price in London, and over ten times the amount he'd originally paid in New South Wales.

"You drive a hard bargain, *señor.*" Jerrold lifted his glass, carefully scrutinizing the man before him. Four and a half kilos of gold. What he wouldn't give to have that amount of gold, especially after his heavy losses this past year in those damnable colonies. But perhaps he could bargain the price down. He smiled as he thought of various methods he'd used in the past. Every man has his weaknesses. He had only to find out what this man's were, then use them to advantage and perhaps acquire the gold for substantially less.

"Nonetheless, I'm certain we can arrive at a mutually satisfying agreement," Barrington assured the Count de Cuervo. He pulled a watch from his vest pocket as if only just realizing the time. "I hadn't realized the lateness of the hour. I hope you will excuse me. I have another appointment. But I would like to discuss this further. I'll be getting together with a few friends, evening after next, at my private club. If you're free, we could do so then."

Zach smiled graciously, masking his keen satisfaction. Barrington had reacted just as he'd thought he would by stalling for time. The man wanted to see what he could find out about the Count de Cuervo and a cargo of four and a half kilos of gold.

Jerrold rose, extending his hand. His cool smile stiffened when the Count de Cuervo only nodded curtly.

"Until Thursday evening, *señor.*"

Pulling on his gray gloves, Zach smiled as he stepped down onto the cobbled sidewalk. His meeting with Jerrold Barrington had gone just as planned. Barrington was careful, but he was also greedy. If he looked up now to the sixth floor set of windows, he would find Barrington watching him. He tipped his hat to a fashionably dressed lady who passed by. The trap had been baited.

He nodded a greeting to Sandy, across the cobbled street snarled with coaches and hansom cabs. The second mate from the *Tamarisk* looked faintly out of place atop the elegant gleaming black coach sitting around the corner. He'd given him instructions to be there promptly at twelve noon, when he'd sent him out before dawn on specific errands. As Zach threaded his way through the congestion of conveyances, the mate jumped down to greet him.

"Mornin', Cap'n." He tipped his hat with an awkward gesture that would have been out of place aboard ship.

Zach corrected him. "Not Captain, Sandy. We must be careful."

"Sorry, your grace." He beamed as he got it right.

"Did you get the information I wanted?"

"Yessir." Sandy opened the door to the coach, lowered the folding step, and stood aside. To anyone observing, they seemed to be exchanging only the customary greeting and response of employer and servant.

"What did you find out about Miss Winslow?"

"I went to the house just as you said, Cap'n." He winced. "Sorry about that."

"Go on." Zach climbed the step, paused to adjust his hat, and took a seat inside.

"With the weddin' only a couple of weeks off, there's all kinds of people comin' and goin' at the house, but I talked to their coachman. He was a real talkative fella. Miss Winslow has been real busy with all the plans."

"What about Barrington?" Zach discreetly watched the street to make certain he wasn't being followed.

"He hasn't been around. But one of the maids at market first thing this mornin' said it's common knowledge Barrington's keepin' a mistress. Some actress I think. He's been spendin' most of his evenin's with her or at that private club of his."

"Does Miss Winslow ever leave the house? She must have appointments to keep. Most ladies do." For days Zach had been trying to find some way to meet with her again. But after their last encounter, he knew it would have to appear to be an accidental meeting. He was certain she wouldn't accept an invitation. Still, he mused thoughtfully, he did have something she wanted to have back.

"No appointments the last two days, but she left the house anyway. She went out ridin' again this morning, just like yesterday."

Zach looked up from beneath the brim of his hat. He swept it off, glad to be rid of it. "Where did she ride?" An idea was beginning to take shape. He knew it was reckless; still, he wanted to see her again, felt almost compelled to see her.

"A place called Kensington Gardens, usually. There's a big fella always follows along behind."

"Protection?" Zach mused with a smile.

"So it seems. But she usually manages to give him the slip. He's not very good with a horse."

"You've done a good job, Sandy. Does she ride at the same time each morning?"

"Same time every day. She slipped outta the house before dawn this mornin'. I never seen a proper-born lady who likes ridin' that time of day. And you wanta know somethin' else real strange?" Sandy refolded the single step into the coach. "I almost missed her both times."

Zach's gaze narrowed. "What do you mean, missed her? She's not exactly the sort of woman you'd overlook."

"Right ye are, sir," Sandy quickly agreed. "She's one beautiful lady. But that's just it. Both times when she left the house, it weren't no lady I saw. It was a man!"

He had Zach's full attention now. "What are you talking about?"

"Just that. She weren't a lady at all. She was a man."

"Sandy, what the devil do you mean, she was a man?"

The second mate from the *Tamarisk* shrugged. "She was dressed up just like a man, with fancy breeches, jacket, and fine leather boots. And she had her hair all tucked up inside a black cap. Darnedest thing I ever did see. But she sat astride that horse like she knew what she was doin'."

Amusement deepened Zach's gray gaze. "Astride?"

"Yessir! Full astride just like a man. You don't think maybe . . . ?" He left the implication unfinished.

Chuckling deeply, Zach met his questioning stare. "No, Sandy. I don't think so at all. She's a woman all right. In every way possible." He sobered. "Let's get going. There's lots to be done

123

before tomorrow morning. Suddenly, I have need of a horse."

He came to her in the darkness of night. No words were spoken. None were needed. It was as though any words would only give unnecessary voice to that which they knew in their hearts. Elyse turned to him, her questions falling away before the answering promise in his eyes. This moment was as it had been a thousand times in the past and promised to be in the future. But now they came together slowly, almost as if they both feared it might be gone again too quickly.

Her eyes were filled with love as he reached out to her. Hands touched, fingers slowly entwining as he drew her to him. All the fears and the emptiness of yesterday slipped away as her body brushed against his. Slowly his arms enclosed her, and the shadow of his face fell across hers. Her lips parted in silent longing. And then, in a whisper of time, his mouth closed over hers, filling her with tender warmth. His breath slipped through her, freeing her from the aching loneliness of the past.

"Sweet Lis," he whispered against her mouth, his lips beginning an impassioned journey that followed the column of her throat to the soft, taut flesh of full breasts. The restraints of her clothes fell away beneath those familiar hands as they swept away eons of loneliness. Elyse cried out softly to him as her breasts crushed into the planes of his hard, muscled chest, his nakedness slipping across hers with the promise of tender possession. Memory as infinite as passion engulfed them, taking them once more into that void where only they existed.

"I knew you would come back to me," she whispered, knowing an aching need as they slipped to the soft coverlet across the bed. They might once have been lovers carried on a barque bound for ancient Thebes, or a knight and his lady in a flower-strewn meadow far from the conflicts of war. Or they might have lain beneath a night sky on a high plain, watching as stars burst overhead in a magical shower of light and promise.

They came together slowly, his body enfolding hers, his lips whispering against her fevered skin, as they explored all the planes and valleys of this woman he'd loved through eternity and lost many times. Her cries against his golden skin were softly sweet with the pleasure of his name, then urgent with loving him. She'd waited a lifetime for him and could wait no longer; an inexplicable urgency was compelling her to that moment of fulfillment. Crying

124

out his name, she let her slender hands slip down his back, her lips brushing the hard curve of his shoulder, her pleas desperately soft against his muscular chest.

They turned together, their bodies entwined as her slender hips moved against his. Her fingers burned across his flesh as they slipped down over the hardened muscles of male buttocks. She rose over him, her long hair a wild torrent amidst their passion. His name broke from her lips as he pulled her down over him, the hardened maleness of him surging into her. And as the burning heat of his engorged flesh seared her, Elyse cried out for the bittersweet ecstasy of loving this man once more, of feeling him deep inside her, touching her soul. It was like the first time and the next time all as one, fulfilling a promise made countless lifetimes ago.

The heat of the sun burst in the sky, stars showered down over them, and the wind echoed their promises as his love filled her. And after the light came the darkness.

Loneliness filled her even as she struggled to hold onto the dream. Passion and desire slipped into the far place of memory and unspoken thought until she couldn't remember at all. *In time,* his voice echoed back to her, aching in its tenderness. *In time, dearest love.*

Elyse sobbed as the dream slipped further from her grasp, playing across her thoughts in fleeting images that made her ache with longing. In the darkness that remains just before the dawn, she threw back the covers of the bed, feeling the staggering jolt of morning air against her bare flesh. She sat up, eyes wide with something very near fear as she wrapped her arms around her naked body. The pale blue gown she'd donned only hours ago as she'd dressed for bed lay on the floor. The covers were in wild disarray and her pulse still raced.

She stared across the room as if she could see the apparition from her dreams, almost hoping she would. Instead, the shapes and forms silhouetted in the early gray of dawn were dearly familiar. Elyse struck a fist against the pillow, venting fear, anger, and frustration. The dreams came every night now.

"Who are you?" she cried desperately into the half-light knowing no one remained to answer her. She flung back the covers. With something very near desperation she swung her feet to the floor. Crossing the room on shaking legs she seized the cloth beside the pitcher and bowl on the commode. With almost vengeful desperation, she scrubbed the clamminess from her skin, then drew the cloth down over her stomach, inhaling sharply at the lingering ache that remained at the tops of her thighs.

She whirled around, almost expecting to see her phantom lover watching her from the bed. Everything remained as she'd left it, including the throbbing pulse of passion deep in her woman's softness. How was it possible for her to feel these things when she'd never lain with a man? How?

It was three nights since the ball, and each night the dream came back to her with a persistence that was becoming frightening, almost as if it was connected to something, or someone. And now this last dream had seemed so real, so intimate . . . She shuddered with the longing that still remained.

"I think they call it bats in the belfry." She essayed a feeble joke, her faint smile fading as she probed her temple where the telltale ache that always accompanied the dream still lingered.

"My mysterious phantom lover." The feeling of helplessness shifted to growing anger. "Who the devil are you!" She tossed the cloth into the basin, sending a wave of water sloshing over the side. She needed a ride more than ever this morning! If she left now, she'd be back before anyone was aware she'd been gone. Elyse whirled around. Stark naked, she crossed to the wardrobe.

A driving restlessness made her impatient. Three days! It was three days since she'd met the Count de Cuervo and lost her pendant. And each day, she'd sent Katy to market to try to find some bit of gossip about the elusive man who'd mysteriously appeared at the engagement party without invitation or acquaintance among her friends, and then had disappeared just as mysteriously.

Elyse silently cursed each button at the closure of the slim men's pants. She shoved the buttons of the shirt through maddeningly small holes and then tucked the voluminous tails in at the waist. Barefoot she crossed back to the bed, riding boots tucked under one arm while she struggled with the loose ends of the tie. Her fingers tangled hopelessly. Tossing both ends of the tie, as well as her heavy mass of her hair, impatiently over one shoulder, she pulled on first one boot and then the other, wriggling her toes into the soft leather. Grabbing a man's cap and riding jacket, she then slipped out of the bedchamber.

The hall was dimly lit by one gas lamp at the far end. One of the maids put it out when she came upstairs to wake her grandmother each morning. The space under Katy's door was still dark. She had been completely exhausted the night before, after spending the last

126

three days in the marketplace, trying to learn something of the Spanish Count. Elyse knew Katy wouldn't be up for at least another hour.

She tiptoed softly down the hall carpet, to the door leading to the servants quarters on the first floor. It was much closer to the back of the manor and the carriage house beyond. Stepping over a creaking floorboard in the middle of the top step, Elyse stole down the narrow stairway. Upon reaching the bottom, she stopped, inhaling the delicious aromas that drifted from the kitchen as cook prepared food for the day. Her stomach grumbled a nagging reminder that she'd been able to eat very little the last three days.

Checking to make certain no one was about, she ducked inside to steal a handful of warm rolls pungent with buttery cinnamon. Taking a fortifying nibble of one, she quickly slipped to the outside door and stepped into the fresh morning air.

A short walk along the hedgerow took her to the far end of the carriage house where Mr. Quist and the stableboy slept. Quimby's room was across the hall; stables, coach, and day carriages were housed at the far end. She could easily slip by undetected, leaving Quimby to follow her as she knew he was instructed by her grandmother, but today she desperately wanted him along. She'd decided on a different route for her ride this morning. She knocked lightly on his door. A loud snorting was the only response, followed by incoherent mumbling.

"Eh? What's that? Who's there?" he finally grunted, obviously not wanting to know.

"Good morning, Quimby." Elyse poked her head inside his quarters, giving his rumpled countenance a tremulous smile. "It's time to be up and about, if you're going riding with me this morning."

"Good God!" was his only discernible comment. The rest were muffled by a mound of bedcovers.

"I'm not decent!" Quimby roared, coming more fully awake against the remonstrances of good judgment.

Leaning against the doorjamb, Elyse popped another bite of cinnamon roll into her mouth. Cook's splendid pastries always seemed to cheer her up.

"You're never decent, Quimby," she quipped. "But you'd better hurry if you want to catch me. After all, Grandmother has ordered you to follow me on all my morning excursions." A playful smile finally appeared at the corner of her mouth. She dearly loved Quimby. He was gruff and a bit uncouth, but he was a steadfast friend and a trustworthy confidant. On top of that, she owed him her life.

"See you in the stables." She left his door open, knowing he'd turn over and go right back to sleep if she closed it, and she very much needed him along today. She had something she wanted him to check up on for her, or rather someone.

"I have fresh cinnamon rolls from Mrs. Halverson," she called back over her shoulder, bribing him. That ought to do it, she thought, as with a knowing smile she grabbed bridle and blanket.

"What's that!" Quimby came up off the bed. He wasn't wrong. He had smelled fresh pastry! "Be right with ya, lass." He rolled out of bed, reaching for pants and boots.

Tightening the cinch strap on the saddle, Elyse slapped the rump of the large roan gelding. Quimby always rode the roan, while she preferred the more spirited bay, aptly named Deliverance.

Quimby found the roll she'd left for him on the small table in his room. Licking buttery syrup from his fingers, he shrugged into suspenders as he strolled down the length of the stable.

"What's this?" he grunted suspiciously, eying the saddled roan.

"I've saddled him for you." Elyse smiled.

Quimby was immediately wary. Hot rolls, no doubt stolen from Mrs. Halverson, for which they would both suffer a good tongue-lashing, and now she'd saddled his horse as well. He shifted his massive bulk uncomfortably. She'd long ago given up trying to slip furtively into the stables. And almost as long ago, she'd taken to calling a morning greeting to him as she passed his door. From there, it was often a contest to see if he could dress and saddle his horse in time to catch her before she reached the end of the lane on her own mount and tried to leave him behind. One eye narrowed speculatively. Unless he missed his guess, she was up to something this morning.

"Cinch strap tight?" He grumbled, not putting anything past her. She could be as devilish as they came when she wanted to put something over on him.

"Check it yourself, if you're uncertain," she offered, an amused smile playing at the corners of her mouth. Stepping beside the bay, she reached for the reins and nimbly pulled herself into the saddle. "I think I'll ride in the Woods this morning. If you don't hurry, you'll get left behind," she teased playfully. Devilment danced in her soft blue eyes.

"The Woods? You haven't ridden there in a long time. Why today?" He was immediately suspicious. It would be just like her to

128

tell him where she intended to ride and then choose another location.

"Quimby!" She pretended to be terribly hurt. "I don't think you believe me." Then she grew very somber. "I have to ride as much as I can. My future husband doesn't approve of such things."

"Neither does yer grandmother," Quimby observed with a grumble. "That never stopped you."

"True enough," she admitted. "But today I have need of some company. Honest, I'll wait for you," she pledged, her mouth suddenly solemn. "Now, are you coming, or are you going to argue with me all morning?"

"Aye, I'm comin'." Satisfied she hadn't deliberately left any of the harness loose, he unsteadily swung his mountainous frame atop the tall roan.

"Damned fool beast!" he roared as the roan side-stepped practically unseating him. "They're stupid, foul smelling and unpredictable," he yelled at her. "Couldn't you settle for a carriage?" While trying to bring his horse under control, he threw her a beseeching look.

"Good heavens, no. We'd look far too conspicuous." She favored him with the devastatingly beautiful smile that invariably got her what she wanted. "The whole idea is not to draw attention to our little ride." Laughter bubbled inside her. Conspicuous indeed! What could be more conspicuous than an oversize giant astride a horse whose sole purpose in life was to be riderless?

On more than one occasion, Elyse was forced to double back from her ride in search of Quimby. Once she'd found him painfully extricating himself from a bramble bush. Then there'd been the time he'd landed in a stream and moss was clinging to his head like tendrils of green hair. Another time she'd found him dangling in midair, frantically clinging to a low-hanging branch the roan galloped under to remove him from the saddle.

He gave the roan a murderous glare. "The beast hates me. Sometimes I think you're tryin' to do me in with these mornin' rides."

She leaned over, patting his arm lovingly. "You know perfectly well the roan is the only horse capable of carrying you. Grandmother selected him especially for you."

"With a little help from a certain young lady, I'll warrant," he accused.

Elyse turned the bay toward the open doors. "Well, I will admit I did influence her decision. I assured her he was a strong, intelligent animal."

"Intelligent!" Quimby spouted. His mouth clamped shut as he was practically unseated before even leaving the stables. "Cursed, good for nothing—"

His description of the roan was cut off as the lunging horse whirled first in one direction then the other, trying to unseat him. Elyse guided the bay into the soft gray light of early morning, smiling to herself. Sooner or later, Quimby would follow. She pulled her horse up, turning about just as the roan emerged alone from the stables. She snatched at his reins as he tried to dart past her.

Following on foot, Quimby mumbled something inaudible, as he massaged his backside. He fixed both Elyse and the roan with a withering glare, and, without a word, took the reins from her and swung into the saddle.

"There," Elyse announced. "Now, do you think you can behave yourself?" Her words were as much for Quimby as the horse. Her eyes widened at the irregular shape of his long coat. "What is that?" She pointed to the flat protrusion.

Quimby flashed open the coat, revealing a short length of board. "It's me persuader." He informed her with a satisfied nod. "If he gets outta hand again"—he retrieved the board, waving it about like a club—"I'll merely persuade him to behave." For added emphasis, he waved the board over the roan's head. The gelding's ears were immediately laid back, but the beast didn't so much as take a step.

"Very good, Quimby." Elyse nodded, urging the bay forward. "I think you're getting the hang of it." And then she was gone down the lane, leaving him in a wake of early morning mist.

Chapter Six

Elyse guided the bay past the Winslow house, down the cobbled lane that ended at Pont Street. Actually it wasn't a lane at all, but a square enclosing several of the more stately London homes. Pont Street led to the heart of London, including Victoria Station. They took the train when her grandmother decided to close the London house and retreat to the country for the warmer months of the summer. Uncle Ceddy's small stately manor house was near the business district and the Houses of Parliament. An elegant day carriage passed, the occupant nodding a stiff acknowledgment, one man's greeting to another.

"Good day, Lord Chetterly." Elyse fixed a somber expression on her face, one that was faintly disdainful, and nodded a greeting to her grandmother's acquaintance. Then she promptly broke into a giggle after he passed by. He'd have a devil of a time trying to decide just who the "young man" coming from Lady Winslow's drive was.

Instead of following the carriage down Pont Street, she cut across the end of the lane, guiding the bay down an embankment, and across a narrow strip of Regent's Park. Skirting the perimeter, she urged her horse across the footbridge that spanned the Boating Lake. The Woods bordered the park to the north. Crossing the indefinable barrier that separated the two was like stepping into another world. One moment she was traversing meticulously manicured grass, the next she'd slipped into shaded, lush greenery allowed to grow unrestrained. It was almost primitive, dark and secretive; and she loved it.

She preferred the overgrown, unkempt trails of the Woods. Footpaths crisscrossed several hundred wooded acres, filled with wild game, rippling creeks, streams, and hidden hollows. Rail fences intersected at unpredictable locations, testing a rider's ability to jump them, relegating those incapable of doing so to taking a long circuitous route back to one of the main trails. The Woods was a magnificent overgrown maze. There were rumored to be three paths that led into it and exited on the far side, but Elyse had been able to

131

find only two of them.

In years past, the Woods had been a hunting preserve for members of the royal family. It dated back to King Henry VIII, and according to legend, that robust king liked nothing better than to lead a party of friends into the park, declaring they must find their own way out.

And of course there was Jane's Folley, the source of an even more outrageous story that dear old Henry, contemplating a new wife, had deliberately sent young Jane Seymour down a badly marked trial in the Woods. Mistress Seymour was not known to be the brightest of Henry's wives. Needless to say, she failed to find her way out, but good old Henry managed to find her. From then on, Jane's Folley referred to the trysting place of the third queen with old Henry VIII. It was a secluded glen, where the King supposedly first bedded his future wife. Hearing of the episode, the Queen, Anne Boleyn, lost her temper, and within a very few months, her head.

Elyse had found the Folley two years ago. Whenever she rode in the Woods, she dared Quimby to find her. And each time she was forced to double back over the path in search of him. It was on one of those occasions she found him picking himself out of a thicket and cursing a blue streak.

The Woods was secluded, and was now frequented only occasionally by more adventurous riders. She knew she was unlikely to see anyone except for Quimby, if he ever managed to catch up with her.

She heard the faint staccato of hoofbeats behind her and smiled. "Very good, Quimby," she mused out loud. "You're getting better." A soft smile turned up her lips. She would be glad for his companionship this morning. As the dream from her childhood occurred with increased frequency, she found herself filled with inexplicable loneliness. She slowed her horse to a walk. Faint smudges of sleeplessness rimmed her eyes, and a restlessness thrummed along her nerve endings; lingering reminders of haunted nights. Three times the dream had come to her in greater detail, each night until last night . . .

And it was exactly three nights since she'd lost the pendant. Her hand wound more tightly around the reins. It wasn't exactly lost, she thought, her irritation mounting. Stolen was a more accurate description!

"Fool!" she hissed at herself, causing the bay's ears to flicker back and forth. She soothed him by running a calming hand along his well-muscled neck. Just how the devil was she to get her necklace back without her grandmother or Jerrold finding out about the incident.

The hoofbeats were closer now, a rhythmic pacing. Elyse frowned. Quimby wasn't an accomplished rider. It occurred to her that he was taking the trail much too fast. She pulled the bay to a halt and turned in the saddle, but was unable to see anyone on the overgrown trail behind her.

A flash of black streaked through the distant trees and then disappeared, but the hoofbeats continued, drawing closer with each passing moment.

A prickling of uncertainty caused the hair at the back of her neck to stand up. Tightening her grip on the reins, she urged the bay on, keeping watch behind her. The sounds of an approaching rider were closer now. She'd given Quimby ample time to follow, but it wasn't like him to take unnecessary chances with a horse. He simply wasn't that confident astride. And the rider bearing down on her at a steady pace was competent as well as confident.

The subtle pressure of her ankle sent the bay ahead at a faster pace. At the intersection of trails, she took the one to the left. As the hoofbeats continued with unrelenting determination, she decided to leave the trail. Only a fool would dare follow her through the densely wooded forest.

Elyse reined the bay hard, sending him down an embankment to the right of the trail. She checked him only once as they crossed a stream and plunged up the far side. Not more than a few paces behind, she heard the faint splashing of another rider crossing the water. Whoever it was, it wasn't Quimby, and he was gaining on her. Flattening herself low over the saddle, Elyse ducked a low-hanging branch. Such a bough would've been Quimby's undoing. Still the rider persisted.

Ahead, the undergrowth broke, revealing a span of crisscross fencing. The jump was not a difficult one, but Elyse knew a hedgerow loomed less than a full stride on the other side. She smiled determinedly as the bay nimbly took the jump. Only a rider experienced in the Woods, or a very lucky one, would know he must cut hard left as soon as his mount touched down to avoid careening into the hedgerow.

The bay cleared the fence, his ears immediately pricking forward at the familiar jump. She guided him hard left, negotiating the turn with ease. Here another surprise waited. The trail sloped up sharply. It took a strong, agile mount to recover from the jump and the hard turn, and to possess enough energy to make it up the incline of the softly mounded embankment. They were very near

Jane's Folley now. At the top of the embankment, Elyse pulled the bay to a stop and whirled in the saddle.

She smiled victoriously at the lingering rush of distant hooves, waited out the momentary silence as the other horse left the ground, breathlessly expecting a telltale crash into the hedgerow. Instead the relentless beating resumed.

"Damn!" she said under her breath, and whirled the bay hard about. Fear tingled down the length of her spine, and beads of moisture slipped down between her breasts. As her mount lunged down the trail, Elyse glanced back over her shoulder, unable to resist a glance. She hesitated a moment too long, waiting for the rider to appear, then felt the sudden tensing in the taut muscles beneath her thighs. The bay's even tempo had changed abruptly. A moment too late, she checked his pace. She gasped at the sight of the large fallen oak that loomed before them across the entrance to Jane's Folley. A brief thought flashed into her mind: Elyse's Folley. It was too late to do anything except cling to the bay and pray he made the jump.

At one moment the morning sky held the promise of a brilliant golden day, the next it exploded in a burst of blinding light. Elyse felt the bay stumble beneath her. Instinctively, she released the reins and relaxed her body. There was nothing more she could do as the floor of the clearing seemed to reach up for her.

Elyse roused slowly, her eyelids unusually heavy. There was a dreadful pounding in her head, and she felt as if a great weight were on her chest. She couldn't seem to breathe. She tried to move her head, only to have the pressure at the back of her neck increase, immobilizing her.

"Not yet," a masculine voice instructed. "Don't try to move. Keep your eyes closed."

She felt the faint pressure of hands moving slowly over her entire body. When the man whose hands they were seemed satisfied that nothing was broken, he instructed her again.

"You took a pretty nasty fall. Just relax and breathe deeply."

Elyse couldn't move if she'd wanted too. Her arms felt as if they were attached to lead weights. And something else prevented movement. As her vision cleared, the ground seemed to come up at her with amazing swiftness. She closed her eyes again.

"You just had the wind knocked out of you. It'll take a minute to get it back. Breathe slowly," the voice commanded again, and she obeyed, the shadows in her immediate vision disappearing as the world seemed to right itself again. She blinked, confused by what she was looking at. Her eyes finally cleared as she focused on a large, brown woolly caterpillar inching its way along between her booted legs. She tried to pull back but felt the firm pressure once more at her neck.

"Not too fast or you'll faint. Breathe."

"I am breathing!" Her response was oddly muffled. Her head was buried in her knees for God's sake! "At least I'm trying to breathe." She pushed back against that strong hand and this time felt gentle release. Everything tilted crazily as she moved too quickly. She snapped her eyes shut in an attempt to stop the unsettling motion. Her head seemed to think it was still astride the horse, while her body was firmly earthbound.

"You had quite a knock on the head. Take another deep breath . . ." As the command came once more, Elyse gritted her teeth. Eyes flashing open, she fixed the source of it with a less than steady gaze.

"If you say that one more time—" The threat ended abruptly. "You!"

"I've been called a great many things," he admitted with faint cynicism, "but usually something more memorable than that."

Elyse groaned as she tried to sit up. "Give me a moment, I'm certain I can come up with something."

"Undoubtedly you can," Zach assured her.

"What are you doing here?" she groaned, her sudden movement sending pain knifing through her head.

"It seems I'm picking you up off the ground."

He was dressed all in black, the only contrast being windblown waves of golden hair that spilling recklessly over the collar of his elegant shirt. Elyse jerked away as the Count de Cuervo reached down to help her stand.

"I can do quite nicely for myself." She struggled to her feet, then suddenly thought better of her remark as the ground tried to come up to meet her again. Gloved hands immediately seized her arms and guided her to the tree she'd jumped only moments before.

"You seem to have a penchant for being unsteady on your feet, Miss Winslow." A smile produced a faint dimple at the corner of Zach's mouth. She'd given him a scare with that jump, but she was obviously feeling much better now. "Everything seems to be in its right place," he said, his gaze warming appreciably. "There don't seem to be any broken bones."

Elyse's head came up. "I suppose you're going to tell me you're a

135

physician as well as a Spanish count and a pirate," she chided, remembering their argument the night of the ball.

Devilment danced in his gray gaze. "I haven't been one recently." He was playing along and with maddening charm. "But then there hasn't been the need until now."

Elyse's eyes narrowed. There was something different about him. She couldn't quite put her finger on it. Or maybe she had taken a worse knock on the head than she'd thought.

Retrieving a handkerchief from his coat, Zach wiped at a smudge of dirt on the end of her nose. "Are you always so reckless when you ride?"

"Do you always run people down?" Elyse responded tartly. Just speaking set her head to pounding.

"I didn't exactly run you down. Until that last jump, you seemed to be doing quite well. You almost lost me at that hedgerow." His smile flashed white amidst dark, bronzed skin. "At any rate, you didn't seem to be about to stop, and I did want dreadfully to see you again."

He was being a perfect gentleman. But the teasing light in his eye hinted at something else. "I don't suppose it occurred to you to call on me at my grandmother's house," she suggested brittlely.

"That thought did occur to me," he admitted with a rueful smile. "But it also occurred to me that after the other evening you might not see me."

"That depends." She looked up at him from beneath the curve of the hand still at her forehead.

He leaned forward, resting his weight on one arm propped against his knee. One booted foot was braced beside her on the fallen tree. His smile softened dangerously, and there was a languorous air about him that could only be described as unsettling.

"On what does it depend?" His voice was faintly husky as he leaned very near her, his gray gaze holding hers with subtle persuasion.

Elyse tried to swallow. She'd been afraid of whoever might be following her, then vaguely relieved to find it was someone with whom she was acquainted. Now the fear returned as a faint warning that tingled across her skin. But this was an entirely different fear. Letting out a slow steadying breath, she moistened her lips.

"It would depend on whether or not you returned the pendant."

The Count de Cuervo drew back, a faint glimmering of something unreadable in his eyes. "Ah yes, the pendant." With maddening calm he stepped away from her and went to check his horse. The bay was nowhere in sight. Elyse placed a cool hand on her aching forehead. At least now she was seeing only one of everything.

"I assume that's the reason for this little encounter." She watched him closely as she waited for his answer. Yes, a pirate, she thought as she watched him check the cinch strap. An elegant, handsome pirate with that flash of black eyepatch covering one eye. He swung effortlessly up into the saddle.

"I'll see if I can find your horse. Stay where you are." Not waiting for a reply, he whirled his mount around and headed down the trail.

"Of all the . . ." Elyse groaned. She couldn't move if she wanted to. There might be nothing broken, but every muscle ached from the strain of the fall. Still her gaze warmed as she watched him. His hand was sure on the reins, and the firm angle of his boots in the stirrups denoted a man who accepted nothing less than perfect control. With a faint snort of disgust, she acknowledged that a man such as the Count de Cuervo would never have allowed himself to be thrown from his horse.

Zach guided the sleek stallion past the next twist in the trail, then turned back. The bay Elyse was riding had cleared the jump and had kept right on going after her fall. Eventually he'd find his way back to his stall. There were two of them and only one horse. A faint smile twitched at the corners of his mouth when he returned to find her standing a little unsteadily beside the fallen tree.

She was just as beautiful as he remembered, but so completely different from the elegant young woman he'd met the night of the ball. Sandy would have no doubts if he saw her now. Soft brown pants were snugged over slender thighs, glistening boots encased her calves. Her jacket was unbuttoned, exposing the flowing softness of a white shirt left open at the collar. And the black riding cap was gone. A disheveled mass of glistening sable-colored hair cascaded over her shoulders and down her back. And her eyes . . . large and soft, with secret shadows that betrayed a woman's thoughts, they were a haunting blue that seemed to go right through him, almost as if she were seeing inside him. The skin across her high cheekbones was pale, the color only now just beginning to return to it. Her mouth was full, too full for her to be anything but a woman, and faintly downturned in the beginning of a frown as she watched him. The illusion of the clothes ceased where the collar ended and soft femininity began.

"It's a lovely day for a ride," he teased, knowing full well by the look that sparked in those magnificent eyes that she was in no mood for jollity.

"Won't you join me, Miss Winslow? It seems your mount is nowhere to be found." He held out a hand, offering to help her astride his own horse.

Elyse hesitated. "What about my pendant?" she persisted, regarding his outstretched hand as if it were a snake.

"You certainly are single-minded." He deliberately avoided a direct answer.

"Do you have it with you?" Provoked by his maddening evasiveness, Elyse felt color rise in her cheeks.

"Actually, there is just one tiny problem." His gaze took in the finely chiseled planes of her face, then slipped down the elegant column of exposed throat to the voluminous man's shirt left open at the collar, plunging to the alluring darkness between the thrust of her breasts. He wondered if she was aware of how beautiful she was at that moment, her hair in wild disarray, twigs clinging to her pants, and a faint scratch across one cheek.

"I see no problem." Elyse's voice quavered. "Simply return the pendant." She tried to disguise her amazement. My God! He was practically undressing her with his eyes, or rather, quite effectively with his one eye.

"I would really like very much to return it to you, but I haven't got it with me."

A look of such boyish innocence came to his face that for a long moment Elyse was caught off guard. But the throbbing pain in her head gave her focus.

"If you don't have it, then what are you doing here!" She stomped a booted foot.

"It seems I'm rescuing a fair maiden."

Her head came up, her gaze locking with his. All the anger and pain seemed to seep out of her. *Rescuing a fair maiden.* A flash of something from her dreams returned and was quickly gone. Shaking her head, Elyse tried to brush away her confusion.

Zach dismounted. "I think you'd better take it easy. And since there is only one horse, we'll have to ride double."

Elyse frowned up at him. "I don't suppose you'd consider lending me your horse since you are responsible for my being without one," she suggested, as his arm slipped around her waist and he guided her to the tall stallion.

"That's right, I won't." When she stubbornly tried to pull away, he nimbly placed her one foot in the stirrup and gently boosted her into the saddle.

For a brief instant, Elyse considered leaving him right where he stood. As her gaze locked with his, she realized he knew exactly what she was considering.

"I wouldn't try it if I were you." He swung up behind her. "You wouldn't want a bruised backside to match your head." He pulled her back into the curve of his body, then smiled as he felt her stiffen in response.

"You wouldn't dare!"

"Wouldn't I?" A smile teased at his lips, which were very near her cheek, but in his gaze was a steely promise. "I always get even when someone tries to pull something on me. And I pay back in triplicate."

Elyse swallowed back a stinging remark. He was just arrogant enough to leave her there without a horse. As for the spanking he'd threatened . . . she didn't really believe he would do it. Still . . .

"What is this place anyway?" He cast a speculative glance around them as his arms encircled her waist, and the reins were gathered in his maddeningly strong hands.

"It's called Jane's Folley. It was named after Jane Seymour, the third wife of Henry the Eighth."

"Henry the Eighth?"

His breath whispered faintly against her ear. She turned to him. "He was the king of England," she reminded him.

"Oh yes, of course," Zach responded vaguely. "And this place was named after his third wife?"

"Well, actually it was named before she became his wife," Elyse informed him matter-of-factly.

"Really?"

There was the faintest hint of disdain in that maddeningly rich resonant voice. It was almost familiar as it slipped over her senses.

"I suppose there's a reason it was named Jane's Folley."

Elyse glanced up at him, so close behind her that his body seemed wrapped around her like a protective shield. "Henry was determined to have a son and when his previous wives had not produced one, he'd gotten rid of them. Jane was his third wife. It's said he courted her here in secret while he was still married to the second Queen."

"Didn't he have six wives?" Zach mused, trying to remember what he could about the English royalty. Tobias had seen to it that he had a rudimentary education in such things.

Elyse frowned. "Yes. And I suppose someone like you would approve of such things." She bit at her lower lip, unable to understand what caused her to be so outspoken with a man she hardly knew.

Zach chose to ignore her comment. "Did he ever get it right?"

"Get what right?" Elyse turned to face him. She immediately realized her mistake. She had thought him dangerous the night of the ball; he was still dangerous, only more intensely so. She quickly turned back around.

Merriment twinkled in his eyes. "Did he ever get the son he wanted, or did he merely wear out six wives?"

Elyse exploded. "You are beyond a doubt the most arrogant, insufferably rude man I've ever met. Yes, he got his son. Jane gave him a son, but she died shortly afterward."

"Ah, I see, and left Henry to take three more wives. I wonder why he didn't just set up a harem. He'd have had his son in much shorter time, perhaps two or three. And English history might have been different."

"What did you say he should have set up?"

"A harem." Zach guided the stallion over fallen limbs toward the trail. "The chieftains of the desert tribes have harems. They choose women they like and make them their concubines. They can claim as many women as they can provide for. That way a man increases his chances of producing many sons." He watched her out of the corner of his eye. "Of course, there are several very pleasant advantages to such a system," he added, forcing back a smile.

"I see!" Elyse fumed. If he was trying to shock her, he'd succeeded. She did see exactly what he meant. Crimson patches spread across her cheeks as pain throbbed in her head. "You really are the most maddening man. For someone who claims to be a Spanish count you have no manners. You're—"

"I think we've been over that already." He cut her off, and urged his horse onto the main trail.

"Please stop!" Elyse breathed out angrily. "I want to get down."

"I don't think so." Zach urged the stallion on at a gentle pace.

"I do want to get down!" she demanded, twisting around in the saddle and practically slipping over the side of the horse. His hands gently prevented her falling.

"And take your hands off me!" she informed him icily.

Zach inhaled the windblown freshness of her hair as it gently blew against his cheek. "I can't do that, Elyse. You see," he began to explain, "if I let go . . ." For emphasis he did just that.

As she fell backward from the saddle, Elyse grabbed at his riding jacket. An arrogant smile immediately flashed across his lips.

"You'll fall," he announced as his arms closed once more around her. "At any rate, it's really not safe for you to be out here alone."

"Not safe!" She turned to looked up at him. "And I suppose riding with you is safe?"

Her coolness at their first meeting returned. It was like an invisible barrier.

"Perhaps you could best answer that question, Elyse. Is it unsafe to meet a man in a secluded place? After all, you are to be married soon. What would people say if they knew you were meeting me like this?" He smiled maddeningly. "And don't forget about Jane's Folley. She ended up marrying the King."

"Meeting you!" Elyse flung back at him. "You followed me!"

"Actually, you're right," he conceded. "I did follow you. And it was fortunate I came along when you needed me."

"I did not need you. If you hadn't pursued me, I wouldn't have fallen. Exactly why did you follow me?" Her fingers slowly entwined about the reins. If she could just get control of the stallion . . .

His gloved hand closed over hers. "I explained that before; I wanted to see you again. After all that was quite a memorable greeting you gave me the other evening. It intrigued me. Where was it you thought we might have met?"

"I explained that it was all a mistake."

As Zach easily loosened her fingers from the reins, something very like a memory filled his thoughts. "You should never ride without gloves," he said, and carefully spread her fingers, exposing lightly callused skin. Tenderly he kissed the palm of her hand, his lips brushing the raised flesh.

In spite of the growing warmth of the morning sun, Elyse shivered. Her fingers curled tightly as something deep inside knotted and tightened at that innocent contact.

All thought, all anger fled. Dear God! What was the matter with her?

She'd been kissed before. But never in her life could she remember being kissed with such infinite tenderness. It was like a breath of wind across her senses, like a whisper of something once remembered but now forgotten. As her startled gaze met his, her fingers clenched protectively over her exposed palm.

"I'll ride whenever and wherever I please, and without gloves. I certainly don't need your approval," she informed him coolly. "Now, if you don't mind"—she drew her hand from his—"I should be getting back. If my horse returns before I do, my grandmother will be terribly worried."

Zach snapped ramrod straight in the saddle, saluting her. His gaze darkened and became unreadable. "Absolutely! And if anyone

141

questions me about this morning, I'll deny anything happened."

"Deny what? For God's sake, what are you talking about?" Elyse turned, her hand still tingling where his lips had touched it. Her breath caught at the nearness of his face. As her gaze fastened on that slash of black satin across his eye, she was suddenly seized with a desire to pull it away and see him fully. She stared at the arrogant sensuality of his mouth, only inches from hers. She wet her lips, for they were suddenly dry at the memory of the exquisite heat of his mouth when he'd kissed her the night of the ball.

The arrogance in his gaze shifted to something equally unsettling. "I'll never tell a living soul that I took advantage of you in a secluded, dark place. I'm afraid your reputation could never stand the rumor and speculation. Nor could mine for that matter."

"Took advantage?" Elyse almost laughed at him. She would have if she could have breathed. She fought to control the wild hammering of her pulse. "I think your reputation will survive anything you do, señor," she whispered, mesmerized by the downward turn at one corner of his mouth, forgetting whatever else she'd intended to say.

Staring into those wide blue eyes, her lithe body against his, Zach felt everything about him slip into some nether world as if everything had ceased to exist except for this moment, except this woman whose slender body enticed even when disguised in masculine clothes. He wanted to kiss her and then walk away from her without regret, just as he wanted to believe he had done the night of the ball. He needed to prove to himself that she was nothing but a pawn he would use to get to Barrington, that she meant nothing to him. But staring into her soft blue gaze he felt something quicken deepen inside, betraying all his well-intentioned plans. Never before had he lost control with a woman—never, until this moment and this woman.

Everything suddenly seemed changed. They were no longer in a shaded hollow of the forest, nor were they in any dimension of time or reality. *There were just the two of them, as there had always been.*

Elyse's eyes closed at the touch of his gloved hand against her cheek.

"Lovely Lis." The mocking laughter was gone from his voice. It was as if the game were suddenly over and they the last two players. The stallion stood quietly beneath them. And time seemed to stand still. Zach ran his fingers through her disheveled hair, caressing the silken mass. "You promised you'd always wear your hair long for me."

Her startled gaze met his. He'd said that once before. Or had she

142

dreamed it?

An inexplicable fear made her shiver. "Please don't."

"You don't mean that," he whispered softly.

She tried to pull away from him. "Yes, I do mean it. I don't want—" Any further protest was cut off as his mouth captured hers in a brief, searing kiss.

Elyse jerked away as if she'd been burned. "Damn you!" She tried to retreat further but there was no escape in the small saddle. She was trapped and she knew it.

He reached up, his fingers slipping behind her neck, twining in the soft thickness of her hair. His other arm encircled her waist, pulling her to him as he gently drew her head back. "I'm going to kiss you as you were meant to be kissed, and want to be kissed." His mouth caressed hers with excruciating tenderness.

Some invisible force compelled her to him. It had nothing to do with the strength of his arms around her, or the demand of his mouth against hers. It was a deep raging need, a hunger that had lain too long unsated. Mindlessly, she clung to him, feeling need and desire knife through her. A soft sound escaped the back of her throat as the kiss deepened, his lips tender ravagement against hers, his tongue plunging between, invading the innocent depths of her mouth.

She cried out softly as her arms slipped around his waist. Yes, her heart echoed. *I knew you would come back to me.* She didn't try to understand how or why the thought came to her. She only knew that it had, like a litany from her soul. There was only this man and the lean, hard strength of his body bruising hers with such tenderness.

Desire slammed through Zach, unexpected, like a blow to the senses. He was out of control and he knew it. It angered and frightened him at the same time. He didn't like being out of control, or vulnerable. And instinctively he knew the one went along with the other. He'd never allowed it with any woman. He especially didn't like that feeling now. She was betrothed to Barrington, as off limits to him as England itself.

Holding her in his arms, Zach knew it was all a lie. But he needed the lie as a barrier between himself and this young woman. She was as good as a Barrington, and because of that she was the same as Barrington, not to be trusted any further than it might serve his purposes.

Even when he was certain he believed that, it took every last shred of control he could call up to close his fingers over her slender wrists and pull them from around his waist. Slowly he pushed her from him. When he looked down at her passion-filled eyes, his gaze once more held the sting of cold mockery. His fingers cut cruelly into her wrists as he pushed her away. The change in his mood was swift, like a cloud engulfing the sun. Coldness replaced the smoldering desire in the Count de Cuervo's shadowy gaze, and the corners of his mouth lifted in a twist of cruel smile.

"It that what you wanted, my lady?"

The cold brutality of his words cut through the fog that seemed to engulf Elyse's senses. She flinched at his stinging words, and inhaled sharply, choking on pain and humiliation. "I was right about you. You're no gentleman. Damn you! You're nothing but a—"

He cut her off. "I'm certain you'll think of the words in a moment, Miss Winslow."

"You . . . pompous . . . overbearing—!"

"Of course." His smile was cruelly mocking. "I get the general idea of what you're trying to say. Now, if you don't mind, I don't think I care to hear the end of your tirade."

Elyse couldn't think of anything bad enough to call him. Cheeks aflame with humiliation and embarrassment, she blazed with cold fury. Jerking one wrist free of his grasp, she drew back her arm, intending to strike him as hard as she could. Instead, the sudden movement completely unbalanced her.

She gasped as she landed on the trail with a sickening thud. Then she raised smoldering eyes to the Count de Cuervo. "You bastard!" she shrieked, so loud she sent a covey of doves rustling from their perches in a nearby tree.

Equally stunned by her sudden fall, Zach checked his first instinct to dismount. He certainly hadn't intended this. But the murderous look in those vivid blue eyes told him she wasn't about to listen to any explanations. Inhaling deeply, he forced back regret and a feeling of self-loathing. She had every right to be angry.

"Obviously, you're not seriously injured," he commented, more coolly than he'd intended, as he turned his mount about.

"Injured? I might have been killed! Where are you going?"

"I'm certain you can manage quite well on your own. You seem to be a young woman of great resourcefulness."

"What about my pendant, you thief?" Elyse demanded. She held her breath when he hesitated, turning back in the saddle.

"As I explained to you I've been called a great many things, but thief isn't one of them. You may have your pendant back whenever you like. You have only to call at my house for it," he announced.

"That will be a cold day in . . ."

Zach shook his head as if he were reprimanding a small child. "Miss Winslow, soon-to-be Lady Barrington, whatever will people think of your choice of words?" And with that, he turned back around. The faintest pressure of a gleaming booted heel sent his mount down the trail, leaving her behind with her bruised ego and an equally painful backside.

"I don't give a fig about what anyone thinks!" Elyse yelled after him. For emphasis she pounded the ground beside her bruised hip. Mud splattered into the air, peppering her pants and jacket. It streaked the white shirt and plastered her hair and face.

She groaned as she looked down at her soaked pants. Of all the places for her to fall. The entire trail was dry except for this one place where rainwater from the light shower just before dawn had pooled.

"Of all the damnable luck!" She struck at the mud puddle again, completing the damage. Then she rose slowly, wincing at the pain in her bruised backside as she walked toward the stream.

If Lucy could see me now, she thought morosely. "And he still has my pendant." Tears pooled in her vivid eyes. She hated him. Oh, how she hated him!

Her head came up at the sound of hoofbeats on the trail. She hastily wiped her tears with the back of her sleeve, excitement sending her heart racing. It quickly died as Quimby rounded the bend in the trail.

"Damn!" she whispered, to no one but herself.

Chapter Seven

It was adding insult to injury.

"Great balls of fire!" Elyse fumed as she slammed the heavy door on the heels of the servant who'd delivered the message from Jerrold.

Swirling into the parlor in a wave of crackling, sea green silk, she flounced into a chair, wincing painfully. She looked up, meeting her grandmother's bemused gaze.

"Was that Jerrold's man, Chivers, at the door?"

"Yes! Honestly, he has some nerve!" Elyse crumpled the elaborately scrawled note, at the bottom of which Jerrold had signed his initials with a flourish.

"Chivers?" Regina Winslow looked up from her cup of morning tea, unable to comprehend why a meek toad of a man such as that amiable servant had sent her granddaughter into such a fit of ill temper.

"No, of course not!" Elyse bounded out of the chair to pace the width of the parlor with restless energy. It was preferable to sitting; she was still smarting from that fall she'd taken in the Woods two days earlier. Actually, she'd taken two falls. And the Count de Cuervo was responsible for both of them. Now this! She waved Jerrold's note through the air like a challenging banner.

"God's nightgown! Does the man think I have nothing better to do than wait for him to come calling. Of all the nerve! We were supposed to attend the opera tonight!"

Lady Regina set down the delicate bone-china cup, giving her granddaughter a long look. "You're speaking of Jerrold, I take it."

Elyse looked up. "Of course I'm talking about Jerrold." She resumed her agitated pacing.

"I seem to remember you sending round word yesterday that you didn't feel up to social functions," Lady Winslow delicately reminded her.

"That was yesterday." Whirling about in front of the manteled fireplace, Elyse tapped a foot in vexation and rested one hand on her hip. Quimby had done his work well. He'd managed to find out a few very interesting things about the Count de Cuervo. Just that morning she'd sent Jerrold a message stating that she wanted to see him about something important, and now his return missive informed her that he was attending his private club that evening, with none other than the Count de Cuervo. And there was some vague reference to a business matter they were to discuss.

She sent the loose fall of her hair back over one shoulder with a decidedly impatient air.

"I take it Jerrold has canceled your plans for the evening," Regina said.

"Precisely. He's invited the Count de Cuervo to attend his private club. Of all people!" Having unfolded the message and read it for the second time, Elyse tore it into a multitude of tiny pieces, which she scattered on the cold hearth. The flames in her eyes were sparking sufficient heat.

She'd learned from Katy's excursions at the market that the count was staying at the London town house of Lord and Lady Vale. Supposedly he was related to them. But of even more interest was the information Quimby had acquired at the docks. It seemed the Count de Cuervo had arrived only days earlier, and though his ship was flying a Spanish flag, there was something very peculiar about an entire crew that spoke not a trace of that language. The harbormaster was unable to provide any further information except that the *Tamarisk* carried a cargo of wool which had been brought ashore and was now stored in warehouses at the docks.

"I think it's very generous of Jerrold to be so hospitable to the count. After all, he is new to England. And I did find him to be such a charming man," Lady Regina confessed.

"Charming!" The word exploded from Elyse's lips. "The man is nothing but an arrogant, rude, ill-mannered . . ."

"Yes?" Her grandmother watched her skeptically. "You were about to call him something?"

"Impostor!"

Lady Winslow's eyes danced with merriment as soft laughter came from her throat. "Impostor? My dearest Elyse, I can name several things he is, but impostor is not one of them. Why, anyone can see that the man has exceptional breeding. His manners are impeccable. I have it on good account that he speaks several languages including French, which you failed miserably at, my dear. And"—she paused for effect—"you cannot deny that he cuts a dashing figure with that eyepatch covering one eye." She tapped an elegant, bejeweled finger against her chin. "I wonder how he came to lose it."

Arms folded below the sweep of a daring décolletage, Elyse rolled her eyes heavenward. Please, not her grandmother, too. Ever since the night of the ball, it seemed every woman in London was virtually agog over the mysterious Count de Cuervo. Eyepatch indeed!

Elyse's mouth dropped open as her eyes widened. "Of course! That's it!" she announced triumphantly.

"What is? Elyse, honestly, you must quit speaking in riddles. I can't understand a thing you're saying."

Ever since she'd encountered the Count de Cuervo on the morning ride that had ended so disastrously, she'd tried to put her finger on just what it was about him that seemed so different that morning. Her grandmother was right about one thing; he did cut a handsome figure. And he was always impeccably dressed. His clothes fit as if molded to him. And the man exuded a sense of power and energy that was both exciting and a little disconcerting. But something else had caught her attention that morning, and she'd been unable to put her finger on exactly what it was. Now her grandmother had given it to her. The damned eyepatch!

The night of the ball, he'd worn the patch across his left eye; she was certain of it. But the morning of their meeting at the Woods, the black silk was bound across the right eye. She was right, the man was an impostor! And she was determined to prove it.

Gathering her grandmother in her arms, she pulled her from the chair and spun her joyously about. "You're wonderful! Have I told you that lately?"

"Not lately," Lady Regina answered, a bit fuddled as she pressed her fingers against her head, trying to stop the dizziness. "Elyse, please! What the devil are you talking about?"

"Eyepatches!" Elyse announced triumphantly. "Eyepatches," she mused aloud, "in all the right places." Her brilliant blue eyes sparkled as an idea took hold. Whirling about, she returned her grandmother to the chair and planted an affectionate kiss on her cheek.

"Where are you going? I thought you were distraught over the idea of not seeing Jerrold this evening," Lady Regina called after her.

Elyse whirled in the doorway. "Jerrold?" A few moments earlier she was talking of nothing else. Now it was as if she'd completely forgotten all about her earlier disappointment.

"Oh, of course." She tilted her lovely head thoughtfully. "But a day to myself will give me the chance to catch up on a few things. I'd like to do a bit of shopping." She cocked a lovely brow. "And I think I'll see what Lucy has planned for the day."

"What do you think?" Elyse turned from the mirror at the dressing table in her friend's bedchamber. She put the finishing touches to the makeup she'd artfully applied. It was late afternoon and she'd just been to the costumer's shop. Lucy's house was her second stop of the day. Fixing her friend with a coolly disdainful look, she tried to smother a fit of laughter.

"The honest truth?" Lucy shook her head, a skeptical expression on her lovely face.

"Of course, my dear." Elyse lowered her voice.

"I think you've absolutely gone round the bend," Lucy informed her.

Elyse choked back more laughter. "Do you mean I'm one brick shy of a full load?"

Joining in the fun, Lucy made a face at her in the mirror. "You simply don't have both oars in the water, my dear." She collapsed onto the brocade coverlet on the bed. Throwing herself back into the downy softness, she giggled.

Elyse tried to go her one better in their verbal sparring. "How about no wick in the candle?"

Tears rolled down Lucy's cheeks. "Or there's a light in the window, but no one's home." She shrieked with laughter.

"Here's a good one." Elyse was determined to outdo her. "Only three wheels on the wagon."

"Stop! Please stop!" Lucy begged, coming up off the bed. She wiped tears from her eyes between gasps for air. "I can't stand it."

"But the question is, my dear"—Elyse fastened on her an expression of pure devilment—"can we pull it off?"

"We?" Lucy shot back a look of complete amazement. "You can't mean . . . ?"

"Of course that's what I mean." Elyse turned back to the mirror. "It won't work unless we both go."

"My God, Elyse! You are crazy!" Lucy gulped back her astonishment. "No woman has ever been inside White's before. At least

149

no woman who's a lady. The only women allowed inside are . . ." Her voice dropped. "And that's only rumor."

"Yes, I know." In the mirror, Elyse caught the reflection of Lucy's startled gaze. "Don't you think it's about time a lady did see just what goes on in an exclusive men's club? Or maybe two ladies?"

"Elyse, we can't. Andrew would never allow me—"

She cut Lucy her off. "Which is precisely the reason you're to say nothing to him about it. Lucy," she pressed her friend, "haven't you been just the least bit curious to know what goes on at those clubs, or what Andrew does when he goes there?" At the faint flicker of response in Lucy's eyes, she knew she'd already won her argument.

"What time do we go?" Lucy murmured, a slight threading of excitement in her voice.

"Chivers told me Jerrold usually leaves for the club around nine o'clock. We should go about nine-thirty."

Lucy's hands trembled with the boldness of their plan. "Aren't you just a little bit nervous about this?"

Elyse smiled wickedly. "I think it's exciting. A little like that trapeze act we saw at the circus last summer, don't you think? Besides, it's all very harmless. We'll go for just a little while, and then leave. After all, Jerrold claims it's all quite boring. Supposedly the men just play a few games of cards, talk, smoke their cigarettes, and discuss whose horse won at the races. He claims I wouldn't possibly be interested in any of it. Still," she mused thoughtfully, "it does make you wonder why they all go if it's so boring." A mischievous gleam danced in her vivid eyes.

Lucy groaned, knowing full well Elyse would go and that she would go with her. "What happens if we're caught? We need an escape plan."

"We won't be caught. Andrew won't even know about it," Elyse confided. "You'll be home and in bed before he leaves the club. But just in case . . . if anything goes wrong, we'll split up and leave by separate doors. I found out there are two doors as well as an employees' entrance out the back alley. What do you think?"

"Think!" Lucy gaped at her reflection in the mirror. "I think you've got bats in your belfry!"

"But you will go?" Elyse turned to her friend.

Lucy sighed. "I think we're going to regret this," she predicted, but the light in her eyes matched Elyse's for excitement. Still, I wouldn't miss it for the world! What's your plan?"

Elyse smiled victoriously. "In that case, you'll find clothes for yourself in that." She indicated the costumer's box on the bed. "I was fairly certain about the size."

"And obviously certain I'd go along with your little scheme," Lucy remarked ruefully.

"Of course. Haven't we always been partners in every little escapade?"

"Yes. And I keep remembering the disastrous results of your last plan: exchanging places at my own wedding just to see if Andrew would notice the difference. He was on to us and said nothing, and you practically ended up married to my husband. I would never have forgiven you." Lucy maintained an appropriately displeased expression.

"You have to admit, it was one of my more successful schemes. Andrew kept waiting for one of us to end it, and we kept waiting for him to say something."

"What could I say?" Lucy's eyes widened innocently. "I was the farthest from the altar and the bishop."

Elyse giggled. "Remember the bishop's face, when he finally realized he very nearly married the wrong bride to the groom?"

"I thought the poor man would have apoplexy. And dear Anne almost fainted." Lucy sighed with fake concern for the stepmother she'd never gotten along with. Then her mouth twitched with delight. "But you'd never have gotten through the wedding night, my dear. Even if he were a blind man, Andrew would have known the difference."

Elyse whirled around on the satin-covered bench, her eyes widening at the revelation of a secret she'd not known until this moment. "Lucy! Do you mean to tell me that you and Andrew . . . ? That you . . . ?"

Lucy smiled triumphantly realizing she'd finally managed to shock Elyse. It was usually the other way around. "Yes, of course. How do you expect anyone to endure a betrothal that lasts an entire year? My god! I'd have come unraveled if I'd had to wait a year to make love with him. Certainly, you and Jerrold . . . ?" When Elyse glanced away, Lucy's mouth dropped open.

"Do you mean to tell me that you and Jerrold have never made love?" She was completely aghast.

Elyse's soft blue eyes darkened defensively. "No," she answered simply. "I'm certain Jerrold wanted to; at least he said as much." She shrugged. "There never seemed to be the right moment, or the right place," she ended lamely.

"The right moment?" Lucy watched her thoughtfully. "My dear, when you're head over heels in love with a man, there's no need for the right place or moment. Somehow every place, every moment is the right one. I speak from experience." She arched a brow knowingly.

Elyse's head came up, her eyes narrowing at this side of her friend she'd never seen before. "What do you mean, every place and every moment?"

Lucy stood and walked casually across the room, tilting her blond head, a smug expression on her face. Bracing an elbow on one arm folded across her waist, she tapped a finger thoughtfully against her lovely chin. "There was the time in the stables. Of course I was picking hay out of my clothes for days. And then there was the time in the coach during an afternoon ride through Kensington Gardens. I would caution you against coaches. There's never enough room, and your legs get all tangled up. But where there's a will, there's a way."

"Lucy! You're dreadful! I don't believe for a moment that any of this ever happened." Elyse sat with mouth agape.

"And then there was my cousin Charlotte's country party. Andrew and I couldn't bear to be away from each other for an entire week. He disguised himself as my driver. The entire week was wonderful. I pretended to have a cold so that I could be excused from the family activities. Then when everyone was out of the house, I'd meet Andrew. Do you remember that little gazebo in the gardens at Charlotte's?" She turned inquisitive eyes on Elyse.

"In the gazebo? You made love in a gazebo?" She was incredulous. "The stables and a coach? Lucy, whatever possessed you?"

"Love possessed me, my dear. Surely, you've felt it."

Elyse turned away, not wanting her friend to see the uncertainty in her eyes. "Yes," she admitted truthfully, "I've felt it . . ." She grew thoughtful considering Lucy's confessions of the heart. "Once, a long time ago I think."

Lucy crossed the room, picking up stray garments strewn across the floor. It wouldn't do for one of her maids to see the clothing and guess what they were up to.

"What did you say, dear?" She turned absently, a pair of silk pantalets clutched in one hand.

Elyse smiled sadly. "Nothing important. Now, what about supper? Shall we eat at Winslow House? Grandmother is dining with Uncle Ceddy this evening. We'll have the entire house to ourselves."

Lucy looked at her speculatively, wondering why she lied about what she'd said. "That sounds fine. Then we can play with this threatrical makeup you purchased. I want to get this disguise just right."

"My dear." Again Elyse lowered her voice dramatically. "By the time I'm through with you, no one will recognize you." She laughed, some of her good humor restored. Then she grew quite serious. "Lucy, have you ever smoked a cigarette?"

The streets of London were like silver ribbons in the glow of light from streetlamps. The night air was cool and held an air of expectancy after the warmth of the late spring day. Open carriages passed an occasional closed coach. Drivers called softly to their teams of horses. The faint clip-clopping of shod hooves grew louder as a carriage approached, then diminished with a rhythmic reminder like the faint ticking of a clock.

The distinguished location of White's was known to every gentleman of breeding and wealth in London society. The membership was exclusive, catering to a specific clientele. There was no brass- or gold-lettered name plate beside the discreet door, not even any street number to denote the exact address. Though no plaque restricted members and their guests to the masculine gender, there was no need of one. Anyone who was anyone about London, from the lowliest hack driver to the most impeccably liveried coachman, knew the hand-carved mahogany doors on the tree-lined street just one block over from the theater. This was White's.

The rented black coach pulled to a stop at the curb. Immediately a liveried doorman emerged from one of those impressive doors and efficiently greeted the most recent arrivals.

"Good evening, George." The raspy voice greeted the doorman.

"Good evening, sir." There was a faint questioning note in George's voice.

The first gentleman to alight from the carriage nodded a brief greeting while waiting for his companion. A second gentleman of approximately the same slight stature emerged and stepped down. His face was concealed in the shadow of his elegant silk hat.

"We're joining Sir Jerrold Barrington this evening," the first gentleman announced. "Has he arrived yet?"

George, the doorman, carefully scrutinized the first gentleman. "He and another guest arrived a short while ago."

"Ah yes, that would be the Count de Cuervo, newly arrived from Spain." The young man smoothed his lapel with a gloved hand. "A splendid fellow and quite interesting with that eyepatch."

George beamed, obviously satisfied that these two gentlemen were indeed well acquainted with Sir Jerrold and the count. "This way, please, gentlemen," he announced with a flourish as he stepped aside to allow them through the elegant, carved doors.

"Do come along, Lucien," the first gentleman called to his companion. "It promises to be an exciting evening. We don't want to miss anything." He was answered only by a loud coughing as his companion joined him.

"Lucien!" the second young man whispered discreetly. "Where the devil did you come up with a name like that?"

The first gentleman smiled suavely as "he" reached to lightly dust off an invisible speck of lint from his friend's shoulder. "I couldn't go around calling you Lucy. It might give all these respectable gentlemen the wrong idea about you." A trace of a smirk appeared at the corners of a mouth disguised by an impeccably groomed mustache.

The young man known as Lucien groaned. "We're both crazy. This will never work."

Stepping through the double doors into the foyer of the exclusive club, they were greeted by another man who offered to take their hats and capes. "Lucien" stiffened visibly.

"Come now, old chap." The first young man chided "his" companion. "They'll give it back to you when we're ready to leave," he said aloud for the benefit of the butler and the departing George.

"Which just happens to be right now!" Lucien muttered as coat and hat were surrendered, revealing a pate of gleaming black hair and flowing muttonchop whiskers, both elegantly groomed.

The first young man looked down at the polished toes of shoes emerging from the line of perfectly fitted trousers, and tried to smother back a fit of laughter. Tears filled *his* eyes, but were gone from those devastatingly blue eyes when he again looked up. Together, they followed the butler to a single door across the hall. And together, like the two perfectly proper young men they appeared to be, they entered the elegantly furnished, faintly smoky, male domain of White's Exclusive Club for Men.

"We're both out of our minds!" Lucy grumbled into Elyse's ear. "And this damn glued-on mustache is driving me crazy." Her upper lip twitched back and forth.

"Relax. Everything will be fine. No one will ever know it's you underneath all that makeup. Actually, those whiskers look marvelous," Elyse teased, side-stepping a painful pinch as Lucy leaned against her. "Look at this, Lucy. Have you ever seen anything like

154

this?" She gestured to the room.

Gold-embossed paper covered the walls above the wainscoting, while below it was crimson velvet. Several small alcoves were sectioned off around the perimeter of the room with heavy, crimson velvet drapes edged with gold satin and bound back with braided satin cords. In these alcoves were tables with anywhere from four to eight chairs placed around them. In some, gentlemen could be seen enjoying conversation along with their drinks. In others, a lively game of cards was underway. A few were hidden from view, their heavy portiers discreetly closed. Only an occasional movement of the drapes indicated someone was behind them. Immaculately dressed young men wove in and out of the tables in the main room, entering the secluded alcoves, replenishing containers of brandy and whiskey. Gas lamps gave just enough light to the tables but left the remainder of the room in semidarkness.

Elyse recognized several gentlemen. Faint streamers of cigar and cigarette smoke curled into the air to mingle with the fragrance of pipe tobacco. She hardly saw anything to cause any excitement. It all seemed a little boring.

"Oh, my God!" Lucy breathed, whirling Elyse around.

"What is it?" She turned her head, trying to see what it was that had managed to upset Lucy.

"Don't look. It'll seem too obvious. Jerrold is coming this way. Someone must have told him about us. Why on earth did you have to use his name?"

"I had to use a name that would get us in the door," Elyse rationalized. "I could have used Andrew's," she reminded her friend.

Lucy only groaned. "Well, it's too late to do anything about it now. We'll be found out. I just know we will."

Elyse smiled from beneath the sweep of the waxed, blond mustache she'd so painstakingly applied. It matched perfectly the blond man's wig that concealed the hair piled neatly on top of her head. She shrugged her shoulders, padded for extra width.

"Now is as good a time as any to find out if these costumes are any good."

Rolling her eyes heavenward, Lucy seized a tumbler of whiskey from a tray as a uniformed young man passed nearby. Whoever belonged to the drink would just have to ask for another. It was quickly downed, causing her to breathe in sharply.

"Good evening." The polite greeting came from behind Elyse.

155

She hesitated as Lucy was seized with a fit of coughing due to the hastily downed drink. With precise masculine gestures, she clapped her friend heartily across the back.

"I say, old boy, you've really done it this time. You must be more careful." Elyse had lowered her voice convincingly.

"Is there anything I can do?"

She turned around to glance disdainfully at Jerrold Barrington, and held her breath as a long moment passed. If they were going to be found out, it would be now.

Then she smiled. "Not at all. Everything is quite under control. He does this all the time." Leaning forward, she placed a gloved hand on Jerrold's shoulder in a companionable gesture. "He has a tendency to overindulge. I do have to keep an eye on him, promised his wife I'd have him home early." Beside her, Lucy gritted her teeth.

"I don't believe we've met, sir," Jerrold said haughtily.

Turning the full force of her deception on him, Elyse looked coolly down the short length of a nose that was a bit too delicate to be a man's. But the softness of her features was hidden behind the heavy mustache. Her gaze never wavered as she met Jerrold's disdain with equal aloofness. The uncomfortable moment was drawn out as she opened her coat and reached inside, retrieving a gold cigarette case. Her concentration broke for only a second as she saw another man coming toward them from across the room. She hadn't counted on a face-to-face meeting. She would have preferred some distance in which to play out her little game of spying on this man. But there was nothing to be done about it now. If she could hoodwink Jerrold, she could fool a fool. Her fingers tightened over the case as the Count de Cuervo joined them.

There was only the faintest trembling in her fingers as she flicked open the case and retrieved a cigarette. Beside her, she heard Lucy's faint intake of breath. They hadn't rehearsed this part. They'd been too afraid of leaving the scent of smoke in her grandmother's house. Lucy had given her brief instruction on the art of smoking, instructing her not to inhale. Elyse wondered how she knew so much about it. She pulled out an elegantly rolled cigarette and tapped it against the gold case.

"Of course you remember, Barrington. I was with Sir Laughton at the races last month; I'm his cousin from Paris. You said if we had the occasion, we should join you at your club in London." Elyse glanced around as if giving the interior of the club careful inspection. "We've just come up from the country."

Jerrold seemed skeptical, and in truth Elyse was making most of this up. She knew he'd been seen with the Laughtons at the races. In fact, he'd been seen with Lady Laughton on several occasions. Now she delighted in the confusion that registered in his eyes as he signaled one of the club's employees. He'd undoubtedly been so caught up with Lady Laughton he didn't remember meeting any-one at the races. She was counting on just that sort of convenient forgetfulness. The employee appeared at Jerrold's elbow, quickly producing a match and striking it. Elyse smiled faintly.

"Perhaps later." She released a shaky breath as the employee retreated. At least one problem was taken care of. However, a problem of another kind was rapidly approaching. The Count de Cuervo would be her real challenge. An impostor would be much harder to fool.

"Ah yes, of course the races." Jerrold responded vaguely. He turned as the count appeared at his side. "May I present the cousin of an acquaintance . . ." He hesitated.

Elyse nodded her greeting. "Étienne Martineau and my com-panion, Lucien de Villiers." She practically choked over the intro-ductions, knowing what her grandmother's reaction would have been to her using the name of an author of one of the French language texts she'd studied with such disastrous results. The French language had practically been her undoing. Lucy, on the other hand, had an impressive command of it. Elyse hoped to God she remembered enough of it in her current state of distress.

Jerrold curtly nodded to them both and introduced the Count de Cuervo.

Elyse inclined her head in stiff acknowledgment as she'd seen gentlemen do when greeting each other. "A pleasure, of course." She held her breath when he seemed to hesitate a moment longer than necessary.

"Have we met before?" Zach's gaze narrowed slightly as he studied the young man.

"I'm certain I would remember, sir. A pleasure nevertheless."

The reply was polite, but the accent seemed a mixture of poor man's French and something that wasn't recognizable. Indeed, the words had a flatness to them, as if the accent were affected. And the second young gentleman seemed to be afflicted with great nervousness. Barrington apparently didn't notice.

"I am very pleased to make your acquaintance." Lucy's greeting was made in flawless French and the count responded in the same tongue, smiling devilishly.

157

"Well" — Jerrold smiled — "since we are acquainted, please join us. We were just about to begin a game of cards. And a little later, there will be some exciting entertainment."

"Entertainment?" Lucy swallowed back her curiosity.

Preceding them across the large room, Jerrold turned and leaned toward them both.

"Several young ladies will be joining us. I think they will prove exciting even by French standards, *monsieur*. Tonight" — he glanced toward the Count de Cuervo — "is a night to forget all other women you have ever known. I guarantee, the young ladies who will be joining us will be like no others you've ever experienced." As they reached Jerrold's table, Elyse felt a twinge of uncertainty. Women?

Elyse had hoped to observe the Count de Cuervo from a distance. This was more than she'd hoped for; they were seated with him at Jerrold's table in one of the secluded alcoves.

"Lord Barrington has been teaching me the basics of a game known as Battle. Have you played before, *monsieur?*" The count reached for the deck of cards and spread them fanlike across the table.

Swallowing back her own uneasiness, Elyse shook her head. "I don't believe I've had the pleasure."

The count smiled warmly. "Then you must learn. It's a fascinating game, filled with all manner of traps and deceptions. One must be very careful." He deliberately fixed on the young man across from him that penetrating gaze. Something was amiss and he was determined to find out what it was.

Elyse quickly learned two things. The first was that she had to pay quick attention to the rapid exchange of cards as the hands were dealt; and the second was that she'd worried needlessly that Jerrold would recognize her. There was far more danger with this man who played cards as if he were out for blood.

She'd dreamed up this mad scheme to expose the Count de Cuervo for what he really was — an impostor. But through the course of four hands of Battle, she felt as if the tables were turned. He seemed to be the hunter and she the quarry. And now she was uncertain whether her suspicions were correct. This evening, just like that morning in the Woods, the eyepatch covered his right eye.

The count laid out the cards of yet another winning hand. "I believe that is my game once more. Shall we try something else. Your friend seems to have found other diversions."

Elyse found herself looking for Jerrold. It was almost an hour since he'd disappeared, saying that he must see to the evening's entertainment, whatever that might mean. She followed the count's gaze to where Lucy stood at a discreet distance from Andrew. She'd been practically hovering over him all evening.

Playing her role of young gentleman to perfection, Elyse sipped at the brandy placed beside her a few moments ago. She was immediately aware of the Count de Cuervo's questioning gaze.

"Is there something wrong with the brandy?"

Startled, Elyse glanced up, then just as quickly looked away. "Not at all."

Zach's gaze narrowed. All evening the young man known as Étienne Martineau had been studying the cards in his hand, the carpeting on the floor, or the velvet table covering; keeping his eyes constantly averted. But in that one betraying moment when he'd looked up, momentarily caught off guard, Zach knew what it was that had disturbed him all evening.

A faint smile twitched at the corners of his mouth. He'd accepted this invitation so he might get to know Barrington better and strengthen their business arrangements. But the evening now offered surprising twists and turns.

Reaching across the table, he pushed the full tumbler of brandy toward his young companion. "Then, drink up, my friend. The evening is still young. And our host would be displeased if he thought you weren't enjoying yourself."

Elyse's startled glance met his briefly, then fell to the tumbler. She swallowed uneasily, knowing she had no other choice but to drink. Bracing herself, she quickly downed the amber-colored liquid as she'd seen the other gentlemen doing all evening. The brandy seared a fiery path down to her stomach and back up again. If she breathed, Elyse was certain flames would leap out of her mouth. Her eyes watered. She tried to swallow. She tried to breathe. When air finally rushed into her lungs, it came out just as quickly in spasms of coughing.

In an instant the Count de Cuervo was beside her, heartily applying his hand to her back. Again and again he clapped her between the shoulder blades, until she thought she was being pounded to death. She clasped a gloved hand over her mouth as she tried to draw another breath. When she pulled her hand away, her eyes widened in horror. There in the middle of the table was the immaculately groomed curl of mustache that had taken such a painstaking amount of time to apply. It had been dislodged by a simple cough and lay glaringly on the rich velvet like a giant raised eyebrow.

159

She quickly reached across the table and snatched it up. Bending over as if still seized by that fit of coughing, she pressed the mustache back into place and prayed it would stick. Then she looked up. Across the room, the other gentlemen seemed oblivious to her. They rose, one by one from their chairs and gathered at the far end of the large room.

Elyse rose from her chair as she composed herself. "What is all the excitement about?"

The Count de Cuervo turned to her. "It seems . . ." He stopped in midsentence and looked at her, an odd expression on his face. Then it was his turn, the violent coughing seemingly contagious. He quickly recovered.

"It seems the entertainment is about to begin. I've met these people before. I think you'll find this most unusual." With a faint bow, he motioned for her to precede him across the room.

Smiling uncertainly, Elyse looked across the room for Lucy, but her friend seemed to have disappeared. Strange music, unlike anything she'd ever heard before, filled the room. The buzz of expectant conversation around them dimmed. All eyes were focused on the source of the music. Pushed forward by others equally eager to see what was transpiring, Elyse was helpless to do anything but move with them.

Her eyes widened in stunned surprise. Under the glow of light from a massive chandelier, a young woman danced and whirled to exotic rhythms. But it wasn't the music that held Elyse fascinated, or even the woman's movements. It was the scanty costume adorning the dancer's voluptuous figure. Nothing more than several transparent silk scarves that whirled in the air with each undulating movement, threatening to expose various parts of the woman's anatomy. Elyse stared, enrapt.

Amusement danced in the Count de Cuervo's silver gaze as he watched the brilliant display. But actually he was fascinated by the young creature beside him. True, Fatima of the Thousand Veils, did promise exotic and tantalizing pleasures. She claimed to be from a Bedouin chieftain's harem, but she was in fact a Portuguese Gypsy. He'd seen her perform in Lisbon.

He leaned over his young companion's shoulder. "Rather interesting muscle control, wouldn't you say? I've heard it said she can hold that gem in her navel indefinitely." Merriment sparkled in his silver eye as he watched both the dancer and his companion.

Elyse's gaze remained fixed on Fatima; she was wondering just how the woman moved her body like that. So this was how Jerrold managed to entertain himself when he came to White's! Card games indeed! A half-dozen other dancers joined Fatima. They whirled and gyrated around the room in frenzied abandon. Their lithe bodies soon glistened with a fine sheen that only seemed to heighten the men's appreciation. The decorum of distinguished gentlemen was gone, replaced by loud hoots of encouragement and some rather vague comments Elyse thought she was probably better off not understanding.

At that moment, as Fatima whirled around right under her nose, the gentleman to Elyse's left decided to add his own interpretation to the dancing. He joined the silk-clad girls, rousingly displaying his ability. One by one, the girls continued their rhythmic flight about the room. With each full circle, every dancer selected one scarf from the myriad assortment attached to the wide waistband that circled low over her hips, yanked it from the band, and wantonly cast it over a bare shoulder. As filmy scarves floated to the floor, the dance continued, more and more silk covering the floor until it seemed to make a thick, waving carpet at their feet.

Elyse gasped as the music ended and the performers posed silently before the leering men. Only two scarves remained about each performer. One dangled between her legs, from the front of the waistband. The other dangled from the center of the back of the band. Absolutely nothing covered the women's breasts. They stood in a circle of gleaming flesh, each exotically clad in two silk scarves, completely naked from the waist up.

"My God!" she exclaimed, fascinated by the performance and the unabashed sensuality of the young women.

The Count de Cuervo waited expectantly. "I told you Fatima possessed captivating talents." His mouth twitched with suppressed amusement that was quickly masked behind a socially correct façade as soft blue eyes met his.

"She certainly does!" Elyse declared, in her own voice. Realizing her error, she quickly cleared her throat. "I really must find my friend. It's quite late; we must be leaving."

"Leaving?" The Count de Cuervo looked absolutely stunned. "You can't! The evening is just beginning." He seized his companion's arm and quickly steered "him" through the circle of gentlemen who mingled with the dancers. Elyse noticed that several other young ladies appeared, their garb as scant as the dancers. Just as quickly, each disappeared, a gentlemen's arm gently looped through hers.

"As you can see, everyone else is leaving. It seems the entertainment is through for the evening," Elyse insisted as she searched the room for Lucy. She caught sight of her friend's black wigged head, and started to make her way across the room.

"Not at all." The count gently restrained his young companion. "The entertainment has only just begun." He gestured across the room, to where the distinguished man, whom Elyse knew to be the husband of one of her grandmother's acquaintances, disappeared through crimson velvet drapes that led to a stairway. A scantily clad young woman clung to his arm. The pair stopped abruptly, the woman leaning forward to wantonly press her body against the elderly man. His appreciative laughter could be heard across the room as he climbed the stairs with her.

"Where are they all going?" Elyse kept her voice deliberately low as she watched several other gentlemen disappear with similarly clad young woman.

"To be entertained, of course. You are rather young and inexperienced in the ways of the world, aren't you?" the count speculated. "I think I know just what's needed in your case."

Before Elyse could turn around to respond, the Count de Cuervo disappeared. She immediately seized the opportunity his absence offered. Crossing the room, she wound her way through the assorted tables and chairs, now completely deserted. Stepping around a man and his female companion, she caught a glimpse of Lucy moving toward the main entrance with a great deal of urgency.

"Lucy . . ." Elyse winced, hoping no one had heard her. She didn't care to stay for the evening's entertainment. They had to get out of here.

"Lucien!"

Elyse gasped as Lucy turned around. Another head turned simultaneously, and she stared straight into the infuriated gaze of Andrew Maitland.

"Come along, *Lucien*." Andrew's hand closed over his wife's arm. "It's been such a long time since we last saw each other," he added for the benefit of those around them. The expression on his face was one of suppressed rage.

Andrew didn't wait to ask to escort Elyse home. Throwing a murderous glare in her direction, he pushed Lucy out the door and into the darkness of night.

"Of all the . . ." Elyse muttered. Then, squaring her shoulders, she struck a more masculine stance and headed for that same door. She was brought up short by a familiar voice. Jerrold stood very near the exit. Beside him was one of the dancers she'd just watched. The woman, completely unabashed in her attentions, was pressing the fullness of her large, bare breasts against the front of his jacket. Disappointment knifed sharply through Elyse, disappointment in many things, far too many for her to even comprehend at that moment. Jerrold laughed at something the woman whispered as he bent low. Then he glanced briefly over her head, his gaze scanning the room before he pulled her into his embrace. At last he turned, drawing the woman with him up the stairs that led into darkness.

Elyse's disguise had really worked. Jerrold had looked straight at her and not recognized her. She almost wished he had so that she could see the reaction on his face at learning he'd been found out.

Elyse whirled around. Several other "gentlemen" lingered inside the foyer. She started for the door. If her disguise had fooled Jerrold, it was good enough to fool these last few men.

"You can't leave now."

Before she could check herself, Elyse collided with the Count de Cuervo. He must have been standing right behind her. Dear God! How much had he heard of her brief exchange with Andrew?

"As I said"—he fixed her with an unreadable gaze—"you seem rather inexperienced in these matters. Therefore"—reaching behind him, he drew the woman known as Fatima from the shadows—"I've arranged for you to enjoy some very special entertainment tonight."

She stared at him, at first not comprehending what he was saying. Then a warning sounded in her mind. "Special entertainment?" Elyse's voice almost failed her. All that came out was a dry, hoarse whisper.

"Exactly so." The count smiled graciously. "Fatima will show you to a chamber. She's very accomplished in these matters. I assure you, it will be a night to remember."

Elyse laughed uneasily as she took a small step backward. "You can't mean . . . ?" Her gaze locked with that of the seductive Fatima. The woman seemed to radiate sensuality. My God, she'd heard rumors of this sort of thing, but she couldn't possibly . . .

Good heavens! If she went with this woman she'd be exposed. Great balls of fire! Lucy! Why wasn't Lucy here when she needed her? Because Lucy's husband had discovered their little masquerade and had taken his wife home, leaving Elyse to the lions.

A hasty idea sprang into her mind. If she went with Fatima, she might be able to find a way out of this place. She glanced at the count. He seemed to be enjoying all this, maybe a little too much. She wondered if he had overheard her conversation with Andrew. No, it just wasn't possible that he suspected the truth. He would have said something before now.

Elyse smiled in what she hoped was a genuinely masculine way as she turned to the count. "I only meant, that you should take advantage of the . . . entertainment for this evening yourself, since you are a visitor to England."

"And you are a visitor as well. Isn't that correct? Therefore, I insist you escort Fatima upstairs. I've told her a great deal about you."

"That's most generous of you, but I couldn't possibly . . ." Elyse backed away one step.

"Of course you can." He seized her by the arm and propelled her toward the stairway.

"I've taken care of everything," he assured her as she turned to protest. "It's the least I can do after winning all those games of Battle." He turned to Fatima, conversing with her briefly in a language Elyse couldn't understand. Their exchange was brief, the woman smiling agreement to something. Her parting words, spoken softly in English, were obviously meant only for the count. "I will take care of everything, darling, as usual."

Elyse's eyes narrowed. *Darling . . . as usual?* What the devil did all that mean? She hardly had time to think about it for Fatima turned to her, seizing her arm with a strength Elyse found it hard to credit. She now had only one choice that wouldn't draw attention to herself.

As Fatima led her firmly up the stairs, her only escape was blocked by a man she found herself hating more with each passing moment. When they stopped before the door at the end of the hallway, Elyse turned to Fatima.

"There's been a dreadful mistake. You don't understand . . ." Further protest was cut off as Elyse was thrust inside the room.

"You will wait here, darling. I promise, you won't be disappointed." The woman drew out the last words, her meaning unmistakable even for someone of Elyse's innocence. Then she disappeared, locking the door from the outside.

Elyse flew across the room, vainly trying the door. Then, collapsing back against the unyielding portal, she quickly took in the darkened room, lushly appointed with more crimson velvet and gold satin braid. A single gas lamp cast golden light onto the room, flooding across the large, bed covered in crimson velvet.

Brothel! The word sprang into her head. White's Exclusive Club for Men was nothing but a high-class brothel!

"God's nightgown!" Elyse breathed out. "What am I going to do now?"

Somewhere a clock ticked with maddening slowness. A door opened and closed down the hallway. Damn! She'd really done it this time. Of all the harebrained ideas she'd ever come up with, this one was the worst. Pacing the room, she fought fatigue and strain and the effects of the brandy. She had to find a way out of here. Jerrold! Where the devil was he when she needed him? But she already knew the answer. She gave out a very unladylike little snort. He'd been one of the first of these so-called gentlemen to disappear with the "entertainment."

Elyse flung aside the elegant drapes that swathed the windows on the far wall. For a second she considered going out a window, but one look at the drop to the street below convinced her otherwise. Eying a second door, she flew across the room. It opened onto a closet filled with an array of garments and other items she chose not to inspect. After trying the first door once more, she paced the room.

Chapter Eight

Zach downed another brandy as he stalled for time. He wondered just what the young "man" was thinking right now. Several minutes had passed since Fatima had led the startled "fellow" up those stairs. His eyes narrowed as he saw the dancer return. She was preceded by several of the girls who'd performed earlier. She didn't look at though she intended to stay for the remainder of the evening. A heavy black shawl was wrapped about her meagerly clad body, and she seemed more than a little nervous as she glanced in first one direction and then another, urging the girls on to the back of the club. Zach set down the empty brandy glass.

"Just where do you think you're going?" His hand closed around her dark-skinned arm. Fatima whirled around, her relief immediate as she recognized him.

"I am leaving, and you should do the same if you're wise," she cautioned, her eyes darting about the empty foyer.

"What is it? What's happened?" Zach was immediately wary. He knew the Gypsies well. They lived by cunning and stealth. Over the past few years he'd acquired those traits himself. He'd learned them quickly; it was a matter of staying alive.

"One of my girls found out the local constable is on his way here! Right now!" she added for emphasis.

"This is a private club. The membership is exclusive. What would the authorities want here?"

Fatima leaned closer, her words urgent. "It seems these rich men are not so exclusive. There was trouble earlier this evening, down near the docks. One of the girls who works there was found badly beaten, and she'd been cut." She made a slicing motion across her throat with her hand. "Before she died she gave certain information about her attacker. He was a very rich man, and a powerful one."

"There are many rich men in London." Zach watched her skeptically. He doubted he could believe much of what she was saying. Fatima had a habit of changing a story to suit her own needs.

"Yes, but how many rich men strangle a woman with this." Reaching around Zach to the heavy velvet drapes, she jerked at the distinctive gold satin braid bordering one. "The boy told my girl, this was especially designed for this place. There is no other like it." She waved the braid in his face. "Take a look around you, my handsome friend. It is all woven the same, in an identical pattern. A piece of it was found around the girl's throat. And your host for the evening was gone for several hours before you arrived."

"Barrington?"

She shrugged, looking past him with startled eyes as a brusque pounding began on the heavy front doors. "I'm leaving!" she announced. "You'd be wise to do the same, Señor Cuervo."

Zach ignored her familiarity. "What about my young friend?"

"Leave him. He is too innocent to come to harm."

"Where did you leave him?" Zach insisted as he started up the stairs.

"The last room on the left. But there isn't time," she hissed at him. Waving her hand in exasperation, she called after him. "At the back of the kitchen is a cupboard, and I was told the brick wall at the back is fake. It leads into a passage that adjoins the next building."

He leaned over the balustrade as the knocking came more insistently. Already, the doors upstairs were being thrown open. George, the ever-present doorman, was nowhere to be found.

"Thank you, sweetheart," Zach called after the dancer.

"Look me up the next time you're in Lisbon," Fatima shouted over her shoulder. Then she disappeared down the long hall toward what was obviously the kitchen.

Zach took the remaining stairs two at a time. Pandemonium broke loose as some unsuspecting fop opened the front door. He reached the top landing as the alarm went out to the rest of the club members. This would be a night to remember. He was relieved that Tobias had insisted on staying at the town house. He was going to have enough problems getting his young card-playing companion out of here. At the moment he had no idea how he was going to get both of them back downstairs to the kitchen.

Elyse whirled around at the sound of the bolt being released.

Then she stood, feet braced. If necessary she'd force her way out of this room!

The door opened briefly and closed just as quickly. Almost immediately she heard sounds others were making in the hallway. But the figure that emerged from the shadows was not that of the lithe Fatima. Elyse stared at the tall man, with golden hair, slightly too long, hanging over his elegant collar. A swath of black eyepatch slashed his face.

"I told you this evening would be special, lovely Lis," he remarked wryly.

Her mouth fell open at the sound of her name. "You know?" she whispered incredulously. "But how?"

Amusement danced in his eye as Zach crossed to her. "There are vast differences between men and women, my dear Elyse. No matter how you tried to disguise your walk or flatten your breasts"—he gestured to her jacket front—"there are still differences. You, my dear, have a very curvaceous bottom. I remember it well, from our little ride the other day."

"Of all the nerve!" Elyse blurted out. But she took a step backward as he walked toward her, immediately wary. His hand snaked out. Fingers closed over her wrist in easy restraint. Then he seized her by both shoulders.

"Let go of me!" Elyse tried to jerk away. She gasped as he whirled her around, and her head snapped up, eyes livid with rage. A multitude of curses died on her lips as she stared at the small mirror on the opposite wall, and her mouth gaped open. Their images were reflected in the glass. Positioned precisely below her nose and above her lip was the blond mustache, its bristly waxed tips curved downward like ridiculous handles at either side of her mouth. It was upside down!

"Oh." She swallowed.

Zach whirled her back around. "Is that all you have to say for yourself?"

Elyse shrugged as all the anger seeped out of her. The long evening, the brandy, and now this. It was all too much. She could think only of how ridiculous she must look with that mustache. And Jerrold hadn't even noticed? The giggling began faintly as she swung back around to inspect those misplaced curves of blond hair. "You have to admit it was a pretty good disguise."

"You can compliment your self later." Before she could react, he reached up and stripped the mustache from her upper lip. She let out a shriek of pain.

"Damn you!" Her eyes watered as the skin above her lip reddened.

"I think you'll survive," Zach informed her, and then because he couldn't resist the soft pout on her mouth, he bent over and kissed her, slowly and thoroughly. "For medicinal purposes only." Seizing her by the hand, he pulled her toward the door amid loud protests.

She came up short behind the broad expanse of the Count de Cuervo's back as he looked out into the hallway.

"What about Fatima?" Elyse snickered, then rubbed the tender skin above her lip. "Shouldn't we wait for her?" she added sarcastically.

He jerked around, fixed her with that maddeningly secretive gaze. "Were you thinking of a threesome?" he quipped with a trace of irritation. "Sorry to disappoint you, but Fatima's already gone. However, we're about to have other company, if I don't get you out of here first."

"Company?" Elyse shrieked with wide-eyed innocence. "Did you invite others as well?"

His patience now gone, Zach turned back to her. "No. I didn't invite the authorities. It seems there's someone here they'd like very much to take in."

"Who? What are you talking about?" Elyse started past him, through the door, only to have herself flattened against the inside wall.

"Dammit! This is not a game." He looked at her hard. "It seems Barrington wasn't here all evening."

She looked up. She didn't trust him for a moment, but she was aware that Jerrold had been conspicuously absent during a good part of the evening. "What are you talking about?" She watched him suspiciously.

"I'm talking about a bit of trouble down at the docks. It seems a certain young lady of questionable reputation managed to get herself killed tonight," Zach informed her coldly.

"What has that to do with Jerrold? He spent most of the evening with someone else." The laughter was now gone from Elyse's voice. But no matter how angry she was at Jerrold, she didn't see how he could be connected to such a thing.

Zach watched for her reaction. "It seems the girl wasn't quite dead when he attacker finished with her, and Barrington was gone for a few hours."

An uneasy feeling slipped down Elyse's spine. My god, it wasn't possible that Jerrold had had anything to do with that.

"The authorities just arrived. It seems they have proof the man who killed the girl was a member of this club. They intend to question everyone."

Elyse's eyes widened. "Everyone? My God, you can't mean . . . ?"

"Everyone." He glanced once more out into the hallway. "That is unless you're willing to leave with me now."

Sneaking into White's in disguise was one thing. But this was an entirely different matter. If she was questioned, she would be found out. She couldn't afford to be caught. And she couldn't risk Jerrold knowing she was here. But depending on this man to get her out didn't sit well with her. He was completely unpredictable and, as she had pointed out on more than one occasion, certainly no gentleman. That little prank with Fatima had proved it. She wondered just how long he would have left her in this room if circumstances hadn't changed so abruptly. Clearly, he didn't want to be questioned by the London police any more than she did. Which only piqued her curiosity all the more. He obviously had something to hide.

"All right. I'll go with you," she announced tightly. "Do you know a way out of here?"

Zach smiled. She might be angry as hell at him, but she'd go along to keep from being questioned by the police. He nodded. "Fatima told me about a way out. But we have to get downstairs." He took her hand and led her out into the hallway.

It was a mass of confusion. Up and down the hall, doors stood ajar, like so many alarmed mouths. The respectable and wealthy gentlemen she'd seen hours earlier now scampered about in varied states of undress. Elyse turned her head, suppressing a giggle as a man she recognized hobbled past them. He was grumbling about being harassed by the constabulary while trying to shove his foot into a pantleg at the same time. A young woman cursed in one of the rooms and then emerged from it with her partner. Everyone was scampering about in different directions, trying to evade the authorities.

"Damn!" Zach glanced up and down the hallway, then pulled Elyse in the opposite direction from the staircase.

"I thought you knew a way out of here," Elyse complained.

He pulled her into one room and then another, frantically searching the closets. When they again emerged into the hallway, it was clear that time was running out. Voices came from the bottom of the stairs.

"It's got to be here somewhere."

"What has to be here? What the devil are you talking about?" He jerked her around and pulled her toward the stairway.

"What are you doing? They're coming up the stairs. We'll be caught!"

Reaching the end of the hallway, Zach ran his hands over the paneled wood. It had to be here. The voices below them grew louder. They were coming from very near the top landing.

"What are you looking for?" Elyse bit at her lower lip as she watched the landing. She could just see the look on her grand-mother's face at hearing she'd been taken in for questioning after being found disguised as a man at White's Exclusive Club. She groaned.

"This!" Zach announced triumphantly as a section of paneling swung away from the wall, revealing a small compartment. "Every respectable establishment has one. After you." He gestured.

Elyse stared. A set of cables ran the vertical length of the compartment. It was approximately two feet deep, of the same width, and perhaps four feet high. At the moment it was occupied by a silver service cleared from one of the rooms. It was a servant's lift.

She began to protest. "You must be joking. There's no way we can both fit in there."

"Then you can wait until I send it back up," Zach informed her as he climbed inside, ducking his head.

Panic seized her at the sound of voices, much closer now. She knew perfectly well there'd be no time for her to escape if she didn't get in immediately. Whoever belonged to those voices would be at the top of the stairs within a matter of seconds. And she was certain they weren't club members returning to resume their activities.

Quickly climbing into the lift, Elyse found herself sitting upon the Count de Cuervo's lap. He immediately tucked her legs in and closed the panel, plunging them into complete darkness.

When he pulled on the wooden handle attached to the release, the compartment immediately began a slow downward descent.

In the cramped darkness of their cocoon, Elyse fumed. "Please move your hand," she said sharply, and tried to shift her position. "There's no need to hold onto me. I can't possibly go anywhere."

"I was merely trying to reassure myself that you weren't a man." Zach smothered a deep chuckle. "And please quit wiggling around."

Elyse tried to sit up straight so that they had as little physical contact as possible, and cracked her head on the low ceiling of the lift.

"Great balls of fire! I must be crazy to have let you talk me into this."

"Crazy perhaps, but I assure you that I had nothing to do with it. You managed this all by yourself." Zach shifted, bringing himself closer to her, enjoying the pressure of her soft curves. He smiled, trying to visualize the expression on her face as she let out an exasperated sigh. He knew there was no question about the way her eyes looked at that moment—a brilliant blue. And undoubtedly they were ablaze with the tiny lights that gave her mood away. The lift gently bumped to a stop.

"I think we've arrived," he announced with maddening humor. After hesitating a long moment, he asked, "Shall we stay in here the rest of the night, or take our chances on the outside?"

Struggling from her cramped position, Elyse braced both feet against the door and pushed decisively. "Outside," she announced, holding her breath in apprehension. What if someone had seen them crawl into the compartment and was waiting for them even now? She tumbled out into the dimly lit kitchen.

Zach crawled out after her, feeling a twinge of regret that their intimate ride was over. Confined quarters in total darkness did have its advantages. His eyes quickly adjusted as he looked for the storage closet Fatima had spoken of. Locating the brick wall, he leaned his full weight against it. The wall groaned faintly as it moved aside.

"Isn't that convenient!" Elyse remarked from behind him. "An escape tunnel for the members of the club. I wonder how many times they've had to use it."

"Evidently not all the members were informed about it," he remarked wryly, thinking of the mad scurrying of the half-naked old men upstairs.

"Where does it lead?" Elyse poked her head inside, sniffing the air that was oddly dry. There wasn't a trace of the damp coolness she'd expected.

"Hopefully a safe distance away." Zach turned to her. "By the way, do you usually prefer dressing in men's clothes?"

"Only when it suits me," she replied tartly. "Actually, I find it's a great advantage when I want to move about unnoticed."

"In disguise," he added with a faint trace of humor.

"Exactly."

172

When she tried to move past him, Zach reached out and snatched the man's wig from her head.

Elyse gasped as her thick mane of hair tumbled past her shoulders.

"Impostor!" he accused, a devilish smile curving his lips as he moved past her into the passage.

Behind her, the brick wall groaned back into place. Elyse scampered after him.

"Great balls of fire, he's an impossible man!" she declared as she proceeded into pitch black darkness, feeling her away along. "And he has the nerve to call me an impostor!"

She came right up behind the Count de Cuervo, and like it or not, it was impossible to deny the relief she felt when he reached behind him, finding her hand. With the sure-footedness of a cat, he moved stealthily through the narrow passage. Elyse tried to count their steps.

"You're very good at this," she remarked, her words spoken into his back as he came to an abrupt halt. "I'd almost think you'd done it before. This is not exactly the sort of skill a Spanish count would come by in his usual activities."

Although it was hardly necessary, Zach drew her to his side. "Or a proper English lady for that matter," he countered wryly. "And be quiet. I'm listening."

"For what?" Her response was immediately muffled by a hand across her mouth. She jerked it away. "I can't breathe!"

Zach smiled under the cover of complete darkness. "I think I found it."

"What?"

"The other door, of course. This passage has to come out somewhere." His hand closed over hers in alarm. "What was that?"

Elyse swallowed back her own panic at the grating sound. "It came from behind us."

"Come on, my little impostor. It's time to get out of here." Releasing her hand, Zach felt all along the end wall for some sort of release mechanism. His fingers brushed against a steel handle. Applying all of his strength, he released the lever and emerged into a subchamber of another building. Elyse quickly scrambled after him, blinking uncertainly in the meager light.

"We've got to get out of here." Zach abruptly swung the heavy door shut, and shoved a thick bolt into place. He was glad that Fatima and her people hadn't done that. Whoever was behind them wouldn't be able to follow from this end, but it might be only

173

a matter of minutes before the constables entered this building through the front door. He seized her arm, and headed toward a wooden stairway that led up to the next floor.

"Wait!" Elyse hissed frantically, pulling back on his hand.

"What the devil?" Zach whirled around.

"I'm caught!"

Sure enough, the seat of her pants, a little too big for her slender build, was caught fast in the bolted door.

"There's no time." Zach rushed back to help as she frantically tried to free the woolen fabric. "If I unbolt that door, they'll be through it in an instant." He pulled on the back of her pants.

Fear shafted through Elyse. "Don't you dare leave me!" she cried out.

Zach's head came up, and their gazes locked in a brief moment of vague recognition. It was ridiculous. This whole thing was ridiculous, yet inexplicably her words touched something deep inside him. He smiled softly as he reached up to stroke her cheek. She was so beautiful. Unbidden, words came to him, seemingly from nowhere.

"I'll never leave you, lovely Lis." His heart seemed to speak the words from long ago. "Don't you know that?"

"Who are you?" Elyse whispered, trying to see beyond the fog of half-forgotten memories.

Just as quickly as it came, the moment was shattered by the sounds their pursuers made on the other side of the door.

"You'll have to take them off."

Mesmerized by his closeness and the confusion of the preceding moment, Elyse blinked uncertainly. "Take them off?"

Zach smiled. "Your pants. And I'd suggest right away by the sounds coming from beyond that door. It'll only take them a moment to figure out we locked it from the other side."

"Take off my pants?"

Zach clamped a hand over her mouth. "Off!" he hissed against her cheek. "Or I'll take them off for you." When he felt fairly certain she wouldn't scream, he drew his hand away.

And so he would, Zach thought with a vengeance. But she had little time to dwell on her anger at him, for the pounding on the door became more persistent. She gasped as she pulled frantically on her trapped pants in a last effort to free them. Then she looked up with startled eyes as the Count de Cuervo turned and headed for the stairs.

"I thought you said you would never leave me," she hissed at him, meanwhile jerking wildly on the wool fabric. Instead of firing some stinging comment back at her, he hesitated at the first step.

"What do you hear now?"

"Nothing!" she spat back at him. Her eyes widened.

Nothing. They were gone. That meant they would be here in a very short time. She'd never doubted that whoever had followed them into that passage would be clever enough to search this building. She groaned, knowing there was no other choice.

"Lis!" Zach growled at her.

"I'm coming! I'm coming." Much more quickly than she had donned them earlier that day, Elyse slipped out of the pants. She winced as she glanced down at her bare legs. Refusing to go without undergarments, she'd worn a pair of the skimpy silk pantalets she'd improvised for wearing on her early morning rides. The seamstress had practically had a fit when she'd insisted they be made for her. They were only one layer of thin silk, cut to just the top of her thighs. With a narrow strip of ribbon drawstring securing them at the waist, they left little to the imaginition.

"Don't you dare look!" she commanded as she kicked off the cumbersome shoes and stripped away the men's garters and socks. She refused to be seen in such ridiculous attire. Barefoot and barelegged, she came up behind the Count de Cuervo.

Zach glanced briefly in her direction.

"Don't peek, just walk! I'm right behind you."

"That is a very intriguing notion." He forced back a smile. He hadn't been wrong. Miss Elyse Winslow was a very beautiful young woman and she had exceptionally long, slender legs. He'd seen many women in varied states of undress, including the voluptuous Fatima just that evening during her performance, but none could compare with the winsome beauty who now clung to him like a shadow.

"Have you thought about what you're going to do when we get out of this building? The night air can be quite cool," he quipped, ducking as she aimed a fist at his head.

"Just get us out of here."

Actually, getting out of the building was easy, much easier than either of them had expected. Judging by the offices they passed in the hallway, it was obviously some sort of professional building. Light from the streetlamps outside filtered through windows, creating vague shadows in the halls but easing their passage. In a matter of minutes, Zach guided them away from the front of the building and out through a service entrance at the back. Elyse stepped out into the darkness after him.

"What now?" she whispered.

"You're going to stay here," Zach informed her, stepping away from the back of the building into the alleyway.

"What? You're leaving me?" She was aghast.

"Only for a few minutes. I have to see about a coach. I don't think you really want to be seen parading about the streets of London at this time of night in your silk underwear."

She threw him a murderous glare. "If you'll remember, it's your fault I don't have my pants. Wait!" she called frantically after him when she realized he really did intend to leave her.

Zach turned and quickly retraced his steps. Without a word, he stripped off his jacket. Slipping his arms about her waist, he wrapped it around her hips. He lingered for a moment, and then, as if he'd suddenly decided something, tilted his head down, lightly brushing his lips against hers. Fleetingly, they recaptured the earlier feeling that everything between them seemed dearly familiar.

Instead of protesting, her lips parted softly under his. Zach groaned. If he stayed neither of them would get out of there. He gently pushed her away.

"I'm going with you," she informed him, not trusting him in spite of that kiss. To a man like the Count de Cuervo, it meant nothing. After all, he'd left her in the Woods without a horse. What was to stop him from leaving her now?

"You're staying here. There's no telling what I'll find out there." He indicated the street that fronted both buildings. "I'll be back."

"Promise?" she whispered after him, trying to make light of it. There was nothing light or playful in his smoldering gaze when he briefly turned back to her.

"Promise." And then he was gone, blending into the shadows as if he were nothing more than an apparition.

Elyse shivered faintly, and drew the coat more closely about her. It wasn't cold out; hardly a breath of a breeze stirred. But inexplicably she felt as if she'd been touched by something out of a memory. It frightened and fascinated her.

It seemed an eternity before he returned. She'd almost believed he had gone off and left her again. But like the cat he'd reminded her of earlier, he suddenly reappeared at her side.

"Come with me." Seizing her hand, he led her in the opposite direction.

"Did you find a coach?"

Without answering, he pulled her down an adjacent alley and then another. It seemed they wound their way blindly for several minutes before they turned into another alley and almost came face to face with two uniformed officers, gas lanterns in their hands. He jerked Elyse into the shadows of a recessed doorway, and they both held their breath as the officers passed by without noticing them.

Elyse only had a moment to catch her breath, for they then ducked down another alley. Emerging at its end, they rounded the corner and practically ran right into a team of horses. She froze.

"That you, Cap'n?" came the soft whisper.

"Aye, Sandy. Thank God you're here."

Captain? The greeting caught her by surprise. And he'd responded with such easy familiarity. Elyse tucked that little bit of information away as she followed him to the waiting carriage. The man called Sandy turned up the wick on the coach lantern to light their way.

"That's the last of em, Cap'n. I heard one of them fellas say they was returnin' to that fancy club."

"Very well, Sandy." Zach stood aside and held the door open for Elyse.

As she reached up to take the handle, Sandy let out a low, soft whistle, and Elyse's startled gaze fell to her exposed legs. She was quickly assisted the remainder of the way into the coach. Just as the Count de Cuervo was about to enter behind her, a warning shout came from down the street.

"Get us out of here!" Zach ordered, pushing her unceremoniously to the floor.

Elyse felt the forward lunge of the coach, and then she was smothered by a strong male body as the count fell full across her. Anything she might have said was buried in his shoulder as they lay together on the floor, pinned sideways between the seats.

Something Lucy had said flashed through her mind as she struggled to right herself and was rewarded by the pressure of shoulder against her breast. She wondered if this was what her friend had meant when she'd referred to making love in a coach.

Their legs and bodies were certainly hopelessly entangled. She should have been angry. At the very least, she should fear that they might still be stopped and questioned. Instead all she could do was laugh at the ridiculousness of it all. The evening hadn't turned out at all as she'd expected.

"What the devil are you laughing at?" Zach tried to untangle his

177

long legs from hers and instead became more hopelessly enmeshed with her as the coach careened sideways down the street.

Any response was muffled against his chest. Grabbing the edge of the seat, Elyse struggled to sit upright and immediately realized the danger in doing so as she came up fully astride the Count de Cuervo.

"I can't say much for your methods, but I applaud the results," he quipped, a devilish gleam in his eye.

"You would say something like that!" Elyse flashed at him, just before she was thrown full-length against his body.

Instinctively, Zach's arms closed around her slender waist even as her hands flattened against his chest, trying to wedge distance between them.

"I'm afraid it's no use, lovely Lis. Sandy is not the best driver in the world. You might as well give up and enjoy the ride."

"Let go!" She struggled further, only to be flattened against his body at the next corner. Finally she gave up, deciding there were worse things than being in close proximity to such a maddeningly arrogant man, worse things such as the broken bones she would surely have if she tried to move around.

The coach turned sharply left, then quickly right, then ground to a bone-jarring stop. Elyse groaned as she tried to push away from him. But she wasn't quick enough. The driver jerked open the door.

Sandy coughed loudly as he whirled back around. "Er . . . ah . . . sorry sir," he apologized.

Elyse wanted to die. She wanted to crawl into the nearest hole and pull the sides in after her. As it was, she could do neither.

"Let me up!" she ground out, her mortification complete for she could well imagine the full view the driver had been given.

"I'm trying to." Zach winced at the sharp edge of the seat cutting into the back of his shoulder. By moving one arm he could twist over, wedge a knee in between her legs, and push himself off the floor of the coach.

"What are you doing?" Elyse gasped at the intimate thrust of his knee between her own.

"Trying to let you up. Lie still!" he commanded.

"Oh no!" She twisted under him, only managing to wedge their hips more tightly together, aware that the coachman stood just outside, probably enjoying the best performance he'd seen in years.

Leaning over, Zach fastened on her a mesmerizing smile.

"Lovely Lis, I'd like nothing better than to lie with you like this for the rest of the night. But there is the matter of your reputation."

"And yours!" she snapped.

"Precisely so. Now if you will please move your bottom." For emphasis, his hand closed over her hip, bare except for the filmy silk pants, and he gently lifted her, freeing his pinned knee. "There. You see, easily done."

Intent on pushing him away, her hands found his shoulders. When his fingers had closed over her hip, her grip had involuntarily tightened.

"Easily done," she whispered shakily, still affected by that intimate contact, her anger now replaced by something far more dangerous.

His hand lingered at her hip, the fingers fanning out across the gentle curve of her bottom. Zach breathed out slowly. Damn! What was happening? What was it about her? Every time he was near her, he found it impossible to keep his hands off her. His voice was tight as he rose up on one knee, cool air rushing between their bodies as he offered his hand.

"Good God! What's happened?" A voice greeted them.

Elyse emerged from the coach as a portly gentleman came down the steps of an imposing house, lantern in hand. She immediately recognized the residence as the London home of Lord and Lady Vale.

"What in the name of . . . ?"

The man was immediately cut off by the count.

"There was a bit of trouble this evening. Don't ask any questions. I believe you've met Miss Winslow." He made the cursory introduction as he pulled Elyse along behind him up the steps of the impressive entrance to the large house.

"Winslow?" The older man was left to ponder in their wake. "Good God! You don't mean Barrington's fiancée?"

She could have died right then and there, but she wasn't even given the time to contemplate doing so. Instead she was whisked up the stairs and through the front doors.

"Where are the servants?" the count demanded.

"Asleep at this time of night," the portly man answered. Elyse remembered he'd been introduced as the count's uncle.

"Good. I want nothing said of this to anyone." After giving his instructions, the count turned toward the wide sweeping staircase.

Any objections she might have voiced were quickly forgotten as Elyse struggled to keep her feet under her and to navigate the

stairs without falling. As they reached the top landing, the Count de Cuervo paused, then pulled her along behind him, opened a closed door, and propelled her into a room. She immediately whirled around.

"What do you think you're doing?"

He turned up the gas lamp on the wall, his disconcerting silver gaze locking with hers and then slowly lowering to take in slender bare legs before traveling back up to her face.

"You'll have to spend the night here," he informed her matter-of-factly, as if it were nothing unusual for him to return home of an evening with a woman and then drag her up to one of his bedrooms.

His long slow perusal had done nothing to improve Elyse's humor. She squared her slender shoulders. "No. I won't," she responded with equal determination. "I appreciate your getting me out of there this evening, but I now insist upon returning home."

"Home?" Zach mused thoughtfully. "Dressed like that?" He gestured to her odd costume.

"I can't believe that you're concerned for my reputation."

"Not at all. I'm concerned for mine."

"Of all the . . . !" Elyse's eyes flashed. "I don't give a damn about your reputation. I want to go home. Now!" She stamped a bare foot for emphasis.

"I assure you, I'd like nothing better. But under the present circumstances it's impossible. Unless, of course," he added, with a maddeningly arrogant tilt of his golden brows, "you have made other arrangements for the evening."

Elyse shifted uncomfortably.

"Just what were your plans for returning home this evening, Miss Winslow?"

She stiffened at the condescending note in his voice. "Lucy and I were to return to her house," she announced archly. "But that was before you intruded with that ridiculous scheme involving Fatima."

"I see. And I suppose you hold me to blame for everything else that happened this evening."

"Well, not exactly everything, but if you hadn't interfered, I would have gotten out well ahead of the police."

Zach leaned back against the doorway. "Is that so?"

She gave her head a defiant toss. "Yes, that's so." A maddening smile curved his handsome lips, and despite their tumbling about in the coach the eyepatch was still firmly in place over his right eye.

"That's where you're wrong, my dear," he informed her calmly.

"When I arranged that little trick with Fatima, Maitland had already discovered his wife's part in this little charade of yours."

Elyse swallowed. He had heard their little exchange at the front door as Lucy and Andrew were leaving.

"He didn't seem very amused by your little escapade. I'll warrant you won't be a welcome guest in his home this evening."

He was right of course. It would be weeks before Andrew spoke to her again. The evening was a complete fiasco. She'd have to make it up to Lucy. But tonight was definitely not the time to do it.

"Then you'll just take me home," she announced coolly, aggravated by his arrogant attitude and by the fact that he was absolutely right about the outcome of the evening.

"And return you to your grandmother's loving arms dressed like that?" He gestured to her bare legs and the once-immaculate evening jacket, now soiled from their crawling along hidden passages and running through dingy alleyways.

"I hardly think so. She'll take one look at you and Barrington will be over here with a pistol to defend your honor. No thank you. I have business with Barrington, and I'll not see it jeopardized simply because you haven't more sense than to go where you're not invited."

"Not invited!" The words exploded from her mouth.

"And furthermore," he continued with aggravating calm, "the streets of London are crawling with police. They're questioning everyone they see, trying to find that murderer. If I tried to get you home at this time of night, I guarantee we'd be stopped, and I don't want to have to explain your current state of undress to the authorities. So you see, lovely Lis, you have no choice but to remain here for the night." He turned in the doorway, one hand resting casually on the knob.

"I think you'll be comfortable, and we'll see what's to be done about you in the morning."

With that, he turned on his heel and left, the door closing behind him, ending their conversation. Or rather his conversation, she thought angrily. She'd hardly been able to get a word in edgewise.

Hands planted firmly on her hips, Elyse mimicked his parting words; " 'We'll decide what's to be done about you in the morning.' " Morosely, she flounced onto the brocade coverlet on the bed. The most aggravating part of it was that he was right. Arms folded, she pulled her knees up, drawing herself into a tight ball. She groaned at looking down at her bare legs. The room was

181

cool, causing her to shiver faintly. But she wouldn't get under the covers! She wouldn't!

Elyse almost laughed out loud at the absurdity of the entire evening. She'd really gotten herself into a fine mess. And like it or not, there was no one else she could blame for the way everything had turned out, not even the Count de Cuervo.

"Impostor!" she grumbled into the silence of the room. And he had the nerve to call her one! Morosely, she wondered what had become of Jerrold, then snorted out loud, as she recalled that he'd seemed to be doing very well for himself right up to the point where she'd been forced to go upstairs with Fatima. He'd been far too occupied with the young dancer in his arms to give her a second glance, and he hadn't been among the half-naked men running about when the police had arrived.

No, she thought, experiencing a feeling that was part disappointment, part anger; Jerrold was far too clever to be caught in a compromising position, either by the authorities or herself. And with that thought, Elyse was forced to confront something she'd ignored during the past months.

She remembered the day Jerrold had asked for her hand in marriage. He'd been calling on her for several months to the exclusion of practically every other woman, except his mistress. Her grandmother had been certain a proposal was imminent, and it had been clear Lady Regina was ecstatic at thinking her granddaughter might marry the son of her dearest friend. And Elyse had to admit that at first she'd been flattered by Jerrold's constant and lavish attentions.

But that had ended the day he'd taken her riding in Kensington Gardens and finally tendered his offer. He'd spoken of family honor and duty, and of all sorts of ridiculous notions about preserving the Barrington lineage. She'd ignored most of it, but the part she hadn't able to ignore was that fact that he'd never once said he loved her. Oh, he cared for her, and as she'd learned on several different occasions, he desired her. But love was an entirely different matter.

Love came slowly, gradually, her grandmother had assured her. Lucy Maitland had refused to comment, but Elyse knew her feelings. Worse, she had the nagging doubt that this marriage was a business arrangement, clear and simple. Jerrold needed a wife, a lady suitable to bear the title of Lady Barrington and the sons he wanted.

She should have been stunned, but she wasn't. This was how

many marriages came about within the circle of her grandmother's acquaintances; alliances were made for the convenience of inheritance. And she'd grown terribly bored with the endless rounds of balls, garden parties, and outings to the country—all for the sake of finding her a proper husband. In the end, when Jerrold had proposed, she'd almost found it a relief to think she wouldn't be subjected to them any longer. As Lady Barrington, everything would be different. But as the months passed and rumors of Jerrold's romantic dalliances continued, Elyse had realized not everything would be different, but eventually she'd come to accept it.

In spite of the promise she'd made herself, Elyse curled up on the satiny coverlet. She didn't want to think about any of this now. After all, it didn't matter. In just a little over a week, she and Jerrold would be married and it would be done with. She closed her eyes for just a moment, thinking what a devilish turn of events it was that she was spending the night in this house with another man.

Then fatigue washed through her and she snuggled deeper into the coverlet. She had to think of a way to get home.

"What are we going to do with me in the morning?" she murmured sleepily.

Having said good night to Tobias and Sandy, Zach paced the room he'd taken for his own. After tossing down a third brandy, he reclined in a chair, rolling his head back against its upholstered back. Tonight could have been disastrous for his plans if he'd been stopped by the authorities and questioned. He smiled faintly as he thought of their escape. Staring up at the ceiling, he tried to imagine what Elyse was doing and thinking at that moment.

Would she be angry? Yes, he was certain of it. He'd seen fire leap into her eyes when he'd delivered his little speech upstairs over an hour earlier. Admittedly, he hadn't given her any choice. He hadn't wanted to, knowing she'd probably have wakened the entire household if he had.

Dear God, what was he doing here, hobnobbing with Barrington and the men who daily made the decisions that virtually controlled his life and had controlled his father's?

The answer was in the question, but it seemed he was no closer to learning the truth than when he'd first arrived in England. The only thing he knew for certain was that Jerrold Barrington's

183

mother had once known his father.

Zach tossed down a fourth brandy, trying to ease the tension from his muscles. Felicia Barrington.

Through the faint glow brought on by the brandy, some vague thought teased at him. Felicia.

Lis. Her name slipped across his senses. Eyes closed, he could hear the soft whispers. He was on the deck of a ship, the mist parting and rolling out to sea. The sun was bright overhead; sails billowed against a cobalt sky.

I knew you'd come back to me.

She reached out to him and her words were like the breath of the wind, a promise of faith and eternal love. Her skin was velvet soft beneath his fingers as he caressed her cheek, living again some moment he knew in his soul they'd shared before. She stepped into his embrace, her slender body molding to his. Her face was upturned, her lips parted to voice some soft endearment. He kissed her, time and place slipping away from reality as he surrendered to the desire. Every moment he'd lived, all the loneliness of endless days without her—these were obliterated in that one instant of surrender. He drank of her, breathed of her, and felt life begin again in her arms. *I'll never leave you.* He whispered the timeless promise against her throat.

Hands shaking, sweat beaded across his forehead, Zach came up out of the chair. He was as cold as ice and yet his shirt was plastered to his skin. Raking his fingers through his hair, he realized he must have been dreaming. But it was so real; she was so real. Damn! He hurled the empty brandy glass against the far wall. Who was she?

Zach whirled toward the door. He was tired, confused, and angry. Every fiber of muscle and sinew felt like a gaping wound. Since that first meeting she'd haunted him. Not a moment passed that he didn't find himself thinking of her, wanting to see her again and knowing the danger if he did so. She represented everything he loathed, the nobility and England.

Liar, he said to himself. He knew she'd haunted him since he'd discovered the pendant, and perhaps had haunted him forever. Truth warred with his emotions. *She's the reason you came here.*

"Damn you!" Zach shouted and, going to the door to her room, threw it back hard on its hinges.

Startled awake, Elyse cried out. She stared at him wide-eyed. She was slow to react, sleep drugging her senses. Fascination was now laced with fear. He was silhouetted in the doorway, like some

ghostly apparition. Her heart hammered, her blood roared in her veins.

"No!" she whispered desperately, backing away on the bed. "You're not real," she choked out, tears pooling in her eyes. Silver light shafted through open windows, illuminating his gold hair, the hard planes of his body, the cold anger in his gaze. She shook her head in denial.

"I know you're not real. You can't be!"

"Who are you?" His voice ached with pain. "Dammit! Who are you?" Zach tore across the room, descending on the bed, fury glinting in his gray gaze.

"You know who I am," Elyse whispered brokenly.

"No!" he roared, grabbing at her as she tried to crawl further away. His fingers closed over her hair and twisted around it, pulling her back cruelly.

Elyse's hand instinctively flew to his. "You're hurting me," she cried out. Then she said defiantly, "Let me go!"

A trembling in her voice reached through the cold wall of his anger; the glistening depths of her eyes melted his pain.

Suddenly his questions didn't matter. Nothing mattered; not the uncertainty, the haunting questions, or the anger. She was here, warm and soft within his grasp.

"I don't care who you are," he whispered achingly, all traces of anger slipping away. His hands trembled through her hair. "I don't care." He bent over her upturned face, his mouth drawn to the tears wetting her cheeks.

Each breath was an ache in her lungs. Her lips quivered as his face shadowed hers. "Please!" she cried softly, "I can't bear it if you're not real."

Zach's fingers grazed her cheek with aching tenderness. Her tears pooled at his fingertips.

"I am real. And I'm damned," he breathed. Leaning over, he gently stroked her hair. Burying his hands in soft sable tangles, he gazed wondrously at her upturned face, feeling the magic of those magnificent eyes stealing into him.

"I know it's wrong," he whispered achingly. "But I can't leave you, my lovely, lovely lady." He groaned helplessly as his mouth closed over hers.

Restraint shattered, and Elyse's hands twisted in the soft fabric of his shirt. She feared holding onto him, feared letting go. A sob escaped her as he cradled her face, caressing the corners of her mouth with his lips, kissing the tears from her eyes.

185

Zach's hands trembled as they slipped over her shoulders. "Lis . . . Lis." Over and over again he whispered her name, like a pleading prayer. His breath caressed the hollow at her throat as he savored the sweetness of her skin. She was forbidden to him. He knew it. But none of that mattered. Those first words she'd said days ago echoed in his mind again and again as he plundered the sweet softness of her mouth.

She cried out at the exquisite pleasure of his mouth bruising hers. "You weren't supposed to be real," she whispered, her voice thick with passion. "You're from my dreams, a phantom. Nothing more."

His lips caressed hers. "I'm as real as you are, flesh and blood." Taking her hand, he pressed her palm against his heart. "Touch me. For God's sake, Lis, touch me." His voice was harsh with emotion, and then inexplicably tender. "I've come so far to find you." The words tumbled mindlessly from him between kisses. He couldn't get enough of her, couldn't seem to touch or taste her without wanting more.

Elyse shuddered as passion wakened in her. Her vivid blue eyes shaded to darkest smoke. So long. It had been so long, and now he was here. And he was real! Her lips ached for his kisses, her hands longed for the touch of his skin. She swept the shirt from his shoulders in a gesture of almost desperate longing.

"Yes," she whispered against his throat as desire rocked through her. "Yes! You are real. I knew you'd come back to me," she whispered fiercely against his bared shoulder. Now there was no fear or uncertainty. Only the passion that swept it all away on the breath of a timeless wind. Her hands moved over him with loving familiarity. Her fingers slipped possessively across the gleaming planes of his chest and she followed their path with her lips, tasting, renewing, remembering.

Reason was obliterated. There was no need of it with this man she'd loved through countless lifetimes. She shuddered as his fingers trembled across her heated flesh, kneading, massaging, stroking. Hands capable of such strength caressed with such infinite tenderness. With passion-filled eyes, she placed her hand over his, closing his fingers over her breast.

"Yes," Elyse breathed as her other hand slipped behind his neck, her mouth hungry beneath his. "Yes, my love." Slowly, they drifted down onto the bed, her slender body welcoming his hard strength.

Time slipped away as he began loving her with his hands and mouth. Everywhere he touched her, his lips followed, and when his

mouth returned to hers she pleaded for something she could never have understood in this lifetime.

When she was certain she could endure no more, he stunned her with new awareness. She lay like a leaf trembling before a mighty wind as he feathered kisses down her throat, in the hollow below her shoulder, his lips teasing at the taut fullness of her breasts. He trailed a wet path around each, his tongue moving in increasingly smaller circles until she cried out.

With a hungering of the soul, Zach drew first one tautened bud and then the other between his teeth, teasing with his tongue, tasting the creamy sweetness of each throbbing, hardened peak.

Her hands moved possessively over ribs encased by hardened muscles. Then lower, exploring his body, needing to feel flesh and muscle, reacquainting herself with every corded sinew, each contour of taut skin.

"You are real, so real," she whispered, her eyes closing at the exquisite pleasure of his body against hers. Desire fanned white-hot across her every nerve ending. She hungered, thirsted for him.

Curse or destiny? He only knew some invisible force had brought them together. Like a madman he felt himself being consumed by desire, and was powerless to stop it. Her words echoed over and over in his soul. He'd lost all reason, all comprehension of time or place. He caressed, teased, and tormented until she was soft and damp and crying out for him.

Her fingers traced the prominence of his cheekbones, then his soft gold lashes and straight brows. Hands tangled in his hair, stroked his shoulders and back, nails dug into his flesh.

Every last shred of his control disappeared as her hand lowered to his abdomen. Muscles leaping in response, Zach groaned, closing her slender fingers over his engorged flesh. Her soft whispers ignited a fire in him.

"Please," she begged against his lips, not comprehending what it was she asked for, knowing only that she was compelled to love this man completely.

Zach moaned, his fingers bruising her soft skin as he lifted her hips. Gently he parted her soft wetness, the probing hardness of his flesh pressing into her waiting heat. Even as desire spiraled through him, some indefinable need to be gentle guided him. He felt the tensing hesitation, her body's resistance, and the slow molding of her young muscles around him, easing him deeper inside her.

Elyse cried out at the burgeoning ache. But the momentary flash

of pain was obliterated as his mouth came down on hers and her soft cries became gentle whimpers of longing. His fingers stroked damp hair back from her forehead as he whispered tender endearments.

His lean thighs were entwined with hers as he slowly stroked deeper inside her. He kissed tears of lost innocence from the corners of her eyes. Then he kissed her lips, tasting the wondrous sweetness of her mouth.

"Lis," he whispered against her throat as her breathing came more quickly. Her back arched, and she braced her hands against his shoulders as he withdrew then entered her again, and again.

Elyse gasped as he stroked hard within her. His mouth crushed down on hers, caressing her until pain became pleasure. Again and again his glistening flesh shafted into her, purging the loneliness. The muscles of her young body quickened deep inside, and she writhed at the exquisite torture that was both pain and pleasure. Each time he withdrew she feared it was ended, and each time he entered her was like the first time, only sweeter. An inexplicable urgency swept through her carrying her toward oblivion.

In her soul, she knew this lover who came to her from across the millenniums of time. They were not bound by the stars in the galaxies. They were travelers who transcended this world, and worlds beyond. She'd searched her dreams for him. He was her guide through the darkness to the fiery light of passion, found before and now renewed with each kiss, every caress, each hard thrust into her. The heat of his hands on her skin was an awakening memory. He rose above her, the muscles in his arms heavily corded, beads of sweat like drops of gold on his skin as her body welcomed him, bathed him. For a brief instant he was suspended above her, like the bright sun in the universe, and then he was earthbound, his body plunging into hers.

Elyse cried out. It began as a flickering flame then burst into an inferno that spread its fury along every nerve ending. She felt as if she were dying and being reborn in the same instant. If I'm dreaming, she thought, let me never awaken; if I'm awake, let me never sleep.

The desire was mindless, insane, and it was his master. His hands closed over hers, their fingers entwining. With aching need, his lips silenced the cry that tore from her throat. He wanted to deny the desire, deny her and the intangible force that had driven him to her.

But he could no more deny what built between them than he could deny the wind. She would hate him tomorrow, and he would hate himself for being the cause of it. But now all barriers were stripped away. He would take these few hours of love, like a beggar; this one night would be a bulwark against all the empty nights that had passed before and would come again.

She was his until the dawn.

Chapter Nine

"Have you completely lost your mind?" Tobias confronted Zach in the library of Lord Vale's home. "She's Lady Winslow's granddaughter, engaged to young Lord Barrington, and you bring her here? Good God, man! What were you thinking?"

Zach slammed the china cup down so hard on the saucer that it shattered beneath his hand. He never even winced as blood seeped between his spread fingers. "And where exactly was I to take her? The streets were filled with police. It was after midnight. I couldn't simply take her home and explain to Lady Winslow that her granddaughter had spent the evening with me at an exclusive men's club."

For the first time in many weeks, Tobias was sober, just when Zach wished his friend were upstairs sleeping off the effects of the night before.

"And what do you presume to do this morning? How do you think you can explain to her grandmother and Lord Barrington that she spent the night in this house? Yer gettin' in too deep, lad. This whole thing is too tricky. And do you think Miss Winslow will play along with whatever explanation you come up with?" He bellowed at the younger man, not caring that lack of sleep and this new problem made Zach's mood dangerous.

"And what good will it do if you bleed to death?" Tobias raged. Seizing a linen handkerchief from the silver service he'd brought in earlier, he bound Zach's hand.

Zach smiled faintly despite the old man's grumbling. Then memories of the night before made him grim. Regret was sharp. He must have been insane to go to her last night. Even now he didn't understand it. He was angry, angrier than he could ever remember being before. Angry at her and her intrusion into his life.

But not even anger could explain everything. It was as if a madness had come over him, driving him to her. If he could only

190

have those hours back . . .

No, if he had them back, he'd make love to her again. And if he did, he knew he'd never be able to walk away from her. He pressed his fingers into his temples, trying to drive the memory of those last hours from his thoughts. What was it about her that haunted him?

He looked up, pain lining his face as Tobias deliberately jerked the makeshift bandage tighter.

"She'll cooperate because she doesn't want anyone to know she was at that club last night." His eyes hardened. "She especially doesn't want to jeopardize her betrothal to Barrington. The man's wealth and title mean far too much to her. That's why I want you to talk to her."

"Me?" Tobias's gaze narrowed. "What makes you think she'll listen to me?"

Zach fixed his eyes on the distant wall, images of the recent hours of passion playing across his thoughts. "She'll have her reasons for not wanting to see me this morning." His gaze whipped back to Tobias's, but he did not quite cover his emotions quickly enough. His smile was ironic. "She thinks I'm an impostor."

He didn't need to say what he was thinking. It was written all over his face.

Tobias scrutinized his young friend. "Just what did happen between you and that girl last night?"

Zach's gray gaze leveled with his. "That, my friend, is none of your business," he said curtly. He was tired, this mess with Elyse had only made the stay in London more precarious, and he still didn't have the information he wanted. Somehow he had to meet with Barrington again. He was confident the man had managed to elude the police the evening before. He pushed aside his own suspicions about Barrington's possible involvement in that girl's murder, telling himself that meant nothing to him.

Tobias shook his head silently, knowing it would do no good to press Zach further. "What do you want me to do?"

"When she awakens, I want you to make arrangements for her return to Lucy Maitland's home. She was to spend the night there. Explain to the Maitlands that I entrusted her to your care and spent last night aboard my ship. That should protect Miss Winslow's reputation." Zach crossed the room and poured coffee into a cup. He hadn't slept the entire night. He hadn't wanted to. His hands shook faintly at the memory of her silken skin and of the passion that came alive when he touched her. Afterward all he wanted was to hold her, forever. As he might have held her before, but not in a very long time.

Seizing a decanter, he added a liberal amount of brandy to the steaming coffee. "I'll be leaving shortly. As far as any of the servants are concerned, I returned to my ship last night." He reached inside the pocket of the pants he'd worn the night before, then threw several hundred-pound notes down on the table. "She'll need clothing, the finest you can buy." His voice was harsh. "After all, a lady must look the part." A lady. Yes, she was a lady; in spite of the man's clothes, in spite of her independent nature. And she was as far removed from him as the truth about his father.

"I will," Tobias replied. "I don't like it, but I'll do it. And pray she goes along with the idea. I'll go up and check on her myself. The sooner she returns home the better, for everyone." He treated himself to his first drink in over twenty-four hours, then shuddered. "I must be getting old. I swear that stuff doesn't taste like it used to." With that he turned, leaving Zach to his tormented thoughts.

Even now, she seemed to possess him. His thoughts were filled with the memory of her in that massive bed, her slender body curled up as when he'd left her. He ached to be the one going to her, felt the heat of her skin against his.

Lis! Damn you! Why do I want you even now? he silently asked.

"No!"

Elyse cried out as she jerked awake. Wide-eyed she stared into the silvery gray of dawn, then ran a hand through the disheveled tangles of her hair. Eyes closed tightly, she tried to hold onto the images that played across her mind.

He'd come to her last night. He was real!

She could still hear his impassioned words, feel the trembling of his hands against her flesh, smell her own fragrance in the heat of their mingling, taste the fierce sweetness of his mouth . . .

Her eyes flew open, a sob catching in her throat. She was alone. He'd seemed so real . . . she'd almost thought she would find him standing there.

Elyse clutched the satin coverlet to her naked body as she fought the frantic beating of her heart. Slowly, like the mist in her dreams, the night before receded until there was only herself and this room. A clock somewhere about chimed softly five times.

As her senses cleared, uneasiness replaced the lethargy of sleep. Her gaze darted about the unfamiliar room, the events of the previous evening coming back to her. Elyse bolted from the canopied bed, gasping as cool morning air slipped over her bare skin.

She seized the tangled bedcovers, jerking them apart in her search for clothing. Then she gasped at seeing the light stain on one sheet. She hadn't been dreaming! She whirled toward the door, as if she expected to find him standing there coolly appraising her with that mocking gaze.

"Damn you!" She hurled the words at the door. "What did you expect to do with me in the morning?" Tears of humiliation and anger welled in her eyes; humiliation at knowing the truth, anger at herself for having allowed it to happen. She tore the sheets from the bed and wadding them into a ball, tossed them against the far wall. Then she stopped, an idea glinting in her emotional blue eyes. She stood completely still and listened.

The house was completely silent except for the ticking of the clock. Five o'clock. Everyone, including the household staff, would be asleep.

"I've got to get out of here," she whispered to herself determinedly. Her gaze fell to her bare legs. She couldn't very well go through London dressed like this, no more than she could have last night. Elyse flounced down on the edge of the bed, trying to sort out her jumbled thoughts.

She needed clothing and a way to get home. But even if she were dressed she couldn't very well hire a hansom cab and alight at her grandmother's front door. Or could she?

Bounding off the bed, Elyse crossed the room. An idea began to take shape. Whenever her grandmother traveled she only took the clothing she needed for the trip. The rest of her things remained behind. She knew Lord and Lady Vale were spending the summer in France, visiting their married daughter and her family. And though they would be away for an extended period of time, Lady Vale wouldn't have taken all her clothing with her. If she had a woman's penchant for new gowns, she'd take only the necessities and purchase whatever else she needed in Paris.

With that hope firmly in mind, Elyse searched the large armoire. It was empty, as were the dressing table drawers. As she looked about the elegant room, she realized the lack of personal items indicated it was probably one of the many guest rooms. Squaring her shoulders, she turned to the door. She would just have to find Lady Vale's room.

Elyse winced as the door creaked. She stepped silently into the hall, flattening herself into the shadows along the wall. Holding her breath, she listened for any sounds of movement on this floor or on the main floor downstairs. After a moment, she let out a sigh of relief and then slipped down the hall in which there were least a half-dozen closed doors.

The fourth room on the far side of the hall brought a triumphant smile to her mouth. This was obviously a lady's room. Early morning light peeked through the slit between closed drapes, spilling on mauve and pink carpeting. There was just enough light in the room to illuminate the outline of the mauve-canopied bed and the dressing table with elaborate gas lamps topped by etched pink chimneys. The lingering sweetness of perfume still clung to the air. Two chairs occupied the sitting area, decorated with pink, lace-edged pillows. Lady Vale certainly preferred pink and mauve. Elyse tiptoed to the large wardrobe.

Lady Vale didn't disappoint her. The closet was overflowing with gowns. She chose one of a light fabric suitable for this time of year. In the meager light it was difficult to select accessories. She took a hat from a hatbox, and selected shoes, obviously several sizes too big, from the bottom of the cabinet. After locating stockings in a nearby drawer, she made a hasty retreat to the room she'd occupied the night before.

Pulling the drapes open wide, Elyse inspected her bounty. She groaned. Pink was obviously Lady Vale's signature color. Gown, slippers, hat, and stockings were all of the same pale color that decorated the room in which she'd found them.

"Why couldn't it be something subtle, gray or blue?" she whispered aloud. "Anything but pink. But I suppose beggars can't be choosers." Sitting on the edge of the bed, she quickly dressed. As she adjusted the neckline of the silk day gown, she looked down at the sagging waist. Obviously she and Lady Vale weren't built quite the same. The garment fit well enough across her breasts, but hung misshapen at her waist and hips. She felt like a child playing at dressing in her mother's gowns.

"This is awful. If I only had a belt." Her eyes rose to the clock. She had to get out of there. In spite of the Count de Cuervo's words the night before about not wanting anyone to know of her presence in the house, she was certain servants would soon be coming upstairs to attend to their daily household chores. She might easily be seen. She dare not risk returning to Lady Vale's room.

Sitting at the dressing table, she stripped off the pink stockings and twisted them into a belt. Securing it about her waist, she smoothed the skirt. It would just have to do. The shoes were another matter. They were entirely too big. Tucking them under her arm, she glanced about the room. Her eyes narrowed. She wasn't about to leave any trace that she'd been there.

Moving quickly about the chamber, Elyse smoothed the bedcovers back into place, minus the one incriminating sheet. She rolled that up and tucked it and the man's shirt under her arm, along with the shoes. She fluffed the pillows, straightened the richly woven rug and pulled the drapes discreetly closed. Satisfied with her quick last inspection, Elyse jerked around at the sound of footsteps outside the door.

After last night, she couldn't imagine the Count de Cuervo bothering with such formalities. It must be a servant. Last night there'd been no one about when they'd arrived at the house. But this morning was an entirely different matter. It would be just like him to humiliate her by informing the household staff he'd had an overnight guest. By midday all of London would know of it. Elyse bit at her lower lip. Knowing she couldn't afford to be seen by anyone, she slipped into the corner beside the tall armoire and held her breath at the light knocking.

As she flattened herself against the wall, she imagined what it must feel like to be a hunted criminal. As if it would make her invisible, she closed her eyes.

She slowly opened them after several moments had passed. Light pooled from the doorway into the shadowy room. Peeking from her hiding place, Elyse saw a short, stout man with graying hair. His hand rested hesitantly on the doorknob as he looked about. Glancing down, she quickly stepped back, pulling in the hem of the oversized gown. Panic seized her as the portly man walked into the room.

Tobias first looked to the bed. It was neatly made, with no trace that anyone had slept in it the night before. The drapes were drawn across the windows. Everything was neat and tidy, completely undisturbed by any occupant. His first thought was that he had the wrong room. He stepped back into the hallway, then realized he'd been right. This was the first door on the left at the top of the stairs. He shot back into the room. Empty. Whirling on his heel he slammed the door hard behind him. She was gone!

Elyse winced as the door rattled in the frame, but she quickly stepped from the corner. If she was correct, the marquis had been sent on a diplomatic mission, and at this very moment, he undoubtedly was on his way to inform the Count de Cuervo that their guest was nowhere to be found.

There was no time to lose. She had to get out of this house!

The rolled bedsheet secured under one arm, the shoes clenched in her hand, Elyse quickly stepped out into the hallway. The main staircase was her only escape. Running to the landing, she leaned over and listened. Downstairs, a door slammed, the echo reverberating up to her. It was foolhardy and she knew it, but there was no other choice. She quickly swept down the staircase, past a formal parlor on one side and a set of closed double doors on the other. Her bare feet were silent against the inlaid wood parquet floors.

"Thunderation!" The word exploded behind her. "I tell you she's gone! Gone!"

Panic-stricken, Elyse raced across the entry. There wasn't time to try the front doors. If they were locked, she was caught. As the marquis emerged from a doorway, his back to her, she ducked around the massive, elegant sideboard inlaid with marble and decorated with a fresh vase of flowers, and hid behind a profusion of late irises, day lilies, and fern fronds.

"That's impossible!" a voice barked sharply in response.

"Then I suggest you see for yourself. The room is empty and spotless. It's as if no one has been there at all," the marquis insisted.

A curse split the air as the Count de Cuervo emerged from the library. "She has to be there!"

Elyse jerked back against the wall, closing her eyes. Dear God! He was just as she remembered—the soft gold of his hair and the sharp planes of his handsome face, defined now by anger. And his visible eyes . . . that same startling shade of gray that was as cold as ice at one moment, like molten silver the next. Her eyes flew open against her will as she stared from the shadows.

Both men raced up the stairway, the Count de Cuervo's longer stride taking the steps two at a time. Elyse didn't have time to consider what she'd seen the night before. As soon as both men were out of sight at the top of the stairs, she crossed the entry to the front door. The latch was quickly thrown, and she escaped into the early dawn.

She found a hansom cab only a half-block from Lord Vale's home. The driver looked at her strangely but said nothing. For the next four hours he obligingly drove practically the entire length and breadth of London. When the shops opened, Elyse purchased a hat that she didn't even bother to try on, and stuffed the sheet and the man's shirt inside the large box.

Just before ten o'clock she waited down the street from Lucy's house. Andrew Maitland was punctual to a fault. Unless she missed her guess he would leave the fashionable abode at Bainbridge Square for his offices in the business district at any moment. Unless of course, he was still so angry with Lucy that he spent the day at home. Looking up, she smiled as the elegant maroon and black coach passed by, the Maitland crest emblazoned on the door.

Thank you, Lucy, she silently breathed and then instructed the driver to pull up to the Maitland house.

Elyse waited impatiently in the front parlor. There'd been no way to slip past the servants. She whirled around at the sound of frantically rustling skirts.

"Good heavens!" Lucy flew into the parlor. Glancing quickly about, she discreetly shut the cream white doors, then immediately crossed the room and took Elyse's hands in hers.

"I couldn't believe it when the butler announced you. I've been frantic all night. Good heavens!" she exclaimed again, taking in Elyse's rather odd costume.

"Not one word!" Elyse threatened. "Don't say a word about what I'm wearing." She pulled back from her friend's embrace.

"All right." Lucy smothered laughter. "At least, not right now. But you'll have to tell me later."

"You have every right to be angry with me." Elyse was determined to clear the air.

Lucy stood back. "You're right. I should be," she admitted. "But it was my own fault for letting you talk me into such a ridiculous scheme. It's a good thing Andrew just left. I don't think he's ready to see you just yet."

"I know," Elyse confessed. "I waited until he'd gone. Do you think he'll ever speak to me again?"

"Maybe in forty or fifty years." Lucy shook her head and then burst out laughing. "I tried to convince him we should go back for you last night, but he thought being left was just what you deserved." She drew Elyse to a nearby settee. "I argued until I was in tears. Finally he turned the carriage around, but when we returned there were police everywhere."

"I know." Elyse reached up to pull Lady Vale's pink hat decorated with satin ribbons and lace flowers from the top of her head. Shuddering, she shoved it aside. "We only got out just ahead of them. I don't know how I would have explained that to grandmother."

"I'm so glad you found Jerrold," Lucy said. "Was he terribly angry?"

Elyse swallowed uneasily. Lucy was her dearest friend and she loved her dearly, but how could she possibly explain where she'd spent the night. It was obvious by her dress that she hadn't been home. She didn't want her friend to know the truth, but the alternative, to allow her to think she'd spend the night with Jerrold, would be even worse, especially if something was accidentally said to him.

"I didn't see Jerrold last night after the police arrived," she confessed.

"But you said he got out. I assumed . . ." Lucy's eyes widened. "He didn't get you out? Do you mean to say you spent the night at the police station?"

"Great balls of fire! No, I didn't spend it at the police station." Elyse came up off the settee and began to pace the floor. She turned to her friend, a ghost of a smile on her lips. "I really could use a bath and clean clothes," she hinted. "And since you are to blame for my being left there—"

"Me!" her friend exclaimed. "If you hadn't talked me into going there neither of us would have been caught." Lucy's gaze narrowed. "There's something you're not telling me," she said accusingly.

"Lucy . . . about that bath? And I'm absolutely starving," Elyse persisted.

"All right. You can bathe in my room, and I know I can find something for you to wear." She made an awful face as she glanced disapprovingly at Elyse's borrowed, pink gown. "That looks like something Lady Vale would wear. Honestly, the woman has the most atrocious taste in clothing." Then she disappeared through the doors to inform the servants to bring a late breakfast upstairs.

On Lady Vale's taste, Elyse couldn't have agreed more.

"The Count de Cuervo?" Lucy Maitland looked as if she were going to faint. It was the first time Elyse had ever seen her friend stunned speechless.

Waiting for Lucy to recover, she closed her eyes in sheer rapture over a mouthful of fresh ham. Hunger had clearly won out over the necessity for a bath. The bath could wait.

"Elyse!"

She swallowed another sip of tea, knowing Lucy would be intolerable until she heard the entire story.

The teapot was empty when she finished almost a half-hour later and rose to eye the bathing chamber off Lucy's room. She'd deliberately left out any details about what had happened after the Count de Cuervo had taken her to Lord Vale's residence.

"Great balls of fire!" Lucy exclaimed, using her friend's favorite phrase. She then collapsed back into the upholstered chair. Just as quickly she sat upright again.

"What's he really like?"

Tea cup in midair, Elyse gulped back her disbelief. Lucy Maitland wasn't at all shocked that she'd spent the night in the house of a stranger. Now she wanted details about the man!

"He's arrogant, overbearing, and impossibly rude!" Elyse set the teacup down with a rattle, then began to untie the stocking belt at her waist. Stepping into the bathing chamber, she quickly shrugged out of the tasteless pink gown. Till now, there'd been absolutely no secrets between her and Lucy. How was she going to keep her friend from finding out what had really happened? She turned the handles atop the wood-encased brass tub. Water rumbled, then burst through the metal pipes. Elyse poured fragrant crystals into the bath from a glass carafe, knowing Lucy wouldn't mind. They burst into luxurious lather, surrounding her aching body as she slipped into the frothy water. She leaned back, closing her eyes, blocking out what had happened the night before.

"Arrogant, overbearing and rude?" Lucy's voice echoed back from the room beyond.

"Exactly," Elyse responded. "I can't stand the man."

"Is that so?" Lucy stood in the doorway to the bathing chamber, a somber expression on her face. She held the incriminating sheet Elyse had taken from the bed in Lord Vale's guest room in her outstretched hands.

"What are you going to do?" Lucy pinned her friend with an insistent gaze.

"Nothing!" Elyse informed her as she sat wrapped in a soft bath sheet.

"Are you in love with him?"

Elyse looked at Lucy as if she'd lost all sanity. "Of course not! How can you think such a thing?"

"Because in all the time you've been engaged to Jerrold, you've never once made love with him. Now the Count de Cuervo comes along and in a matter of weeks—"

"Lucy, please! I don't want to talk about it anymore."

Her friend wasn't about to be put off. She crossed the room, grabbing Elyse by the arms. "I saw it the first time you met him," she said firmly. "And what was it you said? Oh yes. 'I knew you'd come back to me.' Elyse, for God's sake! What is going on? Have you met the man before?"

"Of course not. I never met him before the night of the ball." Elyse shrugged out of her grasp. "And nothing is going on. It was all a mistake. I want to forget it, and I want you to forget it too."

A thought suddenly occurred to Lucy. "My God! Did he force himself on you? If he did—"

Elyse groaned. "No! It wasn't that way at all!"

A strange look appeared in Lucy's eyes. "All right. We won't talk about it after this unless you want to. But there is something you may have to face whether you like it or not."

"What?" Elyse asked, though she already sensed what it might be.

"If he . . ." Lucy began uncertainly. For all their candor with each other and their years of friendship, they'd never discussed this particular aspect of an intimate relationship before.

"That is, when you . . ."

"For heaven's sake. What are you trying to say?"

Her patience gone, Lucy declared bluntly, "If a man stays inside a woman until he's through, there's every chance you could get caught."

Elyse released a shaky breath. "I know," she whispered. "But it doesn't happen every time, or every woman in the world would be constantly with child. You and Andrew have been married for nearly two years and you haven't had a child."

"That's true," Lucy admitted, "but there are certain measures that can be taken when a man and woman don't want to have a child. I have to admit, they sometimes fail, but usually they work. Elyse, I know this is hard." She tried to put it as delicately as possible. "Did he remain with you?"

Elyse shook her head. "Yes. But surely just once . . ."

She breathed out slowly. "It will just have to be all right. And remember, you promised you wouldn't tell anyone. Grandmother would be heartbroken if she knew."

"I'll keep my promise," Lucy solemnly reassured her. "But I think you're making a mistake in going ahead with this marriage. It's not just because of what happened. I've always thought Jerrold was such an odd fish. You're not in love with him, and he won't change his ways. Men like him never do."

"Lucy, please!" Elyse begged. "I don't want to talk about it."

Lucy held up her hands in surrender. "Anyway, I'm glad you

spent the night with the Count de Cuervo. It serves Jerrold right!"

"Lucy!"

Her friend changed the subject. "Now, what are we going to do about today?"

Elyse smiled weakly. "I have to get home. I left word with Katy last night that I intended to spend the night here, but it's late and there's packing to be done for the trip to the country with Jerrold's family. His father is planning a round of parties for all the local people before the wedding."

"Then we must get you home, and act as if nothing unusual happened," Lucy declared.

"What about Andrew? He won't say anything to anyone, will he?"

"Not a chance. He's too worried I might slip and mention something to the wife of one of his friends. I must say, I love the man desperately and he was completely faithful to me even before he found out my disguise, but I'll hold this over his head for a few weeks. It makes him so much more attentive." She smiled confidently. "He won't tell a soul."

Late that afternoon, Elyse bid her friend farewell and swept into Winslow House as if nothing were amiss.

Chivers delivered a message just before dinner that evening. It seemed Jerrold had missed her dreadfully and was looking forward to their trip to his family's country estate the following day. There was nothing to indicate he might have seen through her disguise the evening before at White's. She wondered who he'd spent the night with, and then realized she no longer had the right to criticize him. Nonetheless, she almost gasped aloud as she read part of his note that said how boring the past evening had been for him. He briefly mentioned that he'd spent several hours with the Count de Cuervo, discussing business.

Elyse paled as the name seemed to leap off the paper at her. But that was nothing compared to her reaction to Jerrold's brief postscript; he'd invited the count to join them at Fair View. It seemed there were some final matters to settle in their transaction. Holding the note, her hands shook visibly.

"Was that Chivers, my dear?" Lady Regina swept down the staircase and greeted Elyse at the landing. At her granddaughter's brief nod, she continued her chatter, adjusting a coil of silver hair. "I swear that man comes and goes without being heard or seen. I think he must have been a thief in another life."

Elyse looked up, paying only vague attention to her grandmother. "What were you saying?"

"Chivers," Lady Regina went on to explain. "He moves about so quietly, it's sometimes frightening. I was thinking he must have been a thief in a past life. Are you feeling all right, my dear? You're as pale as a ghost. There's nothing wrong, is there?"

"No!" Elyse blurted out a little too quickly. She tried to smile casually. "Jerrold has invited some other guests to the country, that's all. He says he'll call for us around ten tomorrow morning so that we'll arrive early at Fair View."

"I'm so looking forward to seeing it again." Lady Regina stepped down the last two steps to the main floor, looping her arm through Elyse's. "It's been almost twenty years since I was last at Fair View, and of course you've never seen it at all. It's a grand place. Jerrold's mother was so happy there. She loved going to the country. I think it held special memories for her. She once confessed to me that she would have stayed there year round, but Jerrold's father wouldn't hear of it. His business interests and friends were here in London. You'll love it, my dear." Lady Regina patted Elyse's hand, missing the distracted light in her granddaughter's eyes.

Elyse only murmured a distracted response. She didn't want to discuss either Fair View or Jerrold. Dear God, what was she to do now? Her wild scheme of the night before had ended in disaster, and she'd hoped to avoid all further contact with the count. There would be a great many guests of course. Perhaps she could avoid him completely, or at least avoid being alone with him. Great balls of fire! How was she going to get through the next three days?

She changed the topic of the conversation. "What were you saying about Chivers? Something about his past life? I didn't know you believed in such things." Elyse forced a gay smile as they entered the dining room and took their places at the elegantly set table.

"Past lives?" Lady Regina looked up. "Well, of course there's no proof of such things, but there are people who believe in them." She chatted gaily about a notion popular among certain of their friends.

"Naturally the church condemns such thinking, but I've always thought it to be a most fascinating notion that we don't die but merely pass from one life to another. A lot like cats with their nine lives." She placed a damask napkin across her skirt.

"I wonder if that's how the saying came about? Maybe someone had proof of multiple lives. Wouldn't that be marvelous?" Regina continued, taking a sip of wine. "Think of all the people you could meet. I suppose a person might love someone different in each lifetime. Good heavens! I had a marvelous marriage to your grandfather, and now I have Ceddy. If I kept that up through several lifetimes, it could be quite confusing trying to keep track of all those men."

In spite of the shock she'd had over Jerrold's note and her uneasiness about the next few days, Elyse found herself laughing until her eyes watered. Past lives, future lives . . . and lovers in each one. It was an interesting notion of course, and her grandmother managed to make it all seem quite hilarious. She lifted her wineglass, offering her own suggestion.

"Or perhaps it's the same person in all those lifetimes, just seeming different. Did you ever consider that?" she proposed.

Lady Regina thought long and hard about that one. "Then that would mean I might possibly find your grandfather again in the next life," she concluded. "Oh, dear!" Regina looked faintly bemused. "However am I going to explain to him about Ceddy? He just won't understand at all."

"It seems, darling, that you may just have a problem with that." Elyse smiled. The wine was having a calming effect on her badly shaken nerves. "But I think it's an interesting thought. Once you've found the person you truly love, you would never have to be parted. Such lovers would just find each other again."

"Of course, the opposite might also be true," Regina suggested. "You might keep meeting up with the wrong person and never be happy. Good heavens, that is a dreadful thought."

Elyse had suddenly become very quiet. "Yes, there is always the possibility that we could just go on and on, through one lifetime after another, never finding the person we truly love."

Inexplicably her eyes welled with tears. What if it were true? What if people were destined to meet over and over again, time after time, and never find real love? Did that mean that she and Jerrold were destined to be together not only in this lifetime but in others? And if so, would her feelings always be the same? Dear God, she hoped it wasn't true. She prayed that if she couldn't have the special exhilaration of passion in this lifetime, perhaps she might have it in another. It was a silly notion, but she found herself hoping for thatpossibility.

If she couldn't have what Lucy shared with Andrew or what she knew her grandmother felt for Ceddy, then she didn't want to go on to another lifetime.

The trip took over five hours by coach, but the time passed quickly. Jerrold rode with Elyse and her grandmother. He kept up an animated conversation, pointing out places of interest as the city gave way to rolling green countryside. He seemed to be in a particularly amiable and attentive mood. Elyse vaguely wondered if the events at White's had anything to do with it. Nothing he said or discussed gave any indication that he knew she had been anywhere except at Lucy's home that evening.

Andrew Maitland had chosen not to discuss the matter with anyone, and for that, Elyse was immensely grateful. Though she would dearly love to see the expression on Jerrold's face at finding out she was at the club, that would lead to other questions she couldn't afford to have asked. Even with Jerrold's past indiscretions, she couldn't risk his knowing where she'd actually spent the night.

She wasn't fooling herself. It wasn't because of any regret that he should find out. Like her grandmother, she didn't give a fig about what other people said or thought. What did matter to her was her grandmother. She wanted only to make her happy, and if this marriage would accomplish that, then so be it.

Gazing out the window of the coach at the lush countryside, Elyse hoped she would be more fortunate in love in the next lifetime. Her thoughts wandered: What might it have been like with a man like the Count de Cuervo if the circumstances were different?

Early in the afternoon, they passed through a small town lined with shops and houses and cobbled streets. The horses' hooves clopped rhythmically, like a drum that brought everyone from their cottages and businesses. Heads nodded in acknowledgment of the gleaming coach and the accompanying carriages and wagons. It was obvious the Barrington family held a position of great importance in this area.

Beyond the town, the coach turned off the main road and swung up a long drive lined with mulberry and yew trees, then swept past a lazy stream and lush meadows.

"Elyse, you must see Fair View from here." Lady Regina urged her from the corner of the coach from which she'd carried on a lively conversation with Jerrold for most of the journey.

"It is rather magnificent, darling," Jerrold boasted, insistently taking her arm and drawing her forward so that she could look out the window.

Fair View, the Barrington family's country estate, lay like a magnificent crown at the end of a small, verdant valley. Elyse stared at it as if transfixed. It was a massive Tudor creation of stone and leaded glass. Intricate pathways crisscrossed gardens and led to sprawling lawns, while the house seemed to go on forever in wing after imposing wing, each like a different facet of the crown.

A glass-walled conservatory lay to the right; it was attached to the main house. To the left, the lawns rolled to the stables and beyond them was open pastureland and a heavily wooded forest. They circled a large pond to reach the main entrance. It was filled with graceful black and white swans and inquisitive geese. This was by far the most impressive house Elyse had ever seen, easy rivaling any of the great estates in London for size and magnificence.

Their coach slowed and came to a stop before the wide stone steps. Jerrold's father had preceded them by two days, and he now came down the front steps followed by several servants. Jerrold was the first to descend from the coach. After greeting his father, he turned back to assist Elyse's grandmother. As she gazed at the imposing stone façade of the house, Elyse realized that several guests had arrived earlier. They appeared from the gardens. Atop horses, they called greetings to the new arrivals.

For some inexplicable reason Elyse hesitated, held back in the cool seclusion of the coach. She wanted just a moment longer to look at this wondrous house before the peacefulness and beauty of her first moment here was completely shattered.

Her gaze wandered over the intricate stonework and the expanse of leaded glass that formed the massive front wall of the main part of the dwelling. The bottom rows of glass were made up of the smallest panes, probably only two feet by three feet. The next rows were made up of panes that appeared to be twice those dimensions. And the very top pane of glass spanned the entire width of the opening.

Brilliant sunlight glistened, in prisms of color, off the glass. Shading her eyes, Elyse realized the profusion of colors wasn't caused by the sun at all. In several panes stained glass could be clearly seen. And the largest pane was of such intricate design it could only be considered a work of art. It was by far the most impressive thing Elyse had ever seen. Without conscious thought, Elyse found herself searching the bottom row of smaller panes. At this distance the smaller designs of stained glass were almost indiscernible, and yet her gaze was drawn to the bottom left corner.

It has to be there, she thought to herself. It has to be! Her gaze fastened on the last pane. She held her breath as wispy clouds passed before the sun, momentarily darkening the entire wall of glass to a somber, slate shade, obliterating the colors. Like an expectant child she held her breath, waiting for the sun to emerge and light the wall of color. And, as if moved by her desperate hopes, the clouds skittered past and the sun illuminated the windows once more.

"It is there!" Elyse whispered joyously, tears coming to her eyes. "The rose. I knew it would be there." She stared, transfixed, as the image of a single crimson rose appeared in the leaded design of that last pane. It was like a gift, just waiting to be found by her, a gift of memory and something more.

"Elyse?" Her grandmother looked back at her hesitantly. "Are you coming, dear?"

"Yes!" she breathed out, her heart quickening. An almost uncontrollable exhilaration ran along her nerve endings. Home . . .

It was insane, or perhaps it was fatigue after the strain of the last two days; but for some unknown reason, Elyse felt she had truly come home. It was as if she'd returned from a very long journey, and now the house welcomed her. But that was impossible. A house wasn't like a person, with feelings and emotions. Yet she felt it just the same; a sort of beckoning in the craggy stones and shining glass, a warmth of familiarity that left her almost weak. Even before she'd looked out the window, she'd known exactly what the house would look like.

"I've been here before," she whispered to herself, convinced of it.

She heard Jerrold's impatient reminder and reached for the handle of the door. Inexplicably, she felt angered by the intrusion. Then she silently chided herself. Of course she knew what Fair View would look like. Surely Jerrold or her grandmother had described it to her. As she stepped from the coach, her gaze immediately went to the paned window and the crimson rose patterned in the glass.

The rose was his promise to me. Unbidden, the words filled her thoughts.

"You promised," she whispered, staring transfixed at the single fragile bloom. Without knowing the reason, it occurred to her there was something wrong with the design in the glass pane. She stared up at it, trying to understand what it was that bothered her about it.

"Elyse, please. My other guests are waiting!" Jerrold reminded her impatiently.

"Yes, of course," she murmured in response, reaching down to lift the hem of her gown as she stepped forth. All at once, she remembered what it was that disturbed her about that single pane of glass. Her head came up, vivid blue eyes fastened once more on the simple leaded design.

"There was supposed to be a white rose," she said aloud, causing several heads to turn in her direction.

Jerrold quickly retraced his steps and firmly seized her elbow. "What the devil are you talking about? Everyone is watching." He leaned close, and his voice was tight.

"Elyse, please come along. Now!" he instructed from between thinned lips.

Memory, bittersweet and illusive, whispered across her soul. A red rose was symbolic of passion. A white rose represented love that was true and enduring.

There should have been a white rose entwined with the red one. He promised me the white rose, symbolic of his love.

"Elyse! Try to get hold of yourself. Are you feeling ill?"

"Ill?" She looked at Jerrold as if she were only just seeing him for the first time. "No." Emotion filled her voice.

Jerrold forcefully pulled her up the steps.

It was hardly necessary. She wanted to see everything. This land, this house, the ancient stones and glass were somehow all dearly familiar, were reaching out to her with illusive memories from another time and place.

"Then, do come along," he muttered under his breath.

"Yes," Elyse whispered, her eyes again going to that glass pane with the single red rose, almost as if she were looking for something . . . or someone.

Chapter Ten

Elyse clamped her eyes tightly shut. I must have bats in the belfry! She thought as she hid deeper in the thick downy coverlet of the bed.

She could hear Katy moving quietly about the room, putting away the last of her clothes, straightening things, and then the faint clink of the silver service from last night's dinner as it was picked up for removal from the room.

Great balls of fire! Why did the woman have to be so slow. Usually she flew about like a whirlwind, accomplishing in a very short time what normally took anyone else several hours. Elyse silently ground her teeth. If Katy didn't finish soon she'd come right out of that bed and give everything of her well-planned charade away.

Then where will you be? she chided herself. The answer came quickly enough. You'll be out with everyone else, riding to hounds this morning and very possibly meeting up with the Count de Cuervo. That possibility was the only thing keeping her snug in bed, pretending to have a dreadful headache and a case of the sniffles.

Earlier, when she'd had Katy inform her grandmother that she wasn't feeling at all well, the response from all camps had been predictable. She'd never lied, discounting little childhood fibs, and hated deceiving her grandmother. Lady Regina had immediately come to her room.

Elyse had seen the worry and concern on her lined face, and had felt dreadful for it. But Jerrold was an entirely different matter.

He'd insisted on seeing her to express his concern. Now, she might be good at disguises, but outright lying was a different matter. Jerrold was attentive and solicitous, yet underneath the pleasant demeanor she'd sensed his irritation. And while they were alone for a few minutes, when her grandmother went downstairs to find Katy, he'd very bluntly informed her that he was disappointed in her. After all, he'd said, she was always so healthy and vital. With a disdainful sniff, he'd told her in no uncertain terms that he sincerely hoped this wouldn't continue after the wedding. His mother had been sickly for a long time, and he openly admitted that suffering through the same thing in a wife was completely unacceptable.

The nerve of him! Standing there in her room and handing down edicts like some pompous, imperious ass! A thought flashed through her mind; the shorter the time until the wedding, the more overbearing and downright supercilious he was becoming. In short, he was almost rude to her now.

If she felt any twinges of regret for her deception of Jerrold, they went right out the window at that moment. She would pretend to be at death's door for the next three days just to irritate him!

But as Elyse lay in the bed, wrapped in her downy cocoon of deceit, she heard the muted sound of the call to the hunt, and she wondered who was more irritated at that moment. She'd give anything to be out of this bed and riding with them, to feel the wind rushing against her face.

Only one thing kept her bound to the bed now as she listened to Katy moving about — the presence of the Count de Cuervo. Three days!

The thought of staying cooped up in this room for that amount of time made her want to scream. She seized the opportunity Katy provided by closing a drawer a little more loudly than she'd intended. With a performance that would have rivaled any on the London stage, Elyse turned over slowly, letting out a long, low sleep-filled murmur.

"I'm sorry, darlin', I didn't mean to wake you. Did you manage to get more sleep after Master Jerrold was here?"

"A little." Elyse almost winced as she forced pretended weakness into her words.

"You seemed restless last night," Katy observed. "I heard you movin' about in here long after everyone had gone to bed. Was it the dream again?"

Caught off guard by the woman's comment, Elyse opened her eyes. The dream. No. For the first time in months, she hadn't had the dream! She quickly recovered and resumed her charade, dropping her eyelids wearily.

"It's just this dreadful headache." She sighed heavily, turning back

209

over under the covers so that she faced away from Katy. If she had to look the woman in the eye, Katy would know she was lying. Biting her lower lip, she risked a brief question. She just had to know.

"Have all the guests arrived?" She asked, a tremor in her voice. Even she heard how bad it sounded.

The maid rounded the end of the bed. She frowned faintly as she neatly folded her mistress's dressing gown.

"So it seems. There may be one or two who haven't arrived yet."

One or two! Great balls of fire! Elyse thought. She decided to chance just one more question.

"I think Jerrold was expecting the Count de Cuervo. I've been such a disappointment to him, I do hope the Count didn't disappoint him as well." That was really stretching a point. She was on thin ice and she knew it, but she had to know if that man was at Fair View. "Has he arrived yet?"

"The Count de Cuervo? Oh, that Spanish fellow her ladyship is always talkin' about. I think there was a message came from London. He wasn't able to make the trip at the last minute. Master Jerrold seemed quite agitated about that. But don't you go worryin' your pretty little head over it," Katy said soothingly.

"Now, I'm going downstairs and give the cook the recipe for that special soup of me mum's that you always liked so well. It'll fix you right up. After all, we have to get you well. You can't be ill for your wedding." She fixed the disheveled lump under the bedcovers with a speculative gaze, then shrugged her shoulders. It was probably just a mild case of the sniffles compounded by a case of the jitters, what with the wedding this close. She frowned at that last thought. As long as she'd known her young mistress, Elyse hadn't had a sickly or weak bone in her body.

"That would be wonderful," Elyse murmured gleefully into her pillow.

"I'll just leave these dishes with the morning breakfast. And I'll be back as soon as I can with that soup."

With a mission and a purpose now, Katy was not a woman to be deterred. The door bumped softly closed behind her, and Elyse immediately shot out of the bed.

"Thank heavens!" She whirled about, driving the lethargy from muscles and limbs. Streaking across the room, she threw open the heavy drapes and the filmy sheer underlinings. Then she pushed open the windows and leaned out into the morning air. Her room opened out onto an expansive greensward that swept down a faintly rolling slope to magnificent gardens and the conservatory. The sweet air of a brilliant June morning beckoned her to the freedom of the outdoors.

"That soup will take at least an hour," she said out loud. Unless of course, Katy decided to come back and check on her. In that case, there was no time to lose. She had to get out of that room!

Elyse whirled around, her eyes glinting with suppressed merriment. So, the Count de Cuervo wouldn't be coming to Fair View after all! She felt reprieved, like a man doomed to the gallows and then given a last-minute pardon. It was wonderful, it was exhilarating! A miracle that she'd recovered her health so easily. And she would just have to convince Katy of that. She whirled to the closet and seized the small bag she'd secreted at the back. Katy had packed her clothes for the trip, but Elyse had known she would deliberately omit these particular garments.

She lifted out gleaming black riding boots, sleek pants, an immaculate man's shirt with stock, and the brown jacket, its cut far too slim for any man. With a mischievous gleam in her eye, she quickly dressed, Yes indeed, she thought with uplifted heart. She'd had a most miraculous recovery. It was probably just the mention of the soup that had done it.

Her stomach growled at the thought of the soup. She descended on the silver service that still remained from breakfast. Removing its domed cover, she made a face at the sight of solidified eggs awash in a faintly greasy sauce that could only be described as gray gruel. The cook at Fair View was reputed to have exceptional culinary skills. Elyse vaguely wondered who might have made that judgment as she bypassed the cold eggs in favor of lean strip of ham, some fresh fruit, and a cold but deliciously flaky pastry.

Eyes closed in rapt delight. Jerrold and his guests had already left for the hunt. Though he liked to leave before dawn, she knew he deferred to his guests when entertaining at Fair View, extending the hour to a more respectable time. It must be somewhere near nine o'clock in the morning. No wonder she was famished. She hadn't eaten since yesterday morning before leaving London. She hastily wiped butter from her fingers. Sweeping her long hair atop her head, she then donned the small, man's cap. There, she thought, inspecting her appearance in the mirror. Now to find herself a horse.

From a distance she would look like one of the men. Only the older guests would still be at the house, and many of them wouldn't yet be downstairs. It would be easy enough to sneak out. She smiled ruefully at her reflection in the mirror.

"Impostor," she said accusingly to her reflection, a smile tilting her mouth. The smile quickly faded as she remembered who had called her that. Turning to the door, she slipped from her room and out of the house. En route, she encountered only an older gentleman who nodded to her with a decidedly masculine gesture and then proceeded to the gardens. Giving him a faint salute with her riding crop, Elyse walked straight out the front doors and headed for the stables.

She might be sneaky and a bit devious, but she wasn't foolish. Those who rode to the hunt that morning would be gone for several hours. It was in her best interest to cut her ride short and return early.

The ride helped dispel some of her restless energy, and after returning her horse to the stables, she headed toward the manor.

The morning had grown quite warm. No one was in the gardens as she rounded the corner of the house. She cut through the hedgerow and crossed the stone terrace, slipping quietly into the house.

Stepping into the cool shadows of the great room of the old manor, she released a breath. The massive doors across the room opened onto the main entryway. Just beyond she could see the wide sweep of the stairway. As music drifted faintly from another part of the house, she smiled to herself. At this time of morning, those who'd remained behind would be entertaining themselves with a round of cards, an impromptu concert, or perhaps a walk through the conservatory she'd seen earlier. They would all gather for the midday meal when the others returned from the hunt. Stepping lightly across the deep burgundy-colored carpet, Elyse crossed the great room.

It was heavily paneled with rich, dark woods that gleamed with the faintly odorous elegance attributable to care with lemon mixed with oil. Trophies of mounted boar and deer heads adorned the walls high overhead, set apart by ancient gonfalons draped from spears. They were emblazoned with emblems of elaborate design but all with the main theme of an eagle, wings spread, a spear clutched in one set of talons, a rose in the other. Elyse knew the Barrington family traced its ancestry back to William the Conqueror. This emblem must be the family crest. It seemed to be everywhere in this room.

With her sudden "illness," there'd been no time to see the rest of the house after their arrival the day before. Now, fascination pulled at her. Her grandmother had seemed enraptured with Fair View, and from the elegance of this enormous room, Elyse could easily understand that. Standing in the middle of the great room, she turned about. By the position of the main staircase in the hall beyond and the proximity to the main entrance, she knew this must be the room she'd first seen from the outside the day before. Elyse swung back around to look at the far wall, encased in massive floor-to-ceiling velvet drapes. Something indefinable beckoned her to it.

Crossing the room, she found the heavy, braided satin cord in the far corner, then pulled with all her strength and was rewarded as brilliant sunlight cascaded through the wall of windows into the room, splashing on the crimson carpet, gleaming off mahogany-paneled walls. She stepped back into the center of the large room and gasped as her gaze took in the magnificence of the span of stained-glass windows.

Just as she'd seen from the outside, the entire western exposure was a wall of glass. Brilliant light, in every color and hue imaginable, glinted back at her. Intricate designs cast a dazzling rainbow of rays onto every surface of the room. The sight took her breath away. As if commanded by softly whispered words, her eyes sought the one pane of glass in the left corner of the last row. It wasn't there!

Elyse stepped back in alarm. The rose wasn't there! Her gaze flew over the entire span of panes that made up the wall of windows. She closed her eyes and imagined that one glistening pane as she'd seen it yesterday when she'd first stepped from the coach. The first pane in the left corner, at the last row. Her eyes flew open. Fool! Her gaze immediately traveled to the lower right corner. Of course! That was it! She'd seen it at the lower left corner from the outside, but the pattern of the designs would be reversed inside the house.

Like a brilliant crimson promise, that single elegant bloom on a long stem traversed the entire width of the pane of glass. It was breathtakingly simple, and absolutely the most beautiful of all the designs. Elyse stepped to the window. Unbidden, tears welled in her eyes. Reaching out, she traced the leaded design of the rose with almost aching tenderness.

"Driver." Zach tapped the carved ivory head of the walking stick against the roof of the coach. He shook his head; at least there was something this ridiculous accoutrement of a proper Englishman might be used for. He ordered the coachman to halt at the crest of the hill that descended into the small valley, then stepped down from the coach. It was like stepping into another world, another time and place.

The air was cool and refreshing in contrast to the stifling, cinder-filled heat of London.

Something indefinable came over him. He closed his eyes and breathed deeply, the scent of fresh field flowers and pungent grasses stealing through him. He was filled with the oddest sensation that if he kept his eyes closed a little longer and then opened them, he would suddenly find himself home.

Almost as if he wanted to believe it, Zach kept his eyes closed. He breathed and listened and felt the land around him. When he finally opened his eyes, he almost laughed out loud at his own foolishness. There was nothing in this lush, green countryside that even remotely reminded him of Resolute, except perhaps the openness of it, and even then it was a complete contrast to the stark beauty of the wide, flat ranch in New South Wales.

He almost laughed, but not quite. He couldn't rid himself of the feeling he had been here before, had stood in this exact spot and looked down at the spreading greensward dotted with cottages and farms, brown cattle and white sheep grazing in the fields.

"Ya ready guv'ner?" The driver he'd hired to bring him from London broke in on his reverie.

"Aye, I'm ready." Taking hold of the center post, Zach swung back up into the coach. Earlier feelings of uneasiness about this trip came back to him as he closed the door and the coach lurched down the road.

Tobias had warned him against coming here. "Finish the business with Barrington when he returns from London," he'd argued. "Don't go!" It was almost if his old friend feared his going to the Barrington estate. And perhaps Tobias was right. After all, it wasn't necessary to meet Barrington at Fair View to conclude their business. That could be handled when he returned to London. But like the intangible feeling that had stolen over him at the top of the hill, some indefinable force lured him to the Barrington estate. And, if he were truly honest with himself, he knew it was more than that. It was Elyse.

Two nights ago, when he'd taken her back to Lord Vale's London residence, it had seemed he'd crossed some invisible barrier with her. He could no more explain it than he could explain the events that had destroyed his father's life in England, or Nicholas Tennant's connection to Lady Felicia Barrington.

He'd fight it, that strange fascination she seemed to hold over him, that invisible bond that seemed to bring them together time and again. Of all the women he'd known, she was the one he could never, would never, have. And yet, in spite of the fact that she was forbidden to him, or maybe because of it, he'd gone to her that night and made love to her. If he believed in the possibility of a man being possessed by the devil, he would have believed she'd taken hold of his soul.

That night was almost an attempt to purge himself of his need to have her, he thought. He'd almost believed that if he made love to her just once and then walked away, he would be done with her, would have exorcised the power she seemed to hold over him. But he'd been wrong, and when he realized it he knew something of what Adam must have felt in the garden of Eden, having lusted after Eve. Once tasted, that forbidden fruit couldn't be denied. And so, like poor Adam, Zach found himself drawn to Eden and the winsome creature who seemed to have cast a spell over him.

It was almost the same with his compulsion to come to Fair View. Like a sparkling crown, the estate lay in an arc on a bed of rolling green velvet. The coach jarred to a stop. Not waiting for the driver, Zach thrust the door open in sudden impatience to see the estate.

He felt he was stepping into another world, one dearly familiar, a link to some other time. His gaze wandered across the imposing Tudor façade of stone and wood. Late morning sunlight shimmered off the gleaming span of windows, illuminating a rainbow of colors.

Zach stood motionless for the longest time, just staring, his breathing suddenly constricted, the muscles across his chest tight and painful. His hands trembled at his sides as he struggled with the images that leaped into his mind.

"Say guv'ner. You all right, sir?"

Zach's head snapped around toward the driver's insistent voice. He forced himself to draw a deep breath, clearing away the images. His smile was brief.

"Yes, of course. See to the horses and find a place for yourself with the other groomsmen. I'll be returning to London day after tomorrow," he instructed the man.

As the driver saluted, a servant came down the front steps of the manor. Carrying Zach's two cases, Barrington's man led the way to the front entrance. It was then that Zach saw her.

She was walking quickly across the sloping greensward from the stables. He knew her even though with her head was down and she was dressed in that immaculate man's riding outfit she seemed to fill out with such maddening sensuality, the morning sun beating down

215

on the small cap atop her glistening sable hair.

Perhaps he had come here to prove something, to prove that after the night they'd shared she meant nothing to him. But as he watched her affect that longer man's stride, noting the indisguisable sway of her hips, he felt the familiar tightening of desire. The only person he was fooling was himself.

"Sir?" The imperious reminder came from the servant who carried his cases. It was the second time that morning someone had had to jar him from his thoughts.

"Yes, of course," Zach responded vaguely, unable to shake off the feeling that he knew this house, this place, and this woman from some other time.

He was shown to his room and informed that the other guests, and Lord Barrington, would be returning at any time from the morning ride. He smiled faintly at that. So, it seemed that Elyse had left Jerrold Barrington far behind or had chosen not to ride with the others.

Compelled by that same energy he'd first felt on the steps of the manor, he left the servant to do his unpacking. He wanted to see more of the house. Pausing at the top landing, he watched Elyse as she crossed the main entry hall.

She hesitated momentarily and then, as if she'd made some decision, turned toward the large floor-to-ceiling double doors that opened onto what appeared to be the great room.

Zach knew many of these old country manors dated back several hundred years. Fair View was no exception. He was silently impressed by the interior as he followed Elyse.

Instead of a formal parlor, Fair View had a great room that had once sufficed for the main hall, dining hall, and receiving room. Over the years adjacent rooms had taken on the functions of formal dining room and reception hall. But the great room, as it was still called, still could serve many purposes. It was filled with overstuffed furnishings—chairs, and settees—tables, and elaborately decorated lamps. The walls were paneled in gleaming, rich dark wood, and a massive chandelier in which countless tiny candles were mounted hung suspended from the ceiling. An elegant tapestry depicting Lord Barrington in a hunt scene from another era covered an adjacent wall. But by far the most imposing sight was the one that seemed to draw Elyse.

Floor to ceiling, velvet hangings draped the western exposure, casting the room into cool shadows. All at once the shadows fled as she seized the heavy braided cord at the far corner and drew the crimson portiers open.

Zach watched, fascinated by her every movement. She went to the paned glass, and almost as if she were seeing it for the first time, stood before the massive stained-glass panels and stared, with something very near wonder lighting her magnificent eyes.

Without understanding how or why, he knew her exact thoughts as she reached out to that one pane of glass in the far right corner. And like that moment when he'd first glimpsed the imposing manor from the steps, his breathing made his lungs ache. Almost as if they moved as one, his outstretched hand trembled. He could feel the cool image in the glass beneath his fingertips, could trace the leaded design of that crimson rose.

Incomplete, unfinished. Their thoughts seemed to be echoing each other. He could feel the glass as her fingers traced it below the single rose, as if she, too, were searching for the additional design which should have been there.

Once again, their thoughts were one, and Zach knew she was aware of what he was thinking. It was as if they were simultaneously transported back to another time, another memory. And he knew, as did she, that originally there was supposed to be a white rose to complete the pattern in glass.

The red rose symbolizes passion; the white rose is for that which will last an eternity.

His gaze remained fastened on her hand as she traced the glass, and memory shafted through him like a white hot blade. He knew the rose would be there, alone, unfinished. Just like the single white rose that adorned the arch above the entrance to Resolute; a white rose that held some vague meaning lost long ago with the death of his father and not understood until this moment.

Sensing his presence, Elyse whirled around. "You," she breathed. Somehow she'd known it would be him. He was standing so close she could feel the heat of his body.

He reached around her, tracing his fingers along the one pane she'd touched. "A single rose. It seems rather forlorn, almost incomplete."

"Do you make it a habit to go around sneaking up on people?" She bit the words off sharply, trying desperately to bring her emotions under control.

"I didn't sneak up on you. I saw you returning from the stables." He gently fingered the lapel of her riding jacket, amusement twitching at one corner of his mouth now that the spell between them was broken. "But I see you're still *sneaking* around in disguises." As he teased her in return, his gaze softened. She was so close to him, he could see the wild thready pulse that beat at her throat.

Elyse slapped his hand away angrily. She didn't trust her emotions at that moment. Katy had said he wasn't expected, yet here he was.

His smile was almost mocking now. "Didn't you learn the trouble you could get yourself into playing such games?"

"I don't know what you're talking about," Elyse retorted coolly. She knew perfectly well what he meant, but he was the last person on earth she'd confess it to. He was undoubtedly referring to the night at White's Club, but denial was much safer than admitting the truth. She wasn't prepared to discuss that night with him. And besides, she didn't trust him any farther than she could throw him.

They were alone now, but there was no telling when he might choose to bring it up again. It would be just like him to embarrass her in front of Jerrold or her grandmother. He was such a lowlife, she wouldn't put anything past him.

"Please, let go of my arm," she whispered vehemently.

"This arm?" Zach's smile deepened in maddening enjoyment.

"Damn you!" Elyse hissed. "You know perfectly well which arm."

"Then, you do mean this arm." His fingers slipped to her wrist, sending a jolt of energy skipping along her nerve endings as bare skin touched bare skin. With the greatest of ease and almost without her realizing it, he twisted her wrist, slipping her arm behind her back and at the same time pulling her slender body against his.

The air rushed from her lungs in a gasp of surprise. She was pinned and she knew it. Try as she might, there was no escape.

They were in stark contrast; his height towering over her, the soft waves of his gold hair glinting sunlight while hers tumbled loose from them cap, spreading dark warmth across her shoulders. His silken silver gaze locked with defiant blue, the heat of his fingers searing into the coolness of her straining wrists. They were like fire and ice as they stood locked in a battle of wills.

With his other hand, Zach traced her features: the prominence of cheekbones, the arch of sable brows, the fullness of her lower lip.

"You really should be more pleasant, sweet Elyse. Especially when you want something from someone."

"What are you talking about? You have nothing that I want. Let go of me!" Elyse ground out from between clenched teeth. She felt as if she were paralyzed. A heaviness settled in her limbs. She wanted to run away, as far away as possible, but knew her legs would never carry her. Her heart beat frantically. Something very near fear shivered across her skin: fear of this man, fear of what he was doing to her, fear of herself and of her own betraying responses.

"I seem to remember you saying that to me once before," Zach reminded her, his lips caressing her forehead above the arch of one delicate brow. "But I do have something that you want, very much." His gaze darkened to soft smoke. "I have the pendant."

She gasped. "Do you have it with you?"

"I thought that might change your attitude." He scolded her almost as an indulgent adult would a child. "Yes, I have it. But I want something from you in exchange before I'll give it back. After all, you must earn it."

"Earn it! When it's mine in the first place? You can go to—"

"Now, now, sweet Elyse. That's no way to talk. If you won't cooperate"—he looked regretful—"I'll just have to return it to Lady Winslow."

Elyse gasped. If he did that it would raise no end of embarrassing questions. "You wouldn't dare!"

"Ah, but you know I would. Do we have a bargain?"

"It's like bargaining with the devil. I can't hope to win," she fumed, though soundly caught by his hands and his words.

"Has it ever occurred to you that you're an even match for the devil? I seem to remember your flaunting caution several times. Only someone with a devilish good sense of herself would attempt some of the things you've done."

Elyse was caught in a dreadful conflict. Part of her hated him, dreaded the close contact of his body with hers, the imprisoning strength of his arms. But like good and evil, hot and cold, fire and ice, she also had an opposite reaction; it welcomed the thrust of his hard body against hers; the enfolding warmth of arms driving all reason from her thoughts; the soft whisper of his breath against her cheek, igniting a thousand tiny fires just beneath the surface of her skin.

Dear God, she loathed him, because of what he stirred within her, because of the feelings he aroused. She'd never been so stirred by any man . . . except for the phantom from her dreams.

"It's just like you to bring that up!" She swallowed back indignation and rage, knowing neither would gain her the pendant. "Very well," she conceded. "What do you want in exchange for the piece of jewelry? I warn you, I have no money of my own. Everything belongs to my grandmother."

"Ah, sweet Elyse, but you are a very rich woman in what I want." His voice softened as he watched emotions play across her lovely face. Then he sobered.

"I want a kiss, sweet Elyse. And not"—he pressed a cautioning finger against her lips—"one of the devoted, supercilious kisses you reserve for Barrington."

He shook his head adamantly when she started to object. "No, Elyse. That sort of kiss will never do. I want the kind of kiss I know you're capable of giving. The kind you shared with me two nights ago."

"You pompous . . . !" She sputtered, anger choking her. "I wouldn't kiss you if you were the—" She was again cut off.

"No kiss, no pendant. It's as simple as that, lovely lady."

"And just what do you think you'll prove with this one kiss?" she asked sharply.

"I'm not trying to prove anything to myself. I want to prove something to you."

"That's ridiculous. You won't prove anything to me with a kiss," she assured him defiantly.

"I think you're wrong, Elyse. Nevertheless, that is my offer; a kiss, of equal quality to those you gave me that night, in exchange for the pendant. Not a bad deal altogether. Some might be inclined to think that you stand to win everything." Zach stroked back a silken tendril of hair from her face.

Of all the nerve, of all the bold-faced, pompous, aggravating nerve! Now she knew why she hated him so much, and she also knew she had no choice. If she didn't accept his little bargain, she'd never get the pendant back.

"All right. I accept. But I want to add something to the bargain." By the look on his face she knew she'd caught him off guard.

He was immediately wary. "I'll listen, but I won't promise to go along with it."

She squared her slender shoulders as well as she could when in his embrace. "Our agreement is to be kept in a public place," she insisted. That way he could hardly kiss her the way he had the other night. With the other guests about, he'd not dare kiss her with anything more than a brotherly peck on the cheek. He'd be a fool to do otherwise, and she was certain he was no fool. "And," she went on, "when the terms of our agreement are met and I have the pendant and you have your kiss, then I want nothing further to do with you. Is that clear?"

Zach thought about that for a moment. He forced back a smile. He knew exactly what her little game was all about. She was certain if he agreed to a public resolution, the kiss would have to be a fairly innocent one, much like the gesture of a friend. As for the second condition, there was every reason to believe her kiss might change all that.

"Agreed, Miss Winslow."

"Good. Now, since we've settled on a public place, I think after dinner this evening would be an appropriate time to keep our bargain."

"Very appropriate," Zach agreed, amusement dancing in his silver gaze. Then, without warning, he bent over her and caressed her cheek with his lips.

"You promised!" Elyse gasped.

"I promised that after our bargain was met I wouldn't go near you again. I said nothing about now."

"You arrogant, rude impostor!" Elyse almost cried out as her arm was drawn up so sharply she feared it would snap.

"Do you make that accusation as one impostor to another?"

"I saw you without that eyepatch," she said accusingly. "You didn't have it the night . . ." Her voice broke off.

"Yes. What about the night I made love to you?"

"Damn you! You weren't wearing it then."

"It was dark. How can you be so certain?"

Elyse swallowed back a painful cry as she tried to wrench free. "Because I saw you."

Zach smiled wickedly. "I say you're wrong. But perhaps you should visit me again in my bedchamber, perhaps tonight, just to make certain."

Abruptly freeing one wrist, Elyse drew back her hand and, with all her strength behind it, it flashed through the air. But it was quickly blocked, fingers like steel closing around her wrist. She inhaled sharply.

"Lovely Lis."

His fingers bruised her skin, then inexplicably loosened as with the gentlest touch he turned her hand. Elyse inhaled sharply as he bent to kiss the turn of her wrist, his lips caressing her wildly racing pulse.

"I never meant to hurt you."

They both heard the sharp tread of boots crossing the stone entry hall. Zach quickly stepped away from her. It wouldn't do for anyone to see them together like this.

"Elyse darling, here you are," Jerrold announced as he swept into the great room. "I've been looking everywhere for you. I was informed you had recovered from your illness. And I see you've

221

arrived as well." He turned to the Count de Cuervo.

Zach inclined his head at the greeting, a secretive smile pulling at his lips.

One word, Elyse thought with a vengeance as she rubbed her bruised wrist. If he says just one word, I'll kill him.

"I'm so glad you found each other. You two are the only ones among my guests who have never seen Fair View. After dinner this evening, you must take the grand tour of the house. It really is quite magnificent. The land has been in our family for almost six hundred years. Though the house is only about two hundred years old, Barringtons have lived here since the time of William the Conqueror." Jerrold glanced imperiously at the Count de Cuervo.

"Of course, you must be able to trace your family lineage back almost that far," he said to his guest. "After all the Spanish nobility are almost as civilized as the English."

He gave Elyse a concerned look as she was suddenly seized by a fit of coughing. "Surely you don't intend to spend the remainder of our stay locked away in your room, darling," he suggested.

At that moment, Elyse would joyfully have strangled them both. "Not at all, darling," she replied, with a silkiness that belied the anger underneath. "I feel quite well." She wasn't about to leave Jerrold and the Count de Cuervo alone for any length of time.

"Excellent." Jerrold beamed, then his smile faded as he seemed to notice her riding costume for the first time. "Elyse, please, I do wish you would refrain from such outlandish garb." He gestured to her riding pants and jacket, his expression disapproving, and sniffed. "I'm certain we have something else you might wear. Some of Mother's things are still in her rooms. I'll have the housekeeper see that you have something appropriate." His arm slipped possessively through hers.

"Dinner will be at eight. It's to be a costume affair. We're all to dress as some famous person out of history," Jerrold announced to them both as he led the way from the great room.

Elyse turned to him. "I've nothing to wear for a costume party."

They both looked up as the Count de Cuervo was suddenly seized by a fit of coughing.

"Are you all right, your grace?" Jerrold gazed at him uncertainly.

"Yes, I was just thinking that Miss Winslow would make any costume seem appropriate." He glanced with meaning at her well-turned bottom, snugged within the men's riding pants.

"Jerrold . . ." Elyse began to object.

"Not to worry, my dear." He patted her hand indulgently. "We have trunks and closets filled to overflowing with all manner of costumes. This is an annual event at Fair View, as you will learn. I'm certain we can come up with something for you. And the count also, of course."

"Of course." Zach acknowledged, merriment twinkling in his visible eye. He wondered if Elyse would like to borrow his formal jacket and pants for the evening. She did cut such a dashing figure in formal attire.

"Until this evening, Miss Winslow," he called after her, thoroughly enjoying the stiffening of her slender back and the curve of her lovely bottom beneath those men's riding pants. The evening did promise endless possibilities.

"I thought perhaps I'd be an Egyptian queen. What do you think?" Lady Regina stood swathed in yard upon yard of diaphanous silk. A tall, tubular headpiece adorned her head, another length of silk trailing from it. Row upon row of bracelets adorned her arms. She did look positively stately, and very Egyptian.

"Elyse! You haven't listened to a word I've said."

"What?" Her granddaughter looked up from the elegant escritoire set beside a window in her suite of rooms. "I'm sorry." She turned to Regina and gave her a apologetic smile. "I think your costume is absolutely stunning. You'll be the belle of the ball."

Lady Regina's hands fell to her sides. "But you're supposed to be the belle of the ball, not me. I'm just an old warhorse who happens to be the grandmother of the bride. Have you decided what you'll wear?"

"After Jerrold's little tirade this afternoon over my riding costume I thought of going as a sailor or perhaps a pirate," Elyse remarked wryly. She was unable to stir up much enthusiasm for a costume ball; actually, she was rather put out because Jerrold hadn't told her of it so that she could have brought something to wear from London. As it was, all she had were her ball gowns and party dresses.

"Sweetheart," her grandmother cajoled, "you must be patient with Jerrold. He's simply not used to your ideas about things. But that's the marvelous part about marriage," she said encouragingly. "Two people, sometimes vastly different, come together, and they complement each other, like two marvelous halves becoming a splendid whole."

"You're a hopeless romantic," Elyse accused lovingly. "Did it ever occur to you that not all married people share what you had with

Grandfather, or what you have now with Uncle Ceddy for that matter?"

"Good heavens, no!" But her grandmother was brought up short nevertheless and grew thoughtful. "Of course, most matches are arranged, but they seem to work. You certainly don't hear much about divorce. It seems everyone manages to work things out rather well."

"There aren't divorces because the parties involved aren't about to jeopardize the family fortunes," Elyse pointed out. "It's much easier to take a mistress or a lover and to keep the jewels and estates intact."

"Good heavens!" Lady Regina looked scandalized. "Wherever do you pick up such absolute rot?"

"Darling," Elyse said patiently, "please don't play the innocent with me. I know perfectly well what goes on in some of the finest families in England. Taking mistresses and lovers seems to be common practice among our friends."

Lady Regina sat down heavily on an upholstered bench at the end of the bed. "I know it happens, but I believe there are happy marriages. I certainly had one, and look at Lucy Maitland. Her husband is absolutely besotted with her. And the Queen had her Albert."

Elyse rose and crossed to her grandmother. She leaned over, planting an affectionate kiss on a still smooth cheek. "Yes, but what about all the others? The simple truth is that many of my married friends share their husbands with mistresses in Coddington Square. There's quite a colony of kept ladies established there. And of course, Jerrold . . ."

"That is over and finished," her grandmother stated confidently. "He promised his father everything had ended months ago. And, Elyse dear, I do wish you would quit dropping the ends of sentences. It makes it very difficult to keep up with what you're saying."

They both looked up in response to a knocking at the chamber door.

Elyse was silently grateful for the interruption. How could she possibly explain to her grandmother that she desperately wished she could have the devotion and love of the man she was to marry? "That must be Mrs. Evers, the housekeeper. Jerrold mentioned that there were several costumes I might choose from." She was across the room in an instant.

Lady Regina smiled, but couldn't help feeling there was a great deal more she should discuss with Elyse on the subject of marriage.

She frowned slightly as her granddaughter greeted the housekeeper. When Elyse returned briefly, to give her a tender kiss on the cheek, Lady Regina caught at her slender hand.

"You've brought me such joy. I hope you know, all I've ever wanted is your happiness. If I thought . . ."

Elyse smiled. "There you go, cutting off your sentences. It does make it difficult to carry on a conversation." She winked playfully at her grandmother.

But behind the smile and the cheerful façade, she shivered apprehensively. She loved her grandmother. Regina Winslow had been both mother and father to Elyse, giving her unconditional love and care. She would never do anything to hurt or disappoint her. Squeezing her grandmother's hand affectionately, she swept out of the room in the wake of Mrs. Evers, in pursuit of a costume for the ball that evening.

Chapter Eleven

Jerrold Barrington pushed back the leather chair behind the mahogany desk. "When you give this draft to my man in London he will arrange for the transfer of funds" — his smile was brief — "after he's received the gold, of course."

"I'll just keep the draft here in my safe until you leave for London." He looked up, every inch the courteous host. "How long will you be staying with us?"

Zach met Barrington's dark, hooded gaze evenly from across the desk. This man was being very careful. He must be even more careful. "For the next few days, I suppose, if that's agreeable with you, of course," Zach replied, his tone one of faint boredom. "London is so hot this time of year." He favored Jerrold with that lazy smile he'd perfected. "I'm glad to be done with the gold. It's absolutely impossible to purchase anything with it. And there's always the risk that someone might try to steal it." He gave particular emphasis to this last statement, watching for Barrington's reaction.

Jerrold looked up and scrutinized his guest, wondering what hidden meaning he'd intended. "Someone such as the Raven."

"So it seems," Zach agreed, innocently shrugging his shoulders. "You must admit the fellow has played a beastly devilish game in those Australian colonies. From what I hear, no one has caught him yet. He's clever."

"Not clever enough." Jerrold straightened in his chair, just thinking of the Raven tautening his every muscle. "I promise you, the man will hang from the yardarm before I'm through. And every one of his men with him."

Zach smiled slowly. "Ah, my friend" — there was a derisive edge to the last word; he enjoyed playing this game with Barrington — "but first you much catch him. So far, it would seem you've been less than successful."

"Until now, yes. But I have a different strategy. As soon as the fellow shows himself again, he will find out what it is. Until now my ships have been easy victims. But if it is war the Raven wants, then it is war he shall have. And not only he will suffer for it, but the

226

colonies as well." He'd half risen from his chair to lean over the desk, almost as if he were directing these threats at his guest. His eyes gleamed with an unnatural light, his lips thinned across bared teeth, and a muscle in his cheek twitched with barely suppressed fury.

Barrington's fist suddenly came down on the desktop, rattling the feather quill in the inkwell. "I will destroy the Raven, and then I will destroy this trade rebellion of the colonists. The Crown learned a lesson from the American colonies. We will not lose control again. The colonies will submit or they will be brought to their knees."

The atmosphere in the room was electrically charged, like the sky at sea before a storm. Zach's gaze locked with Barrington's. He did not blink as he slowly rose, having decided it was time to end this conversation. "It seems you've already set the example." He nodded courteously. "I'm certain you'll give it your best effort, my dear fellow." Zach was sincere in making that statement. However, he was equally sincere in hoping that Barrington's best effort would gain him nothing.

Barrington followed him to the door of the library. "I do apologize. The Raven has been most elusive. I find the situation very . . . annoying." He chose his words carefully, not wanting to give the Raven too much importance or to appear less than confident of the eventual outcome of his attempts to catch the man.

"I can see that it would be, but I believe the Crown can rest easy. It has the very best man to deal with the situation."

Barrington smiled hesitantly and adjusted his coat front over his expanding chest. "I appreciate your confidence, your grace."

"Indeed." Zach smiled, greatly enjoying this little game. Barrington might be the best, at least in his own opinion, but this was a case where the Crown's best simply wasn't good enough.

"When did you say you were leaving? I do hope you can at least stay for a few days." Jerrold was beginning to like the Count de Cuervo.

"Even now my crew is seeing to the cargo for our return voyage. That should take only another two or three days at the most."

"What a pity you can't remain longer. I should like you to attend my wedding to Miss Winslow. It promises to be the grandest occasion of the season."

Zach stiffened. How the devil could Elyse be interested in a pompous ass like Jerrold Barrington? He almost laughed out loud. She'd called him that very same thing on more than one occasion.

He felt it again, that faint shadow of memory he'd first experienced months ago when he'd discovered his father's journal and the

227

pendant. It was the same feeling that had stolen upon him unexpectedly ever since he'd come to London, as if some invisible force were driving him. It was always there, just beyond his grasp, elusive. Like a beautiful woman, he thought wryly, and his next thought was of Elyse. She was a lovely and passionate creature. But he'd known many equally beautiful and passionate women. What was it about her that continued to haunt him? Why the devil did the fact that she was marrying Barrington leave him with a feeling of disgust, even contempt? It shouldn't matter. A few weeks ago it wouldn't have. Even now, he told himself he'd made love to her that night only to prove to himself that he could do so and not be affected by it, but he was wrong and knew it. She haunted his nights and burned in his memory.

It occurred to him that these spells seemed to be connected to her. First there was the pendant, of which she had an identical copy, and then the way she'd greeted him on the night of the ball. Their paths seemed to be inextricably intertwined. It was ridiculous, of course, and he put the thought away. He had only one goal, to find out the truth about his father and to sell the gold, for the second time, to Barrington. That thought made him smile broadly as he turned to answer the man.

"I'm sure it will. Indeed, I am looking forward to this evening's party. It promises to be most. . . . enlightening." He chose his words carefully.

"Then you've selected your costume," Barrington concluded.

"Ah yes. One that I think you will find especially amusing. I trust Miss Winslow will be wearing a costume as well."

"I'm certain she'll be able to find something appropriate. Could I interest you in a card game or two to pass the time?" He easily extended the cursory invitation. "My other guests seem to have found their own diversions while we were concluding our business."

Zach eyed the open safe and made a mental note of its location, behind the third painting from the left corner. "With your permission, I think I will take a ride about your estate. I didn't have a chance to see it earlier."

"Then I shall see you later." Barrington bowed stiffly.

"Of course." Zach promised, giving his host a cold smile as he left.

Jerrold Barrington jerked on the bell pull beside the desk. He closed the door to the safe, then nodded to the huge man who stepped quietly from a panel behind the heavy tapestry that covered one wall. "You're to go to London. I will keep the Count de Cuervo here. You will need twenty men to get the gold. The ship is the

Tamarisk. Be back by tomorrow night and do not fail me."

There was a grunt from the dark hulk, and then he disappeared back into the shadows.

When Zach stepped into the cool, immaculate stables, he once more experienced the feeling that he'd been there before. Try as he might, he couldn't shake it off.

Selecting a tall, well-conformed jumper for a mount, he emerged into the late afternoon sun, enjoying the lean animal strength of the Westminster gray beneath him. He was familiar with the breed, although at Resolute there was no need for this finely bred an animal. The horses at the ranch were lean and strong but with a different stamina. They were bred for endurance in an unforgiving climate and in a land that took a toll on both riders and horses. They weren't pampered pleasure horses or hunters; they were working horses. But not so the one he kept in Sydney. The stallion Domino was a hellion. Coal black except for the slash of a white blaze down the length of his magnificent head. This gray possessed much the same spirit, dancing sideways beneath him. Obviously the other guests had thought this one too spirited for their ride to the hounds. The gray hadn't been run as the other horses had, and his confinement had heightened his restlessness.

"You sure you want to take him out, sir?" The old stablemaster had said, eying Zach skeptically. "There are very few who can ride him. Master Jerrold takes him out once in a while, but not since he took that last fall."

Zach stroked the stallion's heavily muscled neck appreciatively. "I prefer a horse with some spirit. This one reminds me of a stallion at my home. Ah yes, he has the same fire as my Domino." An expert rider, he kept firm control of the reins.

"Eh, what's that you said? What do you call yer horse?"

Zach looked up. "Domino. He's as black as night except for—."

"Except for a blaze of white down his head," the old man finished for him.

"Yes." Zach gazed down at the man uncertainly. "How did you know that?"

The stablemaster easily dismissed the question. "Just an easy guess. There's very few horses that don't have some kind of distinctive marking. A patch of white here and there is common on blacks."

"True enough," Zach acknowledged as he turned the defiant horse about.

"Still, there is the matter of the name."

"What name? What are you talking about?"

"I knew a horse named Domino once, just like you describe your black. He was a fine, high-spirited beast. He was here at the stables when I first came on with Lord Barrington."

Zach's gaze narrowed. The name was uncommon, and the chance of there being two horses in such diverse parts of the world, both black and similarly marked, was slim. "Whatever happened to this other Domino?"

"Lord Barrington, Master Jerrold's father, sold him off. Said he didn't want him around."

"Who did he sell him to? Was it someone local?" Zach couldn't explain why he felt the need to know what had happened to this other horse.

"No. That was the sad thing. He sold him off to a band of Gypsies that always used to camp out in the meadow during the warm months each year. Sold him for ten pounds!" He shook his head sadly. "And after the old lord had had him special bred for his son. But after Lord Clayton died, young Master Charles insisted on selling him. He had offers for him from several of his friends. Instead, he sold him to the Gypsies. I offered twenty pounds for him meself, but he refused. Said he wanted to be rid of the black devil. That's what he called him — a black devil."

"Did you ever see the animal again?"

"No. When them Gypsies came through the year after, they no longer had him. Such a fine animal," he reminisced. "Sure is a strange coincidence him bein' so like your horse and with the same name." The stablemaster shook his head.

"How long ago did all this happen?"

The man removed his cap and scratched his head where the hair thinned across the top. "Well, as close as I can remember it must be about . . ." He stopped and counted out numbers on his fingers. "Must be well over thirty years ago."

Zach nodded thoughtfully, wondering at the coincidence of names as well. "Thank you for telling me about this other Domino." He turned the gray away from the stables.

"Sir," the man called after him. "You won't be wantin' to go that way this late in the day. The woods get dark early and you don't want to get lost."

Zach looked up. When he'd started from the stables he really hadn't been watching the direction he was taking. The gray responded easily enough for being high-spirited and this direction seemed the natural one to follow.

"Thank you again, for your concern. But I'll be quite all right." He waved to the man and, calling to the horse, set off in the direction of the woods.

Sunlight glinted off the treetops and shimmered like molten fire through pine and oak branches. It cut across his vision, momentarily blinding him and was then gone. When he looked again, everything seemed oddly familiar.

"What is it about this place?" Zach speculated as he guided the gray over fallen trees, across streams, and through quiet hollows. He seemed instinctively to sense where it was he wanted to go. It was as if some unseen hand guided the reins, and he realized he hadn't consciously chosen this course, if it could be called that. "Why do I feel that I've been here before?" There were no answers, only the soft sough of the wind in the trees.

The trail stopped and then started again in several places. The stablemaster was right; one could get lost if he didn't know where he was going. But Zach seemed to know exactly where he was headed.

Heat faded with the sun, and quiet twilight descended over the forest. The only sound came from the horse's hooves as Zach unerringly guided him around rock-filled gulleys, past a hazardous break in the trail, and through secluded glades so dark it seemed as if it were night. He pushed himself and his mount at a relentless pace, one dangerous in the fading light, uncertain why he felt the need to do so. But the harder he pushed, the more reckless he became; it seemed he almost recognized this turn, that fallen tree, or that cluster of rocks.

Both Zach and his horse were completely winded when they finally halted at the crest of the hill looking down over the valley. Myriad lights winked back at him from Fair View.

"Like so many candles . . . and one day it will be yours, my darling." Zach blinked hard at the words that tumbled unexpectedly from his mouth. Everything before him seemed to shimmer in the last purple light of day. The manor, the stables beyond, everything seemed bathed in the light of some half-memory.

"I have been here before," he whispered in awe as he stared at the valley below. It was impossible, but he felt it and knew that somehow it was true.

Give me tomorrow.

It was as if the words came on the wind. He swept the silk eyepatch from his head and turned to listen. It came again, softer, more faintly.

Give me tomorrow.

Mentally, he shook himself. He listened again and this time heard only the wind.

"Tobias would swear I'd taken to drinking if I were to tell him I'm hearing things now. What do you think, my proud fellow?" He stroked the gray's dampened neck.

Zach answered himself. "I think so too. It's time to get back home."

Home? Now where the devil had that come from? Zach frowned. It was time to get home, home to Resolute. He needed only a little bit more time. Here, he might be able to learn something about Felicia Barrington from the people who'd known her. Perhaps they might have heard of a man named Nicholas; he had no last name to go with it. Then he and Tobias would go home. He had part of what he'd come for. He patted his jacket pocket, and smiled at the comforting crackle of paper—the voucher Barrington had given him for the gold. He'd made a very lucrative deal, selling Barrington's own gold back to him. Perhaps that was all anyone could hope for, even the Raven.

Elyse dismissed Mrs. Evers with a grateful smile and stood before the long wardrobe. She pushed aside first one costume, then another. None seemed to catch her interest. She dismissed the gown of a Greek goddess, then considered the dress of a Roman centurion.

"Wouldn't that stop everyone dead in their tracks?" A smile played at her lips. She stood back, unimpressed. Then her gaze fell to the suit of armor standing at the end of the closet. She giggled.

"I really should," she whispered out loud. She could imagine the looks she'd get upon walking into the party and raising the face plate to reveal her identity.

"But Jerrold would never forgive me. And it would be a bit cumbersome when it came to dancing." Her next thought regarding intimate bodily functions canceled the entire idea.

"Still I wonder how they did it?" She tilted her lovely head. "There must be a trap door," she mused as she continued searching the large long room. It was decorated entirely in blue; with odd pieces of furnishings at one end, all covered against collecting dust. She recognized the vague shapes of a chair and several trunks stacked three high. What appeared to be a large painting stood draped and tied in a darkened corner. She'd seen the family portrait gallery earlier in the day, and the other paintings that hung on the walls of the manor. Jerrold's family was brilliantly displayed throughout. She wondered why this one work had been stored away.

Curiosity got the better of her. There had to be some reason why this painting wasn't displayed with the others. Perhaps it was unfinished, or by the looks of some of the Barrington ancestors, someone had decided this particular one was far too homely to put on display.

The painting was enormous, at least eight feet wide by ten feet high judging by its outline. She struggled with the cover, standing on a box to pull it aside with both hands. Upon uncovering the large painting, she turned and stepped down off the box.

Elyse gasped as she stared up at the portrait.

"Lady Barrington," she whispered in awe. She immediately recognized the young woman in the painting as Jerrold's mother. It was a pastoral scene, the gardens beyond the house in the background. Roses were abloom, and Lady Barrington held a long-stemmed red rose in her fingers, the crimson bloom as radiant as the color in her cheeks. Her other hand was spread across the voluminous skirts of the most exquisite gown Elyse had ever seen. It was midnight blue, reflecting the color of her eyes, with a wide row of blond lace flounced at the hem. The shoulders of the gown swept daringly low across her shoulders, and her fair hair was worn long, sweeping down the middle of her back. But what caught Elyse's attention were the earbobs Lady Barrington was wearing. They were an elegant design of pearls and diamonds, exactly like the pendant her grandmother had given her! She read the inscribed name plate at the bottom of the portrait: Miss Felicia Seymour, on the occasion of her betrothal, 1837.

Elyse traced the etched letters, a perplexed frown turning her soft mouth.

"How very strange." She stood back, staring up at the elegant portrait. It was neither incomplete nor ugly. It was breathtakingly beautiful, and she was filled with a feeling of sadness because it was stored away. She promised herself to speak to Jerrold about it.

But there was no sadness in Felicia Seymour's eyes. She looked radiantly, joyously happy. Elyse only vaguely recognized the woman her grandmother had once described to her as unhappy and sickly.

"You're beautiful, Lady Barrington," she whispered. "I wonder why they closed you away in here." She laughed at her foolishness, sensing that she'd almost expected an answer.

"I don't suppose you have a suggestion for my costume for tonight," she suggested to the painting. "I understand these costume affairs are a tradition." She looked up thoughtfully. "I wonder what you would have worn. Well, this is certainly getting me nowhere."

Leaving the portrait of Felicia Barrington to watch her with eyes dancing with a magical, mystical light, she went back to the wardrobe.

"The armor will never do. I'd probably break my neck. And there will undoubtedly be a dozen Greek goddesses. Everyone always wants to be a goddess." She paused with her hand on the centurion costume, then shook her head.

"Grandmother would love it, but I fear Jerrold would be mortified." She closed the massive doors, then turned back to the center of the room, no closer to a solution than when she'd started. Her soft blue eyes brightened at sight of the wall of closets opposite. Surely she'd be able to find something in there.

Elyse pushed back both large doors then stood back to take inventory. She stared in amazement. No centurion costume or suit of armor greeted her. For here, neatly arranged from one end to the other, was the most stunning array of gowns she'd ever seen.

There were voiles, taffetas, satins, and muslins. Every color in the rainbow was there. There were long-sleeved gowns, more daring evening gowns, hats in boxes overhead, shoes lined up precisely along the bottom. Capes, long and short, lightweight and fur lined. And at the far end were drawers, at least a dozen of them, filled with gloves, delicate hand-stitched underwear, satin evening bags, lace netting for veils, shawls and stockings, and linens. She pulled open one drawer that contained delicate handkerchiefs. The one on top caught her attention. Elegant scrolled letters were embroidered in gold threads: F.B. "Felicia Barrington." Elyse stared. This was Lady Barrington's wardrobe. These were her things; everything meticulously cleaned and pressed, as if they only waited for her. She'd never seen anything like it before in her life and she wondered why Lord Barrington had kept everything.

"He must have loved you very much," she murmured to the painting. Still, this discovery left her feeling unsettled. Her grandfather had been dead for years, her parents as well. Portraits of them adorned her grandmother's house, but Lady Regina certainly hadn't kept their clothing closed away. Except for a few infant's garments, her grandmother kept from when her father was a baby. That was quite common; like a lady's handkerchief, a man's pipe, or a child's favorite toy. But an entire wardrobe?

Elyse shook her head, then reached to close the far door. She didn't have time to wonder about Lord Barrington's reasons. She still didn't have a costume and absolutely refused to be one of many Greek goddesses at the party. That centurion costume was beginning to look better and better all the time.

Elyse stopped, her hand at the other door, and her gaze fastened on a particular gown. Opening the door again to allow light in, she pushed aside the other gowns so that she could see this one better.

Her vivid blue eyes lit up, and she whirled around to the painting. "It is!" she breathed ecstatically. "It's the same gown!" She had an idea. Seizing the gown, she removed it from the satin-wrapped hanger and, with the greatest care, held it against her own body.

"We must have been very much alike," she murmured, then looked up at the smiling image of Felicia Barrington. "I hope you don't mind, but I think I've just found my costume." She looked up, almost thinking she saw silent approval in the woman's eyes. She scrutinized the portrait as she pulled the pins from her own hair.

"It will be perfect," Elyse declared, excitement racing along her nerve endings. Then she frowned faintly. The only flaw would be the earbobs.

"I wonder whatever happened to them," she mused thoughtfully before dismissing the thought. There was certainly no need to worry about that now. As it was, she didn't have the pendant either. Her frown tilted into a lovely smile. She intended to wait until the other guests had gone down to the party before making her entrance. Jerrold and his father would be so pleased.

"Thank you," she whispered to the painting.

Zach tied the wide band of silk behind his head. A smile pulled at his mouth as he deliberately positioned it over his left eye. He wondered if either Elyse or Jerrold Barrington would notice. Standing before the full-length mirror in his chamber, he studied the dashing figure, dressed entirely in black silk, reflected back at him.

"Ah yes, a pirate. Especially for you, Elyse." He pulled on black gloves, and in one practiced move placed a steel blade into the narrow scabbard at his hip. Every pirate worth his weight in gold had a sword. But the pirates he'd met up with usually carried a heavier blade. Tonight, however, he wasn't out to rescue damsels in distress or to relieve rich fools of their gold. A wicked smile curved below the silk mask. He'd already lifted the gold of one fool. As he slipped the pendant into his pocket, the smile deepened. He was after a far richer prize from Elyse, something only she could give — a kiss.

Jerrold Barrington glistened in a satin frock coat Louis XIV of France might have worn. Imitating the posturing monarch, he'd affixed a heart-shaped beauty mark to his cheek and he sported a wig of mountainous curls. It was his custom to dress as someone very powerful and wealthy. He considered himself at home among such company.

Now, with agitation, he glanced impatiently at the wide stairs. All his guests were present. Lady Winslow was chatting nearby with his father. He turned as a faint ripple of speculation sifted through the crowd, lifting a thin brow at sight of the tall, lean figure dressed all in black silk. One by one, Barrington's guests parted as the masked man made his way with animal-like stealth across the crowded hall.

Jerrold's first impression was dismay, then shock. This had to be some joke! His fingers spasmed into hard fists at his sides. It was almost as if one of the guests were ridiculing him by posing as the Raven. Jerrold fought to remain calm. After all, it was only a costume party, and he'd placed no restrictions on what his guests wore.

But still, just the sight of that black silk outfit and the mask was enough to infuriate him. He'd never seen the Raven, but his men had, when their ships were scuttled on the Barrier Reef or lured into traps among the small islands off the coast of New South Wales. His losses to that thief over the past two years had practically driven Barrington Shipping to the brink to ruin. But his marriage to Elyse would bring renewed financial stability to the ailing company. And she would eventually inherit substantial properties from her grandmother. It was probably the most sound financial decision he'd made this last year.

Still his quarrel with the Raven wasn't entirely a matter of money. It had become a personal matter. The pirate's escapades had achieved a certain notoriety in England. Indeed, he now seemed almost a folk hero, one that had an uncanny ability to escape the authorities at every turn. And now, for some unknown reason, he seemed to have gone into hiding. The latest word Jerrold had, from the captain of one of his ships newly arrived from New South Wales, was that there hadn't been any raids on Barrington ships for quite some time. But that wasn't good enough. He didn't want the man merely to lie low. He wouldn't rest until the Raven was dead, or at the bottom of the Barrier Reef. He would stop the Raven, no matter what the cost.

The smile Jerrold Barrington fastened on his face as he finally recognized his guest betrayed none of his hatred. His voice was smooth as the silk of the man's mask.

"My compliments, your grace. You've outdone everyone present.

We choose the most elaborate costumes hoping to outdo one another. You dress in a somber color and cause speculation to run rampant."

"I picked this costume especially for you." Zach smiled. "I was certain you could enjoy a bit of humor as well as the next person. Do you think I resemble the Raven? I understand several of your crews have had an especially close look at the fellow." He turned so that Jerrold was given an eyeful of his costume.

"It's very clever, but the Raven would be far *too* clever to be so bold. Still my compliments to you, your grace. And a bit of a warning." Jerrold found that he was almost enjoying the conversation. "My men will have the Raven. Already his activities are greatly reduced. But let me assure you, if and when he chooses to strike again, Barrington Shipping will be waiting for him."

"I think it's only a matter of when," Zach assured his host. "The Raven doesn't strike me as the sort of fellow who would quit so easily, although I can see that he might become bored with it all. There is really no challenge to sinking ships of the line." He was deliberately goading Barrington.

"Ah," Jerrold responded delightedly, "let me assure you there will be far more challenge in the future. I have joined forces with the Crown and made certain provision aboard my ships. And my people have made certain contacts within the colonies. This fellow, the Raven, will find his followers not so loyal. The problem is, he won't know who is the Judas who will betray him. Should he choose to begin again, he will find his days numbered."

"You seem to have considered everything. Undoubtedly, you've taken into consideration the loyalty of the colonists themselves."

"Naturally. And they are true to their convict ancestors. They'd all sell their mothers for a handful of gold coins. Yes, the Raven will learn there is a price for loyalty. It goes to the highest bidder." Eyes hooded, Barrington sneered almost gleefully. "So, my friend," he said to Zach, "do you still think you want to pose as this Raven?"

"It is only a costume. I hope you won't take offense."

"Not in the least. You have an excellent sense of humor. I like that." He turned to his other guests. "Ladies and gentleman, the Count de Cuervo."

There were several raised eyebrows and mutterings of recognition among the gentlemen. An excited titter came from the ladies.

"You have the undivided attention of everyone in this room, and not one of these ladies' husbands will be on speaking terms with me after tonight. My congratulations, your grace." The smile never reached Jerrold's cold eyes.

237

"Thank you." Zach bowed with a flourish that was almost mocking in its exaggeration. "I thought you might be amused." He then seized a glass of brandy from a tray held by a passing servant, knowing full well amusement was the last thing Barrington felt at that moment. He felt a little like a cat playing with a mouse, or perhaps a rat. He raised the glass in a toast.

"To Lady Barrington."

Jerrold joined in the toast as a hushed silence fell upon the room.

"What is it now?" Barrington turned, his glass halfway to his lips. Then he stopped, his mouth gaping open. His eyes widened until it seemed they would pop from his head, and he inhaled sharply. "Good God!"

Zach turned as a sudden hush fell on the large room and he stared, a mixture of wonder and disbelief reflected in his gray gaze.

Elyse stopped midway down the staircase when she found a roomful of people staring at her.

"Good heavens!" a surprised guest exclaimed. "Will you look at that?"

"My word, isn't that . . . ?" The comment was never finished.

"Of course it is, my dear. She's wearing her gown!" This last was almost a hissing.

"You would think she'd have more sense than to wear it. Lord Barrington must be devastated." The whispered comments contained a hint of wicked satisfaction.

Elyse had hoped to make a grand entrance, but this wasn't exactly what she'd had in mind. She felt shock and dismay as rude stares seemed to go right through her. Then she caught sight of Jerrold's father; his expression could have turned the nearest person to stone. Elyse hesitated, her hand twisting in the soft folds of midnight blue velvet. On Jerrold's face was cold fury.

Zach couldn't take his eyes off her. He felt as if a knife had been thrust between his ribs and twisted. He couldn't draw breath. His fingers tightened around the glass he was holding until it seemed it would surely shatter.

I'll wear the blue gown for you, the sweet words leaped into his thoughts.

You must promise to always wear your hair long for me. The words echoed back through some half-forgotten memory.

I promise, my love.

He reached up, certain he felt the brush of cool fingers against his cheek.

Zach's hands shook so badly he set the glass down. My God! Was he mad? And yet, as he stood there staring at her, he knew it wasn't madness. The midnight blue of the gown caught the shimmering color of eyes that accented the pale oval of her face. Sable-colored hair trailed down the length of her back; it was pulled back from the sides of her face and secured with pearl-encrusted combs. The blond lace that circled the skirt at her feet seemed like a cloud she walked on. It was an old-fashioned gown. And yet it was quite simply the most elegant one he'd ever seen, all the more so because she was wearing it, and somehow dearly familiar.

He could feel the tension in the room, the stunned silence, and Jerrold Barrington's anger. Beside them, Lord Barrington looked as if he were seized with a sudden fit. His face contorted, going from vivid anger to a white mask as he stared at Elyse. The older man's hands clenched, unclenched, and clenched again at his sides.

"Who the devil gave her permission to wear that gown?" he growled low. Then the growl became a roar. "Who!"

"Father, I assure you . . ." Jerrold Barrington was equally speechless.

"Oh, my poor dear Elyse." Lady Winslow was obviously as shocked as the others. She started across the room.

Lord Barrington clutched at the back of a nearby chair. "Get her out of here!" he ground out at his son. "Get her out!"

"Charles, I apologize for the indiscretion." Lady Regina was obviously as distraught as he. "But my granddaughter had no way of knowing."

His voice had carried across the room, a booming cannon in the stunned silence. Every gaze was fastened on Elyse. Her hand involuntarily rose to her throat. Confusion and pain were mirrored in her eyes as Lord Barrington slumped, stricken, onto a nearby settee and Jerrold called for one of the servants to bring him a strong drink. An undercurrent of whispering spread across the room.

"This is absolutely ridiculous," Lady Winslow announced. "I think you're all acting abominably. I intend to put an end to this." She turned on them all, only to have her arm seized as she started toward the entry.

Jerrold's face was a stony mask. "I'll talk to her. After all, she is my responsibility."

Lady Winslow began to protest, but he was already walking away from her.

"Perhaps I can help." Zach set down his own glass and followed, his gaze boring into Barrington's stiff back as he walked to the foot of the stairs.

"Good God!" Jerrold hissed under his breath as he reached Elyse. "What the devil are you trying to do!"

She stared at him, aghast. "I was merely trying to join the party."

"In that dress?"

"Yes." Confusion clouded her lovely eyes. "What's wrong with this dress? Why is everyone staring at me like that?"

"It was my mother's dress," he informed her coolly.

"I thought you would be pleased—"

She was cut off when Jerrold seized her by the arm and whirled her around on the lower landing.

"You're hurting me!" Elyse cried out, aware that they were drawing more curious stares.

Jerrold's grasp loosened only a fraction of an inch. "You're to return to your rooms and change immediately into something more suitable. I don't want to see you again until you have. Is that clear?"

"But, Jerrold, what can be the harm? It's a lovely gown, the one Lady Barrington was wearing in the portrait."

"Where did you see it?" he hissed at her.

"In the room where the costumes are stored. The gown was in the other wardrobe. You said I could wear anything I chose. I never dreamed this gown would make everyone so unhappy."

His voice was tight. "Just please, do as you're told. It doesn't matter what you wear, as long as you take off that gown. Do I make myself clear?"

"Jerrold—" Elyse tried as diplomatically as possible to explain, but he would have none of it.

"Now, Elyse!" he thundered at her, his eyes as cold as ice.

Neither seemed to notice Zach's approach. It didn't matter. He only had eyes for Elyse.

"Good evening, may I compliment you, Miss Winslow. You are, by far, the most beautiful woman here." Zach acted as if Jerrold weren't even there.

Elyse looked up, her wounded gaze meeting his, and Jerrold whirled on him, his expression dangerous. His voice quivered as he struggled for control in front of his guests. "I would caution you, sir, not to interfere in this matter. Elyse is to be my wife; therefore responsibility for her behavior falls to me. I would like a few words alone with her." He turned backed to his fiancée, arching a commanding brow.

"It seems, old fellow, you have already had them," Zach reminded him with maddening smoothness, but his gray gaze had darkened and become intense.

Barrington's gaze jerked back to his, confrontation momentarily imminent judging by his livid expression. But Jerrold's glare slipped into a cold smile as if he'd perhaps thought better of such a display.

"You're quite right, and I am neglecting my guests." He momentarily turned back to Elyse, a polite expression frozen into the hardened lines of his face. "I expect you to do as I ask," he said, then turned abruptly on his heel and stalked back across the tiled entry hall, leaving them standing alone.

She blinked, stunned by his coldness and cruelty, and pain tightened inside her.

Zach fought to bring his own wildly churning emotions under control. He'd spoken out of turn and he knew it, but that didn't matter. Nothing mattered except the fragile, wounded expression in her soft eyes. It tore at him. "It seems you've made quite an entrance this evening."

His voice was gentle, soothing after Jerrold's harsh words. Her blue eyes were vivid pools of emotion, her knuckles white as she clutched at the balustrade. "It seems I have. Great balls of fire! What is everyone making such a fuss over?" Her voice trembled slightly, giving away her uncertainty and wounded pride. "I thought it would be such a special surprise. It fits perfectly".

She lifted a shaking hand to her hair. "I fixed it exactly the way it was in the painting. Damn!" She pounded the skirt with a clenched fist. "Nothing is ever good enough for him. He picks the fabric for my clothes because he doesn't like what I choose. He corrects my language because it isn't proper. I ask to spend an evening at the theater and he decides that we will attend the opera. Great balls of fire! What does he expect of me?" She wiped furiously at the tears that spilled from her eyes.

"Do you have a handkerchief? They're usually recommended when one is about to have a crying jag," Zach teased gently as he took her hand.

She gave her head a defiant toss. "I'm not crying," she announced with a sniff. "It's just that he makes me so angry sometimes."

"Good. I'm glad to hear that," Zach announced.

As if she'd truly noticed him for the first time, Elyse eyed him warily. "What do you want?"

"Your grandmother was worried about you. But from what I just heard, I don't think she has anything to be concerned about."

"You were eavesdropping!" she accused.

"It's a little difficult not to overhear a conversation that's practically being shouted across a room full of people," he responded.

He was right, of course. Jerrold hadn't even tried to be discreet.

"It hardly seems the best way to begin a marriage. By the way," — the light in his gaze had changed subtly, becoming teasing — "why are you marrying Barrington? I would think a creature of your passionate nature wouldn't care for a cold fish like him. You're not at all suited for one another."

"In answer to the first part, it doesn't concern you; in answer to your question, that doesn't concern you either; and as for your opinion about Jerrold, you're wrong." Actually if she were to be honest with herself, the Count de Cuervo wasn't the first person to make that comment. Lucy had said the very same thing. She'd dismissed it. Certainly the Count de Cuervo wasn't a reputable person. Still, it was odd that he and her best friend had said the same thing about Jerrold.

Placing one booted foot casually on the lower step, Zach leaned forward. "And what of my observations about your passionate nature?"

"You're wrong about that too!" she announced, refusing to meet his gaze.

He reached up, his fingers warm beneath the curve of her chin as he forced her to look at him. "I don't think I'm wrong at all." His expression was no longer gently teasing but deadly serious. "I seem to remember a very passionate creature in my bed."

Elyse tried to jerk away, but he persisted, his fingers like firebrands against her skin. She bit back several stinging comments, deciding that ignoring him was undoubtedly the safest course at this point. She didn't need to draw any more attention to herself. "Then your memory fails you. I don't know what you're talking about."

"Let me refresh your memory." He traced her full bottom lip with his index finger, and was rewarded by a betraying tremble and the subtle change of color in her eyes.

Damn him! She'd been embarrassed before an entire roomful of people, Jerrold was furious with her, his father would probably never speak to her again for reasons she couldn't begin to understand, and now this pompous fool was reminding her of something she would much rather forget. Worse still, she couldn't deny the shimmer of pleasure his fingers caused against her skin. Her eyes glittered. In one quick movement she bit down on the offending finger.

Zach's reaction was immediate. His other hand closed around one slender wrist, the hand with the wounded finger snaked around her waist. In the breath of an instant, he jerked her from the landing at the bottom of the stairs and into the shadows of the entry hall.

Elyse gasped as she was pulled against his lean, hard body.

"Did I ever tell you about my methods for taking revenge?" His silver gaze sparked dangerously.

"I don't believe we've ever discussed that," she replied breathlessly. She couldn't manage much else.

A silken smile spread across his lips. "For revenge I expect to be paid in triplicate." He coolly handed down the sentence.

"Three times?" She wedged her hands between them, glancing back uncertainly over her shoulder. The last thing she needed at this moment was for one of Jerrold's guests to come through those doors and find her with the Count de Cuervo. Or worse yet for Jerrold himself to do so.

"Yes," he announced. "It makes the satisfaction so much greater."

He was serious! Elyse stared at him. "Three times!" Did he actually mean he would bite her three times?

"Right now you're wondering if that means I intend to bite you as you bit me. Correct?"

"I'm not thinking anything of the kind." He was leaning over her. She jerked her face further away from his, not trusting him one bit. He had an unnerving effect on her at a distance; close up he was absolutely devastating.

Once more, his fingers insistently found her chin. "Don't lie to me, Elyse. I can always see through it," he threatened, but with sweet tenderness. "Is that what you were thinking?"

"Oh, for heaven's sake! What if it was? It's absolutely ridiculous anyway. It was only a simple bite, and you deserved it. You'll recover. I have great faith in your powers of recovery." Her eyes widened as she vividly remembered his powers of recovery when he'd made love to her.

Amusement twitched at the corners of Zach's lips. "But I fully intend to pay you back three times for biting me." When her hand again came up against his chest to block the contact of their bodies, it was immediately seized in his long fingers.

Elyse gasped and closed her eyes. If he was going to do it, she was powerless to stop him, but she'd be switched if she'd cry out. She forced herself to concentrate on something else, anything, except the coming punishment. The waiting was excruciating. Then she winced as she felt the first contact of his teeth against the soft flesh at the tips of her fingers.

Faint shivers slipped across her skin. He nibbled first one finger then the next, then a third. It was the most delicate touch, languorous and teasing, as his lips pulled faintly on each finger, releasing faint flutterings deep in her stomach. Her eyes flew open.

"I should have known," she said accusingly.

"Yes, you should have known that I would never hurt you." Zach continued the sensual assault on her fingers, until she cried out softly, snatching her hand away to safety.

"I think we should be getting back," she whispered shakily as she backed away from him.

"Are you forgetting? You've been banned from the party," Zach reminded her.

"I'm not the least concerned about the party. I just want to make certain my grandmother is all right. Did she seem upset?"

"She was very upset, but not at you. I can see where you get your temper. Actually, I'm quite taken with her. Lady Winslow isn't afraid of anyone or anything. I envision her marching right up to the gates of heaven and challenging St. Peter to his right to be there."

In spite of herself, Elyse giggled. She'd had just that same thought once or twice herself. "You're right of course. I absolutely adore her."

"Is that why you agreed to this marriage?" he asked bluntly. "Because of her friendship with Lady Barrington?"

"No, of course not!" she blurted out defensively, then realized how it must have sounded. "I've known Jerrold for a long time. He's responsible, he comes from an impeccable family, and he cares a great deal for me. Furthermore, I'm not in the habit of discussing my personal life with strangers."

"Your description of Jerrold reminds me of the qualities one might look for in a good hunting dog. And as for our being strangers . . . we are not," he pointed out. "No two people can remain strangers when they've shared what we have."

"Shared?" She looked at him aghast. "Is that why you came out here? To embarrass me?" She seized the fabric of her skirt in one hand and whirled around to leave.

Zach chuckled softly at her flash of temper, and his fingers closed over her arm. She was so beautiful when she was angry. He wondered if she realized it, then decided she couldn't possibly. She'd be vain if she did.

"That's not the reason," he assured her, then looked over her shoulder as music drifted to them from the room across the hall. Someone, probably Lady Winslow, had had the foresight to have the musicians begin playing.

"Actually, I came to ask you to dance with me."

She tried to free her arm. "Why would you want to dance with me? I certainly don't want to dance with you."

"I thought you might say that. But, you see, I understand you, Elyse. You're not afraid of anyone or anything. I know a little gossip certainly won't stop a young lady who parades around in men's pants and rides astride, or steals into a men's club to sneak a peek at what goes on. As long as they're talking about you, why don't you give them something to really talk about."

"Such as?" She couldn't resist the temptation. Jerrold's nastiness had had a terrible effect on her. In truth, she didn't give a damn about what everyone else thought, except for her grandmother.

"Such as dancing out here with me in the shadows," he suggested with a devilish arch of his brows.

"My reputation will be ruined, and Jerrold will be even angrier. I should go upstairs and change my clothes."

"Like a good little girl." There was a faintly mocking tone to his voice. "My dear Elyse, Jerrold is already angry, in case you hadn't noticed, and as for your reputation"—he placed a hand over his heart as if with regret—"I cannot tell a lie; I have already ruined it. What have you to lose?"

She should have been furious with him. Instead, all she could do was laugh. He was right. That was the most maddening thing of all.

"If I have that dance with you, will you leave me alone?"

"You have my solemn vow," he pledged, one hand over heart.

"As what, a pirate?" She couldn't hold back the taunt.

"As the gentleman that I am."

"A Spanish gentleman," she declared blithely, "who has no accent and never speaks his native language."

"Is there anything else you would like to add to your list of observations?" His warm fingers twined with hers as he whirled her into his arms to begin the first steps of a waltz. But instead of dancing, he just stood there, luxuriating in the feel of having her in his arms again.

She met his silver gaze. "Yes, as a matter of fact, there is. You're not old or infirm. You certainly don't seem to be afflicted with gout, dyspepsia or shaking of the limbs. And"—she paused for full effect—"that costume suits you far too well. You seem more comfortable posing as a pirate than as a gentleman."

Zach smiled, flashing an array of even, white teeth. "Did anyone ever warn you about offending a nobleman?"

"I think it's a little late for that." One hand she rested almost hesitantly on his shoulder, as if afraid to touch him; the other was trapped in his. She glanced about, at the guests who had now begun to dance.

245

"It seems I've already offended two people this evening—Jerrold and now you."

"That's impossible." Zach was enjoying the feel of her lithe body as it brushed against his when they turned. Her eyes were an incredible shade of blue, the exact same color of the ocean off the Barrier Reef, equally as deep and mystifying, and a bit dangerous in their secrets.

"Impossible that you're offended, or that you're a nobleman?" she quipped, some of the gaiety returning to her magical gaze.

"Perhaps a little of both," Zach hinted, drawing her against him. He held her close, watching her eyes subtly change color at the intimacy of their contact.

"You have the oddest way of saying things, almost as if there are hidden meanings." She laughed a little uneasily. "And you certainly don't seem to have much respect for the nobility."

"I have complete respect, when it's necessary." He qualified his statement. "But I'm not fooled by titles. They're just so much decoration and illusion."

"Like a mask?" She arched a lovely brow.

"Precisely." He smiled, enjoying their verbal sparring.

Her smile deepened with her sense of victory. "I knew you were a pirate. It fits so much better than that ridiculous title you carry around. What does it mean—Count de Cuervo? Is it a family name?" She fixed an appropriately innocent expression on her lovely face as if they only shared idle chatter.

Zach wasn't the least fooled by the inquisitive widening on her beautiful eyes or the polite smile that turned her lips. She was an intoxicating, beguiling little witch and she was subtly prying for answers.

"I'll tell you someday." At the moment he chose not to satisfy her curiosity. "Are you going to dance or talk?"

"Both," she announced; then she recalled something that was bothering her. "I do hope you brought the pendant with you. There is still the matter of our little agreement."

"Ah, yes," Zach looked as if he truly hadn't given the matter much thought. "I believe it was something about a kiss in exchange for your pendant."

"You know perfectly well what the agreement was," Elyse quickly proclaimed. "I would like to have the pendant now."

"Is that right?"

"Yes, that's right." They both looked up at the sound of voices, to see a costumed couple emerge from the great room and walk in their direction.

Elyse struggled to free herself from his embrace. It would never do for Jerrold to find out she had been dancing with the Count De Cuervo when he'd thought her to be upstairs changing her clothes.

Amusement danced in Zach's silver gaze as his fingers lingered possessively at her wrist. She pried them loose and quickly stepped away from him so that it looked as if they were only indulging in conversation. The other couple walked past them, nodded some brief greeting, and continued on through large double doors at the end of the hallway that opened onto the magnificent lawns at the back of the house.

"Don't do that!" Elyse whispered.

"Don't do what, my lovely Elyse?" He seized her wrist and pulled her back into his arms, not the least concerned that they might have been seen.

"You know what I mean. This!" She tried to put more distance between their bodies.

"You were saying . . . about our agreement?" he completely ignored her glare of disapproval.

"I want my pendant back."

"I understand that."

He was being maddening. Elyse gritted her teeth to keep from saying something that might jeopardize his returning it to her. It had happened once before, that day he'd followed her into the Woods. She glanced worriedly over her shoulder to where the others danced. "Do you have it with you?"

Zach stopped, a stunned expression on his face.

"You don't have it?" Elyse gasped. Just as quickly as he'd looked appropriately stunned, a devilish smile turned his handsome lips. He was teasing her! She could have joyfully taken that sword at his hip and run him through with it. The only problem was, then she would have to explain the body in the entry hall to Jerrold.

"Damn you!"

"Elyse"—there was a warning tone to his voice—"I refuse to keep bargains with ladies who speak like sailors. I do have the pendant, and if you will just behave yourself and act like a proper lady, you might get it back."

"A proper lady!" She couldn't believe the unmitigated gall of the man.

"You do want it back?"

He was treating her like a child. Well, if a lady was what he wanted, a lady was what he would get—the most proper, dignified lady she could manage to project, in spite of herself. She fixed him

247

with a cool glare. "Of course I want it back."

"Then I am prepared to accept proper payment," he announced. His arm tightened around her waist, pulling her slender body full-length against his.

He towered over her, his face not more than a few inches from hers, his lips coming closer. Elyse panicked. If anyone else were to come out of that room, they'd surely be seen.

"Not here!" she gasped, flattening both hands against the black silk across his chest.

"But you specifically set the terms of the agreement," he reminded her. "It was to be a public place." His face lowered, his lips almost brushing hers.

"No!" Elyse struggled from his arms. "Not here. Someone might see us."

"That generally happens in a public place."

He was trying to trap her, using the conditions she'd set for the agreement.

"I don't care what I said. It can't be here. I've changed my mind."

"Ah, the fickle mind of a woman." Zach shook his tawny head, mischief gleaming in his gray eye. "Where do you suggest we consummate this agreement?" He chose his words very carefully, thoroughly enjoying the play of emotions on her lovely face.

Having sufficiently separated herself from his unnerving embrace, Elyse glanced up and down the hallway. She'd been down it earlier in the afternoon.

"In here," she announced, taking him by the hand and leading him to the reading room. Pushing open double doors, she pulled him inside and turned up the lamp on the side table.

"What is this place?" Zach's gaze narrowed as he peered into the soft pools of light cast by the ornate lamp. Several pieces of heavy furniture were arranged in a conversation area. Framed pictures of every size almost obscured the walls. Obviously this was some sort of gallery.

"It's called the formal reading room. Hardly anyone ever comes in here."

"Oh, that's good, very good." He complimented her, trying to keep the smile from his lips. She'd unwittingly played right into his hands. He studied a portrait just over her left shoulder, noticing the Barrington name on the brass plate affixed at the bottom.

"I wanted a place where we couldn't be seen. Jerrold just wouldn't understand if he were to intrude on us." For some reason she felt the need to explain.

"So, you chose an entire roomful of Barringtons to witness our little 'agreement.' "

"What are you talking about?" She looked in the direction of his gaze.

"This seems to be some kind of family portrait gallery." He indicated the wall behind her. "All those paintings are of Barringtons. Very discreet."

Elyse turned back around. "Are we to keep the agreement or shall I leave?" Her voice was very proper, very ladylike.

"We shall keep the agreement," Zach announced, his gaze fastening on her lovely face.

"I should like to see the pendant first, to make certain you do have it with you."

"Of course." He reached inside a boot and produced a small leather pouch. The diamond and pearl pendant tumbled into his hand. He suspended it from his fingers, turning it slowly. "It really is very lovely. None other like it in the world." He tested her, because he'd switched the pendants just to see if she could tell the difference.

Elyse snatched the pendant from his fingers. She carefully inspected it in the soft light. The clasp was intact as were the stones.

"Does it meet with your approval?" He watched her carefully.

"Yes. It's perfect." She turned to go and immediately felt the pressure of his hand on her arm.

"There is the matter of your part of the agreement," he reminded her.

Elyse slowly let out the breath she'd been holding. She'd hoped to escape before he had a chance to remind her. No such luck. She slowly turned around.

"All right. I'm ready." She forced herself to relax, and fixed an appropriately unfeeling expression on her lovely face.

He almost burst out laughing. She looked like the condemned being led to the gallows instead of a beautiful young woman about to be kissed.

"This shouldn't take long." He stepped forward. Slipping one arm around her slender waist, he pulled her against him. He forced back a smile as he felt her body soften into his. When she continued staring up at him with that abstractly bored expression, the light in his gray gaze changed. He wanted to wipe that expression from her face, to replace it with something far different.

Reaching up, he caressed her cheek, then his fingers stole into the softness of her long hair. As his palm circled the delicate curve of her ear, his thumb grazed the prominence of her cheekbone. Heat was

249

ignited everywhere he touched her. He sensed rather than felt the subtle change in her breathing, the struggle for control that went on in her. With the greatest tenderness, he bent over her, following his fingers with his lips. It was like a game, a delicious, wonderful game. He wanted to prolong it so that when he finally kissed her, it would be so much sweeter.

He loved watching her reactions as his fingers moved to her temple, across a lovely brow, and then over each eye, their touch slowly building in intensity as they traveled the wondrous planes of her face. When he'd kissed every place except her soft, full mouth, he hesitated, then smiled victoriously. Her eyes were closed, her lips were parted expectantly, her breathing was fast and softly sweet. She reminded him of a young girl waiting for her first kiss.

Without knowing why, his gaze went to the wall behind her, to the array of portraits. He chuckled to himself. And she'd thought they wouldn't be seen. His gaze narrowed as he read a nameplate.

Lord Clayton Barrington. From the stablemaster he knew him to be Jerrold's grandfather, the man who'd had the black stallion Domino bred especially for his son. Seated beside Clayton Barrington in a portrait of him as a youth was a young woman with an infant in her arms—Lady Amicia Barrington and son, Alex.

His gaze shot to the next picture—it showed a towheaded child about three or four years of age—then the next—Lord Clayton Barrington again and the blond child, but with a different woman cradling an infant.

His hands dropped from Elyse's face, and he stepped around her, his silver gaze fastened on the family portraits. Two sons. He'd heard nothing about Lord Charles's brother.

Elyse recovered slowly. Her eyes blinking open uncertainly, she turned around and stared openmouthed at the Count de Cuervo who was now completely engrossed in the paintings on the wall.

"Of all the—"

He cut her off. "Who are these people?"

"What?" She was incredulous. One minute he was kissing her, well almost kissing her, and the next he was staring at portraits.

He seized her wrist and pulled her to the wall. "Who are they? he insisted.

"I suppose they're all Barringtons," she announced coolly.

"I can see that." He moved along the wall, reading the nameplate under each painting. He stopped at the one that showed two young boys; the fair-haired one older by approximately four or five years than the dark-haired toddler.

"Alexander Nicholas Barrington and Charles Farragut Barrington. Of course. Lord Charles." But his gaze fastened on the older boy with sun-bleached hair and soft gray eyes.

"Alexander Nicholas Barrington." Zach said the name over and over, slowly.

"Alexander Barrington." Somehow it wasn't right. He said it again, turning it over and over, unable to comprehend why it should seem familiar to him.

One moment he was kissing her and the next he was staring at those paintings like some sort of crazed madman. Well, that was perfectly all right with Elyse. She had what she'd come for. But she couldn't ignore a touch of pique, he was completely ignoring her.

"Whatever happened to the older brother?"

Elyse's gaze turned heavenward. She couldn't believe this. "I think he died very young. No one has ever said very much about him." She opened her fingers to look at the pendant; small lights twinkled in the diamonds, the pearls glowed.

"He was called Nicky," she said simply, her voice suddenly soft with memory.

Elyse gasped as her arms were suddenly seized in a viselike grip.

"What did you say?" Zach ground out. The soft smokiness was gone from his gaze, replaced by something hard and cold. His fingers cut into the skin of her arm like bands of steel. He was completely transformed, everything about him suddenly black, sinister, and forbidding.

She swallowed back the panic that congealed in her throat. "I don't know . . . I . . ."

"His name!" Zach insisted, the bands on her arms tightening, threatening to cut off the flow of blood.

"I can't remember." In truth she couldn't. Panic and the pain of his fingers had driven everything from her thoughts.

"Nicky!" he growled at her. "You said he was called Nicky as a child."

Tears pooled in her eyes; fear cooled her skin. She'd never seen anyone quite so angry, not even Jerrold in his worst shows of temper. And she never cried, not for anyone.

"I don't know why I said it. It just came to me!" That was true. She knew little about the Barrington family, except what her grandmother had told her of Felicia and, of course, Lord Charles.

"Tell me!" he raged at her like some wild thing.

"I don't know," she cried out, her breath coming in great anguished sobs now. She practically fell as he whirled from her, suddenly releasing his bruising hold.

"Alexander Nicholas Barrington. Nicky." Like a massive puzzle with thousands of pieces it began to come together. He fought it, tried to force it back, but he couldn't.

"Nicholas Barrington," he whispered brokenly. "It can't be."

Tears coursed down Elyse's cheeks as she leaned against the table edge for support. At the sound of the name, she looked up. It reached out to her, wrapped around her in some vague half-memory.

"Nicky?" she whispered, the name sounding very far away, like an echo. Slowly, she shook her head. She didn't understand.

"My God." Zach stared at the painting. "Is it possible? Is it?" He whirled on her, his gray gaze stricken. There was something in his voice, in the shaking of his hands clenched at his sides. "I have to know," he rasped, near desperation. "I have to know."

He stalked from the room, leaving Elyse stunned and shaken. In that one brief instant, when he'd turned to her, there had been something in his gaze. It had seemed she was looking at another man . . . someone she knew. One hand flew to her throat as she choked back the truth that struggled painfully to escape from some darkened corner of consciousness. It flashed across her mind like lightning, white-hot, blinding, there one instant, gone the next.

She raced to the door, propelled by something she didn't understand. He was gone, as if he'd never been there at all.

Staring into the empty hallway, she slowly opened her fingers. He was real, very real.

The pendant lay in her palm, its diamonds and pearls still warm, a glistening, shining promise.

Chapter Twelve

Zach stormed from the reading room. He had to know about Alexander Barrington, and there was one person who might tell him. Getting the man to talk would be another matter.

Everything was obliterated from his thoughts: Elyse, the pendant, everything except that name that kept echoing through his mind, as if someone were standing behind him, saying it over and over again. As long strides took him past the room where Jerrold Barrington entertained his guests, his gaze narrowed on Charles Barrington. The second son!

The room was gay, sparkling, in contrast to his chaotic thoughts. People costumed, like himself, were attempting to play out some charade. It all seemed to pass before him disjointedly — a kaleidoscope of movement, color, and sound leaping at him. He turned and practically collided with the bewildered butler, a decanter of amber liquid almost tipping from the silver tray the servant held. Instinctively, Zach reached out to steady the man, his gaze slipping to the cut-crystal decanter. He snatched it from the tray.

Then he hurried down the hallway to the doors that opened onto the gardens. Like a phantom, he slipped out into the night.

Unless he missed his guess, the stablemaster was an Irishman. He'd recognized the soft brogue that matched the accent he'd grown up with at Resolute. It was soft and caught on certain letters. Megan had spoken just that same way. His boots crunched on the gravel that lined the driveway; then his steps were muffled by the soft lawn. A single light gleamed from one end of the stables.

The stablemaster was bent over a saddle, rubbing the leather to a soft sheen. A pipe hung from his lips, fragrant tobacco smoke encircling his head. As the gentle night breeze blew faintly, a sound caused him to look up.

"Good evenin', sir." The other man stood, wiping his hands on his worn pants. "Is there somethin' you'd be needin', sir?"

Zach forced his churning emotions down. "Some night air, a little conversation, and fine whiskey, perhaps." He held the decanter aloft and saw the gleam that leaped into the man's eyes.

"Aye, 'tis a fine summer night."

"Then you'll join me?" Zach entered the stables, placing the decanter on the small table with the brushes, rags, and polish the stablemaster used. He'd bargained that the man was Irish through and through. The gleam in the stablemaster's eyes as they lingered on the gently sloshing liquid in the decanter proved him right.

"The master doesn't approve. . . ." The old men wet his lips as if he could almost taste the amber liquid.

Zach smiled slowly, leaning forward conspiratorially. "But the master isn't here, and this fine whiskey was cast aside. I'd hate to see it go to waste." He stretched out in the chair beside the one the old man had occupied when he'd come in. "I'd like to hear more about that fine black stallion you were telling me about."

The man's greedy gaze lifted momentarily from the bottle. "Oh yes, Domino. That was a long time ago."

"But I'm sure there must be a fine story to tell about him." He appealed to an Irishman's storytelling abilities.

"That there is." The stablemaster wet his lips as if he could almost taste the silken fire of the fine whiskey he knew his master kept. "It might take a long time."

"It might take a long time to enjoy this whiskey," Zach countered.

"It would be a pity to waste it." The old man passed a gnarled hand over the stubble of beard at his chin, as if torn by some great dilemma. It was quickly solved. "I have some clean glasses in me room. I'll be right back." He shuffled off in search of the glasses, and Zach forced himself to relax back into the chair. Now all he had to do was remain sober while luring the old man into enough of a stupor to loosen his tongue.

"Aye, I remember the time when that black devil first came here to Fair View. He was almost two years old, but only partly saddle broke. The young master took it upon himself to ride him that very afternoon."

Zach shifted uncomfortably in the chair. For the last two hours, he'd listened to the man's ramblings, plying him with whiskey and questions. When he'd felt his backside grow numb he'd walked, now he slumped wearily in the chair. Two hours, and the man had told him virtually nothing.

"You're speaking of Lord Charles," Zach inserted. The stablemaster's name was Rooney, and outside of Tobias, he'd never seen anyone capable of talking so much and saying so little.

"What's that you say?" The old man blinked several times to focus. "Lord Charles? Saints preserve us, no! He was afraid of the animal almost from the moment the old master brought him to Fair View. Could've been because he was younger."

"Younger?" Zach sat up, trying to keep the tone of his voice casual and faintly slurred like the old man's even though he'd consumed far less whiskey.

"Master Alex, it was." Rooney leaned forward, one eye closed, the other narrowed. "Aye, the boy was a fine rider, could sit any horse. He had a way about him."

"I've heard little about this Barrington," Zach prodded.

The old man shook his head. "He was the Master Clayton's first son, Master Alexander Barrington. And a finer young man there never was."

"Ah yes." Zach nodded. "There was a portrait in the house of two young boys. His name was Alexander Nicholas Barrington according to the name plate." He betrayed emotion only by a subtle tightening of his fingers around the glass.

"That be the one. And as I said, there was never a finer lad."

Zach leaned forward on the table, bracing himself on his arms. He poured Rooney a healthy draught of encouragement. "I've heard little said about him," he declared casually. "You'd think a father would be proud of such a young man as that."

Rooney grunted as he accepted the glass and took a healthy swig. "You would," he agreed. "But that's not the way of it. Because they all want to forget." The old man tossed back the whiskey in one loud gulp. His glass was quickly refilled.

"What is it everyone is trying to forget? Was he wild and rebellious?"

Rooney shook his head, staring into the soft glow the amber liquid reflected through the glass. "If that were only it, it would have been an easy matter. Such a sad, sad thing."

Zach's fingers constricted about the glass. "What could be so bad?"

255

The old man looked up, fixing Zach with bloodshot eyes. "Murder."

The glass shattered.

Zach leaned against the frame of a tall window that opened onto the balcony outside his room, trying to think. He exhaled slowly, smoke from the cigarette searing his senses. The empty decanter sat on the table beside the window. It had taken more than half of its contents to get what he wanted from Rooney. The old man finally had slumped over his table in a drunken stupor. Zach finished the rest of the liquor, desperately needing something to dull the painful truth.

He inhaled, the tip of the cigarette glowing fiery red.

Murder, two sons born of different mothers, childhood resentments that festered into manhood, a favored firstborn son, jealousies, rivalry for a father's love, and hatred. Then the untimely death of Lord Clayton Barrington. According to Rooney, some said it was an accident, others claimed it was murder. There had been a dreadful quarrel. The house servants heard it. Then there was silence and a young servant girl supposedly found Alex Barrington standing over his father's body.

The trial, and the ensuing scandal. Alex Barrington was brought up on murder charges. The evidence supplied by the servant girl was damning, but there were rumors about her, too. Ah yes, there were rumors. Rooney knew for a fact the girl was caught more than once sneaking out to the stables with young Master Charles. She testified against his brother, then disappeared shortly after the trial.

The sentence: servitude and exile. Because of his place in society Alex Barrington was spared hanging. He was ordered by the courts to serve a minimum sentence in prison and then be sent into permanent exile. In the span of a few short weeks, Alexander Nicholas Barrington was transformed from the heir of one of England's wealthiest families to a convict. His title, his lands, his wealth were all forfeit.

Nicholas Barrington. The words from the journal swam before him:

I began this journey into hell. One day I will return and have my day of justice for the crime of which I am accused.
. . . I shall now be called Nicholas Tennant.

His sentence became his hell. Nicholas Barrington was a man stripped of family, country, and ultimately his name.

It seemed impossible, yet in his soul Zach knew it was true. The connection to the Barrington family had been there all along. He vaguely wondered about Felicia Barrington and quickly dismissed such thoughts. They no longer mattered. He had the answers he wanted. Nicholas Tennant and Alexander Nicholas Barrington were one and the same.

I will reclaim my birthright from those who have accused me. I will return and have my day of justice.

The words from the journal haunted him. They were not words of regret or even denial; they were words of revenge. Was it possible his father had been falsely accused? But why? And who would stand to gain the most if he were dead or prevented from inheriting? Charles Barrington? Rooney had hinted as much, but had quickly let the matter drop and then wouldn't speak of it again. And there was the matter of the servant girl who'd testified at the trial, then disappeared so quickly afterward.

Nicholas Tennant had vowed to return. And what did it all have to do with Felicia Barrington? Zach ground the heels of his hands into his eyes.

He stared painfully into the blood red dawn. His head ached, but the pain helped clarify his thoughts. The hand he raised with a cigarette shook, but not with fear or weakness. The anger had begun hours ago in the stable and had slowly built until it was like a live animal clawing at his insides. Slowly the sun rose in the east, the light piercing deep into his silver eyes.

The mask was gone, as was the black silk shirt. He was clad only in black pants that clung to him like a second skin. A fine sheen of moisture spread across the rippling muscles in his shoulders and back, in spite of the cool night air that lingered. His hair was wild, unkempt, almost afire as the dawn fell in golden waves about his head. There was nothing of the elegant, sophisticated Count de Cuervo to be found in the lean, animal hunger that emanated from him.

As the walls seemed to close in on him, Zach threw the cigarette over the balcony and turned back to the room. He was like a madman, slamming drawers and wardrobe doors. He had to get away. If he remained another moment, he would go mad. There was nothing more to be done here. These people were powerful and respected. They would keep their secrets, because the truth

257

carried too high a price.

No, whatever he chose to do had to be done away from here, where the odds were more evenly balanced. He stopped mid-stride, his chest rising and falling rapidly. He stared at the walls that surrounded him. This had once been his father's home. He might have slept in this very room.

He turned and left, telling himself that Fair View meant nothing to him, held no meaning for him. It was only so much brick and mortar; rooms, hallways, and paintings. It had been part of his father's life, but not his. Those very same walls seemed to throw the lie back at him.

Zach hesitated outside the room at the end of the hall. He leaned into the door, the palm of his hand flattened against the smooth wood, and instinctively he knew. This was her room, Elyse's. She was just beyond that door.

Memories of her in his bed flashed across his mind; memories of sleek, pale skin against his, the struggle in her slender body that melted to passion as they came together. The anger that could flash in her eyes, then simmer to another emotion he knew she would deny—desire. She belonged to Barrington, like one of his ships or Fair View; a possession he'd acquired by right of his title and position. Whatever they might have shared began and ended that one night. His hand dropped to his side.

Downstairs, he found the library easily, and the safe behind the third painting. And just as he'd memorized them, the numbers fell into place beneath his fingers; the small, thick door swinging silently open. He clutched the draft in his hand, leaving behind odd pieces of jewelry, a thickly wrapped bundle of pound notes, and several documents. It would be enough.

"Where did you find this?" The black eyepatch fluttered in Jerrold Barrington's fingers, fingers that trembled with suppressed rage.

Mrs. Evers shifted uneasily, glancing up only briefly. "It was in his room, sir."

"And nothing else?"

"As I said, your lordship. It's as if he's disappeared. Vanished." The well-worn, rounded hands twisted, and the woman's smile disappeared at the look in his eyes.

"A man doesn't simply vanish without a trace. We're not talking about ghosts or spirits, Mrs. Evers. What about the stables?"

"His coach and coachman are gone as well."

"Did Rooney say when he left?"

"He saw and heard nothing, sir." She didn't dare tell him Rooney had been found slumped over a table, snoring through a drunken stupor as if he were trying to summon all the saints in the heavens.

Jerrold slammed his fist down hard on the table, causing the silver tea service to rattle ominously. His eyes narrowed.

Why would a man who'd lost an eye leave behind the item that covered that affliction? He'd thought the man a bumbling fool to be taken advantage of. It seemed he might have been wrong. But who was this mysterious stranger if not a Spanish nobleman? A muscle ticked in his cheek.

He looked up at the housekeeper, his voice causing her to jump. "I want to see Mr. Lash."

Mrs. Evers's gaze widened until it seemed her pupils were nothing but pinpoints in the vast white of her eyes. She didn't like Mr. Lash, no one did. He was a big silent brute of a man employed to handle "private" matters. Her hands twisted into white knots.

"He's not here, sir."

Jerrold whirled on her, his eyes dark and piercing. "What do you mean he's not here? He should have been back hours ago." He stopped to think. It wasn't like Lash to be tardy. The man had an unnerving ability to attain perfection in anything. If he hadn't returned yet, then something must have gone wrong.

"I want to know the moment he returns," he bellowed at the woman.

"Yes, sir." She bobbed into as much of a curtsy as her stout, round body would allow and quietly left the room.

His thoughts churning, Jerrold Barrington paced the library. Suddenly he whirled around, his gaze fastening on the painting, the third from the left corner. It stood a fraction of an inch away from the wall, but he knew.

Elyse stood before the portrait of Felicia Barrington. Restless, unable to sleep after the dream had driven her from her bed, she'd found herself outside the door to this room. Now she looked at the portrait, her fingers gently clutching the diamond and pearl pendant that rested at her throat. It was of the same design as the earbobs Lady Barrington wore.

She studied the painting, watching those eyes that stared back at her, reaching for her from every angle no matter where she stood.

"1837." She repeated the year inscribed in the brass plate.

"Your engagement portrait. What could have so drastically changed your life? You seem so happy?" Elyse whispered to the silent walls.

"She was."

Elyse whirled around, her eyes wide, She laughed. "Grandmother, you scared me. I thought the walls had started talking to me, or perhaps she had." She looked over her shoulder to Lady Barrington.

"Katy said I could find you here. I wanted to see the painting again."

"You've seen it before?"

Lady Regina crossed the room, her smile softened by memories. "Ah yes, just before it was finished. And she was happy then, as radiantly happy as she looks in that painting."

"You said she was a very sad woman. She certainly doesn't look like it here."

"She wasn't when this was painted. I've never seen a more vibrant woman or one more in love. But that was a very long time ago."

"Look at her earbobs. They're exactly like my pendant."

"Yes," Lady Regina answered without elaborating.

"She's so beautiful in that gown. I wonder why Lord Barrington was so very upset last night."

Lady Winslow sighed heavily, thinking it was perhaps time for Elyse to know certain things about this family she was marrying into. Of course she'd known that must be done one day, but she'd put it off. Now it seemed her dear friend Felicia had somehow brought it about.

"You may as well know. You'll hear bits and pieces of it anyway, once you're married."

Elyse turned back to her. "Know what? Family gossip?"

"I'm afraid it's a great deal more than that, my sweet." Regina looked up at the painting.

"She was so very happy. Her parents were friends of your grandfather's, and she was only a few years younger than your father. Naturally, I suppose I hoped that one day . . . Well at any rate that was not to be. Your father went off to America and met your mother. And Felicia met and fell in love with Alexander

260

Barrington."

"Alexander . . . ?" Surprise gave way to shock, and Elyse's startled blue gaze shot back to the portrait. "There were two sons?" She stared unbelievingly, as if she could see something in the image caught so breathtakingly on canvas. Then she whirled back to her grandmother.

"Yes. Alex was Lord Clayton's son by his first marriage. He remarried after his wife's death. I suppose Alex must have been about four or five at the time."

"Why was I never told?" Elyse's dark eyes were troubled.

"It never seemed to matter. It all happened so long ago. It was so dreadful then, but time has a way of changing things. I thought perhaps it had changed Charles's feelings as well, until I saw his reaction at seeing you in that gown." Lady Regina came closer to stand before the portrait. "I never knew much about the boys' childhood. I supposed it was like those of others. But as they grew older, there were rumors of problems. Alex was the firstborn, heir to Lord Clayton's title, lands, everything. Charles as the second son would inherit also, but to a much lesser extent. Of course it was all kept very quiet."

"Alex grew to be a handsome young man. It was easy to see how Felicia fell in love with him, and he with her. This portrait was painted to celebrate their engagement."

Elyse shivered. It was warm in the room; nevertheless, she felt as if something cold had brushed against her. It was like walking through a veil of mist.

"She was engaged to Charles's brother," she whispered incredulously. Her gaze came up to meet her grandmother's. "But how . . . ?"

"It was such a sad thing, all of it." Lady Regina slowly shook her head. "The wedding was to have taken place just before Christmas of that same year. To this day, I don't think anyone knows exactly how it all began."

Her hands closed around her grandmother's. "Tell me!" Her breathing was shallow. But even as she said that, somewhere deep in her soul, she already knew.

"There was a violent quarrel. There were conflicting stories on how it began, or even who was involved. When it was over, Clayton Barrington was dead. He'd been struck with a very heavy object. Alex was found standing over him, an andiron in his hand."

Elyse's hand flew to her mouth. Her throat constricted, closing off any sound. "No!" She felt the denial rather than heard it. Her grandmother's words seemed to come from very far away. And yet they came at her, like shards of glass tearing the skin.

"The evidence was damning. Alex was brought before the magistrate on a charge of murder. There was a dreadful scandal. I read about it in the American newspapers. Your mother and father had just married, and I had gone to New York for the wedding and a long visit with distant relatives. It was all over when I returned."

"Was there a trial?"

"Alex was found guilty of murder, on the testimony of a servant girl who claimed to have found him standing over Lord Clayton. Alex denied everything, but it didn't matter."

"What happened?" Elyse's voice was a strangled whisper as she stared, transfixed, at the portrait of Felicia Barrington. Without understanding how or why, she somehow sensed what this beautiful woman must have gone through. Elyse felt weak, drained, almost incapable of movement.

"He would have been hanged, but Charles pleaded for the court's mercy. In the end, Alex was given a sentence and exiled."

Elyse's fingers tightened. "Where?"

Lady Regina shook her head at the memory. "He was sent to the convict colony at New South Wales, and forbidden to ever return to England. Felicia was devastated. I hardly recognized her when I returned from New York. It was as if she had suffered everything with him. I've never seen two people more in love, or two lives more shattered."

Elyse looked up, her vivid blue eyes brimming with tears. "And she tried to go with him." Reality slipped from her. It was as if she were dreaming, but everything seemed so very real and her grandmother was there with her. It was real.

"She would have endured anything to be with him," Elyse whispered in a voice that seemed to come from a million miles away. "She didn't go."

The expression on Lady Regina's face was troubled. "Yes, of course. He wouldn't allow it," she said.

Pain tightened deep inside Elyse until she thought she couldn't breathe because of it. Her voice had softened to hardly more than a whisper. "He asked her to wait for him. He said he would come back."

Lady Regina stared at her granddaughter. "For two years she lived with that hope."

"Two years," Elyse murmured, feeling time weigh heavily on her slender shoulders.

"And then without anyone knowing of it, without any plans or announcement, she married Charles Barrington." Lady Regina shook her head. "I never understood it. When I spoke to her once about it, she refused to say anything, only that she'd been a fool. But she never explained that statement. A few years after that, word finally came to the family that Alex had died in New South Wales. It was as if she died too. I think it was then she finally gave up all hope that he would return. She had Jerrold within a year or two after that, but she was never really well again."

Elyse was staring at the portrait. She thought she could almost see something alive in Felicia Barrington's eyes, something that wasn't in any of the other portraits at Fair View. And she was certain if she reached out, she would feel warmth in those long, elegant fingers wrapped around the Remembrance Rose. Elyse blinked uncertainly. How had she remembered that? And where had the knowledge come from?

Lady Regina gasped, her hand coming to her lips. For just a moment . . . looking at Elyse standing below the portrait of her friend . . . No! It wasn't possible, she told herself. And yet, she had seen something . . . it was the way the sunlight from the window caught the light in her granddaughter's eyes, it was the turn of Elyse's head, the faint angle of her chin. She breathed in deeply to calm her nerves. For just an instant she saw something that left her stunned. She would have sworn her dear friend was standing before her in that pale green dressing down. But that was impossible. . . .

"Grandmother? Are you all right?" She crossed the room and took Regina's hand. "I'm sorry. I didn't mean to be unkind. It must make you very sad to think of it."

"What?" Lady Winslow slowly recovered. She waved a hand through the air. "No, not at all, really. It is true that I thought of her as a daughter, but she was a dear friend as well. I was saddened by the loss."

"She was so beautiful." Elyse turned wistfully back to the portrait. "And Lord Charles must have loved her."

"Yes, I believe he did, in his own way. But you must understand, she was like a bright, sparkling ornament when he first knew her. And Charles Barrington has always liked to surround himself with bright, pretty objects."

"A possession," Elyse murmured, understanding only too well.

"Perhaps, but I think he was always secretly in love with her. She loved only one man, however, and when she couldn't have him, her life became an empty shell. The woman you see in that portrait ceased to exist. It was as if she died when Alex died."

"You've never told me about how it happened." Elyse's voice was soft, almost a whisper.

Her grandmother's fingers closed lovingly around hers.

"It was expected. And to be very honest, it was almost a blessing."

"A blessing? How can you say that? I think it's dreadful when any living thing dies. But especially someone so beautiful."

Her grandmother stroked her cheek. "I know you do, my sweet. But that's because you're full of life and hope, and love." She added this last tentatively, then quickly went on. "Life is not the same when a person doesn't have that. It's what gives it all a purpose, a meaning."

"I remember how I felt when I heard the news. It was just after the shipwreck. Ceddy and I were at Land's End. Everything seemed so hopeless. No survivors had been found in two days. The weather was frightful." Her eyes misted as she remembered that day fifteen years earlier.

"Everyone said it was no use. It was the worst storm anyone could remember in years. But I knew." She smiled lovingly at Elyse. "I knew if they just kept looking . . ." Lady Regina composed herself. "I didn't realize it at the time of course."

"Realize what?" Elyse held her grandmother's hand tightly.

"It was afternoon. But I remember the sky was dark as night. The coachman had lit the lanterns. Ceddy tried to get me to go back to the inn. It was then that Quimby came over the edge of that cliff with that bundle clutched in his arms. The poor man was half-dead himself. But when they pried that bundle from his frozen hands I knew I'd never seen anything so near death."

"Quimby had found me," Elyse provided, her eyes going back to the painting.

"Yes. Everyone thought he was too late. There didn't seem to be a breath of life in you. But I wouldn't let them take your from me. We took you back to the inn. The doctor from the village looked at you." Lady Regina hesitated, her voice catching oddly.

Elyse soothed her grandmother. "You don't need to go on, if it's too painful."

"I want you to know. Perhaps it will help you understand how very special you are to me." Lady Regina looked up at the por-

264

trait, and Elyse followed her gaze.

"The physician said you might as well be dead." Her voice was hollow with remembered pain. "He said it was impossible that anyone could be in the water that long and survive. But I refused to believe it. I knew I'd lost my James and your dear mother. I wasn't going to lose you as well. To this day I don't know how it happened, whether it was a miracle or just your determination to live. But within days there was a change in you, and I knew you were going to live."

"I kept watch over you and I said countless prayers. You were still terribly weak, but by the next morning the fever had broken and you were much stronger. It was then that we had the news from London that she had died." She looked up at the portrait.

"It happened at the very same hour that you first began to recover." Lady Regina looked at her granddaughter. "I'm not a superstitious woman, but I do believe that something happened in that moment when she was lost and you began to live. It was almost as if your life was beginning just as hers was ending." She patted Elyse's hand tenderly.

"Somehow it helped ease an old woman's grief. I'd lost a dear, dear friend, but I'd gained someone very special as well."

Elyse looked up at the portrait. "Do you believe in love that lasts forever?"

Lady Regina pondered that question at great length. "I know I continued to love your grandfather after he was gone. A part of me still does."

"That's how I feel about mother and father. I don't remember very much about them. But I know they loved me and that I loved them. I'm talking about a different kind of love, one that happens only once in a great while but lasts forever."

"Well, certainly when we're young we tend to believe we will love forever. And perhaps some do. There are no certainties about what happens when we leave this life. I'd hate to think there's nothing at all." Lady Regina smiled thoughtfully. "Good heavens! That's a dreadful thought."

"I wonder if they found one another." Elyse's eyes softened as she stared at the portrait of Felicia Barrington.

"My goodness, what are you talking about?"

"Do you think Felicia and Alex ever found each other again?"

Her grandmother's eyes misted with love as she pondered her granddaughter's romantic notions. "If it's possible, they would find each other. They loved each other that much." She smiled at

Elyse.

"And he promised he would come back."

"Yes." She stared at her granddaughter. "He did promise her to do that." Lady Regina smiled uncertainly, while Elyse held onto her hand as if in her mind she had gone someplace far away and only that bond held her to this place.

"Darling?" There was a note of alarm in Regina's voice. "Whatever is wrong? I never meant to upset you."

Slowly, Elyse composed herself. "I'm just tired. I didn't sleep very well." She gave Lady Regina a reassuring smile.

Her grandmother eyed her skeptically. Elyse did look tired; there were faint circles under her eyes. And she'd seemed so remote, distant. It wasn't like her to be overemotional or moody. Yet for a moment she'd seemed a million miles away, and almost unreachable. A chill of uneasiness ran through the older woman. She remembered that same expression on the face of a child many years ago. It had made her feel as if she'd glimpsed something else very briefly. She had that same feeling now and shivered. "You haven't had the dream again, have you?"

Elyse smiled faintly. "No, of course not," she lied, not wanting to alarm her grandmother. How could she tell her? How could she possibly explain that it had started again; only it had changed somehow, leaving her feeling an overwhelming sadness and sense of regret. It must be a little like dying she thought, then tried to push that idea from her thoughts.

"I'll be fine really. Don't worry," she reassured Lady Regina. But twin blue pools mirrored her uncertainty.

Lady Regina lovingly wrapped an arm around her granddaughter's shoulders, taking Elyse's hand in her bejeweled one as she'd done when Elyse was a child. "It's probably just nervousness, with the wedding only a few days away. I thought it might be better for us to remain in London so that you could rest. Sometimes I question Jerrold's judgment."

She felt Elyse's forehead, her own wrinkling in concern. "You do feel a bit feverish. If you're not feeling well I can have Jerold summon the physician from town."

"I'm fine." Elyse smiled. "I'll be all right."

Lady Regina was unconvinced. Elyse had never been a very good liar. She was much better at braving out the truth no matter what the consequences. But Regina knew that whatever she said, Elyse wouldn't tell her what was so bothersome. Her granddaughter had a decidedly stubborn nature.

"Come along then. What you need is a good strong cup of tea. It will fix you right up." She slipped her arm through Elyse's and together they walked from the room.

Elyse stopped and looked back over her shoulder at the portrait. She couldn't rid herself of the feeling that somehow, somewhere, she'd known Lady Barrington. It left her feeling confused and uncertain. How could she possibly have known a woman she'd never met, a woman who'd been dead for almost fifteen years? And yet . . . .

Damask linen, in a shade of soft gold, decorated the walls, and a pale cream-colored carpet covered the floor. The long dining table extended twenty-five feet, elegant Queen Anne lace trailing from its sides and ends, twenty-five gold place settings laid precisely on it. The mahogany chairs, all twenty-five of them, were richly upholstered in deep gold velvet, and hundreds of candles lit the room winking forth from the multi-tiered chandelier overhead and from the three magnificent gold candelabra on the table. At its center was an elaborate floral arrangement of delicate white rosebuds and yellow forsythia.

Indeed, the dining hall at Fair View, opulent and ostentatious, was aglow. Lord Charles Barrington sat as host, Jerrold on his right. Elyse sat next to Jerrold, and her grandmother was to Lord Barrington's left. It was all very elegant, very proper, and she wanted to scream.

For the last hour, she'd listened to the casual conversation of those present. The local magistrate and his wife were there, along with the vicar, Mr. Beebe, and some neighbors and other notable townspeople. For what must have been the dozenth time she found herself watching the entrance to the dining hall. Then her gaze darted back to the conspicuously vacant chair in which there should have been another guest.

Her head ached and her skin felt icy. She smoothed her hands over the skirt of the pale yellow satin gown Jerrold had insisted she wear. It was one of many he'd personally selected the fabric for. She knew the reason he'd picked it; he'd said it would make her "a yellow bloom in a golden room."

At the time Elyse wasn't certain whether he was complimenting her, the room, or his own good taste in selecting the fabric. She hated yellow and never chose to be seen in the color, at least not until tonight. She had the distinct feeling that in the future she was going to be wearing a great deal of yellow.

Damning herself didn't help; she knew who it was she waited for. Lord Barrington's voice shafted through her thoughts.

"I am of course delighted that you could all join us in that celebration."

As he droned on, she nodded some vague response to the vicar, Mr. Beebe. He was an ancient man with a monstrous bulbous nose and two tiny close-set eyes that seemed to be forever peering up, as if he couldn't see over that great nose. His thinning thatch of white hair was combed in a whorl around his head, to cover the bare spots. So much for godliness outshining vanity. But he seemed a kindly man, and he patted her hand often, remarking more than once that he'd performed several marriages for the Barrington family. This was his unsubtle way of saying that he felt slighted because she and Jerrold were not to be married in the chapel there at Fair View with him performing the ceremony.

Elyse had only smiled vaguely in response. As always, Jerrold had made all the arrangements. She remembered his cool look when she'd suggested that the wedding be small. And then he'd continued to carry out his own plans, determined his wedding would be the grandest affair in all of London.

As the magistrate commented on some local poachers who were finally caught, Elyse noticed that her grandmother was involved in a lively conversation with a man she remembered only as the colonel. He was resplendent in a red uniform with epaulettes and rows of gold braid. The sword belted at his waist had continually tripped him up, but he seemed fairly safe from it at the dinner table, plying her grandmother and the other guests with his adventures while in Her Majesty's service. His gestures were wide, his voice booming. She almost expected him to seize his sword and handily fillet the meal as it was delivered. The remainder of Lord Barrington's guests were no more than a blur to her.

Pheasant stuffed with apples and chestnuts was served. Baron of beef and poached salmon followed. Then there was roast dove with cream sauce and onions. The vegetables, fresh from the gardens at Fair View, were thinly sliced and had been briefly cooked in an herbed butter sauce. As a finishing touch they were sprinkled with slivered almonds and rose petals. And there were hot spiced peaches, sherried apricots, and imported melons. Also lush strawberries. Butter scooped into balls the size of walnuts was served individually; into each serving a delicate rosebud was carved. Red and white wine sparkled in crystal decanters. It was an elegant feast. But Elyse had little appetite. She took only the smallest portions, knowing if she refused anything she would offend Jerrold's father. However, if she took more than she could eat, and left something untouched, she would also offend. She tried to swallow but found it difficult. She felt Jerrold's hand cover hers.

"Your grandmother mentioned that you weren't feeling well earlier. I hope it's nothing serious."

She looked up, surprised that he seemed so concerned. "I think it must be the excitement of the wedding. I'm just a little tired."

Jerrold lifted his wineglass and took a sip. "I was beginning to think it might have something to do with our missing guest." His gaze indicated the conspicuously empty chair at the far end of the table. "Did he leave without saying goodbye?" A faintly wheedling note came into his voice. "He seemed quite captivated by you. And what was it you said the evening of the ball in London? Ah yes, 'I knew you'd come back for me.' Really my dear, making such a fool of yourself."

"Jerrold, please." Elyse pressed ice-cold fingers against her temples, trying to drive away the ache that had begun earlier and now throbbed with vengeance.

"I've been meaning to speak to you all day. Especially after that little episode last evening."

"Jerrold, must we talk about this now? I apologized to your father." Elyse closed her eyes against the pain.

"You've been shut away in your room practically the entire time, what with one excuse or another. I just want to be sure you understand certain proprieties. There are many things that will be expected of you when you become Lady Barrington and are mistress of Fair View. I shouldn't want a repeat performance of last night. And as for dancing out in the hall with the Count de Cuervo . . . well it just isn't proper! At any rate, I will no longer have that fellow to worry about."

Lord Barrington's voice boomed as he rose at the end of the table. "I propose a toast. To my son and the future Lady Barrington." As he raised his wineglass in tribute, his guest did likewise.

Elyse whispered to Jerrold, "I don't know what you're talking about."

He watched for her reaction to his next words. "The Count de Cuervo, my dear. He's gone. I'm told he left very early this morning, before dawn. It seems he left this behind." His fingers

269

uncurled from around the black eyepatch. "Obviously, your friend is not all that he appears, or perhaps he is more. The man is an impostor. I'm having the local magistrate look into the matter, as well as the proper authorities in London."

Elyse gasped, and the crystal goblet fell from her fingers, shattering against the gold plate. A sea of white wine sloshed across the cloth.

"Elyse, for God's sake get a hold of yourself!" Jerrold hissed as he came to his feet beside her. "Last night, and now this! What is the matter with you?"

She felt the scrutinizing stares of the others as they gaped at her in stunned silence. Then the room clouded and a mist engulfed everything, until it seemed she wasn't there at all but someplace she'd seen only in her dreams.

He was gone!

"No." Elyse came to her feet, leaning heavily against the edge of the table. She felt a warm stickiness and raised her hand to stare unblinking at her cut fingers. There was no pain, only silent wonder as brilliant crimson droplets fell on the pristine white of the tablecloth, looking like small, perfect rosebuds. Roses . . . red and white roses. She blinked back the tears that pooled in her eyes.

"You promised," she whispered, her stricken gaze meeting the curious glances, seeing confusion and disapproval on the faces around her. But most of all seeing Jerrold's silent rage and obvious disappointment.

"I can't . . ." Elyse mumbled some vague excuse as she turned, gathering her skirts in her hands, and fled the dining room and the gaping stares.

Zach flexed his fingers against the sudden tingling. Elyse . . . Odd that he should think of her now. Memories of her flashed through his dark thoughts, like shooting stars in a night sky. How different things might have been had they met under other circumstances. But she was a member of London society, born to a title and betrothed to another.

Barrington. The name and everything it stood for tore like jagged glass, across his senses. He'd come to England for the truth. During the months at sea and the weeks in London, he'd prepared himself for whatever the truth about his father might be. He'd tried to imagine what he might discover.

A convict, yes, according to those papers locked away for so many years. But what crime had he committed? Embezzlement? Tax evasion? Zach had lived under English law and domination his entire life, and he knew a man could hang for merely stealing a loaf of bread.

Murder? He refused to believe it. The man Tobias and his mother had known was not a murderer. But then the man they'd known was not Alexander Barrington. He was Nicholas Tennant, a man who'd been convicted of, and had suffered for, a crime. Innocent or guilty, Zach knew no man could remain unchanged by what his father must have endured, first aboard the convict ship and then in servitude in New South Wales.

Convicts were no longer deported to the colonies—the practice had been abandoned several years earlier—but the stigma remained. Even as the colonies struggled to become a land of merchants, farmers, and tradesmen, they were branded by this dark part of their history. But many good men had once been convicts, and Zach needed to believe his father was one of them.

Zach rested his head against the seat back. He was bone tired, but his churning thoughts made sleep impossible. As the coach lumbered and rolled along the road, he was immersed in darkness, sightless, sensing only the rhythm of the wheels eating the distance. Eyes closed, he concentrated on the grinding of those wheels, each turn taking him closer to London.

He drifted, not into sleep but numbness. The old stablemaster had said there was a witness, a servant girl who'd disappeared after the trial. Rooney had given him her last known address in London. Zach wondered if she might still be alive.

As the coach clattered across the heavy-timbered dock, Zach pounded against the roof, signaling the driver. When the equipage rolled to a stop, he vaulted out.

The driver cringed at seeing his passenger emerge from the coach. The man was transformed without the black eyepatch he'd worn when he'd left London. Two haunted, deadly gray eyes pierced him through.

Zach paid the man well and sent him on his way. He'd been traveling all day, and it was after midnight when he walked up the gangplank of the *Tamarisk*.

"State yer purpose or lose yer head." The warning call came sharply.

Zach smiled in response to the familiar voice, but it wasn't a smile anyone would have recognized. There was an air of danger

271

about him; it caused the man on guard to lay the heavy wooden spar across his arm, in preparation to strike.

"At ease with you, Tris," Zach ordered.

"Is that you, Cap'n?" The man on watch aboard the *Tamarisk* squinted into the glow of lantern light that fell across the deck, relief flooding his shadowed face.

"Aye, it's me," Zach acknowledged as he reached for the rope railing and stepped down onto the deck. The sights, sounds, and smells were dearly familiar to him. This was the *Tamarisk*. The gentle roll of her deck, the creaking of mooring ropes, the slap of water against her hull reminded him of who he was. In the last days, he'd almost forgotten.

But something wasn't right. The light from the lantern pooled across boxes and crates of supplies to be stored in the hold. But they were scattered across the deck, splintered open, their contents spilling across planking. A rope from the rigging was slashed, its frayed ends dangled.

"What happened here?" He crossed the deck, then came back. Barrels of fresh water were smashed. Sacks of grain, beans and flour were cut open their contents making lumpy masses in combination with the water. He whirled on the night watch.

"What the devil?"

"They came at us from seaward, sir." He jerked his head to the opposite side of the ship. "Must've been two dozen or so, and they were armed. They were after the cargo and cut down anyone who got in their way. But we gave 'em a good fight, sir. We put at least a dozen or so overboard. Some preferred to jump." The man stroked the wooden spar that was crusted with dried blood.

"There's a good many won't be returnin' home tonight, or any night for that matter."

Zach's brow furrowed into a frown. "But there's no cargo aboard." His head came up in alarm. "The warehouse?"

"They hit the warehouse after they were here. We tried to warn Sandy and the others but we were too late."

"The wool?" Zach's face contorted as anger built in him. It wasn't the wool he cared about. It had been only a disguise for what was hidden deep inside several specially marked bales. The only ones who'd known about the gold hidden inside were himself, Tobias, and Sandy. Neither man would betray him, he'd bet his life on it.

The seaman nodded. "Seems they weren't after the wool at all. They set fire to several bales, then tore open the rest."

"Damn!" Zach cursed. While he'd been in the country playing social games with Barrington, the man had been clever and had struck first. Barrington had been stalling, keeping him away from London long enough to steal the gold.

The money will be paid as soon as my man has the gold.

Barrington's words rang in his ears. Without the gold, the draft was worthless. That had been Barrington's game all along.

Zach fought for control He had to have time to think of an effective counterattack. "What about the men?"

"A few injuries. Nothing that won't heal, sir."

"Have you heard from Tobias?"

"We sent word round to the house. Mr. Gentry got here right away. He's in your cabin, sir."

"Good." Zach turned toward the gangplank. He intended to talk to Sandy, to find out if there was any hope of finding the men who'd attacked the warehouse.

"And there's the man we got down below." The night watch informed him matter-of-factly.

Zach whirled back around. "What man?"

The seaman grinned, his smile crooked in the roundness of his badly swollen and bruised face.

"He doesn't talk much. A big giant of a fella. But he seemed to be the leader. I had him taken below. I thought you might want to ask him a few questions." The bruised smile deepened.

The light in Zach's eyes darkened to something deadly. "Indeed I do. Send word to the warehouse. I want to see Sandy as soon as he comes aboard." He turned and went below. He would have his answers, and he'd have his gold. Then he would repay Barrington several times over.

Zach called out in response to the knock on his cabin door as Tobias sat, red-eyed, in a chair beside his desk. The second mate came in and stood silently before him.

"I've got men searching every street and back alley of London right now, sir. We'll get your cargo back." Determination gleamed in the man's visible eye. The other one was no more than a white slit in a mass of black soot.

"I hope you gave them equal to what you got," Zach observed, pouring a full glass of brandy and shoving it across the desk to his man.

Sandy eyed him skeptically, then took the drink, tossing it back

273

in one quick motion. "That we did, sir."

Zach nodded. Sandy had been with him for a long time. He was the best there was. He would keep his promise. "What is the damage to the ship?"

"There's very little, sir; a few broken crates and smashed barrels. There was some riggin' lines cut."

"I want an exact accounting of the damage and of the injured men. Replace any lost supplies. Make all necessary repairs. I want her seaworthy by nightfall. And I'm going to need at least a half-dozen able-bodied men, the strongest among the crew."

"Sir, I . . ." The second mate started to apologize.

"Save it. I should have expected as much. Barrington is a sly wolf."

"Yessir," his man agreed.

"But the wolf has been careless. I know where his lair is."

"Sir?" Confusion clouded Sandy's gaze.

He smiled at his second mate. "I know where the gold is to be delivered." Zach flexed his bruised and swollen hand. He was lucky he hadn't broken every bone in it. But the prisoner had given his name and a great deal more. Mr. Lash had held out a long time, but they had finally come to an agreement.

Zach knew where the gold was to be taken and hidden until Barrington returned from an extended trip after the wedding. By then, the man probably assumed the furor over the stolen cargo would have died down. But Zach had something else in mind.

"The gold is to be stored at a prearranged location. It's to be delivered there tonight under cover of darkness, and we'll be waiting for it when it arrives."

Sandy let out a long, low whistle. "The gold and the money?"

"Yes. Just payment, I think, for Barrington's treachery. After all"—his smile turned into a lazy smirk—"a gentleman must abide by his agreement or pay the penalty. Wouldn't you say, Sandy?"

"Aye, aye, sir." Sandy's eyes narrowed appreciatively. "But what if the bastard gave you the wrong information?"

"I think it's safe to say the man now believes in telling the truth. But if he's lied, then he dies," Zach stated coolly. Then he glanced at the ship's clock. It was nearly four-thirty in the morning. It would be daylight in another hour.

"It's a full day's ride back to Fair View. When Barrington's man doesn't arrive within a reasonable amount of time to tell him of their success, he will send someone to check up on Mr. Lash or perhaps come himself. I'll wager he'll do the latter since the wedding is scheduled for day after tomorrow. That means the earliest Barrington could possibly arrive back in London would be tomorrow morning. And by then the gold will be safely back in our hands, as will full payment for this." Zach carefully inspected the legal bank draft.

"He'll send someone to the docks. But the *Tamarisk* will be gone. As soon as the gold arrives, I want her out of the harbor." He rounded the desk and approached the map on the far wall. He pointed to the English coastline.

"You'll sail to this point, then anchor offshore at Dover," he instructed his second mate. "According to Tobias, there's a small cover, here." He indicated the meeting place. "It's secluded and not used by anyone."

"What about you, sir?"

"There's someone I must find before I leave London. I may not even be able to locate her. She disappeared over thirty years ago. But if I'm not at that cove by first tide two days from now, you're to sail without me. Is that clear?"

Zach saw the momentary glance that passed between Tobias and his second mate. "That is an order," he said firmly.

The two men muttered that they understood.

"Good." Zach turned to Sandy. "See to the provisions to be brought aboard. Then we must plan how we're to retrieve the gold. We don't have very much time." His mate nodded curtly and left. Then Zach turned to Tobias. "You look like hell. Get some sleep."

"What about you?"

Zach shook his head. "I have to make plans."

"What about Lord Vale's house?"

"Go back only for what you can carry inside your coat. The rest stays. No one is to be suspicious. I want everything to seem normal. The servants must know nothing. Tell them you have several appointments and a dinner engagement, then return to the ship. I want you aboard when the gold arrives."

"You think you can get it back?"

He turned to his friend, laying a hand on his shoulder. "I'll get it back and I'll get Barrington's money as well."

"That's not the real reason you risked all this. Did you find out what you came for?" The old man scrutinized him carefully. In the three hours since Zach had returned he had not spoken of what he'd found out about his father.

"Aye, I did." There was pain in his light gray eyes. "It's not what

275

I expected, Tobias." He stood, staring at the new dawn through the porthole window. "But then, I suppose life is never what you expect." He turned and smiled at his old friend. "I'll have everything I want before I leave."

"What about the girl?"

Zach's anger resurfaced, tightening inside him. "What about her?"

"You can't just leave—"

He cut his old friend off, not wanting to discuss Elyse. "She belongs to Barrington. I'm certain they'll be very happy together."

"You need to talk about it, boy, all of it, whatever you found out about the Barringtons and her."

"I don't have time to talk now." Zach bit the words off curtly.

Tobias clamped his mouth shut, knowing Zach wouldn't tell him anything until he was good and ready. "All right, but you'll have to talk about it sometime. You can't just hold everything inside, eatin' yerself up with it."

"Tobias!" Zach ground out the warning, his patience gone.

"I'll get back to Lord Vale's." Tobias crossed the cabin. He paused at the door, one hand on the latch. "Try to get some sleep," he added, with a gruff smile. "You look like hell."

Chapter Thirteen

He had a name, and an address that was almost thirty-five years old.

And like a man possessed Zach searched through the squalor and stench of a London far different from the one he'd known as the Count de Cuervo. He saw pain in the eyes of the beggars who stretched out their hands to him, and he wondered what had brought them to this existence. Mindlessly, he stalked the streets and back alleys, driving off more than one thief with only a glance. It was as if some unseen force goaded him, pushing him on to the next address and the next while disappointment nagged at him hour after hour.

He began to think it was hopeless, and time was running out. He'd started just after dawn, no longer dressed as a titled nobleman but like the sea captain he was. Rich clothes and a title would only have put these people off. They would close their doors and mouths to him because of the barrier of fine silk, satin, and jewels.

Zach spared no amount of money in trying to find Lydia Roberts. If he didn't find her today, he would have to leave without knowing what she had really seen happen between his father and grandfather that day so long ago. As it was, if he did find her, there was every possibility she might refuse to tell him.

"Hey, Cap'n."

He whirled around in response to the insistent tugging on his cuff. The toothless beggar he remembered from earlier that morning grinned up at him revealing not teeth but gums. He was bald, the knitted cap pulled down over his shining pate full of holes. He looked as if he probably wouldn't remember the last time he'd bathed, and he smelled rank. Zach had paid him a full half-crown that morning for information about Lydia's most recent whereabouts. Like the other addresses he'd been given, it had produced nothing. He'd felt certain that the man had lied because no one at that place had known anything about Lydia. But it wasn't the half-crown that had imprinted the man on Zach's memory, it was the deformed lower half of the wretch's body, which was strapped to a platform fixed with wheels to allow him mobility on the streets and sidewalks.

"What do you want?" Zach ground out. London was like Sydney. No different. Thievery, hunger, and poverty could be found in any city. He'd seen enough today to make him ache for the pristine wildness of Resolute. God, how he wanted to be away from all of this!

"A half-crown, Cap'n. No less," the man demanded with all the audacity of the thief he was.

"I paid you this morning and got nothing for it."

The man squealed as if he'd been stuck. "I gave what ye asked for, no more and no less. It's not on me head if it gained ye naught. Didn't find her, did ya?" His tiny beady eyes looked up at Zach.

Definitely a bandicoot, Zach thought. With his pointed nose and sharp dirty claws, the wizened little man reminded him of the rabbitlike creatures found in abundance in the valley at Resolute. He idly wondered if the beggar used that snoutlike nose to sniff out his next meal, then dug it out with his clawlike hands.

"No, I didn't find her, but then you knew I would not, didn't you?" Leaning down, Zach seized the little creature with both hands, twisting the front of his moth-eaten coat. Just as quickly, he let him go with a grunt of disgust, aware of the diseases he might pick up from touching the man.

"You didn't find her, because she weren't there." The little man gloated from his wheeled platform.

"I'm in no mood for games, beggar. Do you think me fool enough to give you more money?"

The man drew back at the dangerous glint in the stranger's eyes. He had the look of a sea captain, but there was in his bearing something that suggested he was more than that. And the bulge of coin at his pocket suggested wealth. The beggar knew he couldn't physically take the money from this stranger, so he'd decided on a different tactic, though he'd cringed at the thought of being honest.

"You can insult me all you wish, Cap'n. Words never hurt the Snipe." He pounded his chest for emphasis. "I've learned to survive without kindness. This isn't exactly the sort of body that draws friends, or ladies for that matter. I came after you 'cause I knew you wouldn't find Lydia this mornin'. I found out where she's been hangin' out the last year."

"And, of course, there is the matter of that other half-crown," Zach suggested sarcastically, keeping a careful eye to the street about him. It wasn't unusual for a cripple like the Snipe to work with someone else in his thievery. Often the cohort was a street urchin. Without family or the ability to work, the child became a willing accomplice.

"Ain't nothing free in this here life, Cap'n. But then I suppose you're a man who would understand that. A half-crown will do, but I really ought to charge you more." He ran a gnarled hand, minus two fingers, across the grizzled chin that slacked away below his lower lip.

Zach studied the beggar carefully. Undoubtedly the man was lying, but what did he have to lose. He'd followed every lead, knocked on the door of every store, eatery, and whorehouse within a twelve-block radius. He'd begun with faint hope this morning, telling himself that people rarely moved far beyond their beginnings. But as the hours wore on, he'd been forced to admit that after thirty-five years Lydia Roberts had disappeared.

It was late, time was running out. In another hour he'd be forced to return to the *Tamarisk* to make the final plans for the raid that evening. After that, everything would move quickly. There would be no time to search again. Having done what he had planned, he would have to leave London forever. Like his father, he would be an exile, but a willing one.

"All right. But you had better be telling the truth." Holding his breath against the stench, he leaned over the beggar's twisted body, his fingers sinking into the front of the man's jacket, and with hardly more effort than would be needed to lift a small crate aboard his ship, Zach hoisted the man into the air—platform, wheels, and all. "If you lie, I'll take you back to my ship and chain you in the hold. Then, when we are well out to sea, I'll cast you to the sharks. They're not picky about their next meal."

In all his years, the beggar had never known fear. The pain and ridicule he'd suffered because of his deformity had taught him to fear nothing. But he did fear this man, and the unnatural light

279

that glinted in those steely gray eyes. If ever he'd looked death in the face, he was doing so now. The Snipe had no doubt that this man, whoever he was, would carry out every threat he made.

The beggar clawed to free himself. "Hey, Cap'n. If you do me in, how can I take you to Lydia?"

As silent understanding passed between them, Zach set the man back down. "Take me to Lydia and there's a full crown for you; lie and I just may save myself the effort and cut your throat."

"Aye, aye, Cap'n." The Snipe passed a salute across his forehead. Then with all the agility of a man with two good legs, he swung the platform about. Using his hands in oarlike motions, he propelled himself with amazing speed down the sidewalk.

Zach was hard pressed to keep up as the man wove his way expertly through the mass of humanity at the open market they passed. The Snipe navigated around a flower stand, two vegetable bins, and a barrel of apples. Jockeying for right of way with a mule hitched to a cart, he easily passed below the animal's belly and careened around a corner, the left front and rear wheels coming clear of the street.

They passed a tavern, several brothels, and a smithy's shop. Zach was certain he'd passed this way earlier, but quickly realized most streets had at least one tavern, two brothels, and an odd assortment of small shops. He was so intent on the storefronts they passed he almost fell over the Snipe. He staggered and recovered his balance.

"Here we are, Cap'n."

He gave the bandicoot a look that could have split a man's head in two. "Why didn't you tell me about this place, this morning?"

"Because I didn't know of it. Lydia moves around. She has to."

Zach eyed him critically, wondering what line of business Lydia had taken up over the last years. The beggar indicated a long flight of outside stairs leading up the side of the building that housed what was obviously a fish market. With his other hand, he indicated it was time for payment.

"Stairs," Zach grunted out. "Very clever. And by the time I return, you're gone. Not likely, my friend." He spoke the last words coolly. Amidst loud protesting, he snatched the Snipe off the ground, wheeled platform and all, and carried him up the stairs. He was breathing hard, and could only nod to the Snipe, indicating the man was to knock, when they finally reached the top step.

After several minutes, a slender young girl peeked from behind a curtain. They heard the bolt at the door slide back, and she poked her head out.

"Gawd almighty, Snipe. What yer doin' here?" The girl's words hardly resembled those of any known language.

The Snipe was breathing heavily due to the tight constriction of Zach's arm about his midsection. "This here's the one I was tellin' you about. He's come here to see Lydia."

"Gor!" the girl breathed out. "I thought you was twistin' me arm. But Snipe, she can't see no one. She's real bad today. You know how she is when she gets one o' her spells. It's all I can do to keep her quiet. I can't afford to be put out of this place if they hear her cryin'."

"He's got gold coin, Tilly," the Snipe informed the girl, his eyes widening for emphasis. "Lots of it. He just wants to ask her some questions. That's all. What harm could it do the poor soul?"

"Well, awright." The girl named Tilly stepped reluctantly aside.

In spite of her language and manner, the small room was clean though sparsely furnished, and what smelled like a Mulligan stew simmered at an open fireplace. A small cloth decorated with hand stitching covered the table set with two chairs, a rocking chair with two slats missing from the back was set before the fireplace, and a door at the back led to another room.

Much to the Snipe's surprise, Zach carried him into the room and set him in the middle of the floor. But the finagler quickly recovered.

"I'll take that full crown now."

"Not so fast. I want to see Lydia." Zach turned to the girl, not wanting to frighten her. "I just want to ask her some questions about someone she knew a long time ago. That's all, and I'd be more than willing to pay her for her time, if she can spare it."

The girl's eyes swept appraisingly over his wide-shouldered frame. "Spare it?" She laughed. "That's all Lydia has nowadays. She's a good soul, but I warn you, it's a bad bargain." She made a circling motion at her head. "She's not herself, know what I mean?"

Zach looked from the Snipe to the girl, Tilly. "You mean she's crazy?"

Tilly shook her head. "People think she is. She likes for them to think it. But I see a look in her eyes sometimes — not dangerous or anything like that. She has some strange ideas, but yer welcome to talk to her if you like." The girl's gaze again traveled down Zach, taking in the simple but immaculate cut of his seaman's

281

pants, shirt, and coat before they fastened knowingly on the bulge of coin in his left pocket, then on the other bulge beneath the tight-fitting pants. Her eyes gleamed at the first; she wet her lips in unabashed appreciation of the second.

"I'll be right back. Then maybe we can find something else you'd be likin', Cap'n." She hinted, faintly swaying her hips as she disappeared into the other room.

"Cap'n?" the Snipe prodded.

"You'll have your money when I've spoken to Lydia."

The Snipe grumbled something about not being able to trust anybody you found on the street, then rolled himself across the small room to the stew. He was sitting on his wheeled platform, stuffing his toothless face with food, when Tilly came back in.

"It's awright. She'll see ye." She smiled up at Zach with a sweetness that wouldn't survive the streets of London more than another few years. As he passed her by, her hand dropped to the second bulge, caressing him knowingly.

Zach's fingers closed gently over her wrist, setting her aside. He stepped into the room and let his eyes slowly adjust to the half-light admitted through drawn curtains. An hour later he emerged. He wasn't surprised to find the beggar still there. The girl looked up at him expectantly.

"How long has she been like that?"

"Long as I can remember. Her memory comes and goes, always in bits and pieces. I can't make much out of her ravings," Tilly answered with a shrug.

"Are you her daughter?"

"Daughter? Gor! No!" The girl made a guttural sound, then softened her words. "Me and Lydia teamed up about three years ago. She weren't so bad then. Lived in this little place over a few blocks. I needed a place to stay and she needed somebody to help pay the rent. Her money didn't cover expenses. How do you say it? She lived beyond her means, always puttin' on fancy airs like she was some kinda grand lady or something'."

"How did she live?"

"Oh, you mean money." The girl brightened as she understood. "Lydia never worked the streets if that's what ye mean. She has money that comes in, but she was always spendin' it as fast as she got it. On all them fancy satins and beads and things."

"Satins and beads?" Zach didn't understand what this had to do with anything.

"Yeah, like she was a grand lady or something. Called herself

Lady Barrington."

Zach's head came up, his eyes as cold as death. *Barrington!*

Zach sat in the chair before the small desk in his cabin aboard the *Tamarisk*. He'd made his final plans for that night with Sandy and his crew. Now he tried to sleep, but found it impossible. He rested his head on the desk. The ship was cool and quiet, his men either topside seeing to last-minute details before they put to sea or ashore with Sandy. Tobias would come aboard later.

The shipped creaked as it rolled restlessly in calm harbor waters. It was as if she were as eager as he to be at sea again. Soon, he thought as he closed his aching eyes. He'd had no sleep in the last two days, and he'd have none for at least two more. But instead of fatigue, he felt the listlessness of the ship around him, the straining at the mooring ropes.

Lydia Roberts. A madwoman who fancied herself Lady Barrington. He'd been doubtful at first just how much he could believe. But the girl Tilly had confirmed enough.

Perhaps Lydia was mad, or perhaps she'd only retreated to a safe haven where she knew no one would bother her. But as long as he lived he'd never forget the look in her eyes when he'd entered the room and opened the curtains to let in light.

Bedridden, clinging to the elegant satin shawl about her shoulders, she'd stared at him, a half-lucid, half-crazed expression frozen on her face. Then her hand had flown to her mouth.

"It's you," she'd cried. "It's you." And immediately she'd begun to cry, tears streaming from darkly decorated eyes, and trickling down brightly painted cheeks until the colors of her heavy makeup ran together, making her more pathetic than she'd first seemed.

"You've come back!"

As long as he lived, he'd never get over the shock of it. She'd stared at him, her mouth moving, but no words coming out for the longest time. And when she finally spoke, she was in another time and place. She clung to his hand, begging his forgiveness, vowing her love, telling him things too fantastic to believe.

But Tilly had known the truth. She'd heard it countless times from Lydia in the woman's more sane moments, and then, of course, there was the stipend that appeared each month, hand carried by a uniformed servant. He arrived, delivered the envelope into Lydia's shaking hands, then disappeared. And they lived for another month. Tilly supplemented the income from sewing she took in and from other more obvious activities. She'd grown fond of Lydia. She listened to the stories, the rantings and ravings, and held the older woman when the tears came. One day she'd followed the uniformed servant back to his employer—Jerrold Barrington.

From Lydia's fragmented memories and from what Tilly had told him, Zach knew he had the truth at last.

Lydia was a naïve young girl of fourteen when she went to work at Fair View, the Barrington country estate. There she was trained as an upstairs maid by her aunt who'd long been in the family employ. A pretty little thing, it was not long before she came to the attention of both Barrington sons, Alexander and Charles.

The older son, Alex, was favored by Lord Barrington. He had fair hair and eyes the color of quicksilver. Lydia loved him the minute she saw him. It was not so with Charles, who was four years younger. Perhaps that was the reason Charles pursued her. He seemed to be almost unnaturally competitive with his older half brother.

So while Lydia longed for a glance or a touch from her beloved Alex, she received those and more from Charles. With the ruse of a note purporting to come from Alex, he lured her to the stables and there took her innocence and her dreams. With youthful naïveté, Lydia had hoped for Alex's love and had suffered for that with Charles.

The younger son turned her love for Alex against her, viciously blackmailing her into his bed. When he summoned her, she was forced to go to him or have Alex and Lord Barrington confronted with the truth. That she could not bear. She thought her heart would break when she learned Alex was to marry Felicia Seymour. . . .

Zach shook his head. Felicia had once been betrothed to his father. That explained the passages in the journal. Lydia had remembered the pearl and diamond pendants, and the day Alex called her in to see them so he might ask her opinion of them. They were to be a gift for Felicia. Lydia had fled the room in tears, Alex not understanding the hurt he'd brought to the servant girl.

But Charles Barrington wasn't satisfied with luring Lydia away from Alex. He was driven by jealousy, anger, and the consuming greed of his own mother, Lord Clayton's second wife. Alex was the favorite son, the firstborn. He would inherit the business, all the land, the title, practically everything except the small estate in Northumberland Lord Clayton had set aside for Charles. And Alex was to have the lovely Felicia as well. It was more than Charles could bear.

At this point in her tale, Lydia had gazed guardedly at the door, as if she feared someone would do her harm. But then she'd again lapsed into the past. Clinging to his hand and calling him by his father's name, she'd begged his forgiveness for her lies.

Every muscle taut, his thoughts churning, Zach had faced the truth. This woman had given evidence against his father regarding a crime he hadn't committed. Her testimony had damned his father to imprisonment and permanent exile. Zach had wondered if he could believe her, if he wanted to believe her?

In the end, Zach had known Tobias was right; he'd come too far, risked too much not to see it through after he'd found the one person who could tell him what had happened.

Lydia had sobbed out her grief, her tears falling onto his hand as she'd clasped it to her breast. That fateful day, she'd begged Charles to meet her in the library at Fair View. She was with child, and needed desperately to talk to him about what was to be done. She'd stepped into the shadow of a bookcase as she heard him approach with Lord Barrington.

She heard the argument that followed, the violent words, the threats and recriminations. She knew the moment the argument became physical, Lord Barrington striking his son for accusing him of favoring Alex. And she heard the final blow and saw Lord Clayton fall across the carpet.

She'd watched, horrified, as the young man bent over his father. Looking up, his gaze had locked with hers, and Lydia had been certain she'd seen her own death in those dark, evil eyes.

Terrified by what she'd witnessed, she was easily convinced to keep quiet. The bribe Charles had offered was marriage and respectability. And so, Lydia had become his accomplice. Her statement had convicted Alex. For her reward, she'd expected to be Lady Barrington, but Charles had other plans. He had acquired almost everything once promised to his brother but he wanted it all, including Felicia.

Sobbing, Lydia had collapsed back against her pillow, unable to tell him more. But Zach was now able to fit in the missing pieces.

When the trial was over and Alex was exiled for life, Charles Barrington had set out to win Felicia's hand. And he had. It seemed one Barrington was as good as another to that mysterious lady. As for his father, Zach knew that he'd never stopped loving her. Why else would he have kept that journal and the pendant all those years?

Now it was Jerrold Barrington who kept the family secret, paying Lydia handsomely every month for her silence. The child Lydia had conceived by Charles Barrington had died shortly after birth. She'd never mourned its loss, feeling that was really a blessing. And she'd continued to live her sad life, half-insane because the lie she'd told had sent the man she truly loved into exile.

Zach didn't begrudge Lydia her existence, or even hate her. He pitied her. Her life, like so many others, had been irrevocably changed by Charles Barrington's greed. And Jerrold Barrington was a willing participant in the coverup of his father's crime. Why not, when the entire Barrington fortune and his right to inherit depended on his cooperation?

Zach had left Lydia to her memories and her madness. He'd paid the Snipe handsomely for taking him to her, and he'd given the girl, Tilly, enough to put food on the table and coal in the stove for some time. She would no longer have to sell herself to make ends meet. Whatever was left to her in this world or in the shadows of her mind, Lydia could now afford to live in peace, free of Charles Barrington.

Zach was certain he'd dozed only a few minutes, but the dreams came anyway. In the last weeks, he'd been haunted by images out of his father's journal: the trial, the first months in New South Wales, the struggle to build a life at Resolute. The journal was his only link to the man his father had once been. And the dreams were so real, Zach felt he could almost reach out and touch the things his father had described.

It came again. A faint clanking sound, metal grating against metal. He could feel the bite of the metal cuff at his ankles, the dragging weight that hampered movement, the cold dampness of the ship's hull. He could smell the stench of human waste, of vomit; could feel the damp, slime-covered ship's walls. But one bright, shining hope made his suffering bearable.

Lis. She'd become his focal point in a world gone mad; the

promise of her love was balm on the open sores that festered on his body. She was the very air he breathed.

Zach jerked awake, the dream slipping into the dark corners of his mind. His senses cleared slowly. He felt drugged from fatigue and too little sleep.

He rose and stretched, frowning at the time on the ship's clock as the sound came again. Sandy and the others must be returning early. He'd thought it would take them longer to make the necessary arrangements.

Stepping into the passageway outside his cabin, he heard it once more. The sound seemed to come from the forward hold. He walked to the end of the passage. There were two storage areas—one forward, one aft—to give the *Tamarisk* more even keel in the water. With the loss of the wool, both were now empty except for supplies. The ship rode much higher in the water since their arrival. But still the sound came from inside.

Zach unbolted the door and pushed it open, shining the lantern into the hold. It was cool, dark, and faintly musty. Light pooled on the smooth sides of the ship, and made a shadow ladder of the real one that reached high overhead to the closed hatch. He frowned at the sight of neatly coiled ropes used to lash down cargo. There were no chains to be found in this hold. His gaze fell on the heavy iron rings placed at regular intervals along its sides. His men had once reported a rat swinging from one. That was probably the noise he'd heard. There were always rats in the holds of ships.

He closed the door and bolted it. The gold would be stored in that hold when it was safely aboard. As he turned back to his cabin, the sound came again. It had been distinct at first, but now was faint as if it came from far away. Zach turned and cocked his head. It was the sound from his dreams, the clanking of the chains that bound the wretched souls in the hold of the prison ship.

Returning to his cabin, he splashed cold water over his face. He stared into the small mirror above the washstand, searching for answers in the haunted eyes that stared back at him. Ever since he'd begun his voyage, he'd felt compelled to pursue something. It went beyond finding out the truth about his father. There was more; he sensed it, but didn't understand it. Feeling frustration as well as fatigue, he threw the cotton cloth down beside the basin of

287

water. By morning he would have taken the first step in gaining revenge against Barrington Shipping, but what of revenge for his father?

Zach looked up as something intangible slipped across his senses, and he knew. Somewhere between facing the reality of what he'd learned that afternoon and experiencing the haunting memories of his dreams, he'd made a decision.

The night was bathed in blackness, the moon being obscured by clouds. There was no light to mark the passage of the two heavily laden transport wagons bearing the markings of the Argosy Freight Company. If there had been it would also have illuminated seven silvery shadows moving silently around the back of the building bearing that same name.

They moved quickly, one man slipping over each side of a wagon as it drew to a halt at the loading bay. The guards that rode in the back were quickly silenced, their limp bodies slumping to the street. The fifth man and the sixth each took care of a driver, disposing of him without the team of horses so much as flicking an ear.

He emerged from the shadows with his men, only the flash of a wicked smile revealing any of the emotions of these pirates of the night. When one guard roused, he stepped in to assist his men, rendering the guard unconscious with precise pressure at the neck.

Quick, efficient hands affixed new signs over the company emblem and name. And six unconscious forms were bound, gagged, and placed into the two identical Argosy crates sitting in a third wagon. A new driver climbed aboard, two new guards took their places at the back of each wagon. It was a curious scene.

The seventh man gave a silent signal, and watched as each wagon took off in a separate direction, disappearing into the cloaking veil of darkness. Their destination was the same, but for safety they would take separate routes. Satisfying himself that they were well out of sight, he pulled on the bell rope at the loading dock.

The Argosy foreman had been expecting the signal. He opened the small side door and peered outside, a frown lining his forehead.

"Eh? What's this? There were supposed to be two crates."

The seventh man, tall on the straight wagon seat, dressed all in black, nodded and gestured back to the two crates.

The foreman came down the steps and looked into the back of the wagon. He grunted his satisfaction, then gestured to a man inside to set the pulley of the large gate in motion. It creaked open.

Urging the horses forward, the driver reined them to a halt beside the interior loading platform.

"Have any trouble?" the foreman inquired.

"None." The reply was merely a grunt.

"Where are the others?"

"Tavern. It was a long night." This was an equally curt answer.

"Can't say as though I blame 'em. I don't like workin' late meself. All right, just sign here that you delivered the shipment." The man handed the driver the bill of lading. He chuckled at the description of the contents—building materials.

A signature was quickly scrawled. The foreman looked up as the man jumped down from the wagon and silently walked toward the big door.

"Hey, you! Where you headed?"

"Tavern."

For the second time in as many minutes the foreman shook his head. He didn't understand where the boss got people like that, and furthermore he didn't want to know. He vaguely wondered what had happened to Mr. Lash, not that he particularly liked the man. As a matter of fact, he was glad he hadn't come this time.

The foreman looked down, his brow wrinkling. "Hey! What kinda signature is this?" he yelled after the man, but the driver had already disappeared into the darkened street. He looked back down at the scrawl. The man must be joking with him; he couldn't even pronounce the name. Then his eyes widened. Of course, that was it. It was a code name of some kind, to keep everyone's identity secret just like the boss wanted. He turned the bill of lading in three different directions and frowned at the elaborate scrawl of the Count de Cuervo.

"Yeah, and I'm the Archbishop of Canterbury," the foreman mumbled sarcastically.

Within hours, the second mate on the *Tamarisk* had the cargo secured in the hold. As the still night air gave way to the whisper of a good sailing wind just before dawn, mooring ropes were cast aside. The harbor tugs labored to turn the majestic clipper about, nudging her graceful prow toward the open channel. Gulls cried overhead in a lavender sky as Tobias stood beside the man at the wheel. He was glad to be putting London behind him.

At a sharply barked command the sails were unfurled. They billowed and caught the new wind. Their course was set, south to Dover to wait.

Elyse rubbed her throbbing temples. The dream had come again last night, but she didn't remember very much of it. And what she did remember, she didn't understand. She'd slept badly after their hasty return to London two days earlier.

Pleading important business that simply couldn't wait until after the wedding, Jerrold had insisted they return immediately. With the wedding only two days away, Elyse had gratefully agreed. But she hadn't been prepared for the ride back.

The driver had practically ruined the team of horses, and Jerrold had pushed him to such a dangerous pace on bad roads, they'd broken an axle. She'd never seen Jerrold so furious, as if the driver and horses had been to blame. And now this.

She threw the stack of legal papers down on the escritoire in her grandmother's drawing room. The wedding was this afternoon. There were still countless things to be done, including the final fitting of her gown. Now Jerrold had sent his solicitor round with a stack of legal documents she'd never seen before.

"Mr. Chambers, I simply can't read through all this. There isn't time. If you'll just hold onto them, I'm certain I'll have more time after the wedding."

After the wedding. The words stung her. What the devil was wrong with her anyway? Her grandmother was treating her like some sort of invalid, and Katy was avoiding her altogether. Chagrined, she thought of how sharply she'd spoken that morning and suspected that might be the reason. Then, too, she'd heard Lady Regina talking to Katy in the dining room before she'd joined them the evening before.

Bride's blues, her grandmother had called it, attributing it to fragile nerves. God's nightgown! She'd never had a fragile nerve in her life, and she deplored people who did. If everyone didn't quit treating her like some innocent lamb about to be led to the slaughter . . . Elyse tried to shake off her mood. Her choice of comparisons was odd. Did she really feel like a lamb being led to the slaughter? That was ridiculous, of course. She was marrying the most eligible man in all London. He had an impeccable family background, she'd known him practically all her life, and he cared a great deal for her.

The Count de Cuervo's mocking words came back to her: *sounds like something one might look for in a good hunting dog.*

"Miss Winslow."

She turned around. "I'm sorry. About the papers . . ." Once more, she tried as diplomatically as possible to explain. Her grandmother had raised her to be astute and well informed. She simply would not sign these intimidating documents until she had thoroughly perused them.

"I quite understand your concern, Miss Winslow, but I assure you, a dower agreement is quite normal when two families of substantial means are being united." The solicitor was presenting the argument Barrington had instructed him to use.

"Dower agreement?" Elyse fastened on the man a penetrating blue gaze that could even unnerve someone as unmovable as Jerrold Barrington. "I'm sorry. I have no dowry. To me, that practice is archaic."

The solicitor tried again, meanwhile pushing his wire-rimmed glasses back up the length of an incredibly crooked nose.

Elyse found herself staring at that misshapen nose wondering how the glasses navigated it. She closed her eyes, praying for divine intervention as the man repeated his instructions.

"It is customary for the bride to sign over her dower properties, or in this case any properties you will inherit, prior to the marriage. According to English law, everything shall revert back to Master Jerrold."

"I have no properties," Elyse tried to explain for the third time. "What is this about?"

Both turned as Lady Winslow swept imperiously into the room. A radiant beauty even in advanced years, she cut quite a figure in her formal dressing gown of rose taffeta, a large rose, feather boa trailing behind her. Elyse reflected that prayers had a way of being answered.

The solicitor cleared his throat and began again.

Lady Winslow held up a bejeweled hand. "My granddaughter's wedding is in just a few hours. She must dress, and has no time for legal matters. I'm certain my solicitor can take care of everything if you will just leave those with me."

The man shuffled the papers uncomfortably. His instructions were explicit; he was to have Miss Winslow sign the documents. He'd been further instructed that Lady Winslow was not to see the documents. They'd merely be an unnecessary bother for her,

291

Barrington had said.

The man backtracked. "I am in complete agreement. Miss Winslow is far too busy to be bothered by such trivialities. I'm certain this can wait until another day." He quickly stuffed the documents inside his leather case, donned his hat, and made his way to the front door.

"No. Don't bother to show me out. I can find my way. And my best wishes for your happiness, Miss Winslow." The door slammed shut behind him.

"Well!" Lady Regina stood, the feather boa trailing behind her like magnificent plumage. "I wonder what that was all about. I certainly would like to have seen those documents. Dower agreement, indeed! What could Jerrold possibly be thinking? I've never heard of anything so outrageous."

"I wonder too." But Elyse didn't have time to ponder, for Katy charged past the room, stopped, and retraced her steps.

"Here you are. You gave me a fright. I was afraid you had decided to take a late morning ride, today of all days." Katy bustled across the room.

"I tried, but Quimby threw me out of the stables." Elyse planted her hands on her hips. "I don't suppose you would know anything about that, would you?" She fixed Katy with a penetrating gaze. Already, it seemed her freedom was fast disappearing. What would it be like when she actually was Lady Barrington?

Katy was undaunted. "Undoubtedly he and Mr. Quist are trying to get everything ready for this afternoon. They've been polishing up the coach for days, and the groomsman has been working with the horses. They've promised to be ready on time. I can't say the same for you."

"Katy, darling," Elyse gave the maid a soft smile, "did it ever occur to you that you might make someone a good wife?"

"Me? Whatever on earth for? I've got everyone I need right here. Besides, I haven't found a man good enough yet." She nodded as she seized Elyse by the arm and propelled her up the stairs. "When I decide to marry it will be to a man who offers me the sun, the moon, and the stars, takes me breath away and makes me toes curl — a man who steps right out of my dreams."

Elyse stopped in the middle of the doorway. "Makes your toes curl?" A teasing smile turned up her lips. "Katy, I had no idea you thought of such things."

The maid drew back with feigned shock. "I have me dreams too, little one. Just like you."

"Dreams." Elyse spoke with such wistfulness that the maid looked at her with concern.

"Why are you suddenly so sad? This is supposed to be the happiest day of yer life."

The soft shadows in Elyse's eyes betrayed the smile on her lips. She didn't believe in dreams anymore. "Yes, I know."

Lady Winslow followed them to the foot of the stairs. She frowned at the exchange. Today should be the happiest day of Elyse's life. Why did she have the feeling it wasn't?

Three hours later, the coach pulled out of the long drive of Winslow House. Pinned into her seat by layer upon layer of elegant, pale blue, embossed satin, Elyse struggled to sit forward. This was the last time she would look at that house and feel that she belonged there. When she saw it again, she would be Lady Barrington. That thought pushed her back onto the cushioned seat, and made her silent for the remainder of the ride to the church.

When Zach refused to be seated in the office of the agent of Barrington Shipping Company, Lionel Hodge, the young man behind the desk, smiled and waited a moment.

Once more Zach had donned the elegant clothes of the Count de Cuervo; the black eyepatch was firmly in place. He gazed at Hodge when the man's reedy voice broke his train of thought.

"My instruction were that I would honor the draft only when the shipment was delivered."

"Precisely." Zach nodded his agreement. His eyes scanned the office, noting the dust motes glittering in the late morning sunlight. It was still comfortable in the bookkeeper's office, but beads of moisture were popping out along the man's forehead. Zach was cool as ice.

"My man should be here any moment," he said, forcing a pleasant expression. "Would it be possible to have a cup of coffee while we wait?"

The nervous little man jumped up, practically upsetting a pitcher of water. "Of course. I'll just inform my assistant. I'll be back immediately." As if relieved to have an excuse, Lionel Hodge rounded the desk and disappeared through a glass-paned door.

Zach could hear lively discussion behind the glass. Seizing his opportunity, he immediately went to the file drawers along the opposite wall. Unless he missed his guess, he'd find what he wanted in them.

The third drawer contained leather-bound ledgers. Seizing one, he began a quick review of the entries. His silver gaze gleamed with cold satisfaction as he scanned the last ledger and found what he was looking for. Argosy Freight Company was a subsidiary of Barrington Shipping. Entries had been made for an impressive list of shipments. Undoubtedly, this was a little side business Barrington had gotten into. He tore one page of entries from the ledger. Quickly folding it and placing it in the inside pocket of his daycoat, he replaced the ledger just a moment before the pasty-faced Lionel Hodge stepped back into the office.

"My assistant will bring coffee. Our offices are closing at noon today." Hodge's lips twitched into a smile and his eyes darted about the office, looking anywhere except directly at the imposing man standing before his desk. "Master Barrington is being married this afternoon."

"Yes, the social event of the season, I understand." Zach replied, his eyes glittering. Both men looked up as a knock sounded on the outside office door.

"Ah, that should be my man now," Zach announced smoothly. He stepped across the office before Hodge could round the desk, opened the door, and stepped back, allowing Tris to enter, a reluctant companion in tow. The foreman for the Argosy Freight Company gave Tris a sullen glare. His arm was twisted at an odd angle behind his back, preventing escape, and he didn't immediately look at Lionel Hodge. Indeed, he seemed reluctant to do so.

"What is the meaning of this?" The bookkeeper was flustered. He'd obviously recognized the foreman from the Argosy Freight Company.

Zach smiled innocently. "You have the draft signed by Jerrold Barrington for payment in full for the gold. This gentleman can verify that two cartons for that shipment were delivered to his warehouse." He turned to the discomfited foreman. "I believe you received that shipment last night."

The stricken man seemed to have been rendered momentarily speechless. "I, ah . . ."

Deciding the foreman had temporarily lost the power of speech, Zach supplied the necessary information. "Last night a shipment was delivered to the Argosy Freight Company. Is that correct?"

The foreman looked helplessly to the bookkeeper. There'd obviously been no plan to cover this unusual development. Tris jerked the man's arm upward when he answered too slowly.

"Yes!" the foreman grunted out painfully, his face shading from pale to crimson.

But Lionel Hodge wasn't about to be so easily outdone. After all, he had his instructions. If he failed, he'd never work again in London. "What has any of this to do with Barrington Shipping, your grace?"

Zach smiled. He'd been waiting for Hodge to ask that question. "Isn't it true that Argosy Freight Company is part of the Barrington holdings?"

Hodge smiled like a victorious little mouse who'd just grabbed the cheese out from under the cat's nose. "I know nothing of this Argosy Freight Company. You are mistaken, sir. And since the shipment has not been received, I cannot honor the draft," he announced with thin-lipped satisfaction.

"I see." Zach nodded to Tris. A copy of the Argosy bill of lading was presented. He laid it on the bookkeeper's desk. "This proves the gold was delivered last night."

Hodge was undaunted. "That proves nothing." He gave the paper a perfunctory glance. "Only that Argosy Freight received a shipment of gold."

The cat's paw came down on the mouse's tail when Zach retrieved the piece of paper from his coat pocket. "And this is a page from a ledger of accounts. Notice the lettering at the top." He indicated the gold-embossed Barrington name at the heading of the page. "Barrington Shipping Company, and the name of the subsidiary company—Argosy Freight. I believe, Mr. Hodge, we have established that Barrington Shipping, in fact, has received the gold."

Recognizing the ledger page, Hodge swung around toward the file drawers. The third one sat conspicuously open. He whirled back to Zach, the whitening of his face beginning around his mouth and stretching up to his hairline.

"You sir, are—"

Zach cut him off with an impatient wave of his hand. "I am quite correct, Mr. Hodge. Now, if you please, affix your signature to the draft and come along with me. I believe the bank will be open for the remainder of the day. But I do wish to be quick about it, though it's been pleasant doing business with your employer."

"I'm sorry. I will have to notify Lord Barrington." Hodge nervously shuffled the papers on his desk. He reached for the bell pull that would summon his assistant from the adjacent office.

Zach's fingers closed steel like over the man's wrist. "I don't think you'd really care to do that. After all, Lord Barrington is to be married today. He would be most displeased if you were to interrupt him with such a small matter."

The flustered bookkeeper looked from Zach to Tris and back again. The perspiration along his upper lip glistened. "I suppose you're right."

Zach smiled. "Now if you will come along with me, we can conclude this business." He donned his hat, and seizing the book-keeper by the arm, pushed him out the door and down the steps to the waiting coach.

In less than an hour the transaction was completed. Several hundred thousand pounds sterling of Barrington money were transferred to an anonymous account at the small Bank of Zurich.

Zach approached the coach, shoving Hodge onto the seat beside the Argosy foreman. Tris sat opposite them, a pistol leveled at his prisoners, a long-bladed knife across his lap.

"What should I do with em, Cap'n?"

Zach removed the watch from his vest pocket and checked the time. It was one o'clock in the afternoon. In another hour it would all be done.

"Leave them where they won't bother anyone for the next several hours. Then get to the ship."

Tris nodded. "What about you, sir?"

Zach looked up. The gold was safely aboard the *Tamarisk* at Dover. It could be sold to any buyer. The money was safe at the Swiss bank, though some of it had been placed in an account under the name of Lydia Roberts. He hoped the money would in part make up for the woman's suffering. She'd been cruelly used by Charles Barrington, then set aside with a small pension to guarantee her silence. That she should have some of the money was part of the planned revenge.

Zach should have been pleased. Everything had gone according to his well-laid plans. He'd outfoxed the fox. Like the others in the colonies, he would continue the fight against Barrington and the Crown when he returned to New South Wales. But there was a hollow feeling deep inside him. He'd wanted the truth about his father and had found it. But the large amount of Barrington money he'd put in that bank account could never make up for what his father had lost. That was more than gold or money. Alexander Barrington had lost his identity, his family, his honor. What price could be put on that?

His gray eyes hardened, and the muscles in his jaw worked back and forth. He wanted revenge, God help him. Barrington had to pay for what his father had suffered. And no amount of gold would equal the cost. In any case, Barrington would merely send more men and more ships to try to recover that precious metal. Zach looked at Tris, his expression hard. There was something of far greater value to be had from Barrington, he decided.

His men had instructions to sail from Dover on the next tide. There was still time to achieve the ultimate revenge. He nodded icily to Tris and slammed the coach door shut.

"I'll join you at the appointed time. But first I have a wedding to attend."

Chapter Fourteen

The Anglican church was small. It had been the site of royal weddings since the time of Henry VIII. Elyse vaguely wondered if Jane Seymour had once stood in this same small anteroom contemplating her fate.

At least Elyse wasn't plagued by the thought of a former wife going to the guillotine as Seymour had been with Anne Boleyn. Still, she felt an overwhelming uneasiness, almost as if her life were ending. In a way it was. After today she would be Jerrold's wife, Lady Barrington. Strange, in all the months of their betrothal, she'd never consciously thought about that. She'd pushed back her nagging doubts.

She silently tried to bolster her confidence, telling herself all brides must feel this way. Then she looked over to Lucy and experienced a wave of envy. Lucy hadn't been nervous the day of her wedding; she'd been ecstatic. Elyse wished she could at least feel happy excitement, but she just didn't.

Lucy turned from the door, her blue gown a shimmering dark contrast to Elyse's pale blue one. "Jerrold sent this. He would like you to wear it."

Elyse took the long velvet case and opened it. She gazed down at the perfect blue sapphires and diamonds in the gold necklace, and groaned.

"Good heavens! It's beautiful." Lucy sucked in her breath.

"They're gaudy," Elyse declared with a touch of pique.

"They go with your gown," Lucy reasoned.

"They should go with the gown. Jerrold insisted on approving the fabric as well as the design." Snapping the lid to the case shut, Elyse sank down onto a nearby chair.

"Oh, Lucy! What's wrong with me? Why am I so critical? Everything Jerrold says or does irritates me. It shouldn't be this

298

way," she moaned hopelessly.

Lucy sank down in front of her, grasping her hands. She smiled with more confidence than she felt. "Maybe it's just a case of jitters. Want to talk about it?"

"About what?" Elyse rested her forehead on her arm.

"Oh, handsome mysterious strangers, an unexplained night that you didn't spend at my house, and lightning bolts," Lucy suggested vaguely.

Elyse's head came up. "I'm marrying Jerrold. That's all there is to it. The rest is over, done with. Good heavens, it never even existed. It was just a . . ."

"An affair?"

"Lucy, please!" She stood and paced the floor. "Tell me it's just a case of jitters."

"All right, it's just a case of jitters." Lucy was less than convincing.

Elyse gave her a look of complete exasperation. "Tell me I'm doing the right thing."

Lucy hesitated.

"Lucy!"

"If that's what you want to hear, then I'll say it. You're doing the right thing."

Elyse repeated the words she'd been reciting to herself over and over again all morning. "And everything will be just fine."

Lucy shook her head at this foolish game Elyse was playing with herself. "Everything will be just fine."

With a panic-stricken look on her face, Elyse whirled around. "When?" Tears pooled in her lovely eyes.

Lucy crossed the room and put her arms around her friend. She wanted to be truthful and say probably not as long as Elyse was married to a man like Jerrold Barrington. But she didn't, instead she lied brilliantly, knowing that was what Elyse wanted her to do even as she knew her friend was too smart to be deluded by lies, even the ones she'd been telling herself all these months.

"You'll feel better after the wedding. It happens to all brides, and bridegrooms, too, for that matter."

"You weren't nervous," Elyse said accusingly, remembering Lucy's and Andrew's wedding. It had been such a joyous occasion.

"I was marrying someone I loved completely," Lucy hit her smack between the eyes with that one.

"You certainly don't hold anything back," Elyse retorted.

"You wouldn't want me to. Now, are you still going to go

through with this ridiculous sham of a wedding?"

"Oh, Lucy, I must. There's a church full of people, and Grandmother—"

"Wants only your happiness," Lucy finished for her. "Why are you being so damned stubborn about this? For God's sake, you don't love Jerrold Barrington!" She was practically screaming at her friend. They both turned in surprise to the insistent knocking at the door.

"We have to go," Elyse whispered softly.

Lucy threw up both hands in frustration. "If you're determined to ruin your life I might as well be there with you. I've been with you through every other crisis in your life. But if you ask me—"

"Lucy, please." Elyse hugged her friend. "Just be happy for me."

"I guess I have enough happiness for two." Lucy squeezed her hand. "But you should have your own. You deserve it."

"Lucy!" Tears again pooled in Elyse's eyes.

"All right." Lucy turned her around, not able to meet her friend's eyes. "I'll fasten the necklace for you." She picked up the discarded case.

Elyse shook her head as she stepped away. "No. I prefer to wear the pendant Grandmother gave me." When she turned to Lucy, her eyes spoke volumes.

"Jerrold will be upset." Lucy knew him only too well.

Elyse smiled an ironic smile. "Perhaps he'll leave me standing at the altar as punishment." The smile faded.

"I'm ready."

"Elyse . . ." Lucy's brow wrinkled into a rare frown.

Elyse cut her off and started for the door. "I know what I'm doing."

Lucy could only follow or be left behind. "I sincerely doubt that," she muttered under her breath, then expelled a very unladylike expletive that brought a startled look from the two young priests passing the door.

"What the devil is happening?" Jerrold Barrington's explosion caused everyone in the small room to jump. He whirled on the hapless employee of Barrington Shipping, who'd arrived only moments earlier.

"Mr. Lash was found only about an hour ago." The man twisted his hat in his hands as if he were trying to strangle it.

"Where?" Jerrold snapped.

The man swallowed hard. "At a tavern called the Hog's Breath Inn, down by the waterfront." He smiled as he made a feeble attempt at humor. "He was with the innkeeper's daughter."

"Fool! Three days! Three days and not a word from him. What did he say?"

Barrington's minion, reduced to incoherent mumbling, was immediately seized by his jacket front. "Where is the shipment?"

"I'm gettin' to that part. He said they got the shipment just like you ordered. He had the men deliver it, and Jones reported the ship is gone. They must have left early this morning. Everything has gone as you wanted."

Jerrold threw the man from him. "I'm surrounded by incompetent fools. Lash tells you the shipment was delivered?"

"Yes, sir!" The underling straightened his coat. "I verified that with the foreman this morning, just like you said. I saw the two crates myself, sittin' there pretty as you please."

Jerrold's fists slowly relaxed at his sides. Perhaps everything was working out in spite of what had happened to Lash. Still . . . But there was no more time to consider checking further; a knock on the door signaled that the ceremony was about to begin. He turned to his employee.

"Get back to the warehouse and have the crates inspected. I want the contents verified. When that's done, report to me here. Do you understand?"

"Yes, sir!" The man nodded, then went out a side door.

Jerrold turned to leave by the other door. Of course everything had gone as planned, he told himself. Lash had merely taken it upon himself to do a little celebrating after the success of the raid. And yet, even as he stepped from the room and walked the short distance to the door that opened near the altar, he felt a prickling of uncertainty along his nerve endings.

At the back of the church, Elyse smiled only faintly as she took Cedric's arm. He'd been father and grandfather to her for as long as she could remember. It was only right he should stand at her side now. Her hand was ice cold, her fingers trembling as he placed his large hand over hers.

"Ready, sweet?" He gazed down at her quizzically, perhaps sensing some of her own uncertainty.

"Of course." Elyse smiled bravely though her face was pale and drawn.

Lucy followed behind as they walked down the long aisle, passing row upon row of guests, friends and acquaintances and relatives turning discreetly to catch a glimpse of the bride.

Elyse saw her grandmother amidst the sea of colors and faces. She focused on that one beloved face, and forced herself to be strong. What was it she saw in her grandmother's eyes? Was it sadness? Regret? Be happy, Grandmother, she thought. I love you so very much.

She felt the faint pressure of Uncle Ceddy's hand, and looked up. They'd reached the end of the aisle. Jerrold was waiting for her. He inclined his head faintly as Ceddy extended her hand to his. She looked for a smile, something in his eyes, a look or a glance. Anything to show that he was pleased. She saw only a momentary flash of disapproval as his gaze fell to her neck where the sapphire and diamond necklace should have been. Inwardly, she felt a small door close on her feelings. Nothing was ever good enough for the Barrington name. It angered her, causing vivid color to spread across her cheeks, in what would undoubtedly be mistaken for bridal radiance.

Damn! her heart protested; it should have been so different. Her gaze locked with Jerrold's and she immediately looked away, not wanting him to see her true feelings. How had she become so certain of them, and so late? It wasn't a matter of knowing what she wanted, but what she didn't want. But now it was too late. What could she do, turn around and inform everyone present that it was all a mistake? Laugh it off as a foolish charade? *I don't love him!* She wanted to scream it at the top of her lungs. But she didn't. She couldn't bear to think how such a scene would affect her grandmother.

Everything swam before her as the Anglican priest's words droned on and on, intoning the ancient rite that would join her to this man forever. *Forever.* The word screamed forth within her. She couldn't breathe. It was as if a great weight were pressing against her. All feeling seemed to seep out of her, and it occurred to her that if she fainted right now, they'd be forced to stop the ceremony.

Zach watched from where he stood, for a moment caught by the solemnity of the marriage ceremony. God, she's beautiful, he thought, his gaze fastened on Elyse. Her gown was pale blue, tightly cut across the bodice and slender waist before falling into a voluminous skirt. The sleeves were tight fitting to the wrist, the neckline cut low across the swell of her breasts. This is what you wanted, lovely Elyse, he sharply decided. But even as he felt anger over her greed and obvious scheming to be Lady Barrington, he couldn't repress his faint surprise as his glance fell on the simple diamond and pearl pendant she wore.

"You play the part to perfection," he muttered bitterly from the shadows.

The church was softly lit by row upon row of white candles, many of them set before the altar which was draped with a crimson tapestry embossed with the sign of the cross. The priest's words lifted to the rafters, echoing off stone walls as light shimmered throughout in intricate patterns created by the stained glass it filtered through. All eyes were focused on the somber beauty of the bride and the stoical confidence of the groom. Behind the altar, all was cloaked in darkness. No one saw the shadows shift and move.

A robed, hooded figure emerged from the left of the altar, bearing the rings that were to be blessed. It will soon be over, Elyse thought. She briefly wondered why the man had the hood pulled so low over his face. Just as quickly that odd coincidence was forgotten. She heard the priest call for the rings a second time, and looked up. Her gaze meeting Lucy's, she frowned.

Elyse saw the flash of steel but was slow to comprehend. Candlelight from the altar glinted off the long, curved blade pulled from beneath the heavy robe. The sword made a deadly singing sound as it slashed through the air. She was too stunned to move. She heard Lucy's startled gasp. Beside her, Jerrold muttered a curse and was slow to react.

As lean, brown fingers stole from the folds of the robe, clamping down over her wrist, Elyse's gaze snapped up. Before she could think, however, she was pulled forward, past the surprised priest; and before she could breathe, she was turned and pinned against the hard wall of a heavily muscled chest. One of her attacker's arms crossed in front of her, immobilizing her left arm while his hand clamped down over her right. With his other hand, her assailant pressed the blade against her throat.

"No one moves!"

At the hoarse command, a stunned cry rose from the congregation.

Quick to recover, Jerrold took a step forward as if he meant to pursue Elyse's abductor. Despite his stunned expression, his lips curled as he voiced a hoarsely whispered threat. "Let her go."

"One step further, Barrington." At the warning, the blade was pressed deeper into Elyse's throat.

The strong arm pressing beneath her ribs was cutting off her

303

breathing. She could feel the faint sting of the blade pressed into her flesh, but she had no fear. Whoever this man was, if he intended to kill her, he would already have done so. The thought of ransom flashed through her mind.

"My son, please," the priest implored with outstretched hands. "Let the girl go. Surely you can't mean to harm her."

"I respect you, sir," the intruder replied, "but you are not my father." Zach hesitated, his eyes glinting. Yes, he thought with wicked delight, it would be the perfect revenge against Barrington. He turned and waved the blade at the priest.

"Continue the ceremony."

The priest was stunned, his confusion evident on his face. "You can't mean . . . ?"

He immediately ceased protesting when the blade returned to the slender column of Elyse's throat. "Finish it!" The order was hissed. "But . . . with one small change. I will take Lord Barrington's place."

Lady Winslow gasped, coming to her feet. Knowing the danger if any interfered, Cedric quickly restrained her.

"Do it!" The hiss had become a hoarsely barked command that all present could hear.

"I ca-cannot." The priest stuttered. "What you ask is sacrilege."

"Listen to me, priest," Zach warned in a cold voice. "I don't give a damn for your rules. She's coming with me, and neither you nor anyone else can prevent it. If you're so concerned with honor, consider hers once I take her from here. With or without the marriage vows, she will perform her wifely duties. It's up to you, priest."

"You wouldn't dare . . . it would be a sin in the eyes of the church." The priest was incredulous.

"I wouldn't risk so much unless I was prepared to carry out my promise." Zach waved the sword at the priest. "What will it be?"

The priest's hands trembled as they fell to his sides in defeat. He couldn't condone what was happening, nor could he allow this girl to suffer what the man threatened, not knowing shame and dishonor that would be her lot. "You're mad!" he whispered brokenly. "May God have mercy on your soul for what you do."

Jerrold let out a strangled cry. "No! You can't!" He lunged forward, then abruptly halted, his widened eyes fastened on the blade pressed against Elyse's throat. His anger was almost tangible.

"You do this and there is no place on Earth where you will be safe. I'll find you! No mask will protect you!" he choked out. "I will hunt you down and see you hanged for this!"

Zach was undaunted. "Now, priest!" The command hissed through the air, sending a chill of fear across those assembled and pinning Jerrold where he stood.

Within seconds it was done, the priest ending the marriage rites begun such a short time before.

Elyse had whispered a faint yes in response to the blade held against her neck. Her captor had given his assent, and the final seal had been placed on the vows. She thought she was going to be ill.

This couldn't be happening! It wasn't real. But that deep-timbred voice was very real, and the hands holding her immobilized were solid and very frightening.

Zach motioned with the blade. "Everyone stand away! And don't attempt to follow." His meaning was clear.

Elyse was jerked backward, forced to cling to the arm that imprisoned her to keep from falling over the tangled hem of her gown. She stumbled, instinctively flinching as she expected to feel the blade press painfully into her throat. Instead, that arm tightened around her waist, preventing the fall with a strength that was almost gentle. They stopped a moment, and hope flickered that her captor might release her. It died in the next instant as he reached inside his robe, momentarily letting down his guard. Jerrold took that opportunity to advance on them, and the blade immediately returned to her throat.

As her captor laughed, Elyse shivered. Dear God, what was going to happen to her? She stared at the folded paper he'd pulled from inside the robe and thrown at Jerrold's feet. She saw Jerrold's silent fury, saw humiliation spread across his face. And she also saw that he would do nothing to save her.

The hooded assailant raised his head briefly as he threw the message down like a challenging gauntlet. For one brief moment, his gaze locked with that of Lucy Maitland, and she gasped at the bold arrogance in his gray eyes, the cruel twist of a smile on his incredibly handsome lips. She saw what no one else had seen. And then they were gone, Elyse and her captor disappearing into the darkness behind the altar. Lucy scooped up the message as Jerrold, Sir Cedric, and a half-dozen others rushed after them.

Elyse fought the strong arms that pulled her so easily through

305

the long, darkened passage. She couldn't see anything, and wondered how her assailant moved so unerringly. She wanted to scream, but the moment she drew a breath, a hand clamped firmly across her mouth.

Her shoulder bumped into a sharp corner, her shins were scraped from stumbling over the stone flooring, and she almost fell. Elyse gasped as she was pulled through an archway, a door creaking shut behind them. She struggled, she fought, she clawed at those hands that seemed to be everywhere. She half stumbled, half fell down a short flight of wooden steps, gasping as her knee was bruised painfully on the bottom step. It was all happening so fast she didn't have time to think, much less attack this madman.

Suddenly she was jerked around a corner and then abruptly flattened against a wall, uneven stones poking painfully into her back as she was pinned to them by that long, muscular body draped in priest's robes.

His one arm was pressed across her breasts. A warm hand smothered any sound that might come from her mouth. Elyse's eyes widened at the intimate pressure of his hips grinding against hers, of one muscular thigh riding between her legs. She was hopelessly trapped by some deranged maniac who seemed to be taking great pleasure in the close contact of their bodies.

Voices came from the passage, and Elyse jerked her head to the side, trying to free herself to call out. She could vaguely make out the shapes of barrels and boxes in the small chamber. It was a storeroom at the back of the church. Straining against the arms that pinned her, she felt exhaustion seep into her arms and legs. It was hopeless to fight him.

Elyse slumped back against the wall as the voices receded. Gathering her strength, she jerked back around to face her captor. Her brilliant blue eyes glittered dangerously in the pale, gray light that seeped in through the one small window up near the ceiling.

The one thing this man hadn't allowed for was her hands. They were momentarily free and she made one last desperate attempt to break away. She grabbed for the hood that covered his face and jerked it back hard. A pained curse split the air. She had also grabbed a fair amount of his hair.

His hand came away from her mouth as he struggled to capture her wrists. His hips rode hers into the unyielding surface of the wall. With one hand, Elyse slashed at that shadowed face, her nails removing a goodly amount of skin. Her wrist was immediately seized by strong fingers. While his hands were momentarily busy controlling hers, Elyse quickly drew in a deep breath. There would be only one chance. The scream died in her throat.

The priest's hood fell back and Elyse stared up into a face now shadowed only by the single patch that covered one eye. She was too stunned to react. Golden hair fell, unkempt, about his head. The planes of his face were sharply etched, by shadows and an odd, unreadable expression. Small beads of blood appeared where her nails had raked away skin. It couldn't be!

Then the expression on his face shifted dangerously, his handsome mouth curving into a mocking smile that revealed a flash of perfect teeth.

"You!" Elyse choked out. But before she could say more, his head came down, the shadow of his face closing over hers, his mouth bruising hers to silence.

"Damn you!" he hissed, jerking away from her. His lip bled where she'd bit him.

Fingers constricted bruisingly over her wrists as he jerked her arms high over her head, pinning them to the wall. In one motion she was completely helpless. "Let me go!" Elyse seethed. "Just what do you think you're doing!"

Holding both of her wrists with one hand, Zach wiped the trickle of blood from his lip. His gaze locked with hers. "Exactly as I please," he informed her, his fingers bruising her chin as he jerked her face up. "Exactly as I please."

His mouth crushed down on hers, cruelly; his lips forcing hers open, his tongue plunging between in punishing ravagement. He lowered one hand to her waist, letting it ride her hip. Then his fingers pressed through the layers of fabric until they dug into the curve of her bottom. This too was ravagement, but of a different kind—restricted by clothing, teasing at the desire that lay just beneath the anger.

Elyse felt as if she were drowning. What was happening? What was the Count de Cuervo doing here? Why had he abducted her and why had he insisted on that ridiculous ceremony?

Questions flashed, but no answers came. His body pressed hers into the wall, her hands were imprisoned by his, her mouth was a willing victim of his lips. His tongue stroked her mouth to velvet heat, darting to probe deeper until taste was not enough.

Confused and shaken, betrayed by her own body, Elyse was slowly slipping out of control. She gasped out a sound very near disappointment when the kiss was abruptly broken.

His voice was achingly cold. "I'm certain it would be far more enjoyable staying here with you all afternoon, Miss Winslow. But we really must be going."

Elyse's protest was quickly muffled beneath his hand. She groaned out her despair against his faintly salty skin.

"Lovely, lovely Elyse. You wanted so much to be Lady Barrington. Sorry to rob you of that moment, but if Barrington is the fool I think he is, he may still want you when I've finished with you. For the time being, you serve a better purpose as my wife." He momentarily released her wrists.

Confusion filled Elyse's eyes. What was he talking about? Surely he didn't mean to hold her to that farce of a ceremony.

"You make a lovely bride, but this will only slow us down." Zach was quicker than she as he seized the bodice of her gown and viciously jerked downward.

The fabric separated with a sickening tear, leaving her clad only in the thin silk chemise. Elyse's confusion gave way to humiliation, then anger. Her choice words were cut off by his hand, however.

He reprimanded her. "You must really do something about your language, Elyse." Then as if he understood exactly what she was saying, he added, "But you may be quite right. I hope you are. If Barrington is half the man I think he is, he'll come after you. And that is exactly what I want. Of course, that will be after I've finished with you."

Now she felt the fear. It spread, cold, across her skin. Why was the Count de Cuervo abducting her? Where was Jerrold? What would happen to her? What must her grandmother think?

Dear God! This had to be some sort of nightmare. Please, Elyse begged desperately, her thoughts on her grandmother, let this be a nightmare.

But it was frighteningly real. She tried to twist away, but his hand was quickly replaced by a cloth stuffed into her mouth. The coarse material scraped against her cheek. Then she was plunged into complete darkness as something was drawn over her head and shoulders, then pulled down to her ankles. A grain sack! And like so much grain, she was lifted, then settled over one strong shoulder, and carried off. Where?

"Nothing? What do you mean you found nothing? I want results and I want them now! They must still be in the church!" Jerrold stormed about the small anteroom where those closest to bride and groom had gathered.

Sir Cedric squeezed Regina's hand reassuringly. "This is getting us nowhere. We've searched every passage, room, and chamber in this church. She's not here. I think we would do better to notify the authorities."

"Ceddy is right." Lady Regina slowly came to her feet. "While you're standing here ranting and raving, that lunatic has fled with my granddaughter. Something must be done now!" She turned to the stricken priest.

"There is no point in keeping the guests here any longer. There will be no wedding today."

"I think there has already been a wedding." Lucy Maitland seemed the only person not greatly alarmed by the afternoon's events.

"What do you mean, there's already been a wedding?" Jerrold turned on her. "That ridiculous little charade is completely meaningless." He turned to the priest for confirmation. "Tell them."

The priest shook his head tragically. "I'm afraid I can't."

Jerrold strode to him. "What are you talking about? Elyse didn't participate willingly. Everyone saw that."

"Everyone saw a wedding ceremony, performed by a priest. It appeared that Miss Winslow was reluctant and yet . . ."

"Damn you! What do you mean by that?" Jerrold leaned threateningly toward the priest.

"Jerrold!" Lord Charles stepped between the man of God and his son. "You go beyond yourself. You would do well to remember where we are," he hissed. He then swung about and apologized to the priest for Jerrold's outburst.

"Under the circumstances, it is understandable. But the truth is the ceremony is binding."

"What!" Jerrold screamed. He envisioned the entire Winslow inheritance slipping from his fingers.

"If you will allow me to explain," the priest continued, "the ceremony is binding. But if coercion can be proven or if one of the parties should petition for annulment, under these circumstances the marriage would be set aside. But there is the matter of intent . . ." His voice was heavy with regret.

"Intent? What the devil do you mean by that?" Jerrold's voice was filled with cold rage.

"If the man who abducted Miss Winslow is determined to carry out this marriage, then it may prove harmful to her to pursue annulment."

"You can't mean . . ." Jerrold fumed, then whirled to the door. "I'll take care of this myself."

Lucy Maitland's words halted him. "I think what Father Winston is trying to say is that the man who abducted Elyse may have every intention of consummating this marriage." She drew in a steadying breath as a half-dozen pairs of eyes stared at her. "And it would seem Jerrold, that instead of charging off like a raging rhino with no clue, no trace, not even the barest hint of where to look, you might want to read this." She held out her hand, in it was the message dropped by the man in the priest's robe.

"What is that?" Jerrold's eyes narrowed venomously.

"Read it." Lucy handed him the paper, then stepped back to Andrew's side.

Unfolding the message, Jerrold scanned the contents.

Sail the sea; fulfill the quest
of men long dead, who never rest;
Find the jewel, priceless and rare,
in waters only fools would dare;
Prove you're coward or brave 'n'
wear the blade to face the Raven.

His face went ashen, a strangled gasp almost choked from him. He whirled on Lucy Maitland, the fingers holding the note shaking with rage. "Where did you get this?"

"It was left by the man who took Elyse. If you hadn't been in such a hurry, you would have realized you couldn't catch him. His escape was undoubtedly well planned. You've only wasted valuable time. As the note states, he plans to leave by ship. I should think, Jerrold, that you would first want to search the waterfront."

"Thank you, Lady Maitland!" Jerrold snapped. Before he reached the door, a timid voice called out to him.

"Sir?"

Jerrold whirled around. "Hodge! What are you doing here?" Not waiting for an answer, he abruptly said, "It will have to wait."

"I'm sorry sir, but I thought you would want to know this. It seemed important to you before you left London, and I did try to follow your instructions."

"My instructions? Good God, man! Why are you standing there like a weak-kneed sister? Speak up, and be quick about it."

Hodge's thin lips twitched into a weak smile. If he were to have any hope of saving his job or his reputation, he must speak. "It's the gold," he whispered to Jerrold, remembering his employer wanted as few people as possible to know about it.

"The gold? What has that to do with this? It will have to wait."

"I . . . uh . . . I don't think so, sir. You see, that fellow came for payment."

"What fellow?" Jerrold's face went from an ashen hue to embarrassed crimson as he crossed the room and drew his man aside.

"That Spanish count you told me might come by," Hodge explained, making frantic little gestures with his hands.

Jerrold closed his eyes in an attempt to control his urge to kill the man for bursting in at this awkward time. "And of course you handled it just as I instructed."

The man nodded, but the nod quickly turned to a weak shaking of the head.

Throwing the note down on a side table, Jerrold seized Hodge by the arm and jerked him out into the hallway beyond the anteroom. "What are you saying?" he was already beginning to sense what was coming.

"He came for payment, just like you said he would. . . ."

"And?"

"He forced me to sign the draft, then to go to the bank with him . . . to transfer the money."

"What!" Jerrold's strangled response exploded in the stately church. His grip about the man's arm tightened. He longed to feel bones snap, but he felt a restraining hand on his arm and looked into Lord Charles's face.

"Get a hold on yourself."

Jerrold refused to release his employee. "Tell me!"

"I had to do it. He brought along the foreman from the Argosy company. Right there in the office, he proved Argosy had received the shipment; then he proved Argosy is a Barrington company. He threatened to bring in the authorities. What else could I do? I knew you didn't want anyone knowing about the gold," Hodge simpered.

Jerrold thrust him away. The Count de Cuervo had made off with his gold and his money, and now it seemed that the Raven had abducted Elyse.

"What proof did he give you?" Jerrold demanded. He was determined to ruin the accountant's future, to destroy any hopes the man had of working again.

"This is the proof of delivery." Hodge handed the bill of lading to his employer.

Jerrold's eyes narrowed as he looked down at the elaborate scrawl at the bottom of the receipt. Anger constricted in his throat, and he tore like a madman, back into the small anteroom, causing everyone to stare at him. He seized the note supposedly left by the Raven and held the two slips of paper side by side, his gaze darting back and forth.

"It's not possible!" And yet the signatures were amazingly similar. He turned to Lucy Maitland and thrust both into her hands. "Read this!"

Lucy stared down at the boldly written note and then at the signature on the bill.

"They're similar," Jerrold hissed.

"Possibly. But what does that prove? You have one note signed by a man claiming to be the Raven, and another signed by the Count de Cuervo." Lucy stopped short. She then studied both signatures carefully. Slowly her head came up, her eyes growing quite large and round. Lightning indeed. "Oh my!"

"What the devil is wrong now?" Jerrold thundered, taking a threatening step toward her.

Andrew Maitland immediately stepped forward to protect his wife. Lucy tenderly laid a hand on his arm. "It's all right, my love. It really is." She turned triumphant eyes on Jerrold and held both notes out to him.

"This note was written by the Raven." She thrust one note at him, and could see he still didn't understand. "And this was signed by the Count de Cuervo, a Spanish nobleman." The smile began at her lips and quickly went to her eyes. She was going to take great delight in seeing Jerrold's reaction to what she was about to say.

Lucy smiled triumphantly. "Cuervo is Spanish for Raven. It seems Jerrold, that your Raven has been here in London all along, right under your nose for the past several weeks. And now he's made off with Elyse."

"The Count de Cuervo!" Jerrold roared. It was unbelievable, it was insane, and yet thinking back over the last weeks, he knew it was true.

"By God, I'll hunt him down," he vowed, rage darkening his eyes. "There'll be no place on Earth where he'll be safe, no place where he can hide. And when I find him, I'll take great pleasure in seeing him hang."

He stopped before Lady Winslow. "I promise you, I will find Elyse. And no matter what she is made to suffer, I will honor our

312

agreement. She will be Lady Barrington."

Zach checked the ropes that bound Elyse. He'd pushed the horses hard; they needed a rest.

Inside the church, he'd pulled the grain sack over Elyse's head easily enough.

Carrying her to the waiting cart had been another matter. He'd be bruised for weeks where she'd kicked him. At one point, just as he'd ducked out of the church with her across his shoulder, she'd abruptly leveraged herself up, cracking her head against the solid beam over the small doorway. With a muffled groan, she'd gone limp in his arms, so he'd positioned her upon the sacks, and had removed the rough burlap long enough to assure himself she hadn't done herself any great harm. It had turned out she'd have a knot on her head but no permanent damage.

He'd followed his planned route, patiently sitting behind the team of sorry-looking horses that plodded along the road taking them steadily south and then east to the outskirts of London, in the opposite direction from that in which a search would be conducted.

It was just after dark when the cart lurched uncertainly. Zach reined in the team and jumped down to inspect the wagon. With a soft curse he found they'd lost a rim. They continued on, but their pace was greatly slowed. Indeed, it was close to midnight when they reached the small inn. Not a light was shining, but a sharp knock quickly roused the innkeeper. If he saw anything odd in this stranger dressed like a beggar, with a sack slung over his shoulder and an impressive amount of gold in his pockets, he said nothing.

As he paid the man for a room and for stabling the horses, Elyse started to come around. He'd bound her hands and feet, and muffled her mouth, but that didn't seem to slow her down. She thrashed and squirmed until Zach almost dropped her on the stairway.

He merely shrugged at the man. "Me sister ran away from the man she was to marry. I'm takin' her back home. Pa is goin' to wear the hide off her backside," he explained. That provoked an enraged grunt, but Zach merely whacked his "sister" a good one on her nicely curved bottom and continued up the stairs.

Once inside the room, he tossed Elyse, sack and all, onto the bed. She lay alarmingly still, and he foolishly thought he might have hurt her. The undoing of one end of the sack was practically his own undoing. Elyse had doubled up her body as she'd fallen. She swiftly straightened, trying to butt him with her head. He barely missed being knocked unconscious. As he came upright, Zach saw that Elyse had tumbled to the floor. Again she lay frighteningly still. Fear knifed through him; she might have hurt herself. Fool that he was, he quickly knelt beside her and pulled the sack up over her head.

Struggling free of it, Elyse screamed at the top of her lungs. "You lop-eared, swaggering son of a—" She twisted away from him. "You bastard!"

Somehow Zach managed to get the gag back into her mouth, but she continued to struggle, lashing out with her feet until she was breathing hard and practically choking on the gag.

Everything swam before Elyse's eyes, and there was a dull aching at her temples. It was stiflingly hot in the small room, then bone-achingly chilly and she broke out in a cold sweat. Elyse felt her throat constrict as she tried to breathe. Everything went gray and the walls of the room seemed to collapse inward. She had no strength left to struggle, the pain in her head overruled everything else and she fell back into that dark void.

Zach watched her warily, thinking it was another trick. Slowly, cautiously, he stroked her cheek. Her skin was like ice and deathly pale, her breathing was shallow. Carefully, he removed the gag, ready to replace it if she cried out. When she didn't so much as open an eye, Zach knelt beside her. His fingers measured the pulse at her neck. It was rapid and thready. She'd fainted. He checked the darkening bruise against her temple. It wasn't serious, and by what she'd called him only moments before, he had a good hunch she hadn't suffered any loss of memory.

He made her as comfortable as possible, reluctant to replace the gag. And, for the first time since that last night at Fair View, he allowed himself to look at her, really look at her.

Dear God, she was beautiful. Try as he might to hold on to it, he felt the anger seep out of his achingly tired muscles and bones. He stroked the satin smoothness of her cheek, touching the sable tendril of hair curled loosely about the soft shell of her ear.

Damn! Silently cursing, he pulled his hand back as if he'd touched fire. The gag was gently replaced in her mouth. Then he carefully bound her feet to the bedposts in case she might regain consciousness and try to escape. He took the chair opposite the bed, sinking his weary frame down onto the hard wood. Just a few hours' sleep . . . But he found they were not to be his. Restlessly, he paced the room, his eyes constantly turning back to that bed and the softly curved body he remembered from that one night weeks ago. She was clad only in the thin chemise, and even though she was exhausted, she was having a devastating effect on his senses and his control.

"I'm just tired," he mumbled unconvincingly and then stormed out of the room, locking the door behind him.

He allowed them both only two hours' rest; then he returned to the room. Somehow, Elyse had managed to turn herself onto her right side. Her legs were pulled up as far as the ropes would allow, her head was turned up, and her arms were pulled into an incredibly awkward position. Zach found himself standing beside the bed, staring down at her. He reached out, his fingers tracing the curve of a winged brow, the soft spiky length of dark lashes that lay like a stilled butterfly wing against her cheek, hiding those twin pool of shimmering blue light. From his dreams he knew he'd memorized her every curve, every indentation; the texture of her skin; the silkiness of hair now disheveled and in long tangles. He ran his thumb along the full outward thrust of her lower lip, and remembered the wet heat of her mouth against his. It was dry now and faintly chapped from the cloth. He gently removed the gag, and in the stillness of the night allowed himself one small confession.

"If only things had been different for us, Lady Barrington."

From the innkeeper, he'd learned they were still some distance from Dover. Well before dawn, he rebound Elyse's ankles and wrists, then he pressed a cloth moistened with water against her parched lips. "I'm sorry, lovely lady," he said softly as he slipped the gag back into place. They had to get moving. He knew that everything afloat in London harbor would have been searched by now. Barrington would realize he'd chosen another route, or would think he still remained in London. Zach couldn't afford to have Jerrold guess he'd headed for Dover.

The wheel on the cart was hopelessly damaged. Leaving ample payment and the two horses, Zach took two fresh mounts from the innkeeper's stables. He threw a blanket across the saddle of one to soften the ride, then gently laid Elyse across it, snuggled in the sack. He secured ropes so that she wouldn't fall even if she awakened and began to struggle, then mounted the second horse.

They'd been on the road several hours now. He'd just let the horses rest. It couldn't be much further. The sky began to lighten, a faint breeze stirring. Aboard the *Tamarisk*, his crew would be making ready to be underway. He turned in his saddle at the unmistakable sound, but restrained Elyse's horse too late.

So much for ropes he thought as the horse pulled back, jerking the reins from his grasp. He cursed as he lunged for them and grabbed short. It was the strangest sight he'd ever seen, and if he weren't so angry he'd have laughed.

The poor horse seemed to have suddenly grown a hump. As Elyse regained consciousness and struggled, despite her awkward position, to free herself, she rolled and pitched across the back of the frightened animal. Eyes rolling, the horse lunged down an embankment, and for the life of him Zach would have sworn it was a camel that rapidly headed back in the direction of the inn.

The chase was long and grueling. Zach was afraid Elyse would be thrown off and killed by the fall. Eventually, she was thrown, and as he vaulted from his own mount, panic seized him, his only thought being that he was responsible. Never in his life had he known such an overwhelming sense of fear and helplessness.

He quickly stripped away the sack and immediately regretted it. Elyse was fully conscious and angry. She lashed out with both feet, catching him just to the left of the groin. It took all of his strength to subdue her and reach for the chloroform he'd brought along for just such a situation as this.

As he carried the drugged Elyse to the top of an embankment, he began considering alternative plans. His horse was gone, hers was hopelessly hobbled in the ropes that had once held her to its back, and dawn was fast approaching. He freed her horse and, with Elyse across the saddle before him, pushed on as fast as he dared. Afoot, they'd never reach Dover in time. Just as the sun rose over those majestic white cliffs that jut from the sea, Zach pulled the horse to a stop. In the small cove below, the *Tamarisk* rode the gentle swells of the restless tide. Glancing at the small stretch of beach, he saw a longboat and guided the winded horse down the path in the sea wall.

Sandy and Tris ran up the beach toward them. Zach dismounted.

"We thought you might not make it, Cap'n." Sandy fixed a scrutinizing gaze on him. "We heard that was quite a wedding you attended."

Zach looked up through bloodshot eyes. "What else did you hear?"

"Seein's how it's goin' to be a long voyage home I let some of the crew stay in town last night." He winked with obvious meaning. "We got word just a little while ago that Barrington is sendin' search parties to every port up and down the coastline. You wouldn't happen to know anythin' about that now, would ya, sir?" Sandy smiled broadly at him.

"Not a thing," Zach answered gruffly as he gently lifted the sack down from the saddle. "See that this gets aboard will you, Sandy? And be careful." He winked back at his second mate. "It's a very special cargo of delicate fruit. I wouldn't want it bruised any more than it already is."

"Aye, aye, Cap'n." Sandy saluted as he carefully carried Elyse to the rowboat. Zach removed saddle and bridle from the horse and turned it loose. He then turned to Tris.

"Is Tobias aboard?"

"Yessir, he is. And he's none too happy about all this."

Zach nodded. There'd be a confrontation once he was aboard. "I expect he's not." His weary gaze scanned the ocean. Sandy signaled from the longboat as they approached the ship. The tide was fast running out. Shading his gaze against the rising sun, he scanned the *Tamarisk*. She looked like a proud, powerful bird momentarily at rest, her wings slowly expanding, ready to take flight.

"What flag do we fly, Tris?"

"The Spanish flag, sir."

Zach nodded. "When we get aboard, set our course south by southeast with the wind. And run up the Portuguese colors."

"Lisbon, sir?"

"Lisbon." Zach nodded. "There's a man I want to see about some gold on our way home."

Chapter Fifteen

"No mercy! No mercy! Lash 'em to the yardarm!"

Elyse groaned as she slowly awakened, the words jarring through her.

"Keel haul the bloody swine!" was followed by a string of colorful curses.

This must be part of a nightmare. And yet, as the colorful words pushed their way through the haze of her senses, she had a nagging suspicion it wasn't.

Her throat was so dry it was paralyzed, and something was bound across her mouth. Coming more fully awake, Elyse jerked her head to the side, and immediately winced.

Oh God, she hurt! It seemed as if every muscle, every bone throbbed.

"Lash 'em to the yardarm!" The guttural screech helped her focus despite the pain. She felt as if she had been lashed to a yardarm and left for days. She couldn't move. She forced herself to relax. Whoever had been shouting had stopped.

It's all right, she told herself. It's just a bad dream. In a few minutes you'll wake up and you'll be in your room.

It didn't work. She tried moving her arms, but it was useless. Her wrists were bound together. Great balls of fire! Where was she?

Elyse twisted onto her back. She could feel the padded support of the narrow bed beneath her. Staring overhead, she tried to make out shapes in the meager light, but all blurred into soft gray. A thin sliver of light a few feet away and down low caught her attention; light from beneath a door!

She tried to swallow and practically gagged; her throat was so dry. Trying to sit up, Elyse felt the restraint of the rope across her shoulders. She was tied to the bed! She twisted and turned as much as the ropes would allow, then fell back panting on the mattress.

As she breathed in slowly, her senses sharpened. Now she remembered—the Count de Cuervo! He'd been the one in the shadows at the church. That phony ceremony, being abducted at knife point! Where had he taken her? And why? What had he meant when he'd said she would serve his purposes better as his wife?

Wife? Oh God, no, she thought miserably. Please, let this all be a dream. Instinctively, she knew it wasn't.

She jerked sideways as she sensed something else. The slow, back and forth roll, like that of a baby's cradle. Closing her eyes, she listened. There it was, almost like a muffled sigh that broke and then came again. It was oddly familiar.

Lying there in the darkness, she suddenly knew the source of it. It was the sound of water, that caressing gurgle she remembered hearing when she'd swam as a child. Water surrounded her. A ship?

"You can't just leave her in there!" Tobias argued, in spite of the threatening glare that could have cut a man's head in two. "It's been hours since we left Dover. Has she eaten anything in all that time? And what about water?"

"She's all right!" Zach heaved the ship's log down onto his desk. "Tris removed the sack. She's tied because I didn't want to risk her trying to escape while we were still so close to shore. At any rate she's still sleeping. Tris checked on her just a little while ago."

"Three hours ago, to be exact. For God's sake, what are you tryin' to do to the girl?"

"I think you underestimate Miss Winslow. At any rate, it's none of your concern! Leave it be!" Zach hadn't slept. He was weary of arguing, but Tobias wasn't about to let the matter rest.

"As this ship's doctor, I demand she be treated well!"

"That is a situation that can be changed! We'll be putting ashore in Lisbon in a few days' time. If you don't like the way I run this ship, you're free to leave." Zach immediately regretted his sharp words as he saw his old friend stiffen.

He conceded. "I'll have the ropes removed. She'll be given everything she needs to make her comfortable. It was never my intention to mistreat her."

"Is that so? What about bringin' her here? I'm certain you just didn't walk into that church and extend a formal invitation for an ocean voyage. And I'm equally certain if you had, she would have refused!"

"Enough!" Zach's fist came down on the desk.

Undaunted, Tobias tried another tack. "What are you goin' to tell her about all this?"

Zach never looked up. "As little as possible. I think it's better that way."

Tobias stared hard at him. "Is that all there is to it?"

Zach's head came up. He fixed Tobias with a penetrating stare. "That's all. There's nothing to explain. She's aboard this ship and confined to her cabin until I say otherwise. It's safer for everyone."

"You'll have to talk to her sooner or later, Zach. She doesn't strike me as the type to calmly accept bein' shut up in that cabin. She's undoubtedly goin' to have a lot of questions and she's goin' to want answers."

"I'll take care of it when the time comes." Zach put him off, at the same time knowing full well he was only delaying the inevitable. He couldn't very well keep her drugged for the entire voyage to New South Wales, if that was how long it took Barrington to find them.

Tobias eyed him carefully. "Have it your way."

"I intend to. I am captain of this ship," Zach reminded him.

"Aye." Tobias nodded thoughtfully. "Now, I think you'd better tell me what you found out." Something had happened when Zach was at the Barrington estate, and he meant to find out what it was. He didn't understand the change in his young friend. There was something frightening in Zach now, in the way he just sat there taking everything in. And what part did the girl play in all this? Why was Zach goading Jerrold Barrington into a confrontation he probably wouldn't survive.

"It's about your father, isn't it?" Tobias speculated "It has to do with whatever you found out about him and Felicia Barrington." He waited.

It began slowly, then built. Zach rolled his head back wearily, his eyes closed. Then laughter rumbled deep in his chest. It was mad, insane. Hadn't Elyse said that in the church? He came out of the chair, slowly pacing the cabin, laughter rolling out of him, until his shoulders shook, leaving him weak, unable to talk. He'd come to England for the truth. Well, by God, now he had it.

He came up against the far wall of the cabin and braced his hands on either side of the open porthole. Tobias had a right to know. His head hung between his outstretched arms, he just stood there, letting the madness wash over him. Zach didn't know how long he stood thus, giving in to the fatigue and anger.

Slowly he told what he knew; a story of half brothers, a story of greed and betrayal that led to murder, a trial, and the destruction of many lives. And he told of Felicia Seymour Barrington, the beautiful, innocent pawn of one man's hatred against his own brother.

His head came up, and when he again looked at Tobias, the anger had won. It was there in the hardened line of his mouth, the coldness of eyes devoid of anything except the burning light of revenge.

"Alexander Nicholas Barrington was my father." His voice was ravaged by hate.

Tobias shook his head incredulously. "I can't believe it." All at once he felt old, very old. He rubbed his fingers against his forehead. "All those years I knew yer father, and not a word. Not one! There was only that letter from her. I should have known." Tobias sat back heavily in the chair. "I think I need a drink."

Zach stood, staring out the open porthole. Rolling waves spread away to the disappearing coastline in the late morning sunlight. He frowned slightly at the sight of dark clouds on the horizon. Then he came away from the porthole.

He was tired, deathly tired. His body screamed for sleep, but his mind refused it. He wished a drink were all it would take to wipe his mind blank. Then maybe he could sleep.

Tobias reached for the bottle between them. He held it poised over the tumbler and hesitated, his hand shaking. Without warning, he came out of the chair with the energy of man half his age and hurled the bottle against the far wall, the best brandy that could be stolen or bought slipping down it in a dark liquid stain.

"You're mad! You know that, don't you?" He turned on Zach. "Bringin' her aboard will see us all hanged! What in God's name were you thinkin'?"

In all the years he'd known Tobias, Zach couldn't remember seeing him quite so angry, drunk or sober.

"This will bring the Crown down on us. Barrington will come at you with everything he has."

Without so much as drawing a breath, Tobias continued his tirade, emphasizing his remarks with jabs in the air, as if he were striking at somebody or would like to. Zach had no doubt as to the imaginary target.

321

"Suicide! Plain and simple. That's what it'll be. Don't you know that Barrington has ships and men in damned near every port in the world? He controls everything. He gets things done with just the snap of a finger." He snapped his for emphasis. Red-faced, he then turned on Zach and leaned against the edge of the desk, bracing his weight on white-knuckled fingers.

"Where can you hide?" he shouted to the heavy beams overhead.

"I don't intend to hide. I want him to find me."

That brought Tobias around. He could only stare dumbfounded. He was quickly finding out he didn't know Zach Tennant at all. He had once, when they'd begun this voyage. Could the man have changed so much?

Zach's voice was low, deathly quiet. "He has to be stopped."

"And you're usin' that girl for your revenge," Tobias accused.

"Yes!" Zach bit the word off. "Charles murdered his and Alex's father, but Alex paid the price!" He came away from the porthole in long angry strides. "He paid with his life, with everything he valued. Oh, Alex paid!" he stormed, his fists coming down again and again on the desk as anger washed over him. "But even that wasn't enough for Charles Barrington. He had to have her.

"Dammit! She was nothing but a possession to him." Zach was losing control; he could sense it but couldn't stop it.

He stood, hands gripping the desk as if he were in great physical pain, and laughed incredulously. "He took her just as he took everything else. She didn't love him! He knew it, but it didn't matter. And in the end he destroyed her, too."

He seemed wrung dry of any emotion. "She loved Alex. She died loving him, believing he would go back for her someday, just as he'd promised he would. But he never went back. And she died alone, thinking that he didn't love her!" Zach's eyes were stark. There were no tears in them, only pain.

"And now you want revenge, no matter who it hurts," Tobias finished for him.

Zach never looked at him. "Someone has to pay for what they did to him." He turned and stared at Tobias as if he wanted some kind of approval yet knew there would be none.

"Well, I won't be part of it," Tobias announced. "That girl is innocent. She had nothing to do with this, and I won't be part of your scheme. Neither would your father if he were alive." The old man turned toward the cabinet. Opening it, he seized a bottle of brandy and tucked it beneath his arm.

"I'm going to get drunk, very drunk. And I hope like hell you've come to your senses when I'm sober again."

The cabin door slammed hard as Tobias left. It bounced against the latch and creaked open slowly with the rolling motion of the ship. The companionway was silent and empty. In frustration, Zach doubled his fist and drove it against the cabin wall. He welcomed the pain. It forced the numbness from his body. Turning, he braced his shoulders against the cabin wall, and dug the heels of his hands into his weary eyes.

Then he dropped his hands to his sides. Tobias was right. For hours he'd refused to go near that cabin just across from his, unwilling to face her and confront what he'd done. He'd used one excuse after another—that he had to be topside as they got underway and left the coast of Dover, that he had to be at the helm as the storm set in crossing the channel. . .

Coming away from the wall, he seized the key from his desk and crossed the companionway. Key in the lock, he hesitated. Then, thinking better of this move, he called down the companionway for Tris.

Elyse strained as she worked the rope binding her wrists to the sideboard of the bed. She had no idea how long she'd been doing this. She lay back, panting as she tried to breathe through the gag that cut into her bruised mouth. The motion of the ship had changed. Closed as she was into this dark corner, and bound, she knew they'd encountered rough weather. That could only mean they must have put to sea.

She thought of her grandmother and Uncle Ceddy. Dear God, what must they all think? Her grandmother was a strong woman, but she'd already suffered the loss of a husband, a son, and Elyse's mother. Tears of frustration pooled in her eyes. She remembered how happy Regina had seemed on the ride to the church. And Uncle Ceddy had looked so handsome, his face fixed and grave as he'd walked down the aisle with her during the ceremony.

That ceremony! Elyse thought of Lucy Maitland. She could almost imagine Lucy might have had something to do with all this. She'd been so opposed to the marriage to Jerrold. But Elyse had to admit, even Lucy wasn't capable of so elaborate a scheme.

Her thoughts were scattered due to pain, fatigue, and overwhelming thirst. She tried to concentrate and found it easier willed than done. Don't panic, she instructed herself, over and over again.

Was it only minutes, or had hours passed? Elyse didn't know. She opened her eyes, staring through the darkness as the sound came again. It was the grating of metal against metal. A key in a lock? Her head jerked toward the door.

She breathed in deeply and mentally braced herself as the huge figure of a man was briefly illuminated in the doorway. She heard another sound; then light flared briefly in the small cabin — a match held in the man's hand. A lantern was lit and then he turned toward the narrow bed. Elyse instinctively shrank back into the shadows.

As the man approached the narrow bunk, Elyse could see he wore the clothes of a sailor. He leaned over her briefly, his large, callused fingers scratching against her skin as he untied the ropes. Elyse was too stunned at this sudden freedom to pull away from the heavy odor of sweat and salt sea air that emanated from him.

Trying to rub feeling back into her wrists, Elyse cautiously sat up. Clad only in the thin, silk chemise, she gasped as a rush of cool air struck her exposed body. Grabbing for the coarse woolen blanket that had covered her only moments before, Elyse quickly scrambled into the darkest corner of the bed. She clutched the blanket to her like a protective shield.

"Get out of here!" she ordered indignantly. Then as the man turned, seemingly to follow her request, she came up off the bed. "Wait!"

Elyse wrapped the blanket around her. It would do her no good if the man left. Who could know how long it might be before someone returned? If anyone did . . . And she wanted some answers.

"Where is the Count de Cuervo?" she demanded, bravely tilting up her chin. "I demand to see him at once."

The man turned slowly, his dark eyes watching her speculatively. "Who?"

Elyse shifted uncomfortably. "The Count de Cuervo. He brought me here."

The man's gaze slipped over her head to toe. "I don't know any count. Captain Tennant is captain of the *Tamarisk*."

"The *Tamarisk?*" Elyse repeated slowly. "This is the *Tamarisk?*" Her eyes snapped back to the sailor's unreadable expression. It told her only that he was completely loyal to his captain. This man would reveal only what the ship's captain wanted her to know.

"Very well." She squared her slender shoulders, her composure momentarily slipping as the blanket dipped off one shoulder. She returned the covering to its discreet position just below her chin. "I demand to see Captain Tennant at once."

"No."

Not "it's not convenient at this time," not "he'll gladly see you later." Just no; definitely, unquestionably, no. Elyse wasn't about to be put off.

"I'm afraid that's unacceptable," she informed the sailor in her haughtiest tone.

It brought only the faintest shrug of indifference from him. "The captain doesn't want to see you." The sailor gestured to the tray he'd set on the small table by the bed.

"You have water, food, and clothes." His gaze remained discreetly positioned on a point somewhere over her head.

That was all. Water, food, clothing—and no answers. Elyse crossed the small space separating them, the blanket wrapped around her body like a protective shroud. She stared down at the tray.

Seizing the clothing, she scattered them to the far side of the room, saying, "I don't want your clothes." Then she seized the pitcher of water. It crashed against the wall, soaking the clothes. "And I don't want water." Actually she regretted the loss of water more than the loss of the clothing. But she was in a high temper. Her hand went next to the bowl of thick, pasty-looking gruel. No loss there. Her eyes gleamed.

First Zach heard the curses, in an angry but feminine voice, then the crash of dishes, followed by more curses. Only this time they weren't feminine. Tris emerged from the cabin across the companionway as if he'd been catapulted out of a cannon. He whirled around, meeting his captain's questioning gaze.

Emerging from the far end of the passageway, Tobias stared at the large Tris, who was plastered, head to foot, with a sickening-looking lumpy liquid.

Another crash reverberated against the wall, quickly followed by another. The curses were muffled but nonetheless distinct. All three men were treated to a very colorful tirade.

"Sir, I—" Tris tried to explain, but he winced and stepped away from the door as a loud thump jarred the wall of the cabin.

Zach came out of his chair, throwing the pen down on the

desktop on which he'd been trying to work. "That does it! Stand aside!" he commanded his man. Taking the key from Tris, he inserted it into the lock.

"This should be interesting." Tobias nodded to Tris as the man squeezed by him to head toward the crew's quarters in search of clean clothes.

"I want out of here! I demand to see your captain! You coward! You lumbering ox! I won't be kept prisoner any longer! Do you hear me!" Screaming at the top of her lungs, Elyse whirled about the small cabin, making it a shambles. She turned next to the bed, and when it wouldn't give way, she set upon the table and chair. She'd just seized the water pitcher when the door was thrown back on its hinges. She whirled around, murder in her eyes.

"You bast—" Her arm stopped in midair.

"You!" she gasped incredulously. Then, as realization set in, she took deadly aim.

"Elyse! Stop this, now!"

In quick, easy strides, Zach was across the cabin, his fingers closing over her wrist.

"Stop it!" he warned. "I can break it with one simple twist."

Elyse slowly recovered from her first shock. The Count de Cuervo! "This is your ship?"

"My ship! And I don't particularly want it broken to pieces."

She was stunned to speechlessness for a moment, livid with anger the next. "Damn you!" She lashed out. "It was you all along!"

"Yes! Now if you'll just behave yourself."

"Behave?" She was furious. My God, the man must be mad. Behave! Elyse pulled back her free hand. Without thinking, she doubled her fist and punched him as hard as she could. A loud resounding smack drew her up short. She stared at him wide-eyed, equally shocked.

Stunned by the blow, Zach immediately released her, his hand going instinctively to his injured eye. The look he fastened on her could have turned rock to molten lava.

"Elyse!" As she backed toward the door, his free hand snaked out, catching her by the arm.

"Great balls of fire!" she breathed out.

His fingers were bruising her arm, but the open door was too tempting and she'd been closed in too long. Elyse abruptly changed direction. In one quick movement, she lunged, pushing him back against the far wall. Momentarily thrown off balance, he instinctively reached out to break his fall. Elyse darted through the door.

She flew past someone else in the companionway. She didn't have time to see his face. Not wasting a moment, she scrambled up the ladder. Quickly struggling with the latch, she pushed hard, wincing at the pain in her shoulder as the hatch gave way. Then she gasped, her hair whipping across her eyes, wind and rain blinding her.

"Elyse!" Panic drove Zach to his feet. He dove into the companionway, just in time to see her bare feet disappearing over the top rung of the ladder.

"Why didn't you stop her?" he yelled at Tobias.

"How?" Tobias growled back at him. "I didn't have a rope," he added sarcastically.

Zach vaulted up the ladder. Rain pelted him through the open hatch. It blew across the ship in great billowing gusts, making the decks slick and dangerous. Water ran over them, pooled, and then spilled down the open hatch. There was only a minimal crew up on deck; Sandy, who had relieved him earlier, and the two men keeping an eye on the rigging. He saw Sandy at the wheel, gesturing, and turned in the direction his second mate indicated.

Elyse stumbled along the deck, rain plastering the chemise to her body, her hair whipping in the wind.

She was only a few feet away, but on the slick rolling deck of a ship that seemed like miles. Zach lunged after her, fear knotting deep inside him. If she slipped, she'd be swept overboard.

Elyse heard her name called, and then the wind whipped away from her. She turned and saw him coming after her. She wanted to run, to crawl, to do anything to get away from him. But the wind and rain lashed at her, stinging painfully against her skin, making it impossible to see. Dear God, it was a storm just like this . . .

She cried out as strong hands closed over her shoulders. She turned on him, clawing at his hands, trying desperately to break his hold.

Zach pulled her into his arms. Her long hair stung as it whipped around them.

"No!" She fought and screamed and raged, but finally she collapsed in his arms, fighting for breath, her eyes flashing. "I hate you!" she screamed into the wind.

"Save it!" He cursed as he whirled around, drawing her with

him. He grabbed the taut line at the center mast, his other arm encircling her waist.

There was nothing gentle in him as he pushed them both toward the open hatch. His fingers bit into her as he almost threw her down the opening. Elyse grabbed at the top rung of the ladder and made her way down slowly, her hands cold and clumsy, her arms shaking.

Zach shouted to Sandy, saw his mate's thumb's-up sign, then crawled after her, slamming the hatch into place.

He stepped down into the companionway and turned on Elyse.

She was soaked to the skin, water puddling at her feet. Bruised from being battered about, she was in no mood for his anger.

At that moment, Zach was too furious to speak, but his cold gray eyes could have turned the water she was standing in to ice. He looked first to Tobias, then to Tris and to the half-dozen other men gaping at them from the crew quarters. "I don't remember this being a pleasure cruise. I think all of you have something to do."

Every man except Tobias immediately went about his business. Tris headed for the galley with three of the men. The others ducked back into their quarters, closing the door behind them.

"Well?" Zach turned to Tobias.

The older man was certainly not the toughest sailor aboard, yet he seemed completely unaffected by Zach's temper. His eyes narrowed as he looked from Zach to Elyse. Much to his delight he decided she could probably take care of herself.

"I'll be interested to see who wins this round. If you need any help, just call." He turned back to his own cabin.

"Damn! What does it take to have orders followed on my ship!" Zach thundered, his fingers closing over Elyse's wrist as he pulled her down the companionway. He stopped at the door to her cabin. It was a shambles. Her breakfast was plastered to the near wall. Pieces of glass, china, and a metal tray littered the floor.

He pulled her in the opposite direction, kicking open the door to his own cabin, and thrust her inside. Slamming the door behind them, he turned on her, jabbing a finger at her. "I'm captain of this ship. My orders will be obeyed and that includes you!"

Elyse's eyes grew rounder by the moment. She reached up, slapping his hand aside. "Damn you!" Tears of anger slipped down her wet cheeks. "Who are you?"

He was angry, tired; and she'd just scared the hell out of him

328

with that little stunt. Zach grabbed her by the shoulders. "If you ever try anything like that again—"

"Me!" Whatever else she'd planned to say was cut off by his next words.

"You little fool! Don't you realize you could've been killed!"

"A lot you would care. You abducted me from my own wedding!"

"It was necessary!" he shouted back.

"Necessary? To whom? You? And just who the hell are you?" Water dripped off her, creating an expanding puddle. Feet firmly planted, Elyse propped her hands on her slender hips, silently daring him to come closer. She'd like to blacken his other eye.

"That's of no importance to you!" Water dripped from his hair. He wiped at it angrily.

"No importance?" She was stunned. The absolute nerve of the man! Anger goading her beyond all caution, she pulled back her arm.

"Elyse!" he warned.

"You bastard!" she hissed, taking aim. Her clenched fist shot out and was easily caught.

"I'm in no mood for games," he said coldly.

"Games?"

"No mercy! Keel haul the bloody bastard!" From somewhere down the companionway, that voice she'd heard before screeched above the storm. Elyse blanched at the meaning of those words. Her teeth had begun to chatter violently, but not from the cold.

"I suppose you're going to torture me." Her voice was strained as the screeching came again.

He turned from her. "Damned if that isn't what you deserve. But Sebastian doesn't give the orders around here. I do." Going to the chest of drawers along the side wall, he took out a towel and threw it at her.

"Sebastian?" She wondered what sort of character he might be. Undoubtedly another pirate.

"He's a macaw, and a damned bossy one at that. I may just decide to have him served up for dinner one of these nights. Now, get out of that wet . . . thing and dry yourself off. I won't have you catching your death of cold simply because you were stupid enough to go up on deck in the middle of a storm."

Elyse didn't have time to consider what he meant. She caught the towel, her eyes narrowing, and threw it down on the floor. "I will not. And you can't make me."

He whirled on her, his patience gone. "Elyse!"

There was something dangerous in his voice that made her want to hide. Instead she stood her ground.

He should have known better. But, he was tired, and angry. He saw her challenge only as defiance, pure and simple.

He crossed the cabin and with a single jerk, separated the fabric of the chemise that had clung to her like a second skin, revealing everything.

Shock, and then anger, tore through Elyse. First her wedding gown, now this. She couldn't run, and she couldn't hide. Her eyes blazed as her arms came up to hide her nakedness.

Her defiance was like sand in a wound. Zach pulled her to him, his cold gray gaze meeting brilliant blue as his fingers deftly stripped away the clinging silk. Seizing the discarded towel, he bent down, roughly rubbing her bare legs dry. It was practically his undoing.

Swearing, Zach came to his feet and threw the towel into the far corner. He refused to look at her, at least not below the defiant angle of her chin, but for a long moment his eyes bore into hers. Then he turned to pull a dry shirt from the drawer. The full sight of her struck him when he swung around to bring it back to her. If he could have kept his eyes fixed on her face, he would have succeeded. As it was, that one look sent everything reeling out of control.

Elyse stood there proud and defiant, her arms barely crossed over her breasts. She was angry, color alive in her cheeks, fire glittering in her eyes. But she didn't shrink from him.

Damn! What was happening? The harder Zach fought it, the more hopeless it was. His fingers came up to the buttons at his own shirt.

Her heart was racing as she watched him strip away shirt, belt, and then pants. All were thrown aside. And he was angry, she could see it.

He didn't move until his remaining clothes lay scattered about the floor and he stood facing her, staring at her, light illuminating only one side of his face, the other in shadow. If she weren't standing there naked herself, he might have been able to control himself; as it was, there was no stopping what raged through him.

Seeing the dangerous light that had sprung into those cold gray eyes, Elyse backed away from him. The cabin was so small, she could stay out of his reach only so long. Then what? But he was moving with her now, measuring his steps with hers and, Elyse realized with sudden anger, stalking her!

The unexpected had worked once before, it might work again. She stopped retreating and, turning to face him, lunged forward in the hope of catching him by surprise and darting past him to the door. But it was Elyse who was surprised. When he caught one of her wrists, instead of trying to stop her, Zach merely turned, his other arm encircled her waist, and with one foot, he swept both of hers from beneath her. Elyse landed on the thick carpeting.

She was stunned, the breath knocked out of her. That was all Zach needed. Anger had driven him this far, he wasn't about to stop. As she began to recover and squirm beneath him, Zach wedged a heavily muscled thigh intimately between hers. As his hands pinned hers over her head, he heard her gasp in surprise and saw anger leap into her eyes.

"You should have let well enough alone." Zach moved over her, driven by anger and by something less easily defined. He'd take his chances with her hands. He released them; his fingers bruising her as he caught her small chin and jerked her mouth hard beneath his. She tried to push him back, but his other hand found her hip and his knee pinned her leg. He entered her quickly, brutally, with no care for the pain he might be causing her.

"It's too late, Elyse." His words rocked through her, his mouth bruising hers. The floor was underneath her. In answer, Elyse thrust upward trying to escape him. It only sent him deeper inside her.

She gasped, but not out of anger; out of surprise at the exquisite sensation of him filling all of her. Then there was the heat that expanded inside her, making her want to hold him like that forever. She jerked her head away, tears filling her eyes at the sweet betrayal.

Zach's surprise was equally acute—at the unexpected pleasure that deep penetration sent through him and even because his anger was swept away. He'd wanted to punish her for her pride and defiance. Now he felt only overwhelming desire. His hands turned her face to him and his lips found hers, tasting the tears that slipped to the corners of her mouth. Feeling her resistance, he slowly began to stroke it away.

Keeping his mouth molded to hers, he moved his hips, not withdrawing completely but caressing her until he felt the gently rocking response of her muscles around him.

Unknowingly, Elyse lifted herself to him, opening, taking him

331

deeper still as her anger melted away to need and need gave way to urgency. His entire body was molded to hers; his hips, his stomach, the hard muscles of his chest moved against her in a sensuous stroking. She didn't understand how it began or even when, she only knew the driving need began deep inside her, somewhere below her stomach, and spread like fire.

It leaped out of control, the torturous pleasure beginning as a hungering ache and then growing to the sweet throbbing that overcame every other sensation. Elyse arched against him, sheathing him, a soft moan escaping her.

Zach knew he was lost. The muscles of her young body quickened around him and nothing else mattered. His hands spread beneath her bottom, fingers bruising her pale flesh as he plunged more deeply inside her, her body stroking him beyond simple desire, beyond anything he'd ever experienced. Lips pressed against her forehead, he cried out as his body shuddered, pleasure shimmering through them like a live current, binding them one to the other.

Within moments, Elyse tried to push away from him, but he was still deep within her and refused to let her go. When his arms restrained her, she jerked her head so that he couldn't see the humiliation and self-loathing on her face. How could she have let this happen?

"I hate you," she whispered brokenly, not seeing the pain that hardened in his face, then quickly disappeared.

"Hate me in the morning, Elyse," he murmured against her throat, and felt the deep shudder of lingering desire pass through her body to his. "Not tonight."

He was stronger than she, and Elyse couldn't fight him with that languorous lethargy in her arms and legs. She wanted to; oh God, how she wanted to. Her mind screamed it, but her body refused to obey.

Zach gently withdrew from the soft glove of her body. He pulled her into his arms and easily lifted her. He wanted the softness of the bed when he made love to her again. She began to protest, no doubt to tell him again how much she hated him, but he silenced her with his mouth as he gently lowered her, his lips caressing the anger from her. He stretched out against her slender back, pulling her into his body and their legs slipped together, her hips curving into his as her desire sharpened. Her breasts grew taut beneath his hands, her back arched against his chest.

She filled him with a completeness that was frightening with its intensity. Never had he felt such pleasure with a woman, or the need to know that she found equal fulfillment. Always before, the physical act of lovemaking was just that, a physical act. He wouldn't even call it lovemaking—making love. Because he knew he'd never loved anyone. He'd come closest with Alice, but even then something had compelled him to leave her after the act was done and his basic needs were satisfied.

Now a greater need was inside him. Perhaps it had always been there, waiting for one woman—this woman. Yes, he'd made love perhaps for the first time, to her, and he would again before the night was over. As he'd promised her, she would hate him when morning came, but for now she was his; to love, to hold, and then let go.

Chapter Sixteen

Zach rose before dawn. He dressed and slipped silently from the cabin. He needed time to think, to find some perspective for what had happened during the night, though he would rather have stayed in that bed with her.

He slipped into the galley, grabbing a cup of hot coffee. It churned downward into his stomach, steadying, fortifying. He nodded to Sandy.

"How did we fare?"

"She took the storm real good. I've got Jalew topside at the wheel. We were only a few degrees off course when the storm cleared. I made the adjustments and we've more than made up for the lost time."

"Good. When do you think we'll make Lisbon?"

Sandy shrugged. "Late tomorrow or early the following morning, if the wind holds. I went ahead and posted extra men at the watch, just in case." He stood, shrugging off the fatigue of a long night. "I was just headed topside to relieve Jalew. He's been on for a couple hours now."

Zach drained the cup and help it out for a refill. He knew the "just in case" referred to El Barracuda, Juan de la Vasquez Vimeiro. A Spaniard by birth, he'd turned pirate several years ago and now considered the waters of Spain his private hunting ground. Lisbon was quite a ways north of his usual territory, but they'd heard rumors he'd attacked merchant ships as far west as the Gulf of Cadiz. And with a cargo hold full of gold aboard *Tamarisk*, Zach couldn't risk being foolish.

"You get some sleep. I'll take over." He turned toward the companionway practically colliding with Tobias. His friend fixed him with bloodshot eyes.

"I won't ask how you spent the night." Zach nodded.

"Good. I wouldn't remember anyway." Running a hand over his heavily bearded chin, Tobias forced his bleary eyes to focus. "How's our passenger this morning?"

Zach noticed the curious stares of his crew. He frowned. "No screaming, no broken dishes. I imagine she's still sleeping."

Tobias accepted a cup of coffee, frowning when the cook waved aside his suggestion of a draught of brandy. "Dang fool man. I don't see why you keep him on. He's belligerent and disrespectful," he muttered as he followed Zach into the companionway.

"I keep him on because he's the best damned cook on anything afloat or ashore. And as for respect, I suggest you put away the bottle and try to earn it."

"I'll remember that the next time he comes to me with a burn or cut." He rolled a speculative, red-rimmed eye. "I may just let the wound fester awhile."

"Fortunately for us all, my friend, you enjoy eating almost as much as you enjoy drinking. He'd get back at you by putting something in your food. Not a wise idea."

Tobias nodded, glad to see some of Zach's humor restored. "I'll try to remember that." He hesitated, wondering what kind of response his next question would get. "About last night . . . ?"

Halfway up the ladder, Zach stopped. He waited for the obvious. His words were clipped. "What about last night?"

"I'm not askin' for details, but I gotta tell you, boy, you're playin' with fire."

Zach came back down the ladder with measured steps. "Go on."

Tobias shifted uncomfortably. "She's engaged to Jerrold Barrington. You abducted her and forced her aboard this ship. If you've given her any reason to believe . . ."

"To believe what?"

Damn, Tobias thought, the lad isn't going to make this easy. His gnarled hand combed back sparse hair, then fell to his side.

"Dammit!" he hissed, leaning forward so his words wouldn't be heard by the rest of the crew. "You can't just use her like that and then set her aside. I don't care who she's to marry. It's not right! You can't be playin' with her feelin's."

Zach studied him for the longest time, then turned back toward the ladder. "You're absolutely right." And he knew Tobias was. He'd come to that very same decision when he'd left his cabin.

"Therefore, you may inform Miss Winslow that she may have the use of my cabin for the remainder of the voyage. She'll be more comfortable. I'll take hers." He started back up the ladder.

"But about last night—"

"Leave it be, Tobias." Zach bit off the words. "As far as I'm concerned, nothing happened."

As he stepped out onto the deck, Zach knew full well he lied, but there was a small ounce of truth to what he'd said. He'd made up his mind to forget about that night. It was a mistake, one that wouldn't happen again. In that sense, he gave it no importance. He relieved his man at the wheel and spent the next fourteen hours trying to convince himself of that.

Elyse awakened slowly, her eyes fixing on the opened porthole. It took a few minutes for her to remember where she was, then she wished she hadn't. She scrambled to the edge of the bed, pulling the sheet high over her breasts as she pushed back the tangled mass of her hair. He was gone.

She shrank back on the edge of the bed, trying to remember what had happened and how she'd ended up in this cabin. She didn't need to try very hard. She groaned as she let the sheet fall away. My God, how could she have let him . . . ?

Elyse came off the bed, determined not to think about it. She would put her mind on food, the weather, anything else but that. Her clothes had been picked up, folded, and placed atop the cabinet. Captain Tennant, no doubt. The man was full of surprises.

Crossing the cabin, she quickly dressed. Catching a brief glimpse of herself in the shaving mirror above the basin, she cringed and immediately borrowed the soft-bristled horsehair brush. She carefully worked the tangles from her hair. Then she turned to the bed. She was determined to make the cabin look as if nothing happened the night before.

As if I could make it not have been, she thought with a vengeance.

Elyse pulled rumpled sheets taut across the mattress. She tucked in the heavy quilt that had been kicked to the floor, and replaced the pillows. After pounding the last one, she drew back. The bed hadn't really been the problem. Her eyes immediately went to the thick rug underfoot.

A knocking at the door brought her around. Elyse stared in its direction for a full minute. Captain Tennant wouldn't bother to knock, she was certain of it. That could only mean it was one of the crew, probably bringing her breakfast; and that meant that regardless of the fact that she occupied the captain's cabin at the moment, she was still considered his prisoner.

Anger washed over her. She'd learned how to use it to manipulate Jerrold. But it didn't work the same way with Captain Tennant. In fact, it worked against her. He did what he pleased in spite of her feelings. Last night was proof enough of that. She squared her slender shoulders.

"Come in."

The door opened slowly, a graying head poking tentatively around the edge of it. Elyse recognized the man she'd seen in the companionway the day before when she'd tried to make her escape. Now he looked as if he expected a plate or cup to come flying at his head. In spite of herself, she laughed softly.

"I promise not to throw anything." She decided she'd much rather gain some information before her captor came back. After all, where was she to go in the middle of the ocean? There would be time enough for anger later; first she had to know where she was and where she was going.

"You look trustworthy enough." Faintly reddened eyes twinkled back at her, and the man came around the door and fixed her with a disarming smile.

"Tobias Gentry is the name; ship's physician."

Now that she saw him in the full light of day, Elyse's eyes widened. "I know you."

"Aye, we've met before. But at the time, I was dressed a little fancier than I am now."

Recognition dawned. "You were at my engagement ball. If memory serves me correctly, you were a Spanish marquis at the time."

Tobias winced. "It wasn't my idea. I would've come up with something a little more original."

"Such as Tobias Gentry, ship's doctor?" She flung back at him, amusement dancing in her eyes. It was good to be able to talk to someone without feeling anger or the need for confrontation.

His eyes narrowed, but the twinkling humor remained. "Zach said you weren't the shy type. I can see he was tellin' the truth."

"Zach?"

"I suppose there's no harm in your knowin'. Zachary Tennant is captain of the *Tamarisk*." His foot stomped the planking for emphasis. "This is the *Tamarisk*. And a fine ship she is. If you like ships. I don't care much for them myself. But if a fella has to sail, this would be the one to sail on."

337

The beginning of understanding lit Elyse's soft blue eyes. "So, you're a reluctant passenger as well. Were you were abducted"—she paused—"or did you come aboard willingly?"

Tobias rubbed his chin thoughtfully. "I suppose I would have to say that I came aboard willingly."

"Then you must know Captain Tennant well."

"Fairly well, I darned near raised the boy—me and his mother." He stopped, realizing the game she played. His eyes narrowed.

"Yer a clever one. I'll have to be careful of you or you'll have the whole crew mutiny to yer side."

"I don't see how that's possible since I'm being kept prisoner." She looked up. Oh God, what must this man think of her spending the night with his captain? Elyse breathed in slowly. She wouldn't whine, cry, or beg. What was done, was done!

But he surprised her. "Not at all. You may come and go as you please during the day, so long as the *Tamarisk* is at sea."

Her eyes widened. "Then I'm not locked in here?"

Her meaning was more than clear. Tobias shifted uncomfortably. Then his gaze quickly swept the room. He had a pretty good idea of what had happened in it the past night. But damned if she wasn't a surprise. Zach was right again; Elyse Winslow wasn't the fainting, simpering type. She was as proud as she was beautiful, and stronger than most any woman he'd ever met. She was putting up a good front.

He cleared his throat as he broached the delicate subject. "Zach said you were to have the use of the cabin. He thought you would be more comfortable in here. He's to take the other one." He gestured over his shoulder.

Elyse smiled at him gratefully. He'd tactfully avoided a difficult subject, leaving her with pride intact. She couldn't say the same for the captain of this vessel. She found herself liking Tobias Gentry, in spite of his choice of friendships. In some ways he reminded her of her grandmother. "Well, if I'm free to move about as I please, is there any possibility of acquiring some breakfast?"

He brightened. "I thought you might be hungry. The sea air does that to a person. And cook saved some of his best biscuits and ham for you. I supply him with brandy and sherry for his cookin' sauces and he does me a favor once in a while. Like those biscuits. They're the best outside of Minerva's at Resolute."

She looked up. There was a name she hadn't heard yet. "Resolute? Where is that?"

"Home, darlin' girl. Home for these wanderin' seafarers. And I

338

assure you, it will do these old eyes good to see it again." He took her gently by the arm and closed the cabin door behind them.

"Is it very far away?"

He smiled at her and gave her a secret wink. "Not as far as it once was."

Elyse looked at him strangely.

"In good time, Miss Winslow. In time," he assured her.

"Am I being taken to Resolute?"

That question brought him up short. She certainly did have a way of going right to the heart of matters. He squinted at her in the meager light of the companionway. Lord, but she was a beauty with those large blue eyes that took yer breath away. And she wasn't full of herself like so many proper, Victorian young ladies were. Ah, he thought, Zach is a fool.

Then he wondered what the hell she saw in a pompous ass like Barrington. Zach was certain it was the title and the promise of wealth. But that assessment didn't fit this young woman who was completely unaffected, and quite comfortable wearing a man's shirt and trousers instead of fine satins and laces. And that acknowledgment forced him to face another problem. He liked her, liked her a lot. How the devil was he supposed to let Zach carry out his ransom plan now. Lord Almighty, what had they gotten into? He took the easy way out, avoided a direct answer and felt the coward for it.

"You'll have to ask the captain about that."

"I see." Elyse realized that she and Tobias could share pleasantries and casual conversation, but his loyalty was unquestionable. Great balls of fire! What was it about Captain Tennant that earned him the undying respect of the men aboard his ship, including Tris who would brave flying plates and cups? She cast a glance back over her shoulder in the direction of his cabin. The answers might possibly be somewhere in there.

"What about those biscuits, Dr. Gentry? I'm starving."

Reprieved from the inquisition, Tobias beamed. Now food was something he could talk about and enjoy with her.

Elyse had been up on deck for hours. It was wonderful, exhilarating. And it was freedom of a sort after the last three days of confinement in her cabin.

The weather had cleared. The sky overhead was a brilliant blue, broken only occasionally by the few clouds remaining from the storm. The breeze was strong, almost balmy; and the water slipping past them with amazing speed was faintly tipped with foaming whitecaps. This was far different from the steel gray fury of the

339

storm the night before.

She saw him the first moment she stepped from the forward hatch. His golden hair caught and held the sun; his broad shoulders were loosely covered by a stark white shirt, its sleeves rolled high to expose deeply tanned forearms. He stood at the wheel of the ship, completely absorbed in the sails overhead, the direction of the wind, and the ship beneath him.

She inhaled the tangy sea air, luxuriating in her freedom. In spite of the small cabins below, *Tamarisk* was a large ship. She was astounded by the amount of sail that billowed overhead. Elyse knew enough about sailing to realize they were running before the wind, every last inch of canvas burgeoning in magnificent full clouds. Her gaze swept the center mast.

"A Spanish flag?" She turned to Tobias, her curiosity plain.

Tobias followed her gaze. He smiled with keen appreciation. She was observant. "Aye."

"Then the *Tamarisk* is a Spanish ship," Elyse concluded. "But the crew certainly don't seem Spanish. There are more English accents than anything else."

"There's not an Englishman aboard this ship," Tobias informed her, taking a long pull on the pipe he'd lit earlier.

Elyse turned to him, a quizzical expression on her lovely face. How much would he tell her?

He pointed with the stem of his pipe. "Kimo, the big black fella over there is from Africa. He was nothin' but a boy when he was taken off a slaver fifteen years ago." He pointed to another man. "Mano over there is as close to Spanish as anyone on this ship, but he's from Colombia." He recited backgrounds of a half-dozen other crewmen; including a Chinaman from Whampoa, a swarthy little man from Madagascar who greatly resembled a monkey and the man known as Sandy who was second mate aboard the *Tamarisk*.

"Sandy is from the north countries. Swears his ancestors were Vikings. I believe it. The man has an almost uncanny instinct for water and wind. Like Zach. And Jalew over there is an Abo."

He gestured to a short, stocky man who was almost as dark-skinned as the giant Kimo.

"Abo?" Elyse was well studied, she'd traveled considerably with her grandmother, but she'd never heard of this man's nationality.

"Aboriginal. A native from down under. He was born at Resolute." Tobias took a long thoughtful pull on the pipe. Fragrant smoke caught on the breeze, then was whisked away. He laughed when Elyse looked as if she thought he might have slipped a notch

or two. He decided there was no harm in telling her a few things.

His smile softened. "The land down under, at the bottom of the world." Clamping the pipe firmly between his teeth, he held up his hands and spread his fingers wide, making the shape of a globe. "This is the earth as modern man has come to know it."

Elyse watched fascinated as Tobias Gentry continued his geography lesson.

"Europe is up here." One hand came away. He pointed; then the hand returned to the imaginary globe. "With those insignificant little islands of Her Majesty the Queen, nothing more than little grains. Over here you have India, Russia, China. Down here, you have Africa; Kimo's country."

"And over here, is North America and South America," Elyse interjected, greatly enjoying all this.

"Very good." He smiled, complimenting her. "Up here are the Arctic regions, down here the Antarctic. And here is the continent of Australia, the land down under."

Her startled gaze met his. "Australia? But all these men aren't . . . ?"

"They're from a dozen or more countries, they hold fast to as many cultures; but Australia is the port they call home when they're not at sea. They're a wicked lot. But any one of them would give his life for Zach. Each one is more than a brother to him. He captured them, then gave them freedom, dignity, and a good life aboard the *Tamarisk* or at Resolute. You wouldn't know it to look at these men, but most of them are very comfortable financially. Some have families in New South Wales, but for others the sea is as much woman as they want."

"But what about Zach . . . ?" She caught herself. "What about Captain Tennant?"

Tobias nodded thoughtfully. "He's equally at home on land or sea. He was born at Resolute, in New South Wales."

She considered this latest bit of information. "But he speaks perfect English."

"When it suits him, and thanks to me. Only a faint bit of brogue slips through now and then. That came from Megan."

"Who is Megan?" Elyse felt a nagging curiosity to know more about this mysterious man.

"His mother. She was Irish and a very fine woman. She's gone now."

"You said you helped raise him. But you're not his father?"

Tobias looked at her hard. Was there something behind that

particular question. He forced himself to remember who she was; Elyse Winslow, betrothed to Jerrold Barrington. How much did she know or suspect? Still there was nothing in her unguarded gaze to indicate anything but simple curiosity.

"I did help raise him. But no, I'm not Zach's father. His father and I were friends many years ago, in the early years."

"Early years?"

"Aye, when we first went to the colonies as young men. That was a very long time ago. Zach never knew his father. He died shortly before Zach was born. Me and Megan raised him at Resolute."

"My fiancé always said the colonies were filled with convicts worth nothing," she replied thoughtfully, "But you're a doctor, and Captain Tennant is obviously a well-educated man." She looked at the sea, missing the sobering of Tobias.

"As I said," he replied gruffly, "it was all a very long time ago." He studied the pipe in his hands, then frowned as he knocked the bowl against the railing, loosening the smoldering tobacco.

"It must be somewhat like America," Elyse commented as she digested what he'd told her. She knew England no longer transported convicts to Australia; that practice had ceased years ago. Tobias certainly wasn't a convict, nor was Zachary Tennant for that matter. She realized her impressions of the Australian colonies had been shadowed by Jerrold's contempt for that far place.

"I should like to see it someday. It must be a vast, wondrous place to be filled with so many different people, cultures, and languages. Does Captain Tennant speak other languages?"

Her last comment had the effect of completely disarming Tobias. What a wondrous creature she was, completely uninhibited, with an openness and acceptance that was rare even among men, much less a young woman raised in proper, Victorian England.

"Aye, that he does." He beamed at her, with the pride any father might have. "He speaks any of a half-dozen other languages as fine as English."

"And I suppose that includes Spanish as well."

"A fair amount."

She broadsided him with her next question. "But why a Spanish flag, if the captain and crew are from the land down under." She smiled innocently.

He shrugged. What harm would it do for her to know? There was a great deal she was going to find out before this was all over.

"It serves a purpose. Right now"—he gestured with his pipe again out across the expanse of ocean—"we're off the coast of

Spain."

Elyse's eyes widened. My God! She hadn't realized they could be this far from England. She stole a sideways glance at the helm. Captain Zachary Tennant was completely absorbed in conversation with his second mate.

If they'd come this far in only a few days . . . Father in heaven! Where was he taking her? The slender hands that gripped the heavy railing whitened across their knuckles, but her face revealed nothing of her emotional state.

Tobias's words came back at her. *It serves a purpose.* Now just what the devil was that supposed to mean? Her eyes widened. She'd heard of such ships and crews . . . *Pirate ships!* But surely not . . . Elyse swallowed back her panic. She had no proof; surely there was nothing in anything Tobias had said to indicate . . . And yet as she looked at the crew, it did seem a very real possibility.

"So," she began tentatively, "a Spanish flag off the coast of Spain. Why not an English flag when in England?"

Tobias stiffened. "Never an English flag! Zach would put the *Tamarisk* to the bottom of the sea before he'd allow the bloody Union Jack atop her mast!" As if suddenly remembering himself, his expression softened.

"Australia is a Crown colony." His voice was clipped, almost tight. "But we have our own flag."

Elyse bit at her lower lip. Dr. Gentry was obviously very upset about her mentioning the English flag, but why? She smiled as she tried to smooth over the moment. She couldn't risk offending him when she needed more information.

"And perhaps even an American flag?" She smiled at him, trying to restore their earlier mood.

Tobias glanced up at her, and couldn't resist that smile. "Aye, we've flown it more than once."

"My parents were American. They didn't much care for England either."

Tobias watched her thoughtfully. So, this was something about Miss Winslow he hadn't known before.

Elyse turned, leaning casually back against the railing, her hair catching in the wind. "My grandmother still calls the United States the Colonies, even though they haven't been colonies for almost one hundred years. I was born there, but I don't remember very much about it. I came to England when I was very small. My parents died, and I've lived with my grandmother ever since." There was a catch in her voice; she might never see it all again. She quickly

343

smothered her pain, giving Tobias a brave, bright smile.

"England is the only home I've ever known. It's easy to love something when you've never known anything different." Her smile deepened into sunshiny brilliance. "Being born in the United States, people often think of me as a foreigner." She didn't say that Jerrold once suggested he was making a great sacrifice in marrying her. He'd quickly dismissed her American-born mother, emphasizing her father's side of the family when introducing her to family and friends.

If anyone had accused her of it, Elyse would have denied that she looked sideways to find Zachary Tennant. But no one asked.

Who was he? Why had she been abducted? Why did he seem so changed from the man she'd first met in London? The Count de Cuervo had been gracious, warm, even tender, with flashes of humor in those incredibly gray eyes. She saw nothing of that man in the captain of the *Tamarisk*. It was as if he'd shed all of that along with the disguise of a Spanish nobleman.

It was late afternoon. A pin dot of a shadow swooped across the deck. Elyse looked up.

"Gulls," Tobias informed her.

She frowned. "But I thought they stayed close to shore."

"Aye, they do." He nodded to her.

Her gaze met his. "But I don't see land."

"You won't for several hours. But we'll be there soon enough."

Elyse turned. Shading her eyes she strained to see something other than rolling ocean on the horizon. Tobias pointed over her shoulder. "You'll be able to see it there first. The Spanish coastline. We should make Lisbon sometime tomorrow."

Zach adjusted the wheel of the *Tamarisk* with the subtle change of the wind. Only a seasoned seaman would recognize the offshore wind as different from the ocean breezes. Sails were trimmed, and the ship responded easily, slipping before the warmer wind.

Again he found himself watching Elyse. For the last hours, she'd played havoc with his concentration as well as that of his crew. He should have left her locked in his cabin. But Tobias's request that she be allowed some freedom had seemed harmless enough. He was surprised at how much he knew about her. She loved the freedom of a stolen ride in the early morning hours, dressed as a man so as not to draw attention. He could envision her riding in the Woods, perhaps in search of Jane's Folley, her hair whipping out behind her

in a streaming trail of dark sable. Or sneaking through back streets and alleys with him, in nothing more than a man's shirt and coat and something that passed for delicate lady's underwear. She so loved her freedom, he could imagine her frustration at her imprisonment in that small cabin measuring no more than ten feet square. He found himself chuckling at the memory of Tris emerging from that cabin, trying to muster up some small amount of dignity with gruel slipping down his shirtfront. She'd managed to let them all know just what she thought of her situation.

Instinctively, he looked for her, his gaze searching the deck where she'd just been with Tobias. Her long dark hair streamed in the wind.

Earlier, he'd convinced himself that on deck, among his crew, she would be safe enough. After all, these men appreciated a truly feminine figure in a soft skirt and a low-cut bodice. What could be wrong in allowing her some fresh air when she was dressed like one of them?

Good God! There was everything in the world wrong with it. That damned shirt he recognized as one of his own exposed more than it covered. Its oversized fullness was flattened against her body, stark white against the darkened outthrust tips of her firm, high breasts. The effect was teasing in that it promised rather than revealed.

Pants, much too long for her, were shortened in the legs, exposing trim, bare ankles above equally bare feet. Not so unusual. Several of his crew preferred to go without shoes. It gave better footing on often slippery decks. But even his crew seemed to notice those slender, pale-skinned feet that were smaller than any foot had a right to be.

Damn! He swore silently as his gaze swept back up her fabric-sheathed legs. Pants that were comfortable on him, hung loose enough in the thighs. But they were achingly tight, fitting like skin across the finely curved bottom he remembered so well, the blue fabric hiding nothing of what lay underneath. And the waist, snug on his straight hips, was gathered by a rope belt to fit her incredibly small measurements.

"Damn!" Zach cursed aloud, bringing a surprised look from Sandy. What the hell was she trying to do? He turned the wheel over to his second mate.

"Problem, Cap'n?" Sandy looked up, surprised that Zach would give him the wheel. His captain was the sort who preferred to man the helm. He rarely relinquished control during his time on deck.

345

"Yes!" Zach snapped, turning to the starboard side of the ship. "I'd say there's definitely a problem."

With the lean, balanced stealth of a man who's spent much time on the deck of a ship, Zach approached Tobias and Elyse. He had several well-chosen matters he wanted to discuss with Miss Winslow, beginning with her choice of clothing, regardless of the fact that she had no other garb, and then her position aboard this ship.

Instead, his well-planned little speech was completely undone when the sounds of her soft voice and sweet laughter were carried back to him on the wind. As he came up behind her, his anger was fast slipping away. He hesitated, feeling the sweet betrayal of desire at her nearness, the faint sting of her windblown hair as it caressed him, filling him with sweet memories of the night before and carrying to him the subtle scent that seemed to cling to her. It was disarming, alluring; and released a different anger inside him. His words were as biting as the wind when he spoke.

"Miss Winslow, I'm certain you find all this quite enjoyable," he barked, and was immediately rewarded when she spun around, anger leaping into her eyes, her delicate brows of that rich sable color arching. "My crew has work to do. And this is not a pleasure cruise. You will go below. Now!"

Her mouth dropped open. She'd felt him before she'd heard him, known the exact moment he came up behind her, and had sensed something in the hesitating silence before he spoke. He'd been avoiding her all morning, his eyes always carefully averted whenever she looked in his direction. He'd kept his distance from her, yet had been within her vision no matter where she was. There was some significance in his avoidance of her, as when she'd awakened to find him gone from the cabin without even one word to her. Now he had plenty to say, and it wasn't to be pleasant.

She'd thought, even begun to hope, he might change his mind about keeping her aboard. The picture Tobias had painted was certainly not that of a ruthless, unfeeling man. He was responsible and caring to his men. She'd seen it in the easy camaraderie they enjoyed as he spoke to them and worked alongside them. Tobias had said Zachary Tennant had rescued most of these men from a fate worse than death, had given them freedom, dignity, and a place in the world. It was clear that they respected him. Then what was so different about her? Didn't she deserve those same considerations? Why was she less than they?

It was Tobias who broke the emotionally charged air between

them. "There's no harm, Zach. It's beastly hot in those cabins. You said she could come up on deck."

"Well, I've changed my mind. I want her below."

Elyse stiffened. So, now she was to become a prisoner again. Her chin angled defiantly. "I've done nothing wrong. I won't be confined aboard this ship."

"If you object to my request, Miss Winslow, I can always have you removed, forcibly if necessary. One way or the other you will go below. Make no mistake about it. And if you don't cooperate I can always resort to the ropes."

Elyse paled. Why was he being so hateful to her now when he hadn't so much as looked in her direction all morning?

"Zach!" Tobias muttered under his breath, out of earshot of the crew. "There's no need for this. She wasn't doing anything wrong."

"I'll make the decisions about what's right or wrong on my ship, and about who comes up on deck. Simply because I chose to share my bed with you doesn't mean you can expect extra privileges." With maddening arrogance, he turned toward the open hatch. "Miss Winslow, the choice is yours."

Her color had returned and was staining her cheeks. Glancing around, she could see that the crew members who stood nearby had heard most of what was said. She wanted to slap that arrogant, smug expression off his face. But she remembered only too well where that had gotten her the night before, and she wasn't about to give him the satisfaction of humiliating her in front of his crew.

With stiff-backed dignity she walked past Zachary Tennant and stepped down onto the ladder that led back down to her stifling prison. Her thoughts raced. What did he want from her, besides what he'd already taken? She thought, with bitter remembrance, of the night before. He'd refused to tell her anything until now. And the little she'd been able to learn hadn't answered any of those burning questions.

She had only found out that this man was a mass of contradictions. Not a Spanish nobleman but a sea captain, or so it appeared. And he was clever. Whatever he was about, it was part of a plan that included posing as someone else, so that he could come and go among her friends.

In that long, silent walk back to the cabin, Elyse tried to sort through everything Tobias had told her. Very little of it made sense. She was certain of only one thing, that she was being held prisoner aboard this ship, a ship that flew under many flags, using them as disguises. A pirate ship? And according to Tobias, they were even

now approaching the coast of Spain. She went over things again and again, and each time came to the same conclusion.

She halted at the cabin, refusing to go in willingly. He reached around her, his left arm lightly brushing hers as he seized the handle and opened the door. She had two choices, and in that really no choice at all: she could stand there with him so close his chest pressed against her back, or she could go into the cabin. With haughty coolness, looking neither to left nor right, Elyse walked into the cabin.

"Elyse."

The surprising quiet in his voice jolted her. She stiffened, and her hands balled into tight fists at her sides. She wanted him angry, as angry as she was. But he wasn't. She silently cursed. What was he up to now? A repeat performance of last night? Well, she wasn't about to let that happen again. She'd quickly learned she was no match for him physically. The fact that he'd made love to her and that she'd allowed it was proof of that. He'd found an effective weapon to use against her, her own body, and she had no doubt he would use it again. If he did, if she allowed it, there'd be no saving herself.

So now that she knew her own weakness, she had to find his. There had to be a reason he'd risked so much to abduct her. She didn't for a moment flatter herself it had anything to do with what he might feel for her. Feelings came from shared experience, from a past that two people built with each other. She had no past with this man, and she wanted no future. Only one thing would make anyone risk so much. Elyse took a deep breath and slowly turned to face him, her jaw tight, the slender angle of her chin defiant.

"What is the price?"

Zach hadn't expected this question. He leaned back against the closed door, trying to guess what she was up to. The light in his silvery gray eyes shifted as he came away from the door and, seizing a wooden chair, turned it around and sat down, his arms braced across the back. He'd strategically placed himself between her and the door.

"What is the price for what?" He answered her with a question of his own.

Elyse leveled that brilliant blue gaze at him, fighting back her anger. She hadn't thought for a minute this would be easy, nothing about this man was.

"You know perfectly well what I'm talking about." She went on coolly. "What ransom have you demanded for me?"

So that's it, Zach thought appreciatively. She didn't miss a thing. She was smart and it hadn't taken her long to arrive at the obvious conclusion. But the obvious one wasn't necessarily the correct one.

He studied her; the way she stood, hands planted on slender hips, the shirt too big over her shoulders, the tangled mane of her hair falling in wild array down her back. She'd been stripped of all the fine trimmings of a lady. She'd been bound, gagged, and bruised, regrettably by him. Yet at that moment she was the most desirable woman he'd ever known.

It was more than the curve of her high breasts jutting tauntingly against the fabric of his shirt. More than the tight cut of those pants or the incredible smallness of feet that were no bigger than his hands.

It was something he'd felt the first time he'd met her, when her candid response had shocked everyone within hearing. He'd wanted to hate her for what she was, the perfect, well-bred young Englishwoman groomed and molded to be Lady Barrington. But even then, she'd turned everything against him with that indefinable something that made him laugh at her ridiculous schemes at one moment, want to throttle her in the next, and then crave to make endless love to her. She was proud to a fault, defiant to her own detriment, and desirable to his.

She'd been angry up on deck and he'd prepared himself for the confrontation he'd known would follow. Remembering Tris's experience the day before, he'd quickly made an inventory of all loose objects within her reach when they'd entered the cabin. He was relieved to see that no food remained. Now she stood before him, angry but with a tight control over her emotions. It was time. She might as well know. There was no reason not to tell her.

"There is no ransom, Elyse."

His words sank in slowly. No ransom! She paced away from him, then whirled around. "There has to be. You wouldn't risk so much without thinking you'd get something back for it. Surely you must know that Jerrold and my grandmother will send someone after me," she reasoned. "But if you tell me now what the ransom is, we can get this done with." She waited.

Zach leveled his gaze at her. No more disguises, no more pretense. Everything stripped away between them. Nothing but the truth. Could she accept it?

"As I said, there is no ransom."

She laughed, that soft, smoky laugh that was both incredulous and defiant. "Don't you understand? It doesn't matter what precau-

349

tions you've taken, or how fast this ship is. They'll find you."

"I know."

Elyse stared at him. He must be mad, to just sit there and calmly admit that he knew exactly what would happen and yet act as if he didn't care. She breathed her frustration out slowly, her hands coming up as she tried again.

"How much? Ten thousand pounds? Fifty? Name the price. I know we're to arrive in Lisbon soon. Arrangements can be made to give you your damn money then, and we can be done with this, this . . . ridiculous abduction."

"No, Elyse. I told you once before, it's not that easy."

"What are you talking about? Your kind always asks for money. It's the way you are."

Amusement curved his mouth. "My kind? And just what is my kind, Elyse? I'm curious as to what assumptions you've made."

"A mercenary, a kidnapper." She hissed at him, feeling her hard-won control slip just a little.

"Husband?" he suggested, when she failed to include that in her description.

Elyse blanched. "Surely you don't refer to that ridiculous cere-mony. Why no one . . ." She stopped, trying to bring her churning emotions under control. "It isn't binding. I did not give my con-sent."

His smile deepened. "Of course you did, Elyse. Everyone in that church heard you do so."

"You're insane! I was forced. Everyone saw that," she persisted. "Anyway, what purpose does it serve? You don't want to be married to me, and I certainly don't want . . ."

She was cut off as Zach held up his hand. "I don't really care to hear it. But you're right about one thing, I don't want to be married to you. That's the only part you're right about.

"I don't take money for what I do. I work for no one. And as for kidnapping, you are not a child, nor did I take you forcibly against your will last night." He qualified the last statement with a mean-ingful look.

"I married you, Elyse, because it serves my purpose. Jerrold Barrington has been publicly humiliated; his bride has been stolen right from under his nose, and by a man he hates more than anyone in the world. You, my dear, are the perfect lure for the perfect trap."

"Damn you!" Elyse ground out in frustration. He was deliber-ately trying to confuse her. The perfect lure for the perfect trap, indeed! And why the devil should he hate Jerrold, when they'd only just met? She didn't understand any of this. It didn't make sense. In frustration, she clenched her fists.

"Pirate!" she flung at him, silently daring him to deny it. She straightened her shoulders, enjoying a small victory when he didn't answer immediately.

"Pirate. Now that's an interesting possibility," Zach admitted with maddening calm.

"Then you don't deny it."

"I don't deny or acknowledge anything, lovely Lis. You're the one making the assumptions."

Elyse groaned. This was getting her nowhere. If money didn't seem to interest him, then maybe the thought of hanging from a rope would get through to him.

"There's no place you can hide. You'll be found and made to pay for your crime."

"Elyse, do you really believe I didn't know that when I abducted you?"

She swallowed back the uncertainty that rose in her throat. No, she thought, he isn't the sort of man who does things without knowing full well the repercussions. He'd known exactly what would happen.

"Jerrold will come after you. He'll find you," she whispered, incredulous now.

Zach's gray gaze met hers evenly. "I know that. I want him to find me."

His simple admission practically sent her reeling. He was inviting his own death. She shook her head in disbelief. It was hopeless. Those few words had told her there was no hope for her release.

"I don't understand. Why are you doing this? You could have the money. All you have to do is name the ransom."

"In a way, Elyse, there is a ransom. You are the ransom. I knew Jerrold would come after you. His pride wouldn't let him do otherwise. I've even made it easy for him. I left him a note. He now knows who abducted you and where you can be found."

"But why? I don't understand."

Zach smiled, but his voice was filled with bitterness. "It's a family matter. An old score has to be settled." He turned and started for the door.

Elyse went after him. "You could be killed. Is it worth risking your life?"

He turned at the door. "Would that matter to you?"

She drew back, caught by his words and their infinite meanings. He seemed to be waiting for her to say something. "I don't want anyone to be hurt. I just want to go home."

"Home?" Zach looked down at her. "To be Lady Barrington?" His voice was tight, raw edged.

Elyse ran her fingers through her hair in frustration. "Yes, no . . . I don't know. What does it matter? I just want this ended!"

He jerked the cabin door open. "It can't be ended, not until it's really ended, Elyse."

Now what was that supposed to mean? Her gaze shot to the open doorway. His man Tris obediently stood outside.

"Do you really think it's necessary to have him stand guard?" Her anger returned as she was reminded that she was nothing but a prisoner aboard this ship. "Where can I go?"

"He's there to keep you in, lovely Lis. I don't want to lose you to another storm. You're far too valuable to me."

The iridescent depths of her eyes were lit by her fury. "And who'll keep you out?" she spat out from between tight lips.

Amusement sprang into his eyes. "No one, if I want to come in. This is my ship and" — he glanced around — "my cabin. I am the absolute law—"

"Not over me!" she retorted haughtily, her fingers itching to scratch the arrogant expression off his face.

"Ah, but you're wrong, Not only are you under my authority aboard this ship . . . you're also my wife."

His hand came up, and Elyse immediately stiffened, thinking he meant to strike her.

Zach saw her reaction and winced. Did she really believe he would harm her? He reached up slowly, caressing her cheek with the palm of his hand, wanting to take away the anger between them. There'd been no anger last night when he'd made love to her. He saw the confusion mirrored in her magnificent eyes; they reminded him of shimmering tide pools. Ah, sweet Elyse, he thought with deep regret, if things could only be different between us, if we could truly be man and wife. But your loyalties lie with Jerrold Barrington and I'm sworn to destroy him.

It was all she could do to stand there and not run away, the callused roughness of his hand tender on her skin evoking feelings she didn't want to harbor. How could he be so cruel at one moment and so gentle the next?

Elyse fought desperately to control the wild racing of her heart. Dear God, she mustn't let him know how he affected her. To do so would be putting too strong a weapon in his hands. She lowered her eyes, refusing to meet his gaze, afraid he would see the tender betrayal of her words.

"Surely you can't refer to that farce of a ceremony at the church. I'd never consent to being married to someone like you."

"I do, Elyse."

Her gaze came up and she immediately regretted it. "But that's ridiculous." She tried to back away, not trusting the gleam in those maddening gray eyes. "It means nothing. I was forced into that ceremony." Was that really her voice? It sounded strange to her, strained, deathly quiet.

"But it is binding nevertheless," he calmly assured her. "At least until Barrington comes for you." His thumb, rough and callused, moved across her lower lip, tracing its fullness with maddening slowness.

His next movement was quick, not allowing her time to think much less react. He bent down, his lips grazing hers so lightly he might not have kissed her at all.

Elyse breathed out shakily. This wasn't how it was supposed to be. She wanted to hate him, but he'd taken her anger away and left her only confusion.

"You are mad!" she whispered breathlessly.

"Undoubtedly so. Why else would I sail to England and abduct such a troublesome hostage?" The expression in his eyes changed, making her shiver. "But it will be ended soon enough, Elyse." He started out the door.

Panic seized her. He was leaving and she still didn't know any more than she had before. "Wait!"

Zach turned back to her. "Are you already lonesome for me, Elyse?" The mocking tone had returned. "I could take an hour or so, if you think that would be long enough. Any longer than that and my crew might get worried."

"Oh! You cad!" she shrieked. "It's just like you to think of that. You're the last person on this earth I'd ever be lonely for. Jerrold will kill you when he finds you." That stopped him, but the expression on his face wasn't what she expected. There was no fear. His eyes, the cold gray color of ice, were stark and filled with hatred.

"He'll try. I'm counting on it." Then the coldness in his eyes shifted to something mocking as his gaze raked her slender frame. "You just tell Tris if you want to see me."

"You pompous ass!" It was Elyse who slammed the door. It

closed hard, jumping back open, and she took great delight in slamming it again, this time throwing her full weight against it for emphasis.

She collapsed back against the door and let her breath out slowly. My God, she thought, what am I going to do?

Chapter Seventeen

"Damn!" Tobias muttered as he heaved his portly frame down the ladder.

Zach turned from his cabin to find the older man waiting for him.

"Did you have to be so cruel to her up there?"

"It was necessary. Believe me, it would be far too easy for her to forget her position on this ship."

"And just what is her position?" the old man stormed. "Yer treatin' her like some sort of criminal. Zach, for God's sake, she's done nothing wrong! It's not right that you bring her aboard and then take advantage of her!"

"Tobias!" The warning in Zach's voice was unmistakable.

"You've been like flesh and blood to me, boy. But I can't accept what you've done to that girl. And now you've gone and humiliated her in front of half the crew. The other half will know everything by nightfall. Was it your intention to lower her to the status of whore as well as put her through everything else?"

"Enough, Tobias!" Zach was tight-lipped with fury as he tried to push past his old friend. Tobias wasn't to be put off.

"How long do you think you can keep her on board this ship without answering her questions?"

"I'll not discuss this with you, Tobias. She'll stay willingly or be bound and gagged."

Tobias followed him down the companionway. "Not likely, lad. It's not in her to accept that."

Zach turned to him. "Dammit, Tobias! It's not like you to interfere. Why now? What the devil do you care? If I didn't know better, I'd think you were drunk. You always get this way when you've been drinking."

The old man's hands shook, but from something far different

than the effects of drink. "I wish to God I was; then maybe I wouldn't be considerin' what I am at this moment." His own anger very near matched that of the young man standing before him. He hesitated.

"Ah, what the hell." Tobias's head came up. "You deserve this!"

Quicker than either man had time to think, Tobias's great hamlike fist slammed into Zach's left eye, making him stagger back against the wall of the companionway.

Leaning against the wall, Zach looked up at Tobias, his expression one of complete shock. His handsome features were now marred by a rapidly swelling left eye, the very same eye Elyse had taken aim at the day before.

Zach slowly came to his feet, gingerly probing his already closing eye. The last time Tobias had come at him had been with a switch when he was twelve. "If you were twenty years younger . . ." he threatened.

As if he'd just considered that same point, Tobias looked up a bit sheepishly while he flexed his hand against the swelling across his knuckles. "Damn, I've probably broken some bones." But he smiled with grim satisfaction, thoroughly enjoying the swelling of Zach's eye. "I won't apologize. You deserved it!"

"My left eye!" Zach growled painfully. "Couldn't you have aimed for the other one." He sagged back against the wall.

"I was aimin' for the other. I thought two black eyes would be appropriate. I missed," Tobias grumbled. The part of him that was a physician thought to check the eye; then he made some sort of obscene gesture to Zach and headed in the opposite direction, toward the galley.

Sandy met him in the companionway, and was roughly pushed aside. He stared in confusion after the old man, then looked up at his captain, saw the badly swelling eye, and decided a few hours at the helm were safer than questioning him. He quickly scurried up the ladder.

The swelling flesh only partly concealed the murderous glare Zach threw at Tobias's back. It was probably a good thing his friend wasn't twenty years younger or he might not have been picking himself up. For a man of his age, and a physician at that, Tobias could pack one hell of a punch.

Somehow Zach didn't mind. He'd had it coming, and he knew it. The pain helped define his exact state at that moment — miserable. He headed toward the ladder with long, purposeful strides. They were still several hours out of Lisbon. He had business there. He wanted to be done with it and unload the gold. Then they could be on their way. But he also had to check with the harbor master to find out if there'd been any unusual activity on the part of Barrington ships. At best, he knew he had the advantage of two days' sailing time and a faster ship. He needed that extra time to make Sydney and lay his trap.

He climbed the ladder, his orders reaching the crew before his head emerged. At the helm, Sandy merely shook his head. He didn't like sailing with a woman aboard. It meant trouble, pure and simple.

Elyse paced the cabin for hours. The meal the cook brought her was left untouched, and sleep was elusive, long in coming and then restless, filled with dreams.

She finally did rest, but her mind played back everything that had happened to her in the last weeks. She saw a man with waving gold hair and a slash of a mask. He stood at her elbow smiling down at her, he approached on a horse, he smiled at her mockingly and then made love to her. Elyse tossed, struggling against the ropes that seemed so real at her wrists. She was carried, flung across the back of a horse, and always her masked captor taunted her. Then those flashes were engulfed in mist and other images came.

One was of herself as a small girl. She was in a dark place, and there was water all around her. She was frightened, cold, and terribly tired. She wanted to sleep. If only she could sleep . . . Elyse curled more tightly into a ball, against the cold that crept from her dream, and she drifted through timeless memory, back and back.

Other images spun at her and then just as quickly disappeared. She murmured, tossing fitfully and not recognizing any of them.

They were fragments, disjointed pieces of a larger picture that wouldn't come together no matter how hard she tried to force it. But her other self, that quiet, resting, inner self that was her soul, knew them, and they were dearly familiar.

From a distance, Elyse saw a young woman in a garden. She was laughing, her voice coming clearly across time. Her dark blue gown was cut low across the bodice, and she was running, holding the hem of the gown so that it wouldn't be soiled. At first she was turned away, looking back over her shoulder at something or someone. And there was a teasing gaiety in her voice. The man came after her. He was tall and broad shouldered beneath the silk shirt. He caught up to her, his hand closing over her wrist and pulling her back into his arms, His own deep-throated laughter became a sensual caress. He bent low, his mouth at first gentle against hers, then demanding and promising. She reached up on her toes, molding her slender body to his, returning the kiss with equal passion. The dream seared through Elyse, making her cry out softly.

Then the young woman whispered to the man. Her cheeks were brilliant with color, her eyes alive. The skin above her breasts was flushed. Now they'd returned from that secret place in the woods that was theirs alone. They'd made love, but still the desire shone in her eyes, in the possessive way her fingers lingered at the open V of his shirt and lightly grazed his skin. And then she turned for the first time. Her eyes were a brilliant blue and her hair, which had at first appeared fair, was dark and lustrous in contrast to the man's.

I'll be late. The artist is already here for the portrait your father insisted on. Her words were directed at the man. Still he held her.

I have a gift for you. He'd whispered tenderly.

You've already given me a gift. The young woman accepted his lips in a gentle caress. *I want no other; only you.*

The man reached up to stroke the brilliant diamond and pearl bob that dangled from her ear. Its twin dangled from the other. *This other gift is a promise.* From behind him, he raised his other hand. In his fingers, he clutched two roses; one blood red, the other pristine white.

He gave her the red one first. *This rose symbolizes my passion for you.* Then he gave her the white one. *This one is my promise that my love is forever.* The woman's fingers closed gently over the long stems, and she reached up, kissing him. She then turned abruptly, as if she might have heard someone.

She pulled reluctantly from the man's grasp. *I want the artist to paint them in the portrait, so everyone will know.* She dashed from him, in the process dropping the white rose. She started back for it, but he waved her on knowing the artist would grow impatient. It could always be painted in later.

Elyse murmured sadly in her sleep. "But there was only the red rose." Then the young woman and the handsome man were gone, and she was drifting again.

She saw him, the man, tall and handsome in the saddle. He urged the magnificent horse on across the open field, glancing back over his shoulder. Behind him, another rider rode hard to catch up. It was a young woman, her face alive with the wind and the thrill of the race.

The man cut through the trees, sending his mount over a low fence, across a shallow stream. He looked back for the young woman, to make certain she'd had no difficulty. Seeing her break into the woods, he turned his horse and urged him onward but at a much slower pace.

The young woman was dressed in a dark brown riding habit of rich velvet with gold trim. Her hat was long gone, her hair streaming behind her. It should have been fair, but it was dark with hidden golden lights. She was intent on the chase, and pressed her horse faster. The fence was easily taken as was the stream. She laughed gloriously as she saw him just ahead of her. And then the expression on her face froze. He was looking back over his shoulder and didn't see the fallen tree. His horse hesitated, then lunged across the obstacle, losing its footing and its rider in the same instant.

The young woman reined her horse in hard and practically flew from the saddle, fear constricting her heart. He was a good rider, far better than she. Like a maddened creature, she tore through the brush and limbs until she found him. He groaned, sitting up, and she was beside him in an instant. His arms whipped around her, pulling her beneath him on the soft bed of leaves where he'd fallen, and she immediately knew she'd been tricked. Indignation, then laughter, appeared in her eyes. And then she frowned, her fingers going to the gash at the top of his head where even now blood matted his waving gold hair.

You're hurt. Her words were alarmed. *You're bleeding.*

Is it dreadfully bad? His eyes shone, but not with the pain of his injury.

She pulled back from him as far as the hard ground would allow. *It will undoubtedly leave a dreadful scar.*

He groaned, and the young woman was immediately contrite, her fingers gently brushing back a wave of hair. *Are you in a great deal of pain?*

Nothing that cannot be remedied by your gentle touch. His eyes were the color of soft smoke.

She pulled her scarf from her neck and reached to gingerly blot the blood from the wound. The young man immediately moved over her with far more strength than any wounded man should have.

Touch me, sweet love. His voice was husky, as his face lowered and his lips found her throat. And when she hesitated because of his wound, he touched her with the hands only desire can know.

It is for you, my love.

The words came from a light to her left. Elyse turned, wincing against the glare that instantly softened. The dream had changed. The trees of the forest were gone. It was a room. And the man was standing beside the young woman, before a large table.

I had the architect finish these only yesterday. This will be our house.

The young woman looked hesitantly at the angular drawings and elevations, not truly able to see the finished structure with a feminine eye. *Tell me about the rooms,* she whispered, her arms going around his waist.

If you continue that, I shall show you the rooms upstairs. He warned her with a husky voice.

She drew back, horrified. *In your father's house?*

The man turned to her. *I don't need a house or a bed to make love to you.* He then turned back to the drawings. *But I suppose it would be more discreet.* He kissed her long and passionately and then began to tell her of the house. It was a wood structure, two story, with single story wings on either side. Magnificent lawns and gardens descended to a lake. He pointed out the library, the formal parlor, dining room, and kitchen. Then his gaze warmed as he told her of the upstairs rooms and of the bedroom that would be theirs.

How very charming! The harsh words jolted through the heavy shroud that enclosed Elyse in the dream. Where had the voice come from?

Dear brother — the voice fairly dripped with hatred — *surely you don't intend to build such a trifling structure. It hardly befits the status of man who hopes to one day be Lord Barrington.* Then the voice subtly changed, became envious, full of longing as he turned to the young woman. *And certainly not befitting the lovely woman who will be Lady Barrington.*

Charles, the man greeted him. *What causes you to rise so early when you generally prefer to waste about until noon after an evening spent drinking at your favorite club?*

The younger man stiffened, hatred pouring from his dark eyes. *You assume too much, brother. Be careful, or you may lose it all.* He turned to the young woman, gently raising her hand and kissing the back of it. *Including the lovely lady.* His chilling laughter left them in silence as he turned and stalked from the room.

The young woman turned into the embrace of her betrothed,

something frightening chilling her deep inside. *Why does he hate you so?*

Envy, my love. The young man spoke sadly. *I wish it weren't so. He begrudges everything that is not his, including you.*

The young woman shivered, the chill of her dread reaching through the dream to Elyse.

"No," Elyse whispered softly against the pillow, not understanding what it was she was trying to stop. There was a pounding in her head. She tossed and turned, her eyes clamped tightly shut. But the pounding persisted. Over and over . . . .

She saw a courtroom, and so many faces. But she truly saw only his face and that of the young woman. It was a trial, and the young woman had gone to it against the wishes of everyone. The charge was read—murder. The young man was accused of murdering his father! And there was a witness, a young servant girl who claimed she had seen the young man strike the death blow. It all happened quickly, too quickly. The verdict was given, the sentence handed down: exile and servitude. The young woman looked to the brother, disbelieving that he would let this continue, that he wouldn't do something to stop it all. Then her gaze fastened on the man she loved. They were taking him away. She cried out, trying to reach him through the crowd of curiosity seekers and malicious gossips.

Everything shifted, time out of time. Pieces of images flew at Elyse, too fast to see. Then they slowed: a dock, a ship and countless people; some of them crying, some praying, others clinging to these last moments to say their farewells. She saw the young woman again. Then it wasn't the young woman at all, but herself; and she was running, running through the mist that engulfed the ship and the chained men on board. She was fighting, clawing to reach him, pushing past the guards as the men were taken down, down into that cavernous hold. She saw him, and she cried out. He turned to her and she flew into his arms, her heart beating once more just to have him hold her.

I can't bear to lose you, she cried into his shoulder, mindless of the chains that weighted his wrists or the filth of his once-elegant clothes or the stench of blood and sweat. Nothing else mattered except him and that he knew of her love for him. *Let me go with you,* she begged against his lips.

His heart aching in his chest, he tenderly kissed her, wanting desperately to hold onto her, knowing he could not. They would come at any minute and take her from him. He lifted her chin.

I couldn't bear for you to suffer this. Know that I love you, beyond this moment, beyond everything that has happened, beyond this life. They cannot keep us apart. I vow I will come back to you.

The men had come, had slowly pulled them apart.

Her tears flooded his hands as they slipped from hers. She felt the helplessness, knowing he would never let her go with him. She could only stand there and watch him being taken away. But there was one thing she could give him.

I love you, she called after him. Unashamed despite those who watched, she repeated his words back to him, *I love you beyond this moment, beyond everything that has happened, beyond this life. I know you will come back to me.*

And then he was gone and she was being led from the deck by someone. She watched from the dock, cold mist swirling around the ship. She watched until she couldn't see or hear anything, and her soul felt as if it were dead. But still those arms tried to comfort her.

Come away. You must try to forget everything that has happened.

She looked up, seeing the man who would have been her brother-in-law and she tried to pull back. *I love him. He promised to come back to me. I will never forget. If I die, I will never forget.*

"I will never forget," Elyse whispered through the fog of the dream that lingered briefly, and then lifted, returning her once more to the gentle rocking motion that surrounded her. She awakened slowly, blinking uncertainly in the soft gray light that filled the cabin. None of the images remained; she must have been dreaming.

Zach had sat there for the longest time watching her. She was restless, words coming softly from sleep. They were disjointed, wildly happy words one moment, achingly sad ones the next. He started to go to her when he couldn't bear the soft sobs that racked her slender shoulders, then thought better of it. If she were awake, she would be angry again and he didn't want to see that.

He'd walked the deck practically all night, able only to sleep a few hours ago, and even then it was restless, tiring sleep. He was haunted by the last days and the pain he'd caused her. That pain drove him back to the cabin. He just wanted to be near her, without the slashing words they used against each other. And somewhere between the last traces of night and early dawn, he'd decided to begin anew with her. There were weeks of open sea ahead of them, and like it or not she was his wife.

He refused to think right now about what would actually happen when he and Barrington finally met. He knew what the outcome must be, but he wanted this time with her, these few weeks, to try to tear down the anger and bitterness. She was his wife, right or wrong. He knew what they shared in bed. Could they possibly share something outside it? He wanted to try. He didn't give conscious thought to the hope in the back of his mind, that she might actually come to care for him. It was a foolish hope. And yet . . .

"What are you doing here?"

There was nothing conciliatory in her greeting, Zach noted wryly. Evidently she was still angry.

"You forget, this is my cabin."

That sent her to the far corner of the bed, the sheet pulled to her neck. "Do you always sneak into ladies' bedrooms at the crack of dawn?" She bit off testily, still not completely recovered from the restless night or the even more restless dreams. Then more curiously, "What happened to your eye?"

"I walked into a wall," he shot back at her.

Elyse smiled knowingly. She hadn't done that much damage with her little punch the day before, and Zachary Tennant wasn't the sort who walked into walls. "You seem to be doing that a lot lately."

He stood, going to the desk. She wasn't about to give on anything. He sighed, wishing he weren't right this time. It would have been wonderful to have her greet him with that soft, sweet smile of her dreams. "We made port just a short while ago. I'll be going ashore to take care of some business. I know you prefer the comforts of my cabin, but I did need a few things." He reached for a leather case. Inside he placed papers and a manifest of some kind. Then, reaching inside a smaller drawer, he withdrew a leather pouch that jingled faintly of money. That, too, was placed inside the case.

"Lisbon?" Elyse quickly slid over to the side of the bed nearest the porthole, the sheet gaping away from her lovely naked body. Obviously feeling the draft caused by that exposure, she whipped around toward him, her mood immediately contrite. "Can I go with you?"

Zach chuckled. She could be sweet as honey when she wanted something. But honey was found in a beehive and it was dangerous to extract it. He didn't really care to have her words stinging him again this morning.

"I considered it."

She brightened. "Please." She bit back her regret at begging him for anything. If she could go ashore in Lisbon, she might be able to get away.

"I said I considered it. I changed my mind."

The light immediately left her eyes. "That's exactly like you. Promising something with one hand then taking it away with the other."

"Are you always so grumpy in the morning?"

He fixed on her a maddeningly lazy smile that told her there were other things on his mind besides her morning attitude.

"No!" She bit the word off. "I'm usually a very happy person when I get up. It must be the circumstances of my confinement! That, and the fact that I don't much care for being lied to!"

He laughed as he pulled a clean shirt, pants, and seaman's coat from the narrow closet. "I didn't lie. I did consider taking you ashore. It might improve your attitude." That got him a withering glare. "But I thought better of it. The docks of Lisbon are no place for a young lady. There are too many thieves and cutthroats out there who'd like nothing better than to get their filthy hands on a beautiful, young woman."

Her head came up at that one. He'd never before said anything that indicated he thought her beautiful. "You should know about thieves and cutthroats." She turned away, trying to ignore him as he proceeded to change his clothes. The soiled shirt was stripped away. He splashed water over his face and neck, then his chest and arms, working up a rich lather of soap in his hands. That done he rinsed the water from his well-muscled body.

Elyse groaned, pulling the sheet more tightly about her as she waited for him to pull on the clean shirt. Instead he leisurely unfastened the belt at his waist, then stepped out of his pants to stand before her without the least bit of embarrassment.

And why shouldn't he? she thought, her own embarrassment evident in the color spreading across her cheeks. In spite of herself, her eyes were drawn to the straight line of his back, the hard curve of male buttocks, the sheen of softly curling gold hair that spread down his thighs. Then he turned, reaching for the clean shirt and Elyse stared, her gaze drawn up to darker tawny curls broken by the upward thrust of his hardened flesh. Just as quickly she looked away.

But not before Zach had seen something in her eyes; something that made her next words a lie.

Elyse came off the bed, wrapping the sheet around her like a shield. She held it to her as she looked for her own clothes, exasperation evident in every tense movement of her hands. She whirled on him.

"Please get out of here! Isn't it enough that I'm being held prisoner. Now I have to endure your company when I would rather be alone!"

Zach wasn't aware that he walked to her, he just did, the shirt dropping to the floor beside them. Anger and revenge were forgotten as his hands came up to cup her face. She stood deathly still, afraid to stay, afraid to run.

He brushed aside her tangled hair, caressed the heat in her cheeks, traced his thumbs across silken, sooty lashes. He heard the sharp intake of her breath as she tried to jerk her head away.

"Lis," he whispered against her cheek, slowly drawing her back.

"No! I don't want . . ." She protested, both hands coming up between them, the sheet slipping to the floor forgotten.

"Liar," he hissed as his mouth slashed down over hers.

Elyse cried out at the bruising contact. Her hands came up, striking at him, trying to push him away.

His lips moved brutally over hers. His hands slipped through her tangled hair, holding her still for this exquisite ravishment.

She hated him for what he was doing to her, for the feelings he was forcing her to confront; and the hatred was acute. But she was unprepared for such a violent jolt of desire.

His tongue plunged into her mouth and she drew on it, savoring the velvet wet heat. God help her, she wanted this, wanted it with every ounce of her being, and more. She moaned softly beneath his lips, then she reached up, hands stealing through the soft, damp waves of his hair, fingers twisting in silken gold as she felt the driving need to hold him closer.

It was mindless, insane. They were like live embers fueled by the fire of desire. Zach caressed her back, his hands sliding below her waist, then spreading over the firm fullness of her bottom to gently knead until the tips of his fingers curved lower still, slipping into wet heat.

Elyse's hands fanned across gleaming bronze skin, lightly dusted across his chest with the gold of softly, curling hair. Unable to resist, driven by the fever in her blood, she let her mouth follow her hands, pressing a trail of soft kisses against his skin. She wanted to taste all of him.

His hands cupped her head, twisting in her hair as he jerked her back. "Damn you! What have you done to me?"

Elyse felt as if she were dying of thirst and hunger. Her fingers caressed the pulse at his neck, the sharp angle of his chin, and then stole back through his hair, pulling him down to her ravenous lips. It was the only answer she could give and all he needed.

She cried out softly as his lips left hers, but it was only for a moment as he slowly lifted her above him. Elyse was flying, soaring with the passion of his mouth as it lowered from hers, slipped greedily down her throat, and then closed over the aching tip of her breast.

"Yes. Oh yes, Zach."

The sound of his name on her breathless lips was like wind to fire, spreading passion out of control. Her arms were around his neck, her hands pressing him to her breast as she clung to him. His hands slipped down her back, gently supporting her weight as they cupped her bottom. And then he was lowering her, retracing with his mouth the silken skin above her breast, then the hollow of her shoulder and the column of her throat. Back, back to those softly bruised lips.

She felt his fingers biting into the soft skin across her bottom and instinctively wrapped her slender legs around his waist. It was a delicious, bruising power, and it was driving her mindless with need. Her hands were buried in his hair, her elbows braced on his wide shoulders, and then he was lowering her further, her breasts molding against the taut, full muscles of his chest.

His mouth caressed her cheek, his lips warm at her ear.

"You're mine!" he whispered as the need soared through him. His lips plunged back to hers, and he lowered her fully, completely, over him, driving deep into the warm, waiting glove of her damp heat. Then he lifted her away again, but only enough to tease them both before he thrust inside her again.

Their kiss unbroken, he turned with her to the bed. Very slowly, Zach laid her down, deepening the kiss as he thrust into her.

The ache had begun deep inside, like a hunger only sharper. Now he lay with her, slightly to the side as if he were afraid he might crush her. It wasn't enough for Elyse, not nearly enough. She turned toward him so that she could feel all of him, arching her body into his, the aching crests of her breasts molding into his chest. Still, it was not enough.

Her fingers were fevered against his skin as they slipped over his buttocks, pulling him deeper still into her.

Zach was mesmerized by the sight of her beneath him. A round breast, thrust forward, filled his hand as he lightly grazed his palm across its tautened peak.

The sound she made brought his eyes to hers, and his breath caught in his throat at the heat shimmering in the depths of her brilliant gaze. He groaned, his hands thrusting deep into her hair, his mouth locking with hers in a kiss that was brutal with the passion she roused in him. Their bodies moved together, him giving, her taking then giving back again. He knew the moment her body stiffened with the beginnings of fulfillment. She gasped against his shoulder as her muscles tensed around him. For one breathless moment, she arched against him, and then it burst within her.

Zach felt the constriction of his own body as almost pain, but a sweet, burning pain that couldn't be held back. He thrust hard within her, the cry low in his throat, his eyes closed in that one instant that was both life and death. The force of his body driving into hers increased her pleasure, bringing a moan from her lips. She could feel the hard spasming of his body deep within her and it kept her own sweet throbbing alive.

For long moments afterward, they lay entwined, her body softly molding his. Then she turned her face from him as he slowly withdrew. She bit back the tears, refusing to give him the satisfaction of seeing her humiliation.

Zach frowned as her shoulders shook.

"Elyse?"

"Get out of here! Leave me alone!" she whispered brokenly. The wall of anger was firmly in place.

Zach rolled from the bed. He stood for a long time, watching her, trying to understand what had just happened. They'd made love and, by God, she'd enjoyed it. He knew she had, but she'd never admit it now.

"Damn!" He made a swooping dive for his clothes. Stark naked, he threw the door to the cabin wide open.

Elyse sprang upright, aghast at the sight of his bare backside disappearing through the door in full view of anyone who might be below. Her humiliation was complete as Tris leaned inside the cabin and without even so much as looking in her direction, discreetly closed the door.

She grabbed the first thing her hand found. It was an exotic carving from some port he'd put into. Elyse heaved it at the door.

Tears blinded her aim.

It bounced off the wall to the right of the door, and fell to the floor with a dissatisfying thump, still intact.

"I hate you! I hate you! Go! Go to Lisbon! And don't come back. I hope someone cuts your throat!"

Her head rested on arms folded across bent knees. Words, thoughts, everything that had happened over the last weeks washing over her.

You're the ransom, lovely Lis. He'd admitted it so easily, without excuses or apologies for what he'd done to her.

Jerrold will come after you. Why couldn't he understand?

I want him to come after me.

It's an old score that has to be settled.

Would it matter to you?

Elyse groaned and pounded her fist on the blue velvet comforter spread across the bed. What did it all mean?

She was the ransom, deliberately abducted to bring Jerrold after Zach.

She came off the bed, pacing the cabin restlessly. She'd wanted answers, and in a manner of speaking he'd given them to her. But it was like something her grandmother had once told her: the more you know the more you want to know. In this case, she knew a great deal but it told her nothing. It only raised more questions.

With one arm, Elyse raised her long hair off her neck and blew out in frustration. For the longest time she just stood in the middle of the cabin, eyes closed, feet planted firmly against the gentle roll of the ship beneath her, trying to think. Tobias said where they were going was not as far as it used to be. He'd been around Zach too long. He was beginning to talk like him; in riddles. And, of course, there was the land down under. Zach's home, Resolute, was in New South Wales.

Home for these seafarin' lads, Tobias had said. Her eyes flew open. Of course, that had to be it. She knew they were to be in Lisbon only a short time. Possibly to take on fresh supplies. For a longer voyage, to Australia?

An entire map of the world covered the wall behind his desk, oceans and continents clearly outlined. She quickly found England and Lisbon. Then her fingers wandered across vast oceans and seas. She stopped at the African continent. Jerrold had once explained the advantages of the new canal at Suez, opened little more than a year ago.

Elyse backtracked with her fingers, finding the Mediterranean Sea off the coast of north Africa, then the small jut of land that separated it from the Red Sea. The canal joined the two together with a system of locks. Jerrold had grown impatient with her curiosity, but Ceddy had explained the mechanics of this new passage to her. A cousin of his had traveled the new route from England to India right after the canal had opened. At that point in the conversation, Jerrold had declared that the canal saved over four thousand miles of ocean travel, enabling Barrington ships to reach ports with more frequency.

The Suez Canal. That must be what Tobias had been talking about when he'd said it wasn't as far as it used to be. Still, even at that, she was in awe as she gazed at the expanse of water that lay between India and the Australian continent.

Zach wanted Jerrold to come after him—to Australia.

Her hand flattened on the map in mute frustration. Why?

Anger churned inside her. She had to get away. Dear God, what was she to do?

Elyse bounded across the cabin. Twisting the heavy brass closures, she pushed the porthole open. It was early, not even dawn, yet Lisbon harbor was teeming with activity. Two large frigates were tied up at the dock straight ahead, and smaller craft of every size and description crowded the water. The *Tamarisk*, however, was not moored at the dock. They were several hundred yards away. By craning her neck out the porthole, Elyse could see the taut anchor chain far astern. Scrambling to retrieve her clothes, she decided to test her boundaries.

A few minutes later, shirt neatly tucked in at the waist of her pants, barefoot and with her hair pulled back, Elyse tried her door. Wonder upon wonders, it opened. An even greater surprise was the fact that Tris was no longer positioned outside the cabin. She poked her head out into the companionway and listened for voices.

The busy clatter of pots and pans came from the galley. Cook was no doubt working on an exotic dish for the next meal. She poked her head inside the galley and decided to try her luck.

"Good morning."

Without so much as looking up, the cook waved a ladle in her direction. He couldn't have been less interested. Eyebrows raised in faint surprise, Elyse looked to the heavy, wide ladder that

369

poked skyward through the hatch. She nimbly scrambled up it, hesitating just below eye level to the outside. She heard casual conversation somewhere nearby. Tobias. Almost light-headed with her sense of freedom, she decided to test her bounds further.

"Well, well, are you going to just stand there all day like a bandicoot pokin' its nose out of a hole or are you comin' up?" Tobias's pate momentarily shadowed the light from the sky overhead.

"I'm coming up."

"Good girl. I could use the company." He extended his hand down to her, wincing slightly as he helped her out of the hatch.

She frowned. "You've hurt yourself." Still holding onto his hand, Elyse noticed the abrasions across the backs of his knuckles.

Tobias pulled his hand away, waving it through the air. "It's nothing. I had a run-in with a wall last night."

"Is that so?" Her eyes softened with the beginning of laughter. "Must be that same wall that jumped out at Zach"—she caught herself—"Captain Tennant."

His sharp gaze met hers briefly. "Might just be. But here." He turned to the pot and cup on a crate behind him. "How about a fresh cup of coffee? I usually need several meself in the mornin'."

"Thank you." She accepted the metal cup, holding it gingerly between cradled hands. Then she glanced about the deck, noticing there was one man forward and two were at the stern. "Where is everyone?"

"Ah, funny that you should notice." Tobias's eyes twinkled. "Half the crew has gone ashore." He searched for a delicate way to explain. "As they say, to reacquaint themselves with the local establishments and professional people."

In spite of her mood when she'd first come up from the cabin, Elyse's eyes danced. "Professional people."

"Yes. And most of the others are below sleepin', takin' care of the ship, or gettin' themselves spruced up for their turn ashore."

"Did Zach . . . the captain go with them?"

"Aye, that he did. Quite some time ago. He had some business to attend to. That business is why half the crew stayed aboard. Zach didn't want any trouble, he's got a valuable cargo to unload before we take on supplies tomorrow."

"Tomorrow? Then we'll be leaving Lisbon that soon?" Something died inside Elyse. She'd hoped to have more time to plan her escape.

"We sail on the mornin' tide, day after tomorrow. Zach doesn't want to risk bein' in port longer than that."

"I see." And she did. Undoubtedly, he had a lead on Jerrold and didn't want to risk being caught in Lisbon. No, a man like Zachary Tennant would prefer the open sea or at the very least the familiar waters of Australia for whatever it was he intended.

"I was surprised to find my guard gone this morning," she said sarcastically, and immediately regretted her sharp words. Tobias had come to her defense more than once. It was clear that he and Zach were not in agreement about this whole thing.

"Aye, Zach let him go ashore. As long as we're in port, with no danger of you bein' swept overboard and drowned, I think he felt half the crew were enough to guard you. He said you were free to come and go as you please."

"Free to come and go, so long as it's not ashore," she grumbled, sipping at the fortifying coffee.

"Don't be so hard on him, girl. He's got his faults, God knows he does. And I don't agree with his methods, but he's got his reasons. He's a good man."

"Obviously he had good reason for not wanting me to go ashore."

Tobias nodded, understanding her animosity. "That he did. And that's the reason." He gestured over her shoulder.

Elyse's gaze followed his arm. He was pointing to a large, heavily gunned ship.

"Her name is *Sultana*, and her captain is Juan de la Vasquez Vimeiro, more commonly known as El Barracuda."

"El Barracuda." Elyse shaded her gaze as she took a long look at the *Sultana*. It was obvious that her captain was a different sort from the captain of the *Tamarisk*. Her rigging was intact, but her hull was badly scarred and poorly patched, several efforts at repair overlapping each other. She'd undoubtedly seen any number of confrontations and though she seemed to ride the water surely enough, no great care had been given the wood of her hull or her decks. She was a dingy, mottled green color, and barnacles showed just below her waterline. In contrast, the *Tamarisk* gleamed like a polished black pearl in the rising morning sun.

The sleek schooner's hull was freshly painted, and her decks shone white with varnish. Her tall masts, painted a brilliant red, thrust proudly into the blue Mediterranean sky. Her lowered sails had been lashed down, the booms secured with new rope, the knots so perfect it was impossible to find their ends. The *Tamarisk* was immaculate. The day before, all crew members had constantly been working with buckets and mops. Elyse felt certain she could eat off those gleaming oak planks. Every bit of brass, steel, and wood gleamed, and high above, at the center mast, the Spanish flag fluttered gaily in the breeze. The *Tamarisk* reminded Elyse of a big beautiful bird, a gleaming black bird, hovering over the water. Like her captain, she was lean, strong, and beautiful to look at.

Elyse quickly changed the direction of her thoughts. "Who is El Barracuda?"

"He's one of the worst cutthroats that ever sailed the seas."

Elyse turned to him in surprise. "A pirate? They really exist?"

Tobias gazed at her speculatively. "Aye, girl, they exist. Some bad like El Barracuda, others not so bad."

"I knew there used to be a great many pirates off the coast of South America, but I didn't realize there were any here."

"Here or in any one of a half-dozen oceans and seas around the world. They're nothin' but thieves. They just happen to use ships to go after other ships with rich cargoes."

She nodded. "Jerrold has had a great deal of trouble with pirates, particularly in your land down under." She smiled up at him, missing the guarded look that crept into his eyes. "What makes El Barracuda so bad?"

"He's a man with no honor," Tobias stated flatly.

"Honor? Among thieves?" Elyse was incredulous.

"Aye, even among thieves. Everyone must have a code to live by, even if it's not the same as the next fellow's. Mind you, I'm not condonin' piracy. I'm just sayin' there are those who attack to support themselves or to right an injustice, and then there are thieves like El Barracuda who attack for no other purpose than to destroy. Aye, he's a bloodthirsty fellow. Makes my blood run cold just to see that ship so nearby. That means he's piratin' the Mediterranean."

"What about here in the harbor? Why do the authorities allow him to come in?"

"As long as he's not caught at thievin' and abides by the law inside the harbor, they allow him to come in for supplies. His money spends like everyone else's, no matter how ill gotten it is. Zach had a run-in with him, several years ago. El Barracuda has never forgotten it. That's another reason Zach kept part of the crew here and took some of the men with him."

Elyse's eyes widened. So this was something else she hadn't known about Zachary Tennant. Her gaze went back to the *Sul-*

tana. Why would Zach have had problems with El Barracuda? "What happened?"

"El Barracuda decided he wanted a cargo Zach and some of his men were carryin'."

"He attacked the *Tamarisk?*" Elyse was wide-eyed.

"That was his first mistake. The *Tamarisk* is not as big as most ships, being only a schooner. But she's heavily armed, and fast." He gestured down the long decks to the cannons. "It was the only time El Barracuda ever lost a confrontation. It cost him his ship, his cargo, half his crew, and a great deal of his pride. He swore he'd see Zach sent to the bottom for it. That's why Zach is so careful, especially with you."

"Oh yes, of course," Elyse commented wryly. "He doesn't want to lose his precious hostage." That brought to mind her real purpose. "When will Captain Tennant and the others be returning?"

"The men will probably stay ashore for the night. It helps them unwind a bit before the voyage to Sydney. Zach will probably return after he's completed his business. I'd say in a few hours."

"A few hours." She looked up at Tobias, afraid he might read her thoughts. "Well, that should give me time to straighten up the cabin, since I have nothing else to do. Thank you for the coffee, Tobias."

He looked at her strangely, wondering about this sudden complacency. He wouldn't have expected it. "You're welcome, girl. If you need anything, just give a holler."

Elyse nodded as she turned toward the hatch. "That's very kind of you." She hesitated. "Thank you, Tobias, for being a friend."

"Think nothing of it. I've always had an eye for a pretty lady."

Elyse quickly lowered herself down the ladder and returned to her cabin.

Once inside, she turned to the porthole. Leaning far out, as she had earlier that morning, she made a decision. If she tried to leave from the deck, someone would surely see her. She had to go through the porthole. In line with the excuse she'd given Tobias, she cleaned and straightened the cabin. Everything was put back in its appropriate place, right down to the statue that had had the disgusting good fortune not to break.

Going to the shaving mirror, she inspected her appearance. She'd have to take care or everything would be undone when she slipped into the water. After tightly binding her hair on top of her head, she went through Zach's drawers and found a round, knitted seaman's cap. She yanked it down snugly over her hair. Her shirt and pants would suffice, but she needed shoes. Zach's were hopelessly large. She'd just have to get a pair when she reached the dock. That raised the interesting question of money.

She felt like a thief. But it couldn't be helped. Though she still had her diamond and pearl pendant, she was reluctant to part with it, even to buy her way home. She opened the drawer she'd seen Zach go into that morning. Several gold coins were tucked away in a pouch at the back of it. She had no idea what the currency was, but told herself that gold was gold. Surely someone would accept it.

Tucking the pouch inside her shirt just above the waist, Elyse turned to the porthole. She looked out again. Now that her decision was made, the drop to the water seemed miles instead of only feet. She bit at her lower lip, scanning the cabin. There were several sheets and blankets in the footlocker at the end of the bed. Tying these together, she formed a crude rope. Fastening one end of it to the brass closure of the porthole, she dropped the other end out. It fell quite short of the water, but she quickly decided she could survive a drop of that distance.

Elyse carefully wedged herself out of the porthole, silently giving thanks that she was endowed with small bones and slender hips. Hand over hand, she carefully inched down the makeshift rope. If anyone was going to see her from the deck of the *Tamarisk* it would be now. Reaching the end of the last blanket, she glanced briefly up the way she had come, then back down again. It was a good twenty-foot drop. Holding her breath, one hand flattened against the hat to hold it in place, she let go. To her, the sound she made hitting the water was like a cannon's boom, but in reality it was only a small splash. She'd braced herself for the shock of cold water, and was surprised to find it warm. As she quickly kicked her way to the surface, she thought fleetingly of what else might be down there swimming around and quickly decided it was better not to think about it.

With the smooth, even strokes she'd learned as a child, Elyse swam away from the *Tamarisk*. A smaller ship was anchored not too far away, between the *Tamarisk* and the dock. She stroked into the shadows cast by the vessel, then hesitated, trying to get her bearings.

As a strange sensation slipped down her spine, Elyse turned briefly, feeling that unseen eyes were watching her. At any moment she expected the warning cry to go out from the deck of the *Tamarisk*. But none came. She must have been mistaken. Though she couldn't rid herself of the feeling that she'd been seen, she couldn't waste valuable time worrying about it. She shrugged off the feeling and turned to the matter at hand.

Always a strong swimmer, Elyse found she'd miscalculated the distance to the docks. She did the sidestroke to avoid splashing and held only her head above water. Finally, a small landing with steps leading up to the dock lay just beyond the next small craft. Elyse moved quietly through the water.

Dockside, people bustled about, ships were loaded and unloaded, wagons delivered cargoes and carted other cargoes away. The pier was a noisy, buzzing confusion of workers, seamen, and merchants. No one noticed as a bedraggled figure pulled up onto the landing.

Elyse cast one long, backward glance over her shoulder. The *Tamarisk* was lovely in the morning light, like that large graceful bird she had earlier imagined it. Something tightened deep inside her at leaving the ship. She didn't try to understand the feeling; she knew only she had to go.

Chapter Eighteen

Lisbon reached out to the sea from its sheltered position on the broad, warm estuary of the Tagus River, called the Sea of Straw because of the golden brilliance of its waters in the sunlight. The city, made up of seven coastal hills, reflected the varied influences of ancient cultures. It had long been an international port. Its intricate, winding cobblestoned streets provided access to houses of soft pink, turquoise, and white, with tiled roofs and iron balconies accented with flowers.

This city's heritage was greatly influenced by the Moors, but it dated back to prehistoric times and was rich in history, culture, and trade. Elyse knew this; she had visited Lisbon two years earlier with her grandmother. They'd stayed at an elegant villa high in the terraced hills overlooking the city, and had made trips to ancient castles, fortresses, churches, and museums. The Lisbon she knew was a mixture of cultures, fascinating. She'd enjoyed watching the brilliantly costumed dancers in the *terreira* on warm evenings, and she'd ridden in a carriage through the Alfama district, had seen the lovely Arabic palace, the Catelo São Jorge, used as a fortress by the Visigoths from the fifth century to the eighth.

In the marketplace could be found gold and diamonds from Brazil; ivory from Africa; spices, silks, rubies, pearls, and porcelains from China and the East Indies; ginger and pepper from the Malabar Coast. Elyse had discovered it all with her grandmother. But that was the Lisbon that a privileged traveler saw. It was not the Lisbon she was looking upon.

Still exotic and fascinating, this was the province of merchants, traders, and seafarers. She dodged past tall black sailors that greatly resembled Kimo. Stripped to their waists, they wore great gold rings looped in their ears, and brilliant bracelets adorned their heavily muscled arms.

She dodged away from more than one swarthy merchant fascinated with the "lad" who possessed such fair skin. Following the directions of their gazes, she quickly found out why. The front of her shirt was plastered to her body, leaving nothing to doubt. Arms folded across the front of her shirt, she continued her explorations.

Winding her way through the throng of milling people, Elyse pulled the pouch of gold coins from her shirt. She knew just enough of the language to ask for the local museum. As a result, she smiled radiantly when she found a streetside vendor who spoke something that resembled English and was willing to accept her gold coins.

He was selling all manner of goods, from fresh lobster, prawns, and crabs to brightly woven baskets, hats, and a few items of clothing. Elyse quickly selected a hat with a wide brim and a colorful cape of the type she'd seen some men wearing. It would help conceal her until her clothes dried, and the tentlike shape would make her blend into the crowd. To complete her purchase, she chose a pair of woven sandals.

As Elyse held out the gold coins, the merchant's eyes glittered almost as brightly as the gold. He seized one. Then, after biting down hard on it to test its value, he held out his hand for more. At a definite disadvantage, Elyse hesitated. These coins were all she had. She hoped to send a telegram to Paris, where she might be able to contact friends of Uncle Ceddy's, but it could be days before her departure from Lisbon could be arranged. She handed the merchant one more coin. His fingers automatically signaled for two more.

Her decision was quickly made. Until she knew just how long she might be in Lisbon, she had to hold onto as much money as possible. She always had the pendant of course, which was now concealed in the pouch, but she wouldn't part with it unless it was absolutely necessary. Elyse quickly replaced the sandals, hat, and cape, and held her hand out for her money.

Once a merchant always a merchant, and a meager sale was better than no sale at all. Amusement danced in Elyse's eyes as the man quickly wrapped the items she'd selected in plain white paper and thrust them at her, demanding the original two coins.

Elyse gave him one, fixed a stubborn expression on her face and waited. He hesitated and Elyse firmly shook her head, indicating she would give him no more. He shrugged his shoulders, gave her a withering glare and turned to another customer.

She was ecstatic, and pushed back the nagging suspicion that she'd probably paid double what everything was actually worth. She donned the cape and hat, and strapped the sandals to her feet. Now she had to see about getting out of Lisbon permanently.

Elyse was hot. Her clothing had long since dried from her swim in the harbor, and trickling beads of perspiration now pushed their way down between her shoulder blades. She'd already learned what Zach meant by thieves and cutthroats. Twice she'd seen fancily dressed men attacked by street thieves. She kept out of the shadows. Their obscurity invited trouble, and trouble was the last thing she needed. She'd also learned to watch for the crew of the *Tamarisk*. In one shop she passed, she saw a large African buying some colorful cloth. Kimo. Elyse immediately ducked around the corner when he turned and came out of the store with another crewman, the cloth tucked under his arm. It was amazing how small a large seaport city could be.

And she was tired and hungry. She had walked for miles on the cobbled streets that wound, in a confusing maze, through the area near the wharf. She passed second-story dwellings overlooking shops and businesses, laundry draped along their balconies or hung from lines strung between open windows.

And in countless shops she asked about boat passage. She got everything from disinterested shrugs to blank stares. In one market, she had a pomegranate stuck in one hand, a smelly mackerel in the other, while the merchant held his out for money. He got the pomegranate and the mackerel back.

By late afternoon Elyse collased wearily onto a chair at a small sidewalk restaurant. Too tired to go on, she was also too hungry to ignore the wonderful aromas that came from inside. She ordered food she remembered: ensopado, a rich meat soup with large chunks of fresh vegetables, and a huge loaf of bread still warm from the oven. The Portuguese loved their wine; a request for water would have brought one of those blank stares she was rapidly becoming used to. Elyse chose a cup of the aromatic coffee.

No finely prepared meal at Winslow house or aboard the *Tamarisk* had tasted as good as that one. When she finished, she presented one of the gold coins and was greatly surprised at the change she received back, the waiter informing her in fluent

English that the gold coins were Spanish and easily exchanged anywhere in the city. He had no other customers at that time of the afternoon so he struck up a congenial conversation while Elyse tried to decide what to do next. Since the waiter was friendly, hadn't cheated her for her meal, and spoke such good English, Elypse decided to trust his judgment.

"I'm traveling to London. I need to arrange passage. Do you know of anyone who might be leaving for England?" At first her question brought only a disheartening shrug, but then the man paused thoughtfully. He'd obviously made several assumptions about the way she was dressed, the most accurate being that she didn't have a great deal of money.

"Go to the Green Dolphin," he volunteered in heavily accented English.

"The Green Dolphin?" Elyse repeated it so that she was certain of what he'd said.

He nodded, stroking his chin thoughtfully as he removed her empty bowl and cup. "It is a tavern not far from here, on the Rua do Carmo. My wife's cousin, Santo, works there. He hears things, he may know of such a ship. But he will not be there until later. He works at night and sleeps during the day."

Elyse rolled her eyes. Her passable knowledge of French would do her no good here. But an address should be simple enough. "The Green Dolphin on the Rua do Carmo. How far is it?"

He indicated with outthrust fingers, pointing to her left past the small square. "Three streets. Turn right, middle of the street with a large sign of a green dolphin." He smiled at her.

"Of course, what else?" Elyse returned the smile, feeling as if she'd truly found a friend. She gathered the last of the loaf of bread, and as she rose to leave, she felt gentle pressure on her arm.

"Faça favor." He addressed her in his native language, then, remembering her difficulty, changed back to English, "Be careful, young man."

She was pleased by her successful deception.

He continued with a friendly warning. "Many of the men who go there are captains and sailors from the different ships. There is much drinking, sometimes fighting. It is not a place for someone as young as you. Be very careful. It is not a good place to be if there is trouble. There, a man takes his justice with a knife."

Elyse nodded, thanking him greatly for his information. "I'll be careful," she assured him as Zach's warning of thieves and cutthroats immediately came back to her.

Stepping from the restaurant, she looked at the late afternoon sky. She still had a few hours before she could find Santo at the Green Dolphin. Until then she would just have to keep out of sight.

His sale of the gold concluded, together with the arrangements for its transfer before sundown, Zach stepped out of an office in a building located in the Baixa, the central business district in Lisbon. He'd sold the gold for a substantial sum. Payment would be transferred to his bank in Lisbon as soon as the broker verified receipt of it. He'd done business with Esteben Bautano and knew the man could be trusted, unlike other people he'd dealt with recently.

Zach nodded to Sandy to be quick. He was anxious to get back to the ship, but his second mate wanted to make a few purchases in the open-air market that lined the waterfront. Their last time in Sydney, Sandy had spent most of his time with the daughter of an Irish merchant. Zach suspected his Nordic friend thought himself to be in love. Taking advantage of the cool shade outside the shop, he waited, leaning back against a stone wall. He watched as a beggar worked the opposite side of the street, cup clutched in one bony outstretched hand. The man wandered blindly, tap-tapping along with a cane. Zach smiled as he watched the man, who seemed to have uncanny ability for picking out the most wealthy of passersby. The area was full of passengers arriving from or departing for some foreign port. Several coins dropped noisily into the cup.

The man continued along the street until he rounded the corner. Then he became noticeably more surefooted. His pace quickened, the cane was forgotten as he slipped to the middle of the alley. The cup was upturned, the coins quickly stuffed inside the pocket of well-made pants once hidden beneath the soiled cape. Zach smiled at the well-dressed beggar. After all, it wouldn't do for him to leave too many coins in the cup. It might seem that he was receiving more than his fair share. The man dropped the cape back into place, resumed his hunched, shuffling gait and tap-tapping, and returned. Such was life in the street.

When the man approached, Zach nodded him on. When the beggar persisted, he laid a hand on the knife belted to his waist, and the "blind" beggar quickly moved on. A group of native boys caught Zach's attention. They scattered down the street, begging for money, imitating the blind beggar, and stealing fruit from a sidewalk store. A particularly small lad, undeniably the youngest, boldly approached him.

Feet planted squarely, one hand placed on a hip covered by pants that had obviously known several owners, the boy peeked up with large dark eyes from beneath the brim of a soiled cap. The little beggar mimicked the common street phrases the others had used, holding out his hand. He's getting started awfully young, Zach thought with regret. The little fellow probably had six or seven brothers working the next street over, bringing home a good income for their family. Still, Zach never was able to turn his back on a child, especially not one as young as this.

"Here." He pulled a gold coin from his pocket. Holding it out, he spoke to the boy in his native language. The child snaked the coin from his fingers, mumbling a quick thank you, then starting to dart away, but something about him caught Zach's attention. A wisp of glossy, long hair peeked from beneath the boy's cap.

Quicker than the child could leap away from him, Zach reached out. With one hand he caught a wrist barely bigger than one of his fingers. With the other he swept the round little cap off the child's head. Both gasped as a torrent of long silky hair cascaded down, transforming the smudge-faced little boy into a wide-eyed, solemn little girl.

She was a dark-eyed little temptress, part vixen, part alley cat. She struggled at first, until Zach reprimanded her in her native tongue. Then she hung back warily, bracing herself away from him on firmly planted feet. Her head came around slowly, huge brown eyes like liquid amber contemplating her next move.

Zach dropped down into a crouched position to meet her at eye-level, and slowly drew her to him. He reached out, taking black silken hair between his fingers.

"So, you're not a boy at all," he declared with a stern expression. He smiled faintly when she gave a quick look over her shoulders, seeking the others. But they had already disappeared down the street. Her wary gaze turned back to his.

"Why are you begging in the streets?"

"My mother and sisters are hungry," she blurted out unconvincingly.

Zach shook his head. "I don't think so, little one. Your cheeks are not sunken and your skin is not sallow. You have full cheeks, healthy skin, and lustrous hair. I think your mother and sisters

381

are well provided for and wondering where you are right now," he surmised, his eyes twinkling.

In spite of her initial fear the little girl found herself warming to this tall, gray-eyed Anglo with hair like the sun. And when he smiled, he made her feel very special indeed.

"So, why then are you begging on the streets of Lisbon?"

A somber expression came to her face. She didn't know what this stranger would think or do to her, if she told him the truth. But the soft light in his eyes betrayed his stern expression. She looked up at him from beneath the sweep of long, lustrous lashes.

"To see if I could do it." She shrugged her slender shoulders, an impish light leaping into her dark eyes.

Zach threw back his head and laughed. He laughed until tears filled his eyes. Then he looked at her, really looked at her. It was the same, that slightly brazen stance with small shoulders squared as if she'd take on the whole world if necessary. It was in the cocksure expression in her eyes and the defiant tilt of her chin. All of it, exactly like Elyse; those mornings she would sneak out for an early morning ride, dressed as a man, or the evening she boldly strode into an exclusive men's club dressed in a man's formal attire. It was the same: reckless abandon, the fiery light that smoldered in this young one's eyes, the faint amusement that danced at the corners of her mouth as if she'd just played a joke on someone.

His fingers eased around her wrist, and he felt her relax as well. Impish little sprite. She was sizing him up! Still he crouched on the street before her.

"Don't you know you should be home with your sisters, wearing pretty dresses, learning how to be a lady?"

"Why would I want to be a lady? It's boring. All they ever do is sit and gossip, drink *café* and eat fine pastries. They all grow fat, but I will never be fat." She laid a hand against her chest as if making a solemn promise. "I want to be slender, so that I can run fast like the boys. I do what boys do, I like boats and horses and fighting."

"Ah." Zach sighed, taken by her tiny loveliness. "But you are a girl nevertheless, and that can be quite a marvelous thing. Don't you know you will one day break many hearts?"

She seemed to consider how that might be accomplished. "How could I do that?"

Zach lifted a strand of her hair. "With lovely long hair worn loose about your shoulders, and pretty dresses in every color imaginable."

"I don't like dresses. My mother always makes me wear pink ones with too much lace. It itches." She rolled her eyes disgustedly. "I wouldn't mind if she would let me wear clothes like Antonia."

"Is Antonia your sister?"

"Yes, she's fifteen. She would like you."

"Would she now?" Zach thought on that, thoroughly enjoying such a lovely creature even if she was no more than seven or eight years old. She was laughing and teasing and even a little flirtatious. How he wished someone else he knew could feel that way about him. It seemed so easy for this little one. Her feelings were unguarded, unpretentious.

"What sort of clothing does Antonia prefer?"

Her eyes widened. "Oh, she likes bright things; red, blue, green. Pretty full skirts, and blouses with short sleeves. They're made of satin and silk. My mother has a woman make them for her. They're so beautiful." There was a note of worshipful envy in the little girl's voice.

"What would you choose, if you could have something pretty to wear?" Zach played along, genuinely interested in the workings of this young, but decidedly very feminine, mind.

His little captive thought very long about that. Closing one eye, she placed a finger against her chin and pondered. Then her eyes widened and she pointed over his shoulder.

"That is what I would have." Her eyes sparkled with childish delight, as she slipped from his grasp and darted behind him to the small shop Sandy had entered earlier. She stood in rapt delight, looking up through the glass.

Zach followed her gaze. There displayed in the window was a magnificent silver and white knitted shawl. It was large, meant to be worn long over a woman's dress. But in spite of its size, it wouldn't be heavy. It was woven of most delicate threads in a pattern of interwoven blooms. At first it appeared to be white in color, but as Zach stepped aside, the sun shone through the glass, sparkling on the silver beads that had been intricately worked into the design, making it appear that each bloom was tipped with silvery droplets of water. It was beautiful and obviously very costly.

"That is what you want?"

"Oh, yes." The little girl stood beside him now. "It is something a boy would give a girl he cared very much about. My sister has such a shawl."

383

"Does she now? And does she also have a special young man in her life?"

"Yes, Jorge. They are to be married. I'll be glad. Then I can have a room all to myself."

Zach laughed at her charming innocence, and then he sobered, his smile softening. "Thank you for telling me about your sister."

"Do you have a special lady?" She lifted those large dark eyes that would one day hold a man's fate in their depths. "You should," she decided. "No one who is as handsome as you should be without a lady." Then she looked up at him, struck by a sudden idea. "Would you like to meet my sister Josefina?"

"I don't think so. Thank you anyway." He smiled down at her. He couldn't remember when he'd enjoyed a lady's company so much, except perhaps that morning and the night before with Elyse. Odd how she and this child were so much alike. "But if your sister is only half as beautiful as you are, then she will have no trouble finding a young man." His little captive immediately blushed, but Zach didn't notice. He was staring at the exquisite shawl.

"Come on, little one. You shall have your shawl." Taking her hand in his, he led her across the store.

He ignored Sandy's bemused glance as he approached the shopkeeper's wife. He made several purchases. The white shawl he'd seen in the window was for his little apprentice thief. The second shawl he chose was very similar, with delicate hand-worked yarn and silver beads, but it also had tiny seed pearls woven into the design. He had them wrapped separately. Along with the pearl-covered shawl, Zach chose several brightly colored skirts and blouses. His little companion took great delight in picking the colors.

Zach accepted the wrapped items and paid the woman handsomely. Then he turned back, one last purchase in mind. He eyed the many clear glass jars containing candies of different sizes and shapes. What better way to sweeten a little girl's disposition? He let the little thief select her favorites.

Sandy, who had long since completed his purchases, stood waiting outside, a speculative expression on his big, raw-boned face. Zach held out his hand to his little companion. "I am very glad we met, *senhorita*."

She dimpled, flashing him a devastating smile that surrounded several pieces of candy. *"Muito obrigado."* She beamed at him and turned to leave. His hand delayed her.

The little thief turned, and Zach started to present her with the package containing the shawl she'd seen in the window. For a moment he held it just beyond her grasp. "You must promise you will wear a dress at least one day each week, and when you wear it, you will wear this also."

She nodded, her large round eyes adoring. *"Muito obrigado, senhor,"* she breathed out, and then, like the child she was, she scampered away from them. But a few yards down the cobbled street, she stopped and turned back around, returning slowly.

"What is it, little one?" Zach's eyes smiled his pleasure at giving her such a gift. Truly, he felt as if he'd received the greater gift; he'd purchased something for Elyse, something he felt she would truly enjoy.

"How old are you, *senhor?*" the girl asked with straightforward abandon. In another three or four years she would blush even to speak with him.

Sandy had been watching this little exchange, and he could contain himself no longer. He burst out laughing. "I think, Cap'n, your little *senhorita* has plans for you. You'd better watch out or she'll be taking you home to meet her mama."

Zach glared at his mate, but it was done good-naturedly. He waved to the little girl. "If I were ten years younger and you were ten years older, I would never be able to leave Lisbon, little one."

She thought on that a minute, undoubtedly making mental calculations. Then her delicate little mouth formed an astonished "O." "You are very old, *senhor.* I mean no disrespect, but when I am still a young woman, you will be almost as old as my father. I do not think I would like that. I want a young man who is very strong and handsome. He must at least be able to sneak apples away from old Gonsalves's cart without being caught."

Zach laughed. "You are perfectly right, little one. He must at least be able to do that." Then, becoming very solemn, he placed his hand over his heart as if it were truly breaking. "I will never forget you."

Suddenly the child revealed the breathtaking beauty she would one day be. She smiled shyly, her lashes sweeping low across her cheeks. "I will never forget you, *senhor.*" Then the woman was forgotten as the child scampered away, her bundle clutched tightly under her arm, candy clenched between her teeth.

"Ah, Cap'n." Sandy shook his head appreciatively. "You've a way with the ladies."

Zach frowned slightly, wondering if another young lady would be as pleased with his gifts. He found himself wanting to say there was only one young lady who mattered to him, but he didn't. He merely nodded gruffly at Sandy.

"Let's get back to the ship. I want to be there when that broker arrives for the transfer. The sooner that gold is off my hands, the happier I'll be."

Sandy nodded sternly, but the light in his eyes danced. "Aye, aye, Cap'n."

It was almost an hour later when they crossed from the landing to the *Tamarisk* in the small rowboat. Zach nodded to his man on watch as he swung himself up the ladder. Sandy followed behind. It was already early evening, shadows slipping darkly across the shimmering waters of the harbor. He'd hoped to be able to tie in at the dock to unload the gold more easily, but this was a busy time of year in Lisbon. At any rate, Esteben had two steam-driven ferries he used to transport goods up and down the Tagus River. One was tied up not too far away, having just brought in a shipment of wine casks for delivery to clients in the city. The broker was to meet the ferry captain and they would be along at any time. Zach looked up as Tobias came up from below and walked the length of the deck. At a glance, all seemed orderly and calm aboard *Tamarisk*.

His old friend greeted him warmly.

"Any trouble?" Zach glanced meaningfully back over Tobias's shoulder in the direction of the *Sultana*.

"Not a whisper. I don't think El Barracuda is aboard. A good many of the crew are gone as well. There's just a skeleton crew keepin' an eye on things. The rest are undoubtedly ashore stirrin' things up before puttin' to sea again. They've been takin' on supplies most of the day."

"What about our supplies?" Zach took the supply manifest Tobias handed him.

"Everything's aboard and shipshape. Tris checked off each item as it was brought aboard. He and a couple of the other men just finished securin' the stuff about an hour ago. They're eager to be ashore themselves as soon as the others return."

Zach nodded, scanning the manifest briefly. Tris was trustworthy; he could be certain they had most of what they would need for the voyage to Sydney. Extra stores of fresh water and perishables could be obtained along the way, although he didn't want to be delayed by putting into port too frequently. Their course across the Mediterranean to Suez and through the canal to the Red Sea would take them across the Arabian Sea to India. From there they would skirt the coast of Ceylon en route to Singapore, head on to New Guinea and into the Coral Sea off the coast of Australia. It was not the easiest route, but it was the shortest, if a man knew the waters, the reefs, and the small scattered islands that could offer shelter.

Zach looked up, his gray eyes scanning the deck for Elyse. He'd left instructions she was to have the freedom of the ship, and at this time of day, when the hot sun no longer glared on the decks, he expected to find her enjoying the cool evening air and the panorama of Lisbon harbor.

"Was there any problem today with our passenger?" he inquired lightly.

Tobias shook his head. "She was up on deck earlier, but she's spent most of the afternoon below." He noticed the package Zach held under his arm. "What have you there?"

Zach glanced up, shoving the manifest back at Tobias. "A very pretty young lady in Lisbon reminded me that a gift might help tame an angry lady." He started for the companionway.

"She's been real quiet down there most of the day. I think maybe she's not so angry now." Tobias huffed and puffed as he followed Zach back down the ladder.

"Tobias!"

The loud, bellowing roar stopped him dead in his tracks, then propelled him toward the captain's cabin as if all the demons of hell rode on his heels. He stopped, stock-still, in the doorway as his gaze swept the cabin. All was neat, orderly, everything in its place. Too neat, too orderly, and not quite everything in its place. Elyse was nowhere to be found.

"Real quiet!" Zach whirled on him. "Is this quiet enough for you?" His jerked an arm to the open porthole and the length of knotted sheet, one end fastened to the brass closure, the other disappearing over the side of that long drop to the water.

"Father in heaven!" Tobias muttered with disbelief as he crossed to the porthole and gaped down at the water below. He shook his head. "How on earth did she ever get through there?"

Zach turned on him. "It's quite simple. She's not built like you!"

"Now listen, lad!" Tobias took exception to that rather crude reference to his potbelly, but Zach had already charged past him to bellow orders down the companionway.

Zach was in a dilemma. He assumed Elyse had been gone most of the day, at least since midmorning when Tobias had last seen her. The crewmen who were ashore still had not returned. They were due aboard at any time, but a sailor on shore leave might delay his return. Though he'd given them strict orders to be aboard just about now, Zach knew they would trail back one by one. Ashore, it would be impossible to find them, and with the gold still aboard *Tamarisk* awaiting the broker's finalization of the transaction, he dare not take the crewmen now aboard to search for Elyse. That was much too risky with the *Sultana* and El Barracuda nearby in the harbor.

He quickly made a decision and dispatched Tris to the landing with the rowboat. As soon as any of the crew returned, he was immediately to bring them to the ship. Zach would then return to the landing with him and set out to find Elyse himself. "Damn!" he muttered. Didn't she realize the danger of being alone in a seaport city without protection? A woman was a vulnerable target. That thought brought him up short. His mind filled with images of the little girl he'd met in the plaza, dressed like the little boys who begged in the streets.

Elyse wouldn't be dressed as a woman! The only clothes she possessed were the pants and shirt he'd given her. She didn't even have any money. . . .

A thorough search of the cabin confirmed his suspicions. He couldn't see that any clothes were missing, but the bag of Spanish gold coins he'd kept in the desk was gone. Why had he trusted her? Why had he thought she wouldn't try to escape after the way he'd treated her that morning?

Greetings were shouted over the railings. Tris had returned from shore. The first man over the side was Kimo. Zach quickly ordered Tris to prepare to take him back; then he ordered Tobias to send men, as they returned to help in the search. He brushed past Kimo, not seeing the puzzled expression on the African's face.

"The little girl is gone? I wonder if dat might have been her we see in marketplace."

Zach whirled around and seized the man by the shoulders. "Where?" He was six foot four inches, but Kimo towered over him, and the man was so black his features seemed to disappear into his face, except for the whites of his eyes. But Zach had a special bond with this loyal seaman. He'd taken him off a slaver with almost sixty others, and he'd delivered them to Sydney where they were given their freedom and the choice of returning to their native land or of staying in Australia. Kimo had wanted to stay with the *Tamarisk*. It was as if this large, gentle man had found his home on those oak decks. Zach had taught him English and how to read and write. For his part, Kimo was blood loyal, as was the entire crew. And the huge African knew Zach's secrets, but he would die before he would give them to anyone. There was nothing he wouldn't do for Zach.

"I'm prob'ly wrong, Cap'n. I would know that pretty face and that long dark hair. But today in the marketplace I saw a young man. He was small and I only saw him for a minute, but he had fair skin, almost too fair for a boy, and eyes the color of the water on the Barrier Reef. It made me think if that pretty lady had a brother, it would be him."

"Where?" Zach was frantic. Maybe fair skin wasn't a sound enough reason to think Kimo had seen Elyse, but those eyes. Dear God, he'd never known such eyes. And hadn't Zach's exact thought been that they were the color of the water off the reef?

"You've got to think, Kimo. Where did you see this boy?"

"It was so quick and then he was gone." The African thought for a moment. So much of Lisbon was the same; the shops, the vendors with their carts, the white-washed houses with pastel façades. He rubbed his glistening black hair, then his head came up, a wide smile splitting his face from ear to ear.

"It was outside the shop where I bought this silk for Annie back home." He turned to his companion, but the man only shrugged to indicate he didn't remember seeing the boy.

"Kimo, I need more—the name of the shop, a location, something different that you remember."

The man's smile broadened even more. "The shopkeeper was a black man, like me. Tall, from the Zulu tribe in the north. He was taken like I was and managed to get his freedom and come here."

Zach beamed as he clasped Kimo with genuine affection. It wasn't much, but it was something. There couldn't be many black men who owned shops in Lisbon, much less blacks from the notorious Zulu tribe. Zach went below. When he came back on deck, he was tucking a gun into his belt, and the wide-bladed cutlass was secured at his hip.

"I go with you, Cap'n." Kimo started for his own weapons.

"No, Kimo. I want you to stay aboard with Tobias and Sandy to make certain that shipment of gold is transferred. If there's any trouble, they'll need you." Zach looked up at his friend. "It's all right. I know my way around Lisbon. When Tris and some of the

other men return, send a group ashore to try the usual places."
Then Zach had a thought. "When did you see this boy?"

"It was afternoon. We stopped at a small tavern to eat, then came back here."

"How far a walk from the docks was it, and in which direction?" Zach was trying to get a bearing on the general area where Kimo had seen Elyse.

Kimo turned to look back at the curve of the city as it spread away from the docks. "There." He pointed a long finger to the south of the landing. "We stopped to eat near the shop, then walked to the docks. It was a short walk, just a few minutes."

Conflicting emotions seized Zach. He was grateful to learn that at least in midafternoon Elyse had still been in the waterfront area. That greatly narrowed down their search. But it was a most dangerous area. Something nagged at him. Seeking her out would be like trying to find a needle in a haystack, and he was fast losing daylight. He went to the rail and braced his weight against the ropes.

"I don't know how long I'll be gone. But I want all the men aboard by midnight."

"Aye, aye, Cap'n." Kimo nodded. Tobias stopped Zach's descent. "Why do you bother?" The look on his face was hard, as if he blamed Zach for her escape. "Forget it. Barrington doesn't know that she's escaped and he's not likely to. You'll have that bloody confrontation you've been wantin' and she'll be well out of it."

"What the hell is that supposed to mean?" Zach thundered at him.

"It means that you've brought the girl nothing but grief since you two met. She was nothing but a pawn to get to Barrington anyway, you said so yerself. Why not just leave it be? Save yerself the effort. She means nothin' to you."

That did it. Zach leaped back over the rail, his hand burying in the front of Tobias's shirt. For a long moment they just stood there locked in a battle of wills, one speaking the truth, the other refusing to accept it. Slowly Zach let go of Tobias, regret sharp in his eyes. His hands closed fondly over the old man's shoulders. "I guess she does mean something to me," he whispered, then turned and climbed down over the side. Tobias leaned after him, victory shining in his eyes.

"Be careful out there, lad. Lisbon is a dangerous city at night." Zach looked up at him. "It's a dangerous city at any time, my friend."

He bid farewell to Tris at the landing. Then he made his way along the familiar waterfront, fear nagging at him. She must have been really angry and desperate to leave like this. He silently cursed himself. He'd been a fool to believe she wouldn't try. Hadn't she asked him time and again to release her? And everything had been so bad between them when he'd left that morning. Visions of Elyse taunted him. He saw her dressed in a man's riding pants and jacket, in a man's formal attire . . . in old trousers and shirt, just like the impish little beauty he'd met that day. She was stubborn, defiant, and strong willed.

He'd gotten no less than he deserved, but this time he feared she didn't know what she was getting into. This wasn't London, where her grandmother was well connected and the Barrington name could shield her from danger. This wasn't a morning romp to Jane's Folley in the Woods, or a prank like slipping into a discreet men's club. This was Lisbon, dangerous, deadly; and no place for a young lad, much less a young lad who wasn't a lad at all.

It was dark. An hour earlier, Elyse had found the tavern known as the Green Dolphin Inn. Now she waited outside. The oil lamps at the corner cast soft shadows a few feet down the street, then everything was plunged into darkness. Suddenly a light appeared as if by magic. The Green Dolphin's door had opened.

Actually, Elyse thought with a frown, it had opened frequently, sailors having wandered past her in the shadows to slip into the place. Others had emerged, unsteady on their feet, assisted by friends or alone, had staggered a few feet then become violently ill. Elyse pulled back into the shadows of the building across from the tavern. Above, in second-story windows, lights glowed; families were enjoying their evening meals. Occasionally she heard voices as people passed by, the squall of a cat, or the cackling laughter of the woman whose shadow appeared briefly at a window, then disappeared as a disembodied arm reached for her, pulling her from view once more.

In spite of the warmth of the cape, Elyse shivered. The waiter at the restaurant had warned her this was not the place to be. But it was where his wife's cousin Santo worked, and hopefully the man would know of a captain who might be bound for England.

It seemed to Elyse she'd waited for hours. The cool night air, damp from the sea, had given the wool cape a heavy musty smell. She couldn't wait any longer, and quickly walked across the street, her sandals noiseless on the cobbled bricks.

The interior of the Green Dolphin hit her in a wave of sights and smells. This was life at its lowest, drunken and perverse. If she'd feared the darkened streets of Lisbon, likening them to her worst nightmares, this was like no nightmare she'd ever experienced.

Tables sat about the tavern, surrounded by chairs. All were occupied by men: sailors, wharf riffraff, and a sprinkling of the scourges of humanity. Somewhere in this sea of human flotsam was Santo.

Elyse asked for him at the end of the long bar, keeping her eyes downcast. A burly, black-haired man with a sweeping mustache was pointed out to her. The quickest way to him was to follow the bar across the smoke-filled room, but that was also the most dangerous. She chose to work her way around the darkened perimeter, stealing behind collapsed chairs, darting out of the way of a weaving drunk, pushing another away when he careened toward the wall, and ducking beneath the swinging arm of a balding pirate who had taken aim at his companion's face. His companion was a garishly made-up woman whose stained satin bodice gaped away from mammoth breasts. The man missed, swung himself off balance, and then fell face first into that sea of flesh. The expression on the woman's face went from surprise to unroarious laughter, and she clasped him tightly against her, then dragged him to a room at the opposite end of the bar. The door slammed shut behind them. Elyse quickly decided she didn't want to know what went on behind that door. She inched her way up to the other end of the bar.

"What can I fix yer up with, boy?"

Elyse's head jerked around. "I . . . would like some information, please." She winced, realizing how ridiculous such proper language must sound in a place like this. The man behind the bar obviously was thinking the same thing. His greasy brows shot up. "We don't give that away around here. Whatever you want, ya gotta pay for. If you want a drink, I got it."

Elyse squirmed. "I want to talk to Santo."

The man looked at her carefully, dipping his head slightly to see below the brim of her hat. Elyse lowered her head, shielding her face. The man shrugged.

"Hey, Santo. *Faça favor.*" He shouted in a poor mixture of Portuguese and English. Then he turned back to her. "You can talk, but not at the bar. I got payin' customers I gotta take care of."

Élyse nodded as the man Santo came up beside her, giving her a questioning stare. He wiped his hands on the long, white apron that draped the front of his body. "*Sim?*" He watched her warily.

"Your cousin's husband said I should see you." Again that guarded look. She supposed working in a place like this could cause that. "He said you might know of someone with a ship going to England."

"England?" He reached across the bar in front of her and took from it a tray with glasses and two bottles of dark amber liquid. With a noncommittal shrug of the shoulders he turned away, crossing the tavern to serve the drinks. Elyse drummed her fingers on the bar. Perhaps the man didn't understand. When Santo came back, she leaned over, trying to make herself more clearly understood. "I need passage, on a ship to England." She made the motions of a ship sailing on the water with her hands.

"England," she repeated.

"I understand what you are saying," he replied in faultless English. Elyse held back a choice comment.

"Do you know of someone?"

He looked at her speculatively. "I might. But such a thing would cost a great deal of money. Where would a boy like you get that kind of money.?'

Elyse started to say she had it with her. But looking around she hesitated. Thieves and cutthroats. Santo himself didn't look very trustworthy. She'd liked the waiter, but she vaguely wondered how this man had become a part of his family. "I can get it," she said bluntly.

Santo only snorted as he moved behind the bar, nodding to a customer at the far end. Elyse's gaze followed him as he took a bottle to the customer. Her eyes widened. If there were such things as pirates on the high seas, this man surely was one.

He wore bright red pants, sashed at the waist with a broad black belt that barely controlled a belly that was bulging through the strained buttons of his soiled white shirt. The long, leather vest he wore hung practically to his knees. His girth almost matched his height, and his chubby legs overflowered black leather boots whose cuffs were rolled just below his knees. He was bald on top of his head, but a matted fringe of hair grew around the perimeter of his skull and fell past his shoulders. His gleaming forehead, set far back on his head, lapped over his eyes in a series of folds, and was accentuated by what should have been black, bushy eyebrows. Instead, they were just one continuous, shaggy brow that grew out of the area above his eyes. And those eyes were what frightened her.

They were like narrow slits, pig eyes in the flat, fat plateau of his face, pink rimmed and without lashes. They drew back only slightly over stark white eyeballs broken only by the barest pin dots of blue pupils so pale they faded into the white. And they were cold eyes, gleaming with strange lights in spite of the fact that the tavern was dimly lit.

He reminded her of a great black bear she'd once seen gaily dressed in fine clothes at a country fair. But fine clothes hadn't kept the bear from breaking its tethers in a fit of rage and turning on everyone within striking distance.

Now, as Santo spoke to the man, he shifted those evil eyes to her, looking straight at her but seeming to see through her. Then, if it was possible, those pig eyes narrowed in scrutiny and she felt fear slip down her back.

"So, little man." With this gruff acknowledgment, the bear shifted his weight and came toward her down the length of the bar. "You are looking for a ship bound for England. I might be setting a course for England. If the price is right." He chuckled at some private joke only he understood. Then he leaned toward her, his stench preceding him so that Elyse was forced to hold her breath if she wanted to stand her ground. She knew running would only invite trouble.

He guffawed as the brim of her hat dipped lower, shielding her from his view. "But it doesn't look as though you have the price, little one."

Elyse's head came up. Zach had called her that; the nickname had seemed endearing on his lips, a casual caress spoken as he'd made love to her. Dear God, how far away all that seemed now, and in spite of the anger that had sent her from the *Tamarisk*, she found herself longing for that safe haven. Elyse swallowed hard. She hid her pale, small hands beneath the cape, lest they give her away. She was here, and must see this through.

"I have the price, *senhor*," she boldly informed him, lowering her voice as much as possible.

"Ah! So the boy can speak. I was afraid you might be a mute." The bear roared with laughter. "Like the last one I had." He turned and noded to several men at a table close by. Were they friends, fellow sailors? Their uproarious laughter echoed his. A more dangerous and deadly lot Elyse was certain could not be found, and she couldn't throw off the shiver of uncertainty that warned her she was venturing into something very dangerous. Still, what other choice did she have?

"So what do you say, my little friend." The bear clapped her so hard on the shoulder he almost sent her to the floor. Then he patted her, his hand squeezing down cruelly over her shoulder. "You are soft, little one. I would almost think there was a girl beneath that cape you wear. But I don't mind the softness. So, tell me, if I were to risk my ship and my crew on this voyage to England, what would you pay us?"

Elyse had the wind knocked out of her. She straightened, pulled the hat more securely down atop her head and lowered her voice once more. "I have gold and there would be more when we reach England."

"Ah, more when we reach England." He winked a pig eye at a companion nearby. "But what if you are lying? What if you only have a few coins or none at all? I make the trip for nothing, at great expense to myself and my crew. But if you have something more to offer . . ." he suggested.

Elyse shook her head. "I have nothing else."

A smirk distorted the bear's face. Then he became like a hunter stalking prey. "There is always yourself, little one."

"Myself?" Elyse gasped. Great balls of fire! Had the man seen through her disguise? Was some of her hair hanging below the hat? My God, what should she do now? "I am sorry, *senhor.* I will look elsewhere," she mumbled, backing away from the bar. Neither she nor the grinning bear paid any attention to the shadowy form that moved in a darkened corner of the Green Dolphin.

Zach had arrived in time to hear the last of the exchange. He'd trailed the "boy" with those exceptional blue eyes from the shop where Kimo had purchased the silk to the restaurant and then to the Green Dolphin. Ultimately he would have looked here, knowing from past experience it was a gathering place for sea captains and their crews, and also knowing Elyse would be desperate to find a way back to England. No one had so much as turned to glance in his direction as he slipped in through the front entrance. Those present were too enthralled with the conversation between the slender young "man" in the bright-colored cape and the wide walrus of a man at the bar.

Zach's hand settled over the pistol in his belt, quietly pulling it out. He was dressed all in black, wearing his pirate's costume as

Elyse would say, the better to move about the darkened streets of Lisbon undetected. He knew sooner or later his crewmen would come here in their search. A quick look around the dimly lit tavern confirmed that they hadn't arrived yet. Whatever he decided, he was on his own with Elyse.

If he or she later tried to recall the events of the next few minutes, each would have decidedly different tales to tell.

From Elyse's position near the bar, it seemed the entire tavern erupted at once. Deciding that she would have to look elsewhere for someone to take her to England, she stepped back and tried to get past the bear and make it to the door. She screamed in terror when he lunged for her, drawing back instinctively. From somewhere over her shoulder she heard a sharply barked command that was oddly familiar, then her name cut through to her as the bear tried to pin her to the bar. Zach! She almost cried out his name, she was so glad to hear his voice, though it carried a note of urgency. Looking up, Elyse saw the danger.

The bear was descending on her with large, grimy paws outstretched. She ducked, losing her hat, then heard a loud exclamation as her hair tumbled to her waist. Seizing the momentary advantage, she glanced in the direction from which she'd heard her name called. A stealthy shadow moved there, and Elyse started toward it but found her way blocked. Instead of being pulled back as the bear expected, Elyse used the same trick she'd once used on Zach. She lunged for the bear, cringing as her hands pushed into mounds of lumpy flesh, but it worked. Caught off guard, the bear staggered, teetered off balance, and then collapsed into the middle of a round table, sending it crashing to the floor.

Curses filled the air, punctuated by shouted commands. Elyse was seized from behind, an arm cutting off the air at her throat. Then she saw him, and knew no sight had ever been more welcome. Zach emerged from the shadows, and the expression on his face, the deathly light in his eyes was more frightening than anything she'd ever seen. He raised his gun and aimed right at her. Elyse, screamed as the gun discharged. Instead of feeling a bullet rip into her, she felt the arm at her throat go lifeless, and the weight of the man who'd been holding her fell from her shoulders.

Zach grabbed Elyse and pulled her behind him. For the moment the element of surprise was working to their advantage. He fired at several other sailors who lunged toward them. A few were still pinned beneath the mountainous weight of the table on which the flattened pirate lay. One by one, they struggled out from under that weight as Zach slowly backed Elyse away from them. The others formed a human barricade at the front entrance. With one hand on her wrist, Zach propelled Elyse toward the small room she'd seen at the end of the bar.

"No!" She tried desperately to explain, but Zach only kept pushing her. Then she was alone; Zach had stepped away from her.

"Get out of here!" he shouted. "There's a door out the back, through there." He fired again and again, two men falling at his feet. Then he drew the cutlass.

Elyse felt as if she were fastened to the spot. She couldn't run and she couldn't scream. Then she saw him, the great bear of a man who'd attacked her. He slowly rose from the splintered wood-pile that had once been a table, drew an equally long blade from his waist, and shouted orders. Immediately the wall of men descending on Zach fell back and the bear pushed his way through. A venomous smile appeared below the pig eyes.

"So, Zachary Tennant, we meet again. And now you think to have what is mine."

"Back off, Vimeiro."

"Senseless warning. There is no escape. Even if the girl gets away, I will still have you. There are at least twenty of us and you . . . are apparently alone. A fatal mistake, my daring friend."

"Only for you, Vimeiro. As it was once before," Zach reminded him. If it was possible, the pig eyes narrowed.

"Only you would be so daring to remind me of that. But in truth, I have never forgotten it. Now, you see, the situation is reversed. I am in control here, but I feel I can be generous."

"What are you talking about?" Keeping up the conversation with Vimeiro, Zach slowly backed Elyse to the door of the room.

"I am an honorable man, Zach Tennant. I will give you a chance to fight for the girl."

"Why should I fight for her when she's already mine?"

The bear stiffened at the arrogance of the man caught in a trap. He chuckled. "But only yours if you can succeed in getting her out of here and away from twenty men. On the other hand, if you were to fight for her and win, I would be forced to allow both of you to go unharmed."

Elyse cringed as Zach laughed. He was mad to taunt a mindless giant like Vimeiro. "That is, of course, assuming that you are honorable, which everyone here, including your crew, knows is not the case."

Her knees practically buckled beneath her. What was Zach trying to do, provoke this bear into attacking? Suddenly, he whispered to her, "Whatever happens, you get to that door. Don't stop. Get to the ship."

"I won't leave you."

"You can't do me any good!" Zach hissed at her, his well-muscled body forming a protective wall between her and the man known as Vimeiro. "Just get out of here."

"Right," Elyse muttered, knowing full well she wouldn't. He'd risked his life in coming after her. She might be foolish, but she wasn't ungrateful. She backed up a few steps, glancing over her shoulder to the closed door and praying it wasn't locked.

"All right, Vimeiro. I'll fight you and I'll beat you again."

"Agreed. We'll fight with cutlasses, like true pirates. And we'll both turn our guns over to my men, for safekeeping." The man was already gloating.

"Forget it. The girl gets the gun."

Elyse stared at Zach, wide-eyed. Great balls of fire, she hoped he knew what he was doing. She'd never so much as laid hands on a pistol before. But Zach was bluffing, and wasn't about to give the man any quarter.

"I may as well warn you, Vimeiro. She's a dead shot. I taught her to handle arms."

"As fond as she seems of you, I'm surprised she hasn't used a pistol on you."

"She has no need to do so. I give her whatever she wants."

Elyse almost choked on that last comment. She would have if she hadn't been stunned when Zach thrust the pistol into her shaking hands.

"If anyone moves, shoot them!" he bit off curtly. Then, transferring the cutlass to his right hand, he prepared to face Vimeiro.

The bear had the advantage of weight, and he was surprisingly strong for a man his size. But he was slow to move, and was forced to yield and change position constantly as he lunged and found nothing but air where Zach had been a moment before.

They grappled, they slashed and backed away from each other. Then they lunged, each trying to catch the other off guard and to strike a deadly blow. Zach was strong and much quicker, but he was hemmed in by men who owed allegiance to his enemy. Any one of them would cut him down at a signal from Vimeiro.

Therefore, he couldn't afford to stay in one place; he had to keep moving.

Vimeiro, on the other hand, acted the part of the bear Elyse thought he resembled. He stalked, lumbered, grunted, and stalked some more, wearing Zach down with swipes and lunges that weren't necessarily meant to draw blood. She stared at the men encircling the combatants, and she knew. Honorable indeed!

"Zach, they're all closing in on you!" she whispered to him as he once more crouched before her. Her warning was loud enough for the others to hear and brought an infuriated grunt from Vimeiro.

"Just as I thought," Zach hissed. "You don't know the meaning of the word 'honorable.' Therefore, Vimeiro, I will be forced to kill you." He lunged, missing; quickly recovered and lunged again.

This time, Vimeiro side-stepped at the moment of contact, swung around with surprising agility, and lunged, his cutlass aimed at Zach's shoulder.

Elyse screamed but quickly recovered as the wall of men began to close in on the deadly match. She waved the gun threateningly. "Anyone takes another step and I'll blow his head off!" she said coldly, desperately hoping she could carry out such a threat.

Zach and Vimeiro struggled. They were like contorted dancers now, their movements frightening. Arms slashed out and were blocked. Zach stood, bracing himself against Vimeiro's weight; then he countered a blow and lunged at the bear. But the bear wasn't about to be struck down without a fight. The foes whirled away from Elyse to be lost in the shadows as they stumbled over chairs and bodies. Then Zach lunged back into view and Elyse sighed with relief. But he was moving differently now, his fatigue showing; and he was constantly turning his left side away from Vimeiro's blows. The giant lunged after him, and Elyse screamed a warning. Instead of moving out of the way, Zach side-stepped, agilely spun around, and brought the hilt of his cutlass down hard across the back of Vimeiro's head as the huge man stumbled to the floor.

Vimeiro lay crumpled, unconscious, on the floor. A deathly silence hung over the tavern as his crew stared at his still form, open-mouthed. They found it impossible to believe their leader had again been beaten by this man. Not waiting for them to recover and give chase, Zach lunged for Elyse and pushed her through the door of the small room. They were obviously in some sort of store room. Hundreds of bottles lined the floor-to-ceiling shelves; casks and wine barrels stood about.

Elyse had a quick glimpse of the woman she'd seen earlier. She was sprawled on a wooden counter top, her bright red skirt riding high over her waist. The bodice of her gown had been pulled down, revealing massive, jiggling breasts that fell to either side of her body. Her head came up off the table at the interruption.

"Hey, what's this? Who the hell do you think you are, barging in on a lady?"

The man bending over her wasn't the least disturbed. "Shut up, Consuela," he growled, never missing a stroke as he moved between her legs. His trousers were down around his ankles, his white bottom was as bare as his balding head; yet he thrust back and forth while Consuela let out a string of curses that would have raised the dead. Then her words became oddly muffled.

"Ah, Duffy, you make a girl feel like a queen," she said. Then she started another round of curses as Vimeiro's men ran past.

"They're after us." Zach grimaced, pushing Elyse ahead of him. Another door blocked their escape.

"Go!" Zach ground out.

"I can't! It won't open!"

"Here!" Zach shoved passed her. He tried the lock. It did not give. Drawing back, he threw his entire weight against the door. His face paled as it budged slightly.

Elyse threw a worried look over her shoulder. Vimeiro's men were only a few feet away when Zach lunged at the door again, this time forcing it open.

Again glancing back at the men descending on them, Elyse would have little chance of escaping unless she could stop them. As she went out the door, her gaze fell on barrels stacked on their sides on a dray where they'd been recently delivered. There was no time even for a small prayer; Elyse took aim as she'd seen Jerrold do countless times when she'd gone hunting with him. She jerked back the hammer and pulled the trigger. A deafening roar filled the storeroom, followed by a creaking groan as the rope severed and a mountain of barrels rolled free. They bowled over the first men to rush out the door, knocked others to the side, and still kept rolling. One split open as it crashed into the building and sent a sea of red wine washing over everyone.

"Elyse!"

She plunged down the narrow alley at the back of the tavern, and Zach's hand closed over hers.

"We've got to get out of here."

400

She couldn't have agreed more. If she'd counted right that was the last bullet left in the gun. But Zach hesitated beside her, and she practically went to the ground as he sagged onto her, putting one arm around her shoulders.

"What is it?"

He braced himself against the wall of the building, his breath coming in uneven gasps. Then he laughed, a hard, cynical laugh.

"Either I'm getting slower or Vimeiro has lost some weight and he's getting better."

He pulled her close as footsteps sounded in the alley. Elyse held her breath as someone passed by. Dear God, she hadn't counted on some of Vimeiro's men coming around to the back of the tavern. She could hear cursing from inside the storeroom. They had to get away and quickly. Zach took her hand and pulled her to the street. A lamp overhead pooled soft light on them as they emerged. They could hear voices heading the opposite way. It would take only a few minutes for the men to start searching in this direction.

"Which way is the ship?"

Zach chuckled. "So now you're willing to go with me."

"I hardly think this is the time to discuss it," she said sarcastically, still scared out of her wits. "Come on!" she prodded.

"Not until you say it."

"Say what? For heaven's sake, Zach, they'll find us. Do you want to have to fight Vimeiro again?"

"Say that you want to go with me."

He spoke with a lazy drawl. Great balls of fire! What was wrong with him?

"All right. I want to go with you."

He smiled faintly in the lamplight and reached out to stroke her cheek. "I don't think I'm going to make it." He braced himself against the lamp post.

Elyse's head came up, her alarm sharpening. "What are you talking about? We have to get back to the *Tamarisk!*" His arm was around her shoulders, holding her tightly against him. Elyse pulled away to look up into his face and she gasped. Through his shirt a warm, wet, stickiness was soaking through.

"My God! You're hurt!" She stared at the stain spreading across the vibrant colors of her cape, blending them into that sickening crimson color.

"I have to get you back to the ship," she declared as she secured his arm around her shoulders so she might bear his weight.

"I'll never make it," Zach groaned.

Elyse cried out softly, turning into him. "Dammit, you can't die on me. Not here!" Nothing she'd said made sense, and she knew it.

"There's a place near here."

"Where?" She dashed the tears from her eyes. Now was certainly a foolish time to be crying over this man. But for as long as she'd known him, she'd been doing just that.

"Zamora's," Zach whispered between pale lips on which a smile briefly appeared. "She's an old friend."

Zamora. The name conjured up visions of another friend of his, the one she'd met in London at Jerrold's club—Fatima. She wondered if Zamora was the same type of friend, then quickly thrust the thought from her mind. It was none of her business; they needed help.

"How do we get there?"

"It's not far from here." He winced, inhaling sharply as she took his weight against her. "Two blocks to the left, three to the right. At the place with the sign of the half-moon over the door."

"Oh, so you're familiar with this neighborhood. You really should pick your friends more carefully." That got a rise out of him.

"Elyse, unless you think you can carry me, I suggest you be quiet and start walking. I'm not sure how long I'll be able to stay on my feet."

She shook her head as she slipped her arm more tightly around his waist. "The Green Dolphin Inn and now a place with a damned half-moon over the door. Will my life ever be normal again!" Elyse murmured as she supported his full weight.

She wasn't certain how they accomplished it. They stopped and started many times, night sounds sending them into darkened doorways. But Zach seemed to know where they were going. God, she prayed he wasn't incoherent. He'd lost so much blood, she didn't know how he stayed on his feet, much less whispered encouragement to her.

Now she was frantic. They'd stopped and she'd searched every façade, every doorframe and window molding, all number signs and name plates. Zach kept insisting this was the street and finally she found the half-moon carved over a doorway. She lifted the iron knocker and pounded.

"Elyse, for God's sake, are you trying to tell everyone where we are?"

"No!" she hissed back at him, afraid he would pass out on her at any time. "Just this friend of yours! I hope she's a good friend." Whoever this woman was, Elyse desperately hoped she was home. Zach smiled wickedly back at her from the shadows of the doorway.

"She is." He sighed heavily.

Elyse gritted her teeth and knocked again. Why should it make any difference to her what his relationship was with this Zamora? It shouldn't! But it did.

After what seemed an eternity, a bolt was released inside, the door opened a crack, and a small voice whispered, *"Quen é?"*

Elyse drove frantic fingers back through her tousled hair. "I don't understand what he's asking!"

Beside her, leaning against the doorframe, Zach inhaled sharply against a new wave of pain. "He wants to know who it is," he explained and then groaned to the small voice.

"El Cuervo." Zach suddenly grabbed for the doorframe as he felt himself going down. The last thing he heard was Elyse crying out as he collapsed and fell unconscious through the doorway.

Chapter Nineteen

Elyse stared as a small form emerged from the doorway. It belonged to a dark-haired boy not more than ten or twelve years of age.

"Cristo!" he exclaimed, and whistled softly as he bent over Zach. Then he turned and dashed back inside.

She started after him but then hesitated. She couldn't risk leaving Zach alone. So much for friends, she thought angrily. As soft light struck the walls of the small hallway, she looked up. A bent form in a long shawl crept toward them, followed by the boy and two men who looked no better than the one they'd just left. Great balls of fire, what was going to happen now? Elyse seized the heavy cutlass from Zach's limp hand and protectively stood in front of him.

The bent form halted, holding a lantern up high, and Elyse could see it was an old woman. Zamora? The light from the lantern slipped up Elyse's body until it revealed her face. The old woman mumbled something in her native language, and the boy quickly came around and whispered back to her. Elyse understood nothing of what they were saying, except two words she'd heard before — *El Cuervo*.

At the sound of the name Zach had given the boy, the old woman's eyes came alive. She made a soft clucking sound between her teeth; then, completely ignoring the cutlass, she brazenly pushed past Elyse and once again held the lantern aloft. It spread golden light over Zach's unconscious form and the spreading pool of blood beneath him.

Elyse immediately went to Zach's side. When the old woman held out a cane, poking at the stained black silk of his shirt, Elyse immediately batted the cane away.

"No!" she hissed. It was the one word she knew was easily

understood. It immediately brought a response from the boy as well as the two men she'd forgotten about. Elyse swallowed her fear as they came out of the shadows toward her. She didn't care what they did to her, but she wasn't going to let them hurt Zach. He'd risked his life in coming after her. It was her fault he was hurt. She owed him this much.

One word from the old woman halted the others; her authority unmistakable. Was this Zamora? It was hard to believe. The look on Zach's face when he'd mentioned the woman's name was secretive, almost that of a lover. Surely this woman wasn't Zamora. But Elyse must know if this woman would help them or harm them. It was clear Zach could go no further.

She tried to make herself understood, speaking very carefully and slowly. "I need to find Zamora."

Again that fathomless stare and dangerous silence.

Elyse groaned. Her knowledge of Portuguese was so limited. Her Spanish was hardly better, but she decided to try it. She desperately sought the words she needed. Blood. She pointed to Zach's shirt. "*Sangre. Mucho sangre. Por favor.* I need to find Zamora." She stared at the four mute faces, tears of frustration pooling in her vivid eyes. How could she make them understand? "*Por favor!*" Please, she thought desperately, help us.

The woman turned and Elyse panicked. No! She couldn't just leave them there.

"*Vem!*"

At that word, the two burly men moved in on her. She brought the blade up with both hands, but the first man swatted it aside as if it were no more than a bothersome fly. He moved past her before she could recover, and started to lift Zach. She stared as the other man seized Zach's legs. As they lifted him with great care, her gaze shot to the old woman. The boy had already run on ahead of her, up the small flight of stairs at the back of the hall. He stood on the small landing at the top, holding open a door, the light from inside the room lighting the stairs.

"You are brave, *senhorita*." The old woman spoke perfect English. "Do not be afraid."

Elyse stared after them in confusion. If this was where Zamora lived, then where was she? Zach was carried to a bed in one room of the small apartment. She hastily followed the glow of light, gasping as he was laid on the bed, his face pale and haggard.

405

Orders were given in a rapid flow of the old woman's native tongue. Then the two men quickly left the room, and the small boy took up the lantern. The old woman carefully unbuttoned Zach's shirt, spreading the black silk away from the knife wound.

"Take the lantern," she curtly ordered Elyse. To the boy, she said, "Fresh cloths, hot water. Hurry!" He bounded out of the room.

Elyse held the lantern aloft as instructed, though her hands were shaking. The old woman looked up at her briefly. "He has lost much blood."

Elyse nodded mutely. "There was a fight at the Green Dolphin. Where did those two men go?"

"Do not concern yourself with them." She glared at Elyse. "We must think of him." The boy had returned. "Hold the light steady!" she growled to Elyse. Then she muttered to the boy, "Take the lantern from her before she drops it." She jerked her head toward the lad, and he quickly took the lamp.

"You must help me!" She looked up at Elyse. "And quit shaking. You will do him more harm than good."

Elyse's eyes flashed at the sharp remark. "I got him here, didn't I?"

The old woman chuckled, a deep gravelly laugh. "So you are spirited as well as brave. Amazing for one so small. Are you a girl or a boy?" She gestured to Elyse's clothes.

"I hardly think this is the time to discuss it!" Elyse bit out. "Shouldn't we bandage him before he bleeds to death?"

The woman turned sharp eyes on her. They were old eyes that had undoubtedly seen much, but they were as alive as the boy's.

Elyse panicked as the old woman hesitated, just staring at her. "He's alive, isn't he?"

"Is that important to you?"

"Of course it's important to me!" Elyse blurted out. "Why else would I have brought him here?"

The old woman only shook her head, then began applying bandages. They quickly turned crimson beneath her wrinkled fingers.

"Where is Zamora?" Elyse whispered, her eyes dark and frightened as she stared at the flow of blood that seemed undaunted. "He wanted me to find Zamora."

The woman ordered her to take her place. "I am old and not

so strong. You must do this. I am Zamora."

Elyse moved beside Zach. Her small hands crossed over the thick pad, applying pressure until the muscles between her shoulder blades ached. Still she wouldn't relax. If she did the bleeding would begin again.

"It is no good," Zamora announced, drawing Elyse's startled glance. "The bleeding will not stop. The wound must be closed."

"What are you talking about?" Elyse's startled gaze locked with the old woman's. "You have to help him. Surely there is something else that can be done. Perhaps more bandages?"

The old woman shook her head. "Look. Even now the bandages you hold are filled with blood. If the wound is not closed, he will die. I have done it many times for my own people, but there is great danger." The old woman sat back, more folded bandages in her hands.

"What danger?"

"There is the possibility that the knife may have done more damage inside. If I close this outside wound, he may continue to bleed inside. Then it will be only a matter of time until he bleeds to death." Zamora drew a heavily veined hand across her forehead, smoothing back a strand of silver-streaked shoulder-length hair. "There is only one way to be certain. I have seen this many times. My people are very adept with knives. If the wound inside is not cared for, it could also fester and fill with poison. He will then die a slow and very painful death, long after the bleeding has stopped outside."

Elyse swallowed back the fear that constricted her heart. She squared her slender shoulders, determination glittering in her vivid sapphire eyes. "Then we have to close the wound inside as well."

"Yes." The old woman nodded her agreement. "But I cannot do it."

Elyse paled, her throat going completely dry and making it almost impossible to swallow much less speak. "You have to do it! There is no one else!" Her voice grew stronger. "Dammit, he asked me to bring him here. He said you could help! I thought you were a friend!" she accused, her eyes glistening fiercely.

The woman shook her head. "I am a friend, more friend than you will ever know, little one. But there is only so much old Zamora can do. Do you think I like what I tell you?" She came out of the chair, her long, skinny arms waving through the air in a gesture of helplessness. Gold and silver bracelets flashed through the silence. "I owe El Cuervo my life!" She flattened a hand against her breast. "There was a time when I hoped he would take my Yasmine to wife; she dances, using the name Fatima. But they are much the same, volatile and dangerous when angry. They would have torn each other apart if they married. Still I look upon him as a son. But I cannot do what you ask. I would do him more harm with these old hands."

Elyse hung her weary head, too tired to understand everything the woman was saying. "He'll die if the bleeding isn't stopped. I won't let that happen, simply because you're afraid to try." She fought back tears of fear and frustration. Breathing past the constriction in her tight throat. She thrust her fingers back through her disheveled hair, as she tried to think. Then her head came up. Her eyes were hard and determined.

"Tobias!" she whispered as if the name were a prayer.

The old woman's eyes narrowed. "That old man is here?"

Elyse nodded. "Aboard the *Tamarisk* in the harbor." She breathed more easily as relief washed over her. Tobias would come! He would do what was necessary to save Zach.

Zamora spat out contemptuously. "The old fool is probably drunk. You'd be killing him to let Tobias touch him."

Elyse eyes riveted on the woman. "It seems I have no choice! At least he's not afraid to try." She didn't voice her own fears. It was true. She'd seen Tobias several times when he'd had more than his share to drink. But in his sober moments, his hands were steady. She'd trust him sober or drunk before she'd trust this old woman.

"We must send one of the men to the ship."

"No!" the old woman grunted. "They are needed to guard the door. Whoever did this to him will still be looking for both of you."

Undaunted, Elyse stood up. "Then I'll go myself!" She met the woman's gaze defiantly.

"He might die while you're gone."

"You won't let that happen," Elyse declared with more confidence than she felt. After all, she didn't really know this woman. "You said yourself he is like a son to you. Would you let your son die?"

"You have the fire and spirit of a Gypsy, little one." The old woman cackled. "You are right. I will not let him die. For one with light eyes, he is worth ten Gypsies." Her old eyes darkened. "Stay with him. I will send the boy."

Elyse protested. "You can't! It's too dangerous! He's too young."

"The boy will be all right. He knows the streets of Lisbon. They are dangerous only for those who do not know them. Besides, I would not risk him any more than I would risk El Cuervo. After all, the boy is my grandson." She called to the lad and rapidly gave instructions in her native language. He handed her the lantern, then bounded from the room.

"The boy will bring Tobias, though I think you make a mistake in this."

"No." Elyse shook her head firmly. "He would want it." She looked down at Zach, a silent prayer on her lips. Live! Please, dear God, let him live.

It seemed they waited an eternity. Elyse kept pressure on the wound, until Zamora pushed her aside to relieve her. Then she couldn't keep still. She fussed, she paced, and she constantly checked the draped window. Then she whirled around at the sound of footsteps on the stairs. She flew to the cutlass, drawing a sharp look from the old woman.

"Do you think my sons would let anyone else come into this room?"

Tobias came through the door, followed by Sandy and Tris. Elyse thought she would collapse, so great was her relief. Tobias's eyes immediately went to Zach, then found her as he rounded the bed. "Are you all right, girl?"

"Yes," she whispered brokenly, causing him to look up.

Her eyes were wide pools in the soft oval of her face as Tobias examined Zach. "Can you help him?" Doubt washed over her. Still nothing but silence, and that deepening frown on Tobias's careworn face. "Tobias!" she whispered, desperation in her voice.

He never looked up. "He's lost a lot of blood, lass, and his pulse is very weak." His grave eyes met hers. There was a faint twinkling of hope in them. "I'll do my best." Then, sensing that she needed more, he smiled gently.

"He's strong. I've seen him take worse." He fixed a speculative gaze on her. "Does it matter to you?"

She hesitated, caught off guard. She'd been certain of her feelings at the Green Dolfphin when she'd first laid eyes on him, and she'd been certain when she'd thought Zamora's sons might hurt him. "Yes," she admitted frankly. "It matters."

Tobias nodded and smiled faintly. "Good." It was only a beginning, but it would have to do. He watched her carefully, wondering just how much courage this beautiful girl did have. "I'll need help, and I don't trust that old crone with her herbs and potions." He gestured to Zamora. Obviously their contempt was mutual. His remark brought a withering glare from the old woman, but she held her tongue.

Elyse was stunned but quickly recovered. "I'll do whatever I can."

"Good girl. Step over here and bring my bag, then wash your hands thoroughly. And have that boy step closer with the lamp. My eyes aren't as good as they used to be and we've got some stitchin' ahead of us." He nodded to Tris and Sandy. "Go on back to the ship. I can handle everythin'. here. He's not goin' anywhere for a while." The men nodded and left the small apartment.

As long as she lived, Elyse would never forget the next hours. Zach roused only once, as Tobias made the first incision. Then, as pain engulfed him, he quickly fell unconscious. Rejoining the cut tissues was a time-consuming process, and it required all of Tobias's skill and concentration. Both his hands were bloodied to the wrists in a very short time, and Elyse constantly blotted blood from the wound so that he could see what he was doing. Time and again, she poured disinfectant over the wound as he'd instructed her. And time and again, she was certain she could stand no more — no more blood or cut flesh, no more watching the frighteningly shallow rise and fall of Zach's chest as he breathed.

She fought the screams at the back of her throat, closed her eyes, and could still see blood. How was it possible to lose so much and still live? She couldn't imagine anything worse than standing there, helpless. She wanted to hold Zach's flesh together with her fingers so the bleeding would stop. She'd lost all track of time. Her back ached from standing bent over in one position for so long and her arms had long since lost all feeling. She felt like some sort of mechanical creature, obeying Tobias's commands, handing him scissors or needle, cutting the thread he stitched with, wiping his forehead to keep the perspiration from running into his eyes. If there was a hell, this was surely as close to it as anyone could come.

And always there was the blood. Elyse was certain as long as she lived she would see it every time she closed her eyes. It was as if her own lifeblood were slipping through the cloths and cut flesh, staining everything. And then, miraculously, there was no more blood. She wiped the wound and stared at the bandage as it came away clean. Her startled gaze shot up to meet Tobias's.

"Aye, we're done. It's closed and the bleeding has stopped, for now." He wiped his hands across the front of his shirt, now stained with dried old blood.

"Will he live?"

The old physician straightened, aware of the stiffness in his back. He rolled one shoulder to ease the nagging pains that had set in there. "Ah, now you ask quite a lot. It's hard to say. I hope so, Elyse." Tobias smiled. "He's strong and he's a fighter. But perhaps Zamora could answer that better than me?" He turned gruffly to the old woman whom he obviously held in equal contempt.

"What do you say, old Gypsy? What do you see with those old eyes of yours? Or perhaps you could brew up some tea and ask the tea leaves?"

She came out of the chair where she'd been watching everything with dark, glistening eyes. "Be careful, you old sea turtle, or I will throw you in a pot of boiling water and make soup of you. I've always thought that would do you a great deal of good," she snapped.

"Ah, enough of your threats, Zamora. I'm tired and the girl is about ready to collapse. He can't be moved. So it looks as if you have house guests at least until morning," Tobias informed her, undaunted by the old woman's ravings.

"They're welcome to stay, old man. But I should throw you out for your insults."

"Then who would tend to his wound, should he awaken?"

Zamora's eyes narrowed as she took a step toward Tobias. "My medicine is as powerful as yours, maybe more powerful."

"Then why didn't you use it, old hag." Tobias was weary, his eyes were red rimmed, his even temper was fast fading.

Zamora sniffed indignantly. "Because she repays my kindness by insisting that I send for you. But I understand what is in her heart. It speaks what her words will not say. And because of that, I am willing to do as she asks. Now, plague me no more, you fool!" She thrust a bent finger toward another doorway. "You can sleep in the boy's room. He will not mind, and he will not be inclined to slit your throat." She turned to Elyse.

"I'll stay in here," Elyse announced flatly. She had no idea why such animosity existed between Zamora and Tobias, and she really didn't care to know right then. She just wanted to be near

411

Zach in case he awakened and needed something.

The old woman shrugged her shoulders as if to say it made no difference to her where Elyse slept, but her keen eyes watched as Elyse dropped into the rocking chair beside the bed, then pulled it closer and curled sideways in it, facing Zach so she could see him the moment he awakened.

Elyse must have dozed off. She roused slowly at the pressure of a hand on her shoulder. Confusion clouded her senses; where was she? Then her gaze fastened on Zach and she immediately came upright in the chair. The clawlike hand restrained her.

"He is all right and still sleeps."

She relaxed slightly as her eyes focused on the old woman. A single lantern cast a faint glow in the room. It was still dark. How long had she slept?

Zamora waved toward the small table across the room, where bowls had been set. Streamers of steam curled lazily above each, and Elyse thought vaguely of the tea leaves Tobias had mentioned earlier. She hesitated, wondering if the woman really was a Gypsy.

"You must eat. How can you care for him, if you are weak?" Zamora motioned her to the table. "Come. There is nothing you can do for him right now. More than anything, he needs rest. Soon the fever will start and then you will work very hard."

Elyse rose slowly, a hand-stitched blanket falling from her lap. She picked it up, slightly confused. She didn't remember having the blanket earlier.

The old Gypsy smiled. "You were restless in your sleep, and it gets cold at night when one is so close to the water." She motioned to a chair.

Elyse threw her hair back over her shoulder. "I couldn't sleep. I kept seeing things."

Zamora's eyes narrowed as she placed a basket of bread on the table. "Ah yes, dreams. Sit and eat." She took the chair opposite, positioning her small body on the seat as if she were a watchful bird on a perch.

Elyse rubbed her weary eyes. "What about the fever?" She glanced back over her shoulder to Zach. He seemed to be resting peacefully enough, the rise and fall of his chest indicating even breathing.

"Always it is so with an injury such as this. The fever will come when his body fights off the poison that comes with the wound, no matter the precautions one takes." Zamora smiled as she gestured to the bowl of steaming liquid. "It is not the finest meal, but it will keep the hunger away."

Elyse thought nothing had ever smelled quite so delicious. Chunks of meat and fresh vegetables filled the well seasoned broth. And long strands of noodles and chunks of a rich dough mixture completed the mixture. It was wonderful and made her think of the ensopado she'd enjoyed at the restaurant the day before. My God, had that only been a few hours ago?

She dragged a shaking hand through her sable hair, sending it in a dark fall down her back. As her questioning gaze met the old Gypsy's, she wondered what other ingredients might be in the soup. It was as if the old woman read her thoughts.

"I am a very good cook. My great-grandfather taught me. There is nothing in the soup to harm you."

Elyse blushed in embarrassment. "I didn't mean to imply . . ." She took a large spoonful of the soup. "It's delicious," she proclaimed without the slightest hesitation. "My grandmother's cook would pay handsomely to know what you've put in it." At the thought, a wave of homesickness washed over her. The spoon hung suspended midair as she thought of her grandmother, Uncle Ceddy, and Katy, all left behind in England, not knowing her fate. Her soft blue eyes brimmed with unshed tears.

Zamora watched her with keen eyes, instinctively understanding there was a great sadness in this young woman. "I know you have come a great distance and I would gladly give you the recipe for your cook, but it is not written down. It is made with a little of this and a little of that, a pinch of herbs and whatever else can be found in my kitchen."

Elyse smiled through her tears. What good would they do her now? "No magic Gypsy potions?"

"Bah!" Zamora exclaimed. "That old fool Tobias would have you believe I chant incantations over a witch's brew and fly about on a broom." She gestured about the small room. "Do you see a black caldron?"

"I see a pot of soup," Elyse confessed.

"Yes, and you must remember everything is not always as it seems. Eat before your soup grows cold." Zamora pushed the basket of warm bread toward Elyse.

Aware of the old woman's steady perusal, Elyse said, "Everything is not always as it seems. That pot of soup just might be a

413

witch's caldron."

"Only to that old fool of a man." Zamora laughed with her. "Being a Gypsy is my heritage, not my profession. He would have you believe we ride around in brightly painted wagons, make campfires in the hills, and steal from rich travelers."

"But you don't," Elyse surmised.

Zamora fastened on her those fathomless, secretive eyes. "I am too old to ride around in a wagon, and my bones feel the coldness of the earth around the campfire. Why should I travel about to steal from rich travelers when that can be done right here in Lisbon?" Her mouth spread into a teasing smile so that Elyse wasn't certain whether she lied or played at some joke.

"And you tell fortunes with tea leaves," Elyse teased in return.

"Tea leaves! Bah!" Zamora shook her head, sending silvery, waist-length hair swinging back and forth at her hips. "That is for silly old women with nothing better to do, and superstitious fools. I am neither, in spite of what that old dog tells you." She poured two earthenware tumblers full of sparkling, deep crimson wine. Then her smile returned. "Tea leaves are unreliable."

Elyse smiled as she took a sip of the wine. She liked Zamora. "Do you make the wine as well?"

"This is made by a friend. He brings me more than enough wine to share with friends."

"Is Tobias a friend?" Elyse broke a piece of bread off and dipped it in the heavy broth as was the custom.

Zamora laughed, the throaty sound coming from deep inside. "Yes, in spite of himself. He is a friend of El Cuervo. That is all that matters. And I respect his skills as a physician. I would never have attempted such an operation. His skills have stopped the bleeding. Now Zamora's skills will defeat the poison that will come with the fever. It is not necessary that we like one another, only that we respect each other."

Elyse was surprised by the woman's candor and astuteness. "Does he respect you?"

Zamora nodded. "He would rather die than admit it is so, but whenever the *Tamarisk* is in Lisbon, Zach comes to see me. And he always asks for my special healing herbs. I am not fooled. I know it is the old man who asks for them, but he is too proud to do so himself." She said no more for a long time, concentrating on the soup before her. Nibbling on a piece of bread, she watched Elyse. "He is afraid to admit that an old Gypsy knows more than he when it comes to healing potions. That knowledge is handed down through the generations of Gypsies, unlike the ability to foresee things which comes to only a few."

Elyse's gaze came up, her soft blue eyes darkening and giving her away.

Zamora smiled knowingly. "Even now you are wondering how I know you have come a great distance."

Elyse shrugged. "It's not so difficult to guess. You undoubtedly know I was aboard the *Tamarisk* and we only just arrived in Lisbon. And I certainly don't speak your language."

Zamora nodded. "Yes, there is a great deal that is obvious on the surface, but there is much more that I see in you."

Elyse smiled. "And now you want to tell my fortune." She'd once had her fortune told by a Gypsy in a traveling caravan that camped on her grandmother's country estate. She was only a child at the time, but she'd quickly learned the woman's technique of drawing out pertinent information with innocent conversation, then turning it around to make it seem she actually was able to know about other people's lives.

"What do you see in me?" She slowly drank the wine. "How much money will you ask to tell me my fortune?"

Zamora's eyes narrowed as she realized the girl didn't really believe her. And why should she? Still there was something about this one. "I do not want your money. And I do not tell your fortune. Only you can tell your fortune. I am merely the seer, like a window that you look through to see something. But you mock me. You think Zamora is a cheat, a charlatan." Her eyes narrowed again, then she burst out laughing. "Perhaps you are right!

"I cheat because I refuse to use the talent that I have been born with, the ability to see what others cannot, to predict events. I could be a very rich woman, but as you see"—she gestured to the small room and its sparse furnishings—"I chose not to exploit my gift."

"The ability to see? To read tea leaves in cups?" Elyse was trying to be polite.

"No!" Zamora growled. "That is fools' talk, I know of no true Gypsy who believes in reading tea leaves. I believe in what I know here." She pointed to her head, to her sleek hair bound back by a blue silk cloth. "And what I feel here." Her hand rested solemnly over her heart. "And I know that you have traveled a far greater distance than you did on the *Tamarisk*."

Elyse shook her head. She was tired and in no mood for the

woman's ramblings. "I suppose you can tell me where my journey began and will end."

She immediately regretted her sharp words. Whatever Zamora was or pretended to be, she had been generous with her house, her food, and her care of Zachary. Elyse had no right to criticize her.

But Zamora had known countless people who'd doubted her, at first. She nodded tolerantly. "I cannot tell you. Only you can know that."

A slight frown turned the corners of Elyse's mouth. "But you're supposed to tell." She was confused. This was certainly not how a Gypsy should go about telling her fortune.

"Ah, but you see, you doubt my abilities. So I will let you see for yourself. Here, I will show you what I mean." Zamora opened her left hand and extended it across the table. "Each of us has lines within our hands. And these lines mean something. This one" — she pointed to the one crossing the top of the palm from just below the index finger — "is the line that tells what the course of love will be. As you can see, the line in my hand is long, but shallow and broken in many places. I will tell you what I have told no one else." She leaned across the table as if she were sharing a great secret.

"I have had five husbands and at least as many lovers. My sons do not know this, but they are only half brothers. I have loved many times, but never deeply and only briefly."

Elyse had finished the soup and bread. A warm comfort filled her. She propped her elbows on the edge of the table as she sipped the wine that slipped soothingly over her senses. "Like the broken path of the heartline."

"Exactly so," Zamora concluded. "I knew this as a young girl, but I chose to ignore it. Had I heeded the teachings of my great-grandfather and the knowledge I was born with, I would have taken greater care and loved more wisely."

Elyse opened her fingers, staring down at the palm of her own hand. The exact same line was deeply etched and continuous across her palm, unbroken with no divergent paths.

"That isn't always right," she said, thinking of the divergent path her life had taken in the last weeks. Did the heartline account for abductions?

"It is not for me to say. Only you can say that." Zamora offered no more as she sipped her wine. But she quietly studied the beautiful young woman across from her.

416

"What about the other lines in the hand?" Elyse became more curious as the soft glow of wine spread through her.

The old woman smiled. "There are many. Their significance is matched to different aspects of a person's life; the happiness a person will know is indicated in the line very near the heartline."

Elyse laughed with the old woman. "Are there others?"

Zamora shrugged. "Yes. One indicates health and another indicates whether you will know great riches or poverty." Her eyes twinkled. "But wealth can be measured in many ways. It is not always measured in the amount of gold in one's pocket."

"Please tell me more."

Zamora's eyelids lowered. The girl doubted her. She was merely being polite, thinking to humor an old woman. She sensed this but didn't think badly of Elyse for it. There were always skeptics. Zamora sighed. She brushed fingers across her forehead. Feeling an unusual chill in the room, she stood and moved to place another stick of wood on the fire.

"You think to fool an old woman."

Elyse's eyes opened in appreciation of her ability to know what she was thinking. "Yes, I do."

Zamora stirred the fire, frowning. She'd sensed something in this one the moment she'd laid eyes on her. It was that knowledge of her great-grandfather's that allowed her to see beyond the façade of skepticism. There was something about the girl; something worldly in spite of the innocence, something sad and almost mournful in spite of the bright light in those beautiful eyes. Ah yes, Zamora thought, in spite of the youthful beauty, there is a very old soul in this girl.

"I shouldn't bother with you," the old Gypsy grumbled, knowing it would not be easy to convince this one. "You do not honestly believe, and there is danger in that if I tell you what I see."

Elyse extended her hand. "I won't lie to you and tell you I believe in your abilities. If you have the power you claim, you would see right through that. But I will admit that I believe in the possibility of such powers," she admitted.

The old woman's eyes narrowed. Elyse was being completely honest. She didn't believe in Zamora's powers but she did not disbelieve either. An open mind was a place to start.

"All right." Zamora brought a bottle of wine back with her, and smiled at the young beauty before her. "I will tell you a Gypsy's tale of great love, wealth, and travel to foreign lands."

She filled both their cups, then sat in the chair across the table. With great ceremony, she smoothed back gleaming tendrils of silver black hair from her wizened face and pushed back the ornate bracelets on her arms. She threw back her head, eyes closed, clearing her thoughts. No doubt the girl would think this all quite amusing, but it was necessary, this clearing away of everything around her.

Zamora opened her mind as she opened dark, glistening eyes, closing out everything else except this room, the table, and the young woman sitting before her.

"Give me your hand," she commanded softly, her dark eyes hooded. Her slender, aged fingers were warm from stirring the fire. She cupped Elyse's hand in hers, gently spreading the fingers, until they were relaxed, and then she stared for a very long time, the silence drawing out in the room.

"What is it you see? No riches, travel, or love of a handsome stranger?" Elyse speculated with faint amusement.

Zamora looked up at her slowly. Her black, fathomless eyes were filled with mysterious light. They were old eyes, ancient, and filled with the secrets they saw in those twin pools of sapphire blue. The old woman tried to shake off the visions and whispers that came to her. She wanted to doubt this beautiful girl. It was too impossible, a part of an ancient legend handed down from one generation to another of her people. But as she again looked down at the small hand in hers, she knew it was true, and she also knew that her entire life had been lived for this moment. She must not waste it, and she must find a way to make the girl understand what it was she saw.

"Is something wrong?"

Zamora frowned. Again that feeling of coldness seemed to fill the room. But it wasn't the cold, empty feeling that usually came with the forewarning of something dreadful about to happen. It was like the mist shrouding the harbor in the cold winter months. She stared again at the outstretched hand before her, quickly enfolded the long fingers within her own, and then pushed Elyse's hand back. No, she thought. There is too much doubt in this one. She will not accept the truth.

"I see wealth, happiness, and travel to a distant land," she stated simply and rose from her chair.

Elyse had sensed it too, that vague almost illusive something almost within her grasp; and then it was gone like the visions from her dreams. It was as if it were there for a brief moment and suddenly gone. She'd thought to humor the old Gypsy, but now her own sense of loss was almost unbearable. It was like reading an entire book only to find someone had torn out the last pages. It was a hunger for food that was within easy reach and then was snatched away. It was being lost in a fog and suddenly seeing a light up ahead, only to run toward it and have the mist close in all around. She couldn't disguise the disappointment in her voice. Perhaps it was that she desperately needed answers when there were none, had never been any.

"Is that all? You didn't see anything else?"

Zamora was busy at the stove. She poured water from a huge urn into the simmering pot of soup, then cut up more vegetables and chunks of meat. She turned, fixing the girl with that penetrating stare. Perhaps this one really did want to know. "What more could you want than wealth, love, and happiness?"

Elyse frowned. This was hardly what she had expected. She'd virtually called the woman a fraud, a charlatan who took money from people for the predictions she could give with the second sight all Gypsies claimed to have. But this woman had not asked for money and had now refused to tell her what she'd seen.

"What did you see?" She held up a hand when Zamora repeated the words, feeling a tremor of apprehension. Why was it suddenly so important to know what the woman had seen, or had thought she'd seen?

Zamora shook her head. "I do not think you are prepared to hear the truth."

"Nevertheless, I want to know," Elyse insisted.

The old woman returned to her chair. She took both of Elyse's hands, her dark eyes boring into sapphire blue. "Yes, perhaps you are strong enough to accept the truth. Perhaps it is time for you to understand." Her hand tightened over Elyse's. Slowly she spread the fingers apart, exposing a soft, vulnerable palm.

"This"—she pointed with her finger—"as I told you, is the heartline." She stopped, staring down at Elyse's hand. "That is very strange. For most people it is broken by tiny lines to one side or another. That means they will experience more than one love in a lifetime. But yours runs very deep. It is long and unbroken. That means you shall have one great love in your life, and only one. And you will find great happiness." Zamora hesitated. Her fingers closed warmly over Elyse's hand.

"Go on. I want to know everything," Elyse persisted. After all, what could be so dreadful that the old woman wouldn't want to tell her.

The old Gypsy nodded and continued. "Here is where the lifeline is usually found." She drew her finger in a wide arc from the inside of Elyse's hand just above her thumb down to the heel of her palm. Then she stopped and drew her finger away. Where she indicated, there was no line, only the smooth unbroken plane of smooth skin.

Elyse stared down at her hand. Then, with faintly amused eyes, she looked up at the old Gypsy. "I don't seem to have a lifeline, and yet here I am, very much alive." It was as if to say she'd indeed proven the old woman to be a charlatan.

Zamora looked up at her, those ancient eyes boring into Elyse's, seeing beyond the present moment, into past moments, years, and lifetimes.

"The lifeline does not signify whether a person lives or not, but the length of one's life."

Elyse laughed softly. "How can you measure something you can't see?"

The old woman only stared at her. "You already know the answer. You have always known it. It is only that your conscious thoughts would not let you accept it." The old woman gently released her hand.

"But how can you measure something when you don't know where it begins or ends." A tingle of fear slipped down Elyse's spine. What was the Gypsy trying to tell her? She snatched her hand away, closing out the truth. She didn't want to know.

Zamora continued. There was no other choice, now that the path had been chosen. She must tell the girl everything, force her to confront and accept the truth, or she would be lost forever.

"My great-grandfather told the story of a man he once knew. This man had no such line on his hand. But he had the ability to vividly recall another life in another time and place. Those who knew him said he'd always had those memories since he was a small child, from the moment he'd learned to speak. And he knew of this life, down to the most precise detail; could recall the names of people and places, events that he couldn't possibly know of unless he'd seen them. They would come to him in his dreams, and he would speak of them as if he were actually living and experiencing everything again. He spoke of leaving one life and entering another." Zamora leaned far over the table, her gaze boring into Elyse's. "The lifeline measures the beginning

420

and the end of life. The pattern may be short or long, but always it is there. And it speaks the truth. I know, for I have seen it in many. This man possessed no such line across his hand, because his life had no beginning or end."

Elyse stared at her incredulously. "What you're saying is impossible! A person is born, lives, and dies. That's all!"

"Is it? Can you deny that even now you are troubled with dreams you do not understand?" Zamora went on to tell Elyse what she already knew. "You've had the dreams since you were a child, and always they are the same, over and over again."

Elyse looked up, fear congealing inside her. She was frightened of hearing what the old woman would say, more frightened not to. "Go on."

"There will come a time, perhaps it has already come, when the dream becomes almost real to you. It is merely part of a larger picture, not a dream, little one, but a memory of something that happened before, in another time and place, in a previous life."

"No!" Elyse whispered vehemently.

"You may deny it with every breath, but you know it is true. I see it in your eyes."

"You're wrong. You know nothing about me. You're only guessing, playing at some trick!" Elyse suddenly stopped denying it, memories of her vivid dreams playing back across her mind. She rubbed her fingers across her forehead as if to wipe out the incredible possibility that Zamora had suggested. She wanted to laugh, or cry, most of all to deny this, to call it witchcraft or fanciful imagination. But she couldn't.

"I am not wrong." Zamora calmly confronted her.

Elyse refused to meet that dark gaze, afraid of what she might see. "Are there others like this?"

Zamora nodded. "There is another," she answered simply. "One other that I have known of in my entire life."

Elyse looked up, following the line of the old Gypsy's gaze to the bed against the far wall on which Zach slept.

She whirled on the old woman. "What are you saying!"

"I am saying there are many things in this world that neither man nor God can explain. There are those who live many lives, perhaps searching for something, or someone. It is there in your hand. You have no lifeline because you have lived many lives, and may live many more. The truth is there. Can you deny it?"

"You expect me to believe this?" Elyse demanded.

"I expect nothing of you. You asked me to tell you what I saw and I have explained it to you. Whether you choose to believe it or not is up to you. For some reason only you can know, fate has brought you two together again. But I warn you, if you ignore what I have told you, there is a possibility that the two of you may never find each other again, not in this lifetime or any other."

Zamora rose on unsteady legs, suddenly very weary. It was always the same when she used the gift of inner knowledge.

"I must take food to my sons. You must check his bandages. Make certain there is no bleeding. And then you must make your decision."

"What decision?" Elyse was confused. Great balls of fire! What was the woman rambling on about now?

Zamora nodded understandingly. "You must decide whether to accept what fate has offered you or turn away." She looked to Zach, whose long body was stretched out on the bed against the wall. "He has taken you from your home and another man against your will. I know this. Now, in his condition, you have the opportunity for freedom. If you take it, he will never find you again. All will be as it was before. What will you do, my little cat? Only you can decide." Then she was gone, a bowl of soup in each hand, the door slightly ajar as she made her way down the darkened stairway.

It was impossible! Surely the woman was mad! What she suggested was unbelievable. Incredible. Yet it left a nagging fear deep in Elyse's heart. How was it possible for the old woman to know so much about her when she'd told her nothing, when they'd met only hours ago?

Elyse was unable to sleep after the old woman left. Instead she paced, thoughts turning over and over in her mind. Everything she'd been taught negated what Zamora had told her. People didn't live one life and then simply drift into another. It just didn't happen that way. It didn't!

But even after the old woman returned and made her bed upon a pallet of blankets before the hearth, the doubts remained. It would have been so easy to ignore what the Gypsy suggested, to dismiss it as nothing but foolishness, except for the dreams. Always there were the dreams, filled with visions and images she didn't understand much less recognize. The only thing she was certain of was that those images were not from her own life. They were pictures from another place and time, played back through her mind over and over and over. . . .

Another place and time. My God, Elyse thought, fear taking hold. What if it were possible? What if the old woman's words were true? What if she had lived more than one life and Zach had somehow been a part of it?

There is another I have known in my life.

The old woman's words haunted her. There had been no reason for her to tell such a fantastic story. Zamora had asked for neither gifts nor money. She'd asked for nothing.

Elyse slowly walked to the bed on which Zach lay. There was no chair nearby so she sat on the floor. Gently, so as not to waken him, she turned his hand in hers, exposing first one palm and then the other. She swallowed back the denial. Then she uncurled her own fists, tightened against the truth. The same.

She rubbed at her palms with a vengeance, twisting and turning them, retracing the lines that did appear, staring at the place where another should have been. Elyse closed her eyes and pressed her hands against the throbbing ache in her temples. It was impossible!

Slowly her eyes opened and she stared at his sharply chiseled profile, at the long, straight nose, the golden lashes fanning down over those penetrating gray eyes, hiding them from her. A stubbly growth of golden beard glistened on his cheeks and in the indentation just above his upper lip. She stared at him and would have sworn they'd never met before that first night in London.

I knew you'd come back to me.

The words she'd first spoken that night echoed back to her, and it was true; this man now haunted her dreams. His was the face that looked back at her through the mist, his arms were the arms closing around her. Tears pooled softly in her eyes.

And the Gypsy was right about something else; she could leave now. Zach was powerless to stop her, and she felt certain Tobias would do nothing if that were her decision. She should go, run as far and as fast as she possibly could. It would be so easy to do just as she'd planned when she'd left the ship. She still had the gold coins in her pocket. She could easily slip out before anyone awakened. In her heart, she knew the old woman would never try to stop her.

Only you can decide what you will do.

It could all be done so easily. She would find a ship and return to England, and Zachary Tennant would still have his opportunity for revenge, for she knew Jerrold wouldn't rest until he'd found him.

What was it that made her hesitate? "It isn't possible, is it?" she whispered to no one but herself.

But what if it is true? her thoughts echoed in answer.

"Who are you, Zach Tennant? And who am I?" She rested her head on the bed, against his hand. There would be time enough to decide in the morning.

Zach was certain he must be dreaming. He opened his eyes and everything was blurred to a soft shade of gray. Morning? He tried to sit up and immediately felt weakness and pain wash over him, sending him back down onto the bed. He sensed rather than felt the motion of the cabin around him. Was he aboard the *Tamarisk?* His vision cleared. It wasn't his cabin at all, but a room, and the first light of day was just coming in through the narrow slit between drawn drapes. God, but it was hot in here. He tried to move again and felt the gentle restraint of something very like silk around his fingers. Lis. He whispered her name as memories came back to him. They were in Lisbon . . . at the Green Dolphin. He'd gone there to find her. She was here now, safe, beside him, her head resting on the edge of the bed beside his hand. But what was she doing on the floor? Then sleep washed back over him.

Elyse was wakened by the heat of Zach's hand against her cheek. She drew back gently, untangling her hair from his long fingers. She looked to the window. The first gray light of dawn was just slipping through the slit in the worn drapes. There was still time. She pushed herself to her feet and quietly made her way across the small apartment. As she thrust her hands into her pockets, coins tinkled reassuringly. Except for that faint noise, all was quiet. Everyone was still asleep. She slipped silently out the door. Somewhere between Zamora's ridiculous story and the cold light of day, she'd made her decision.

Still she hesitated. Why? What was it that held her back, like invisible strings refusing to let her go? Run! Run! And she did, out into the street, stumbling through the mist that rolled up from the harbor, beads of moisture mixing with the tears that fell down her cheeks. Run!

Zach jerked awake. His body was drenched in sweat at one minute, burning with dry heat the next. He tried to moisten his lips and found his mouth was dry. His fingers curled instinctively seeking to feel the cool silkiness of her hair, and closed over emptiness. The memory of the night before came swimming back to him across the gulf of pain. He looked around. The small apartment was vaguely familiar. Zamora's! But how? His fingers convulsed into a tight, hard ball. Clamping his teeth against the pain, Zach came up off the bed as he remembered. Damn! She was gone, really gone.

He forced himself to his feet and staggered across the small room, bracing his weight on the small table on which two empty bowls sat. She'd been here, he remembered it. But how long had she been gone?

The dizziness returned, draining away the last traces of strength. He had to find her and bring her back. Seizing the knob, Zach twisted it violently as he lunged against the door. It opened out onto the landing. He stared into the gaping darkness of the stairway. And then everything was dark. Blackness swirled around him, closing in like a silent beast taking everything else away. Taking Elyse.

Chapter Twenty

Elyse ran. She didn't know where she was going, only that she must get to the waterfront. There, somewhere, she would find a ship returning to England. She turned a corner not far from the building where she'd left Zach and Tobias, but ended up in a short alley that led to the rear of the building she'd left. She ducked down it and into the street at the end. Crossing that, she dodged sidewalk vendors, fishmongers, and people emerging from their homes to begin the day's work.

She ran until her sides ached. Twice she thought she saw crewmen from the *Tamarisk*. Each time she darted down the opposite street, looking back over her shoulder, as she ran on.

Elyse screamed as a grimy hand clamped down over her mouth and an arm went round her middle, practically cutting off her air.

"Well, well. Looky what we got ourselves here, Chappy." A grunt of approval came from the shadows as Elyse struggled to free herself.

"Hey, ain't it the boy that started all the trouble at the Green Dolphin?" Another, heavily accented, voice speculated.

"One in the same, my fine friend." A face loomed out of the shadows bending toward Elyse. The sickening smell of filth, fish, and body sweat made her stomach turn over.

She squirmed, groaning helplessly under that hand that prevented her from crying out. Beads of sweat broke out between her breasts and trickled down, molding the dampening shirt to her every curve. If they hadn't already guessed, they'd soon see that she wasn't a boy at all.

She freed one arm and swung hard, hoping to throw her captor off balance. Then she spun away from him.

"Oh, no you don't, you little wharf rat!" the first man grunted as he reached out, seizing her by the only thing he could grab, her cap.

It came away, and in one dark swirling mass, her hair tumbled about her shoulders.

"What the hell?" He stared in amazement at the cap.

Elyse gasped as the realized the most essential part of her disguise was dangling from the man's hand. She lunged away a moment too late, crying out as her hair was seized and jerked painfully.

"Well, well. Look at this, will ya! Either we got ourselves one of those eastern Hindu boys, or this ain't no boy at all!"

Elyse was roughly spun around. Her hand instinctively went to her hair in a futile attempt to loosen his hold. Bile rose in her throat as she was drawn up against the man, her body forced against his.

"Just as I thought. This ain't no boy at all!" The man declared triumphantly as he crudely ran a hand down Elyse's body.

She jerked away from him, causing herself no small amount of pain. "Get your filthy hands off me! You pig!"

"And feisty too. El Barracuda will be real interested to know why you were disguising yourself. But then I always did think he cared for young boys as much as he cared for them whores he visits in port. But yer a bit skinny. Maybe he won't like you at all."

The man's meaning was obvious for he'd run his hand down her back, lingering over the curve of her bottom. She lunged away from him, only to be brought up short by the grip on her hair.

"Hey, Quid, take it easy with her. You may be right. But she may be able to tell El Barracuda what the Raven is carryin' in the hold of that ship he's guardin' so well. You rough her up too much, and she won't be able to tell him nothin'."

"You're wrong. I don't know anything about that!" Elyse spat out.

"Shut up!" the man called Quid grunted as he seemed to consider what his companion had said.

"Yer right." He nodded. "I sure as hell don't want to make him angry. All right, we'll take her back to the ship and let him question her. He'll let me have 'er when he's through."

Elyse cried out as she was easily lifted and thrown over Quid's shoulder. When she tried to kick out at him, he efficiently clamped one arm over her legs. Pounding his back with her fists,

427

Elyse let out a string of curses. They were cut off as a stained, foul-smelling rag was stuffed in her mouth.

"That's just so's you don't draw too much attention before we can get you to the ship."

For a response, Elyse swung at the man called Chappy. Her wrists were seized and quickly tied. All the way to the ship, she was bumped and jostled over that hard shoulder, the air slammed from her lungs as she dangled upside down. Damn the Count de Cuervo, or Zach Tennant, or whoever he called himself. Damn him! This was all his fault!

For two days Zach ordered the streets of Lisbon searched, and for two days his men returned with the same response: nothing. There was no sign of Elyse. She had completely disappeared.

He insisted on returning to the *Tamarisk*. If Elyse were to come back, she would go there. He was fighting off the effects of the wound and of the medicines Tobias had been pumping into him. He tried to stand, felt the floor shift beneath his feet, then heard his friend cursing explosively.

"What are you putting in that brew of yours, old man?"

"Somethin' you've used a time or two yourself. Now, you've got to stay put or that wound will open again," Tobias firmly instructed.

"Is there any word?" Zach winced as he tried to prop himself up. When the dizziness swept over him, he collapsed weakly back against the pillows, cursing ill-tempered Gypsy women and physicians who liked to practice their skills on unfortunate souls.

"Not a word." Tobias frowned. He didn't say that he didn't think there would be any. Elyse had chosen to leave before. It was only by sheer luck that Zach had found her at the Green Dolphin. He looked up as the second mate suddenly appeared in the doorway. He pulled Sandy into the companionway, out of Zach's range of hearing.

"Any word at all?"

"None. The men have returned. There's no sign of her. But we've other matters to consider. There's word along the waterfront that a ship is due in from Oporto to the north," Sandy informed him.

"Barrington?" Tobias's brow furrowed.

"There's been a lot of activity at the Barrington docks. Word has it he's on her himself."

"Damn! And us stuck in port. There'll be hell to pay if Barrington bottles us up in this harbor."

"I was thinkin' the same thing," Sandy admitted. "How's the captain?"

Tobias shook his head. "Not fit for sailin' or fightin'. As second mate, it'll have to be your decision."

Sandy shifted uncomfortably. He'd sailed a good many years with Zachary Tennant, crossed more oceans than most, raised hell in more harbors than many could remember. But never once had he taken over command of the *Tamarisk*. And he didn't like to do it now.

"Is there any chance he can give the orders?"

"He's in no condition. If he so much as goes up on deck, he'll open that gut wound again. You'll have to take over, Sandy." Tobias nodded grimly. "You know better than anyone what his decision would be."

"Aye, I know," Sandy agreed. "I'll give the orders. You just keep him quiet and don't let him move about. If we can get her out of the harbor unseen, we'll have a chance to make it."

The orders were quickly given. The late morning breeze had picked up, and it gently rustled the sails as they were slowly unfurled. Strong backs leaned into the ropes, hoisting the anchor. Lines were drawn taut and ropes were secured as the *Tamarisk* moved like a great majestic bird across the glistening water toward the open sea along the southern coast, the Strait of Gibraltar beyond.

Eyes watched as the graceful ship slipped through the water. The deckhands aboard the *Sultana* winched in their own anchor. Loose sails were drawn taut to catch the late morning breeze, and like a menacing predator, the heavily gunned frigate creaked through the water, slowly gaining on the open sea that beckoned and the rich prize she pursued.

Below decks, Elyse squinted at the glaring light thrust into her face. She cried out as she was jerked forward, tripping over ropes that bound her ankles, falling to her knees in the slime-filled water that sloshed about in the bowels of the ship. She tried to break her fall with her bound hands, cringing as her fingers sank into the filth and sludge that lined the hold. Then she was jerked upright by the back of her collar, the light again piercing her eyes. Always it was the same, slow torture. No food, no water, only the endless questions.

"Now, missy, we'll try again," the taunting voice wheedled from behind the lantern. "What is the cargo aboard the *Tamarisk?*"

Elyse shook her head. The same question had been asked countless times, and she had given the same answer. "I don't know," she croaked from between dry, parched lips as she forced herself to look in the direction of the voice. She was so exhausted, but she'd give them no satisfaction.

"I wasn't allowed in the hold, and no one said anything about the cargo." Her head slumped forward. "I don't know anything."

She was lying, but she'd die before she'd tell them the truth. She could barely stand she was so weak. She hadn't eaten since she'd left Zamora's, and the good crew of the *Sultana* weren't about to offer her anything.

Her thoughts were blurred, but she tried to hold on to just one. If she gave in to the bone-aching weariness she might let something slip. It would have been so easy to tell them about the gold Zach hoped to sell in Lisbon. It might still be aboard the *Tamarisk* for all she knew, but as long as she could still think she wouldn't tell them of it.

El Barracuda. That name, the memory of that face, haunted her. He'd almost killed Zach; she wouldn't give him any information. It was a small revenge, but she was determined to have it.

Zach. In the two days since she'd been taken captive she'd thought of nothing else. Zamora's words swam back to her through the fog of fatigue and hunger.

There will come a time . . . when the dream becomes almost real to you. It is merely part of a larger picture, a memory of something that happened before, in another time and place, in a previous life.

The light glaring in her eyes waned and flickered. She blinked hard, trying to concentrate on the droning voices. Dear God, she was so tired. They'd been at this for hours, never allowing her more than a few minutes' rest before starting in again with their questions. If they would just go away and let her sleep. The faces of the two men blurred into one and then disappeared completely; then she was floating where there was no more hunger or fatigue, only blissful sleep.

Elyse shivered. It was dark all around her and she was deathly cold. Her thoughts drifted, somewhere between the reality of the present and the memories of the past.

Please don't leave me again. A voice echoed back to her from the shadows of dreams. It was her own. *You promised, and I've waited so long for you.*

It seemed so real. Hands, strong and warm, closed over hers, taking away the cold. She saw herself as a child, then a woman, and she was dreaming again. The dream changed and the woman was no longer the same, yet it was she. Like fragmented pieces of a large mosaic, the picture slowly came together—a man and woman. The woman turned and Elyse knew she was staring at herself. The man beside her turned. His eyes were soft gray with hidden lights that seemed to reach into her soul.

I promise I will come back to you. You are my life, you are my soul. Wherever you go, I will find you. I promise.

"Zach!" Elyse jerked upright, her eyes staring into the gaping darkness, her breath coming in great aching sobs. "You promised."

Promised what? Elyse was shaking uncontrollably. She'd been dreaming again. The old Gypsy's words came back to her over and over.

"My god, it's not possible," she whispered brokenly. She wanted to deny it. The Gypsy was wrong! Yet even as she thought it, she couldn't convince herself.

I warn you, if you ignore what I have told you, you may never find each other again, not in this lifetime or any other.

Other memories, more recent ones, flashed through her thoughts. One of them was of meeting Zach on the night of the engagement ball. Even now she couldn't explain why she'd said what she had. And there was the trip to Fair View, a place she'd never seen before yet somehow knew in unerring detail. That feeling when she'd stepped from the coach, as if she'd truly come home at last. The stained-glass windows . . . how could she possibly have known there was to be another rose in the design? And the dreams, always the dreams. And always the same, since childhood. The same, until . . . until she met Zachary Tennant and they'd become lovers.

Was it possible? Could Zamora be right about their link to one another? Had they somehow known each other in another time and place, as lovers. Had they been soulmates sworn to each other for all eternity and then somehow separated?

It contradicted everything she'd ever been taught of life and death. And yet, what if . . . ? What if she and Zachary Tennant had known each other before, in another life? What if the dreams were her memories of that life, a life with him? She couldn't deny the passion she'd found with him. Never before

431

had any man made her feel so alive, so complete, as if the greater part of herself were found in him and the passion they shared.

I warn you, if you ignore what I have told you, you may never find each other again, not in this lifetime or any other.

"I have to get out of here. I have to find him. Somehow, I have to know. If I don't find him, I will never know. There must be a way."

Elyse struggled upright. She was stiff and sore from sitting in a cramped position. But somehow she had to get of there. She tried to move. The ropes were gone, her feet, bare except for the leather sandals, were slipping against something slimy. She tried to crawl up out of the water.

A wall? She could feel the faint rolling motion. A ship! Everything came back to her. She was aboard El Barracuda's ship. Had it only been two days? Or was it more? Submerged in this darkness, there was no night or day. She couldn't be certain how much time had passed.

Elyse stretched her arms and legs, massaging feeling back into unwilling limbs. She was sitting or rather leaning against the sloping hull of the ship, her feet sloshing in a few inches of water. She picked at the cotton shirt, practically fainting from the smell. Small furry creatures brushed against her ankles, squeaking loudly. Elyse screamed as she lunged backward. Rats! Uncontrolled shivering washed over her. God, how she hated rats!

Her shoulder bumped into something stout. A box or crate? Elyse didn't waste time investigating. Although she was half-starved, she quickly scrambled atop it, pulling her legs up underneath her. Great balls of fire! What was going to happen to her now? She tried to think, but loud blasts shattered her thoughts.

Blasting? Dear God, this was El Barracuda's ship, and unless she was greatly mistaken, that was cannon fire! That could only mean one thing; El Barracuda was after a ship. The *Tamarisk?* Despite the confusion of the last two days, Elyse knew in her heart it was true. She had to get out of the hold.

Wide-eyed, she searched the darkness. Finally she spotted what she was looking for, a sliver of light overhead.

"It has to be a hatch," she whispered aloud. A hatch meant there had to be a ladder.

It was quite some distance away, and Elyse shuddered at the thought of sloshing through the water to get to it. What if the ladder wasn't there? What if El Barracuda's men had pulled it up after themselves to prevent her from escaping?

"What if?" Elyse thought miserably. "What if isn't going to get me across the hold of this ship." Inhaling deeply to steady her nerves, Elyse extended first one foot, then the other as she slipped down off the crate. Water came up around her ankles, and floating objects brushed against her legs. Could rats swim? The possibility that they could propelled her through the darkness to that sliver of light, her guiding star.

Several times she bumped into crates or barrels, and had to work her way around them. More times then she could remember, Elyse wanted to crawl atop the next crate and hide from the unseen creatures she was certain were in that hold. But the cannon blasts overhead propelled her onward. She hadn't endured so much these last few weeks to die in the hold of a ship.

She would not die in this hold. Another fragment of memory swept over her, and tears filled her eyes. She was a three-year-old child again, frightened and alone, the chaos of a storm tearing apart the ship on which she stood. Her parents were gone, and she was waiting, waiting . . .

Her shoulder grazed something solid. Elyse grabbed the ladder. Clinging to those solid rungs, she pulled herself up, up from the darkness until her head bumped against the restraint of the hatch.

As the ship shuddered, she struggled to maintain her precarious hold. What would she find up on deck? Would El Barracuda's men seize her and throw her back down into that hold? Another deafening blast exploded somewhere very close, and Elyse wedged her bruised shoulder against the hatch. It lifted easily, and she slipped her hands into the opening. Raising it just a small distance, she peered out onto the deck. Another blast rocked the ship, a heavy cloud of smoke momentarily blinding her. Elyse pushed with all her strength, rasing the hatch enough to allow her to slip through it, the smoke from the ship's guns hiding her escape.

The wind shifted and the *Sultana* came about. Sailors of every size, shape, and description ran past Elyse. She ran to the railing, bright daylight painfully piercing her eyes. Out across the rolling blue-green expanse of water was another ship. The *Tamarisk!*

Dear God, El Barracuda was attacking Zach and his crew.

"Here! Take this." A seaman thrust an ax into her hands, never looking into her face. "Try to free that line." He pointed to the splintered mast that dangled crazily across the deck. A distant roar echoed from the *Tamarisk*. Elyse whirled around, joy leaping in her heart. Then her joy was quelled by an overriding fear. The *Tamarisk* was returning fire, and she was right in the middle of it.

The schooner was lighter, faster, more maneuverable than the bulkier *Sultana*. Elyse watched as the gleaming ship cut across the course of the frigate, immediately trimming sail as she prepared to come back to starboard. Zach was turning the attack, bringing his ship about to bear down on the Sultana. One, two, three. Before she could blink the cannons fired in sequence.

Elyse had never been so scared in her life. One cannonball barely missed the bow of the frigate. Another sliced across the stern splintering through the deck railing. The third fell short, and *Tamarisk* ran before the wind to maneuver for another broadside attack. Smaller and less heavily gunned, the schooner had to rely on speed. Now she was vulnerable.

Frantically, Elyse scanned the deck of the *Tamarisk*. She couldn't see Zach. Dear God, where was he? The ship had sustained little damage that she could see, yet as orders were barked out aboard the *Sultana*, she knew the danger. El Barracuda was in an almost perfect firing position with no less than six cannons on his starboard side as *Tamarisk's* sails momentarily slacked for the waiting wind. The command was given, the cannons prepared, and still *Tamarisk* moved very slowly in the water, like an unsuspecting bird. Everything moved slowly as if in time out of time as Elyse's fingers closed over the ax.

She flew to the center mast. Dear God, did she have enough strength? She drew back the ax, swung high and wide from the shoulder, wincing as pain tore through her. Again and again, she swung, her aim falling short of the mark more than once. With dogged determination she swung again, this time, the ax sliced through the heavy ropes, burying its head in the heavy timber of the centermast.

"You there! What the bloody hell do you think yer doin'?" The roar came from behind her. But already it was too late. The ropes untwined and snapped, the heavy line snaking through the rigging. The sails overhead immediately went slack, fluttering in the wind like so much laundry in the midday sun. The *Sultana* was now the prey, dead in the water, only her momentum carrying her slowly along.

"It's her! That wench we took in Lisbon! Kill her!"

Elyse whirled around, her eyes widening at the sight of three seamen moving in on her. They would surely kill her for what she'd done. A blast from a distant cannon roared overhead as *Tamarisk* came about and gained position.

Attuned to the feel of his ship even through the delirium of fever, Zach was jolted awake at the sudden change in *Tamarisk's* course. They were at sea! Struggling up through the fog of pain, he came unsteadily to his feet. He vaguely remembered returning to the ship. He did not remember giving the order to set sail. He was forced against the post of the bed as the ship heeled sharp to starboard. Someone was maneuvering the schooner hard and fast. That meant one of two things; either they were trying to run before a storm, or they were changing position to elude someone—they were under attack.

Zach lunged toward the door, practically falling into the companionway. He shouted to his crew. There was no answer. Gritting his teeth against the pain that tore through his side, he slowly made his way to the ladder. With great effort he pulled himself up one rung after another, then thrust himself through the open hatch. Bracing his weight against the opening, he swung his long legs through. Then, with great effort he stood upright and whirled to the helm.

"What the hell is happening up here?" he shouted to his second mate, his voice carrying on the wind. Sandy's expression was grim as he nodded over the starboard bow. Zach followed his gaze, his own narrowing at the sight of the heavy frigate. The *Sultana* was dead on their course and closing the distance.

"Damn!" Favoring his bandaged side, Zach moved to the helm.

"Who gave the orders to put to sea?" he roared at his second mate.

"I did, sir." Sandy's expression never wavered.

"I take it you had good reason."

"Good enough. Barrington was two days' north of Lisbon. You were in no shape to make any decisions. I take full responsibility."

Zach only nodded. This was not the time or place to discuss it. As it was, Sandy had made the exact same decision he would have made, except for Elyse. That, too, was something he couldn't think about now.

"When was the *Sultana* sighted?"

"She left harbor right on our tail. The wind was against us or I would have put back into Lisbon." Sandy adjusted their course.

Zach was in no shape to take the wheel and he knew it. His gaze shot up the center mast, checking the trim of the sails. He motioned to Tris to have extra line pulled in.

"They're coming into position, sir. They'll undoubtedly open fire." Sandy heeled the *Tamarisk* hard to port, forcing the *Sultana* to adjust her course. "We could try and outrun her," he barked over the wind.

Zach shook his head. The wind was still against them. There wasn't enough of a breeze this close to shore. "We'll have to outdistance her." He winced against the pain beneath his ribs. Down the length of the deck, Tobias was making his way to the helm.

"Just what the hell do you think yer doin' up on deck?"

"Trying to sail my ship."

"You've an able crew for that! You'll open that wound again!"

Zach didn't ask the question that burned through him. If Elyse had been found and brought aboard, Tobias would have been the first to tell him.

He braced himself beside Sandy. What the devil was El Barracuda after? That crafty old pirate was a cutthroat, but he wasn't stupid. He wouldn't risk his ship unless he thought it worthwhile. Did he intend to attack? Zach had his answer as the *Sultana's* cannons roared, smoke belching from them.

"Damn!" Zach cursed then gave Sandy instructions to evade the attack. He fixed a weather eye on the center mast. Unless the breeze stiffened, they'd be forced to come about and fight or risk losing the *Tamarisk*. She was fast, built for speed rather than cargo. Her hull was of the finest teak, sleek and lightweight. She was outgunned, but each gun on the *Sultana* added unwieldy weight.

Cannonballs burst overhead, cutting a clear path over the *Tamarisk*. The schooner came about sharply, and the command was given to return fire.

Zach refused to go below. This was his ship and his crew. As long as there was life in him, he would stay on deck. Several well-placed shots caught the *Sultana* broadside. Zach didn't wait to glory over the advantage. He gave orders, had the sails trimmed even more and heeled the schooner hard to port, bringing her sharply about to continue the attack. But the *Sultana* had maneuvered as well; her starboard guns were now given a clear target.

Race the wind, Zach thought grimly. Cut sharply, pull in the

436

mainsail, and set her on a dead run across the bow of the *Sultana*. But the wind was fickle. It wavered. *Tamarisk's* sails momentarily went slack, giving the advantage to the larger, heavier ship. Aboard the *Sultana* a victorious cheer went up as the crew manned their guns.

"They'll cut us to ribbons, Cap'n." Sandy's expression was bleak, but Zach was already yelling to his men to turn the guns. It was a shootout on the high seas, the outcome almost certain.

"Look!" Tris gaped, his arm extended. Everyone aboard *Tamarisk* turned to stare at the *Sultana*. The heavy lines to her mainsail had been cut, and her sail flapped loosely in the wind as the heavy frigate tried to come about. Almost instantly, she fell dead in the water. Shouts were heard from her decks as the wind came up and rushed across the open sea, finding the schooner's taut sails and plunging her headlong through the water and away from *Sultana*.

Zach gave the orders and the *Tamarisk* was brought about, hard astern of the frigate. The *Sultana* was hopelessly crippled; her prize, the *Tamarisk* was lost; and her crew was furious.

Elyse thought for only a moment, then she jumped over the side of the *Sultana*. She heard the angry shouts of the crew and the roar of water rushing past as she plunged into the deep, cold sea.

It was a nightmare turned to reality as water pulled at her clothing and her body, refusing to release her, sucking her downward. She kicked violently with all the strength she possessed, pulled with her arms until they ached. And then, mercifully, she was rising, bubbles streaming past her, her eyes stinging from the salt water, her lungs straining to hold in that last precious breath of air.

Elyse burst to the surface. Her hair was a smothering mask over her face, making it difficult to breathe. But she was alive. Something popped in the water very near her head. Gunfire! Taking only long enough to locate the *Tamarisk*, Elyse dove beneath the rolling surface of the ocean and swam hard. Though she'd worried about unseen creatures in Lisbon harbor, she dared not think what might be lying in wait in the ocean. Fear propelled her—fear of the crew aboard the *Sultana*, fear of the water that dropped away hundreds of feet below her—lodging cold and hard between her shoulder blades, driving her through the water, giving her strength when none remained.

"Good God! Someone's gone overboard," Tris shouted.

Zach winced as he turned to Sandy. "Get us out of here while she's dead in the water."

"Look!" All aboard *Tamarisk* turned as a lone figure battled the rolling ocean, stroking arm over arm toward them.

"You can't just leave, Cap'n. Whoever cut those lines, saved us." Sandy had already turned the wheel, bringing the *Tamarisk* about.

"I'll be damned!" Tobias whistled through his teeth as he leaned over the railing. "Throw out a line."

Slowly, *Tamarisk* came about, her guns still aimed at the frigate as her crew scrambled atop the center mast and desperately tried to repair the damage. El Barracuda had begun the attack. By every law of the ocean, *Tamarisk* had the right to finish the frigate off. Zach saw the pirate captain wildly pacing the deck of his ship, trying to anticipate when the killing blow would come.

"No!" he ordered as the cannons were positioned and manned. "Let him wallow around out here in the ocean for a few days, easy prey to any pirate who comes along. It'll take him that long to make repairs. Let him wait and wonder and worry. On another day El Barracuda will meet the Raven. We can't afford to waste time now." He turned as lines were thrown over the side of his ship to take on the crewman from the *Sultana*, no doubt some unfortunate lad who'd been shanghaied.

Sandy made the adjustments in their course, and the *Tamarisk* was already slipping away from the *Sultana* as the sodden crewman was brought aboard. Tobias supported the lad at the railing, and Zach's gaze narrowed as he slowly and painfully approached them.

His hand grasped the fall of sable hair, jerking Elyse around. "What the hell!"

"Zach, for God's sake!" Tobias tried to step between them as he saw the blind fury on Zach's face.

Zach stared in disbelief. This his shock hardened with anger as reality hit him. He'd wondered what El Barracuda could want aboard the *Tamarisk*. What prize could be worth such a risk so close to Lisbon? Gold could be worth such a risk, or the money to be had for it. He'd trusted his crew unto death. They'd never betray what *Tamarisk* carried for cargo. But someone else would, someone who had reason to hate him. "What was the price?"

Elyse was on the verge of collapse, too weak to comprehend. "Zach, I . . ."

"What the hell did he promise you to betray me?"

"What?" She could only stare at him, her jumbled thoughts not allowing her mind to take in his words. "I don't know what you're talking about."

"El Barracuda would never have come after the *Tamarisk* unless he thought our cargo rich enough. But you had no way of knowing that the gold had already been taken ashore."

"Zach, what the devil has come over you? The girl almost drowned out there." Tobias tried to reason with him.

"Did he promise to take you back to Barrington? Was that it? When did you find out he wasn't going to keep his word? Was it before or after you warmed his bed?"

"Zach!" Tobias warned. "I'm dead against hittin' a man when he's hurtin', but if you don't shut your mouth, I'll shut it for you."

Invisible fingers of pain and searing fever goaded Zach beyond reason. "My God, is there nothing you won't do to get back to Barrington? You'd even whore for El Barracuda?" Zach coughed, blood appearing on his fingers as he fought his pain and anger.

Elyse saw the bright crimson color appear and spread on the bandages across his midsection. "Tobias, do something. He'll kill himself!"

"Tris!" Tobias roared to the crewmen. "Calm yourself, girl. He doesn't know what he's sayin'. It's the fever burnin' inside him."

"Damn you!" Zach shoved Tobias aside, swaying against Elyse. His fingers tangled in her hair. He jerked her to him.

"Zach, please!" She was frantic as her hands slipped to his shoulders, trying to brace his weight. "You don't understand."

"I understand enough!" Zach coughed again, the stain spreading beneath the bandages.

"Please, don't!" She sobbed. His grip on her hair was painful. "You'll open the wound."

"Would that matter to you, sweet Elyse?" he ground out.

Tears of pain filled Elyse's eyes. My God, she'd fought El Barracuda to come back to this? "Yes, it matters!" she cried out, frantically trying to convince him, of that before he did himself more harm. "Zach, please!"

"Cap'n." Tris gently seized Zach, pinning his arms to his sides with one arm. With the other, he loosened Zach's grasp of Elyse's hair. Zach towered several inches over his crewman and ordinarily could easily have resisted him, but the wound and the strain of being up on deck had taken their toll.

"Get him below," Tobias quietly ordered. "Be careful of that wound."

He turned to Elyse. "Are you all right, girl?"

Elyse was too stunned to speak. She could only nod.

"Good. Now, let's get you below as well, and into some dry clothes. Then I want to hear where you've been for the last two days, and how you got aboard the *Sultana*." The physician wrapped a comforting arm around her slender shoulders.

"He thinks I betrayed him to El Barracuda." Elyse's voice was unsteady. "I didn't Tobias. I swear, I didn't."

"I know you didn't, lass," he said soothingly. "The man's his own worst enemy. He's headstrong and foolish. And right now that fever has hold of him. Try not to dwell on what he said. If he can shake the fever, you'll have a chance to set it right with him."

Elyse grabbed Tobias's arm, panic darkening her sapphire eyes. "Tobias, he won't die? He can't!" Her fingers were like slender bands of steel, biting through the cloth of his coat. "You mustn't let him!" There was a wild, almost unreal light in her eyes. "He can't die! Not now! Not when I've waited so long for him . . ."

Tobias was staring at her as if she'd lost all reason. My God! What had she just said? He must surely think her mad.

Was it possible? Was Zamora right? Elyse bit at her lower lip as she wearily pushed her fingers back through her wet hair. She was so cold and tired that she didn't try to understand what was happening. She only knew that in those hours aboard the *Sultana,* she'd realized she had to come back to Zach. It was as if she'd been driven by some unseen force, compelled to come back to him. She had to know, she had to find the truth. Because if she didn't . . .

Fate has brought you together again, but if you ignore it you may never find each other again, not in this life or any other.

Tobias shook his graying head. "He won't die. Not if I can help it, lass. Not if I can help it."

For Elyse, the next days all blurred into one long day without end. She was only vaguely aware that they passed through the Strait of Gibraltar and crossed the Mediterranean Sea to the Suez Canal. Her sleep was sporadic, invaded by dreams. Or were they memories? She didn't know anymore. When she was awake, she refused to eat, spending countless hours beside Zach, personally caring for him.

Zamora's words haunted her. What if Zach died? It would be her fault. He'd been wounded coming after her. And then she'd run away again.

The bleeding had stopped, but Tobias admitted there was no way of knowing what damage might have been done inside from the effort of going up on deck. And Zach was now too weak to endure another operation. All they could do was wait and hope the fever broke.

Elyse refused to leave his side. She sponged the fevered sweat from his body, then piled blankets high when the cold chill set in. Hour after hour, day after day it was the same. She didn't understand how he could possibly survive, yet refused to believe that he wouldn't. It was as if her own soul were slowly dying with each precious hour that slipped away.

"Tobias! Dammit, wake up!" Elyse shook the old physician hard.

He jerked awake, fixing her with bloodshot eyes. "What is it? What's happened?"

"He's alive, but barely." She was frantic. "He's got to eat. We've got to get something down him or he will die." She paced away from Tobias and then whirled back around, her eyes wide with fear and determination. "There's got to be something."

He shook his head sadly. "I've done all I can. I've tried everything known to man. The fever should have broken by now."

Elyse tried to think. There had to be something. "Zamora!"

"What?" Tobias fixed unfocused eyes on her.

She came back to him, kneeling at his feet, her hand twisting the front of his shirt as she shook him. "Zamora said you often asked for some of her powders and herbs."

"Herbs? Bah! That's witchcraft, not medicine," he scoffed, pulling his shirt free. "They serve well enough as a poultice or a brew for headaches, but not for this."

"Where?" Stubbornness glinted in her eyes as she came to her feet, hands planted firmly on her hips.

"Yer draft! You'll just as likely kill him with the wrong mixture."

"He's dying now! Dammit, Tobias, we have to try. We have to! If I lose him now . . ."

"All right, all right." Tobias tried to calm her, thinking her distraught. He rose from the chair he'd occupied for most of the last several days. "Come with me."

He headed down the companionway to his own cabin. They

441

were alone below. A somber mood had settled over the _Tamarisk_ with Zach so desperately ill. The crew rarely spoke, and when they did it was only to convey necessary orders or instructions for sailing the ship.

Tobias opened a small cabinet and took down several vials and bottles. "I went through and labeled these myself accordin' to what they're supposed to cure. I couldn't pronounce any of that old woman's words." He indicated one bottle. "That's powder for mixing a poultice. This liquid is made from some root or another. It's supposed to take away pain, like headaches or toothaches. Seems to work."

"What is this?" Elyse picked up a small vial.

"Never tried that. You're supposed to mix it with boilin' water and set it in a room with the patient to relieve chest congestion."

"Damn." Elyse swore softly feeling helplessness wash over her. "There has to be something here."

"There is the mixture of leaves and twigs in this pouch." He held it aloft. "It's supposed to be boiled in water. Makes a kind of tea. I've never used it. Zamora said it rids the body of poisons."

"Poisons." Fever? Zach's fever was caused by the wound. Dear God, she wished she knew for certain. But if it was to be brewed and swallowed, what harm could it cause? She quickly decided to try it.

Elyse thrust the pouch of herbs toward Tobias. "Give this to cook and tell him to mix a strong tea."

The old man's eyes narrowed. "I'm a physician. I don't hold with trying something that hasn't been proven."

"Did Zamora use this?"

"That's what she said."

"That's good enough for me." Elyse's mouth narrowed into a determined line. "Now, Tobias. There's no time to waste." She whirled out of the small cabin, to go back to Zach.

"I don't approve of this one bit," Tobias grumbled as he handed Elyse a cup of pungent steaming liquid a short while later.

"I know, but there's no other way."

With dogged determination, Elyse stayed with Zach. She propped pillows beneath his head to make swallowing easier. She talked to him, coaxed him, not even knowing if he heard her. She kept at it for over an hour with no success. Tobias had gone topside to get fresh air, grumbling about witchcraft, Gypsies, and

442

strange potions. In mute frustration, Elyse slammed the cup down hard on the table beside the bed, spilling the hot liquid over her hands. She whirled back to Zach.

"Damn you!" she cried out. "Damn you! You force your way into my life, coming from God knows where. You lie to me, you lie to everyone about who you really are. Well, who are you? And why do I care?" Her voice broke on a sob as she collapsed at the side of his bed. "Damn you, I have to know. But I can't if you die! I'll never know if it was true!" Her hands the dug into sheet that draped the lower part of his body, her fingers grazing the heated flesh near the bandage. Tears flooded her eyes as she stared at his gaunt face, still so handsome, so strangely familiar.

"Dammit, you can't die! You can't! I love you! God help me, I love you!" She buried her face in the sheets, feeling as if her soul were dying. Her shoulder shook, tears wetting the covers.

"Lis."

It was a faint whisper at first. Like a breath of wind against the sails, or water gently lapping against the hull of the ship. *I love you*. He must have dreamed he heard her say those words. Or had he been awake? God it was so hot in here, and he could feel the rolling motion beneath him. Yes, now he remembered; he was aboard a ship, he and all the others. Everything was dark around him, but he could smell the stench of sweat and blood and death. He could hear the others as they moaned in pain and misery. Four months. Four long months, they'd been closed up in the hold of this ship, allowed up on deck only once in all that time to be soaked with sea water like so many animals and then thrust below again. When would it ever end? When?

His eyes focused on that one lamp, swinging overhead. It was like a single beacon of promise. He fixed his thoughts on that lantern. It was constantly lit. As long as it didn't go out, then he knew he was still alive. It was like a bright sun in a universe that no longer had light. It was the only thing that remained of his sanity; it allowed him to keep going, to hold on. That . . . and his memories of her.

Two roses; one red, one white. *I will love you forever. Forever* . . . The words echoed back across the days, months and years, back across time that couldn't be measured. He tried to mouth the words, his lips so parched and dry. He must be dreaming. He thought he could feel her hair against his hand, so soft like silk, and her tears. . . . *I will love you forever, beyond this lifetime.*

He remembered. He was riding. Lis was far behind him on

another horse. He'd looked back over his shoulder to her and didn't see the fallen tree. Too late he felt the subtle change in the horses' gait, the uncertain hesitation. And then he was falling, and there was pain and blood. Dear God, where was he? What had happened . . . ?

"Felicia . . . Lis?" He tried to turn his head, his fingers moving in her hair.

Elyse raised tear-filled eyes to search that haggard face. She'd heard it, she knew she had. He'd whispered that simple little special name he'd always called her. Lis. But there'd been more. Felicia. He'd called her Felicia!

He had voiced those words from her dreams. No, not dreams—she felt it deep in her soul—they were memories.

He groaned, trying to sit up, his hand reaching for her. "Is it dreadfully bad?" He tried to laugh, feeling foolish at being unseated from a horse. He tried to clear his thoughts. Not a horse, but a ship. The *Tamarisk*. Her words came back to him across time.

"You're hurt; you're bleeding." She tried to pull out of his grasp, then stopped. Elyse stared at him incredulously. She couldn't believe the words had tumbled from her lips, words she knew she'd spoken to him before, that day when he'd fallen in the woods at Fair View.

"It will undoubtedly leave a dreadful scar." Her fingers trembled as she pushed him back against the bed. She already knew without thinking what her next words would be, those same words she'd said on that day so long ago.

"Are you in a great deal of pain?" She held her breath knowing what she wanted his words to be, fearing they wouldn't be the same as they had been on that day. She almost wept as he whispered with great pain.

"Nothing that cannot be remedied by your gentle touch." And his eyes, when they looked at her with a trace of lucidity, were the color of soft smoke, just as they'd been that day at Fair View.

Elyse brought a cloth from the nearby basin and bathed the sheen of fevered sweat from his skin. Her hands shook as her fingers grazed across his chest, above the wound just below his ribs and down his back. He lay on his side, his face cast in shadow. She couldn't see his eyes now, for he'd turned away from her as if he'd retreated to his own dreams and memories. She carefully changed the bandage at his side, swallowing back her fear at the sight of the flesh that had torn anew.

Zach turned slowly, his eyes like molten steel with the heat of the fever. As quickly as she bathed away the sweat, more replaced it.

"Lis," he groaned from between parched lips, watching her in the soft light. All he could see was the shadow of her face and the dark fall of hair that swept over her shoulders. She was different, but the moment she looked up at the sound of her name, he knew. There was something in her eyes, the soft shadow of memory in those sapphire blue depths.

"Touch me, sweet love," he whispered, his hand reaching for hers.

Elyse took Zach's hand. His skin burned into hers. His strength was frightening, almost unnatural, as if he were clinging to a lifeline. She held fast to him, her fingers twining with his. She didn't care what he thought, she didn't care about the anger. It no longer mattered. She was bound to this man. She didn't know where or when the tie had begun, only that it existed. And she was bound heart and soul.

She could have stayed with El Barracuda and ransomed herself to freedom. Of that she was certain. But she hadn't because it would have taken her away from Zach. And although she didn't understand why, she quite simply accepted that she could never bear to be parted from him again. They were bound to each other by a common memory of some other time and place.

"I can't leave you," she whispered. "God help me, I can't."

He seemed to be dozing, his breathing shallow and rapid. She couldn't be certain he was still aware that she was there. Yet he clung to her hand as if he feared letting her go.

With her other hand, Elyse reached for the cup and spoon. With the greatest of care, she gently fed him the brew made from Zamora's herbs. Live, her heart cried out to him.

"Live, and come back to me," she pleaded.

Chapter Twenty-one

The Red Sea, the Arabian Sea, and along the southern tip of India. For weeks they sailed, making port only when fresh water was needed. They'd left land far behind three days earlier. The next land they would see would be the coast of the Australian continent.

The ocean was vast, filled with wondrous things: masses of tiny phosphorescent creatures glowed in the waves at night, forming a soft, blue-green cloud in the water about the ship; flying fish played about the ship, as did porpoises and dolphins, and the exotic Portuguese man-of-war often floated on the surface, and of course there was Sebastian, the brilliant green and red macaw who screeched obscenities. It was a place apart, a small private world aboard the *Tamarisk*, where faces and smiles had become dearly familiar.

No one spoke of it, but Elyse knew by the way Sandy drove the crew that Jerrold couldn't be far behind. In a few days, perhaps more, but he would come. She found herself watching for sails on the distant horizon along with the rest of the crew. And all of this was happening because of a need for revenge she didn't understand.

Zach's recovery was slow. As a physician, Tobias had done all he could. It was now a matter of fighting off the fever. She continued forcing the tea brewed from Zamora's herbal mixture down him, and later the heartier stews the cook prepared for the crew. His gradual recovery was marked by an increased time each day when he was free of the fever.

Somewhere between the fever and delirium, they'd struck a silent truce. She knew in his more lucid moments, Zach watched her in guarded silence. She could sense he was still angry about the attack on the *Tamarisk*, and undoubtedly believed she had betrayed him to El Barracuda. But that would have to be dealt with later. She would make him believe the truth. At least he hadn't sent her away. Even grudging acceptance was a beginning. A small one, but a beginning nevertheless.

In a sense, the fever was an unwelcome ally. Wracked by dreams, Zach tossed and turned as the heat seared through his body. The words that came with the delirium gave a disjointed, fragmented picture of his life. But slowly it came together. Tobias provided some of the missing pieces, and she learned a great deal about Zachary Tennant in those first weeks at sea.

He was sleeping now. Elyse sat at the side of the bed. She'd carefully changed the bandages, then carried the soiled cloths and the small basin of water to the built-in sideboard. It had taken her a while to get used to furniture that didn't move about. But she'd quickly realized that a ship was constantly moving and shifting, and often sailed storm-filled seas.

She stretched and walked about, then sat down at the desk. She'd eaten earlier and taken a sponge bath. It was all that was allowed when water was so precious on the long voyage to Sydney. Watching Zach now, she wondered what awaited her in that foreign land. Would he keep her captive until Jerrold arrived or would he set her free, considering his main objective accomplished?

He'd been especially restless earlier that afternoon as his fever rose. Tobias had sat with him while she'd gone up on deck to get some fresh air. He constantly nagged at her about that. She smiled softly at his gruff demonstrations of affection, much like those of a father. She found she liked them. They'd become very close these last weeks. She hoped that wouldn't change when they reached New South Wales.

She stacked and restacked papers into neat piles on Zach's desk. It was fastened to the wall, like the other furnishings in the cabin. The chair, when not in use, fit into the well underneath it. The shelves above had railings across them to keep books from tumbling to the floor in rough seas. They were filled with a variety of volumes, charts, and the ship's logs.

Elyse was surprised at the variety of books Zach kept. There were two by Herman Melville; *Moby Dick* and *Typee*. She'd read *Moby Dick* years earlier but had only finished *Typee* days ago. She read a lot lately, having much time on her hands.

There were books written in French and Spanish, which she couldn't begin to read, and an entire series on the history and government of England. Not so surprising, since Australia was a Crown colony. But she was surprised at the extensive papers and journals, and the volumes on the American colonies, one entitled *The Birth of a Nation, American Independence*. She was quickly learning there was a great deal more to this man who'd so mysteriously come into her life.

She found the small trunk on the bottom shelf beside a thick dissertation written by Thomas Jefferson. It was very old, with brass closures and with letters that were hardly visible, the leather was so badly worn. She'd never been one to pry into another person's affairs. But instinctively, she sensed this was something very different.

Inside was a leather-bound book. It was small, no bigger than a diary. Upon opening it, Elyse found it was indeed a form of diary, a journal of a man's life. She stared, transfixed, at the articulate words that spilled forth on page after fragile page. The journal was written by Nicholas Tennant.

Elyse's hands shook, and she glanced up. Zach still slept on the wide bunk across the cabin. Dare she read it? A journal was a private thing, containing thoughts, hopes, and dreams not meant to be shared by everyone, much less a stranger. But she wasn't a stranger. Her fingers trembled as they turned the first page, and then there was no turning back.

London, England
June 7, 1839

I begin this journey into hell. One day I will return and have my day of justice for the crime of which I am accused.

I will reclaim my birthright from those who have accused me. And, God willing, Felicia will be waiting for me. I shall now be called Nicholas Tennant.

Elyse stared at the words she'd read at least a dozen times. Felicia. He could mean no other than Felicia Barrington. She didn't want to go on. It was as if she were afraid to know the remainder of what was written on those pages. She stared at the journal, feeling all the desperation and futility that poured forth in those words.

But she read on about Resolute. The struggle, the daily fight to carve a home from the wilderness of New South Wales. She sensed the iron-willed determination of Nicholas Tennant in his descriptions of a harsh life. She saw frustration in his bold, short strokes, and calm acceptance of a small victory when an entry recorded the number of lambs born that first spring.

Zach had spoken of Resolute with something very near reverence. It must mean a great deal to him. She laid her head against the chair back. Eyes closed, she let it all wash over her. Nicholas Tennant was Zach's father.

"I don't understand," she whispered, to the walls of the cabin as a single lantern glowed softly over her head. Her gaze settled on the man in the bed. She did understand, but she was fighting it, just as she'd fought everything Zamora had tried to tell her. She closed her eyes, trying to block out his image, thinking it would be easy. But she was wrong to do so, because Zach was bound up in all of this. It was all there, if only she would allow it to come forth. But deep in her heart Elyse knew she was afraid.

"From this day forward I shall be called Nicholas Tennant."

"He was called Nicky." The name came back to her unbidden. Alexander Nicholas Barrington! Her eyes widened as the name tumbled in her thoughts.

She remembered Zach's exact words that last evening at Fair View. "I have to know." It was the name that had upset him.

Nicholas Tennant. An identity for a new life in a new land. The man Felicia Seymour had been in love with was Alexander Nicholas Barrington. Nicholas Tennant.

"No!" she whispered, pressing her hands against her temples as if she could force the memory back. Then she gasped as it all swept over her.

"My God! It can't be!" But it was. Alexander Barrington was Zach's father!

If she needed further proof, it was there in the small leather pouch at the bottom of the small trunk. Even as her fingers fumbled clumsily with the leather strings, she knew what she would find inside. The pearl and diamond pendant tumbled from the pouch into her hand. It was identical to the one her grandmother had given her.

"My pendant," she whispered, tears filling her eyes as she finally understood. There had always been two. They were the earbobs Felicia had worn for the portrait. Alex had given them to her.

* * *

For the longest time, Zach just stared at her. He didn't know exactly what it was that had awakened him. And then, as he saw her sitting at the desk, he heard it again, soft weeping.

He hadn't been dreaming. She was here, she was real. And she was so incredibly lovely. Lis. Her image was a living dream.

Memories pierced through the fever, memories of another time and place.

The deck of a ship. She'd been crying then as well. He couldn't bear her tears, any more than he could bear to leave her.

He fought the memories, angrily trying to push them back as his gaze fell to the pendant clutched in her fingers and the open journal on her lap.

"Did you find everything you were looking for?" His harsh words cut through Elyse, jerking her back through memory, back to the present time. Her startled gaze came up, locking with cold gray eyes. Her breath caught in her throat.

Zach came off the bed slowly, wrapped only in the bed sheet, pain hard in his eyes. By sheer force of will he groped his way toward her, using the bed post then the desk for support.

"So now you know the truth!" he ground out, his voice ragged as he tried to separate dream from reality. One hand pressed against the thick pad of bandages at his side as he drove himself that last distance to stand before her. It cost him much. His breathing was labored, and a fine sheen of moisture glistened on his skin.

"Alex Barrington was convicted of a crime he didn't commit!" His eyes flashed with silver fire. "The murder of his father. And Charles Barrington knew the truth. He knew because it was he who murdered their father!" His words were cast at her like shards of ice.

Elyse shook her head, in disbelief. "No."

"Brother against brother! Charles made certain Alex took the blame. He knew Alex would never hang. He was spared that because of the godalmighty Barrington name. Spared!" He laughed derisively. "Condemned to a life as a convict." Zach weaved unsteadily as weakness threatened to send him to the floor.

"Zach, please! You're not strong enough—"

He cut her off. "You read the journal. You wanted to know. But there's more you don't know. I planned all of this. Revenge is the name of the game." He laughed, a short, fevered laugh that sent chills down her spine.

450

"An eye for an eye, as the Bible says. Charles Barrington murdered his father and blamed Alex. He took everything. Then he took the one thing Alex valued above everything else."

"Felicia," she whispered.

"You wanted the truth." He choked back the anger. "Well, by God, you'll have all of it!"

Elyse wanted to run, she wanted to hide. This wasn't how it was supposed to be. She loved him, had always loved him. She knew that now. But he was so filled with anger. How could she possibly make him understand? God, she almost laughed aloud at the very idea. Who would ever believe it? She came out of the chair, moving away from Zach.

"Yes, Felicia!" His eyes were wild as he came at her, until their bodies were almost touching. And then he was bending her back over the desk.

"He took her and made her his wife! Then the betrayal was complete. She wanted the Barrington name. Just like you! When she couldn't have Alex, she married Charles!"

"No!" Tears filled Elyse's eyes as his words tore through her. They were coming back at her from across that void of years, her pain acute. She had waited for him. She'd waited an eternity. She clamped her hands over her ears, trying to block out his cruel words.

"It's not true!" she whispered brokenly.

Zach grabbed her wrists with surprising strength, jerking them down hard, forcing her to listen.

"She betrayed him, just as Charles betrayed him!"

"You're wrong!" Elyse cried out. Tears stung at her eyes, blinding her, turning soft blue into limpid pools of brilliant sapphire. She wiped at them viciously.

"That's not what happened!" Her breath was coming in great, choking sobs, her hands trembling beneath the bruising pressure of his fingers. And then it was as if the reservoir of emotion suddenly burst in her, everything tumbling out; the painful secrets that had lain in her heart a lifetime pouring into that small cabin.

"I never loved anyone else. And I waited for you! I knew what you were going through. I suffered everything you suffered, felt everything you felt, because I was with you in my heart. I was always with you and I died the day we parted." She was blurting it all out, between tears and sobs, the secrets Felicia Seymour Barrington had waited so many years to tell.

Her eyes bespoke her torment. "Charles said he knew a way to set you free. He promised he would bring you back. But he made me promise to marry him. That was to be the price for your freedom. And I would gladly pay it again. I loved you too much to bear your suffering."

Elyse was stunned into silence. Father in heaven! What had she just said?

"Damn you!" Zach spat out, his lips trembling with emotion. He released her wrists, his hands plunging into her hair, his fingers closing around her head until she thought he would crush her.

"What are you saying?" His voice was hard, disbelieving, his eyes as cold as slate.

Tears spilled from Elyse's eyes, wetting her cheeks. "You know what I'm saying," she whispered brokenly, her hands covering his, trying to break his painful hold on her.

Zach stared at her, his fingers like bands of steel, as if he could crush the truth from her.

There was no going back. Elyse knew that now. She'd torn away the first stone in the wall between them. Whatever happened, whether or not he chose to believe she was Felicia, she had to tell him everything and tear down the remainder of that wall. She had to believe he would know the truth in his heart.

"A long time ago at Fair View, you gave me two roses. The artist was coming to paint the engagement portrait. I was wearing the blue gown. One rose was red, for passion. The other was white, because our love would be forever. Those were your words to me that day. And I've believed in them always."

He stared at her incredulously, fighting back the truth. "No. It's not possible." But even as he denied it, he remembered.

My God, he thought, what is happening?

Elyse knew she had to give him more, something that wasn't in a portrait or a journal or any dream. It was something only Alex Barrington would know.

"There are roses at Resolute, red and white. Alex planted them; you planted them. Each spring the red roses bloom, bright with color. The white roses have never bloomed."

Zach's fingers tightened. "Damn you!" he exclaimed. "How do you know that?"

"Because, dearest Alex, I've always been with you in my heart. I've always believed in you, believed that you would come back to me," Elyse whispered softly.

His hands shook, yet his face remained hard. He denied it with every breath.

Dammit! Who was this beautiful creature? How could she possibly know things no other living person knew? Zach knew the answers, but they were more frightening than anything he'd ever experienced.

Angry, he buried his hands in her hair. He had to stop her, stop the words.

"It's not true!" he yelled at her.

Elyse bit back the sobs that tore through her. He shook her so hard, she thought her head would separate from her shoulders.

"Say it!"

"I can't! Zach, please! You must believe me. I don't pretend to understand it. I don't know why it's happened. I only know it has. Zamora knew it. She's the one who told me. Before that I never understood the dreams." The tears had begun anew. If he didn't believe her, then what was left to her?

His fingers sank into her hair, and her jerked her against him the instant before his mouth plunged down against hers. It's not true, his thoughts screamed. It can't be!

His kiss was brutal, as if he could deny everything by causing her pain. He wanted to hurt her, force her to take it all back. There was no denial, only the sweet softness of her body taking his weight as he leaned into her.

Her lips were bruised under his assault, and she tasted blood. She tried to hold him away, afraid he would harm himself. But he was frighteningly strong, even when weakened by the fever.

"Please!" Elyse tore her mouth from his. "Don't. You'll open the wound."

"No!" he whispered harshly, forcing her mouth back to his. "I want you to prove it." His cold voice sent fear down her spine. "If you're Felicia Barrington, prove it! Prove how strong your love is!"

My God, she thought, he won't accept it. His desire for revenge is too strong. Instinctively, Elyse knew she was powerless to stop him.

"Prove it, sweet Lis," he breathed into her mouth, his anger slipping away at the taste of that sweet wetness. "If what you say is true, prove how much you love me." It was almost a plea as he pulled her back with him. The high, wide bunk caught him at the back of the legs, and Zach fell onto the bed, groaning painfully against her throat as he pulled her with him. His hands immediately came up, trapping her.

Elyse struggled against him. He was angry and meant to use that anger against her, just as he'd planned to use her to lure Jerrold into a trap. She knew it now. And she also knew it mustn't be this way or it would destroy them both.

She tried to push away from him, leveraging her body against his, but their legs were entwined, pinning her. He rolled over, the bareness of his chest searing her through the soft cotton of her shirt, and then his skin was burning into hers as his fingers deftly worked the buttons.

"No! It can't be this way. You don't believe . . ." She gasped, first at the sudden coolness as the shirt was pushed open, then at the heat as his lips closed over the taut peak of her breast. "No," she whispered with far less conviction, as his tongue began a sensual assault. His lips caressed as his teeth nibbled, taking the nipple full into his mouth, then teasing it to aching anticipation as his tongue swirled a maddening wetness across her skin.

"I want you, Elyse. It has nothing to do with past lives. This is here and now," he breathed against her mouth. "Beyond that it means nothing!"

His fingers slipped down her side, caressing her beneath the snugness of the pants. The skin across her stomach leaped in response as his fingers worked at the closure. Her hands rode his shoulders, intent on pushing him away yet clinging to him as desire tore through her. His bare chest crushed against her, the aching peaks of her breasts swelling against muscles coated in gleaming bronze. His skin glistened with a sheen of gold hair, the soft silkiness setting her aflame.

He took away her will and reason with another kiss, as tender now as the first one had been brutal. Instinctively he knew he wanted her — had always wanted her.

It means nothing. His words stung her, and panic welled inside Elyse. If she let this happen, now, this way, he would never understand and she would lose him forever. She loved him and wanted him. God help her, she wanted him so, but not like this, not with revenge and hatred between them. She moved her hands to stop him, but he thrust them away.

"Who am I?" His voice was harsh in the deep valley between her breasts. He was determined to force it from her.

Elyse arched away from him, frantic because of what he intended, even more frantic because she feared he would harm himself.

454

His voice was ragged, his breath like smoke against her skin. "Sweet Lis. Say it." His fingers stole down across her stomach, slipping through soft dark down. There was no patience left in him. For weeks he'd lain in that bed, torn between dreams and reality, seeing her, wanting her. It was as if she were the fever in his soul. Revenge had set him against her; now desire played a different game where there were no rules. Zach tore the shirt from her arms and then jerked her full against him. His hands moved down the arch of her back, over the curve at her waist, sliding against her skin. The pants were quickly stripped away.

"Please, don't do this!" Elyse cried out; desperate trying to pull away even as her betraying body opened to him. She gasped, then shivered with uncontrolled pleasure, her body coating his fingers with desire as they slipped inside her. He caressed her; withdrawing, teasing, then touching the very core of her until Elyse was mad with desire for him. But she wanted more, so much more from him. This wasn't nearly enough. Her hand slipped to his, guiding him, encouraging him; and then her hand caressed him beneath the thin sheet wrapped around his hips.

"Who am I?" His words tore through Elyse. He'd tortured and tormented her, daring her to say it, yet he'd refused to believe it. Elyse knew he wouldn't, even as she felt her body set afire by his hands. It was complete madness. She'd been mad with wanting him from the first moment she'd seen him again. If he wouldn't believe her, then she must show him, prove to him what she knew in her heart.

It means nothing. She flung the words from conscious thought. It did mean something, and her hands were like cool whispers against his fevered skin as she pushed him back against the bed and carefully straddled his hips. Elyse began to caress him with only the sheet separating them.

And then quite simply, none of it mattered any longer. He was here, and for now, in this moment, she could love him again. And perhaps, in doing so, she could convince him as no words could.

The sheet was swept away, and she rose above him. In his memory she had golden hair, but he soon realized she was all gold. Her skin was like tawny satin; the dark, lustrous hair that fell to her hips and brushed his thighs was filled with thousands of tiny, hidden lights that gleamed in the darkened cabin. But it was her eyes that held him spellbound. They were the softest blue one moment, fiery turquoise the next as desire leaped from their hidden depths.

Elyse leaned over him, bracing her weight on bent elbows, her hands cradling his face as she kissed him. For weeks he'd been the stalker, the abductor, the master; now she turned it all against him. She hunted, tormented, and teased with her lips. The more she tasted of him, the more she wanted. This was a lovemaking not of the body, but of the heart and soul. Her eyes closed in exquisite pleasure as her lips traced the features she'd committed to memory; long, golden lashes that no man should have, masking eyes as unfathomable as the silver mists of her dreams; the strong arch of brows; the straight, aristocratic nose; the maddening indentation above his upper lip. She was mindless with the taste of him as his mouth opened to her, his tongue wrapping around hers in sweet supplication.

With the greatest tenderness, Elyse curled over him, nipping, tasting, licking; at his shoulder, across the heavy collar bone, then downward, her assault on hard, male nipples beginning. He came alive beneath her, his hand slipping up her back, pulling her back to him, until his mouth found her breast.

· Elyse cried out at the exquisite torture of his lips, her fingers caressing his brows, his cheekbones, holding him against her breast. And then there was no patience left within her. She must have him inside her or die for it. The sound that came from her throat was low, animal-like. She rained hot, fevered kissed down over his face, his neck and gleaming shoulders. And then her hand was slipping between them to guide him to her. She felt that first pressure of him pressing into her, and then she opened to him, sliding down over him, slowly, so that she could feel every bit of him surging deep inside her. For one breathless moment, she was suspended above him, her body poised, and then as her lips crushed down on his, the joining was complete, her hips plunging full against him, the searing heat of his erection thrusting to the mouth of her womb.

"Let me love you," she whispered. "Let me love you as I've always loved you." With quiet desperation in her soul, Elyse made love to him. He might believe nothing else, but he would believe this. If they had nothing else, they had the desire that had brought them together before. She stroked him lovingly, her lips caressing his mouth as her body caressed his. Again and again, she took him to the brink of climax and then arched above him, unsheathing him, until beads of sweat glistened across his body. He cried out at the withdrawal, his hands bruising on her thighs, his thumbs sharp over the bones at her hips. Almost brutally, he brought her back down over him.

It wasn't enough for her to know that he wanted her physically. "Who am I?" she whispered against his lips.

"Elyse," he ground out between drawn lips as he forced his way into her slender body.

She shook her head, a curtain of sable hair falling around them. "Who am I?" She was turning it all against him, even as she felt the quickening deep inside where he was hard within her.

"My God, what do you want from me?" Zach groaned.

"Say it!" She licked at the hard bud of the male nipple, crisp golden hair swirling about it.

"Lis, my sweet Lis!" he gasped as his hands closed over the fullness of her breasts. It was enough for now.

Then there was no need for words between them. Their desire had never known boundaries, not of language or time. She moved to take him deeper still, opening herself to him completely, wanting more. Her mouth covered his as she felt that first hard spasming. He groaned against her lips, but still she stroked him, wanting all of him. He thrust hard against her, his hot liquid burning through her with shattering violence. And her body responded, tightening with that first breathlessness of wonder, and then she gasped as wave after wave of fiery heat swept through her.

Even as her lips gently caressed his, even as he slipped into that darkened world of exhaustion, Elyse knew he had traveled part of the way back to her. But not all the way.

For the longest time, she lay beside him, her leg possessively lying across his. "Come back to me, my love," she whispered against the hard curve of his shoulder. And then she, too, slept deeply, her soul at peace.

Zach watched her sleeping beside him. God, she was beautiful. He remembered the darkening of her eyes as they'd made love. Had he only been dreaming about the night before? At the sight of her naked body against his, he knew differently.

Her skin was silken to the touch, like pale gold. Her hair spread across the bed, became trapped under his shoulder. She was turned toward him, on full breast brushing against his chest. He carefully slid away, coming painfully upright. He wanted very much to get out of that bed. It was time. But he hesitated as he turned back to her. Her remembered her slender body poised over his. Never before had a woman made love to him like that, so freely, so wantonly, bringing him to the brink of such complete pleasure and then tormenting him as she held him back time and again.

Zach thrust his hand back through his hair as he tried to remember everything that happened, everything that was said. He needed to be up and about, but as he looked back at her naked loveliness, he couldn't resist a kiss. What other nourishment could a wounded man possibly need? And he wanted to prove something, to her, to himself.

She'd come to him with that ridiculous notion last night and then had seduced him into believing it. But this was now. He cast it aside. Now he wanted to repay her for that seduction. He wanted to prove that he didn't need her or want her except for the revenge. He needed to prove he could make love to her and then leave her, that she meant nothing to him.

He bent over her. His tongue gently circled the tip of her breast, and he smiled as he watched it tighten with desire. She moaned softly in her sleep, her leg moving against his thigh. He turned slowly into her, wondering what it would take to awaken her. He moved his leg between hers, his hand following, as his mouth continued that butterfly assault of her breast. Elyse breathed out slowly, her lips moving without words as she turned over on her back.

With the gentlest of movement, Zach stroked her. His lips followed the downward descent of his fingers, and he was kissing her, stroking her much more intimately, his lips finding and gently caressing that hardening bud at the core of her woman's body. She inhaled sharply, and then her hips began a slow rocking motion against his mouth. Zach slipped his hand under her hips, opening her fully to him. She was sweet. God she was so sweet. He wanted to pay her back for last night, by proving to her that it was only a physical act. But as her sweetness washed over him, her slender body arching to meet the invasion of his tongue, Zach knew he was hopelessly lost.

Her head was thrust back, her shoulders pressed deep into the bed. Mindlessly her head twisted from side to side. Surely she was dreaming; she must be. Then her eyes flew open, and Elyse knew she wasn't. She saw his golden head, felt the exquisite heat of his tongue at the center of her being, and was once more swept away by passionate caresses. There were no words between them, nothing of the acceptance she so desperately needed from him; only desire. She hated herself for it, but she was powerless to stop it. She wanted him as much as she had last night, and was willing to sacrifice her soul to fulfill her need.

It was as if he were trying to torture her, punish her with the weapon of his body. His hands stroked while his tongue spread fiery heat until Elyse was mindless, sensations pouring through her. His assault on her body and senses drove everything else away, his every touch making her mad with desire. Still he punished her, taking her to the brink of complete fulfillment and then, with exquisite tenderness, tasting her fully. The sun burst within her, white hot, her body pulsing with tiny stabs of pleasure.

"Alex!"

She cried out his name, not even realizing that she had.

"Damn you!" Anger tore through him at the name of her phantom lover, yet he gathered her in his arms and thrust deep inside her, again and again, until his heat melted through her, seeping into every corner of her being.

Zach knew she was awake, but he left without a word, dressing quickly in the still-dark cabin and then slamming the door hard behind him.

Elyse curled into a tight ball at the edge of the bed. Tears stung her eyes. Her body had betrayed her once more. But what good was physical love if he denied what was in his heart? She turned into the pillow and wept. Their time together aboard *Tamarisk* was almost over. When they reached Sydney everything would change. He would have his revenge against Jerrold, and would no longer need her. What then? Would he still refuse to accept the truth? Would he simply send her back to England as if nothing had ever happened.

Prove it to me. If not last night or that morning, then how, when he refused to even discuss it with her?

Prove it to me. What if she couldn't? What if the only truth was in her heart and he still refused to accept it?

Elyse moved her few things back to that small cabin across from Zach's, determined to get as far away from him as possible. If he wouldn't believe her, then everything was hopeless. Later that day she found they had been returned to his cabin, laid across the bed with several brightly colored skirts and blouses.

459

She threw them all in the bottom of the small wardrobe, refusing to accept his gifts when he couldn't give his love.

They rarely spoke as the days passed in painful silence, each afraid to talk about what was happening between them. She couldn't bear to hear him deny what she knew to be true, and he dared not risk being confronted with what he feared. They had become intimate strangers.

Zach paced the deck. It was somewhere near dawn. Soft gray streaks shot through the night sky, the beginning of a new day, one day closer to Sydney. Unable to sleep, he'd come up hours earlier. He'd practically taken off Sandy's head when his second mate had suggested he needed sleep rather than an additional watch at the helm.

It nagged at him. For countless nights he'd lain awake, Elyse curled up beside him, unable to drive what she had said that night weeks ago from his mind. Was it somehow possible that Elyse was Felicia?

He laughed it off. It was ridiculous, too fantastic to believe. He could come up with practical explanations for everything that existed between them. The evening they'd met, the strange feeling he'd known her before . . . it was nothing but his appreciation for a beautiful woman. Undoubtedly he'd once known someone who vaguely resembled Elyse.

I knew you'd come back to me. Good God, now there was an original statement if ever he'd heard one. It was a little more inventive than what he usually heard from women when they wanted him to take them to bed. But in that there was complete contradiction. Oh, she'd been very good that night, a regular little actress. She'd pretended to recover quickly, acting as if she were as surprised as he by the statement. Then she'd been angry with him.

The pendant. That was simple enough to explain, too. Her grandmother was a friend of Felicia Barrington's. The pendant had been a gift from Felicia to Lady Winslow, who in turn had given it to her granddaughter on the occasion of her engagement to Jerrold Barrington.

And what of his meeting with Barrington? Those offices, the furnishings had meant nothing to him. He'd felt nothing when he'd met Jerrold. But there had been that etching of the small sloop, *Gypsy Moth.* That was also the name of that first old bucket he'd learned to sail in Sydney Harbor. He'd been twelve at the time and had named the sloop himself.

Fair View. He tried to shrug off his feelings and emotions about the place: his first reaction at seeing the Barrington estate. His driver had surely thought him mad. Perhaps it had been temporary madness. But there was no explanation for his reaction at seeing her again in that blue gown.

"Christ!" Now he was doing it, his thoughts coming forth as if they were memories.

As he stared out over the horizon and the awakening dawn, Zach's eyes reflected the brilliant purple, orange, and blood red colors of the morning sky. Red. As red as that single rose in the stained-glass window. He'd found her in that room, staring at the pane of glass and instinctively he'd known her thoughts.

There was an explanation for everything that had happened since he'd returned to England, everything except the roses at Resolute. Those damned roses that he'd always thought Megan had planted. But she hadn't; Alex had. He'd planted roses for a lost love. The red roses bloomed in wild profusion; but as Elyse had said, the white ones had never bloomed.

As an educated man, he knew the impossibility of what Elyse had suggested. But as a seaman who'd seen countless unexplainable phenomena around the world, he knew nothing was impossible. And quite simply, there was no explanation of how Elyse had known about the roses at Resolute.

He'd descended on Tobias that first morning, thinking his old friend was in his cups again and rambling. But he'd been stunned to find his friend stone-cold sober, as he had been for weeks. Tobias had flat-out denied having told Elyse anything about Resolute, and when Zach had pressed him about it, he'd actually threatened to knock some sense into his head.

Tobias was getting downright testy in his old age. But even if his old friend had told Elyse about the roses, how could she possibly know why Nicholas had planted them? Yet she had.

They'd left the Bass Strait behind the day before. They were only two or three days out of Sydney. Then it would only be a matter of waiting for Barrington, and Elyse would be free to go. Could he let her go?

It was a hard question. And each night as he pulled her into his arms and made love to her, he found the answer less and less clear. With a loud curse, Zach readjusted the wheel of the *Tamarisk* and refused to think about it anymore. It would be over soon—finished, done with! And he wouldn't need her any more.

Elyse stood in the middle of the cabin she'd shared with Zach these last weeks. It was strange how'd she'd become accustomed to the movement of the ship. She could feel a coming summer storm in the subtle change in the way *Tamarisk* slipped through the water. Now, the easy, lapping motion told her they were approaching Sydney Harbor.

She'd been up on deck all morning, watching the coastline to starboard. It was then she'd made her decision to leave at the earliest possible moment. Zach had made it quite clear he no longer needed her, now that she'd served her purpose as hostage, and as whore.

The last thought stung cruelly. But there was no other way to define her position in their relationship. Zach stubbornly refused to talk about what had happened, and she refused to accept his refusal, not that it did her any good. Now she quite simply had to get away from him.

She wished she felt more certain. What would she find in Sydney?

"Hopefully a dressmaker," Elyse murmured morosely, sitting down on the bed. Her meager wardrobe left much to be desired. She didn't need fine satins or velvets. She'd never been one to care about fancy gowns. But she needed something more than sailors' clothing and the colorful native skirts and blouses Zach had given her. There was always her wedding dress, of course. But it was torn beyond repair and lay forlornly on the bed with the other garments. Anger twisted inside her, and she seized the gown. Rolling it into a tight ball, she thrust it through the open porthole. Just let the sharks wonder about that one!

Much as she hated to admit it, that childish antic, throwing the wedding dress into the sea, did make her feel better. It brought back memories of her abduction; not the wedding that almost was, but the ridiculous wedding that had taken place.

Only moments later Elyse jumped up from the bed, as the door to the cabin slammed back hard on its hinges. Zach strode in, the sodden wedding gown, dripping, in his hands.

"Just what the devil is going on down here? One of my men fished this out of the water!" Sea water soaked the front of his shirt and pants, plastering the cloth to his lean, muscular body and playing havoc with her senses.

She backed away from him, taking a safe position across the cabin, and shrugged her shoulders. "I was simply cleaning my things out of your wardrobe. I had no further use for the gown. Disposing of it seemed the best idea at the time. After all, that leaves me far less to pack."

Zach heaved the gown into the corner, where it plopped onto the floor, water from it running across the wood planking. "And just where the hell do you think you're going?"

Elyse took a deep breath, steeling herself for the storm that was sure to come. Slowly her gaze came up to meet his.

"I'm going ashore in Sydney," she coolly informed him. "I want to send word that I'm alive to my grandmother, on the first available ship back to England."

Zach's eyes narrowed. She was being too calm, too quiet. For weeks things had been difficult at best between them. During the day they were strangers, barely talking, and when they spoke it was always the same. Her words were pained, cool, his were angry. The nights were all that remained to them. He shifted, uneasy with this sudden change in her.

"I fully intended that you would go ashore. I've made arrangements for you to go to Resolute," he informed her matter-of-factly.

"That's not necessary," Elyse responded evenly.

Zach's fists clenched at his sides as he tried to restrain an urge to strangle her. She was acting as if he'd extended an offer of hospitality and she was politely refusing it.

"It doesn't seem that you have any choice in the matter, Elyse. You have no money and no clothes. You are entirely dependent on me," he said curtly. "And I don't care much for the idea that you might decide to turn me in to the authorities, for abducting you. After all, New South Wales is a Crown colony." This last he spat out, his contempt obvious.

"I have no intention of going to the authorities. I would merely like to see if I can locate any acquaintances of my grandmother," she stated. There, it was said. And she'd meant it. She had no desire to see him punished. She couldn't handle that. She wanted only to be away from him and the constant turmoil between them. She couldn't force him to accept what he would not. But she couldn't stay with him either.

"No." It came out soft, low, and final. "As I said, I've made arrangements."

Elyse couldn't believe what she was hearing. Just like that, he was making decisions for her again. He was still the captor, she the captive. Well not for long! Her chin angled defiantly, her eyes flashing.

"You have no right to continue to hold me prisoner! You have what you wanted. Undoubtedly Jerrold will be arriving in a matter of days. Holding me would serve no further purpose. I demand that you release me immediately!"

Again that simple, damning answer.

"No, Elyse. You'll do as I say." His eyes were masked now. Like silver mist, they shrouded his emotions.

"But why?" Her control was shattering. She hadn't expected this. "You have no reason to keep me any longer!"

He turned away, his hand resting on the latch of the cabin door. Elyse was stunned. He was leaving. Just like that, without any further explanation. Then he hesitated and she braced herself.

"Don't try to leave, Elyse. I have my reasons."

With that, he was gone, the door closing quietly behind him. It was that quiet which disturbed her far more than the open forcefulness she'd come to know.

"Reasons!" Her eyes swam with tears. "Well I have my reasons too." She whirled back around. Ignoring the wedding gown, she selected a cotton skirt, a bright turquoise blouse and a pair of sandals. She would leave the rest. The pants and shirts belonged to Zach, and she'd die before she'd take any more of the skirts or blouses. That left only her pendant, identical to the one in the leather pouch. She wrapped it carefully in a square of cloth, then tucked it inside the waist of her skirt. Her packing was completed. After all, if she took nothing with her, then no one would be suspicious.

Outside the cabin, Zach waited for a crash, for something to be thrown against the door. There were any number of things she might use. But she didn't. He shrugged as he moved down the companionway toward the open hatch. Still, he would have felt better if she'd broken something. It was the quiet he didn't trust.

Elyse stood on deck, watching, as the *Tamarisk* slipped into Sydney Harbor. She felt gentle pressure at her arm and turned to find Tobias standing beside her.

"It really is beautiful." She breathed in the cool air that caressed her as it blew off the water.

"Aye, and it's a strange and wondrous land. There's a lot to see and learn about. It's far different from England."

"Is Sydney very different from London?" There was more than one reason for her asking. She needed to know what to expect of the city, for she was determined to go there.

"Not so very different. The weather is warmer in the summer, milder in the winter—inland that is. But Sydney is a harbor town and stays pretty constant year round. Although we do have some good storms in the winter, they usually blow over quickly. As for the city itself, it's a lot like any other big city." He smiled at her. "You'll see it soon enough. It's a grand sight."

"Then it's not primitive?" She shaded her eyes, gazing out across the brilliant blue-green water.

"Primitive?" He actually looked crestfallen. "In spite of what you may have heard, young lady, Sydney is a very modern seaport. We have paved streets, streetlamps, constables, and all manner of business and industry. There are hotels and restaurants, cabbies with hansom carriages; a theater, hospitals, a library, an opera house, and a racetrack. And we have a fine selection of ladies' shops as well. We've come a long way since the first convicts sailed into Botany Bay."

"I'm sorry. I didn't think . . ."

Tobias waved his hand in a gesture of dismissal. "No apologies necessary, no offense taken." He smiled at her affectionately. "It's easy enough to understand what you think, what with Barrington feeding you all sorts of wild tales. But I expect you'll like Sydney. And I dare say, it will have its socks knocked off when it sees you." Then he sobered, as if he'd just remembered something.

"There's something I've been meanin' to say to you. I think now is the time."

Elyse immediately looked up because of the solemn tone of his voice.

"It might help you understand things a little better."

Her eyes softened as she looked at him. "And what might that be?"

Tobias shifted uncomfortably. Never in all his life had he spoken out against Zach. He'd always been proud of the boy, and loyal to a fault. That damned fool trip to England proved that. But everything was different now. She was caught in the middle, and he wouldn't see her harmed.

"It's about Barrington," he began hesitantly.

465

Elyse slipped her small hand into his. "I know," she informed him softly.

"What do you know?" he blustered.

What should she tell him? The truth? Would he believe it? Or would his reaction be the same as Zach's? She smiled.

"I know that Alex Barrington was Zach's father." Her voice had become very somber. "I also know that Alex was convicted of a crime he didn't commit, and was sent here. I read the journal and I found . . . Felicia Barrington's pendant." She'd started to say that she'd found her own pendant.

"Good Lord!" He let out a long, low whistle.

"And I know that Zach is the Raven. He abducted me so that Jerrold would follow and he could seek revenge for Alex's fate." She stared out over the water, watching dolphins arc through the water. They were so playful and majestic, so carefree.

He winced. "You've figured out quite a lot."

She laughed softly. "Yes, for all the good it does me." She looked up to find him watching her.

"But I don't understand why Zach became the Raven."

Tobias stared down at the pipe clenched in his hands as he leaned against the rail. "There's been a lot of oppression in the colonies, by the Crown. Barrington Shippin' virtually controls everything comin' in or goin' out of every major seaport. With the blessin's of Mother England, the Crown's representatives levy taxes, set their own prices, buy and sell as they choose, and steal at will."

"We colonists have lived with that a long time. In part it's due to the way Englishmen see the colonies. To most, we're still nothin' but a convict colony. It's a hard thing to live down." There was an edge of bitterness in his voice, as there had been when Zach had spoken of it.

"You seem to know a great deal about that," Elyse replied softly.

Tobias breathed in slowly, the pain of his memories deep. "I should. I was one of the convicts sent here." He was silent for a long time, his mouth working to mask the trembling of his lips.

Elyse slipped her arm through his, gently comforting him. She felt as if her heart would break at seeing this kind, gentle man so undone. "You don't have to tell me."

He shook his head. "Yes, I do. You need to know so that you can understand how it was in the beginnin', and just exactly what it means to be a colonist. Then, maybe you can understand him must a little bit better."

For the next hour, Tobias stood at the rail, reliving things he hadn't thought about in well over thirty years. He told her about Nicholas Tennant as a young man, and through his memories, Elyse recaptured the years she'd been separated from him. He told her about Nicholas's dream for Resolute, of Megan, and about Tennant's untimely death before his son was born.

Oddly, Elyse did not feel jealous of the woman Alex had married. Felicia had married, foolishly, she knew. But that was removed from her now, a brief moment of the past that she couldn't clearly remember. Bits and pieces of it came back to her from time to time, fragments of her life before. Perhaps in time, more of it would come back. And there was the possibility that she would remember very little, only pieces of her life with Alex. She shivered faintly, not certain she wanted to remember, now that she must leave him.

Tobias broke the silence that had settled over them.

"I'm not askin' anythin' about what's passed between you and Zach. He can be hard to live with sometimes." He seemed to be apologizing for something. "I know that firsthand, better than anybody. But he's a fair person and he has a good heart for all his stubbornness."

Elyse almost laughed. Almost. "He still thinks I betrayed him to El Barracuda."

"Did he tell you that?"

"He accused me of it, and then he kept yelling about it when he had the fever."

"Has he said anythin' about it recently?"

She had to admit that he hadn't. "No."

"And he won't!" Tobias informed her. "Because he saw what happened that day, along with half the crew. We all saw the way you cut those lines. You saved the *Tamarisk,* and everyone knows it. We'd never have gotten away if you hadn't done that."

"Then why can't he admit that?" Tears of frustration glistened in her eyes.

"It's part of this whole thing. It's almost like an obsession with him." His eyes narrowed. "Truth is, you've become an obsession with him. And I feel responsible for everything that has happened."

She turned to stare at him. "Why should you feel responsible? You had nothing to do with it. As it is, you've been a good friend." She smiled up at him, then became very somber herself.

"It would have happened anyway. It had nothing to do with you."

He nodded, passing a hand over his whiskered chin. "Aye, maybe. But I still feel responsible. If there's ever anything I can do to help . . ." His words trailed off as he stared out across the harbor.

Her gaze fastened on Zach. He was at the helm of the *Tamarisk*, his head bent as he said something to Sandy, the wind lifting the golden waves of his hair. Elyse swallowed back the tightness in her throat. It had to be this way. She would hate herself if she stayed, and hate him for refusing to accept what fate had given them.

They both stood there, silent and alone with their own thoughts. Elyse remembered everything that had brought her to this place. She watched Zach with haunted, hungry eyes that betrayed her emotions to the man standing beside her.

"What will happen now?" She couldn't get past the tightness in her throat.

Tobias stared hard at her. My God, the lass is in love with Zach, he thought. Then his gaze followed hers and he knew her thoughts.

"We'll put in to Sydney. The men with families will go ashore. The others will stay aboard. I imagine he'll take on supplies."

"Supplies? Then he's planning on leaving again?"

He smiled at the alarm in her voice. She did care. A lot. "Not the supplies yer thinkin'." His expression sobered. "They'll need to take on powder." When she looked at him quizzically, he grimly clarified the statement for her.

"Munitions — cannonballs, explosives."

"Oh." Fear closed around Elyse's heart. "Will he wait here for Jerrold?" Her voice was very small.

"No. Barrington will probably come at him with everything he's got, includin' the Royal Navy once he puts to port and apprises them of the situation. Zach will be outgunned and outmanned. He knows that, so he'll lure Jerrold out where he has the advantage." He gestured over the port side. "There's a chain of islands out there. That's where he'll lead him." He looked up the center mast, to where the Spanish flag fluttered in the breeze. "When the *Tamarisk* leaves Sydney Harbor, she'll fly her own flag."

"My God."

The sadness in her voice wrenched his heart.

"He'll die out there." Her knuckles turned white as she grasped the rail. "Can't you stop him?"

Tobias shook his head. "I wish I could. But even if that were possible, there's no stoppin' Barrington. Not now. Zach knew when he took you that you would insure that Barrington would come here. And there's too much history between them. Now, knowin' what he does about his father, Zach would never back down. Not for anything."

Not even for me, Elyse thought in silent desperation. Because he doesn't understand and he can't accept what's between us. Tears pooled in her vivid eyes, one slipping down her cheek. Zach was determined to have his revenge. It meant more to him than anything. The situation was hopeless.

"I won't stay and watch him die, Tobias. I can't." Her tear-filled gaze met his.

His hand covered hers, communicating love and understanding. "What is it you would have me do, girl?"

"I have to leave, before . . ." As her voice caught, she bit at her lower lip. Before I'm too deeply bound to him, she wanted to say, but it was already too late for that; before he comes to me again; before he says that last good-bye. "I can't bear to lose him again."

A faint frown turned Tobias's mouth down. Again? He didn't understand, but that didn't matter. "I'll do whatever you ask, girl. You deserve that much."

Chapter Twenty-two

Zach was in a dangerous mood.

Three days! How could anybody disappear completely for that length of time?

His finger tightened over the tumbler of brandy. Oh, he knew how it had happened! With the help of a certain old man who'd gotten downright cantankerous these last months.

He should've known better than to leave Elyse aboard with Tobias when they'd reached Sydney. He should've seen the affection the old man had for her, known he'd try to help her if she asked.

As it was, he hadn't needed to confront Tobias when he'd returned and found her gone. The wily old physician had come to him. Throwing the pendant down on his desk, Tobias had told him exactly what he'd done, and why. Then he'd calmly warned Zach not to go looking for Elyse, saying he had no right to her, no claim. Tobias had told him to let her go!

Well, he'd tried. Damned if he hadn't. He knew Tobias was right. Now that they'd reached Sydney, Elyse was well out of it. He'd used her as a hostage to lure Barrington, and in the next days or weeks, no more, he'd know if Barrington had come after him.

But damn, he couldn't get her out of his thoughts, her and that ridiculous notion of hers. Not once, not one minute had he had any peace since she'd slipped off the *Tamarisk*. And the nights were worse. Her tale haunted him; she haunted him.

God knows, he'd tried forcing her from his thoughts. He'd done everything imaginable to get rid of her memory. But it was no good. That was why he'd stayed in Sydney instead of leaving with Sandy when the *Tamarisk* had smiled for the Raven's hideout on Fraser Island the day before. That was why he'd combed

every backwater hotel and boardinghouse, and checked out Tobias's acquaintances.

But the old man had hid her well. There was no sign of Elyse.
She'd wanted to disappear from his life and she had. And that
was why he'd come to Alice, hoping against hope that perhaps
she could make him forget. But it hadn't worked. Memories of
Elyse had become even stronger, more intense. They invaded his
dreams until he had no peace, until he knew only her and the
desire he remembered.

"Goddammit!"

Alice Mulroney jumped as he slammed the crystal tumbler
down on the table. She didn't care about the drinking, which had
been pretty constant since Zach had returned to Sydney, because
it had kept him in bed with her longer than a few hours, even if
he had been too drunk to make love to her. Zach Tennant was a
man who usually controlled his drinking as he controlled his
emotions. But the last three days he'd controlled neither. First,
he'd showed up at her place, roaring drunk, and had invited her
out on the town to celebrate. Although he hadn't elaborated on
what they were celebrating, she'd assumed it was his return. And
she'd been happy enough to celebrate. She'd been eight long
months without him, and as far as she was concerned, no other
could compare with Zach Tennant.

So they'd celebrated high, wide, and handsome, staying out
late, eating at the most fashionable restaurants. He'd even promised to take her shopping today, which she knew he detested.
Whatever was responsible for the change in him, Alice liked it.
Now it was merely a matter of getting him to keep his promise.
She had an entire list of shops she wanted to visit. After all, she
didn't find him in this kind of a mood often.

Alice slowly approached him, wrapping her arms around his
neck.

Zach's head was thrown back against the settee. He felt the
subtle pressure, the soft skin that somehow wasn't quite the same
as he remembered. Lis. Her name came through the hazy mist
created by expensive brandy. Yet something nagged at his senses.
The cologne was too strong, almost overpowering. His eyes
opened slowly, gray heat suddenly turning steely. She hadn't
worn any cologne. She hadn't needed it. His fingers twined in
the long strands of hair that lay across his bare shoulder. They
were coarse and pale, not the rich, vibrant color of darkest sable.
As his senses cleared, Zach released the blond tresses. He

reached for the tumbler, refilling it.

"Zach!" Alice pouted a bit, knowing from past experience she could only push him so far. But then, he was acting quite differently than he had in the past. Her pale blue eyes narrowed as she wondered about the changes in him. Was it possible he'd grown tired of the sea and wanted to settle down? This was the first time he'd ever come directly to her after a long voyage. Usually he'd gone straight to that damned sheep ranch of his. She didn't think much of Resolute. The idea of wasting away on a dirty, stinking ranch didn't appeal to her. That was why she'd had Zach buy her this small house in Sydney. It was perfect for her, and for Zach when he was in town. If they were to marry, she'd convince him to build a bigger house in town. And it would be a grand house. She knew Zach had plenty of money. She softened her voice as a frown appeared on his handsome face.

"You did promise to take me shopping today. Don't you remember?

Zach came out of the chair so suddenly that Alice drew back in alarm. He slammed the tumbler against the bedroom wall, brandy staining the wallpaper to soft gold.

She knew how to soothe his rages, and softly crossed the room, slipping her arms around his bare waist. "Don't you remember? You promised yesterday. Can't we please go? Then we can come back here and spend the rest of the day in bed. We can even have my housekeeper bring dinner up here." Her fingers caressed the hard muscles on his chest, brushing against the new scar, a wide crescent in gleaming bronze skin. Her lips moved across his back teasingly, promising what might come later.

Zach whirled around. His fingers closing like steel bands over her wrists, he jerked her around in front of him. Her eyes were wide.

"I didn't mean to hurt you," she stammered. "It's just that it looks like it's healed. It's such a bad scar. How did you get it?"

"Do you want to go shopping?" Zach asked wearily, pushing her away from him.

"Of course I do, darling." Alice was acting like an excited child, and at that moment was as aggravating as one.

"Then get dressed," he ground out. Seizing his shirt and jacket from the wardrobe, he stalked to the door. "If you're not downstairs in ten minutes, I'm leaving." The door slammed shut behind him.

"Ten minutes! I can't possibly be ready in ten minutes. Zach?" Damn! What had gotten into him anyway. Absolutely nothing about the man was predictable since he'd returned. But she was ready on time quite simply because she wasn't about to pass up the opportunity to spend some of Zach's money.

Ten minutes. Zach prayed like hell she wouldn't be ready. In all the time he'd known Alice she couldn't so much as comb her hair in ten minutes, let alone get fully dressed and presentable. He'd given her the ultimatum because the last thing he wanted was to be dragged along on one of her shopping binges.

But ten minutes brought him something he did want. A smile was on his face when Alice came downstairs within the appointed amount of time. It disappeared when he saw her. He nodded curtly to Tris who'd brought the information he'd waited days to hear. He'd promised to go with Alice and there was no easy way out of the obligation. A lengthy explanation would be necessary and he wasn't about to give her one. Maybe he could accomplish two things at one time. He wanted was to see Elyse again, to say the good-byes she'd robbed him of days earlier. If he knew she was all right, then maybe he could be finished with her.

But his mood was just as dark as it had been earlier when he escorted Alice from the house and gave specific instructions to the coachman to take them to an area where there were many small exclusive shops. It was very near a certain hotel.

Elyse slipped out of the hotel, cautiously looking in one direction then the other. She silently chided herself for her precautions. It had been three days since Tobias had slipped her off the *Tamarisk* and brought her here. And in that time no one had so much as approached her, except for a polite gentleman or two at the hotel; they'd been surprised to find a young Englishwoman unescorted. But Elyse was far from alone.

Tobias had to return to the *Tamarisk* that first day so as not to raise Zach's suspicions about her disappearance. But if she needed to contact him, she could do so through Kimo, who preferred to stay with a young woman in Sydney. Tobias had assured her that Kimo could quickly get a message to him.

It was with little satisfaction that Elyse realized she'd been successful in disappearing from the *Tamarisk*. She'd registered at the hotel under a different name. If Zachary Tennant could do it, so could she. For the past three days, Elyse had used Lucy

Maitland's name. And she was absolutely miserable at being so successful in her escape.

In these few days, she'd accomplished a great deal, however, most of it the first day.

As miraculous as it seemed, Tobias had managed to get her off the ship without being seen. They'd waited until most of the crew had gone ashore, including Zach. Then they'd simply left. She'd hated to ask it of him, knowing his loyalty to Zach, but there simply had been no other way. And he'd agreed without question or argument.

He'd brought her to the St. Charles Hotel. It was one of the better hotels in Sydney, and was located in the center of town. The matter of her finances had been just as easily settled. Tobias was not a man without means. He'd simply agreed to lend her the money she needed until arrangements could be made for her to return to England. Reluctantly, Elyse had accepted his offer, knowing she had no other choice. She'd signed a note, and had given Tobias her pearl and diamond pendant as collateral. He was to hold it until she could repay him; she fully intended to have it back.

The hotel manager was acquainted with Tobias, and his wife had referred Elyse to several shops. She'd purchased two ready-made gowns and a few accessories, then she'd paid a visit to a dressmaker and had been fitted for several more gowns. She'd also purchased a trunk for the return voyage and had visited a shipping company to arrange passage to London. She found it ironic that she would be returning on a Barrington ship. She prayed Zach wouldn't take it upon himself to sink it.

Now she carefully made her way along the sidewalk in Sydney. It was midmorning on a bright, early spring day. She shook her head, marveling at this strange city. As Tobias had promised, it was like other large cities, but it was also very different from London. It was now early fall back home. The days could be crisp and cool there, fog rolling in off the Thames of an evening. But here, down under, as Tobias liked to say, Sydney was enjoying the first days of spring, the weather being bright and balmy.

Elyse had last seen England in the early spring and summer, now she was experiencing spring in Australia. If she was able to get immediate passage to England, she would arrive in time to enjoy spring there again. A whole year of her life would have passed, yet she would have seen only one season.

Those were her thoughts as she stepped into the dressmaker's shop not far from the hotel. They were much safer thoughts than the ones that had haunted her these last three days, and less frightening than the dreams that filled her sleepless nights.

"Just one more shop. Please, Zach." Alice stretched up on her toes, pressing a kiss against his cheek. She was instantly made aware of his disapproval by the hardening of the muscle at his jaw.

"All right! One more." Zach indulged her because he was stalling for time. He closed his eyes a moment against the throbbing pain of a hangover. God, how the hell does Tobias stand it? he wondered. The truth was, Tobias didn't. In the years Tobias had drunk, he'd rarely sobered up long enough to experience a hangover. But the last weeks of the voyage, he'd been stone sober. Whatever had caused him to do that must have been very important, Zach reflected.

Then he groaned. If Alice didn't hurry, he'd leave her in the shop. Elyse, or Lucy Maitland as she was calling herself, had already left the St. Charles. Obviously the hotel manager's wife had been mistaken about Elyse coming this way to do some shopping. He had to find her.

His head was splitting, his eyes felt as if they were being squeezed out of their sockets, his mouth was dry, and his tongue, twice its normal size, seemed coated with fur. It had been a long time since he'd felt this bad, and his failure to find Elyse did nothing to improve his mood.

Alice made this last stop a quick one. She knew Zach was fast losing what little patience he had, and she didn't want to ruin a good thing. She came out of the milliner's carrying two hatboxes and found him where she'd left him. Desire tightened deep inside her. She wouldn't mind staying in bed with him the rest of the day. Just thinking of doing so held the promise of all kinds of pleasures.

"There." She smiled prettily. "I'm all finished. That's the last stop." She leaned against him, her breast pressing into his arm through the satin material of her gown. "I bought something I think you'll especially like. It's the latest lingerie from France. I'll try it on for you when we get back," she purred huskily. She looked up when there was no immediate response.

"Zach!"

But he was already walking away from her in long, angry

475

strides, his hands clenched into tight fists.

"Zach Tennant!" Alice stomped a leather-slippered foot. "Damn you, what is it now?" She bit back whatever else she might have said when she noticed several people looking in her direction. Handing the hatboxes to her driver, she lifted her skirts a bit and went after him. He passed the milliner's, then turned into the dress shop. She smiled secretly to herself. Why of course! Zach intended to buy her something.

Elyse had just stepped out of the ready-made gown she'd worn that morning. Standing in the curtained enclosure, wearing only a lacy camisole and pantalets, her feet bare, she heard the urgent tinkling of the bell over the shopkeeper's door. There'd been two women in the shop when she'd entered, and the seamstress hadn't yet gotten to her. Now it seemed someone else had come in. She hoped the woman would have time for the fittings.

Alice Mulroney waited outside the shop for just a moment, to give Zach the time he needed to make his selection. When she could delay no longer, she followed him inside. She was right behind him, a slight frown wrinkling her lovely brow as he bypassed the seamstress, two customers, and the shop's owner, heading for the back of the shop.

Zach stopped before the enclosure at the rear. The French seamstress, the two customers, the owner, and Alice gaped in stunned amazement as he seized the satin curtains and tore them aside.

Elyse jerked around, gasping as she clutched her gown to the front of her body.

"*Monsieur! Monsieur!*" the seamstress shrieked. One woman fainted into the shopkeeper's arms, and Alice was as shocked as Elyse.

"Good morning, madam!" Anger, surprise, joy, and relief collided in Zach as he greeted her. But only one emotion was reflected in those flashing silver eyes.

"My God!" It was all Elyse could manage as she stood there using the gown as a barrier, trying to spread it across the exposed parts of her body. She failed miserably, and a slow appreciative smile spread across Zach's lips.

"I've been called a lot of things, but never that. Now, get dressed and be ready to leave immediately!"

Elyse's mouth dropped open, but she was already beginning to recover. The first solid emotion she felt was anger. How dare he walk back into her life like this! Her eyes shaded a darker blue, her lips set in a determined line.

"You can't give me orders here, Zachary Tennant. I'm not a prisoner aboard your ship any longer!" Elyse waved a tiny fist at him, but when she did, the gown gaped away from her heaving breasts. She was at a decided disadvantage. She could fight him off practically naked or she could hold the dress to her body. He seemed to be taking great delight in her dilemma.

"Prisoner? Zach, what is going on here?" Alice came up behind him. That was her first mistake. The second was her irritating and demanding tone of voice.

"Get out of here, Alice," Zach growled menacingly. "This doesn't concern you."

"Doesn't . . . !" Alice stared at him incredulously. "It most certainly does concern me." She wedged her way around Zach, planting her hands firmly on her slender hips. "I demand to know what you're doing in here." That was her third mistake.

When Zach turned to look at her, his eyes could have turned a pot of boiling water to ice. "One more time; it's none of your business. Get out. And keep your voice down. You're creating a scene."

"A scene?" Alice's eyes narrowed venomously. "You dare tell me I'm creating a scene when you march in here like some sort of crazed person and assault this . . . this . . ." She fumed as she sought the right word.

"Whore!" That was her fourth mistake.

Zach's hand snaked out with lightning speed, trapping her slender wrist in a viselike grasp that threatened to break it. He bent over Alice, his towering height dwarfing her completely, and drawing out every word, he said deliberately, "The . . . lady . . . is . . . my . . . wife! Get out of here! Now!"

"Wife?" Alice's mouth gaped open as she stared at him. For the first time since she'd entered the shop, perhaps for the first time in her life, she was stunned into silence.

If Zach had wanted to attract everyone's attention, he'd succeeded magnificently. Elyse could only stare at him. Of all the nerve! Of all the bold-faced nerve! Great balls of fire, who the hell did he think he was, humiliating her like this with his . . . his . . .

Elyse groaned. She felt as if she were going to faint. All of a sudden it was oppressively warm in the shop and everyone was shouting.

Then she realized Zach was the only person speaking. Actually, he wasn't shouting; he was merely threatening everyone in sight, everyone except the blond woman who'd come in with him. All at once the small dressing room looked like Victoria Station at the beginning of summer. The only person lacking was a uniformed train conductor. But a man in uniform was just coming through the door. She slumped down onto a chair, trying to gather her wits about her. Damn Zach anyway! How had he found her, and what right did he have to come after her? Unless . . . Oh, God! Was it possible that he'd decided to give up his plan for revenge? Had Tobias somehow managed to convince him of the danger? Her startled gaze fastened on him. Had he somehow begun to believe her?

Alice Mulroney fumed. "This is it, Zach Tennant! We're through. This is absolutely the last time you can do something like this to me. I won't be—"

"Won't be what, Alice?" Zach's voice was a honied blade. "You know I don't like threats," he warned. "And I suggest that in light of your current status, you shut your mouth and get out of here."

The last had the effect of completely taking the wind out of her sails. "You wouldn't," she breathed in disbelief.

"I don't make promises I don't intend to keep."

Alice knew when to back down; when it was a matter of money. And this most certainly was. Her relationship with Zach was tenuous at best; it always had been. If she wanted to salvage anything from this, she had to be careful.

"Of course, Zach." Her voice was tight as she twisted her hands together and slowly backed away from him. "We can discuss it later." He only nodded.

"Zach?" She hesitated too long. One threatening glance was enough to send her flying to the door.

"Uh-hum!" At the loud clearing of a throat, Zach turned around to the uniformed constable.

"Is there a problem here?" the man asked officiously, trying to keep his eyes averted from Elyse.

Zach immediately stepped into the opening of the dressing room, shielding her from prying glances. "No problem at all."

The constable tried looking over Zach's shoulder, but he was at least six inches shorter and could see nothing. "A very distraught woman said there was some difficulty here. She said a young lady was being accosted."

Zach's smile was catlike, and Elyse groaned, almost expecting to hear him purr. "There is no difficulty at all, sir. I'm certain you can understand the situation. My wife came here to buy some new gowns. She just bought a dozen last week."

Elyse groaned. Wife? A dozen new gowns? He was mad.

"This morning she informed me she needed at least a dozen more. Then, not one hour after she left, I received last month's bill from another shop." The expression on Zach's face was one of frustration. "That makes a total of thirty-four new gowns in less than two months. I'm certain you can understand how upset I was."

This had to be absolutely the best performance she'd ever seen. She could tell by the expression on the constable's face that he believed every word. Zach would have him eating out of his hand in another few minutes.

"I understand. I have that same problem with my wife. But she has a thing for hats. It's a crime. You ought to see the awful things she comes home with." The constable smiled agreeably, and then, seeing that the commotion had died down, he gave everyone one last look before turning to leave. He paused at the door.

"Only one cure for it."

"What's that?" Zach looked as if he truly wanted to know.

The constable lowered his voice, making certain the other ladies were out of the range of hearing. "We have four kids and another on the way. She hasn't bought a new hat in over a year. She doesn't have the time. I keep her too busy."

Zach chuckled as the man left. Then he turned back to Elyse.

She came up off the chair as though she'd been catapulted, waving the dress at him as if she were thrusting a red flag in front of a bull. "Damn you, Zach Tennant! What right do you have to come in here and embarrass me and threaten everyone else?"

He knew she'd be angry over what he'd done, but now he had absolutely no idea what he was going to say to her. He wanted to strangle her, yell at her, throw her over his knee and thrash the living daylights out of her for scaring him these last three days. He also wanted to take her in his arms and hold her until she was no longer shouting at him. And he wanted to make love to her. Damned if he did not! He wanted it more than anything else at that moment, wanted her more than he'd ever wanted any other woman. She was beautiful when she was angry. Beautiful in sleep, or in men's clothes, or standing on the deck of the *Tamarisk* with the wind blowing in her hair. And in the last three days he'd come to terms with everything he felt.

But she was furious, and wasn't about to listen to anything he had to say even if he did have it all sorted out, which he didn't. So he quite simply said the only thing he could at that moment.

"You're my wife and you're coming with me." He reached for her arm.

"Bloody hell I will!" Elyse backed away, warning him. "If you lay a hand on me, I'll call that policeman back."

"And tell him what?" Zach watched her with maddening calm.

"I'll tell him everything. I'll tell him who you really are," she hissed at him.

"Who is it I'm supposed to be now, sweet Lis?"

Tears pooled in her eyes. He was deliberately being hurtful. "You know perfectly well what I mean. El Cuervo!"

Zach shook his head, not the least moved by her threats. "I beg you to remember, Lis, under English law, like it or not, we are married. And under English law, a wife cannot testify or speak out against her husband."

When her mouth dropped open, Zach gently slipped a finger beneath her lovely chin, closing it. He brushed her lips with his, in a very tender kiss. "Now, dear wife, please get dressed, or I will be forced to drag you, as you are, out into the streets of Sydney." He turned to step outside the closure.

"You wouldn't!"

"I've seen you in far less, sweet Lis." He looked back at her, his eyes stealing over her like silver fire. "You know I would."

Pain stabbed through her. He hadn't said one word to her about his feelings. Not one word! The dress still clutched firmly in one hand, she planted both hands on her hips.

"I won't go with you, Zach," she calmly declared; her voice low. But he heard and whirled around.

"You are coming with me," he informed her coolly.

"Where?"

"I'm taking you to Resolute."

"Why?"

Her dark lustrous hair, once coiled neatly atop her head, had come undone, tendrils of it escaping to her shoulders. The color in her cheeks was high, and her magnificent blue eyes glistened with anger and determination. Didn't she know how very much he wanted her, know the torment he'd been through these last days while trying to find her?

"Damn!" Zach swore softly. "Because it's safer there."

She almost laughed. "Safe? From whom? Surely not Jerrold. You forget. I'm the reason he's coming after you. He won't harm me.

"I haven't forgotten. I haven't forgotten anything!" His voice was low, almost inaudible. He turned away from her, unable to meet her eyes. "I want you at Resolute because you belong there."

Hope soared within her and she took a step toward him, oblivious of the shopkeeper, the seamstress, anyone except this man she loved so desperately. "Then you do believe it." Her voice was equally soft, slipping over his senses like a caress.

Zach silently cursed. It was back to that. No! He didn't believe it. What she'd told him weeks ago aboard the *Tamarisk* just wasn't possible. Alex Barrington had been his father, plain and simple. The rest of it—the dreams and memories, her knowledge of things she couldn't possibly know, the pendant—that was all coincidence. He didn't believe it was more; he couldn't pretend that he did.

"Elyse . . ."

Elyse this time, not Lis, as he'd come to affectionately call her, an intimate name lovingly used in that other life. Tears welled in her eyes. He wouldn't let himself believe any of it. He loved her, but he still refused to accept the truth. Nothing had changed. Nothing. And if he died confronting Jerrold, he would be lost to her forever. She knew it in her heart.

"Alex," she pleaded, everything within her reacting purely on instinct. Then she caught herself as she realized what she'd called him. It had been so natural, had slipped out so easily, yet it had accomplished just the opposite of what she wanted. She could see the anger hardening in his eyes.

"Damn! I don't want it to be this way between us!" Now he was yelling at her.

And she was yelling back. "It's the only way it can be. I can't stay with you if you go through with this plan of revenge. In the name of God, can't you see it! It's repeating the past; the same anger and hatred that started it all. If you go out there, you're no better than Jerrold or Charles. And I'll lose you forever."

"You can't let it go, can you?" He hurled the words at her, all the anger and worry of the last days pushing him past caution. "Because of some foolish idea, some coincidences—nothing else— you won't let it go."

481

She shook her head. "They're not coincidences. I don't know how or why these things happened, I only know they have. I've had the dreams almost all of my life. They began that night when I almost drowned, the night Felicia Barrington died. Somehow, her life, everything she'd known and felt, became part of my life. You became part of my life."

Zach shook his head, knowing he was losing her. He was a practical person, he believed in what he could see and touch. He couldn't accept the possibility that Alex Barrington lived again through him. But he couldn't bear to lose her either.

"Please come to Resolute." Emotion was hard in his voice, and Elyse knew what it cost him to ask her rather than order her. But it was no use. Those weren't the words she wanted or needed. "I can't."

Zach swore softly as he spun about on his heel and charged out of the dressing room, past the shopkeeper, the seamstress, and one very shocked customer who hadn't been able to tear herself away from all this. The door of the shop slammed behind him, the bell overhead clattering violently.

He was gone, really gone. And so was her last hope that things might be different. Oh, she'd hoped all right. She'd prayed every moment of the last three days that somehow, in spite of using Lucy's name, in spite of sneaking off the *Tamarisk*, in spite of leaving him, that he would come after her. Countless times she'd envisioned the moment when he would finally come to her and admit that he could accept the truth of their previous lives. But it wasn't to be. He really was lost to her.

In a fit of frustration and anger she tore the new dress to shreds. That only brought on an onslaught of tears.

"Damn you!" Elyse said aloud. Then she crumpled onto the chair in the small dressing room. She cried and cried, completely soaking what was left of the satin dress.

Elyse was at the hotel four days later when word arrived late in the morning that Jerrold Barrington had arrived in Sydney. The presence in the colonies of such an influential man wasn't something that could go unnoticed, especially when he'd arrived with an escort of three royal frigates.

She'd given her correct name to the hotel manager, evading his questioning stare, knowing it would now be easy for Jerrold to find her. He didn't disappoint her.

Elyse was waiting for him in the sitting room of her suite when he arrived late that afternoon.

"My God, Elyse." He rushed across the room toward her, quickly taking her in his arms. "You're safe. You can't imagine, all manner of things ran through my mind when that pirate abducted you." He tried to kiss her, but she abruptly pulled away from him.

"You are all right? My God, if he hurt you?" He began to make threats, but Elyse cut him off.

"I'm unhurt, as you can see," she assured him.

He seemed to accept that, and took her hands in both his. "I know all this must be painful for you to talk about, and we don't need to discuss it now. But I want to assure you the man will be made to pay for what he's done. You have no idea of the crimes he's committed. He's responsible for sinking several of my ships. Did you know he's also known as the Raven?"

Elyse pulled her hands from his. "I don't know anything about that," she lied, as she turned away from Jerrold and put distance between them by sitting on the settee. But, undaunted, he followed her, sitting down beside her.

"I have the proof I need. It will be only a matter of time before the fool is in jail or at the bottom of the sea. Either way, I fully intend to put an end to the Raven. But let me assure you, my darling, he'll be punished for what he's done to you."

Elyse almost laughed out loud. Done to me, she thought crazily. What had he done to her? Oh God, her head was spinning. What had he done? He'd come back to her; across time, beyond death. If only he'd accept it. But he wouldn't and now Jerrold was determined to see him brought to trial, or worse. The laughter she'd been trying to hold back came out as a small jerky sob.

"Elyse, my love, I didn't mean to frighten you. I know how dreadful this has been for you. But it will all be over very soon. Of course, your statement will be needed at the trial when he's caught. It will be difficult to prove the crimes he's committed as the Raven. I swear these damned colonists are unfailingly loyal. They've made him out to be some sort of folk hero of all things. But that is about to come to an end. He'll be made to pay for what he's done and then we can return to England together as man and wife."

Elyse sprang up off the settee, needing to put distance between herself and Jerrold. She paced the room. Man and wife? Great balls of fire! What was he thinking? She didn't want to be married to Jerrold. What was she thinking! She couldn't be married to Jerrold, she was already married. And, according to English law, a wife couldn't testify against her husband.

She turned back to him. "Jerrold, I don't want you to do this." Oh God, could she pull this off? Would he do as she asked?

"What are you saying?"

"Just that. I want all this ended." As much as it galled her to ask him for anything, Elyse was willing to try. "I don't want you to go after him."

Jerrold came up off the settee after her. "Elyse, for God's sake. What happened to you on that voyage?"

"Nothing happened. I just want this ended. It's over. Let it go." For a brief moment she thought Jerrold might consider what she was asking. In the next, she knew he wouldn't. Nothing had changed. Jerrold hadn't changed. She saw it in the cruel hardening of his eyes.

"Elyse, I know you've been through a great deal," he said indulgently. "But you must understand, this has gone too far to ignore. The man's crimes are atrocious."

Anger rose in her as she realized he wasn't about to do as she asked. He didn't give a damn about her feelings, had never cared one whit for her.

"As atrocious as the crimes of the Crown against the colonies?" she spat out before she realized exactly what she was saying. Once she'd spoken the words, she wasn't about to take any of them back.

"You know nothing about any of this, Elyse. You've only recently arrived in New South Wales, and undoubtedly you've been under very unsavory influences these past weeks. I can see that you're still quite exhausted from the whole ordeal; we can discuss it later. I've taken rooms here at the hotel so I might be near you when all of this is finished."

"I've arranged for the trial to be concluded quickly, if he's brought in alive. As I said, your testimony will be required. If, by some stroke of good fortune, the man should choose to stand and fight, I assure you he will not survive and then we can be done with this very quickly."

His voice was cold, his manner authoritarian as it had always been with her. With startling clarity, Elyse knew this would be the pattern of her life if she married him. Was it worth it?

She squared her slender shoulders. "You're quite right, Jerrold. I have been through quite a lot. But you may as well know that I won't be testifying against anyone."

"What?"

That one word whipped across the distance between them, stinging at her. It sent fear slipping down her spine, and she shivered in spite of the warmth of the spring day. She placed herself behind the settee preferring the safety of that barrier.

"I can't testify against him, Jerrold."

"You can and will!" he informed her coldly. "I haven't come all this way just to see him escape me again."

So that was it. Now she knew. It wasn't love for her that had sent Jerrold after Zach. That was merely a convenient excuse. He wanted him, but for far different reasons. He didn't care about her; he was protecting the Barrington family fortune, his fortune. Her chin angled slightly.

"A wife cannot be forced to testify against her husband," she stated flatly. The explosion she'd expected came.

"What!" Jerrold roared at her. "Do you mean to tell me . . . ?"

"You witnessed the ceremony yourself. We were married before we left England."

"You can't possibly mean that farce of a ceremony performed under duress on the day we were to be married?" His hard glare bore into her, trying to see the meaning behind her words.

"I meant just that." Elyse knew Jerrold well enough to know exactly how far she could push him. Beyond a certain point, he could be violent, explosive.

"Then I have to ask just one more question." A muscle ticked in his left cheek, his lips thinning into a hard line. "Did he force himself on you?"

Oh God, this couldn't be happening. Force himself on her? She might say yes. But when had that been? That first time in London, the night he'd gotten her out of the club? Or was it aboard the *Tamarisk* when he'd stormed into her cabin? Both times his lovemaking had been almost violent, ravaging. But had he forced himself on her?

"No," she answered simply, and it was the truth. There had been no violation. In spite of everything when he'd come to her that first time, she'd wanted him, wanted him with all the longing of her soul.

"Thank God for that," Jerrold spat out. "You can't make me believe you actually feel something for this man, or that he feels something for you." It was as if he were merely asking to hear her deny it, certain that she would.

485

"No," she responded, but the reply answered only half of his question. He doesn't feel anything for me, her heart cried out.

"Then you should have no qualms about giving a statement to the magistrate," Jerrold concluded. "And we can clean up the messy detail of that ceremony right here in New South Wales. I intend that we should be married before we return to England."

"Jerrold. You haven't heard a word I've said." Elyse boldly stood her ground. "I won't be making any statement."

His eyes glittered as he seemed to understand that there was something behind her words. "I see. As I said, Elyse, you're obviously distraught. I'll leave you now. You need more time to recover from this ordeal. I'll take care of this so that there will be no necessity for you to make a statement." Picking up his hat, Jerrold whipped away from her and stalked across the room.

Elyse flew to the door after him. "Jerrold, please don't do this! Let's leave now and forget what happened. I'll go back to England with you now, today. We can be married when we get there. I always wanted a church wedding." Then she stopped, a coldness sweeping over her at the realization of what she'd said.

It was exactly the same as it had been so many years ago, when she'd bargained for Alex's life by promising to marry Charles. And just as in that other life that ended so sadly, this man wasn't about to keep any promises he made. In her heart she knew it, and she knew the reason. That was it, it must be!

"You know who he is!" she whispered incredulously.

"Yes, Elyse, I know. Zachary Tennant, my cousin. Son of my father's long-lost convict brother."

"Then you must know the truth about Charles and Alex."

Jerrold laughed at her. It was a cold laugh, completely devoid of all feeling. "Yes, I know that as well. I've always known. I was the one who made all those payments to the downstairs maid. She was the only one who actually saw what happened. But the money guaranteed her silence. It kept her quiet for years. Until he came to England and started asking all those questions. I didn't trust him, not from the very beginning, especially after he seemed so drawn to you.

"Then, when I realized who he really was, I knew it would double my pleasure at seeing him dead. Be ready to leave when I return. I have no desire to stay any longer than absolutely necessary in this godawful place."

"You'll never find him, Jerrold," Elyse said desperately. "He knows you're coming. He'll wait until he has the advantage. You

486

don't know these waters."

"That's where you're wrong, my sweet." He managed to make the endearment seem dirty and degrading. "I know exactly where to find him. You see, he hasn't counted on the power of the Barrington name and wealth. Money can buy anything, especially a man's loyalty. I know exactly where to find the Raven. Even now the commander of the royal frigate is waiting for my return. We shall spring our trap at Fraser Island and snare the Raven. Make no mistake about it." His hand was on the doorknob.

He was leaving and she had to stop him. "Jerrold, please! It's not necessary. He doesn't care about the land, the title, none of it. It doesn't mean anything to him. His life is here."

"Your loyalty is very touching, Elyse. And quite revolting. But you're wrong." He whirled back to her, the expression on his face making her blood run cold.

"And the man is hardly worth it. Within hours the Raven and Zachary Tennant will be dead, and you will be my wife." His eyes lit up at the expression of horror on her face. "His life is not here, my pet, only his death."

Chapter Twenty-three

Elyse was frantic.

Jerrold knew about Fraser Island. Tobias had told her that was where Zach and his crew would be hiding out. Did Zach know Jerrold had arrived in Sydney? And how had Jerrold gotten his information? Was there a traitor among the *Tamarisk*'s crew who'd willingly passed it on for a few pieces of gold? Somehow she had to warn Zach. But how?

Her only hope of getting word to him in time was to find the African, Kimo. Tobias had given her the address where the huge dark man usually stayed when he was in Sydney. It was the house of the young woman Kimo hoped to marry.

Elyse dashed across her hotel room. Would Jerrold sail with the naval vessels, or would he merely wait, content to gloat and indulge in visions of victory? No, she quickly decided, Jerrold would want to be in the thick of it. The look in his eyes had told her so. He wanted Zach dead, and wouldn't be satisfied until he'd seen proof of it. Besides, now that Jerrold knew that Zach was Alex's son, his need for Zach's death had increased.

Now the raids Zach had led against Barrington ships and his abduction of her were merely salt in the wound. The heart of the matter, the greatest risk to Jerrold, was the loss of the Barrington empire itself. It was his because of betrayal, murder, and false accusations. He'd do no less to keep it.

Elyse fought back waves of fear as she descended the wide staircase to the lobby of the hotel. Did Zach already know Jerrold was in Sydney? He seemed to know everything before it happened. Had he already returned to the *Tamarisk* after he'd left her, or had he gone to Resolute, thinking Jerrold wouldn't come for several more days? The questions tore at her. But this simple fact was that Jerrold knew the *Tamarisk* was at Fraser Island. He would go there and wait. Then he would close the trap.

Elyse quickly hailed a hansom cab and gave the driver Kimo's address. She promised him double the usual fare if he made the trip quickly.

Twenty minutes later, Elyse descended in front of a modest home. The driver was instructed to wait as she flew to the door. She knocked impatiently, all manner of thoughts flying through her head. The expression on her face must have been revealing as Kimo came to the door, followed by a pretty dark-skinned young woman.

"Thank God you're here!" She was practically in tears. The large African stepped through the door, his heavy brow furrowing.

"What's wrong, Miss Elyse?"

"I've got to get word to Zach. Jerrold Barrington is here in Sydney. Do you know where Zach's gone?" She twisted and twisted at her hands.

Kimo nodded, trying to calm her. "I know, but I can't say."

"Great balls of fire, man!" Elyse exploded and immediately regretted it when she saw the young woman huddle behind Kimo's large body.

"I know all about Fraser Island."

"How you know about that?" His large amber eyes narrowed.

"Tobias told me, but Jerrold Barrington knows as well. He came to see me not over a half-hour ago. Somehow he's found out Zach keeps the *Tamarisk* at Fraser Island. He's laid a trap for him." Tears threatened, and Elyse fought them back. "Jerrold has two ships from the Royal Navy with him. Kimo, we have to do something!" Her voice had risen several octaves, and she could no longer hold back the tears.

"Who told Barrington about the island?"

"I don't know. I only know that's where he's gone! Kimo, please!"

The African nodded. "You stay here with Anna. You'll be safe. I'll go to the island and warn the cap'n."

Elyse's tears immediately disappeared. "I'm not staying here, not on your life! I'm going with you!" she announced with such grim determination Kimo knew it would be senseless to argue and waste valuable time. He only shook his large, handsome head.

"No good in those skirts, Miss Elyse."

"They'll do for now!" she declared. "I'm going. You may need help."

Kimo didn't argue. Instead he reentered the house and almost immediately reappeared at the door, strapping a long cutlass to his waist, a pistol already tucked in his belt. Elyse's eyes widened but she said nothing. By the look she'd seen in Jerrold's eyes, she knew this would be a dangerous affair. Kimo came through the doorway and signaled to the driver. "I know a quick way."

Elyse ran after him, halting when she felt a tugging at her elbow. The shy young woman, Anna, held out a folded shirt and pants. "I sometimes wear them when I go certain places with Kimo."

Elyse took the garments. "Thank you." She smiled gratefully. "I'll try to bring them back to you in one piece."

"Missy!" Kimo yelled, and she ran to the carriage, accepting his big paw of a hand for assistance.

As long as she lived, Elyse would never forget that ride to the waterfront in Sydney. When the driver she'd hired seemed to lag behind in late afternoon traffic, Kimo merely grabbed the man by the scruff of the neck and tossed him out. He then seized the reins and took his own route. As he said, he knew a quicker way. He went right up over curbs and onto sidewalks, weaving in and out of coaches, wagons, and other carriages, taking side streets in which Elyse would've been hopelessly lost. But Kimo was not.

In what was surely half the time it would have taken her driver, he pulled the cab to a halt in front of a warehouse bearing a sign: N.S.W. Limited. Confusion quickly gave way to overwhelming relief as she saw Tobias emerging from the small front office.

"What is it? What's happened?"

Elyse was breathless with fear. "Jerrold is here in Sydney."

"When?"

"This afternoon. He came to the hotel."

"It was expected." Tobias nodded glumly. His brow furrowed. "But there's been no sign of them in the harbor. Only three ships came in today. One of them was the *Sultana*."

Elyse swallowed hard, remembering the hours she'd spent in the hold of that ship. "El Barracuda is here?"

"He's not for us to worry about. It's been quiet out there, and the harbor patrol here is real strict about the laws. If El Barracuda steps out of line, they'll run him up on the reef. His men came ashore earlier, but I haven't seen hide nor hair of him. At the moment, he's not our problem. I wonder if Barrington could have put in farther up the coast."

"Up the coast?" Elyse didn't understand what that meant.

The expression on Kimo's face matched Tobias's. "Fraser Island is up the coast."

Elyse's face drained of all color. "My God, Tobias! Jerrold knows about Fraser Island! He knows that's where Zach has the *Tamarisk*."

Tobias swore between clenched teeth. "Goddammit! How did he find out?"

"I don't know! Tobias, we've got to do something!" She wanted him to say everything would be all right; but his nervousness only increased hers.

He tried to soothe her. "Take it easy, lass. Zach knows what he's doin'. This isn't the first time he's gone after a Barrington ship."

"You don't understand. This isn't just a Barrington ship. Jerrold has brought a commander of the Royal Navy with him. They're taking three ships to Fraser Island!"

Tobias's expression was stark. At that moment he looked and felt every one of his sixty-three years. "God have mercy! They'll be surrounded and cut down. Damn the bloody bastard!"

"Oh God, Tobias! There's got to be something we can do!"

He stood for a long moment, rubbing his gnarled hand across his chin. "Damn! If only some of the men were here, but most every one of them is with Zach. Still, we might be able to round up some of the men from N.S.W."

"N.S.W.? Will someone please tell me what that means?" Elyse looked from one to the other.

Kimo nodded, grinning broadly and pointed to the emblem they'd seen on the building. "N.S.W.: New South Wales, Limited." The smile broadened. "Longshoremen; tough sons 'o beetches."

It took her a minute to understand. She turned to Tobias. "Will they help?"

"Help?" His eyes sparked with the first sign of hope she'd seen. "Zach will fire every one of them if they don't. They're not sailors, but they're good men and they work for him and the consortium. We only need one helmsman." He looked to Kimo.

The tall African nodded. "You give me somethin' with sails on it." He grinned broadly.

"A ship. Now there's the problem. There's not a ship in the harbor with enough guns to do any good, except the ships of the line. And they'll not likely put to sea to help a man they've been huntin' for the past five years." Tobias shook his head.

"There is one ship." Elyse's eyes glinted as her gaze fastened on the lone frigate flying the French flag. It was a deception, as when the *Tamarisk* had flown the colors of Spain while in English waters. The ship should actually be flying the skull and crossbones.

Zach checked the night watch, nodding to his man as he passed by. All lights aboard the *Tamarisk* had been extinguished. They couldn't afford to chance giving themselves away, even though nothing had been seen of Barrington.

Fraser Island was actually a small cluster of islands separated by shallow waterways and inlets that popped up at a moment's notice. The waters throughout the chain could be treacherous, if a navigator didn't know his way through them. Zach knew these waters well. And it was for just that reason he'd chosen to anchor the *Tamarisk* at Fraser when he wasn't in port.

Over the years, the islands had provided an excellent hideaway when he wasn't raiding. All ships leaving Sydney Harbor were forced to turn into the wind, directly in the path of the islands. But Zach knew as few other did, that the sea breezed around the islands could be traitorous. They blew contrary to most winds, causing more than one captain inexperienced in these waters to founder on the rocky shoals that crisscrossed through the chain, or to run up on the deadly reef just a little to the south when the wind suddenly died, leaving sails slack.

Zach had first ventured to these islands with the old sailor who'd taught him to maneuver the *Gypsy Moth*. He'd learned to sail without instruments, gauging direction by stars, currents, and wind. Knowing the sea had become second nature to him. Now, sipping at coffee as he watched the last light of day on the western horizon, he found his thoughts wandering.

He'd certainly made a mess of everything the last time he'd seen Elyse. Damn, but she was angry; and she had every right to be. He'd wanted to take her to Resolute. He felt she'd be safe there. Safe from what? Barrington. It came back to him just that simply.

There were two things he was certain of. He felt more for her than he'd ever felt for any woman. God, she had the ability to drive him to distraction. She could be headstrong, willful, and exasperating as hell. At one minute he'd wanted to strangle her for sneaking ashore into Lisbon, the next he'd been searching every tavern, gambling den, and whorehouse to find her. It occurred to him that he might be well rid of her, but that thought immediately fled before the much stronger realization that he couldn't bear losing her.

When in the hell had she become so important to him? That answer came just as quickly and simply: always, forever.

He'd wanted to tell her that. And then there hadn't been any time left. Not that she would have listened anyway, she was so angry then. And he'd been pressed to get to the *Tamarisk,* because he knew Barrington would show up soon. Actually he'd expected the man before this. Still, all the reports from Sydney were the same; no unusual shipping had entered the harbor, except the *Sultana.*

That gave him a chuckle. So, El Barracuda had managed to make repairs and put into Sydney in fairly good time. He wondered what the pirate's game was.

Suddenly Zach felt it again, that vague prickling of premonition. It was an uneasiness he couldn't quite name. The ship lay quietly at anchor, water lapping gently at her hull. Somewhere below, Sebastian squawked and was then silent, probably silenced with a piece of bread rather than the dull blade he deserved. Most of the men were below. The guards nodded as he passed them by. Nothing seemed out of the ordinary; still, he couldn't rid himself of that feeling.

Over and over again, he told himself this confrontation with Barrington was only unfinished business and after it was settled he'd find some way to make Elyse understand why it had been necessary. God, he couldn't forget the look in her eyes when she'd begged him not to go. But he had to have justice for his father's suffering. Somehow she had to understand that.

He? Christ! Now he was beginning to think of this as if it were his own revenge. Elyse's words came back to him. Did she really believe what she'd said, that somehow Felicia Barrington and his father . . . that they were . . .

He flung the idea away with the last dregs of coffee he threw overboard. He couldn't think about it now. There would be time enough later to try to understand it all. For now, he could think only of Barrington.

I've waited a long time, his heart cried out.

The British commander stood at the bow of the heavily gunned frigate, his feet planted firmly on the gently rolling deck as the vessel slipped through the night. He hoped to hell Barrington was right about all this. If not, they'd come a long way on a fool's errand. And earlier that day he'd begun to believe it was just that. Now it seemed Miss Elyse Winslow was refusing to testify against this man Barrington was convinced was the Raven. Without her testimony the abduction charges were meaningless. He looked at Jerrold Barrington, at the bow beside him.

"You had better be right about this, Barrington. I don't mind telling you the admiralty is gravely concerned about our inability to bring the Raven to justice."

"You need have no fear, Commander," Jerrold assured him with all the confidence of a wolf about to turn on a fox. "He'll lead us right to the Raven." He nodded to the shadowed third man. "Enough gold can buy anything, even a man's loyalty for a time. Isn't that right, my friend?" But Jerrold didn't need an answer.

"Now all we need is a little bit of time to put all the players in place." His teeth flashed in the midnight darkness. But they were overshadowed by the cold gleam in his eyes. Soon, he told himself. Soon.

Word had it that Tennant's ship had been seen in Sydney Harbor only days earlier. And if the man beside him was correct, there was one place where the Raven would be waiting for them, hoping to take advantage of the element of surprise. But surprise would be on their side. And this time there would be no escape. If the man beside him had lied, he would die.

The blood red dawn touched the decks of the *Tamarisk*, its ominous fingers muted by thin vapors of mist. The ship was cloaked in eerie silence. Moments before the guard had changed when the call went out from the watch posted on a nearby island. A sailor rowed back to the *Tamarisk* in the dinghy, scrambling quickly aboard.

"What did you see?"

"It's him, Cap'n. It's Barrington. That ship is sitting pretty as you please a few hundred yards off the mouth of the cove. I saw the flag myself; the Barrington crest along with the Union Jack."

Zach clapped his man on the shoulder. "Good work, Jalew. Did you see anything else?" Again that shimmering of uneasiness slipped down his spine.

"Not a thing, sir. Just one ship. I'd have seen 'em if there was more."

"Unless they came in under cover of night," Zach speculated to Sandy.

"No one would try it at night. It's too dangerous, Cap'n. You're the only one knows these waters good enough to do that."

Zach nodded, hoping his second mate was right. Then he turned to the rest of his crew and give the orders that would get them underway.

Jerrold Barrington waited aboard the Royal Navy frigate. He was using his own ship as the decoy, but he wasn't about to be in the line of fire when all the excitement began. No indeed! He wanted to be in a position to watch the slaughter when the Raven took the bait and came out into the open, thinking they were evenly matched.

The wind was sharp and strong, buffeting Tamarisk's flags against the center mast as she slipped from the hidden cove. The ship was a grand sight, her black hull slicing through the water, the rising sun slanting off bleached decks. Her center mast caught the blood red of the sun, reflecting it in the eyes of her crew, and overhead the red flag bearing the emblem of a jet black raven snapped beneath the colonial flag.

All aboard were ready, their eyes trained on the lumbering Barrington frigate. She rode low in the water, coming slowly about on a windward tack. It was then, as Tamarisk first became fully exposed, with the wind against her, that the cry went up. A blast rocked through the chain of islands, the echoes reverberating off the rocky peaks and cliffs. And in that instant, Zach knew the horrible truth. The frigate had only been the lure, sitting innocently in the shimmering blue-green water, tempting them to a deadly fate.

Tamarisk was running before the wind, Zach's original intention to come about and square off with the frigate. Now everything had changed. He took over the helm, realizing a trap had been laid. Cannons roared from the cloistered islands on either side of them, trying to slice the schooner to ribbons. If the wind held, Zach's only hope was the open sea.

Many times Zach had relied on the fickle winds that seemed to come at the islands from all directions, confusing inexperienced seamen. Now he was the victim of these same winds. *Tamarisk*'s sails billowed, tautened, held briefly, then fluttered wildly.

"Damn!" Zach cut the wheel sharply. They'd never outrun the two light frigates that were bearing down on them, having left from their hiding places amid the smaller islands nearby. *Tamarisk* was on a northerly tack, and came about to try to catch the wind. One frigate approached from the small island to the west, the other from the east. And now the third frigate, the decoy, was directly in *Tamarisk*'s line of fire. But even as they came alongside and Zach gave the command to fire, he knew Barrington was not aboard. Now his only hope was to outmaneuver the three heavier ships, slip past them back to the safety of the islands, and hide there until he could slip away under cover of darkness. It was not to be.

Zach sensed more than saw their game. The frigate poised off the starboard bow came about abruptly, seemingly giving way in the chase. The natural move would be to slip past her port side where even now her crew raced to reload the cannons. But Zach knew in that way lay disaster: shallow, rocky shoals. He might have fought on, the schooner fast and sure beneath him, but heavy cannon fire from the third frigate made the decision for him. One ball caught the center mast broadside. A long, sickening shudder passed through the *Tamarisk*. Canvas and line buckled to the decks.

He jammed the wheel hard to port as the wind caught the smaller sail and slowly carried them forward. They could stay and be cut to pieces by cannon fire, be no more than a target while Barrington proceeded to board and raise the Union Jack and take him prisoner; or there was one other alternative. Zach gave the command all aboard had known might one day come. The faces of the crew were grave as they went to their tasks. They were loyal men and did as bid without question.

Elyse's hair whipped across her face as she leaned over the rail of the *Sultana*. She strained her eyes in the direction Tobias had indicated. Slow and unwieldy, the frigate creaked disapprovingly as rough seas plumed over her bow.

Elyse tried to act as if she hadn't heard about the ploy Tobias had used to lure the remainder of El Barracuda's crew ashore hours earlier. But shouts had been heard clear across the harbor, as the infamous crew of the pirate ship had responded to word that there were a dozen new women at Sophie's down on the waterfront.

She pitied the hapless Sophie, whoever she might be, for having to deal with the rowdy customers descending on her establishment; even more she pitied the women who worked there. They had a full night ahead of them. But Tobias had informed her that Sophie's was actually owned by a mountainous Russian. He'd said the man could handle any number of men from the crew of the *Sultana*: five, ten, or twenty.

They'd put to sea just after midnight and had followed the coastline north. She hadn't been able to sleep. She kept remembering being aboard under far different circumstances. Finally dawn had come.

Beside her, Tobias held out a folded square of red silk. At her questioning stare, he motioned to the center mast where *Sultana's* flag flew.

"It's a bit of deception. I thought it might come in handy. Run up that new flag, girl."

Elyse did as he instructed, her eyes widening as the emblem, a bold, black raven, fluttered on a field of red. Deception indeed. Anyone seeing that flag might be persuaded to believe this was the Raven's ship.

She heard the firing before she could see anything, and sickening dread tightened deep inside her. She'd heard cannon blasts before, in the confrontation between Zach and El Barracuda, and had hoped never to hear them again. She jumped as other blasts came, too quickly, and she knew. The *Tamarisk* had been found.

Rather than skirting the chain of islands, Kimo and Tobias decided their best advantage was to slip through the narrow channel separating them from the mainland. Now they emerged, through the swirling mist to an eerie sight.

Elyse cried out as she saw the *Tamarisk* in the distance. Oh God! They were too late! That beautiful grand bird was crippled, her center mast a huge broken wing. And there were several gaping wounds along her black hull just above the waterline.

"Tobias!"

"Easy, girl. She's still afloat." He turned and yelled to the dock workers who'd come aboard with them. It was a scant crew, only a dozen men, Kimo, Tobias and herself. But they were all that

497

was needed. As every inch of canvas was hoisted, the *Sultana* plowed through the water, the hunters now the hunted.

To the west of them lay the green, swelling coastline of the Australian continent. To the east were the outer islands that made up Fraser Island, and the four ships. Tobias gave the orders as they came within range. With the precision of the physician he was, he executed the maneuver. The cannons on the starboard side exploded with a round of lethal fire, six in all. Four found targets. The element of surprise was now gone.

Zach heard the roar of cannon fire, and his head came up. His gaze narrowed. Damn! The *Sultana.* That was all they needed; El Barracuda had come to pick their bones. But as the cannon fire struck its target he realized there was something wrong, very wrong.

The first frigate to emerge from the islands and fire on Zach was now under siege. Elyse watched with satisfaction as the ship suffered substantial damage. Her crew scampered about, trying to shove fallen timbers out of the way. All the while, Kimo was maneuvering the *Sultana* into position for another broadside. Elyse's gaze swept back to the *Tamarisk.* She thought she saw Zach on deck, but couldn't be certain.

"Tobias!" she shrieked. "What is he doing?" He followed her frantic gesture, and by the expression on his face, she knew. Something he'd once said to her tore through the confusion of smoke and the roar of the cannons. He'd once told her that Zach would scuttle the *Tamarisk* before he'd allow the Union Jack to fly atop her mast. And as she watched, horrified, she realized that was exactly what he was doing.

The second frigate was slowly coming alongside the crippled schooner. They were close enough that Elyse could see those on board: several men in blue uniforms, sailors in their white pants and shirts, and Jerrold. Beside him stood a man she'd prayed she'd never see again.

"El Barracuda." The name was choked from her throat.

"What!" Tobias was instantly beside her. "Why that murderous, thievin' sonofa—He's the one who knew about Fraser Island!"

Elyse whirled on him. "But how? How could he possibly know?"

"Three years ago he tried to interfere when Zach took down a Barrington ship. He followed us here and then chased Zach all through the islands. But he had to give way when the *Sultana* almost grounded on one of those shoals. The *Sultana* has a deeper

498

draft than the *Tamarisk*." His voice was grim. "By God, I'll see him in hell for this." He raced across the deck, giving Kimo instructions to bring the *Sultana* about for another run. So far the wind was holding.

El Barracuda's shock and indignation showed on his face as the mist and smoke parted and he looked across the water at the *Sultana*, the red standard with the black raven flying from her center mast.

"What is that?" he screamed, outraged.

Jerrold followed his gaze, his eyes bulging from his sockets. The commander's eyes narrowed at sight of the flag.

"What is the meaning of this, Barrington? You assured me the *Tamarisk* was the Raven's ship. Yet another ship flies his flag."

"It's a trick!" Jerrold breathed out, fury tightening deep inside him. "I tell you, it's a trick!" The fury exploded as his gaze fell on Elyse standing on that far deck. Her gaze was defiant, filled with loathing and contempt. "Fire on them! Fire!"

The British officer beside him immediately countermanded the order. "Are you mad? At this close range the blast would kill us all!"

And they were close, dangerously close. Elyse was frantic as she watched the English frigate slip closer to the *Tamarisk*. And then she saw Zach's crew going overboard. They slipped over—one, two, three at a time—off the port side, away from the eyes of those on board the frigate. And then the men were swimming toward the closest island. A bright green object fluttered into the air high over the *Tamarisk*; Sebastian was winging his way to the island. She watched for Zach, straining to see through the smoke that now gusted toward them. It was coming from *Tamarisk!*

She never knew exactly what happened next. She never saw the bow of the *Sultana* slice into the frigate as Kimo guided her. It seemed everything exploded around them at once. She remembered holding onto the rail and watching, horrified, as massive explosions tore through the *Tamarisk*. Before she could scream, the very deck below her seemed to explode and she knew the *Sultana* had hit something. From somewhere behind her, she heard Tobias give the order to go over the side. She looked back once and saw Kimo, his teeth flashing in a wide grin, still at the helm.

"Damned fool!" Whether Tobias cursed Kimo or himself she

never knew. The next instant, an explosion ripped apart the deck beneath her feet and she was catapulted into the water.

Down, deeper, deeper, she plunged. Water rushed past her, making strange, singing, gurgling sounds. Bubbles streamed past her face, the salt water stinging her eyes. And her last thought was of Zach.

Please! Please, dear God! Let him live. Let him live. And then she was cold, so very cold, and she was alone.

The narrow channel between Fraser Island and the mainland looked as if a major sea battle had taken place. Five ships in all were lost: three sunk, including the *Sultana*; one ship of the line heavily damaged; and the *Tamarisk* scuttled, rocked by explosions, only her forward mast jutting from the blue-green water.

For years afterward the residents of the small hamlets and fishing villages would tell tales of the battle. For many it signified the beginning of the end of colonial domination by the Crown. For even though the admiralty considered it a victory because of the loss of the *Tamarisk*, none of her crew were ever caught.

Zach staggered along the beach. Men were gathered in small clusters on it. Some helped others from the water. He'd seen the *Sultana* in those final minutes. Kimo had rammed her right into the frigate pulled alongside the *Tamarisk*. The big African was now up the beach. Tobias was with him. Kimo had hauled him through the waves to the shore. The old man was exhausted, he had a deep gash at the side of his head, but he would live. Elyse hadn't been found.

He'd seen her on the deck of the *Sultana* only moments before everything had exploded around them. The first blast on the *Tamarisk* had only opened the hull. Knowing the ship was going down, Zach dove into the water. Only then did he see the *Sultana* bearing down on the frigate. He cried out to Elyse, but too late. As long as he lived, Zach would remember the dying sounds of those two ships coming together, the splintering of wood, the groaning as water rushed into gaping hulls, and the shouts of the crew as they abandoned their ships. He caught one flashing glimpse of Barrington on the deck of the frigate. The man must have been crazy to try to board the *Tamarisk*. Then the explosives Zach had set went off and the schooner went down.

He brushed past someone.

Sandy reached out to steady him. "Cap'n, you've got to rest. I've got some of the men searchin' further down the beach. There's a lot of places she could have come ashore."

"How many men did we lose?" Zach's voice was hollow.

"Everyone's accounted for, but the bloody English sure lost a few." He smiled briefly. "She's a strong lady, sir. She'll show up."

Zach never heard his last words. He was already moving down the beach, across the island to the far side. Maybe, maybe. The anguish inside him was unbearable. Desperation propelled him down that lonely stretch of sand. Oh God, he kept thinking over and over. She's so small, so beautiful. Please! Please let her be alive.

The mist was thick, rolling over the island. Across the channel, he could barely make out the signal lamps that had been lit. Still, he pushed himself, beyond reason, beyond human strength. He would find her! He would!

"Lis!" He cried out her name. "Oh God, please. I can't lose her again. Not again." Pain and grief washed over him. Nothing seemed real. The water, the sand, and the wind tore at him. He turned, trying to get his bearings. How far had he come? If he just kept going, kept looking, he'd find her.

Her words came back at him through the mist.

Dearest Alex, I've always been with you in my heart. I've always believed in you, believed that you would come back to me.

"Lis!" He hurled her name into the swirling mist. She'd believed it and she'd tried to make him believe.

The white roses at Resolute have never bloomed.

Zach stared hard across the gray beach. Everything was gray: the water, the sky, the mist that shrouded everything.

I knew you'd come back to me.

"I'm here! Lis, I'm here. Oh God, please. Don't leave me, Lis!"

Then he saw it. It was a small form, limp and seemingly lifeless in the surging tide.

Zach ran; he stumbled and clawed his way down that stretch of beach. Then he fell into the rolling surf, pulling that small form from the cold water.

His heart seemed to stop as he turned her over. Lis! God, she was so cold and pale. He pulled her against him, carrying her to

501

the safety of the high sand. Then, cradling her in his arms, he looked at her, really looked at her.

Her skin was pale, almost translucent. Long dark lashes fell against her cheeks. Her eyelids, a purplish blue, were closed over those eyes that seemed to look back through his soul. Her long dark hair was heavy over his arm and she seemed completely lifeless. His hands swept down over her arms and back again, as he tried desperately to rub warmth into her skin. He pulled her against him, tucking her small form into the curve of his body, anything to give her warmth. But they were both so cold and wet. Oh God, he thought desperately, she isn't breathing. When he could feel no pulse in her neck, tears slipped from his eyes.

"Live! Dammit, don't you dare die on me!"

Quickly he placed her on the sand, on her stomach. He then turned her head to the side and opened her mouth. Straddling her legs, he pressed open hands against her back, just below the ribs. He did this rhythmically until she coughed and water spewed from her mouth.

Zach stared down at her. "I won't let you go. Not again!" The words came from his soul. He was certain he was mad, but it no longer mattered.

"Lis! I love you! I've come so far to find you!" He buried his face against the pale skin of her neck and his tears flowed, warming them both.

The mist was all around. Then it swirled and parted.

She must be dreaming. It had to be a dream.

From somewhere very far away, she heard a voice; his voice. And she was walking through the mist. She could almost see him. She looked up as she felt the warmth of the sun overhead. And then her eyes came back to him. He was the phantom from her dreams, the lover from the mist.

Always before there'd been sadness, that feeling of emptiness when he'd turned away from her, always just beyond touching, his face obscured in the mist. But the sun overhead was driving the mist away and she could see him.

And she could touch him. He was real! Her tears fell onto his fingers as he caressed her cheek.

Zach's head came up. He stared at the tears on his fingertips, and then at the wondrous blue eyes staring back at him. "Lis?" Her name came achingly from his lips.

"Alex?"

"Yes! Oh, yes, sweet Lis! I'm here and I'm never going to let you go." He pulled her to him, his lips caressing her cheek.

"I thought I would never find you," she whispered as she curled weakly against the strength of his body.

"I knew you'd come back to me," he responded, his lips brushing her forehead.

Epilogue

Among the aboriginals, whose culture was as timeless as the land, it was known as the Dreamtime. In the minds of these people it was an age that existed long ago and yet remained ever present, a timeless experience linking past, present, and future.

Through her belief in Dreamtime, Elyse found the final truth of her other lives. She and Zach had always been together; in other times and places known by other names, but always together. They were soulmates destined to be together once more, in this life.

She still had the dreams, but they were different now: fragments, bits, and pieces she no longer feared, but accepted as memories of those other lives. And he was always part of her memory, just as he was now part of her life.

Elyse walked back alone from the small cottage not far from the main house at Resolute. She listened to the night sounds; she still hadn't gotten completely used to them.

She'd been visiting with Jingo Nymagee's wife, Sara. The power of Dreamtime was strong in Jingo's family. Usually only the men were allowed to sit under the stars at night, building the fires, chanting the ancient messages connecting them to those other lives. But Elyse was allowed to watch from the perimeter of their circle at these times, because it was accepted that she was blessed with the power also.

Afterward she always felt at peace, and content, more of her questions about those other times and places having been answered. These sessions of communication helped her to understand and accept her special gift.

It was more difficult for Zach. On the day of the explosion aboard the *Tamarisk* all his barriers had been stripped away. He refused to talk about what he'd experienced then, but she sensed it was constantly in his thoughts.

Often she would find him watching her, a strange expression on his face, almost as if he did understand. But then he would look away, confusion in those gray eyes.

His bitterness over the betrayal that had sent Alex Barrington to this land so many years ago was over. It had ended when Jerrold had died trying to board the *Tamarisk*.

She now knew the rest of the story: a young servant girl had been forced to lie to the court about what she'd witnessed. They'd received word that Lydia Roberts had gone before the London magistrate shortly after Jerrold had left England, and had told the truth about Charles and Alex Barrington. Alexander Nicholas Barrington was now cleared of murder. Charles Barrington had simply disappeared. The Barrington title, Fair View, Barrington Shipping, all belonged to Zach now. That had been so before Jerrold ever reached New South Wales, but he'd had no way of knowing it. Zach had promised Elyse that his pirating days were over. Now that he controlled Barrington Shipping, he could practice another form of resistance to the Crown, one within the bounds of the law.

Elyse had sent letters to her grandmother explaining everything and promising they would visit her in England. She was anxious about how Regina had taken the news of her marriage, in fact, to the man who'd abducted her. But when Lady Regina wrote back, a letter that greatly resembled a book, she'd been more concerned with receiving an invitation to visit this land "down under" as she now called it. She and Ceddy would be arriving sometime in the spring for an extended visit that was also a belated honeymoon for them. They'd married shortly after receiving Elyse's letter.

About time, Elyse had thought, delighted that Ceddy was now officially part of the family. And by the time the older couple arrived, they would officially be great-grandparents. She ran her hand over the rock-hard firmness of her stomach. She was almost six months pregnant but it was hardly visible beneath the gowns Minnie Halstead had made for her. They were loose and cool, and very accommodating to her expanding waistline. She'd had to abandon the pants she preferred two months earlier when she could no longer fasten the closures on them.

She would have a son, of that she was certain. As certain as she was about her other lives. And she knew the exact moment she had conceived this child. It had been aboard the *Tamarisk*, that night when she'd finally realized the truth, that Zach and Alex were one. Elyse loved the feel of the child within her. He was a reaffirmation of life, this life. In a way she supposed that made all life continual. But she silently wondered if this son of hers, who kicked and somersaulted beneath her ribs, would understand their secret. Would he have the mark of the lifeline strong in his hand or would he, like they, enter one life from another? And what of the future? Elyse could accept whatever it offered, for within her was the certainty that when this life as they knew it ended, she and Zach would find each other again.

She approached the gardens at the west side of the house, and hesitated as she saw a shadow separate from the others. She couldn't see it clearly. Then it lengthened and came toward her. Zach stepped from the darkness into the soft glow of light cast from the windows. Usually he let her go alone to the meeting place of Jingo's people, but tonight he'd waited for her.

"Good evening, little star watcher." He greeted her tenderly, his arm slipping around her enlarged wrist. "Did you travel with the Dreamers tonight?"

He wasn't teasing, Elyse knew that. Zach respected the ancient culture of these people who were so closely bound to the land at Resolute, just as he was.

"Only for a little while." She smiled up at him. "I wanted to return to you." Elyse shivered faintly. The night air had turned cool.

Zach's arm tightened around her as they stopped in the garden beside a large eucalyptus tree, the leaves fragrant with that uniquely pungent smell. He pulled her back against him, his hands sliding from her shoulders, down over her enlarged breasts to the fullness of his child within her. "Are you keeping my son warm?"

Elyse laid her head back on his shoulder, sighing as his mouth slipped down the side of her neck to the top of her shoulder. Heat spread through her, settling somewhere below where the baby now rested.

"He's very warm." She laughed softly as, through the soft fabric of her dress, Zach's hands closed over her disappearing hipbones. He pulled her hips back against him and she felt the hardness of his arousal, longing shuddering through her. God, would she ever be able to have enough of him? How was it possible that with this child large and heavy within her, she could still feel that quickening of desire only Zach could fulfill?

She knew he wanted her. Could she possibly ask him now, when she knew he would promise practically anything?

"Zach?" She called him that now, because it was his name in this life.

"Hmmmmm?" he murmured against the back of her neck, inhaling the sweetness of her long, unbound hair.

"Come with me next time."

Silence.

Elyse bit at her lower lip. Up until now Zach had let her go alone when she felt the need to understand more about the other lives. But always with that silence. Was it the same now?

"All right."

She let out a slow breath. It was a beginning, the beginning of full acceptance. She knew that. Slowly she turned around in his arms, wondering if she dare ask what might have changed his mind.

"You're certain?" Her lower lip trembled slightly.

Zach's finger came up, tenderly tracing its fullness. There was a somber light in his eyes. "Very certain."

"But how . . . why? I don't understand. Always before you never wanted to talk about it."

He reached up, stroking back a tendril of hair from her cheek. She was so beautiful—this woman, his wife, the mother of his child. He smiled. His son. He'd mentally corrected himself because Elyse was certain it would be a son.

Zach didn't know what she wanted to hear. He only knew what he felt in his heart each time he looked at her, that deep, inner knowledge and acceptance that they had been together before. How many times? He didn't know, and he didn't begin to understand how it happened. He just finally knew that it was true. No matter how much he denied it or fought it, no matter what logical arguments he used, he knew they were bound together for all eternity. And he found that more priceless than anything.

Never in this life had he known the complete peace and fulfillment he'd found with her. His obsession with Felicia Barrington was ended, quite simply because he knew she was Felicia Barrington. It was what had drawn him to her that first time so many months ago in London. She had been waiting for him, and he'd been compelled to go to her. But the name didn't matter. It never had. She was the same, as she'd always been the same. She was his soul.

"I first began to accept that it was true when I thought I'd lost

507

you forever. You died on that beach, Elyse. I know that as surely as I'm standing here. But somehow you came back to me." His voice was heavy with emotion as he spoke of that night for the first time.

Her fingers came up to his lips to silence him, knowing how difficult this was, remembering how difficult it was for her when she at last finally understood. But he insisted on going on.

"I'm not a religious man: I never felt the need for it. I still don't. And there are many things I don't understand, may never understand. But I know that there's something stronger than life and death, something that goes beyond and keeps two people together. It's what I feel for you. I've always loved you." He cupped her face in his hands.

"I love you today, I'll love you tomorrow, I'll love you forever." His face lowered and he tenderly kissed her, sealing the promise with his lips.

Her eyes were glistening with tears as she laid her head against his chest, feeling the strong beating of his heart. The arms around her, the strong hands caressing her, they were from her dream and now they were real. She'd found him again. He'd come back to her.

"Zach, look!" she whispered softly against his chest as she pointed across the garden.

There, bright and luminous in this evening lit by the stars of dreams, the white roses of Resolute bloomed among the red, fulfilling his promise to her from that other lifetime: *This rose symbolizes my passion for you. This is my promise that my love will last forever.*

ZEBRA HAS THE SUPERSTARS
OF PASSIONATE ROMANCE!

CRIMSON OBSESSION   (2272, $3.95)
by Deana James

Cassandra MacDaermond was determined to make the handsome gambling hall owner Edward Sandron pay for the fortune he had stolen from her father. But she never counted on being struck speechless by his seductive gaze. And soon Cassandra was sneaking into Sandron's room, more intent on sharing his rapture than causing his ruin!

TEXAS CAPTIVE   (2251, $3.95)
by Wanda Owen

Ever since two outlaws had killed her ma, Talleha had been suspicious of all men. But one glimpse of virile Victor Maurier standing by the lake in the Texas Blacklands and the half-Indian princess was helpless before the sensual tide that swept her in its wake!

TEXAS STAR   (2088, $3.95)
by Deana James

Star Garner was a wanted woman—and Chris Gillard was determined to collect the generous bounty being offered for her capture. But when the beautiful outlaw made love to him as if her life depended on it, Gillard's firm resolve melted away, replaced with a raging obsession for his fiery TEXAS STAR.

MOONLIT SPLENDOR   (2008, $3.95)
by Wanda Owen

When the handsome stranger emerged from the shadows and pulled Charmaine Lamoureux into his strong embrace, she sighed with pleasure at his seductive caresses. Tomorrow she would be wed against her will—so tonight she would take whatever exhilarating happiness she could!

Available wherever paperbacks are sold, or order direct from the Publisher. Send cover price plus 50¢ per copy for mailing and handling to Zebra Books, Dept. 2470, 475 Park Avenue South, New York, N.Y. 10016. Residents of New York, New Jersey and Pennsylvania must include sales tax. DO NOT SEND CASH.